D0509693

THIS PLACE

150 Years Retold

Foreword by Alicia Elliott

Stories by Kateri Akiwenzie-Damm, Sonny Assu, Brandon Mitchell,
Rachel and Sean Qitsualik-Tinsley, David A. Robertson, Niigaanwewidam James Sinclair,
Jen Storm, Richard Van Camp, Katherena Vermette, and Chelsea Vowel

Illustration and colours by Tara Audibert, Kyle Charles, GMB Chomichuk,
Natasha Donovan, Scott A. Ford, Scott B. Henderson, Ryan Howe,
Andrew Lodwick, Jen Storm, and Donovan Yaciuk

HIGHWATER PRESS

Canada Council for the Arts Conseil des Arts du Canada

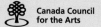

We acknowledge the support of the Canada Council for the Arts./ Nous remercions le Conseil des arts du Canada de son soutien.

Canada Council for the Arts Conseil des arts du Canada

New Chapter 2017 and Beyond Nouveau chapitre 2017 et au-delà

This is one of the 200 exceptional projects funded through the Canada Council for the Arts' New Chapter initiative. With this $35M initiative, the Council supports the creation and sharing of the arts in communities across Canada./Ce projet est l'un des 200 projets exceptionnels soutenus par l'initiative Nouveau chapitre du Conseil des arts du Canada. Avec cette initiative 35 M$, le Conseil des arts appuie la creation et le partage des arts au cœur de nos vies et dans l'ensemble du Canada.

HighWater Press gratefully acknowledges the financial support of the Province of Manitoba through the Department of Sport, Culture & Heritage and the Manitoba Book Publishing Tax Credit, and the Government of Canada through the Canada Book Fund (CBF), for our publishing activities.

Acknowledgements

Thank you to the following people, who lent their time and expertise to the creation of these stories.

Lawrence Barkwell

Jodi Ann Eskritt, Curator, RCMP Historical Collections Unit

Dr. Chantal Fiola

Captain Tim Feick, C.D.

Ellen Gabriel

Shelley Germain

Kawenniiostha Jacobs, Mohawk language consultant

Norma Jean Martin

Theresa Mitchell, Mi'gmaq translator

Aandeg Muldrew, Ojibwe translator

Brody Nanakim (Qəmkʷalał), Wiwēqaýi reviewer and Kwak'wala translator

David J. Parker, Edmonton Friends of the North Environmental Society

Waubgeshig Rice

Dr. Raven Sinclair

Sivulliviniit

Molly Swain, fellow *Métis in Space* world-builder

Sheryl Thompson (Puʎas), Wiwek'am reviewer and Liq'wala/Kwak'wala translator

Frank T'Seleie

Janice Vicaire, Mi'gmaq translator

Marsha Vicaire

Library and Archives Canada Cataloguing in Publication

This place : 150 years retold / foreword by Alicia Elliott ; stories by Kateri Akiwenzie-Damm [and 10 others] ; illustrations by Tara Audibert [and 5 others] ; colouring by Scott A. Ford and Donovan Yaciuk.

Includes bibliographical references.
Issued in print and electronic formats.
ISBN 978-1-55379-758-6 (softcover).--ISBN 978-1-55379-782-1 (EPUB).--
ISBN 978-1-55379-783-8 (PDF)

1. Native peoples--Canada--Comic books, strips, etc. 2. Native peoples--Canada--Juvenile fiction. 3. Canada--History--Comic books, strips, etc. 4. Canada--History--Juvenile fiction. 5. Comics (Graphic works). I. Elliott, Alicia, writer of foreword II. Akiwenzie-Damm, Kateri, 1965-, author III. Audibert, Tara, 1975-, illustrator IV. Ford, Scott A., colourist V. Yaciuk, Donovan, 1975-, colourist

PN6732.T45 2019 j741.5'97108997 C2018-904588-4
C2018-904589-2

22 21 20 19 1 2 3 4 5

Contents

Foreword

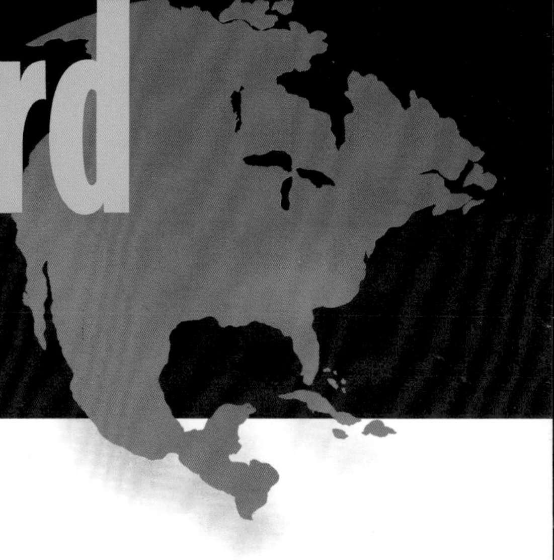

I have never liked the phrase, "History is written by the victors." I understand the idea behind it—that those in power will tell and retell stories in whatever ways flatter them best, until those stories harden into something called "history." But just because stories are unwritten for a time, it doesn't mean they'll be unwritten forever. And just because stories don't get written down, it doesn't mean they're ever lost. We carry them in our minds, our hearts, our very bones. We honour them by passing them on, letting them live on in others, too.

That's exactly what this anthology does. It takes stories our people have been forced to pass on quietly, to whisper behind hands like secrets, and retells them loudly and unapologetically for our people today. It finally puts our people front and centre on our own lands. Inside these pages are the incredible, hilarious heroics of Annie Bannatyne, who refused to let settlers disrespect Métis women in Red River. There's the heartbreaking, necessary tale of Nimkii and Teddy, heroic youth in care who fight trauma and colonialism as hard as they possibly can in impossible circumstances. And there are many more—all important, all enlightening. All of these stories deserve to be retold, remembered, and held close.

As I was reading, I thought a lot about the idea of apocalypse, or the end of the world as we know it. Indigenous writers have pointed out that, as Indigenous people, we all live in a post-apocalyptic world. The world as we knew it ended the moment colonialism started to creep across these lands. But we have continued to tell our stories; we have continued to adapt. *Despite everything, we have survived.*

we are [illegible] have survived the apocalypse. When you think about it that way, every Indigenous person is a hero simply for existing. The people named in these stories are all heroes, inspired by love of their people and culture to do amazing, brave things—but so are the unnamed people who raised them, who taught them, who supported them, and who stood with them. Our communities are full of heroes.

That's why this anthology is so beautiful and so important. It tells tales of resistance, of leadership, of wonder and pain, of pasts we must remember and futures we must keep striving towards, planting each story like a seed deep inside of us. It's our responsibility as readers to carry and nourish those seeds, letting them grow inside as we go on to create our own stories, live our own lives, and become our own heroes. As you read, consider: how are you a hero already? And what will your story be?

Alicia Elliott

Annie Bannatyne was a formidable woman. Little-known outside of Winnipeg and Métis communities, not even known to me until I was an adult, Mrs. Bannatyne is an inspiration who deserves more recognition.

Born and raised in Red River, in what is now Winnipeg's Exchange District, she was the daughter of Andrew McDermot, a wealthy store owner, and Sarah McNab, a Métis-Saulteaux woman. As an adult, Annie married Andrew Bannatyne, another successful store owner. Mrs. Bannatyne was well-educated and community-minded. In addition to running her store and raising her family, she spearheaded many charitable initiatives, and was instrumental in the fundraising and founding of the Winnipeg General Hospital, the first hospital in the region.

Mrs. Bannatyne was not the kind of woman to mess with. So, when Charles Mair wrote disparaging things about Métis women in the Toronto *Globe*, Mrs. Bannatyne didn't just get mad, she got even.

Later that month, Montreal's *Le Nouveau Monde* published an editorial by the mysterious "L.R." that also criticized Mair's remarks. Most historians think this was none other than Louis Riel in his first act of written revolt, inspired by the actions of Mrs. Bannatyne. As one historian notes, "In 1869, Annie stepped outside her gender role and committed a single act of resistance that fired the imagination of a young Louis Riel."[1]

Katherena Vermette

1867
Confederation of Canada.

1868
Canada First is founded. The movement promotes a British Protestant ideology as central to the Canadian identity.

1870
The province of Manitoba is created, with promises to respect Métis land titles. Annie and many others never receive their land due to fraud and delays by government agents.

1868, NOVEMBER
The Toronto *Globe* publishes a letter by Charles Mair containing offensive, racist comments about Métis women.

1869, FEBRUARY
Annie Bannatyne horsewhips Mair. Later that month, a letter signed "L.R." is published in *Le Nouveau Monde*, criticizing Mair and Canadian attitudes towards the Métis.

1869, DECEMBER
A provisional government is established, with Louis Riel as secretary, to negotiate the Red River Colony's relationship to Canada.

Annie of Red River

Katherena Vermette
Illustration: Scott B. Henderson
Colours: Donovan Yaciuk

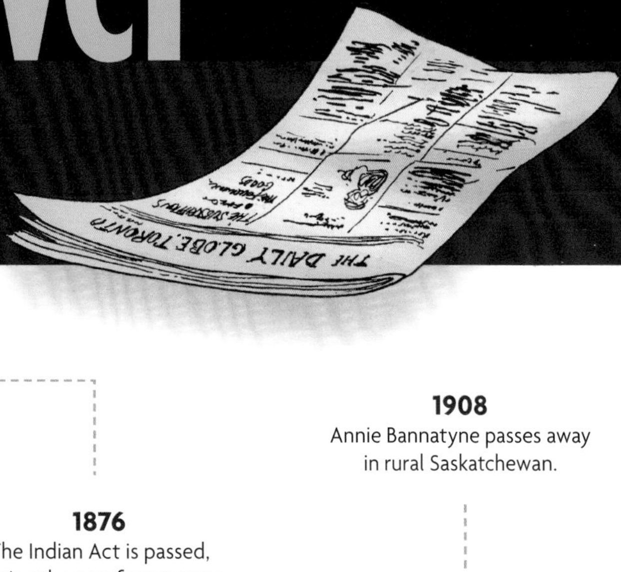
THE DAILY GLOBE, TORONTO

1871-1875
The first five numbered treaties are signed. These secure much of Rupert's Land and the Northwest Territories as Crown property and guarantee federal responsibility for the well-being of the territories' Indigenous inhabitants.

1876
The Indian Act is passed, paving the way for reserves and residential schools.

1884-1885
Canadian encroachment upon Métis and First Nations' lands on the Western Prairies leads to the Northwest Resistance.

1885
The Canadian government executes Louis Riel.

1885
Canada introduces the pass system, confining Indigenous people to their reserves unless they have written permission to leave from the Indian Agent.

1908
Annie Bannatyne passes away in rural Saskatchewan.

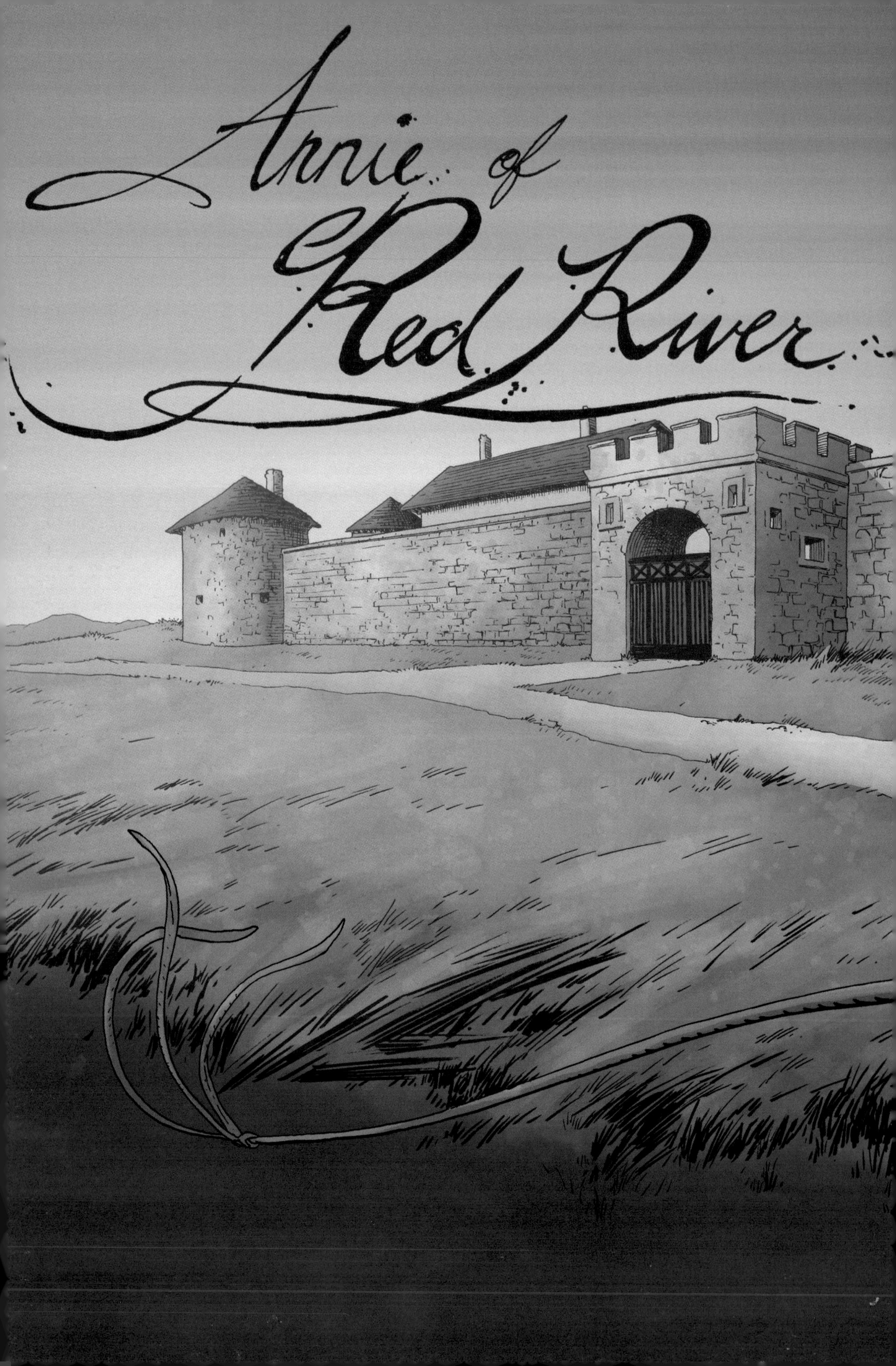
Annie of
Red River

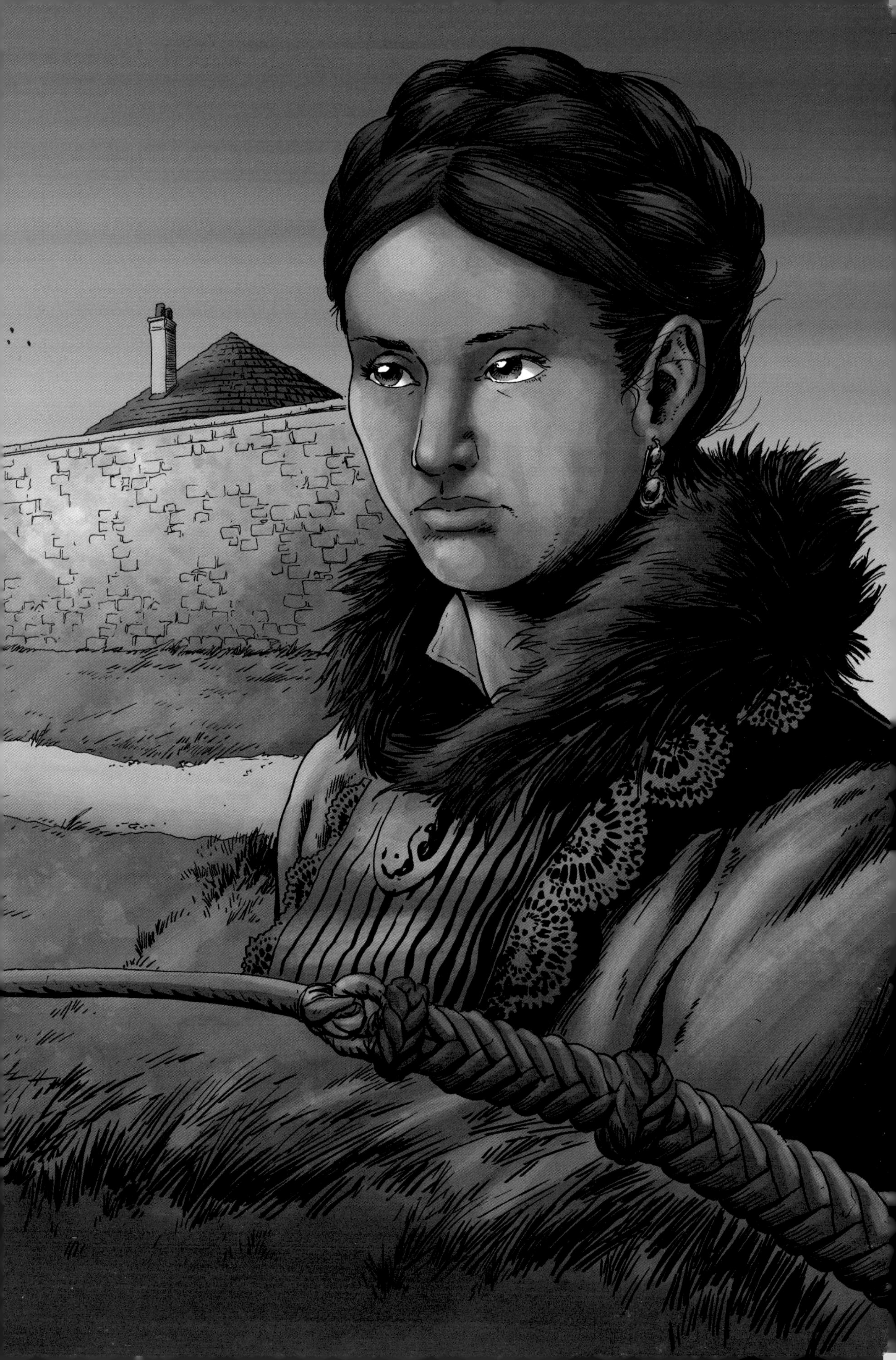

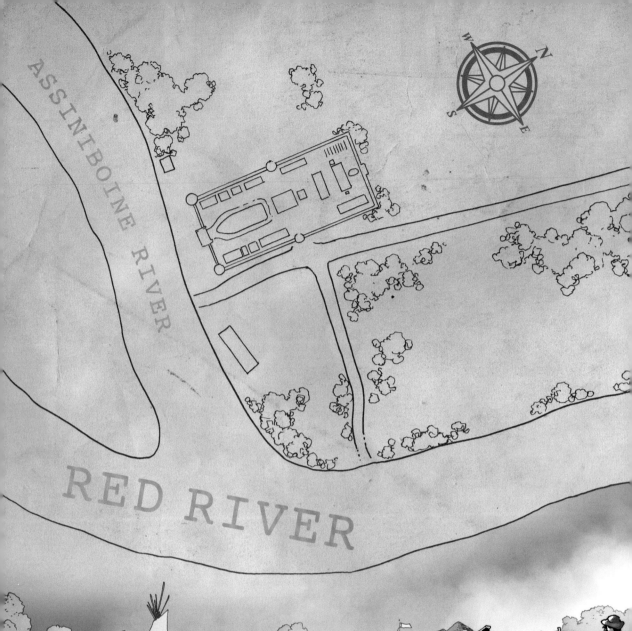

ASSINIBOINE RIVER

RED RIVER

1850

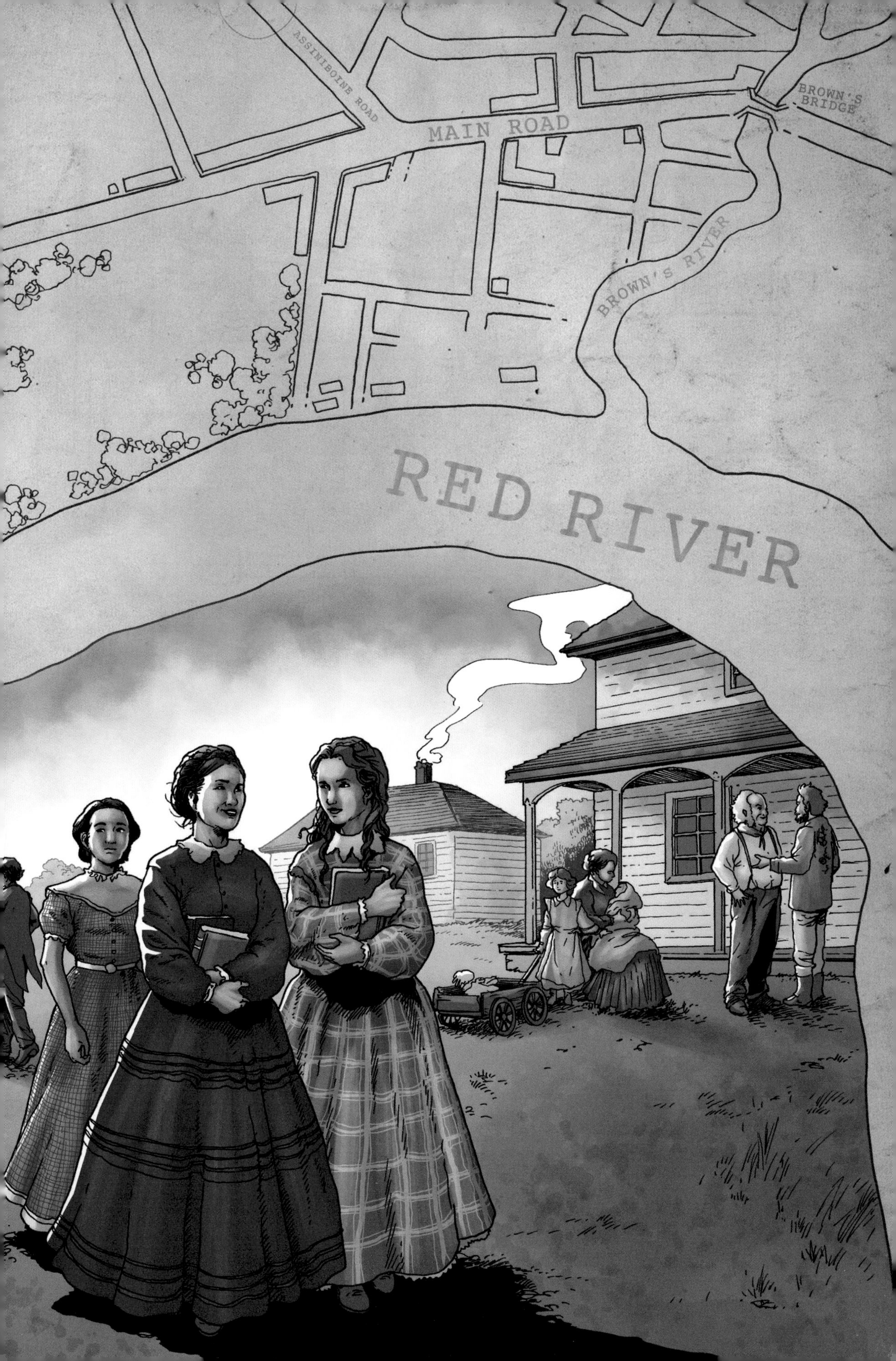
ASSINIBOINE ROAD
MAIN ROAD
BROWN'S BRIDGE
BROWN'S RIVER
RED RIVER

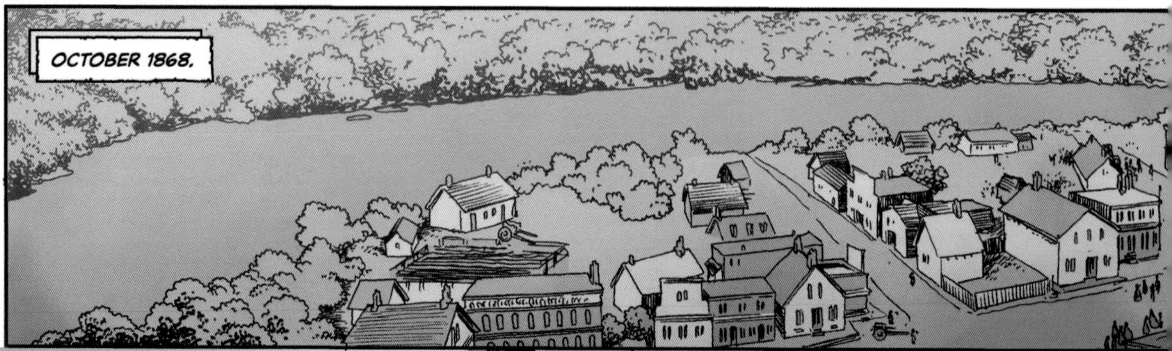
OCTOBER 1868.

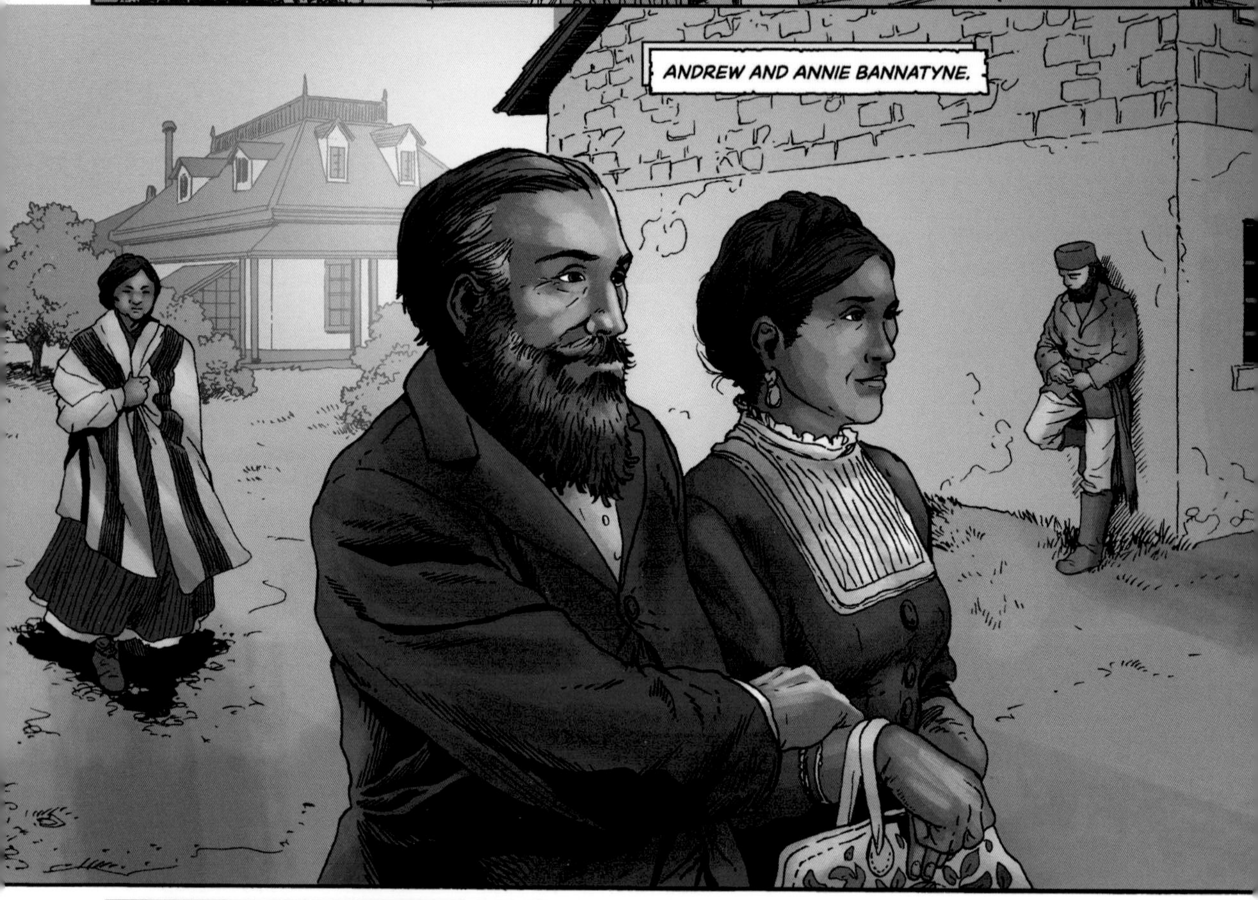
ANDREW AND ANNIE BANNATYNE.

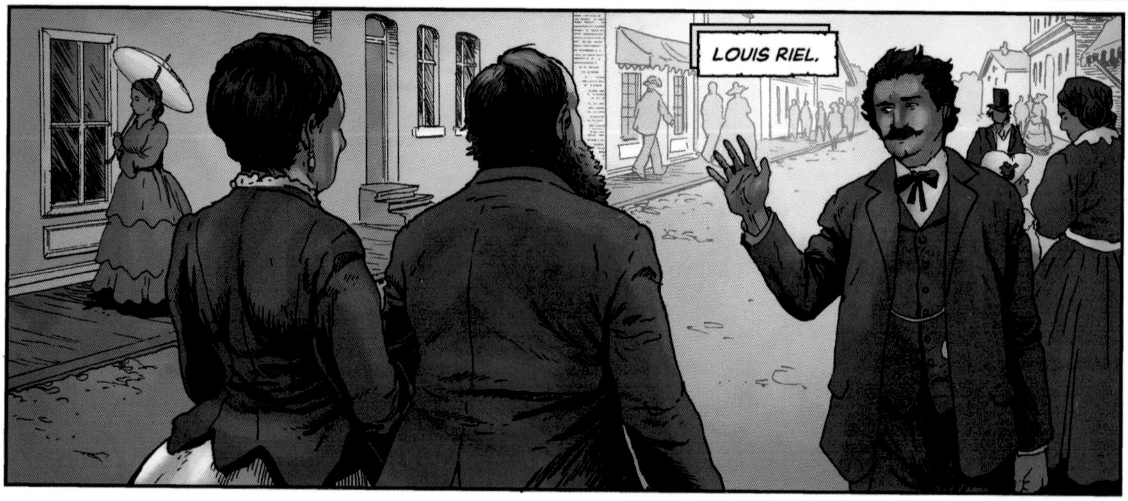
LOUIS RIEL.

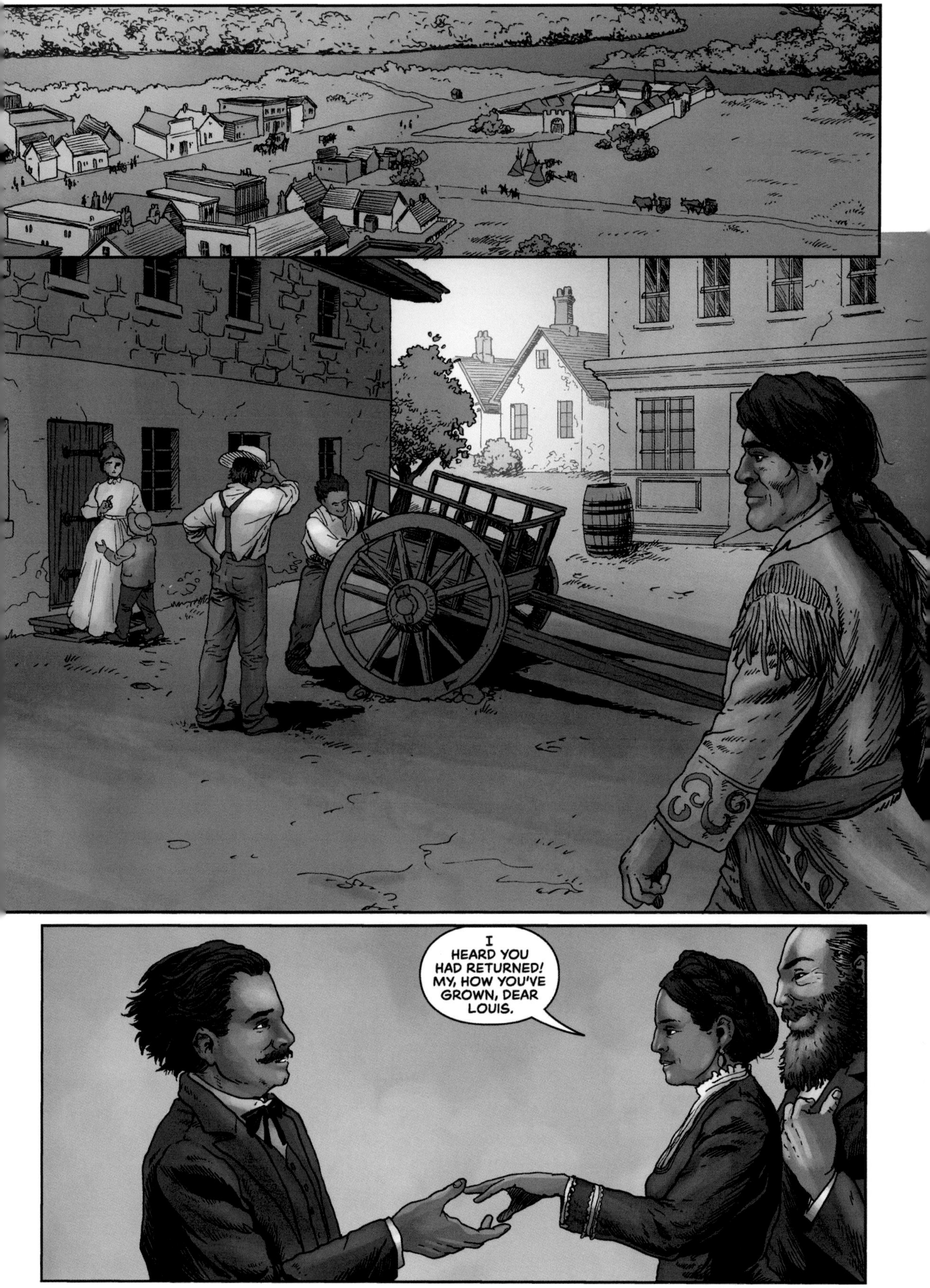
I HEARD YOU HAD RETURNED! MY, HOW YOU'VE GROWN, DEAR LOUIS.

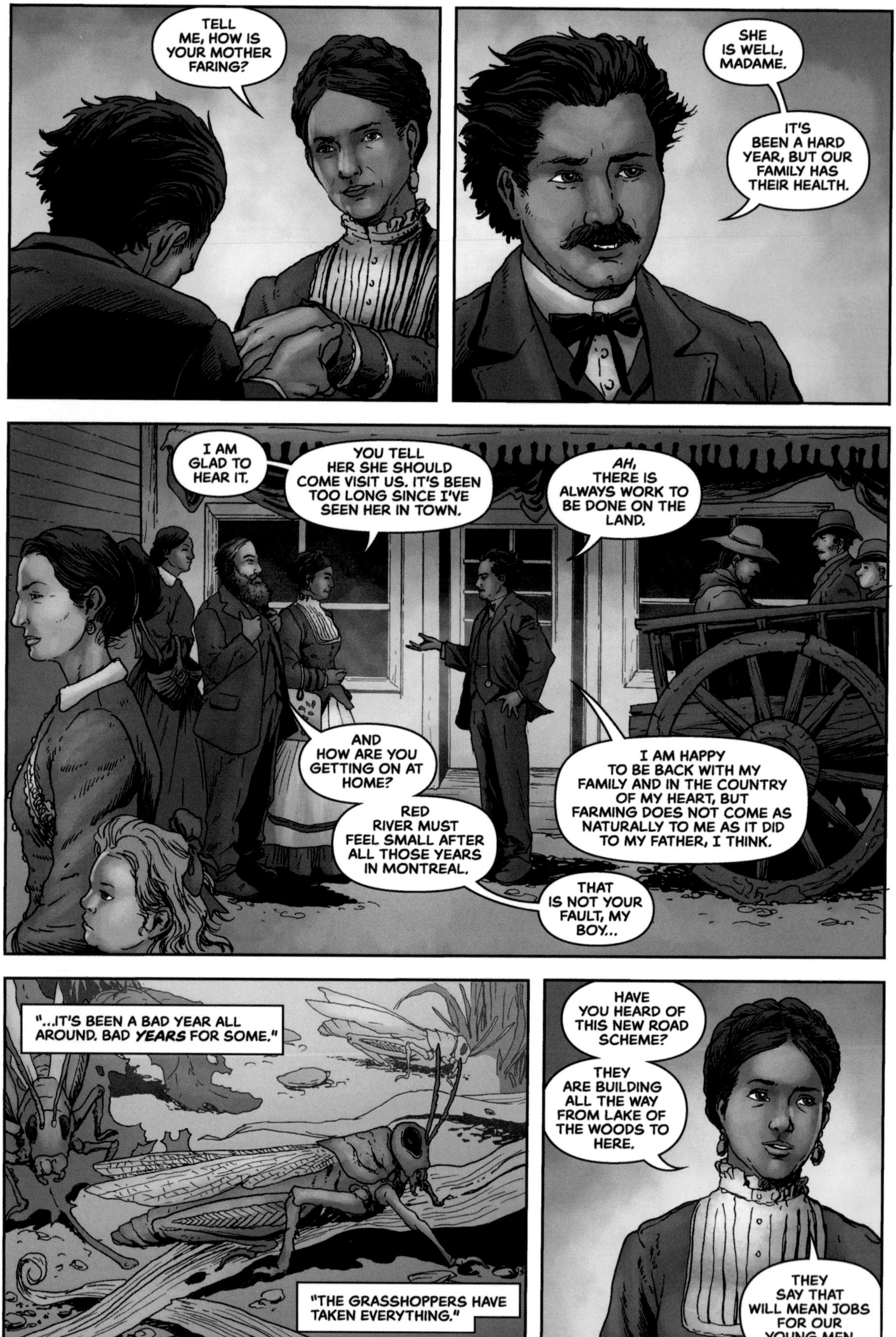
TELL ME, HOW IS YOUR MOTHER FARING?
SHE IS WELL, MADAME.
IT'S BEEN A HARD YEAR, BUT OUR FAMILY HAS THEIR HEALTH.
I AM GLAD TO HEAR IT.
YOU TELL HER SHE SHOULD COME VISIT US. IT'S BEEN TOO LONG SINCE I'VE SEEN HER IN TOWN.
AH, THERE IS ALWAYS WORK TO BE DONE ON THE LAND.
AND HOW ARE YOU GETTING ON AT HOME?
RED RIVER MUST FEEL SMALL AFTER ALL THOSE YEARS IN MONTREAL.
I AM HAPPY TO BE BACK WITH MY FAMILY AND IN THE COUNTRY OF MY HEART, BUT FARMING DOES NOT COME AS NATURALLY TO ME AS IT DID TO MY FATHER, I THINK.
THAT IS NOT YOUR FAULT, MY BOY...
"...IT'S BEEN A BAD YEAR ALL AROUND. BAD *YEARS* FOR SOME."
"THE GRASSHOPPERS HAVE TAKEN EVERYTHING."
HAVE YOU HEARD OF THIS NEW ROAD SCHEME?
THEY ARE BUILDING ALL THE WAY FROM LAKE OF THE WOODS TO HERE.
THEY SAY THAT WILL MEAN JOBS FOR OUR YOUNG MEN.

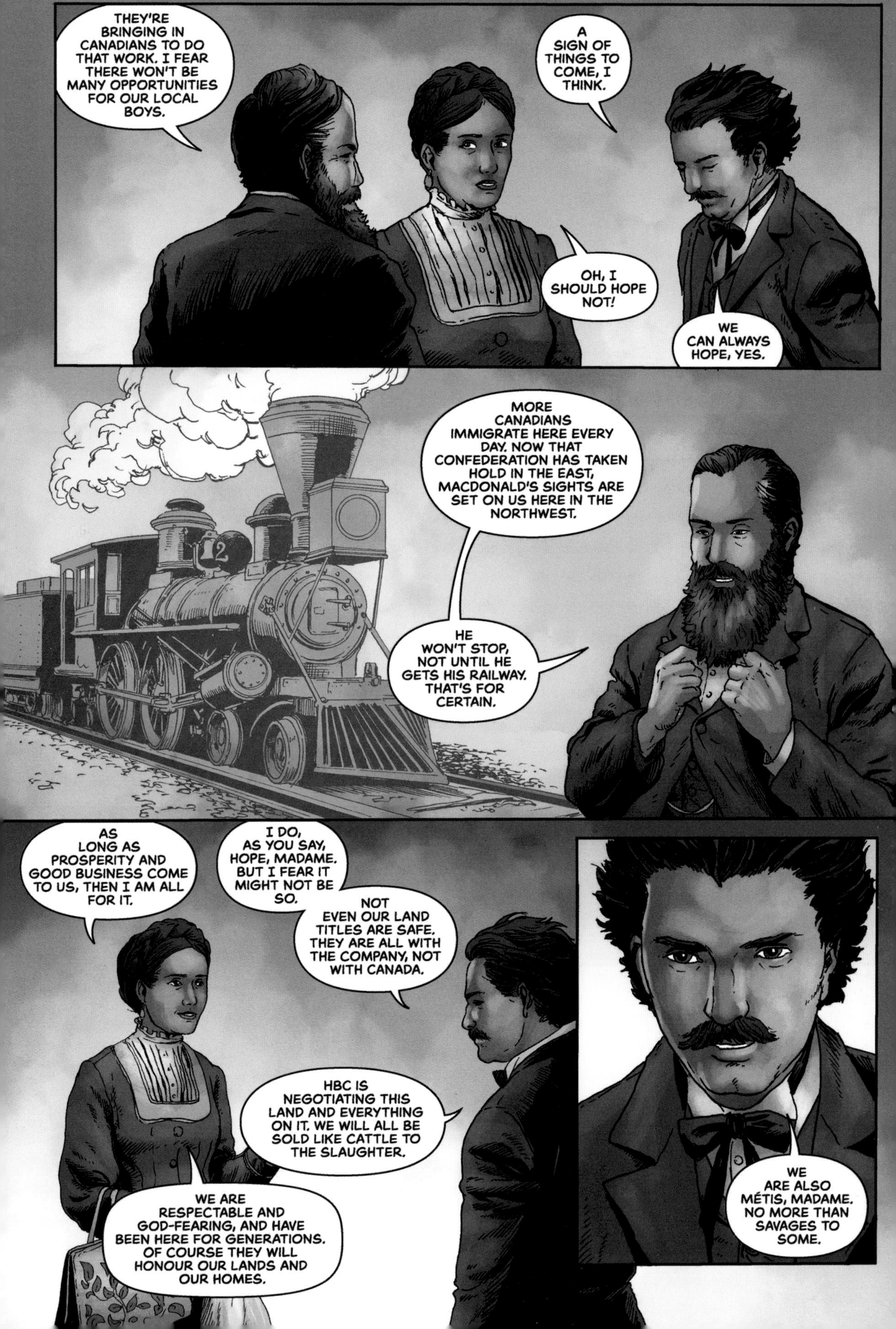
THEY'RE BRINGING IN CANADIANS TO DO THAT WORK. I FEAR THERE WON'T BE MANY OPPORTUNITIES FOR OUR LOCAL BOYS.
A SIGN OF THINGS TO COME, I THINK.
OH, I SHOULD HOPE NOT!
WE CAN ALWAYS HOPE, YES.
MORE CANADIANS IMMIGRATE HERE EVERY DAY. NOW THAT CONFEDERATION HAS TAKEN HOLD IN THE EAST, MACDONALD'S SIGHTS ARE SET ON US HERE IN THE NORTHWEST.
HE WON'T STOP, NOT UNTIL HE GETS HIS RAILWAY. THAT'S FOR CERTAIN.
AS LONG AS PROSPERITY AND GOOD BUSINESS COME TO US, THEN I AM ALL FOR IT.
I DO, AS YOU SAY, HOPE, MADAME. BUT I FEAR IT MIGHT NOT BE SO.
NOT EVEN OUR LAND TITLES ARE SAFE. THEY ARE ALL WITH THE COMPANY, NOT WITH CANADA.
HBC IS NEGOTIATING THIS LAND AND EVERYTHING ON IT. WE WILL ALL BE SOLD LIKE CATTLE TO THE SLAUGHTER.
WE ARE RESPECTABLE AND GOD-FEARING, AND HAVE BEEN HERE FOR GENERATIONS. OF COURSE THEY WILL HONOUR OUR LANDS AND OUR HOMES.
WE ARE ALSO MÉTIS, MADAME. NO MORE THAN SAVAGES TO SOME.

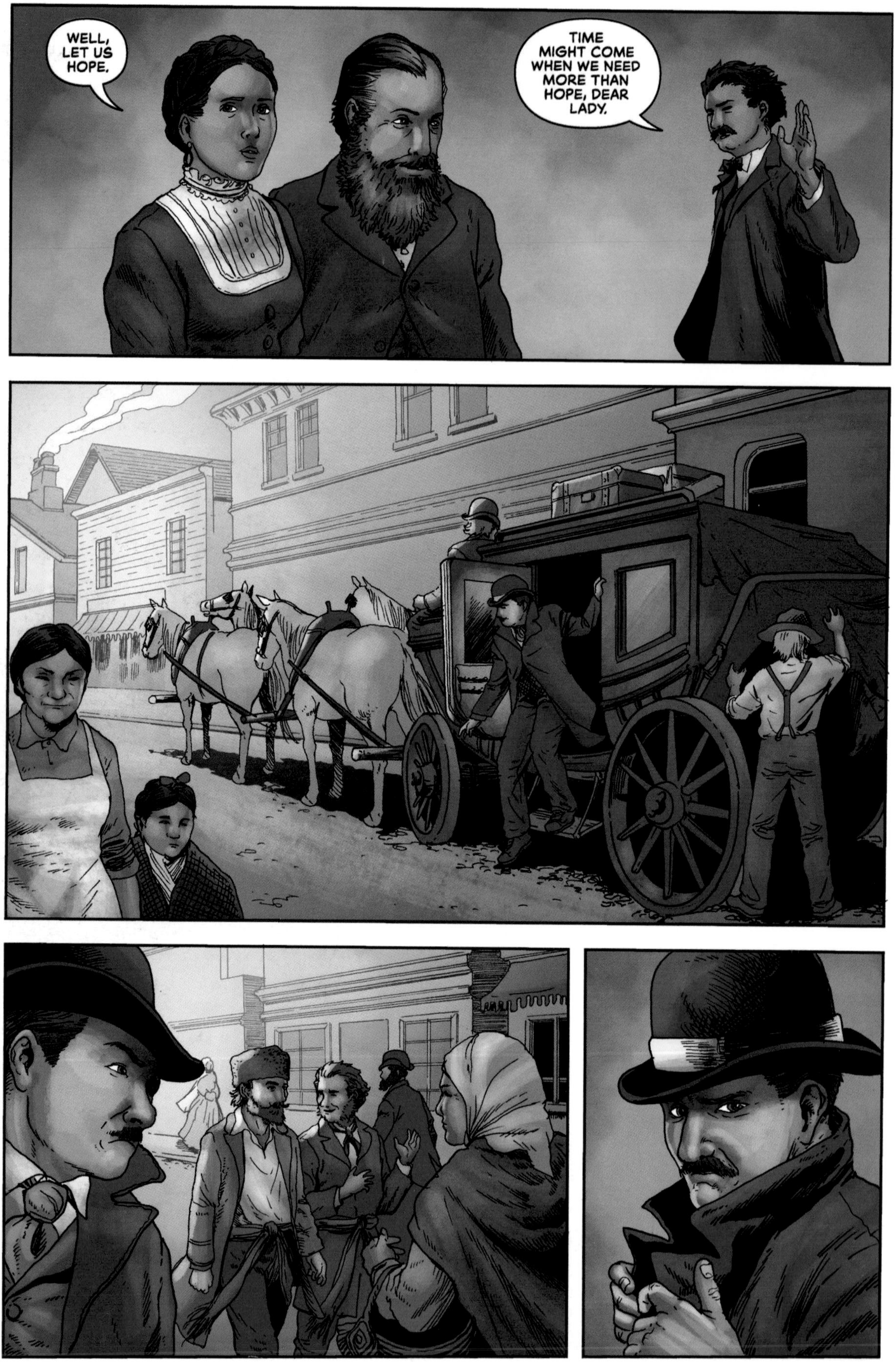
WELL, LET US HOPE.
TIME MIGHT COME WHEN WE NEED MORE THAN HOPE, DEAR LADY.

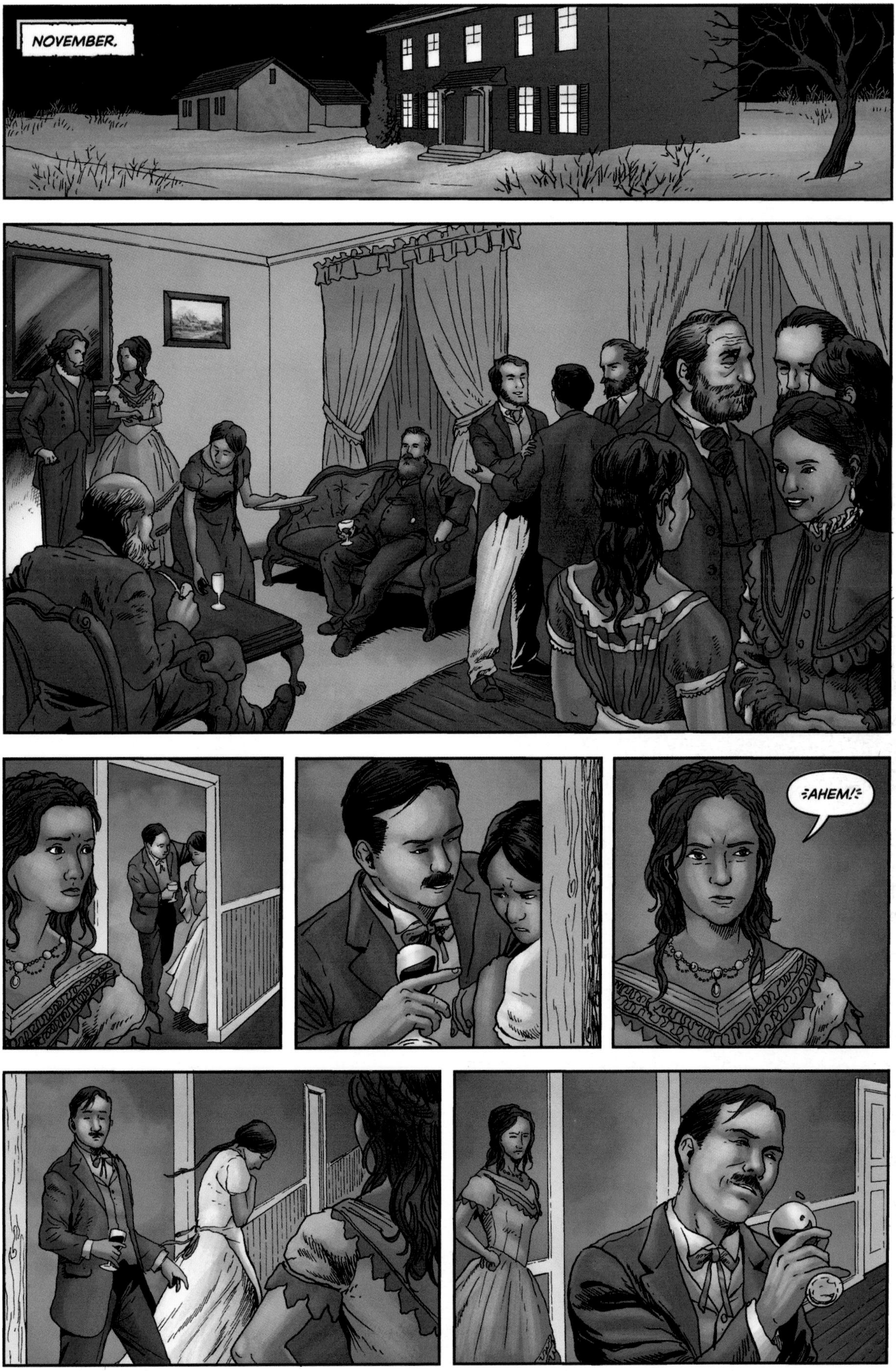
NOVEMBER.
AHEM!

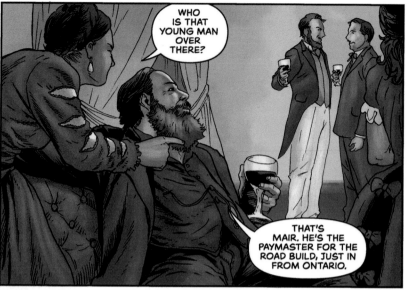

WHO IS THAT YOUNG MAN OVER THERE?

THAT'S MAIR. HE'S THE PAYMASTER FOR THE ROAD BUILD, JUST IN FROM ONTARIO.

MY SISTER JUST CAUGHT HIM BEING *INDECENT* TO ONE OF BEGG'S MAIDS. A YOUNG GIRL, JUST ARRIVED IN TOWN.

THESE ONTARIANS THINK THEY ARE IN WILD COUNTRY HERE.

WITH ALL OUR *WILD WOMEN.*

OH YOU!

WILD WOMEN. THE GIRL WAS A *CHILD.*

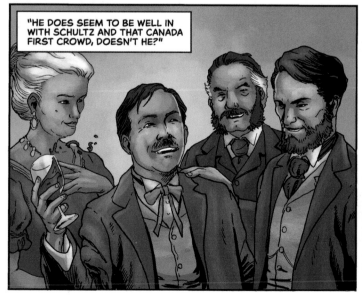

"HE DOES SEEM TO BE WELL IN WITH SCHULTZ AND THAT CANADA FIRST CROWD, DOESN'T HE?"

I DON'T TRUST *THEM* AS FAR AS I CAN THROW THEM.

YOU DON'T TRUST *ANYONE,* MY LOVE.

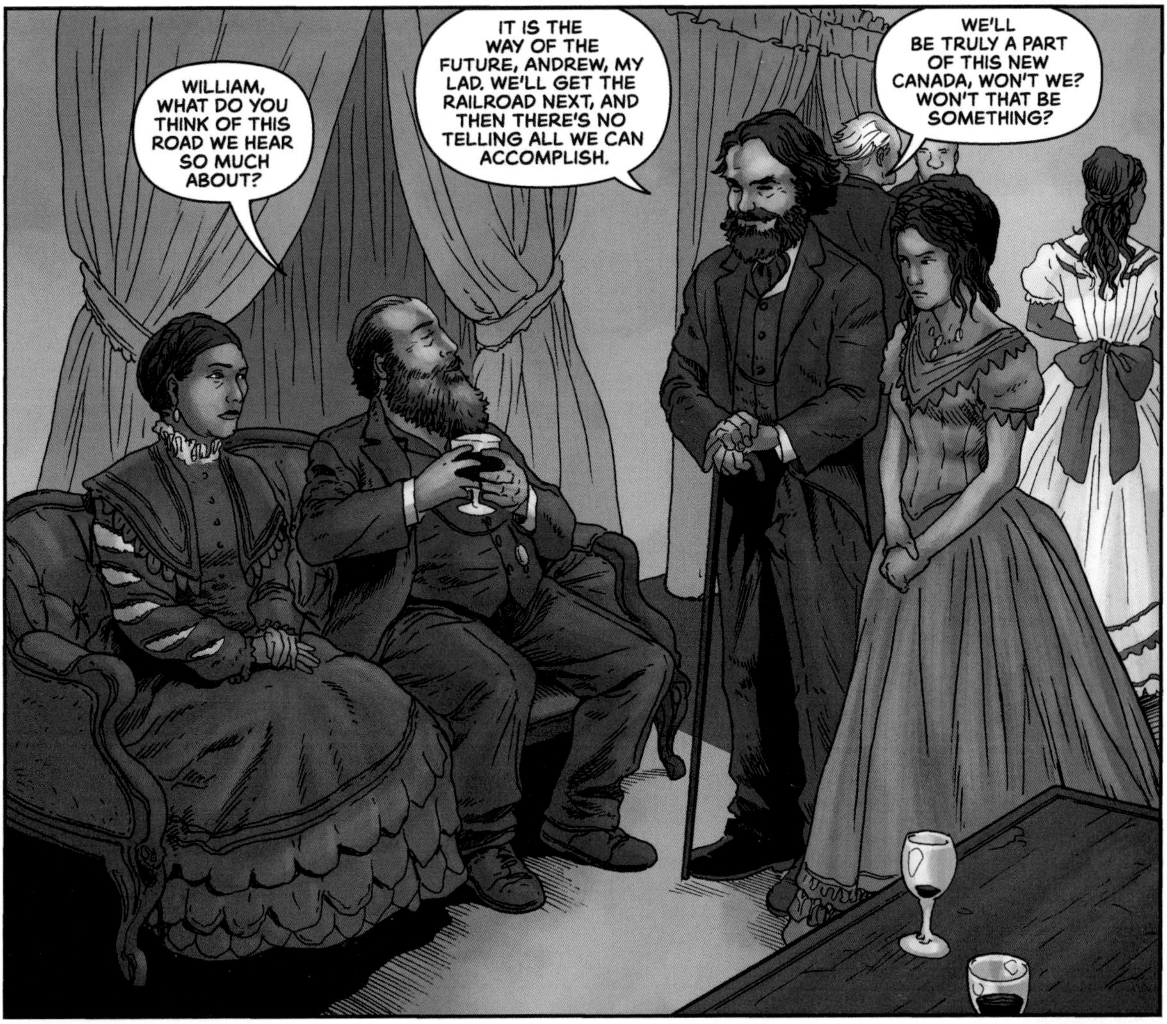
WILLIAM, WHAT DO YOU THINK OF THIS ROAD WE HEAR SO MUCH ABOUT?
IT IS THE WAY OF THE FUTURE, ANDREW, MY LAD. WE'LL GET THE RAILROAD NEXT, AND THEN THERE'S NO TELLING ALL WE CAN ACCOMPLISH.
WE'LL BE TRULY A PART OF THIS NEW CANADA, WON'T WE? WON'T THAT BE SOMETHING?

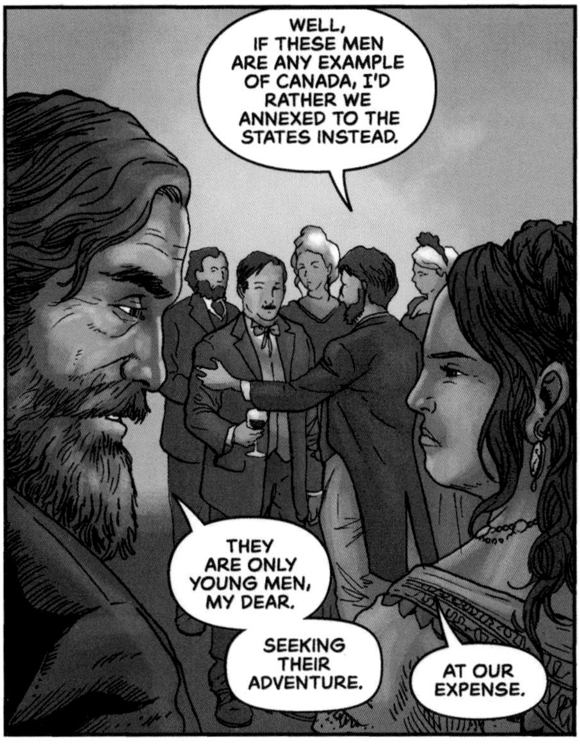
WELL, IF THESE MEN ARE ANY EXAMPLE OF CANADA, I'D RATHER WE ANNEXED TO THE STATES INSTEAD.
THEY ARE ONLY YOUNG MEN, MY DEAR.
SEEKING THEIR ADVENTURE.
AT OUR EXPENSE.

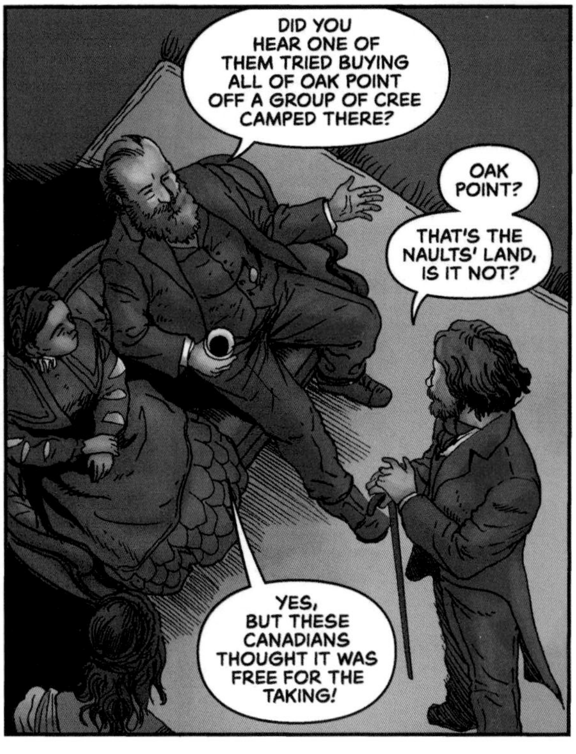
DID YOU HEAR ONE OF THEM TRIED BUYING ALL OF OAK POINT OFF A GROUP OF CREE CAMPED THERE?
OAK POINT?
THAT'S THE NAULTS' LAND, IS IT NOT?
YES, BUT THESE CANADIANS THOUGHT IT WAS FREE FOR THE TAKING!

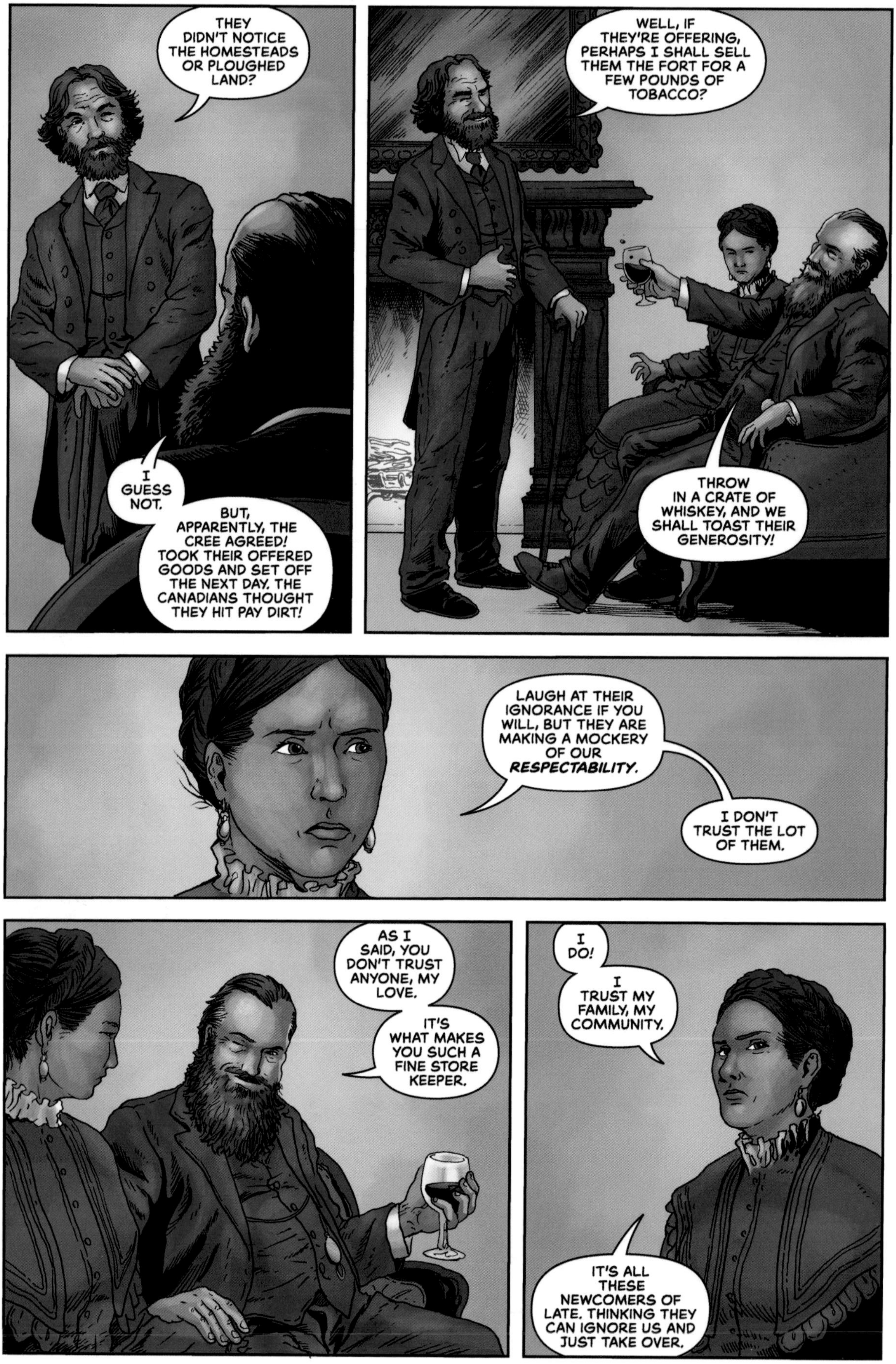
THEY DIDN'T NOTICE THE HOMESTEADS OR PLOUGHED LAND?
I GUESS NOT.
BUT, APPARENTLY, THE CREE AGREED! TOOK THEIR OFFERED GOODS AND SET OFF THE NEXT DAY. THE CANADIANS THOUGHT THEY HIT PAY DIRT!
WELL, IF THEY'RE OFFERING, PERHAPS I SHALL SELL THEM THE FORT FOR A FEW POUNDS OF TOBACCO?
THROW IN A CRATE OF WHISKEY, AND WE SHALL TOAST THEIR GENEROSITY!
LAUGH AT THEIR IGNORANCE IF YOU WILL, BUT THEY ARE MAKING A MOCKERY OF OUR RESPECTABILITY.
I DON'T TRUST THE LOT OF THEM.
AS I SAID, YOU DON'T TRUST ANYONE, MY LOVE.
IT'S WHAT MAKES YOU SUCH A FINE STORE KEEPER.
I DO!
I TRUST MY FAMILY, MY COMMUNITY.
IT'S ALL THESE NEWCOMERS OF LATE. THINKING THEY CAN IGNORE US AND JUST TAKE OVER.

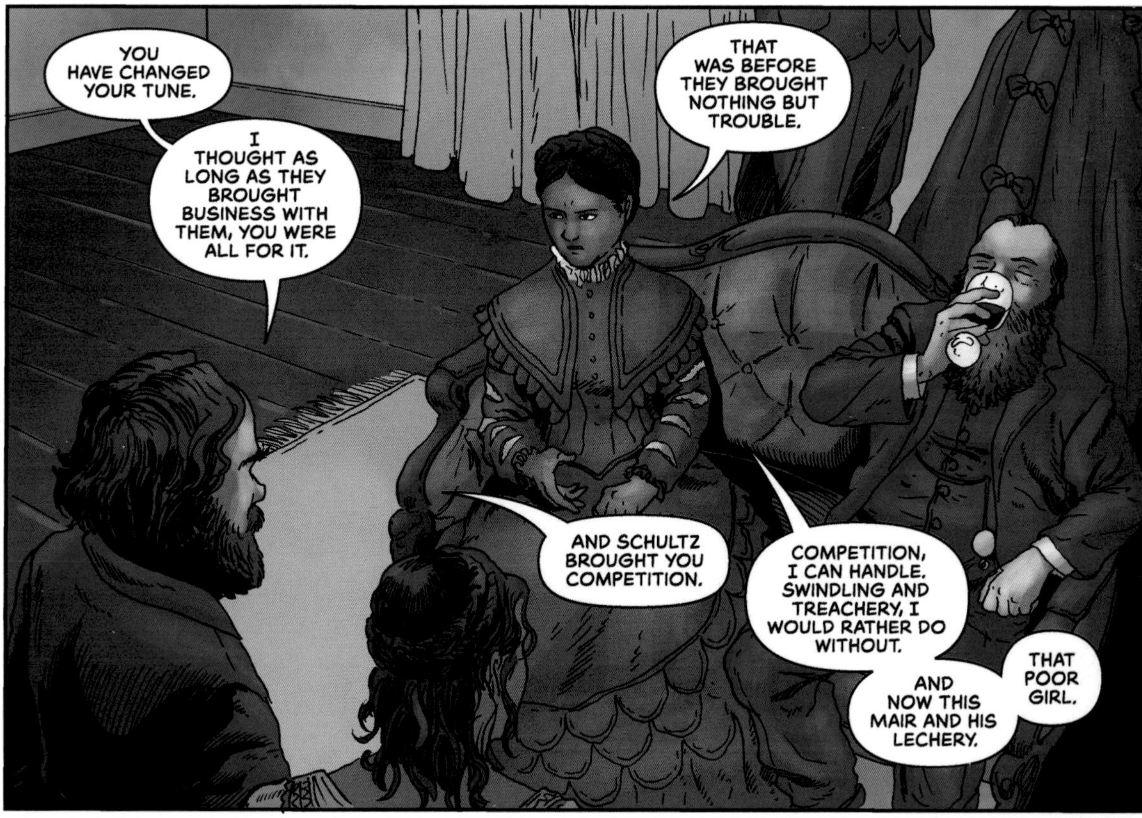
YOU HAVE CHANGED YOUR TUNE.
I THOUGHT AS LONG AS THEY BROUGHT BUSINESS WITH THEM, YOU WERE ALL FOR IT.
THAT WAS BEFORE THEY BROUGHT NOTHING BUT TROUBLE.
AND SCHULTZ BROUGHT YOU COMPETITION.
COMPETITION, I CAN HANDLE. SWINDLING AND TREACHERY, I WOULD RATHER DO WITHOUT.
AND NOW THIS MAIR AND HIS LECHERY.
THAT POOR GIRL.

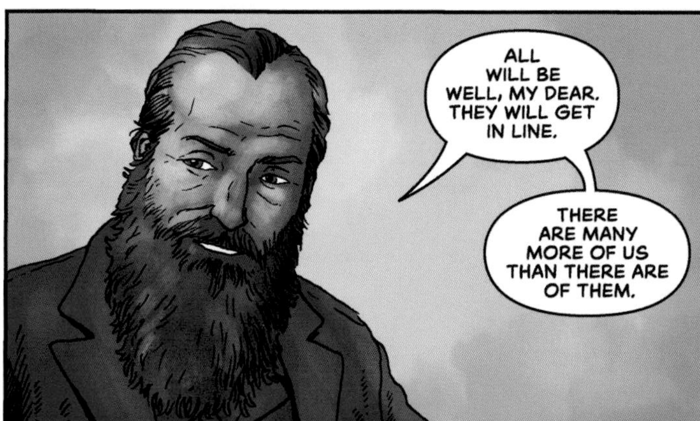
ALL WILL BE WELL, MY DEAR. THEY WILL GET IN LINE.
THERE ARE MANY MORE OF US THAN THERE ARE OF THEM.

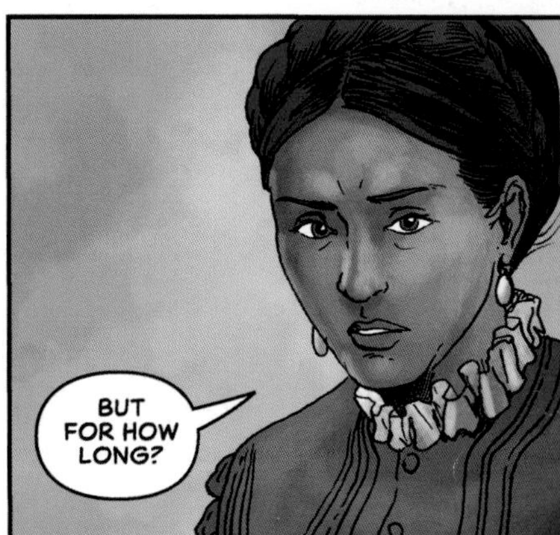
BUT FOR HOW LONG?

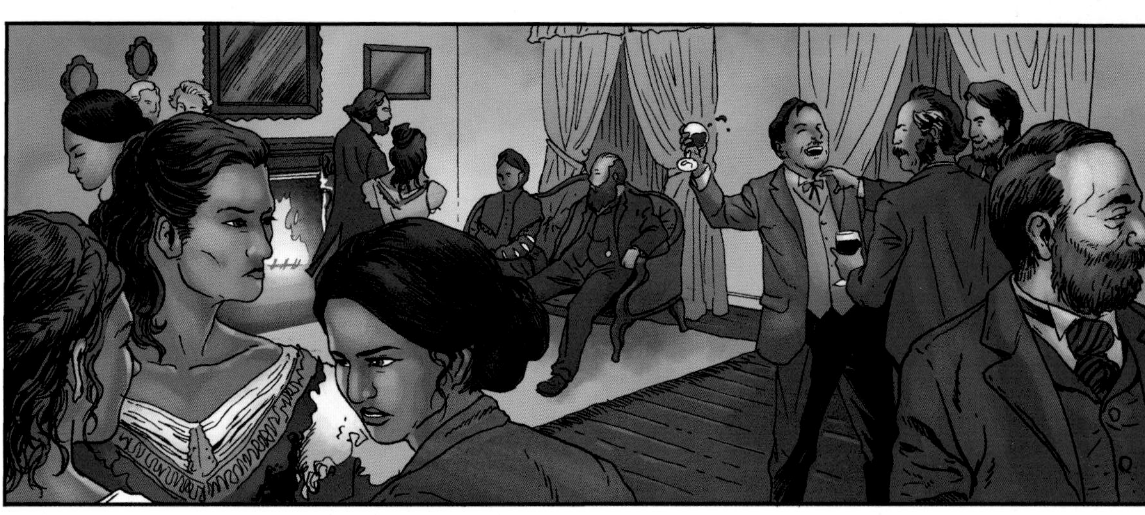

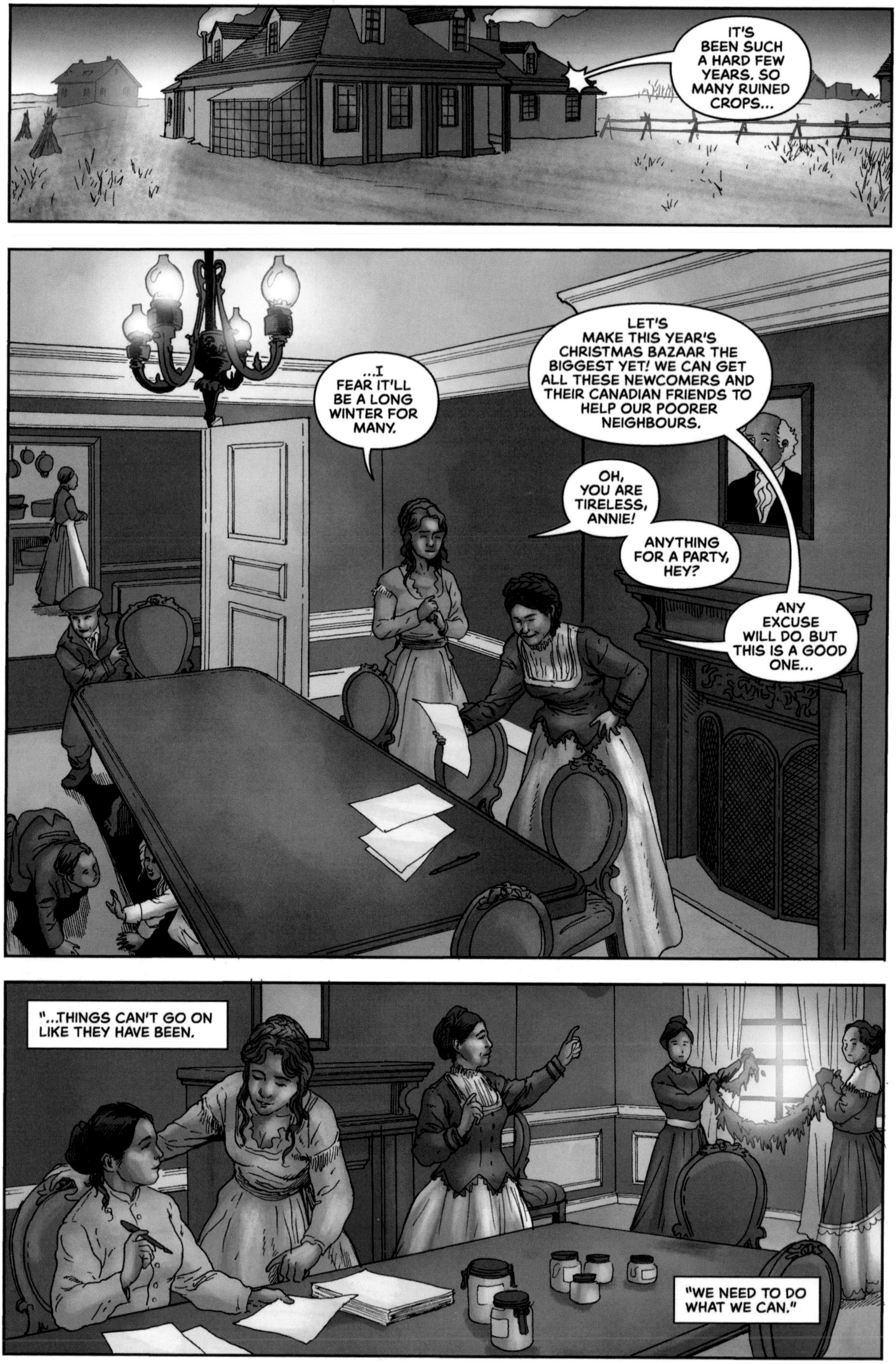

IT'S BEEN SUCH A HARD FEW YEARS. SO MANY RUINED CROPS...
...I FEAR IT'LL BE A LONG WINTER FOR MANY.
LET'S MAKE THIS YEAR'S CHRISTMAS BAZAAR THE BIGGEST YET! WE CAN GET ALL THESE NEWCOMERS AND THEIR CANADIAN FRIENDS TO HELP OUR POORER NEIGHBOURS.
OH, YOU ARE TIRELESS, ANNIE!
ANYTHING FOR A PARTY, HEY?
ANY EXCUSE WILL DO. BUT THIS IS A GOOD ONE...
"...THINGS CAN'T GO ON LIKE THEY HAVE BEEN.
"WE NEED TO DO WHAT WE CAN."

After putting up at the Dutchman's hotel there, I went over and stayed at Dr. Schultz's, after a few days.

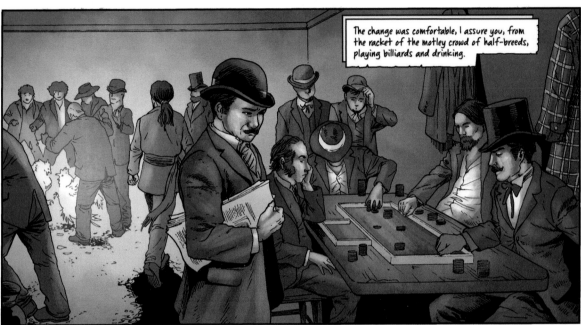
The change was comfortable, I assure you, from the racket of the motley crowd of half-breeds, playing billiards and drinking.

Many wealthy people are married to half-breed women, who, having no coat of arms but a 'totem' to look back to, make up for the deficiency by biting the backs of their 'white' sisters.

The white sisters fall back upon their whiteness, whilst the husbands treat each other with desperate courtesies and hospitalities, with a view to filthy lucre in the background.

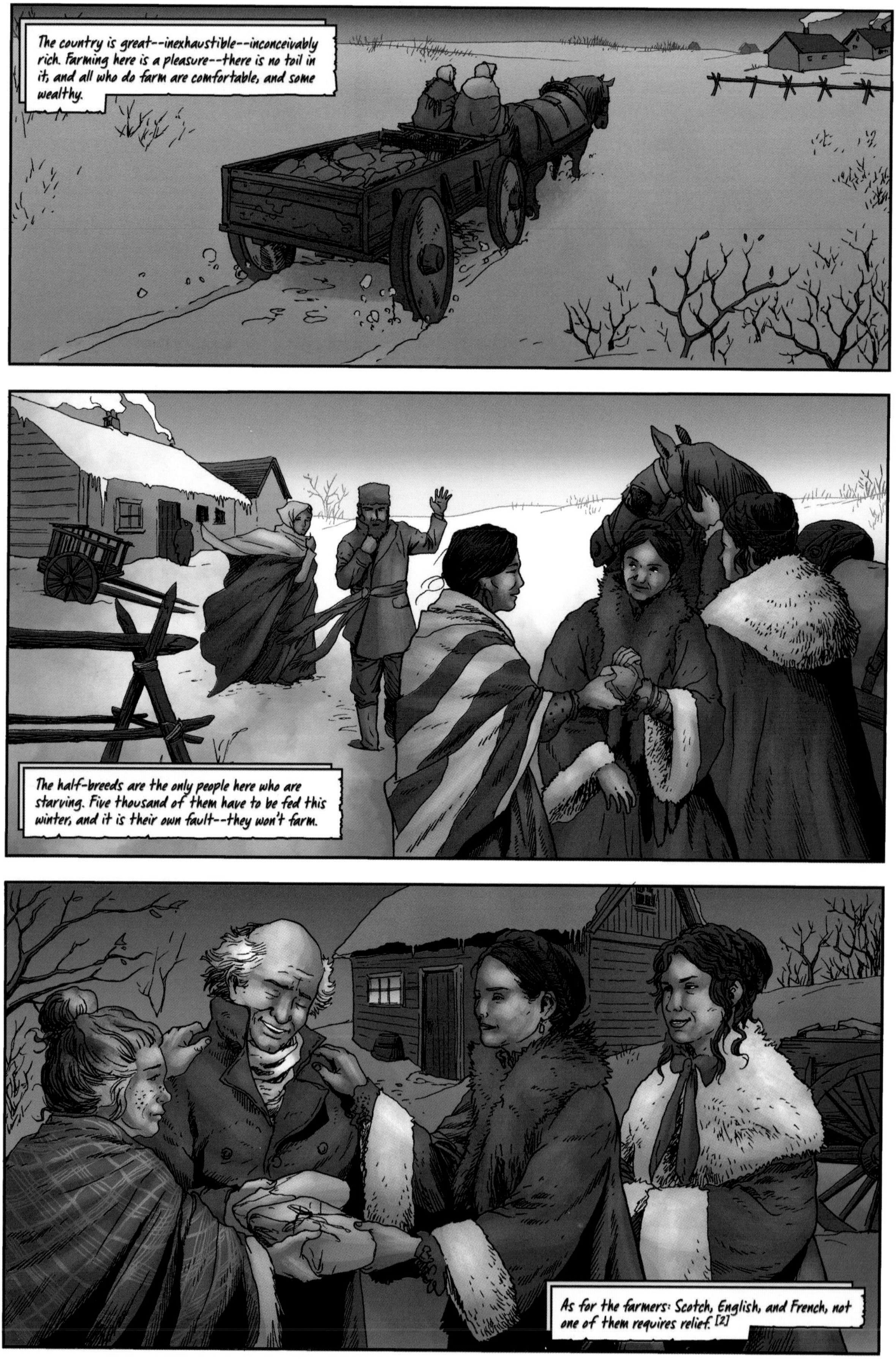
The country is great--inexhaustible--inconceivably rich. Farming here is a pleasure--there is no toil in it, and all who do farm are comfortable, and some wealthy.
The half-breeds are the only people here who are starving. Five thousand of them have to be fed this winter, and it is their own fault--they won't farm.
As for the farmers: Scotch, English, and French, not one of them requires relief. [2]

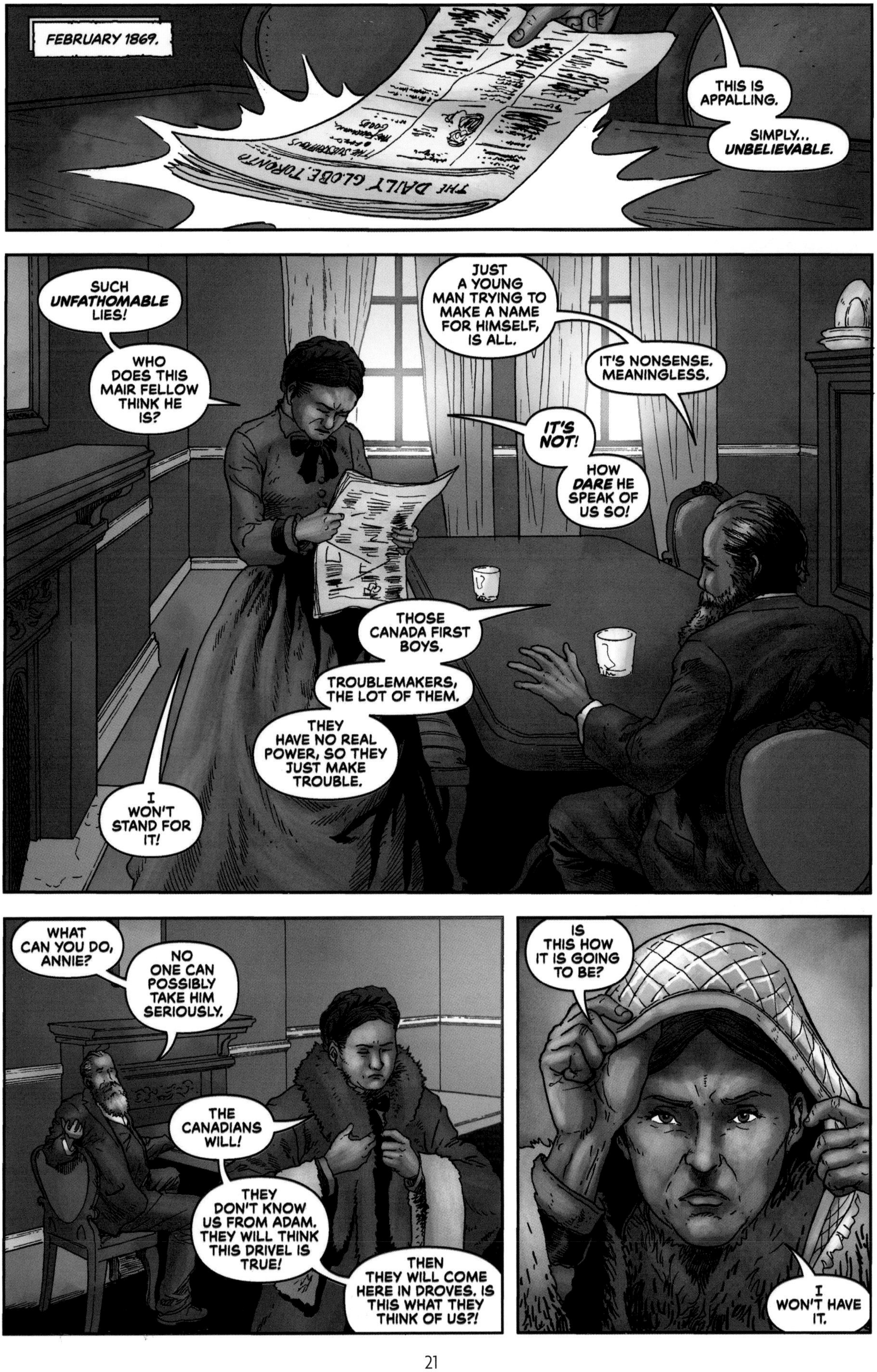
FEBRUARY 1869.
THE DAILY GLOBE. TORONTO
THIS IS APPALLING.
SIMPLY... UNBELIEVABLE.
SUCH UNFATHOMABLE LIES!
WHO DOES THIS MAIR FELLOW THINK HE IS?
JUST A YOUNG MAN TRYING TO MAKE A NAME FOR HIMSELF, IS ALL.
IT'S NONSENSE. MEANINGLESS.
IT'S NOT!
HOW DARE HE SPEAK OF US SO!
THOSE CANADA FIRST BOYS.
TROUBLEMAKERS, THE LOT OF THEM.
THEY HAVE NO REAL POWER, SO THEY JUST MAKE TROUBLE.
I WON'T STAND FOR IT!
WHAT CAN YOU DO, ANNIE?
NO ONE CAN POSSIBLY TAKE HIM SERIOUSLY.
THE CANADIANS WILL!
THEY DON'T KNOW US FROM ADAM. THEY WILL THINK THIS DRIVEL IS TRUE!
THEN THEY WILL COME HERE IN DROVES. IS THIS WHAT THEY THINK OF US?!
IS THIS HOW IT IS GOING TO BE?
I WON'T HAVE IT.

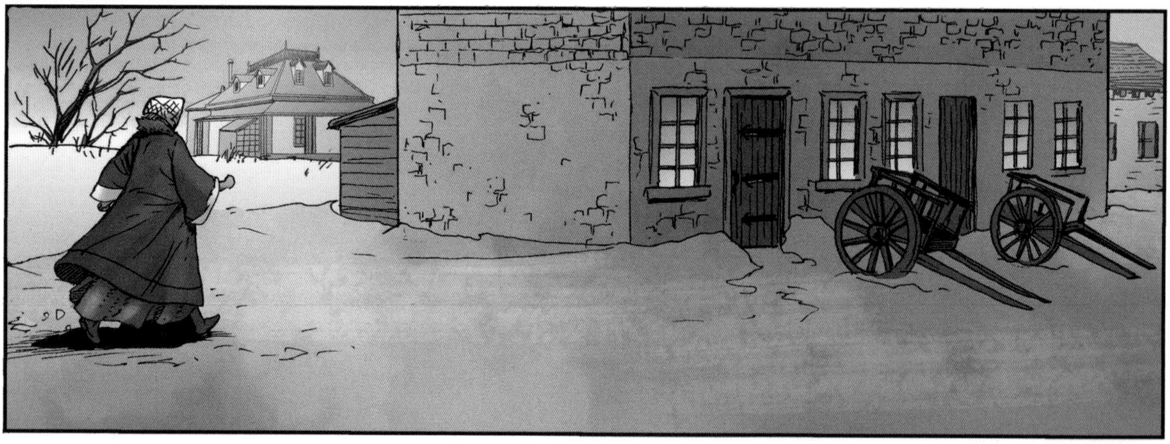

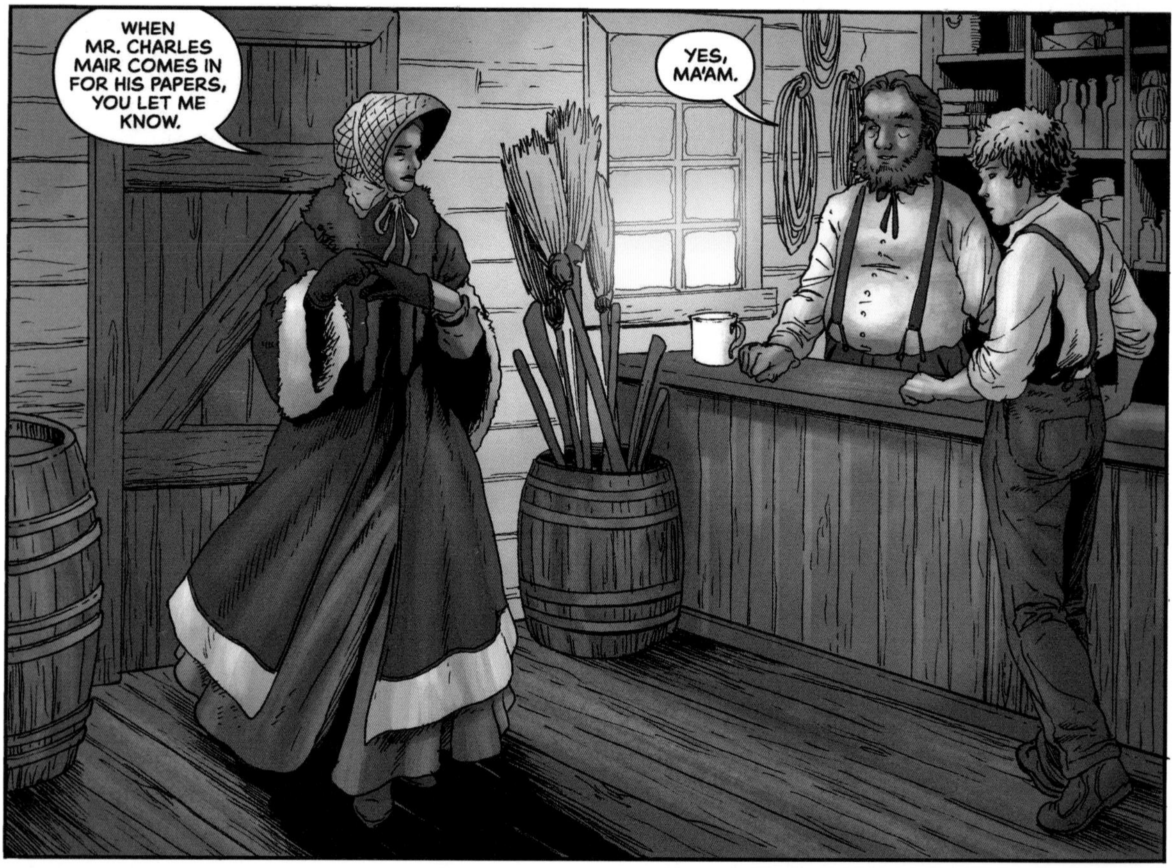
WHEN MR. CHARLES MAIR COMES IN FOR HIS PAPERS, YOU LET ME KNOW.
YES, MA'AM.

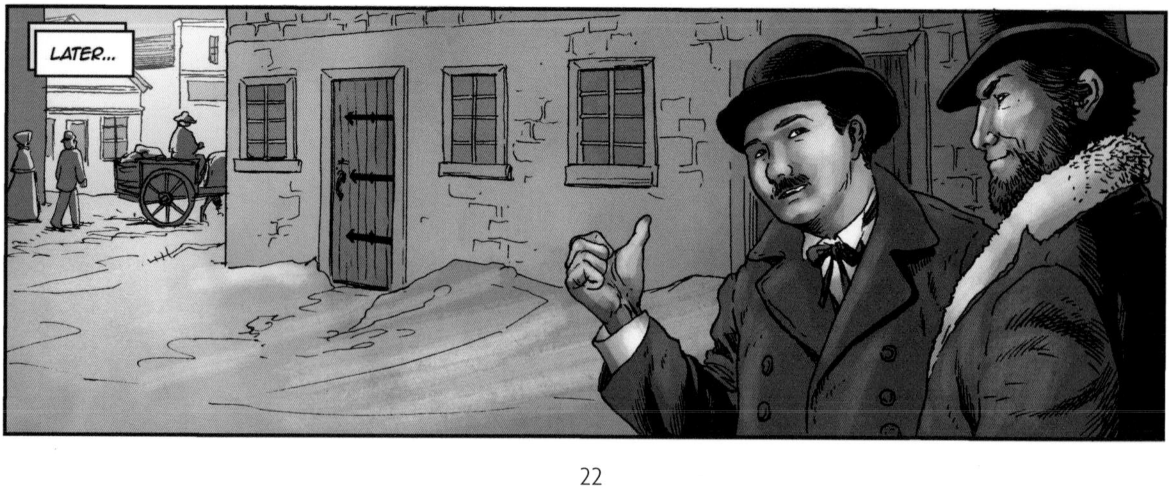
LATER...

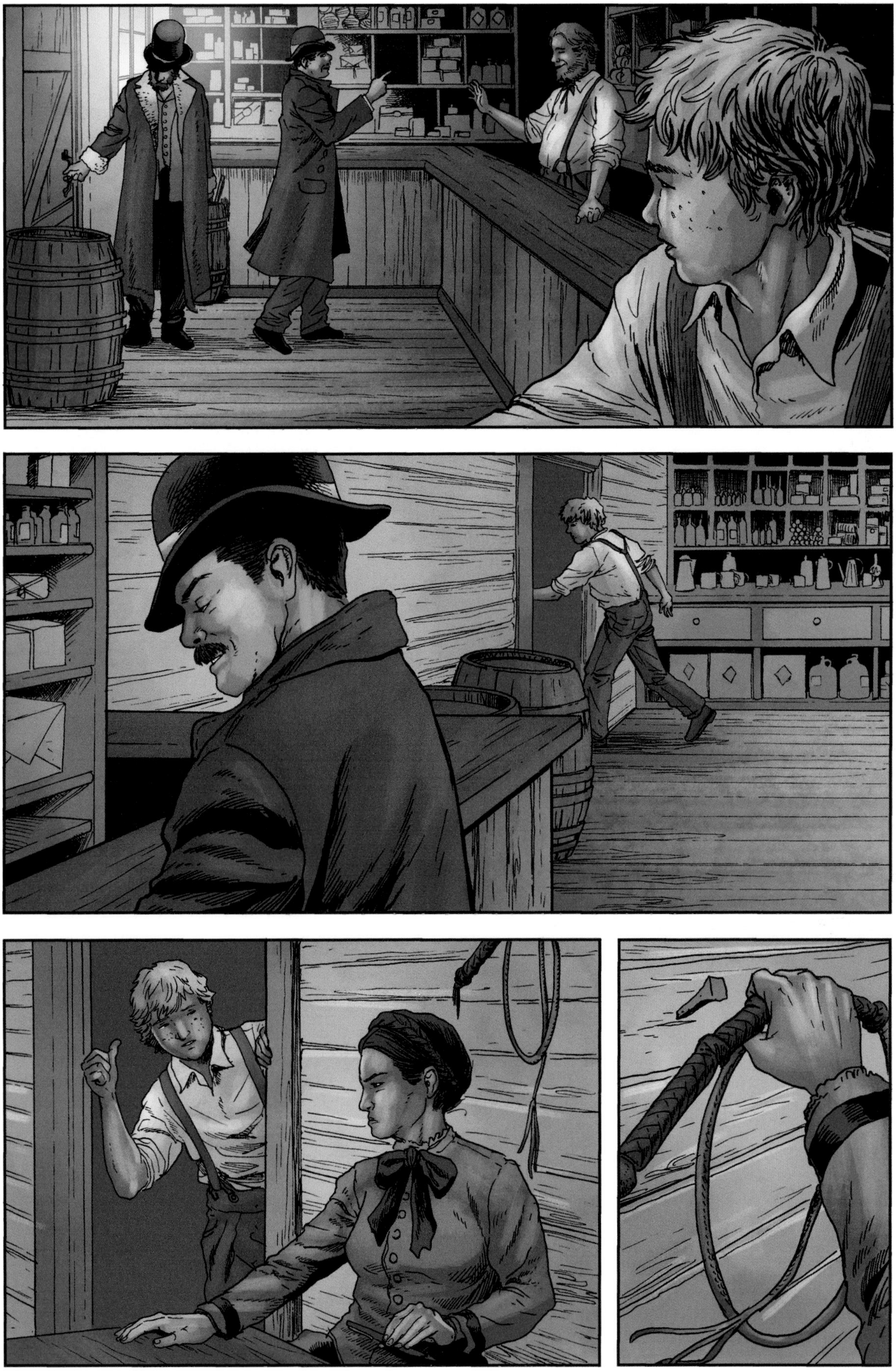

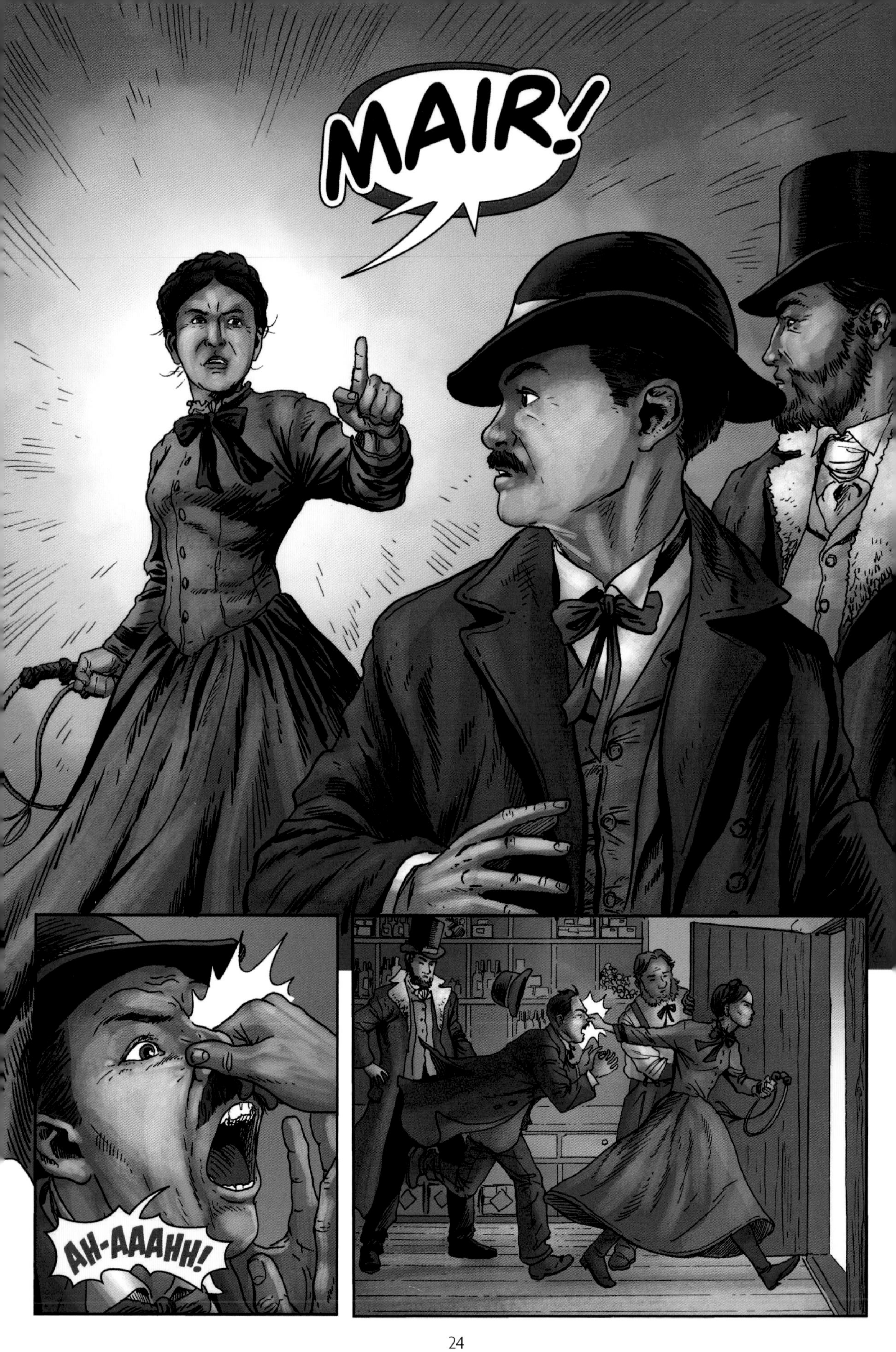
MAIR!
AH-AAAHH!

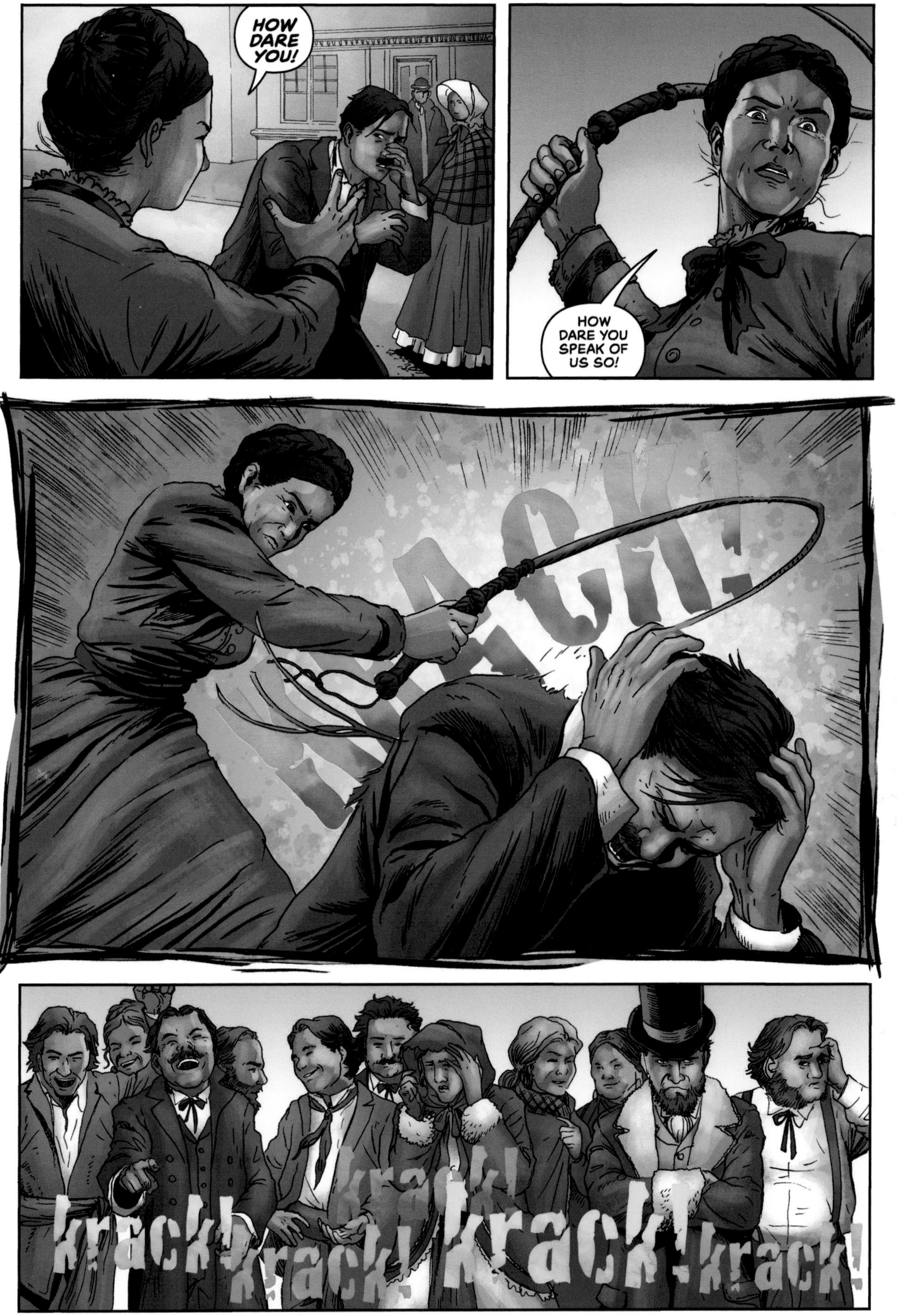
HOW DARE YOU!
HOW DARE YOU SPEAK OF US SO!
krack!
krack!
krack!
KRACK!
krack!

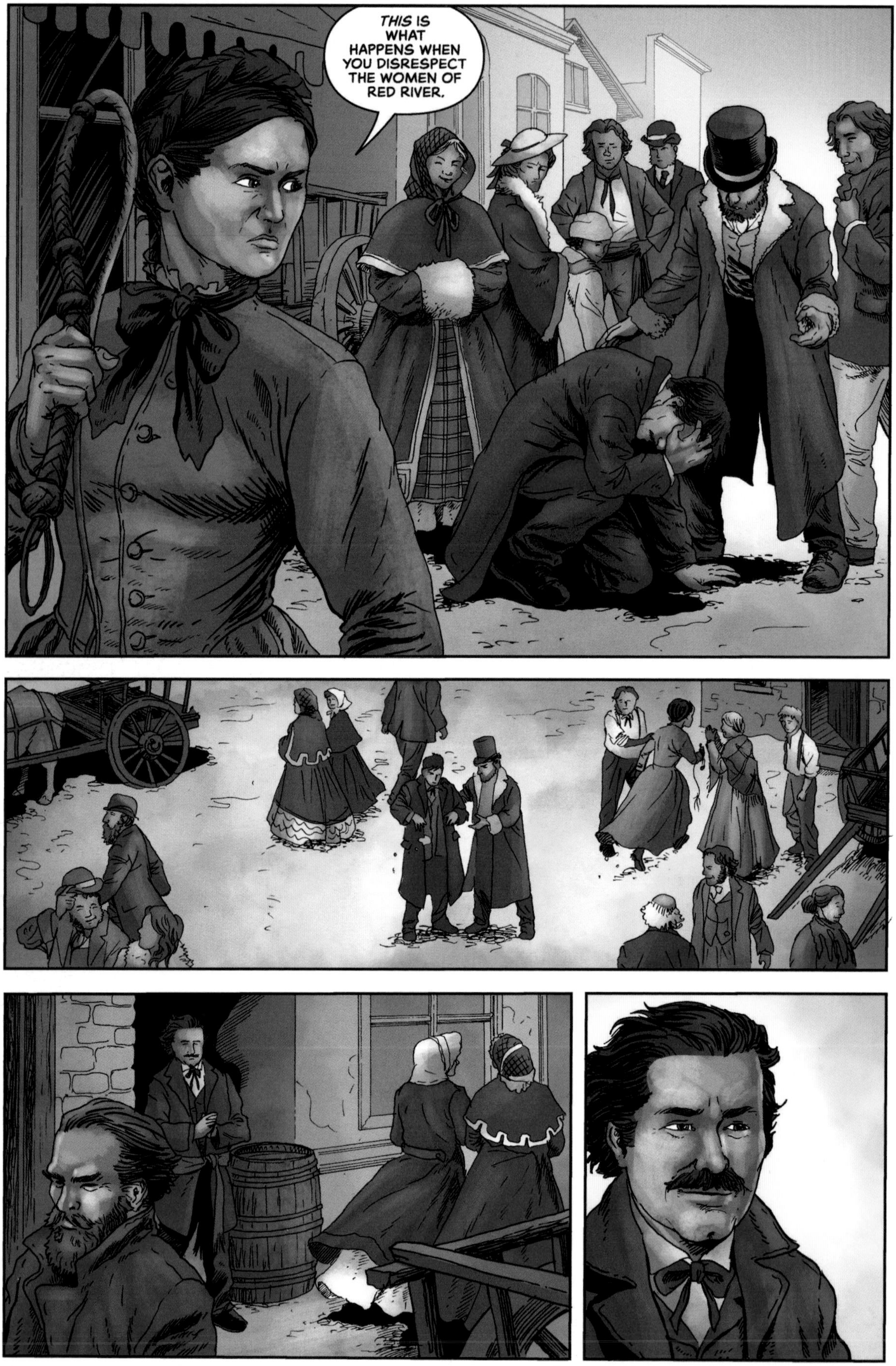
THIS IS WHAT HAPPENS WHEN YOU DISRESPECT THE WOMEN OF RED RIVER.

My great-great-grandfather, Chief Billy Assu, has been an important figure in my life and work for the better part of a decade. He inspired the *Chilkat Series, Ellipsis, Silenced: The Burning, Gone Copper!* and *Billy and the Chiefs: The Complete Banned Collection.* He died in 1966, but I met him in 2010.

I was heading to Ottawa for a reason I can't remember. An exhibit or an art jury, I think. My grandmother, Mitzi, said to me, "You know, your grandfather's regalia is there." I had no clue. "At the Museum of Man," she said, "or whatever they call it now."

She told me the story of how, on his death-bed, Chief Billy Assu passed down his regalia to his eldest grandson, Herbie. "Billy sent someone to get the regalia." Mitzi remembered. "He gave it to Herbie and said, 'It's yours now'."

You should go see it." Mitzi said to me over coffee and those blue-tinned butter cookies. "I'll write you a letter, saying you are my grandson and that you can try it on."

And I did. There I was, standing in an anthropology-white room with a couple of museum folk looking at each other. Then looking at me. Questioning. "Can we do this? Is he allowed? Are we allowed…?"

"Um, yeah, my gramma said. I've got a letter."

When the regalia was placed on my shoulders, the ancestors passed through me. I welled up; I almost cried.

Okay, I did cry a little.

Sonny Assu (Ǧʷaʔǧʷadəx̌ə)

1862
Smallpox epidemic decimates about 60% of Indigenous populations in British Columbia.

1885
Indian Act amendment bans the potlatch.

1885
Canadian Pacific Railway arrives on the west coast.

1887
The Crown declares its ownership of Nisga'a lands, in violation of a previous agreement from 1763. The stolen lands are opened for settlers.

1888
The Federal Fisheries Act bans Indigenous people from participating in the salmon fishery.

1888
Skeena River Uprising

Tilted Ground

Sonny Assu

Illustration: Kyle Charles

Colours: Scott A. Ford

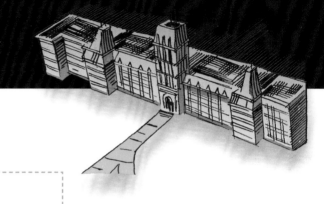

1890s
Missionaries, believing totem poles to be a form of "idol worship," pressure West Coast Indigenous peoples to stop creating them and to destroy the existing poles.

1897
The Klondike Gold Rush begins.

1951
The potlatch ban ends.

1899
By 1899, the first eight treaties are signed.

1900
Tlingit-English ethnologist George Hunt is arrested for dancing with the Hamatsa (a Kwakwaka'wakw secret society). Hunt claims he was just doing anthropology, and with Franz Boas corroborating, he is eventually released.

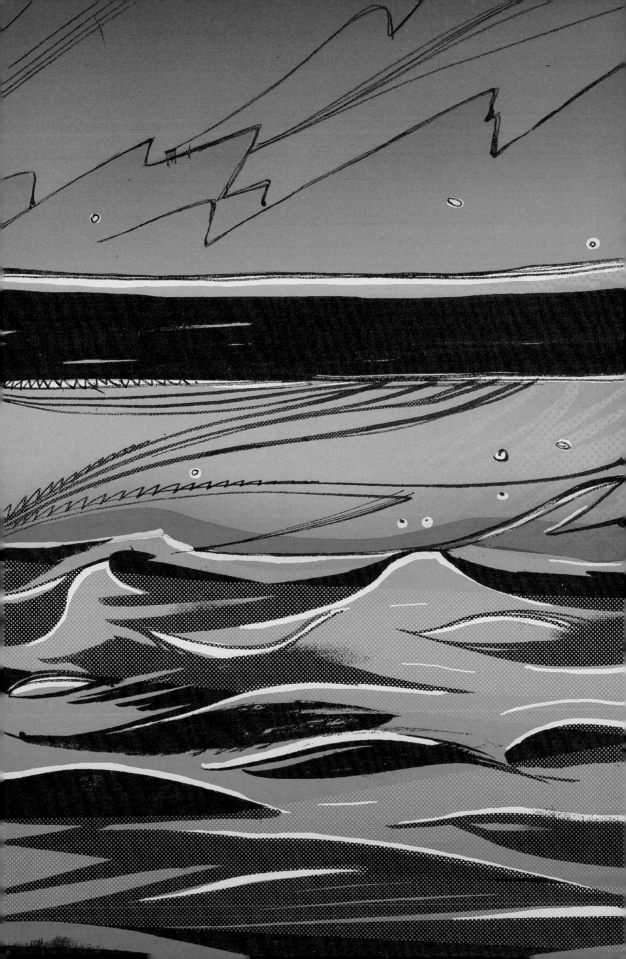

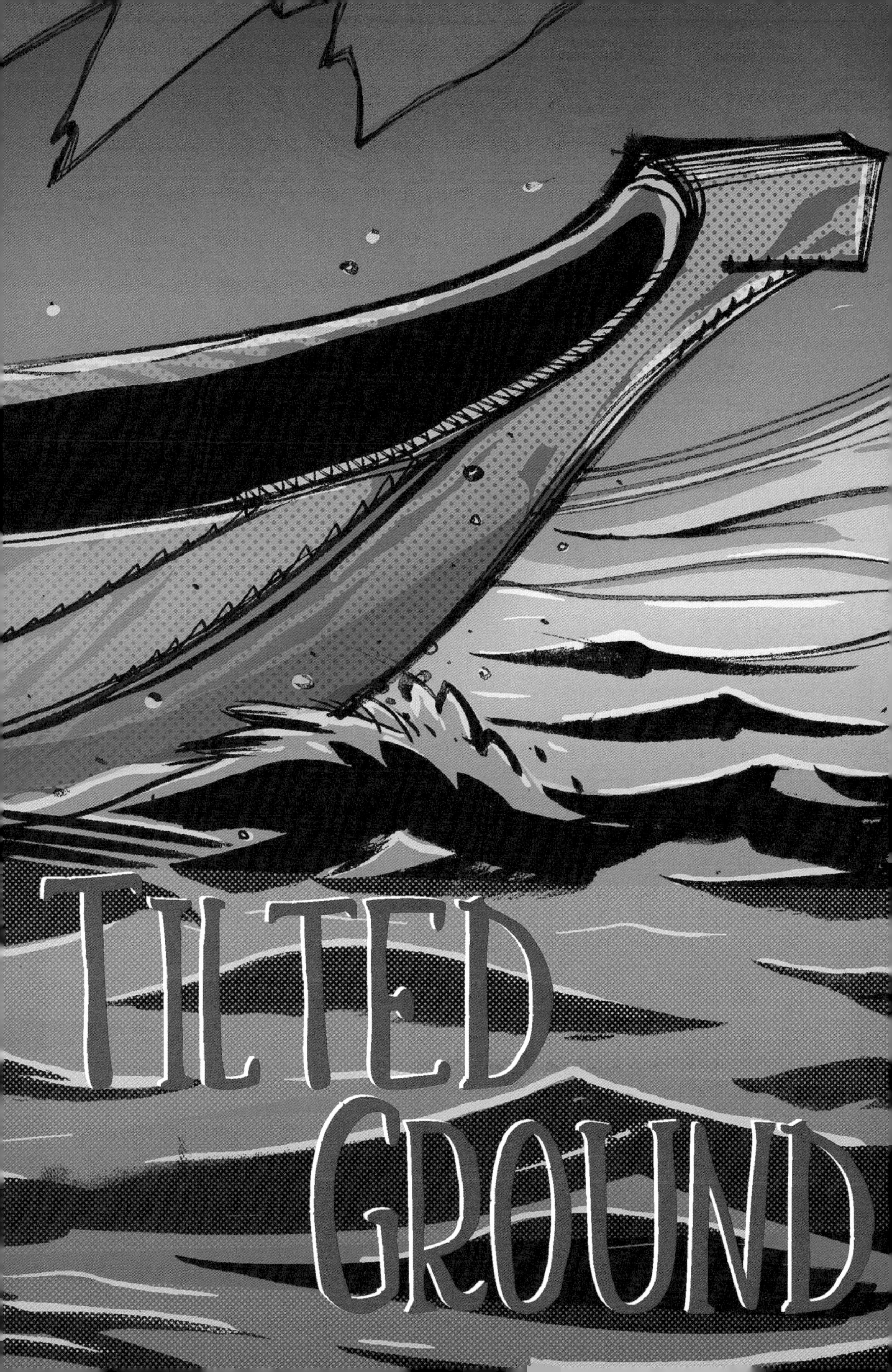
TILTED
GROUND

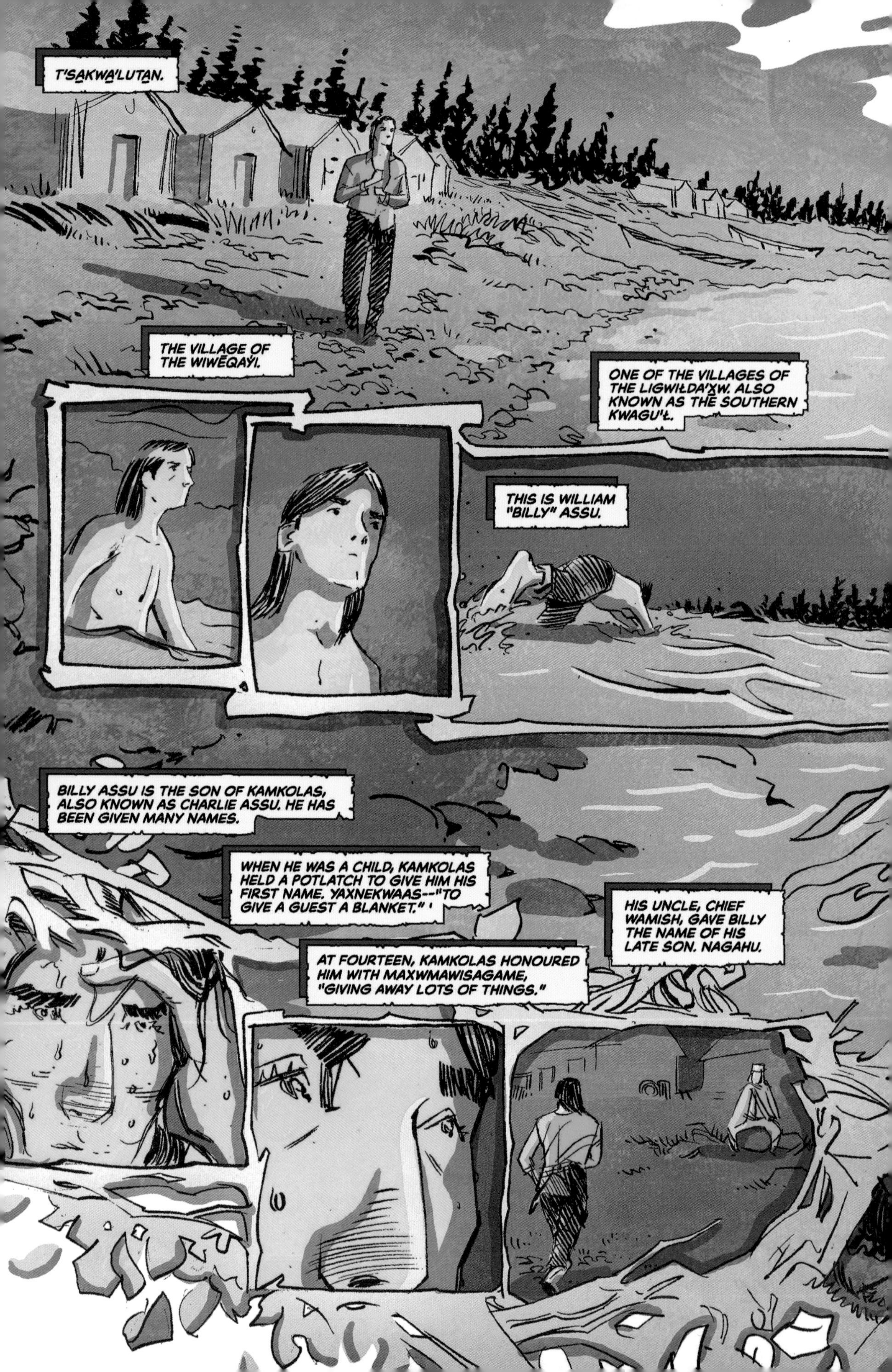
T'SA̲KWA̲'LUTA̲N.
THE VILLAGE OF THE WIWĒQAY̓I.
ONE OF THE VILLAGES OF THE LIGWIŁDA'X̱W. ALSO KNOWN AS THE SOUTHERN KWAGU'Ł.
THIS IS WILLIAM "BILLY" ASSU.
BILLY ASSU IS THE SON OF KAMKOLAS, ALSO KNOWN AS CHARLIE ASSU. HE HAS BEEN GIVEN MANY NAMES.
WHEN HE WAS A CHILD, KAMKOLAS HELD A POTLATCH TO GIVE HIM HIS FIRST NAME. YAXNEKWAAS--"TO GIVE A GUEST A BLANKET."
HIS UNCLE, CHIEF WAMISH, GAVE BILLY THE NAME OF HIS LATE SON. NAGAHU.
AT FOURTEEN, KAMKOLAS HONOURED HIM WITH MAXWMAWISAGAME, "GIVING AWAY LOTS OF THINGS."

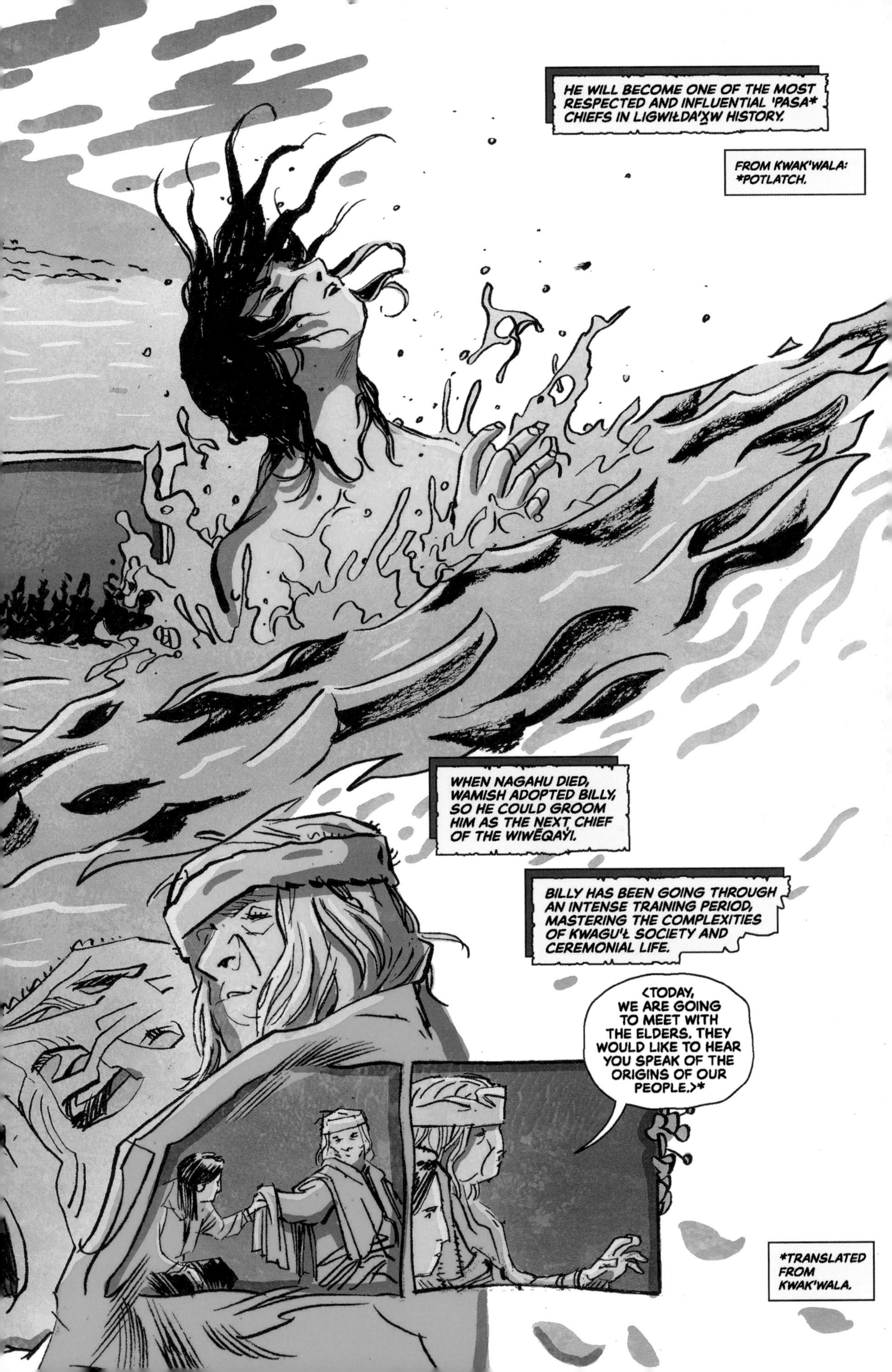
HE WILL BECOME ONE OF THE MOST RESPECTED AND INFLUENTIAL 'PASA* CHIEFS IN LIGWIŁDA'X̱W HISTORY.
FROM KWAK'WALA: *POTLATCH.
WHEN NAGAHU DIED, WAMISH ADOPTED BILLY, SO HE COULD GROOM HIM AS THE NEXT CHIEF OF THE WIWĒQAY̓I.
BILLY HAS BEEN GOING THROUGH AN INTENSE TRAINING PERIOD, MASTERING THE COMPLEXITIES OF KWAGU'Ł SOCIETY AND CEREMONIAL LIFE.
<TODAY, WE ARE GOING TO MEET WITH THE ELDERS. THEY WOULD LIKE TO HEAR YOU SPEAK OF THE ORIGINS OF OUR PEOPLE.>*
*TRANSLATED FROM KWAK'WALA.

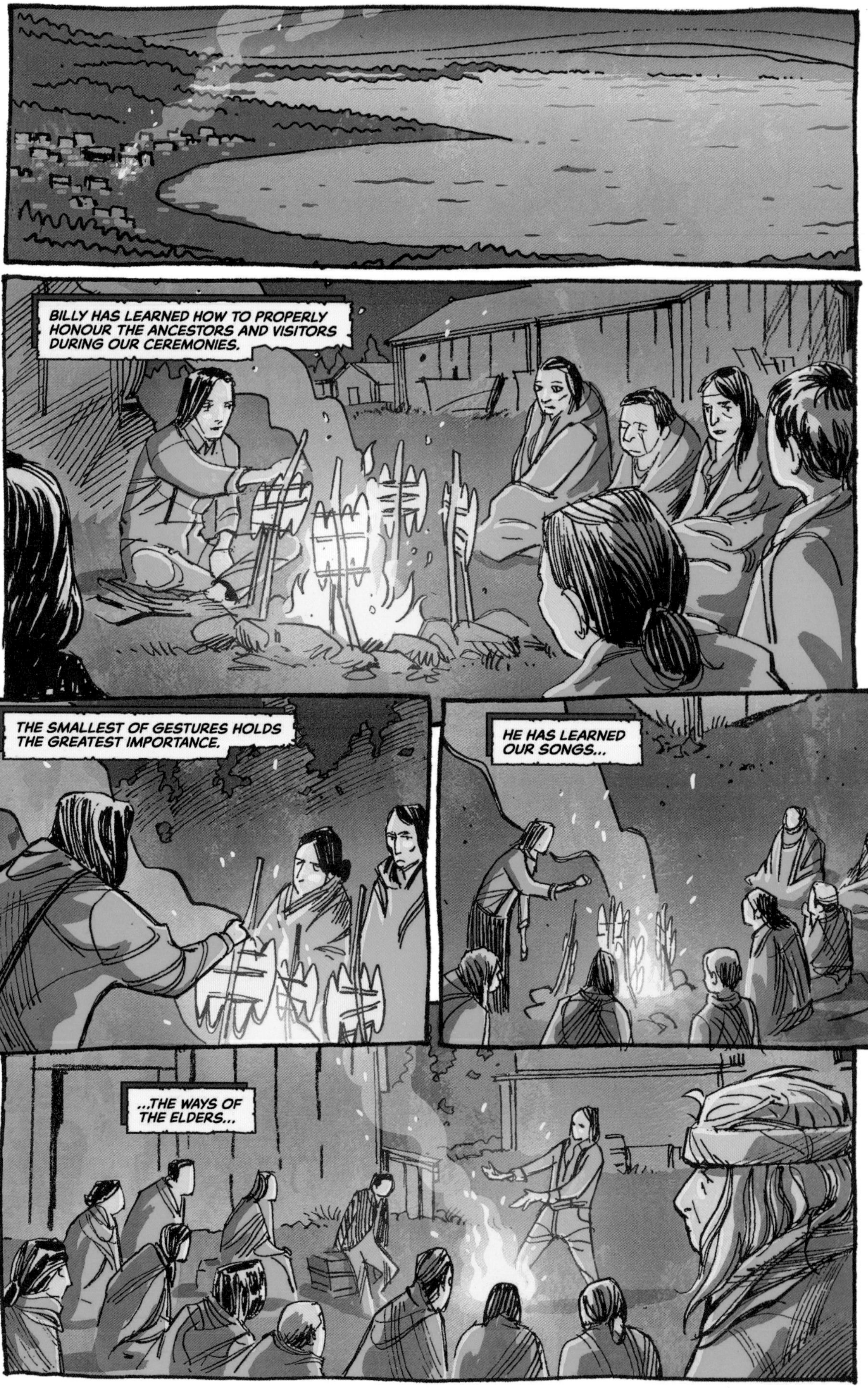
BILLY HAS LEARNED HOW TO PROPERLY HONOUR THE ANCESTORS AND VISITORS DURING OUR CEREMONIES.
THE SMALLEST OF GESTURES HOLDS THE GREATEST IMPORTANCE.
HE HAS LEARNED OUR SONGS...
...THE WAYS OF THE ELDERS...

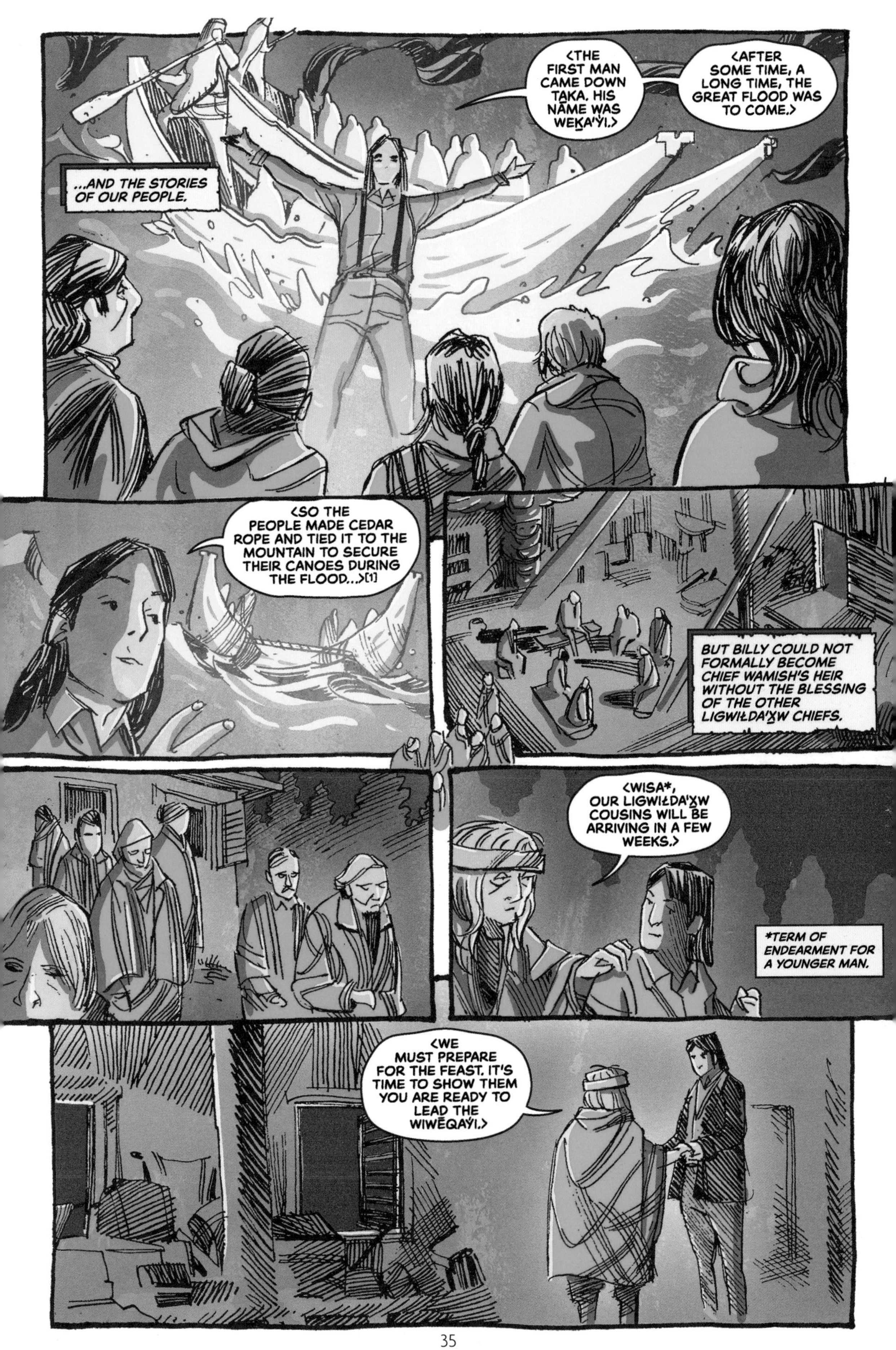
<THE FIRST MAN CAME DOWN TA̱KA. HIS NA̱ME WAS WEḴA'YI.>
<AFTER SOME TIME, A LONG TIME, THE GREAT FLOOD WAS TO COME.>
...AND THE STORIES OF OUR PEOPLE.
<SO THE PEOPLE MADE CEDAR ROPE AND TIED IT TO THE MOUNTAIN TO SECURE THEIR CANOES DURING THE FLOOD...>[1]
BUT BILLY COULD NOT FORMALLY BECOME CHIEF WAMISH'S HEIR WITHOUT THE BLESSING OF THE OTHER LIGWIŁDA'X̱W CHIEFS.
<WISA*, OUR LIGWIŁDA'X̱W COUSINS WILL BE ARRIVING IN A FEW WEEKS.>
*TERM OF ENDEARMENT FOR A YOUNGER MAN.
<WE MUST PREPARE FOR THE FEAST. IT'S TIME TO SHOW THEM YOU ARE READY TO LEAD THE WIWĒQAY̓I.>

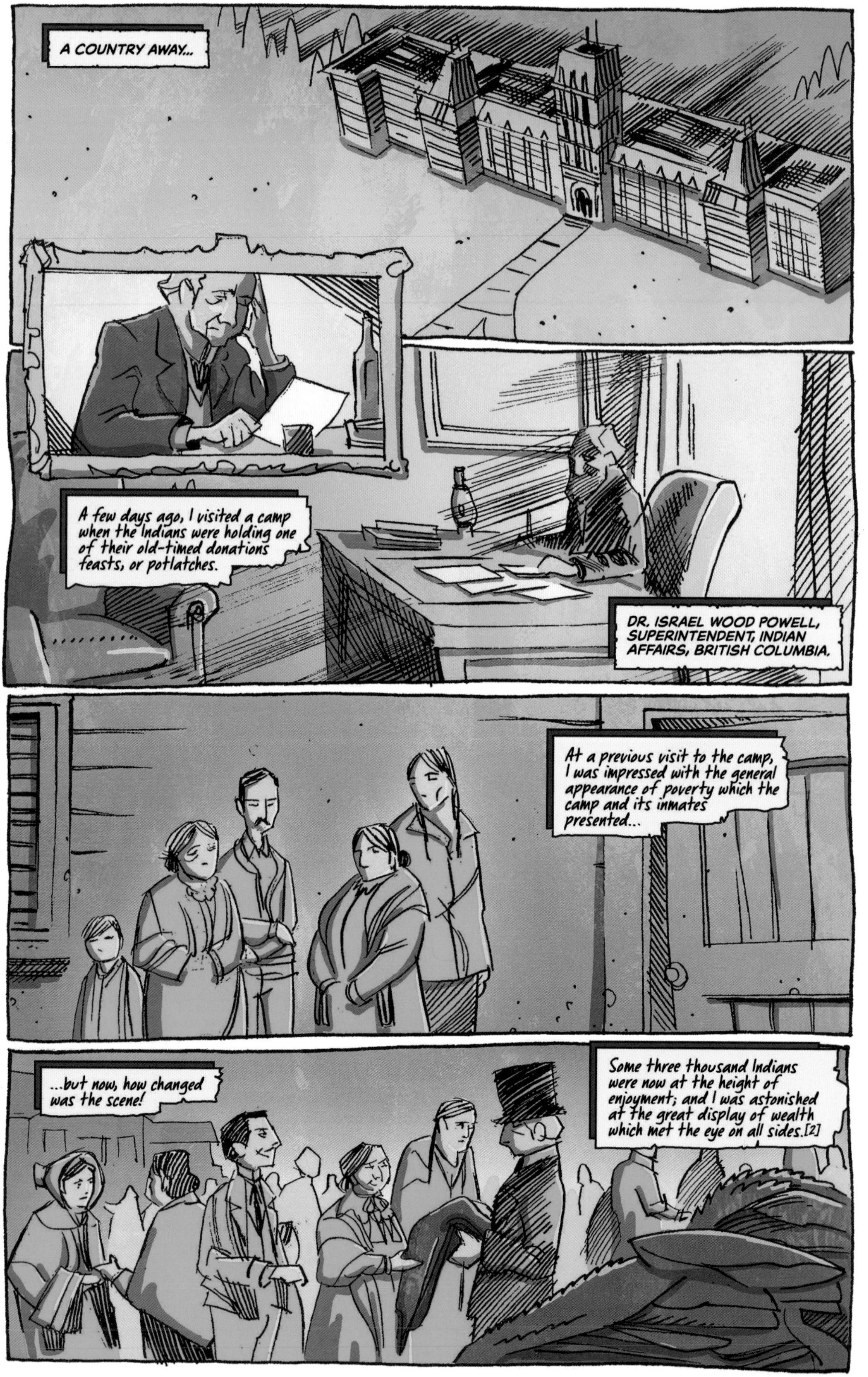
A COUNTRY AWAY...
A few days ago, I visited a camp when the Indians were holding one of their old-timed donations feasts, or potlatches.
DR. ISRAEL WOOD POWELL, SUPERINTENDENT, INDIAN AFFAIRS, BRITISH COLUMBIA.
At a previous visit to the camp, I was impressed with the general appearance of poverty which the camp and its inmates presented...
...but now, how changed was the scene!
Some three thousand Indians were now at the height of enjoyment; and I was astonished at the great display of wealth which met the eye on all sides.[2]

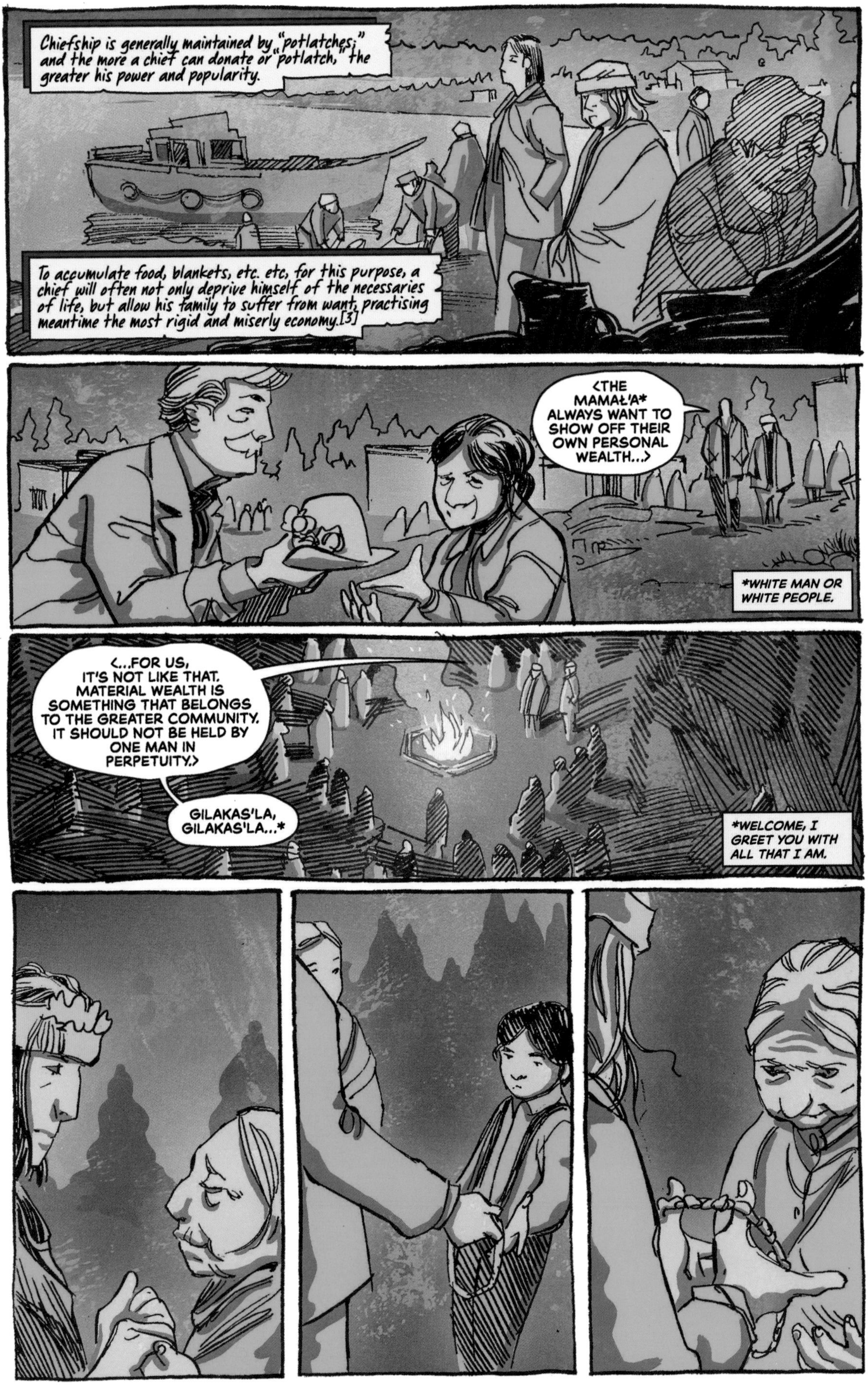
Chiefship is generally maintained by "potlatches," and the more a chief can donate or "potlatch," the greater his power and popularity.
To accumulate food, blankets, etc. etc, for this purpose, a chief will often not only deprive himself of the necessaries of life, but allow his family to suffer from want, practising meantime the most rigid and miserly economy.[3]
<THE MAMAŁ'A* ALWAYS WANT TO SHOW OFF THEIR OWN PERSONAL WEALTH...>
*WHITE MAN OR WHITE PEOPLE.
<...FOR US, IT'S NOT LIKE THAT. MATERIAL WEALTH IS SOMETHING THAT BELONGS TO THE GREATER COMMUNITY. IT SHOULD NOT BE HELD BY ONE MAN IN PERPETUITY.>
GILAKAS'LA, GILAKAS'LA...*
*WELCOME, I GREET YOU WITH ALL THAT I AM.

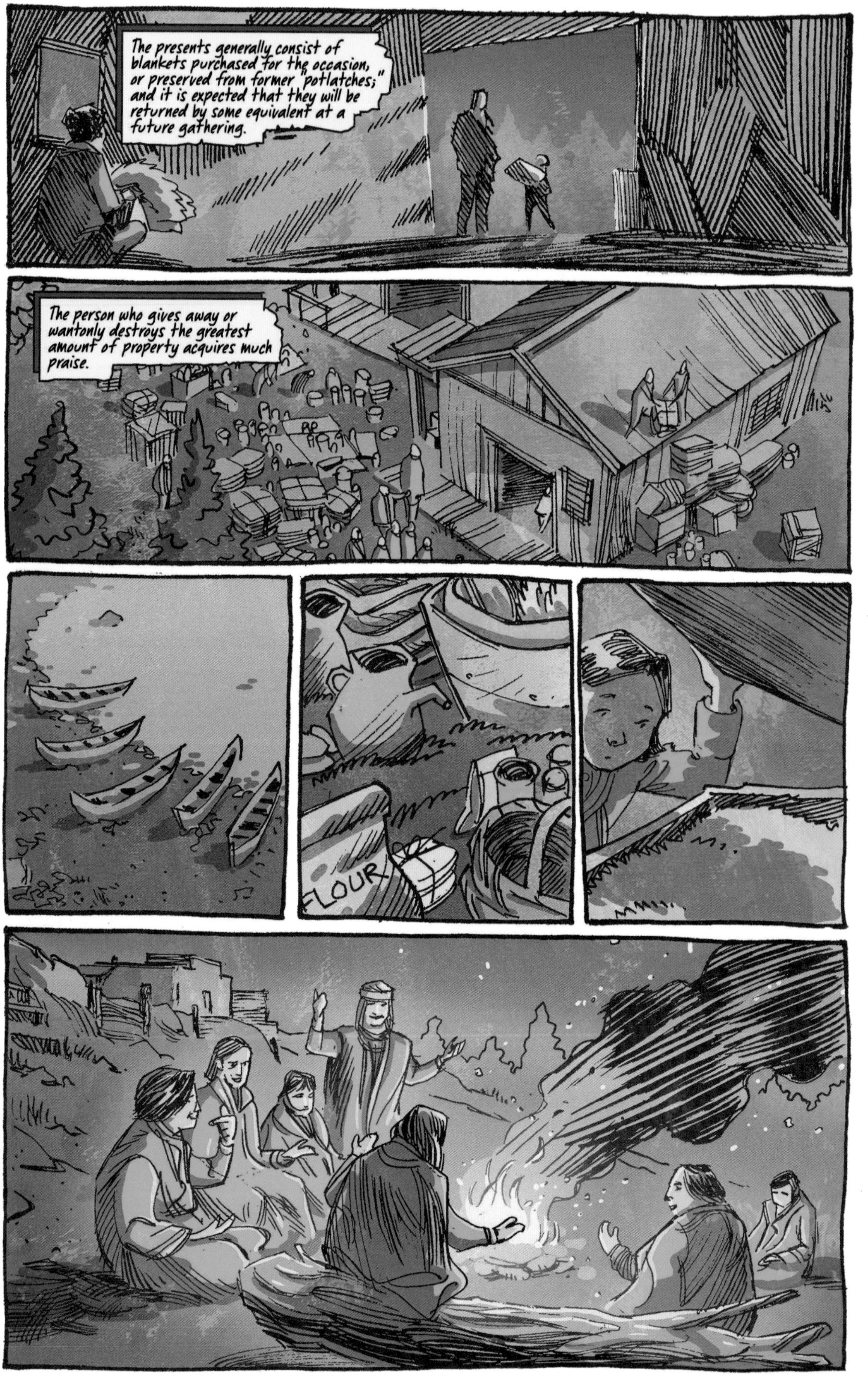
The presents generally consist of blankets purchased for the occasion, or preserved from former "potlatches;" and it is expected that they will be returned by some equivalent at a future gathering.
The person who gives away or wantonly destroys the greatest amount of property acquires much praise.
FLOUR

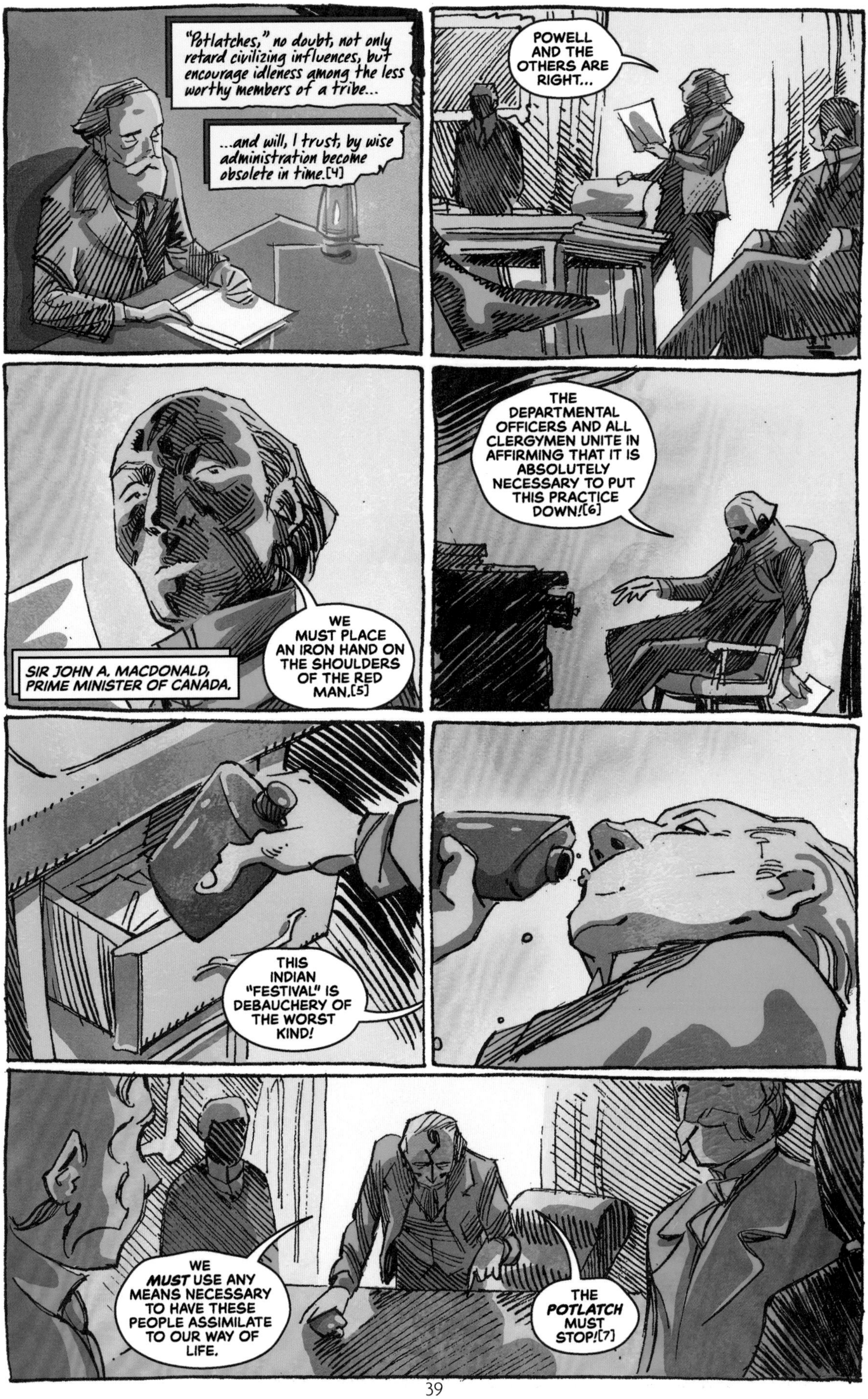
"Potlatches," no doubt, not only retard civilizing influences, but encourage idleness among the less worthy members of a tribe...
...and will, I trust, by wise administration become obsolete in time.[4]
POWELL AND THE OTHERS ARE RIGHT...
SIR JOHN A. MACDONALD, PRIME MINISTER OF CANADA.
WE MUST PLACE AN IRON HAND ON THE SHOULDERS OF THE RED MAN.[5]
THE DEPARTMENTAL OFFICERS AND ALL CLERGYMEN UNITE IN AFFIRMING THAT IT IS ABSOLUTELY NECESSARY TO PUT THIS PRACTICE DOWN![6]
THIS INDIAN "FESTIVAL" IS DEBAUCHERY OF THE WORST KIND!
WE *MUST* USE ANY MEANS NECESSARY TO HAVE THESE PEOPLE ASSIMILATE TO OUR WAY OF LIFE.
THE *POTLATCH* MUST STOP![7]

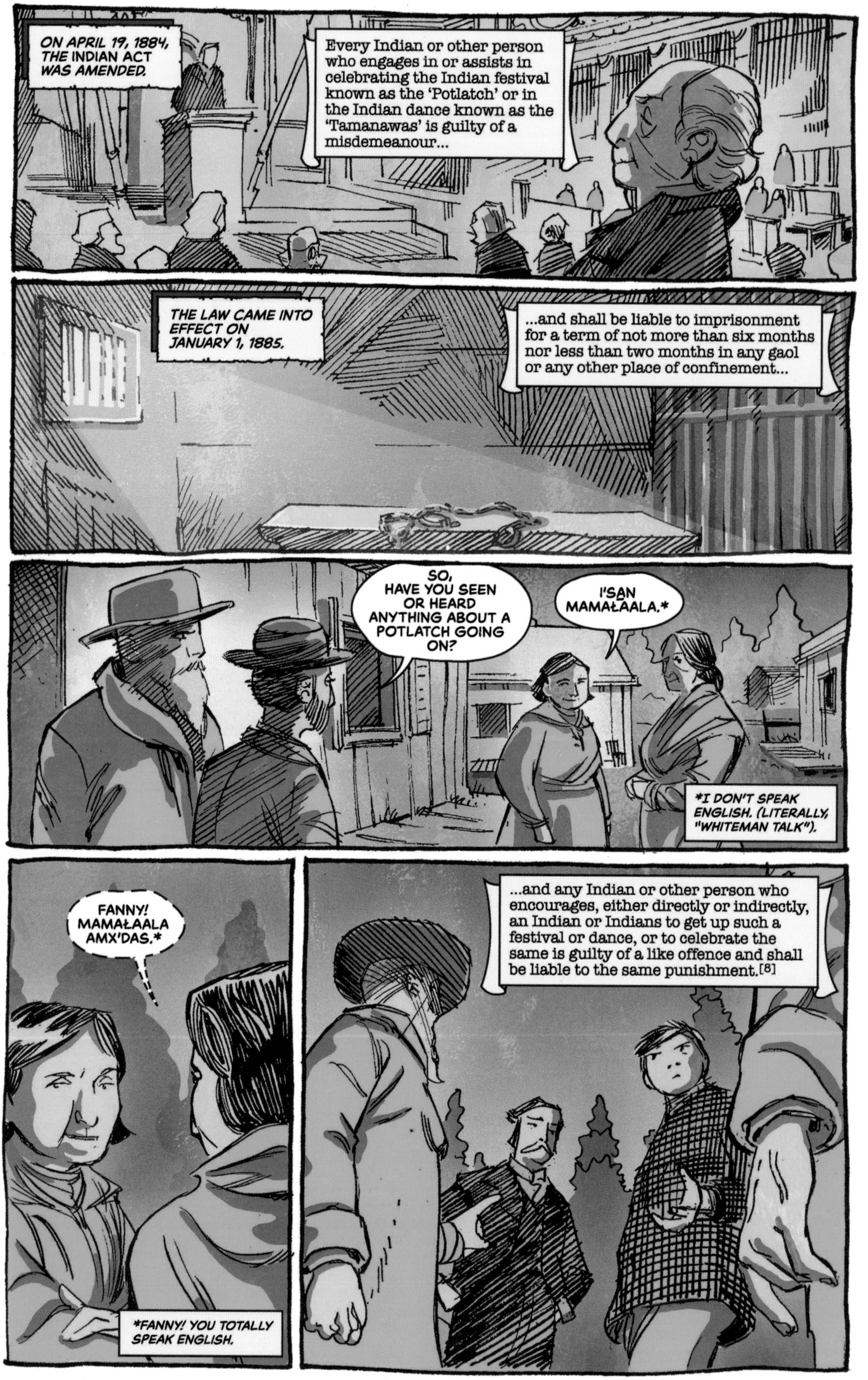

ON APRIL 19, 1884, THE INDIAN ACT WAS AMENDED.
Every Indian or other person who engages in or assists in celebrating the Indian festival known as the 'Potlatch' or in the Indian dance known as the 'Tamanawas' is guilty of a misdemeanour...
THE LAW CAME INTO EFFECT ON JANUARY 1, 1885.
...and shall be liable to imprisonment for a term of not more than six months nor less than two months in any gaol or any other place of confinement...
SO, HAVE YOU SEEN OR HEARD ANYTHING ABOUT A POTLATCH GOING ON?
I'SAN MAMAŁAALA.*
*I DON'T SPEAK ENGLISH. (LITERALLY, "WHITEMAN TALK").
FANNY! MAMAŁAALA AMX'DAS.*
*FANNY! YOU TOTALLY SPEAK ENGLISH.
...and any Indian or other person who encourages, either directly or indirectly, an Indian or Indians to get up such a festival or dance, or to celebrate the same is guilty of a like offence and shall be liable to the same punishment.[8]

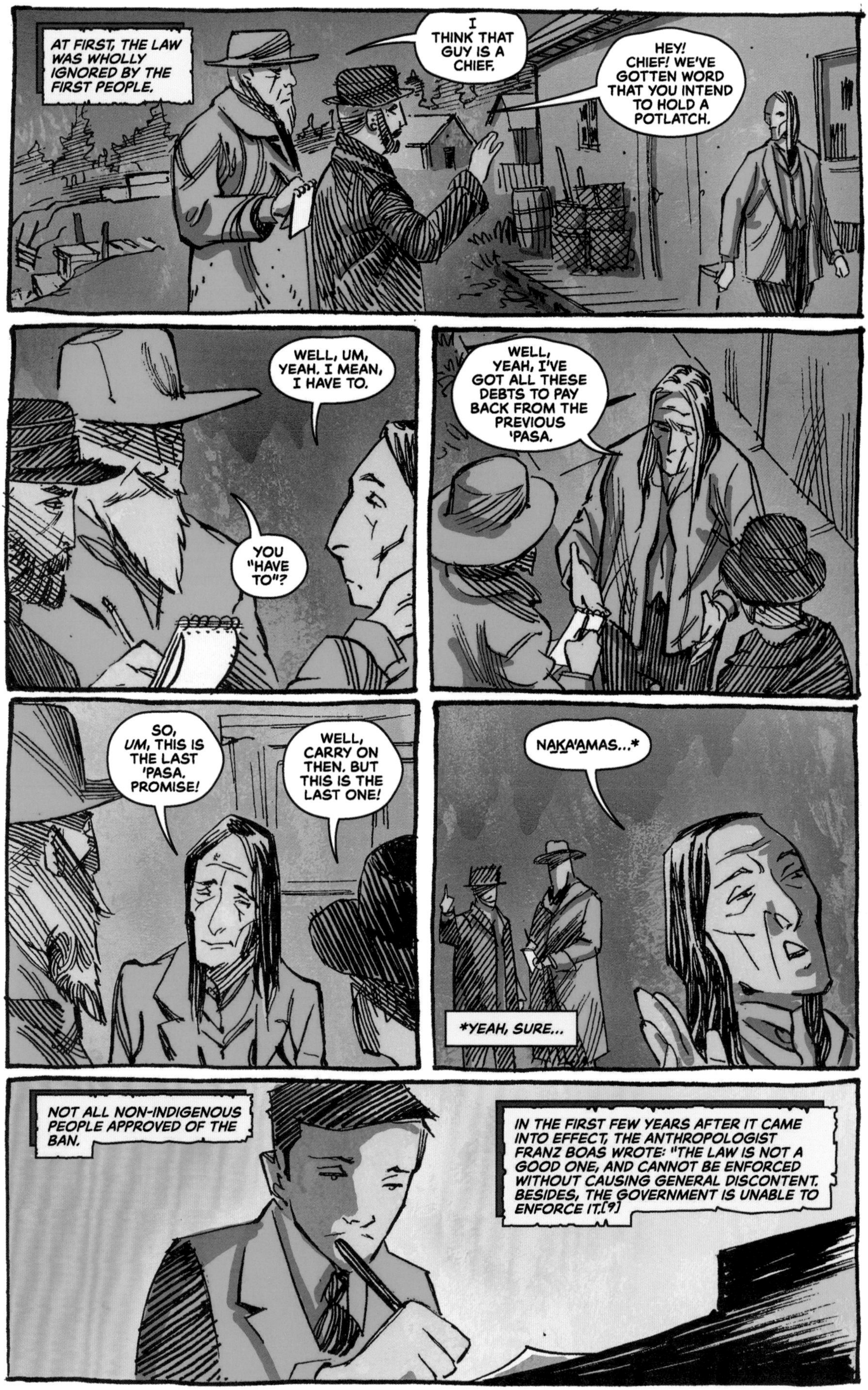
AT FIRST, THE LAW WAS WHOLLY IGNORED BY THE FIRST PEOPLE.
I THINK THAT GUY IS A CHIEF.
HEY! CHIEF! WE'VE GOTTEN WORD THAT YOU INTEND TO HOLD A POTLATCH.
WELL, UM, YEAH. I MEAN, I HAVE TO.
YOU "HAVE TO"?
WELL, YEAH, I'VE GOT ALL THESE DEBTS TO PAY BACK FROM THE PREVIOUS 'PASA.
SO, UM, THIS IS THE LAST 'PASA. PROMISE!
WELL, CARRY ON THEN. BUT THIS IS THE LAST ONE!
NAKA'AMAS...*
*YEAH, SURE...
NOT ALL NON-INDIGENOUS PEOPLE APPROVED OF THE BAN.
IN THE FIRST FEW YEARS AFTER IT CAME INTO EFFECT, THE ANTHROPOLOGIST FRANZ BOAS WROTE: "THE LAW IS NOT A GOOD ONE, AND CANNOT BE ENFORCED WITHOUT CAUSING GENERAL DISCONTENT. BESIDES, THE GOVERNMENT IS UNABLE TO ENFORCE IT.[9]

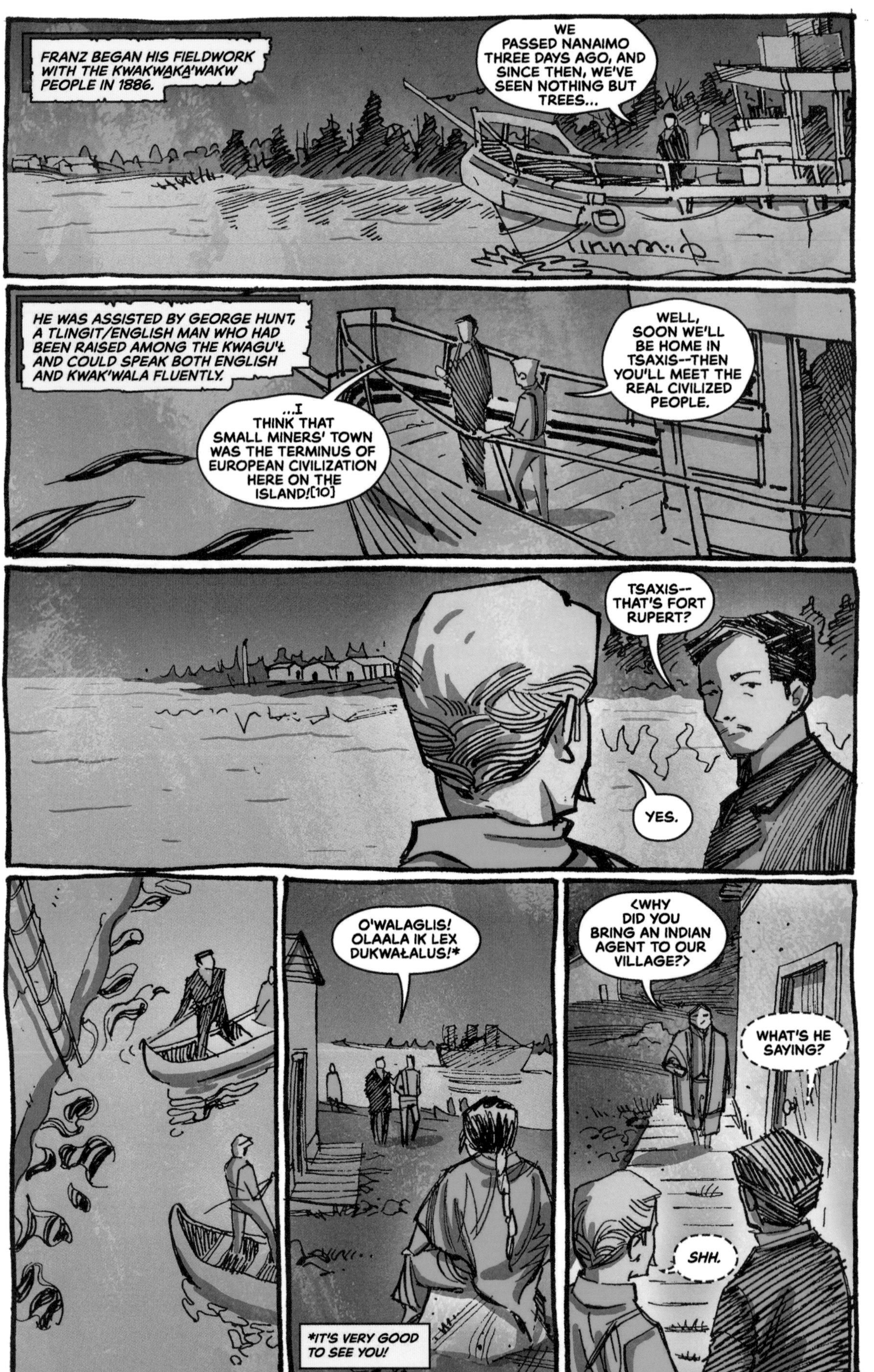
FRANZ BEGAN HIS FIELDWORK WITH THE KWAKWAKA'WAKW PEOPLE IN 1886.
WE PASSED NANAIMO THREE DAYS AGO, AND SINCE THEN, WE'VE SEEN NOTHING BUT TREES...
HE WAS ASSISTED BY GEORGE HUNT, A TLINGIT/ENGLISH MAN WHO HAD BEEN RAISED AMONG THE KWAGU'Ł AND COULD SPEAK BOTH ENGLISH AND KWAK'WALA FLUENTLY.
...I THINK THAT SMALL MINERS' TOWN WAS THE TERMINUS OF EUROPEAN CIVILIZATION HERE ON THE ISLAND![10]
WELL, SOON WE'LL BE HOME IN TSAXIS--THEN YOU'LL MEET THE REAL CIVILIZED PEOPLE.
TSAXIS--THAT'S FORT RUPERT?
YES.
O'WALAGLIS! OLAALA IK LEX DUKWAŁALUS!*
*IT'S VERY GOOD TO SEE YOU!
<WHY DID YOU BRING AN INDIAN AGENT TO OUR VILLAGE?>
WHAT'S HE SAYING?
SHH.

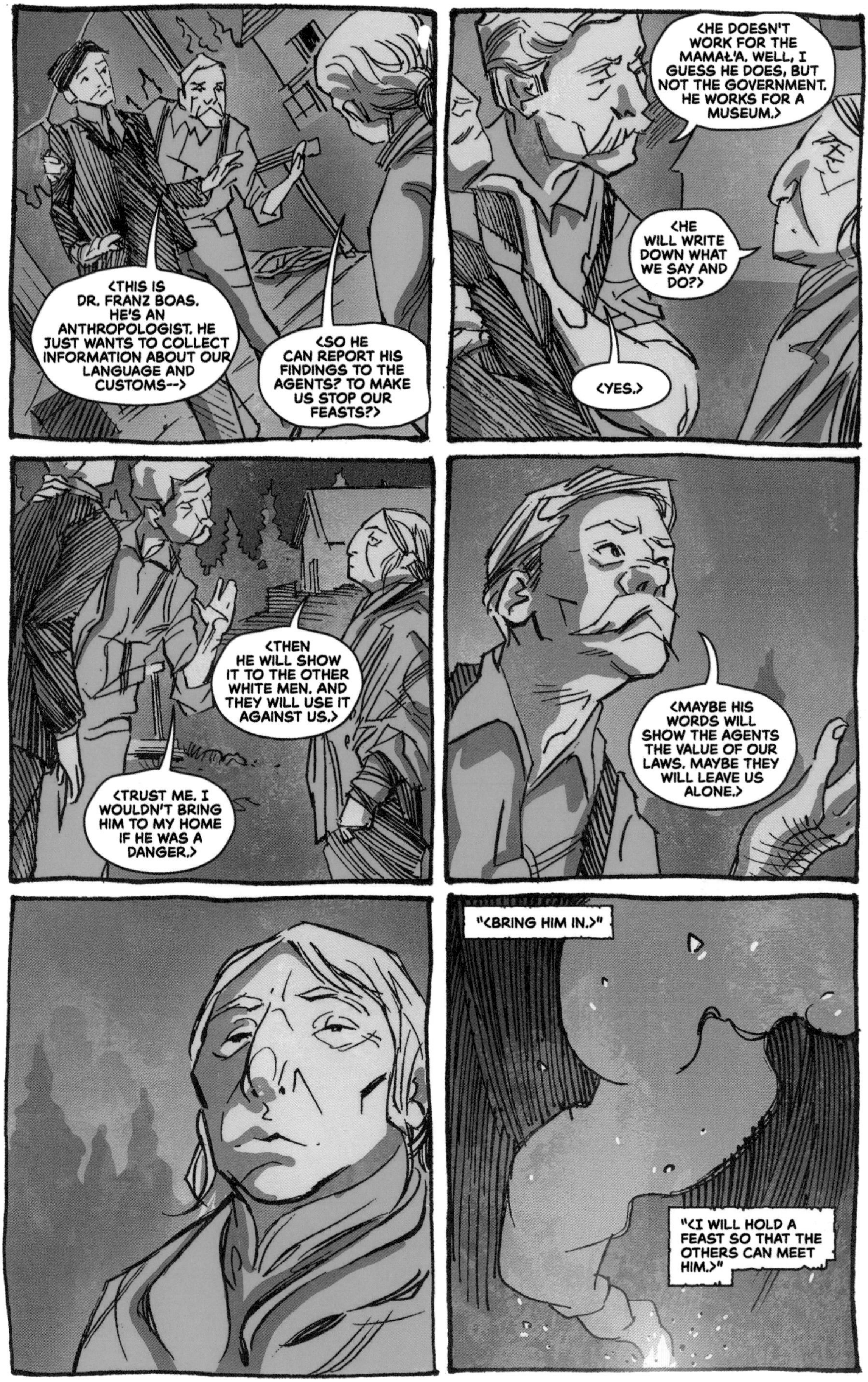
<THIS IS DR. FRANZ BOAS. HE'S AN ANTHROPOLOGIST. HE JUST WANTS TO COLLECT INFORMATION ABOUT OUR LANGUAGE AND CUSTOMS-->
<SO HE CAN REPORT HIS FINDINGS TO THE AGENTS? TO MAKE US STOP OUR FEASTS?>
<HE DOESN'T WORK FOR THE MAMAŁ'A. WELL, I GUESS HE DOES, BUT NOT THE GOVERNMENT. HE WORKS FOR A MUSEUM.>
<HE WILL WRITE DOWN WHAT WE SAY AND DO?>
<YES.>
<THEN HE WILL SHOW IT TO THE OTHER WHITE MEN. AND THEY WILL USE IT AGAINST US.>
<TRUST ME. I WOULDN'T BRING HIM TO MY HOME IF HE WAS A DANGER.>
<MAYBE HIS WORDS WILL SHOW THE AGENTS THE VALUE OF OUR LAWS. MAYBE THEY WILL LEAVE US ALONE.>
"<BRING HIM IN.>"
"<I WILL HOLD A FEAST SO THAT THE OTHERS CAN MEET HIM.>"

‹WE WANT TO KNOW WHETHER YOU HAVE COME TO STOP OUR DANCES AND FEASTS.›

HE SAYS, HAVE YOU COME TO STOP OUR CEREMONIES?

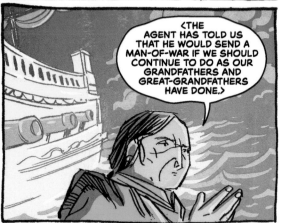

‹THE AGENT HAS TOLD US THAT HE WOULD SEND A MAN-OF-WAR IF WE SHOULD CONTINUE TO DO AS OUR GRANDFATHERS AND GREAT-GRANDFATHERS HAVE DONE.›

‹BUT *WE* DO NOT MIND HIS WORDS.›

"‹WHEN YOUR MAN-OF-WAR COMES, LET HIM DESTROY OUR HOUSES.›"

"‹DID YOU SEE THOSE TREES? WE SHALL CUT THEM DOWN AND BUILD NEW HOUSES, AND LIVE AS OUR FATHERS DID.›"

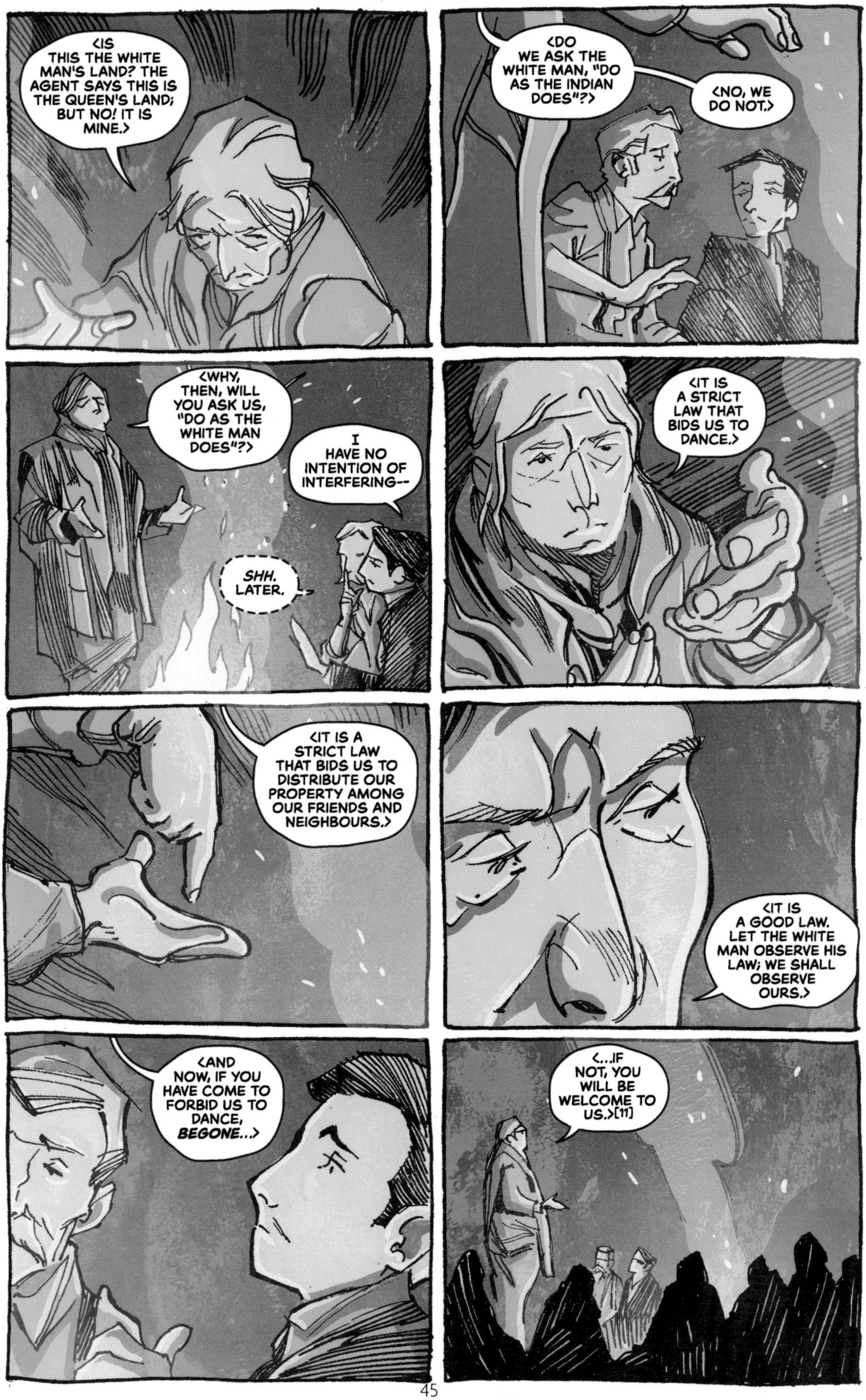
<IS THIS THE WHITE MAN'S LAND? THE AGENT SAYS THIS IS THE QUEEN'S LAND; BUT NO! IT IS MINE.>
<DO WE ASK THE WHITE MAN, "DO AS THE INDIAN DOES"?>
<NO, WE DO NOT.>
<WHY, THEN, WILL YOU ASK US, "DO AS THE WHITE MAN DOES"?>
I HAVE NO INTENTION OF INTERFERING--
SHH. LATER.
<IT IS A STRICT LAW THAT BIDS US TO DANCE.>
<IT IS A STRICT LAW THAT BIDS US TO DISTRIBUTE OUR PROPERTY AMONG OUR FRIENDS AND NEIGHBOURS.>
<IT IS A GOOD LAW. LET THE WHITE MAN OBSERVE HIS LAW; WE SHALL OBSERVE OURS.>
<AND NOW, IF YOU HAVE COME TO FORBID US TO DANCE, ***BEGONE...***>
<...IF NOT, YOU WILL BE WELCOME TO US.>[11]

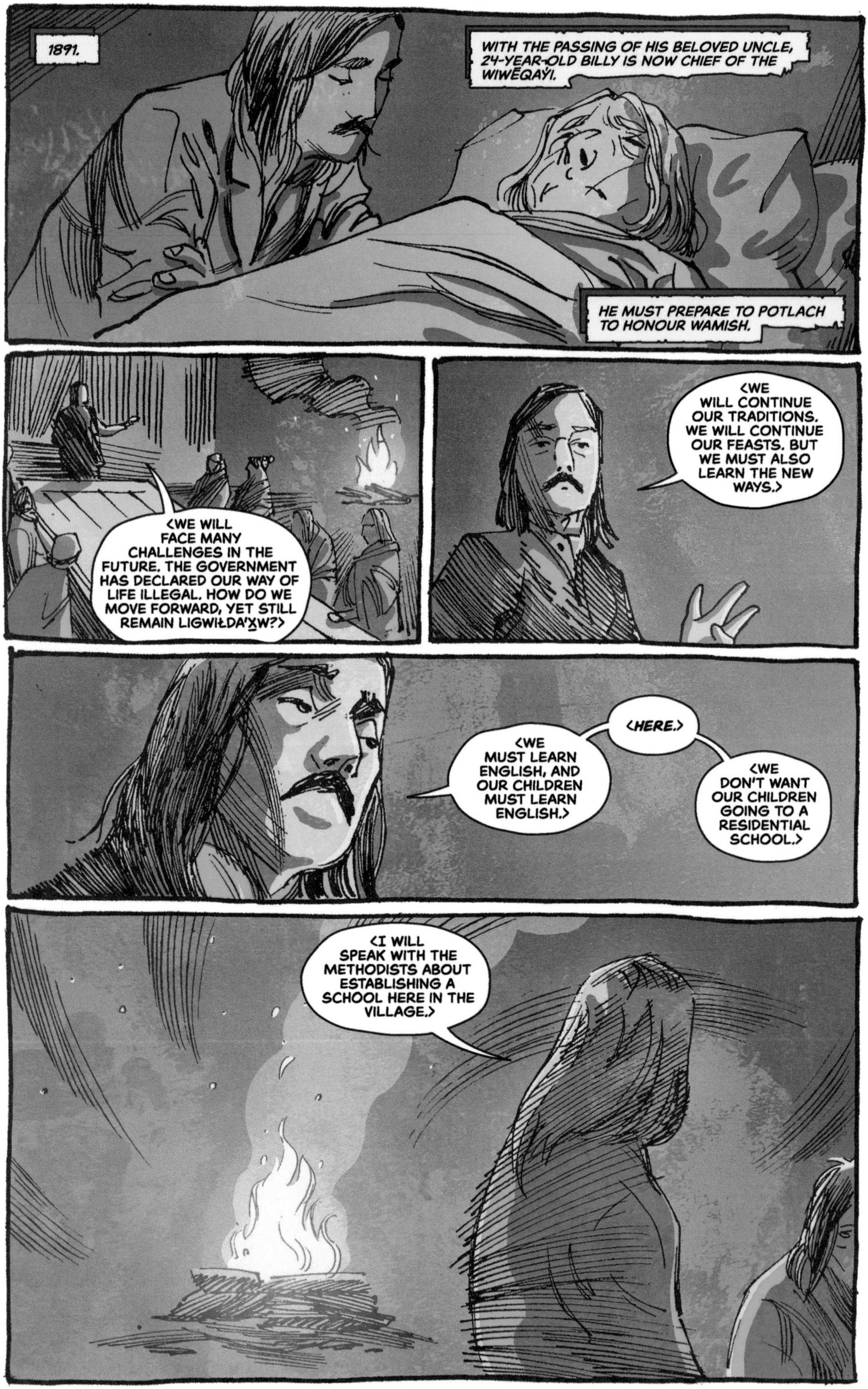
1891.
WITH THE PASSING OF HIS BELOVED UNCLE, 24-YEAR-OLD BILLY IS NOW CHIEF OF THE WIWĒQAY̓I.
HE MUST PREPARE TO POTLACH TO HONOUR WAMISH.
<WE WILL FACE MANY CHALLENGES IN THE FUTURE. THE GOVERNMENT HAS DECLARED OUR WAY OF LIFE ILLEGAL. HOW DO WE MOVE FORWARD, YET STILL REMAIN LIGWIŁDA'X̱W?>
<WE WILL CONTINUE OUR TRADITIONS. WE WILL CONTINUE OUR FEASTS. BUT WE MUST ALSO LEARN THE NEW WAYS.>
<WE MUST LEARN ENGLISH, AND OUR CHILDREN MUST LEARN ENGLISH.>
<HERE.>
<WE DON'T WANT OUR CHILDREN GOING TO A RESIDENTIAL SCHOOL.>
<I WILL SPEAK WITH THE METHODISTS ABOUT ESTABLISHING A SCHOOL HERE IN THE VILLAGE.>

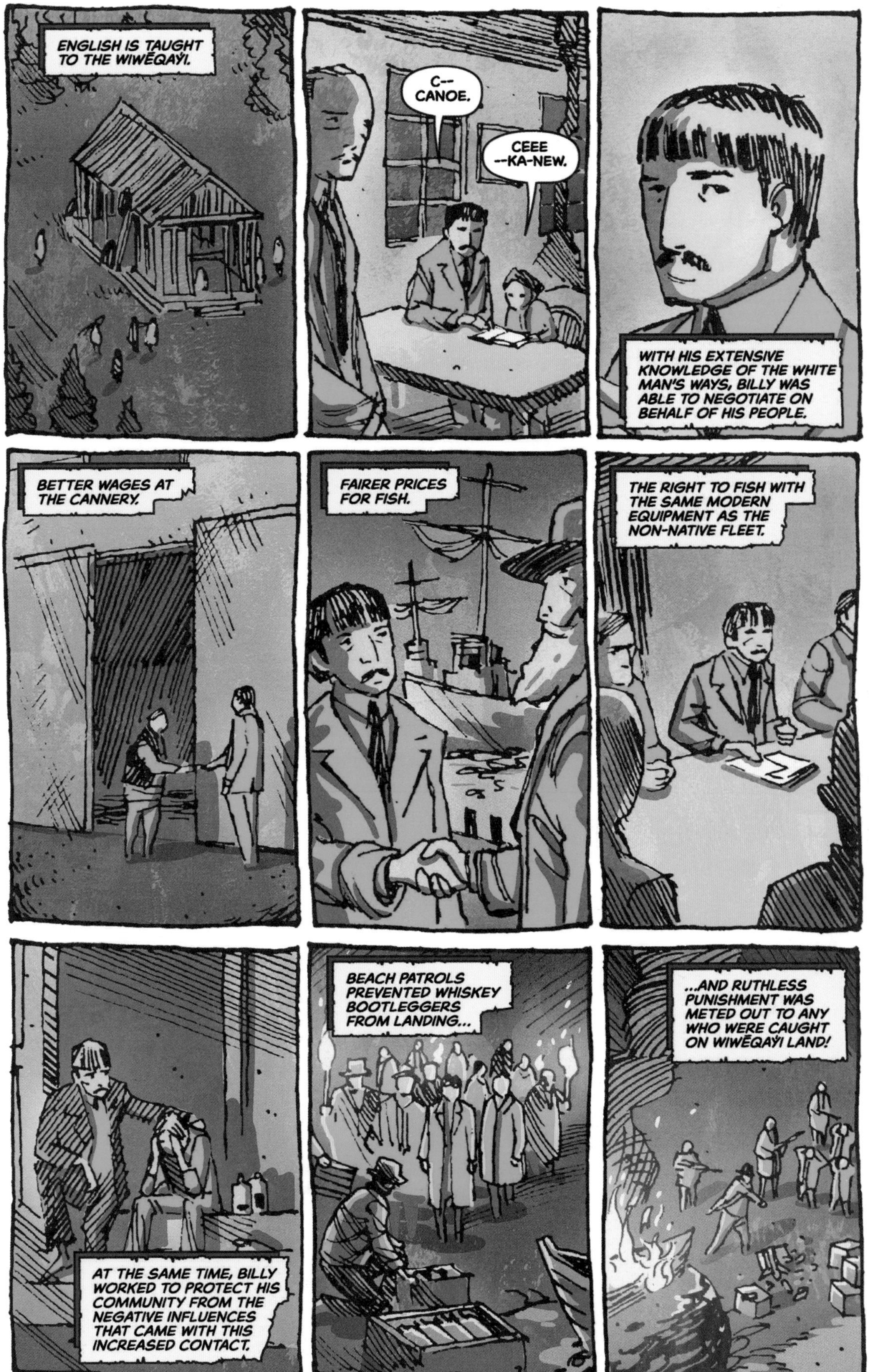
ENGLISH IS TAUGHT TO THE WIWĒQAỲI.
C-- CANOE.
CEEE --KA-NEW.
WITH HIS EXTENSIVE KNOWLEDGE OF THE WHITE MAN'S WAYS, BILLY WAS ABLE TO NEGOTIATE ON BEHALF OF HIS PEOPLE.
BETTER WAGES AT THE CANNERY.
FAIRER PRICES FOR FISH.
THE RIGHT TO FISH WITH THE SAME MODERN EQUIPMENT AS THE NON-NATIVE FLEET.
AT THE SAME TIME, BILLY WORKED TO PROTECT HIS COMMUNITY FROM THE NEGATIVE INFLUENCES THAT CAME WITH THIS INCREASED CONTACT.
BEACH PATROLS PREVENTED WHISKEY BOOTLEGGERS FROM LANDING...
...AND RUTHLESS PUNISHMENT WAS METED OUT TO ANY WHO WERE CAUGHT ON WIWĒQAỲI LAND!

BILLY ALSO ENCOURAGED HIS PEOPLE TO GET JOBS IN THE EMERGING INDUSTRIES.

HIS VISION WAS NOT ABOUT ASSIMILATION...

<COUSIN, HAVE YOU THOUGHT ABOUT WORKING ON A FISHING BOAT? OR IN THE LOGGING CAMP?>

<HMM...>

<COUSIN, HAVE YOU THOUGHT ABOUT WORKING IN THE CANNERY THIS SUMMER?>

<HMM...>

...BUT ADOPTION.

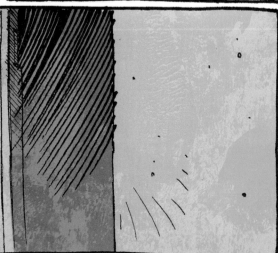

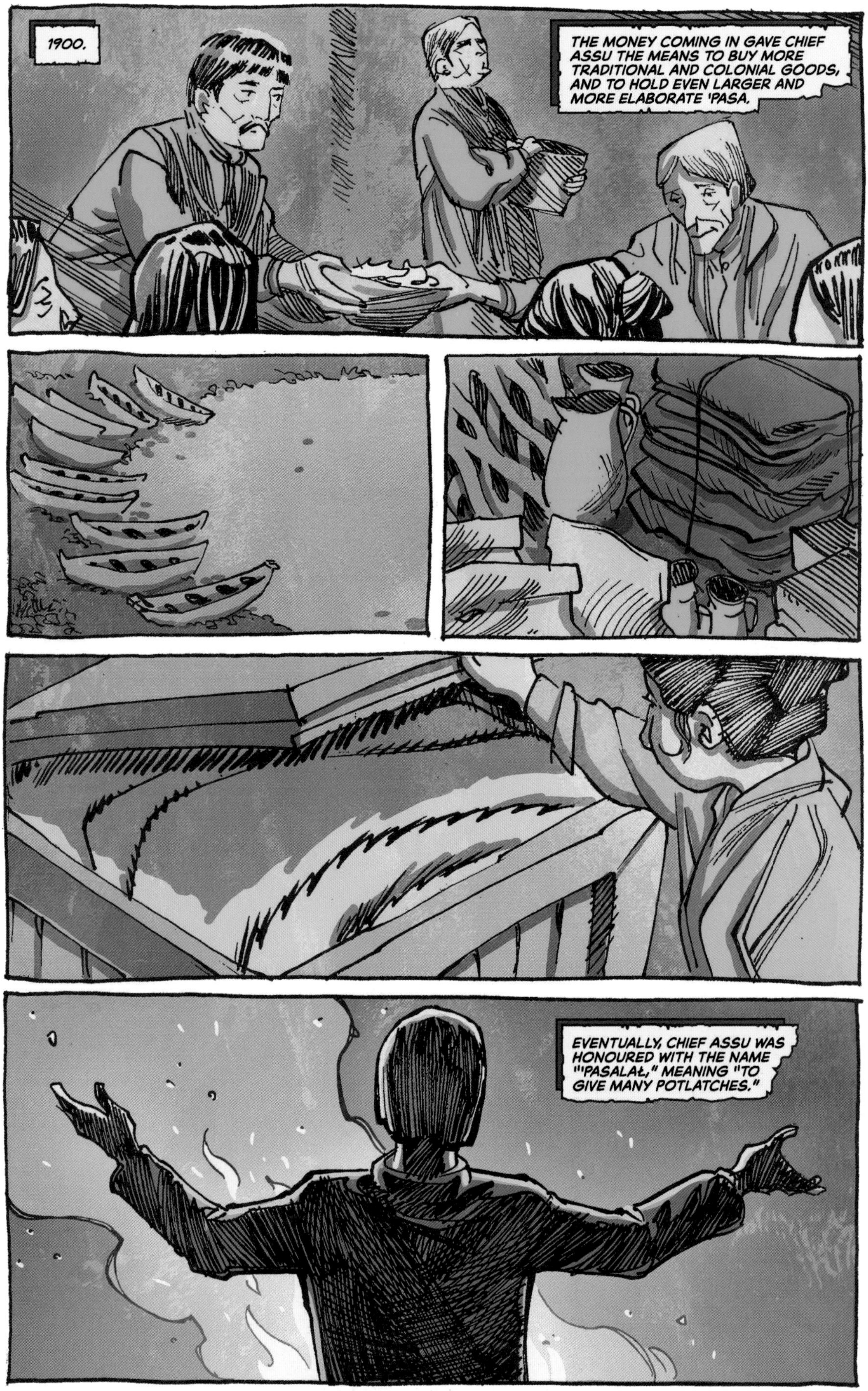
1900.
THE MONEY COMING IN GAVE CHIEF ASSU THE MEANS TO BUY MORE TRADITIONAL AND COLONIAL GOODS, AND TO HOLD EVEN LARGER AND MORE ELABORATE 'PASA.
EVENTUALLY, CHIEF ASSU WAS HONOURED WITH THE NAME "'PASALAŁ," MEANING "TO GIVE MANY POTLATCHES."

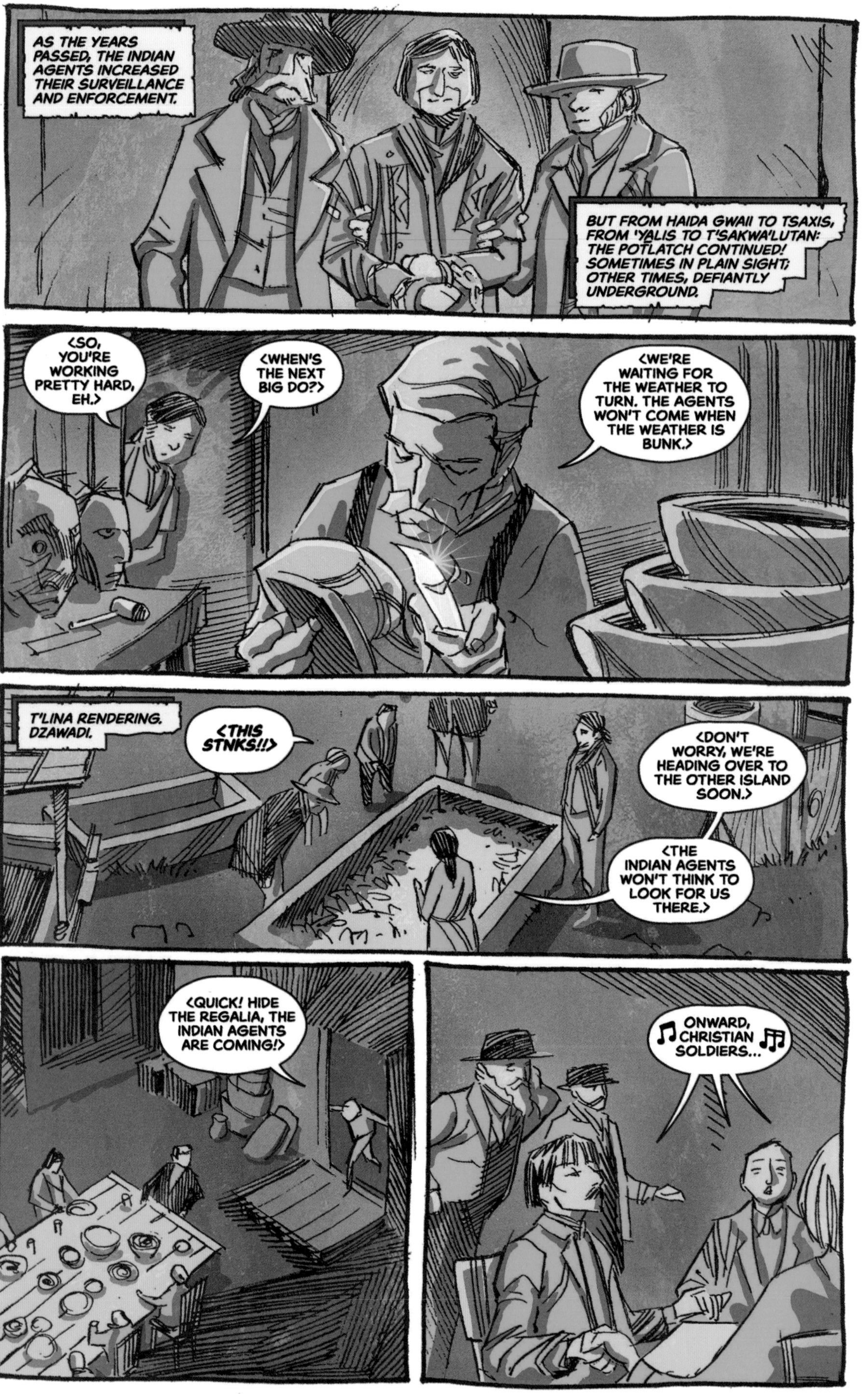
AS THE YEARS PASSED, THE INDIAN AGENTS INCREASED THEIR SURVEILLANCE AND ENFORCEMENT.
BUT FROM HAIDA GWAII TO TSAXIS, FROM 'YALIS TO T'SAKWA'LUTAN: THE POTLATCH CONTINUED! SOMETIMES IN PLAIN SIGHT; OTHER TIMES, DEFIANTLY UNDERGROUND.
<SO, YOU'RE WORKING PRETTY HARD, EH.>
<WHEN'S THE NEXT BIG DO?>
<WE'RE WAITING FOR THE WEATHER TO TURN. THE AGENTS WON'T COME WHEN THE WEATHER IS BUNK.>
T'LINA RENDERING. DZAWADI.
<THIS STNKS!!>
<DON'T WORRY, WE'RE HEADING OVER TO THE OTHER ISLAND SOON.>
<THE INDIAN AGENTS WON'T THINK TO LOOK FOR US THERE.>
<QUICK! HIDE THE REGALIA, THE INDIAN AGENTS ARE COMING!>
♫ ONWARD, CHRISTIAN SOLDIERS... ♫

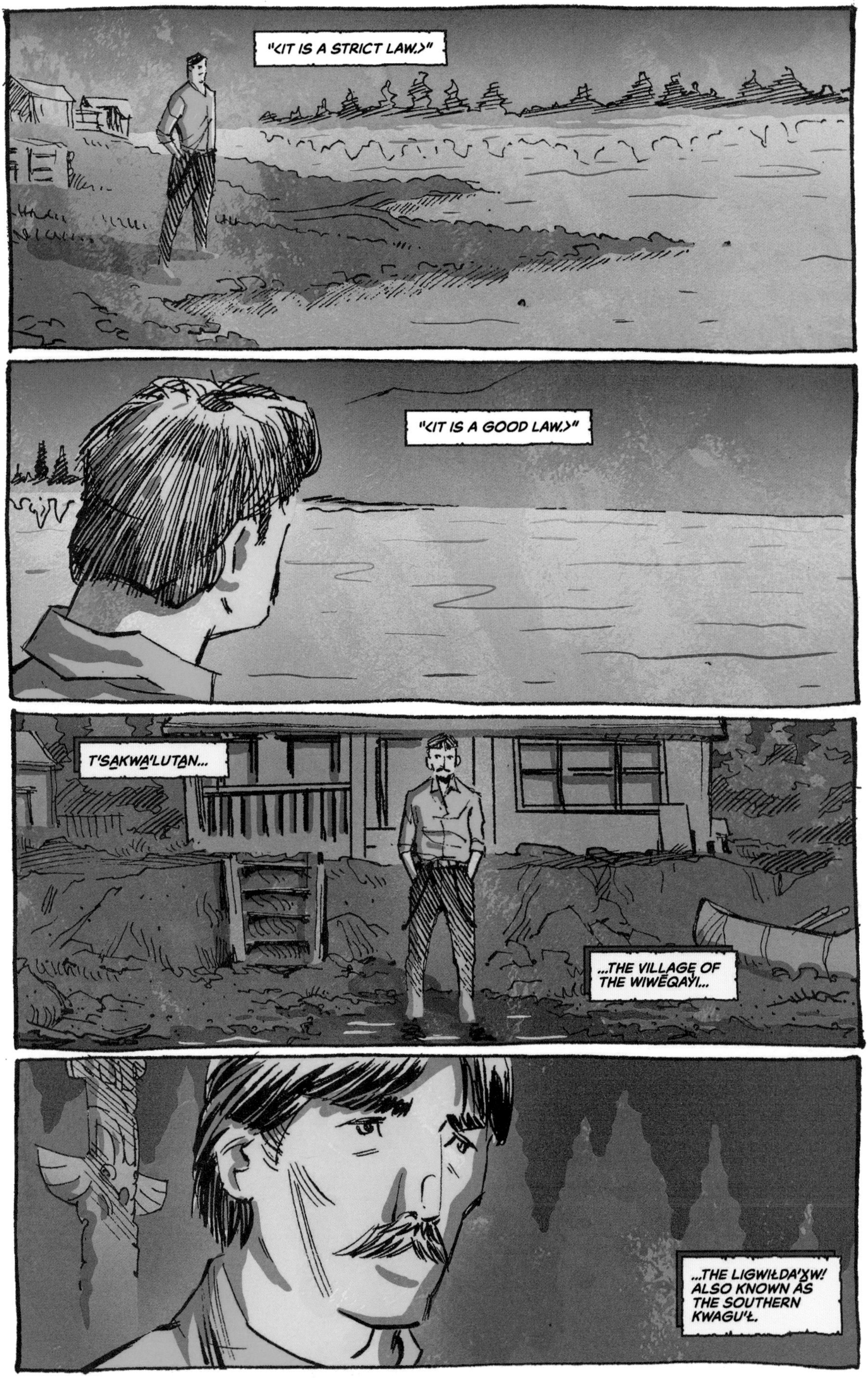
"<IT IS A STRICT LAW.>"
"<IT IS A GOOD LAW.>"
T'SA̱KWA̱'LUTA̱N...
...THE VILLAGE OF THE WIWĒQAY̓I...
...THE LIGWIŁDA'X̱W! ALSO KNOWN AS THE SOUTHERN KWAGU'Ł.

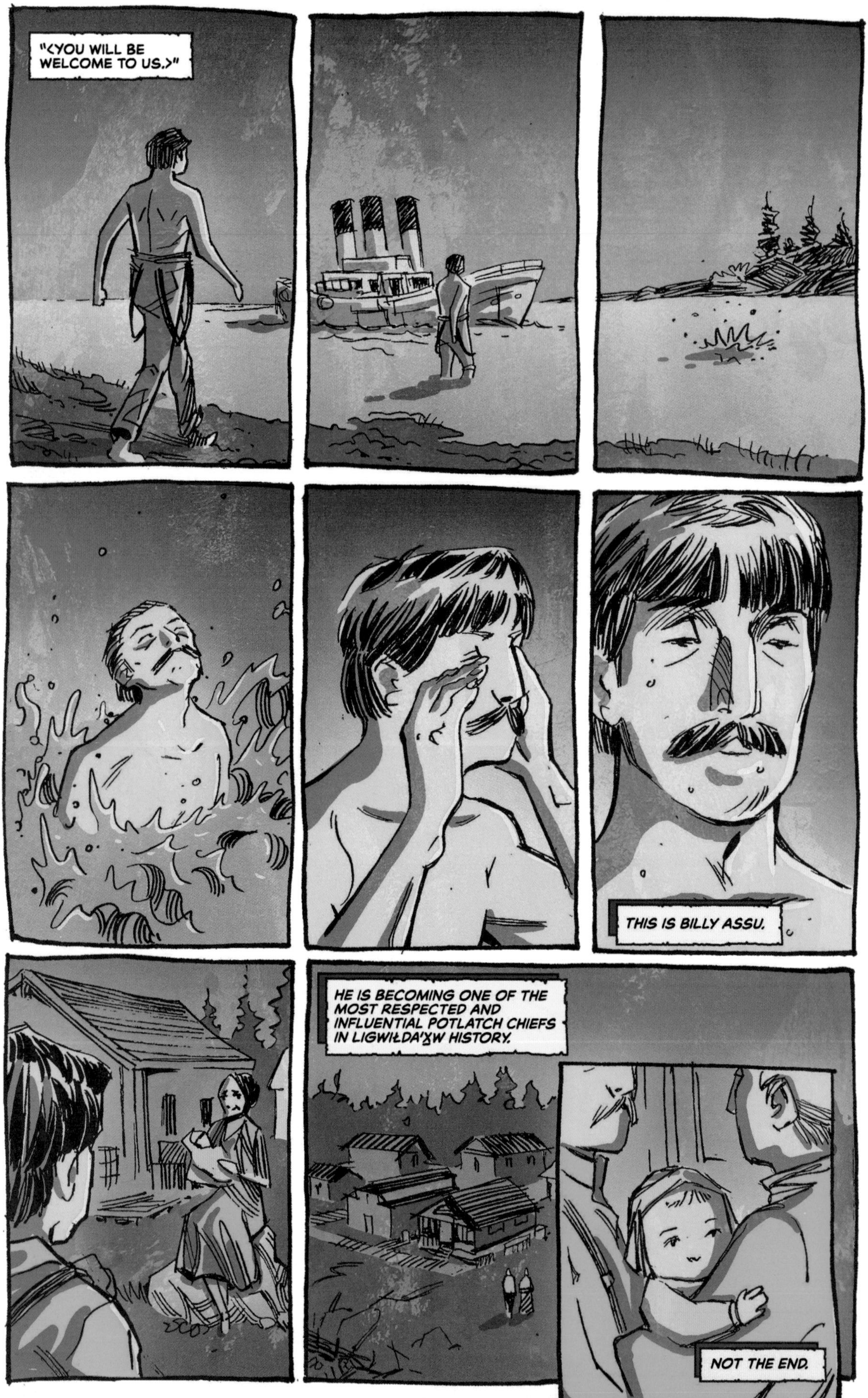
"<YOU WILL BE WELCOME TO US.>"
THIS IS BILLY ASSU.
HE IS BECOMING ONE OF THE MOST RESPECTED AND INFLUENTIAL POTLATCH CHIEFS IN LIGWIŁDA'X̱W HISTORY.
NOT THE END.

In the early 20th century, the indigenous peoples of northwestern Ontario were starving. The fur trade era was coming to a close, and animals had become scarce through over-hunting. During this time, there were notable instances of people becoming delirious and resorting to cannibalism. Indigenous communities took this offence very seriously and had their own laws to deal with it.

There are stories that tell of red clouds appearing over an approaching windigo, as a warning or omen. Some stories say windigos' hearts turn to ice. Some say you can hear the crunching sound of ice breaking in their throats, not unlike the sound of grinding teeth.

In writing this story, I relied heavily on the oral histories, trial transcripts, and other information in the excellent book *Killing the Shamen*, by Thomas Fiddler and James R. Stevens. It was important to me to write this story from a woman's perspective, as it granted me the opportunity to tell a story without retelling the one already written.

Wahsakapeequay is the name of a real woman who was killed by her community's leader, Jack Fiddler, when she became delirious. However, she never ate human flesh. Little is known about her life.

In this story, the character is a fictionalized composite of Wahsakapeequay, Kichi Kakapetikwe, and a number of other windigo accounts told by Fiddler's descendants. The police charged Fiddler and his brother with murder upon hearing of the medicine man who had killed 14 windigos.

This is the story not just of a windigo, but also of a way of life that changed forever.

Jen Storm

1905

Treaty 9 is negotiated between Cree and Ojibwe communities in northern Ontario and the federal and Ontario governments, who share the cost of purchasing Indigenous title to the land. This is the only time a provincial government participates in a numbered treaty.

1906-1907

Treaty 10 is negotiated and signed by the Canadian government and several Indigenous peoples in northern Saskatchewan and Alberta.

1906

A delegation of Squamish chiefs travels to England to petition King Edward, seeking compensation for lands in British Columbia that had been appropriated without payment.

Red Clouds

Jen Storm

Illustration & Colours: Natasha Donovan

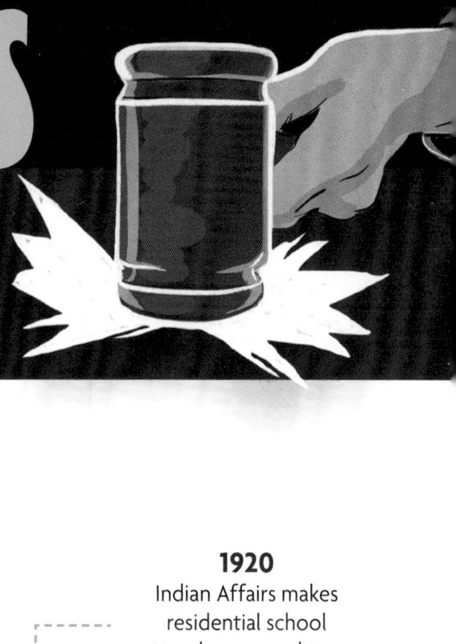

1907
Jack Fiddler, wendigo killer, is the first Indigenous man to be charged as a serial killer.

1907
Dr. Peter Henderson Bryce reports that up to 42% of Indigenous children are dying in residential schools. The report is largely ignored.

1912
The Nisga'a of northwestern British Columbia's Nass River Valley are the first Indigenous group to initiate a land-claim action against the Canadian government.

1920
Indian Affairs makes residential school attendance mandatory for all Indigenous children aged 7 to 16.

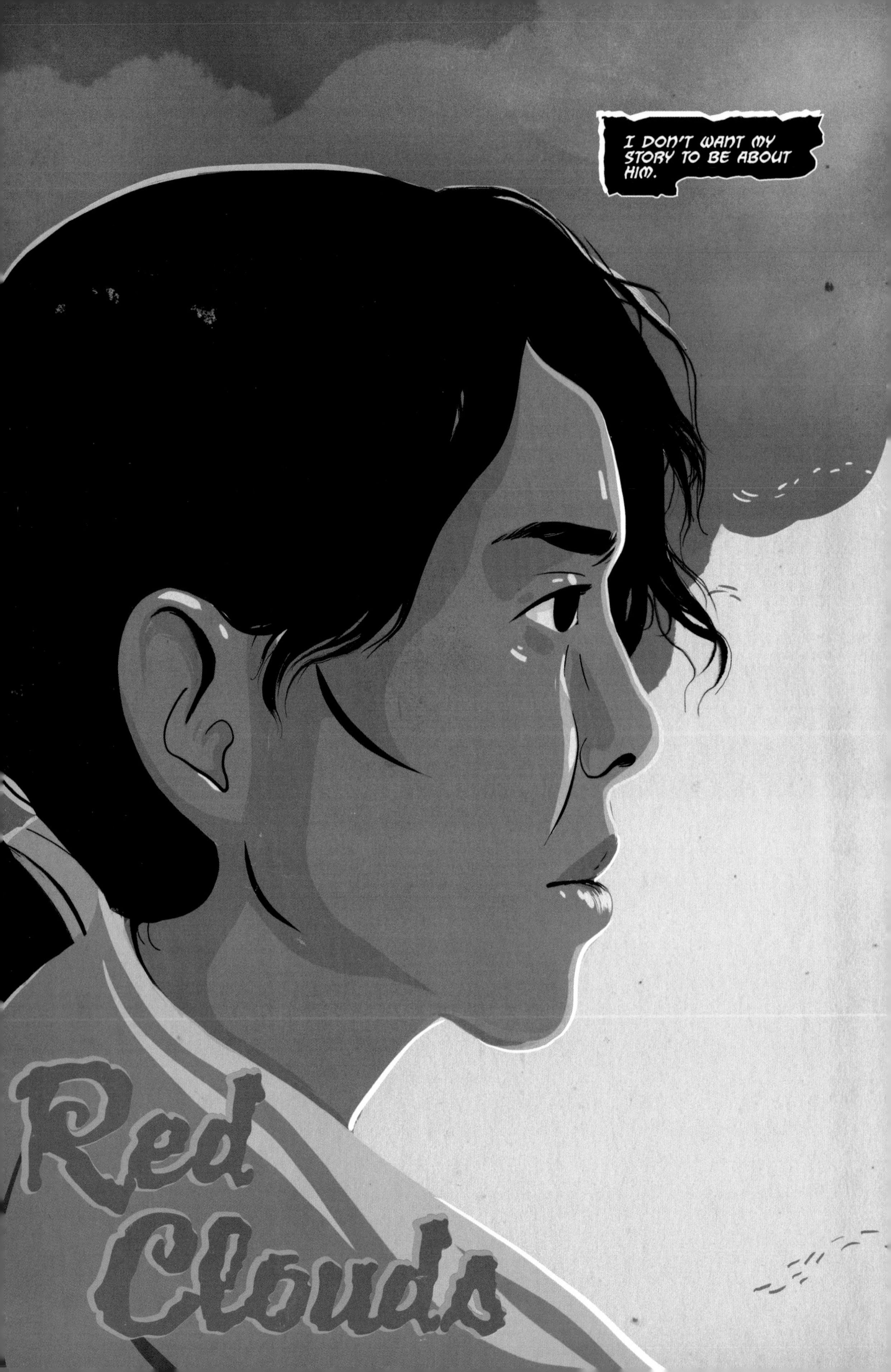
I DON'T WANT MY STORY TO BE ABOUT HIM.
Red Clouds

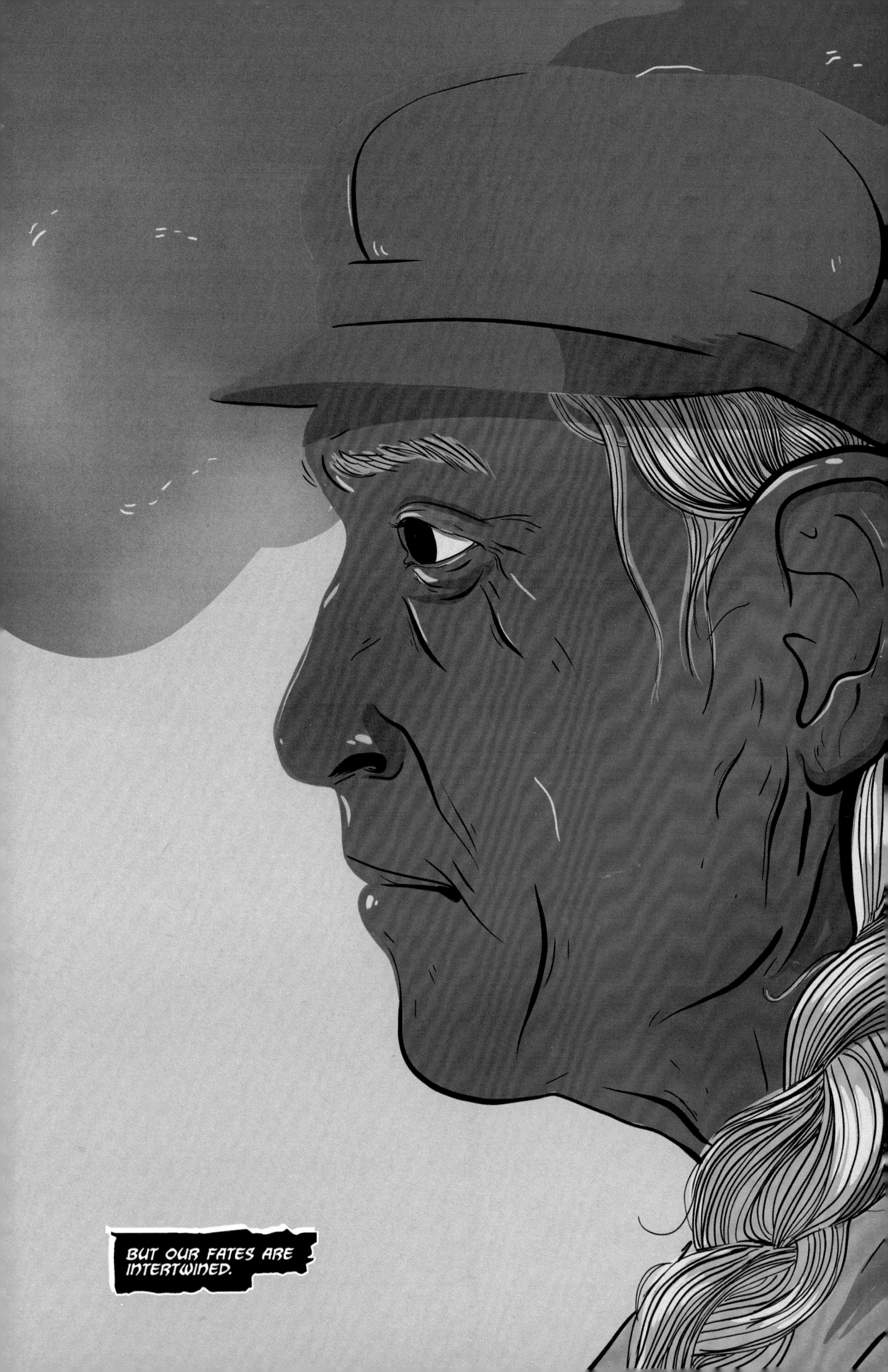
BUT OUR FATES ARE INTERTWINED.

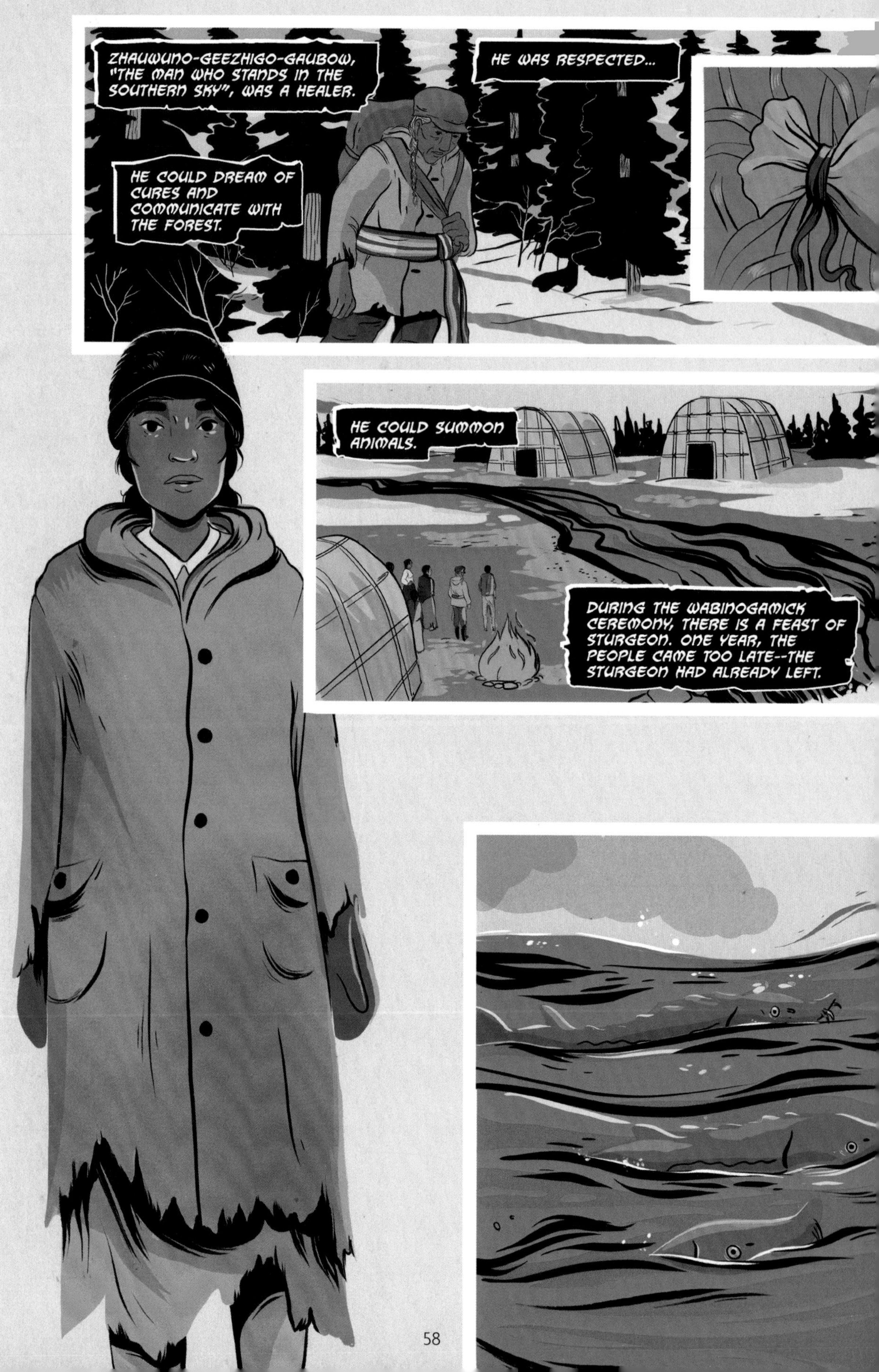
ZHAUWUNO-GEEZHIGO-GAUBOW, "THE MAN WHO STANDS IN THE SOUTHERN SKY", WAS A HEALER.
HE COULD DREAM OF CURES AND COMMUNICATE WITH THE FOREST.
HE WAS RESPECTED...
HE COULD SUMMON ANIMALS.
DURING THE WABINOGAMICK CEREMONY, THERE IS A FEAST OF STURGEON. ONE YEAR, THE PEOPLE CAME TOO LATE--THE STURGEON HAD ALREADY LEFT.

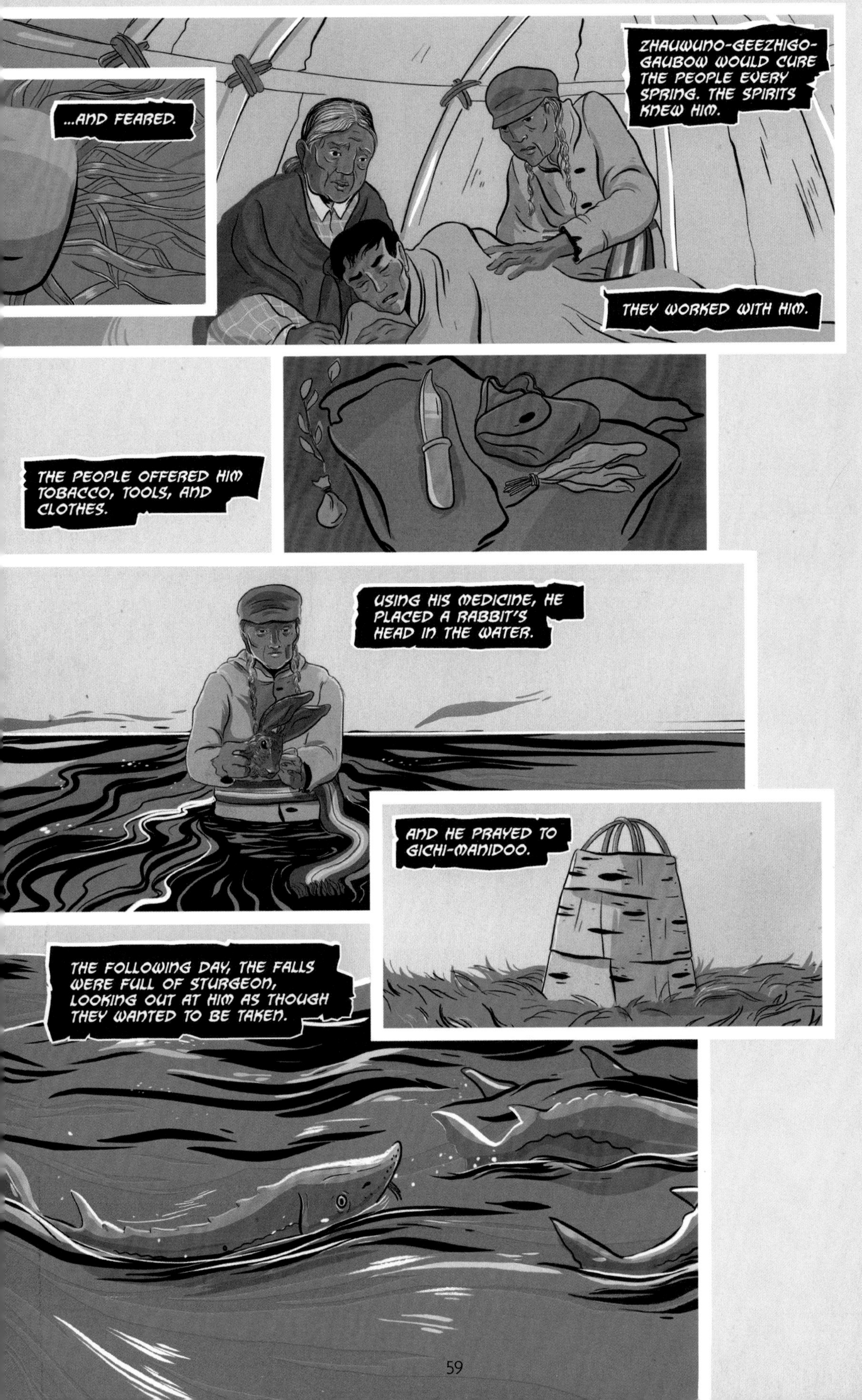
...AND FEARED.
ZHAUWUNO-GEEZHIGO-GAUBOW WOULD CURE THE PEOPLE EVERY SPRING. THE SPIRITS KNEW HIM.
THEY WORKED WITH HIM.
THE PEOPLE OFFERED HIM TOBACCO, TOOLS, AND CLOTHES.
USING HIS MEDICINE, HE PLACED A RABBIT'S HEAD IN THE WATER.
AND HE PRAYED TO GICHI-MANIDOO.
THE FOLLOWING DAY, THE FALLS WERE FULL OF STURGEON, LOOKING OUT AT HIM AS THOUGH THEY WANTED TO BE TAKEN.

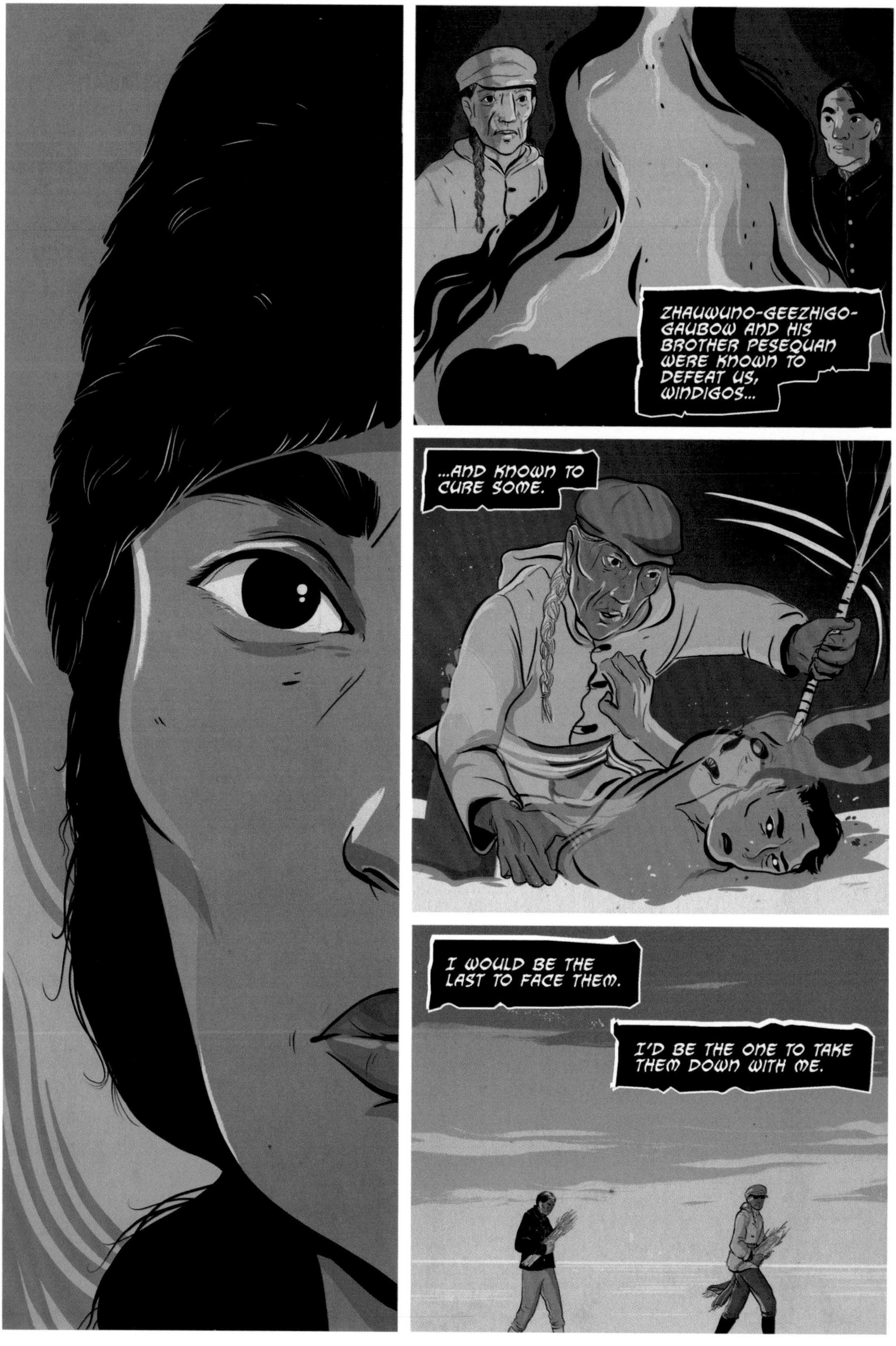
ZHAUWUNO-GEEZHIGO-GAUBOW AND HIS BROTHER PESEQUAN WERE KNOWN TO DEFEAT US, WINDIGOS...
...AND KNOWN TO CURE SOME.
I WOULD BE THE LAST TO FACE THEM.
I'D BE THE ONE TO TAKE THEM DOWN WITH ME.

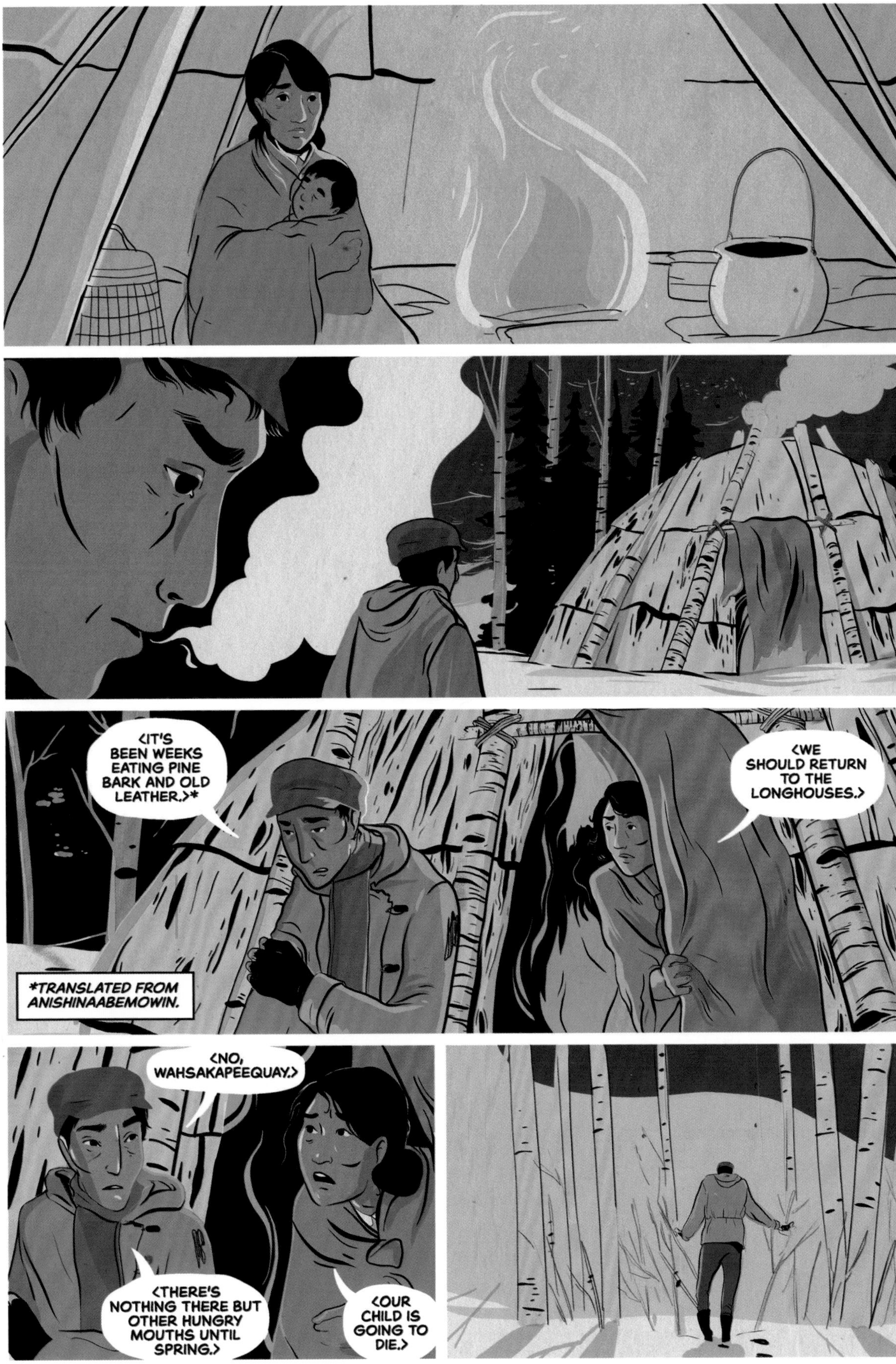

<IT'S BEEN WEEKS EATING PINE BARK AND OLD LEATHER.>*
<WE SHOULD RETURN TO THE LONGHOUSES.>
*TRANSLATED FROM ANISHINAABEMOWIN.
<NO, WAHSAKAPEEQUAY.>
<THERE'S NOTHING THERE BUT OTHER HUNGRY MOUTHS UNTIL SPRING.>
<OUR CHILD IS GOING TO DIE.>

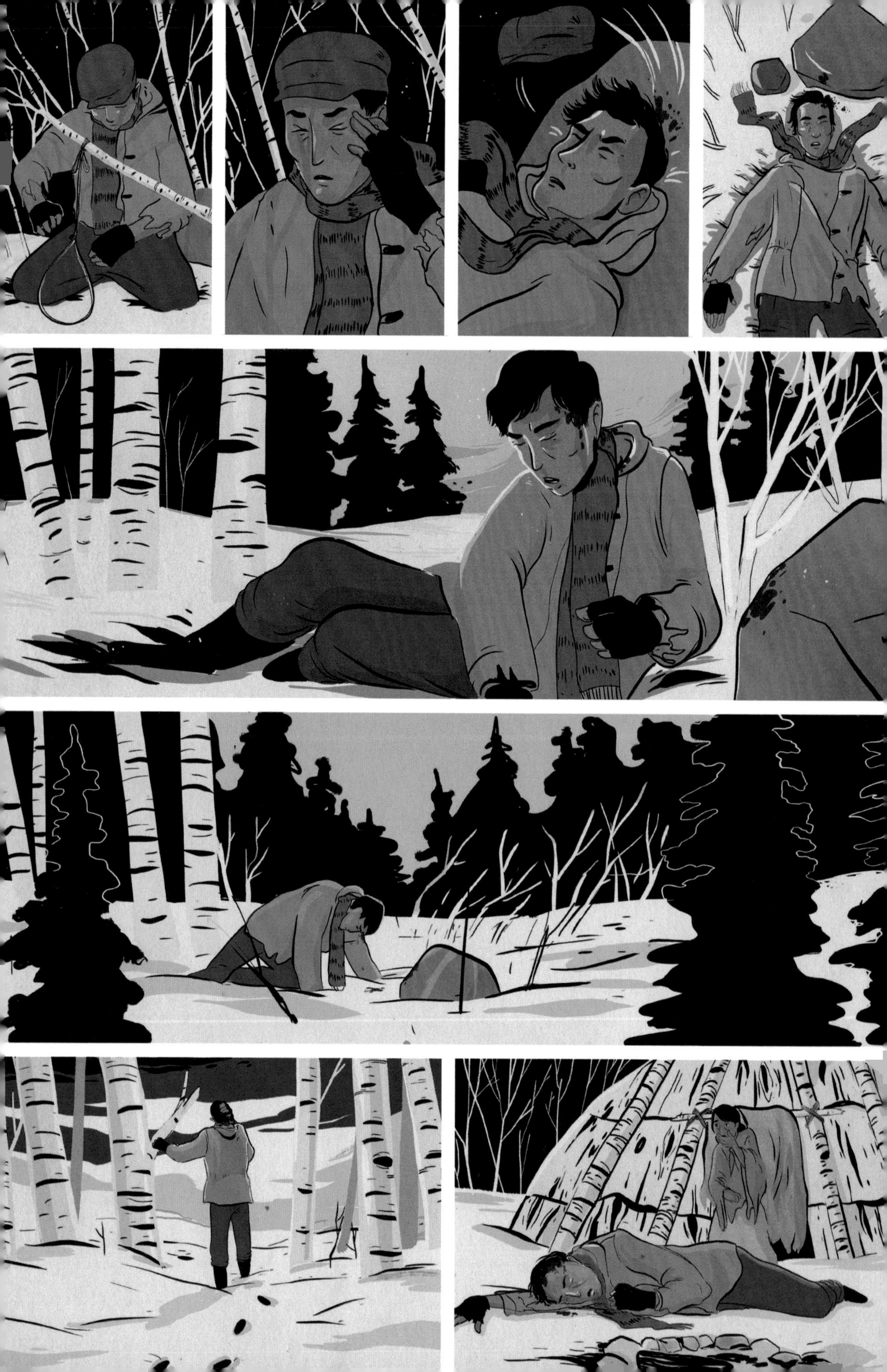

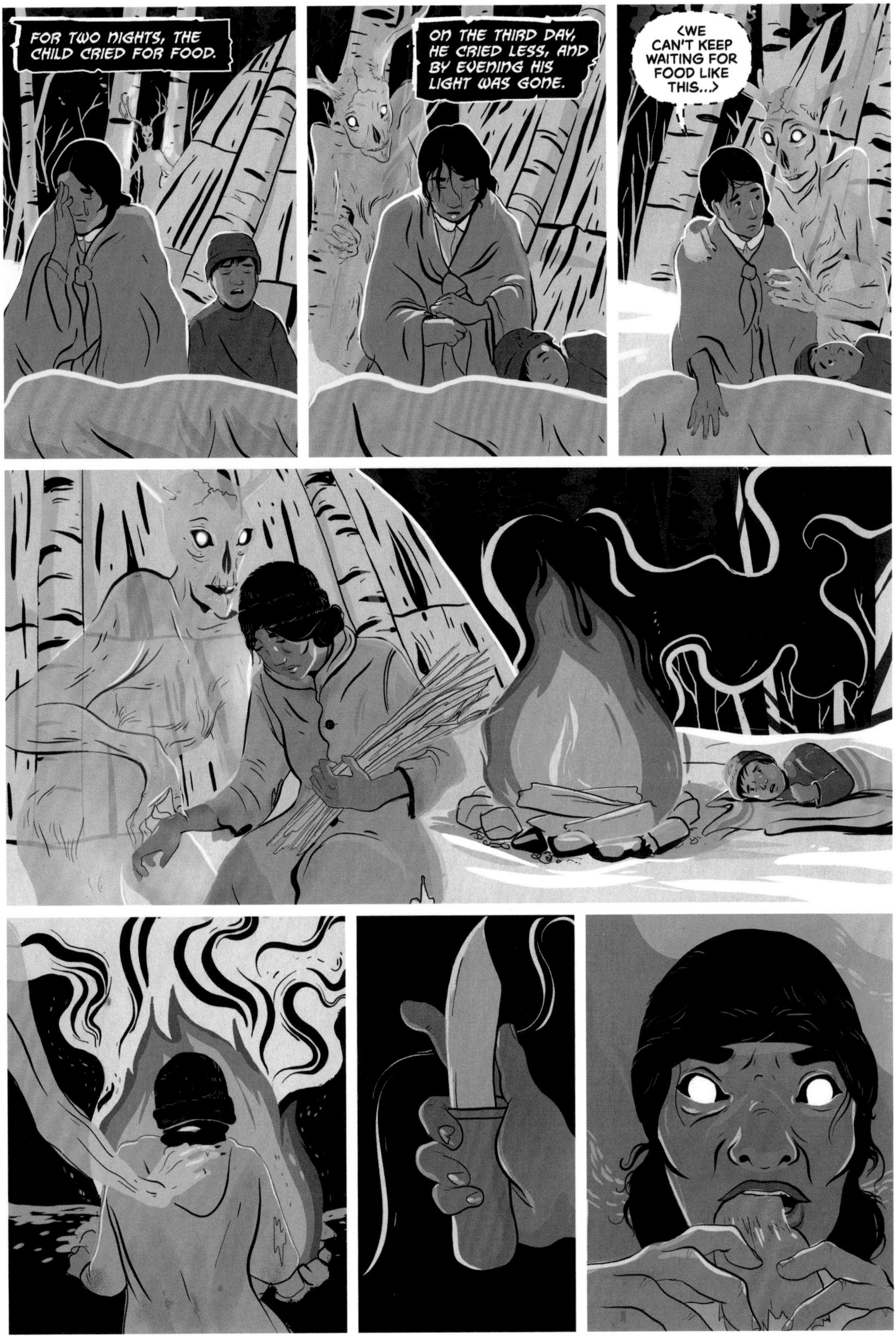

FOR TWO NIGHTS, THE CHILD CRIED FOR FOOD.
ON THE THIRD DAY, HE CRIED LESS, AND BY EVENING HIS LIGHT WAS GONE.
<WE CAN'T KEEP WAITING FOR FOOD LIKE THIS...>

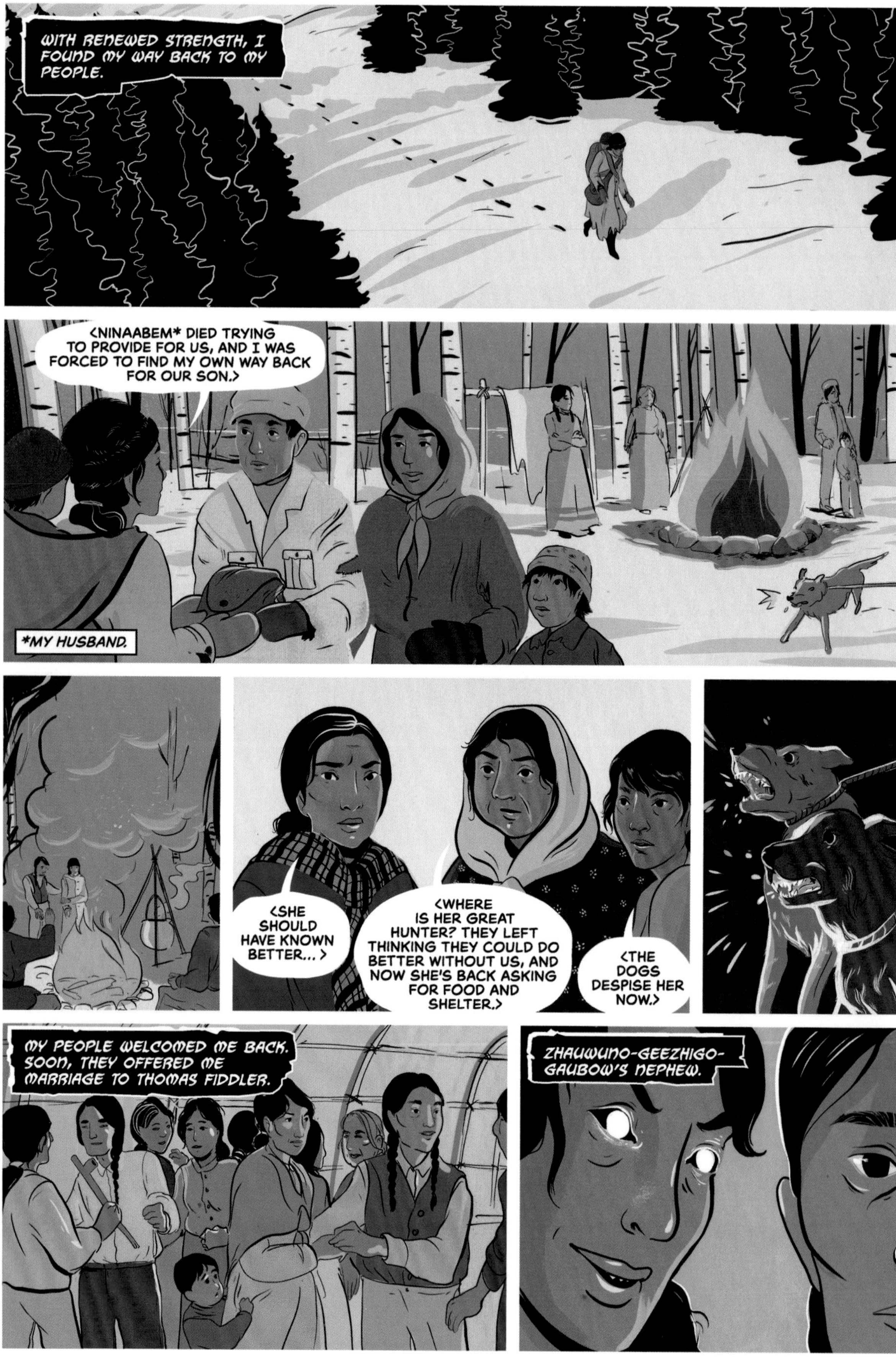
WITH RENEWED STRENGTH, I FOUND MY WAY BACK TO MY PEOPLE.
<NINAABEM* DIED TRYING TO PROVIDE FOR US, AND I WAS FORCED TO FIND MY OWN WAY BACK FOR OUR SON.>
*MY HUSBAND.
<SHE SHOULD HAVE KNOWN BETTER... >
<WHERE IS HER GREAT HUNTER? THEY LEFT THINKING THEY COULD DO BETTER WITHOUT US, AND NOW SHE'S BACK ASKING FOR FOOD AND SHELTER.>
<THE DOGS DESPISE HER NOW.>
MY PEOPLE WELCOMED ME BACK. SOON, THEY OFFERED ME MARRIAGE TO THOMAS FIDDLER.
ZHAUWUNO-GEEZHIGO-GAUBOW'S NEPHEW.

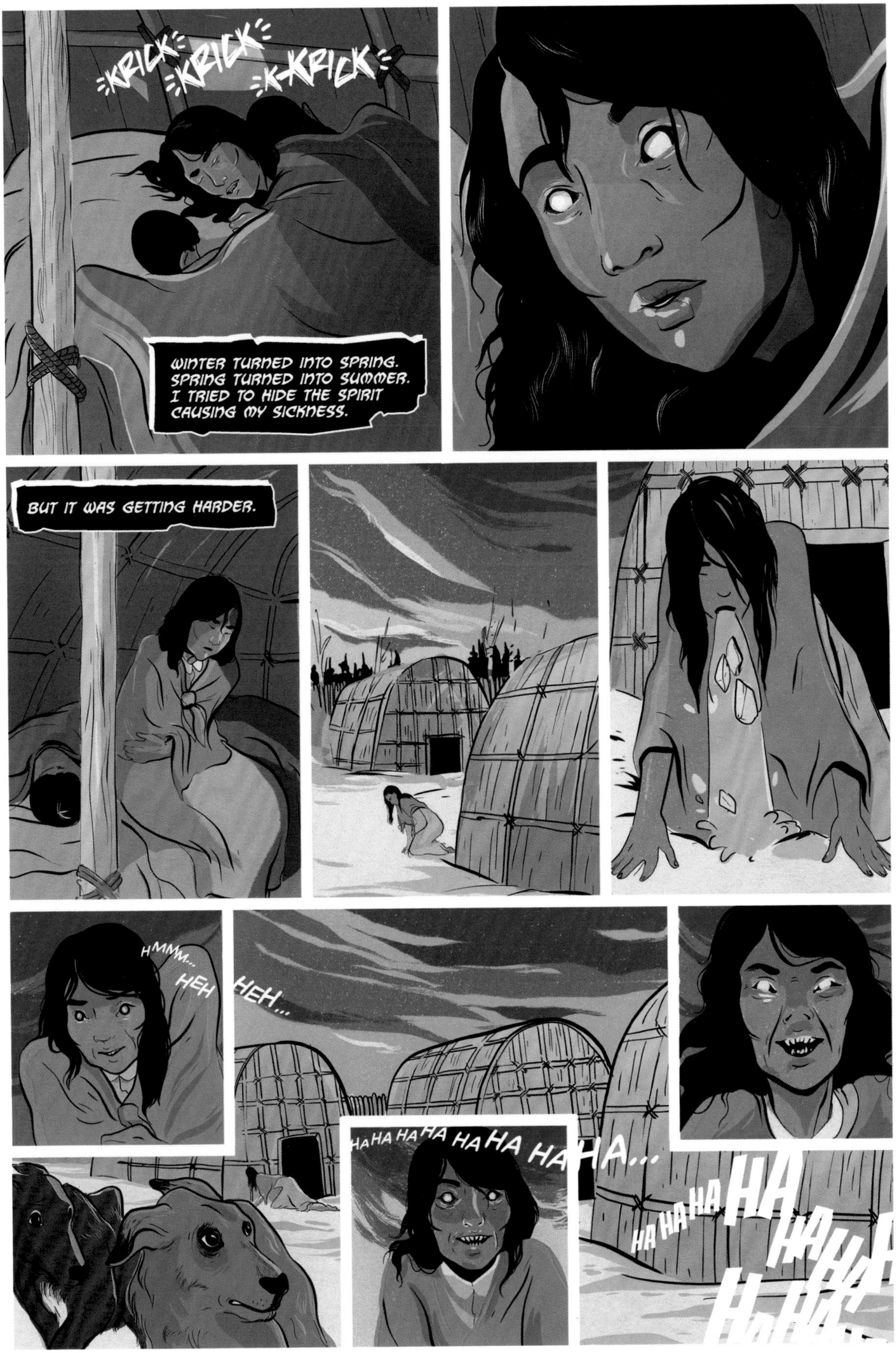
KRICK KRICK K-KRICK
WINTER TURNED INTO SPRING. SPRING TURNED INTO SUMMER. I TRIED TO HIDE THE SPIRIT CAUSING MY SICKNESS.
BUT IT WAS GETTING HARDER.
HMMM... HEH HEH...
HA HA HA HA HA HA HA HA HAHA...
HA HA HA HA HA HA HA

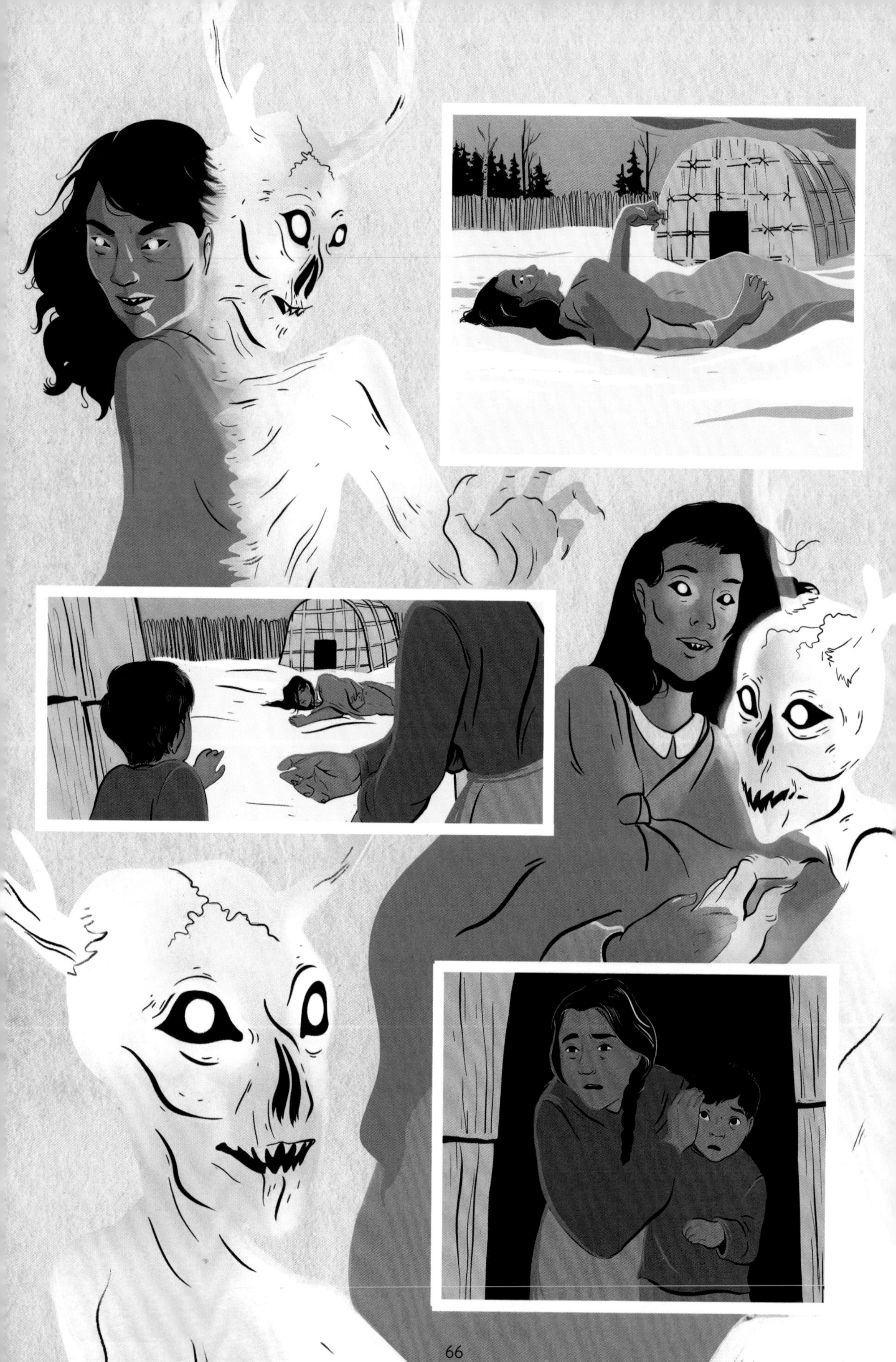

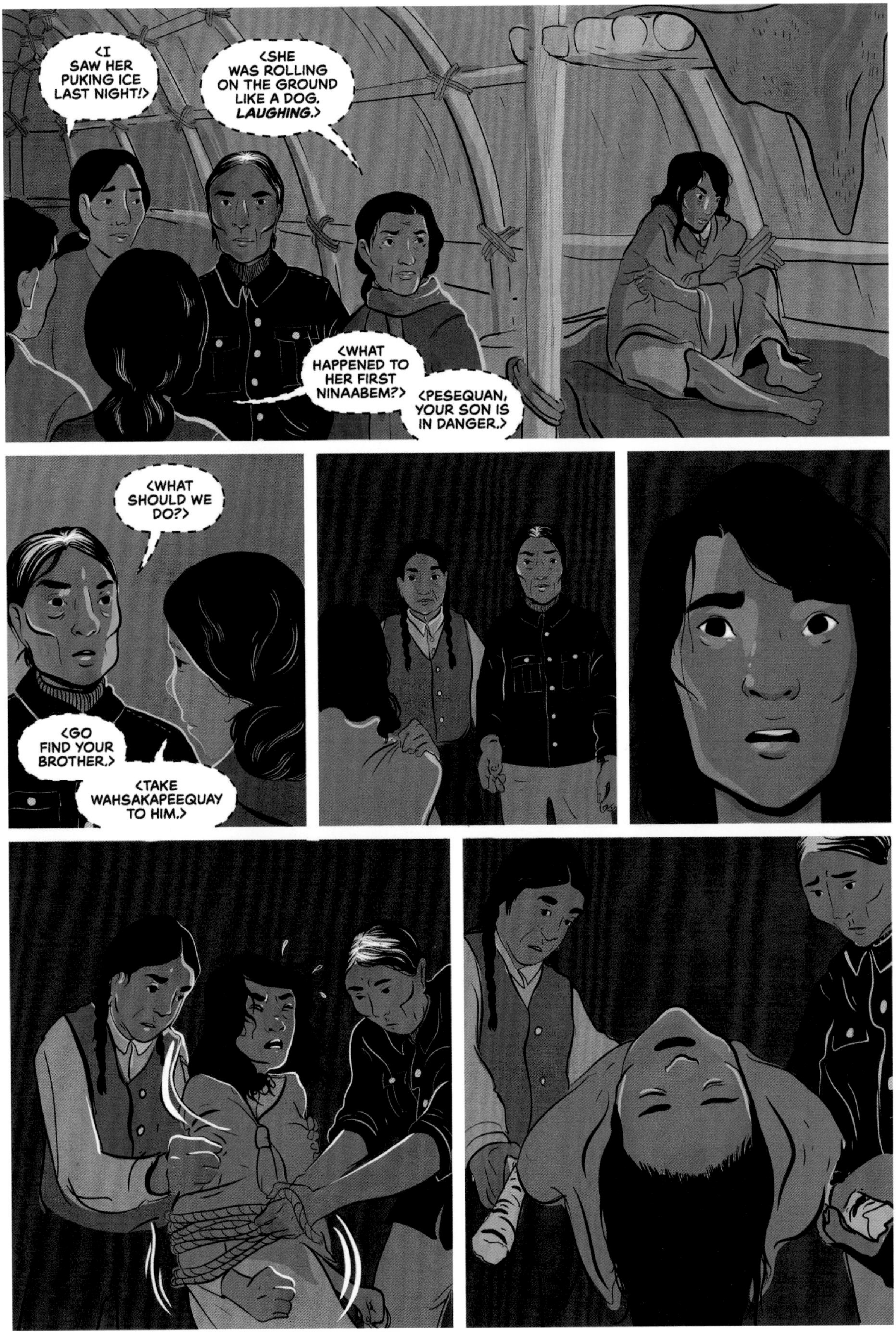
<I SAW HER PUKING ICE LAST NIGHT!>
<SHE WAS ROLLING ON THE GROUND LIKE A DOG. *LAUGHING.*>
<WHAT HAPPENED TO HER FIRST NINAABEM?>
<PESEQUAN, YOUR SON IS IN DANGER.>
<WHAT SHOULD WE DO?>
<GO FIND YOUR BROTHER.>
<TAKE WAHSAKAPEEQUAY TO HIM.>

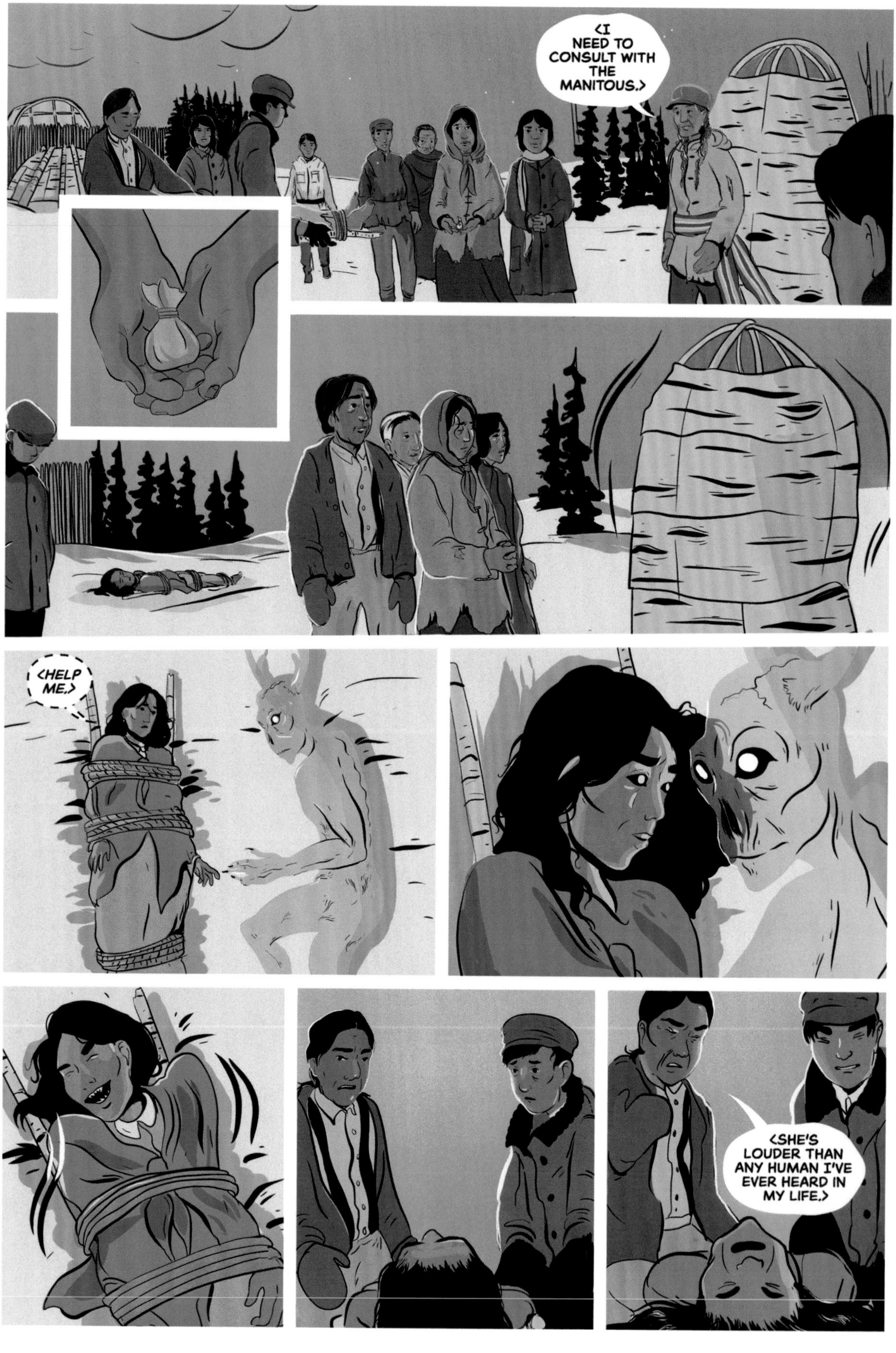
<I NEED TO CONSULT WITH THE MANITOUS.>
<HELP ME.>
<SHE'S LOUDER THAN ANY HUMAN I'VE EVER HEARD IN MY LIFE.>

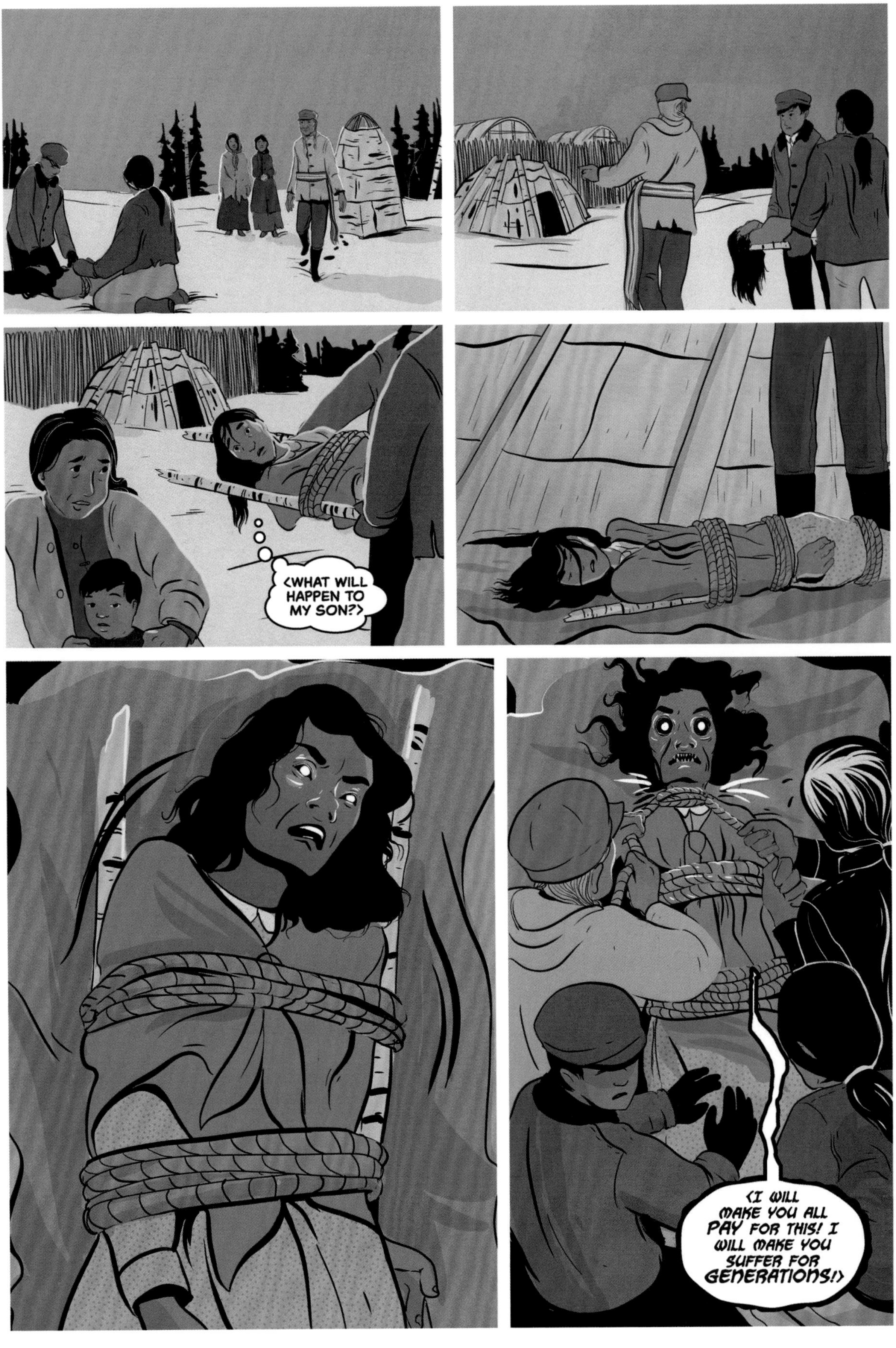
<WHAT WILL HAPPEN TO MY SON?>
<I WILL MAKE YOU ALL PAY FOR THIS! I WILL MAKE YOU SUFFER FOR GENERATIONS!>

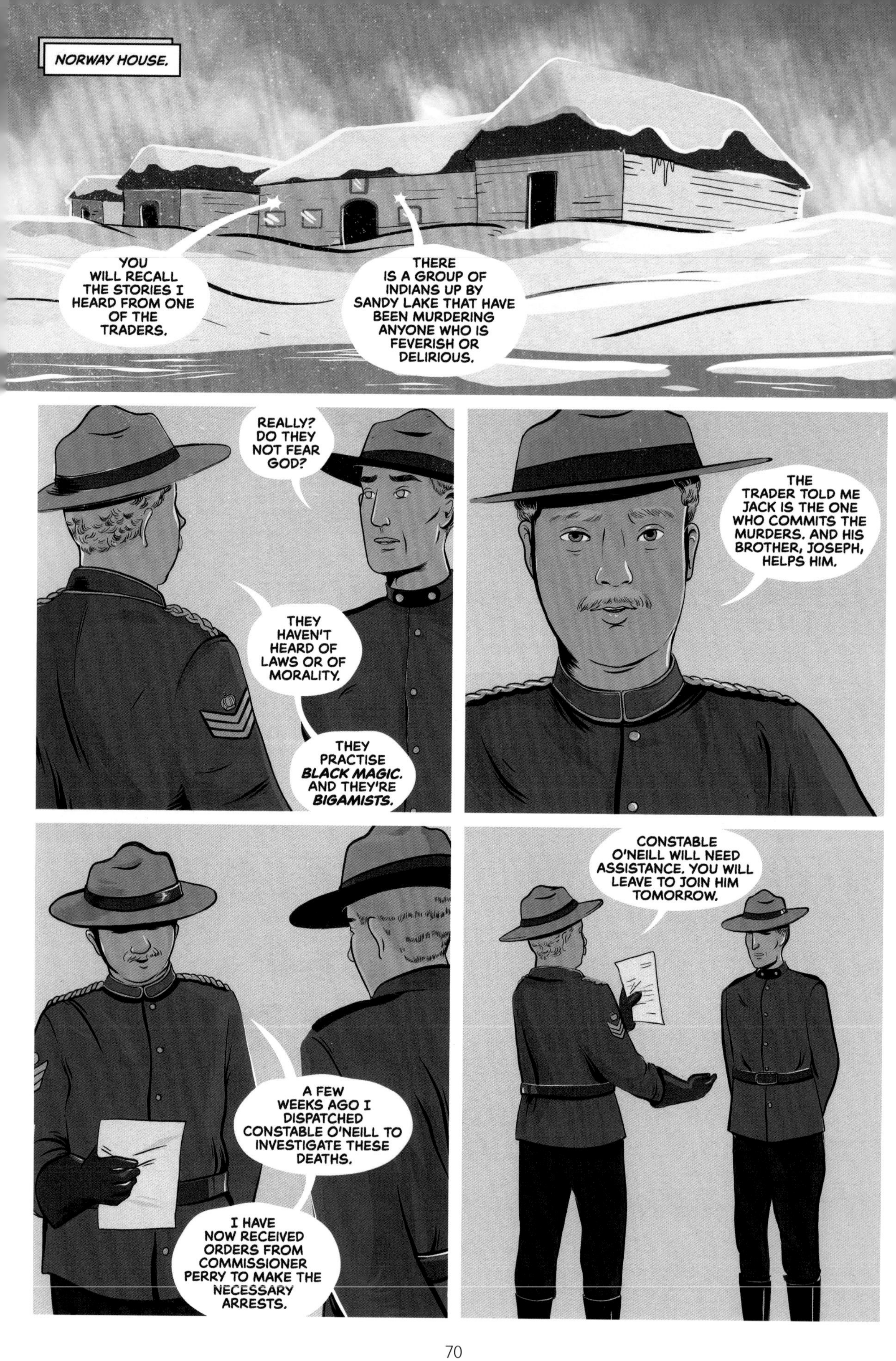
NORWAY HOUSE.
YOU WILL RECALL THE STORIES I HEARD FROM ONE OF THE TRADERS.
THERE IS A GROUP OF INDIANS UP BY SANDY LAKE THAT HAVE BEEN MURDERING ANYONE WHO IS FEVERISH OR DELIRIOUS.
REALLY? DO THEY NOT FEAR GOD?
THEY HAVEN'T HEARD OF LAWS OR OF MORALITY.
THEY PRACTISE BLACK MAGIC. AND THEY'RE BIGAMISTS.
THE TRADER TOLD ME JACK IS THE ONE WHO COMMITS THE MURDERS. AND HIS BROTHER, JOSEPH, HELPS HIM.
A FEW WEEKS AGO I DISPATCHED CONSTABLE O'NEILL TO INVESTIGATE THESE DEATHS.
I HAVE NOW RECEIVED ORDERS FROM COMMISSIONER PERRY TO MAKE THE NECESSARY ARRESTS.
CONSTABLE O'NEILL WILL NEED ASSISTANCE. YOU WILL LEAVE TO JOIN HIM TOMORROW.

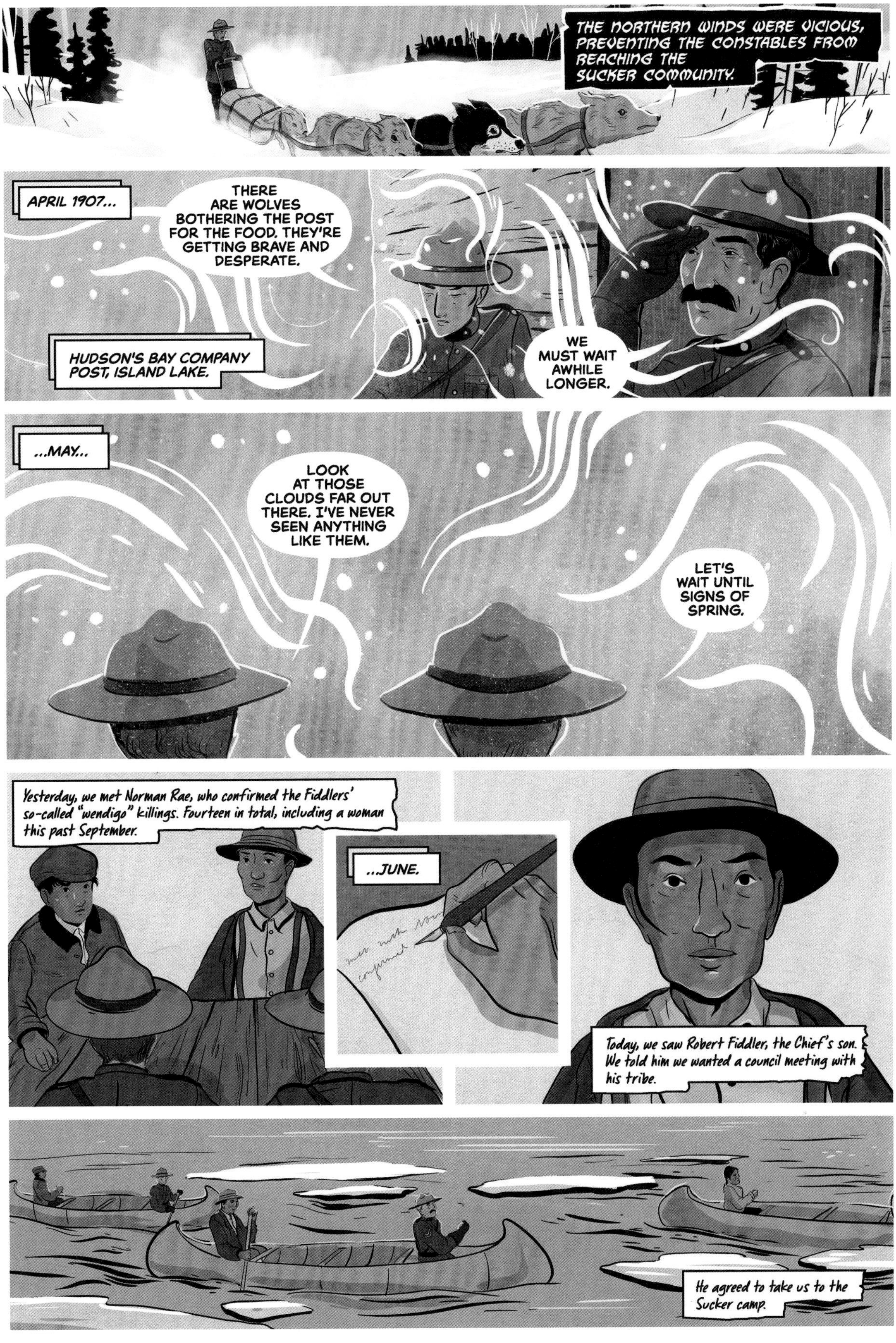
THE NORTHERN WINDS WERE VICIOUS, PREVENTING THE CONSTABLES FROM REACHING THE SUCKER COMMUNITY.
APRIL 1907...
HUDSON'S BAY COMPANY POST, ISLAND LAKE.
THERE ARE WOLVES BOTHERING THE POST FOR THE FOOD. THEY'RE GETTING BRAVE AND DESPERATE.
WE MUST WAIT AWHILE LONGER.
...MAY...
LOOK AT THOSE CLOUDS FAR OUT THERE. I'VE NEVER SEEN ANYTHING LIKE THEM.
LET'S WAIT UNTIL SIGNS OF SPRING.
Yesterday, we met Norman Rae, who confirmed the Fiddlers' so-called "wendigo" killings. Fourteen in total, including a woman this past September.
...JUNE.
Today, we saw Robert Fiddler, the Chief's son. We told him we wanted a council meeting with his tribe.
He agreed to take us to the Sucker camp.

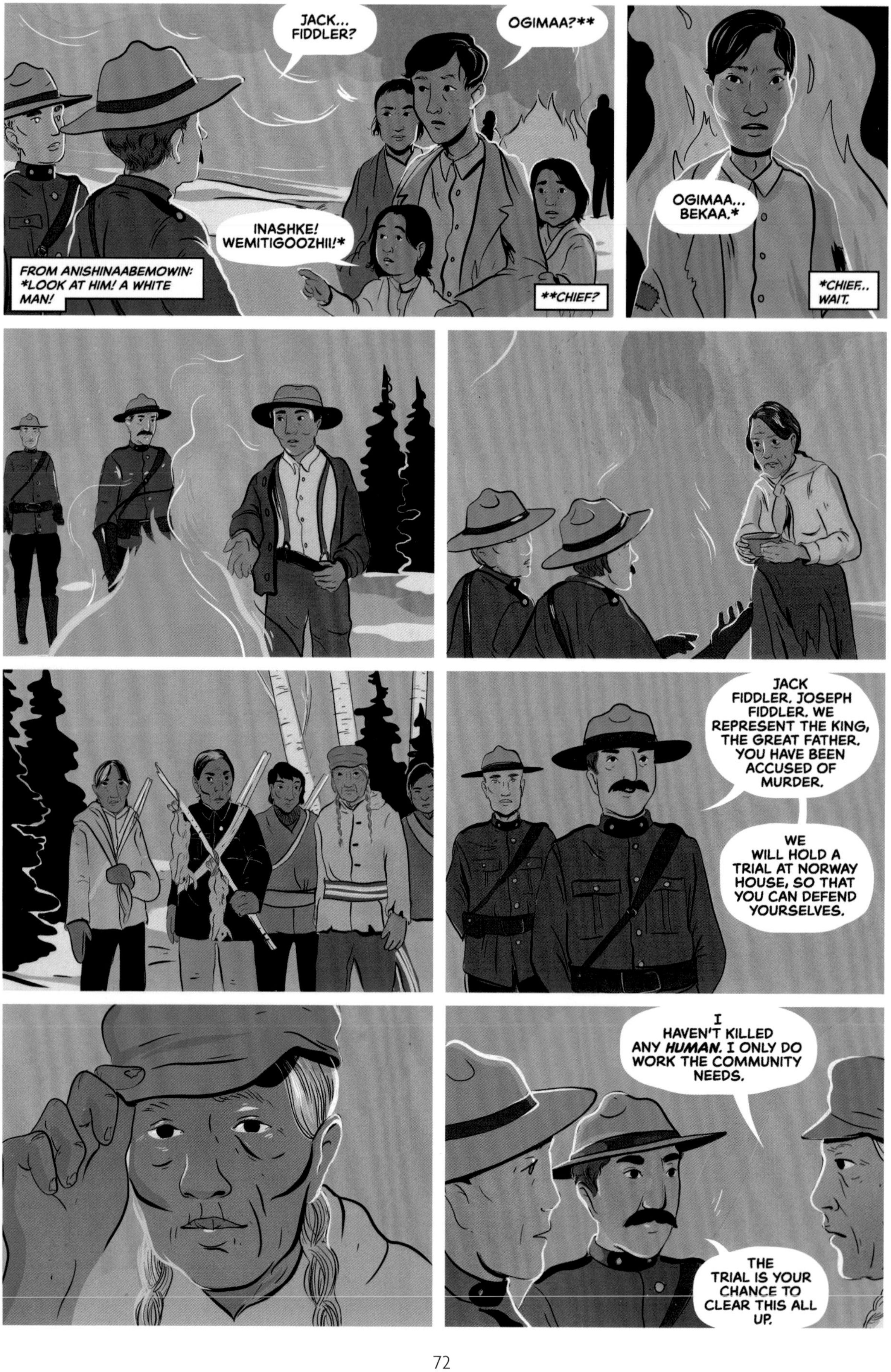
JACK... FIDDLER?
OGIMAA?**
INASHKE! WEMITIGOOZHII!*
FROM ANISHINAABEMOWIN: *LOOK AT HIM! A WHITE MAN!
**CHIEF?
OGIMAA... BEKAA.*
*CHIEF... WAIT.
JACK FIDDLER. JOSEPH FIDDLER. WE REPRESENT THE KING, THE GREAT FATHER. YOU HAVE BEEN ACCUSED OF MURDER.
WE WILL HOLD A TRIAL AT NORWAY HOUSE, SO THAT YOU CAN DEFEND YOURSELVES.
I HAVEN'T KILLED ANY ***HUMAN***. I ONLY DO WORK THE COMMUNITY NEEDS.
THE TRIAL IS YOUR CHANCE TO CLEAR THIS ALL UP.

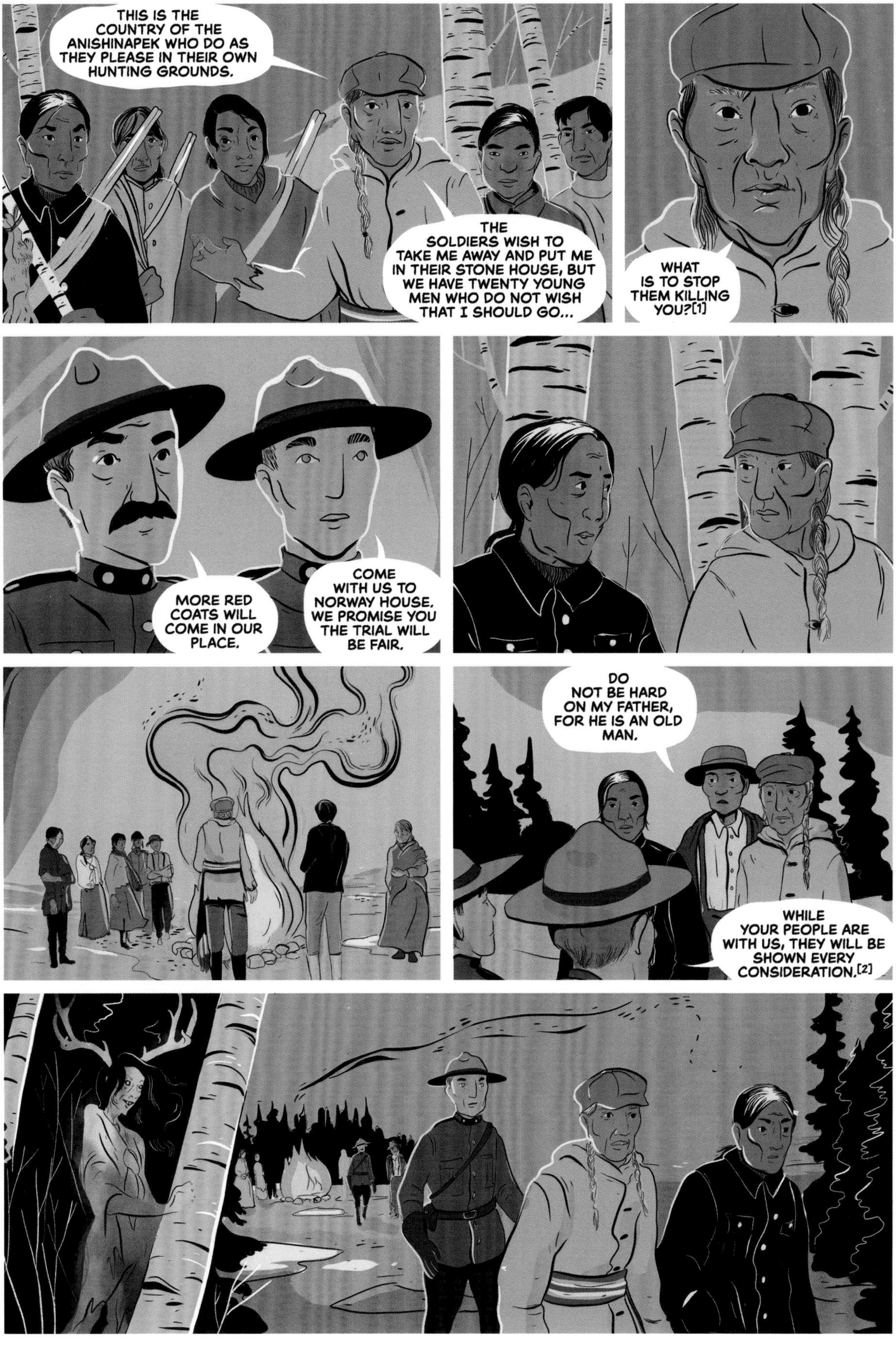
THIS IS THE COUNTRY OF THE ANISHINAPEK WHO DO AS THEY PLEASE IN THEIR OWN HUNTING GROUNDS.
THE SOLDIERS WISH TO TAKE ME AWAY AND PUT ME IN THEIR STONE HOUSE, BUT WE HAVE TWENTY YOUNG MEN WHO DO NOT WISH THAT I SHOULD GO...
WHAT IS TO STOP THEM KILLING YOU?[1]
MORE RED COATS WILL COME IN OUR PLACE.
COME WITH US TO NORWAY HOUSE. WE PROMISE YOU THE TRIAL WILL BE FAIR.
DO NOT BE HARD ON MY FATHER, FOR HE IS AN OLD MAN.
WHILE YOUR PEOPLE ARE WITH US, THEY WILL BE SHOWN EVERY CONSIDERATION.[2]

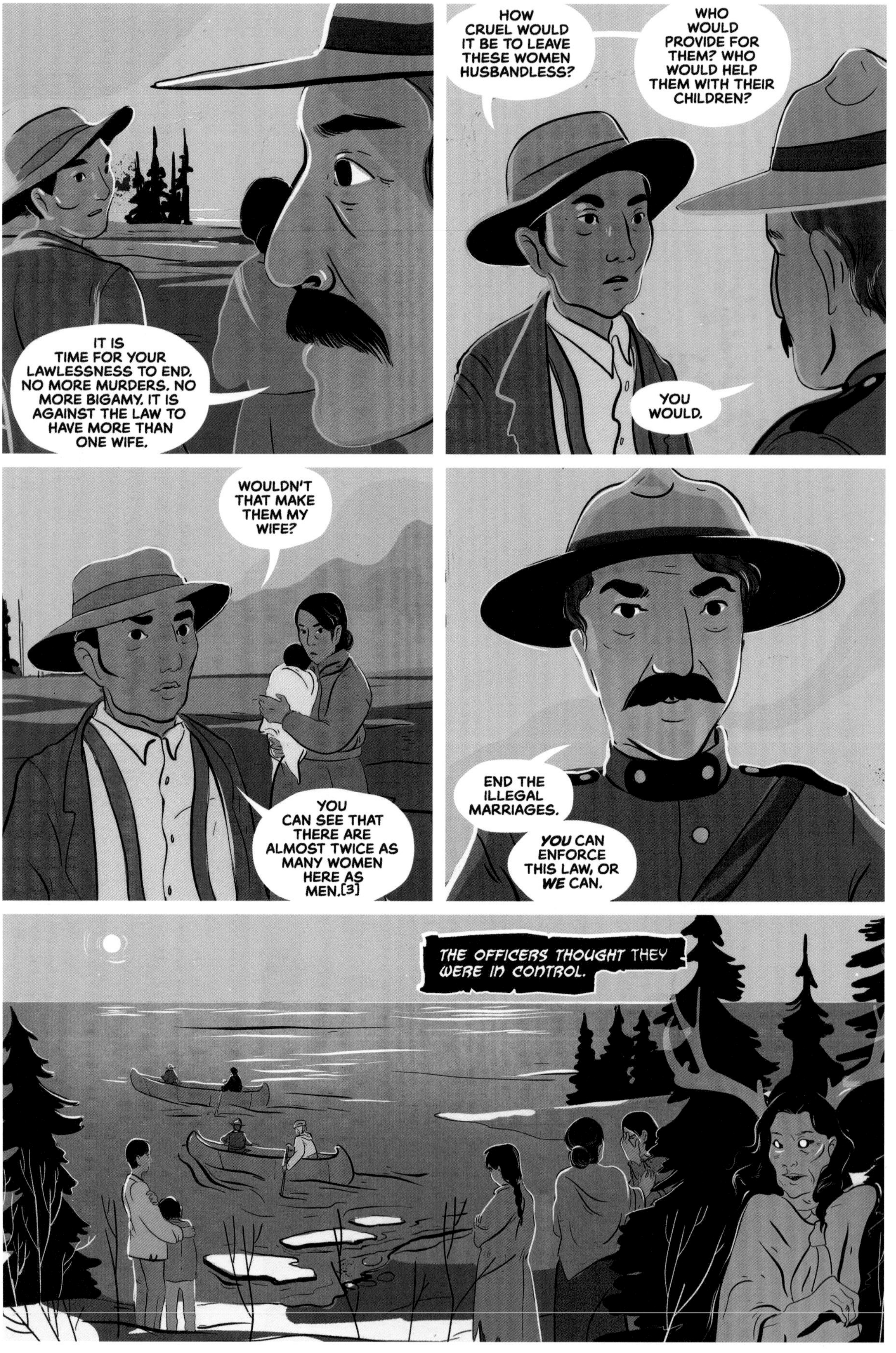
IT IS TIME FOR YOUR LAWLESSNESS TO END. NO MORE MURDERS. NO MORE BIGAMY. IT IS AGAINST THE LAW TO HAVE MORE THAN ONE WIFE.
HOW CRUEL WOULD IT BE TO LEAVE THESE WOMEN HUSBANDLESS?
WHO WOULD PROVIDE FOR THEM? WHO WOULD HELP THEM WITH THEIR CHILDREN?
YOU WOULD.
WOULDN'T THAT MAKE THEM MY WIFE?
YOU CAN SEE THAT THERE ARE ALMOST TWICE AS MANY WOMEN HERE AS MEN.[3]
END THE ILLEGAL MARRIAGES.
YOU CAN ENFORCE THIS LAW, OR WE CAN.
THE OFFICERS THOUGHT THEY WERE IN CONTROL.

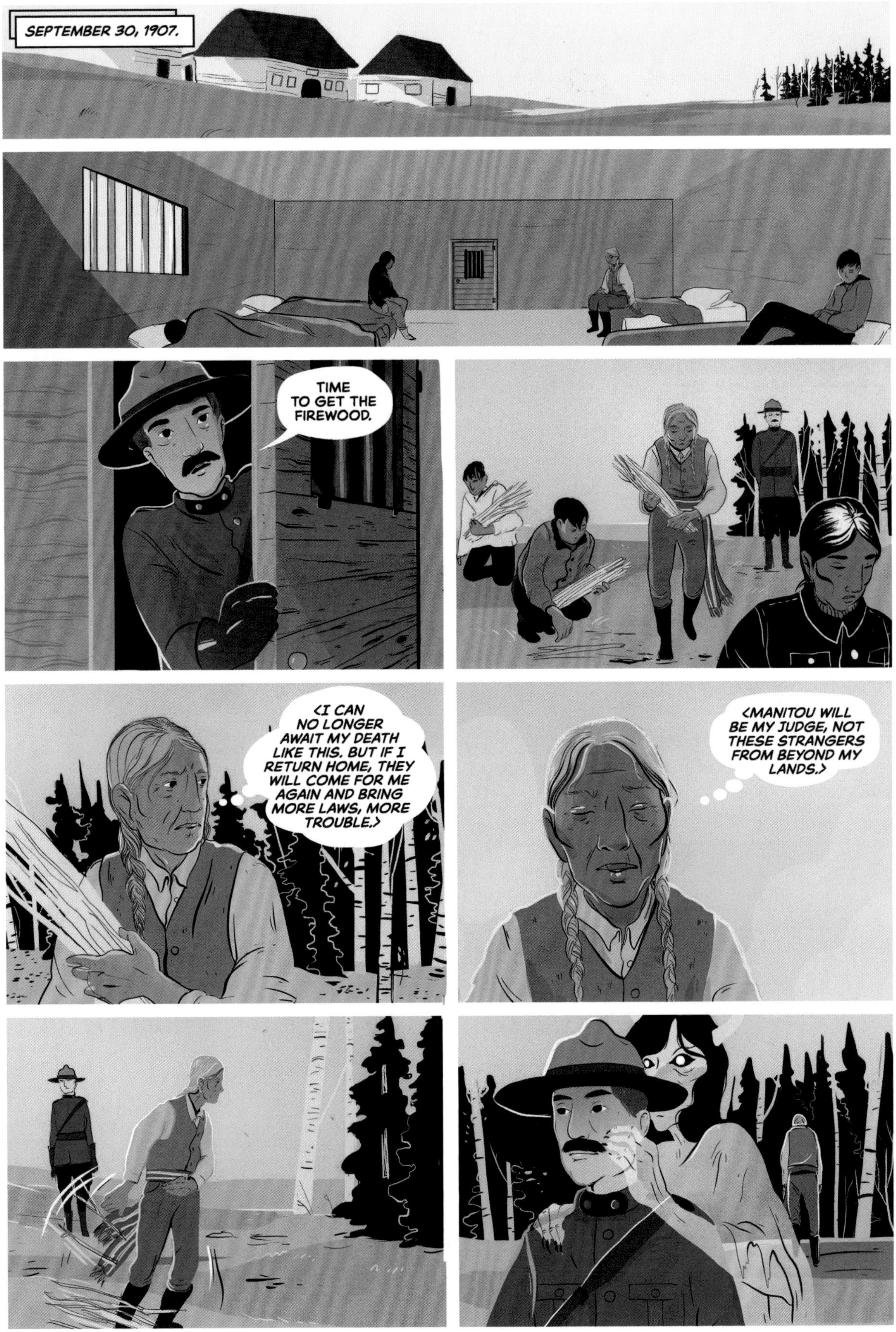
SEPTEMBER 30, 1907.
TIME TO GET THE FIREWOOD.
<I CAN NO LONGER AWAIT MY DEATH LIKE THIS. BUT IF I RETURN HOME, THEY WILL COME FOR ME AGAIN AND BRING MORE LAWS, MORE TROUBLE.>
<MANITOU WILL BE MY JUDGE, NOT THESE STRANGERS FROM BEYOND MY LANDS.>

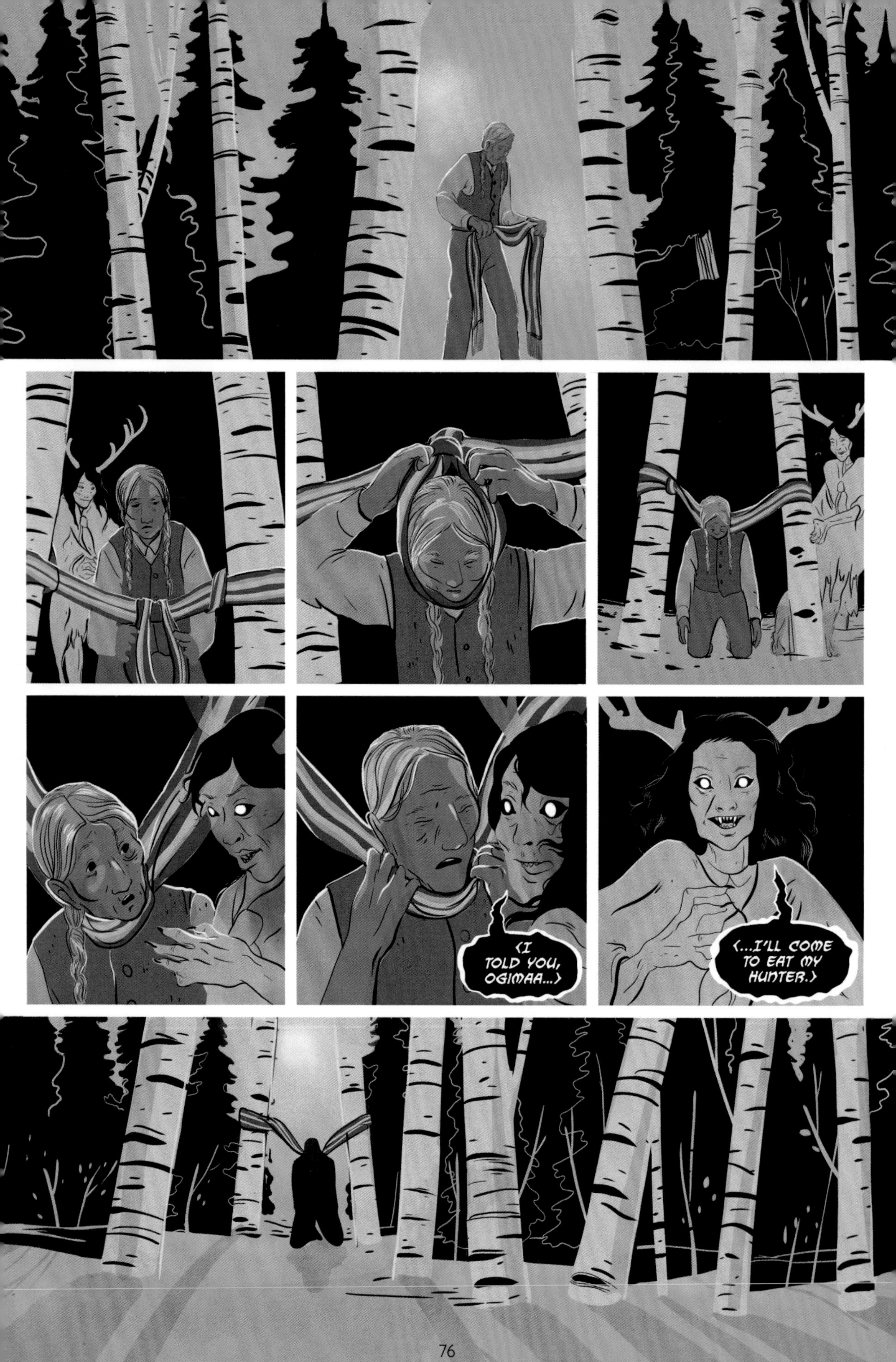
‹I TOLD YOU, OGIMAA...›
‹...I'LL COME TO EAT MY HUNTER.›

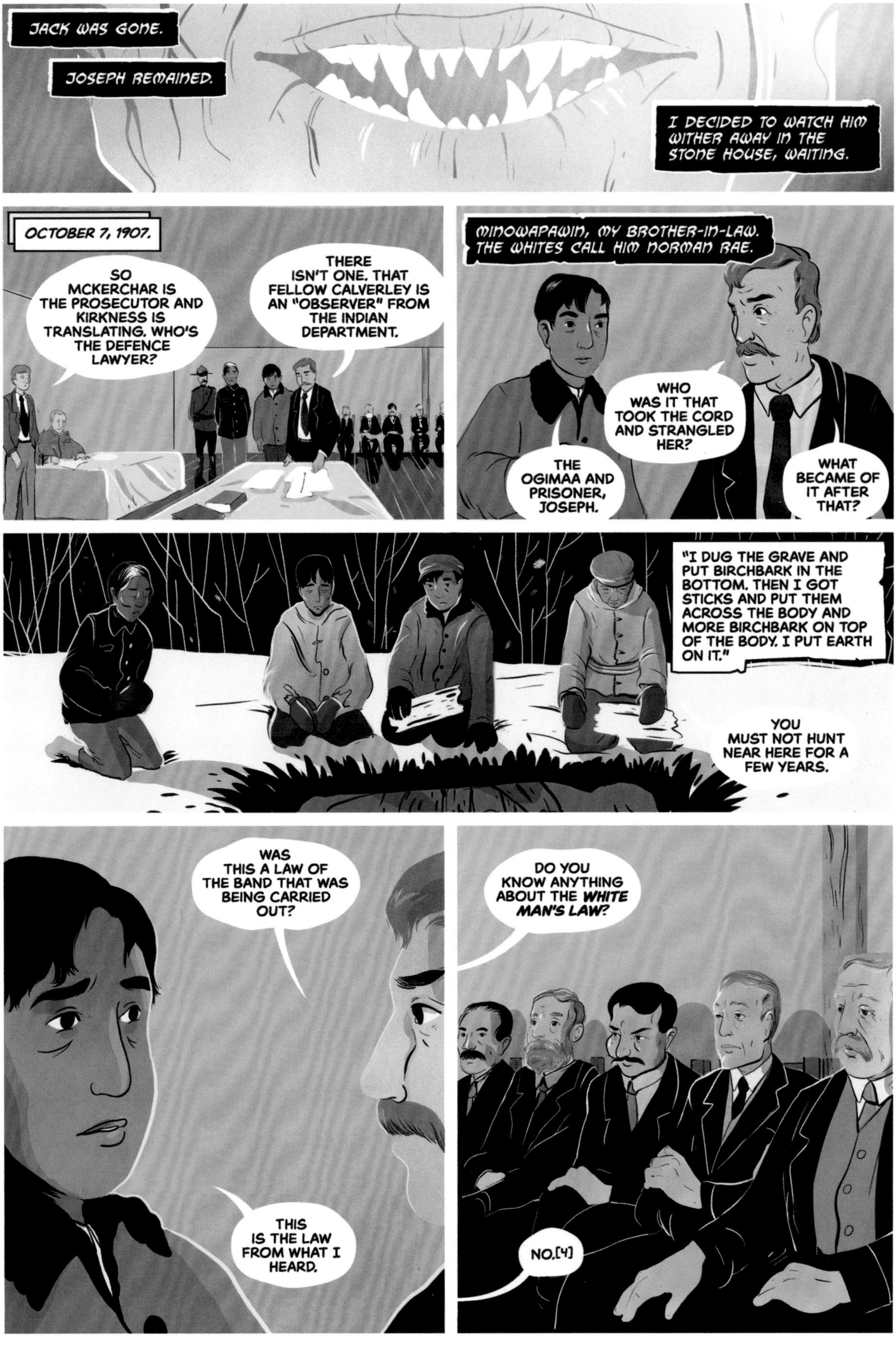
JACK WAS GONE.
JOSEPH REMAINED.
I DECIDED TO WATCH HIM WITHER AWAY IN THE STONE HOUSE, WAITING.
OCTOBER 7, 1907.
SO MCKERCHAR IS THE PROSECUTOR AND KIRKNESS IS TRANSLATING. WHO'S THE DEFENCE LAWYER?
THERE ISN'T ONE. THAT FELLOW CALVERLEY IS AN "OBSERVER" FROM THE INDIAN DEPARTMENT.
MINOWAPAWIN, MY BROTHER-IN-LAW. THE WHITES CALL HIM NORMAN RAE.
WHO WAS IT THAT TOOK THE CORD AND STRANGLED HER?
THE OGIMAA AND PRISONER, JOSEPH.
WHAT BECAME OF IT AFTER THAT?
"I DUG THE GRAVE AND PUT BIRCHBARK IN THE BOTTOM. THEN I GOT STICKS AND PUT THEM ACROSS THE BODY AND MORE BIRCHBARK ON TOP OF THE BODY. I PUT EARTH ON IT."
YOU MUST NOT HUNT NEAR HERE FOR A FEW YEARS.
WAS THIS A LAW OF THE BAND THAT WAS BEING CARRIED OUT?
THIS IS THE LAW FROM WHAT I HEARD.
DO YOU KNOW ANYTHING ABOUT THE WHITE MAN'S LAW?
NO.[4]

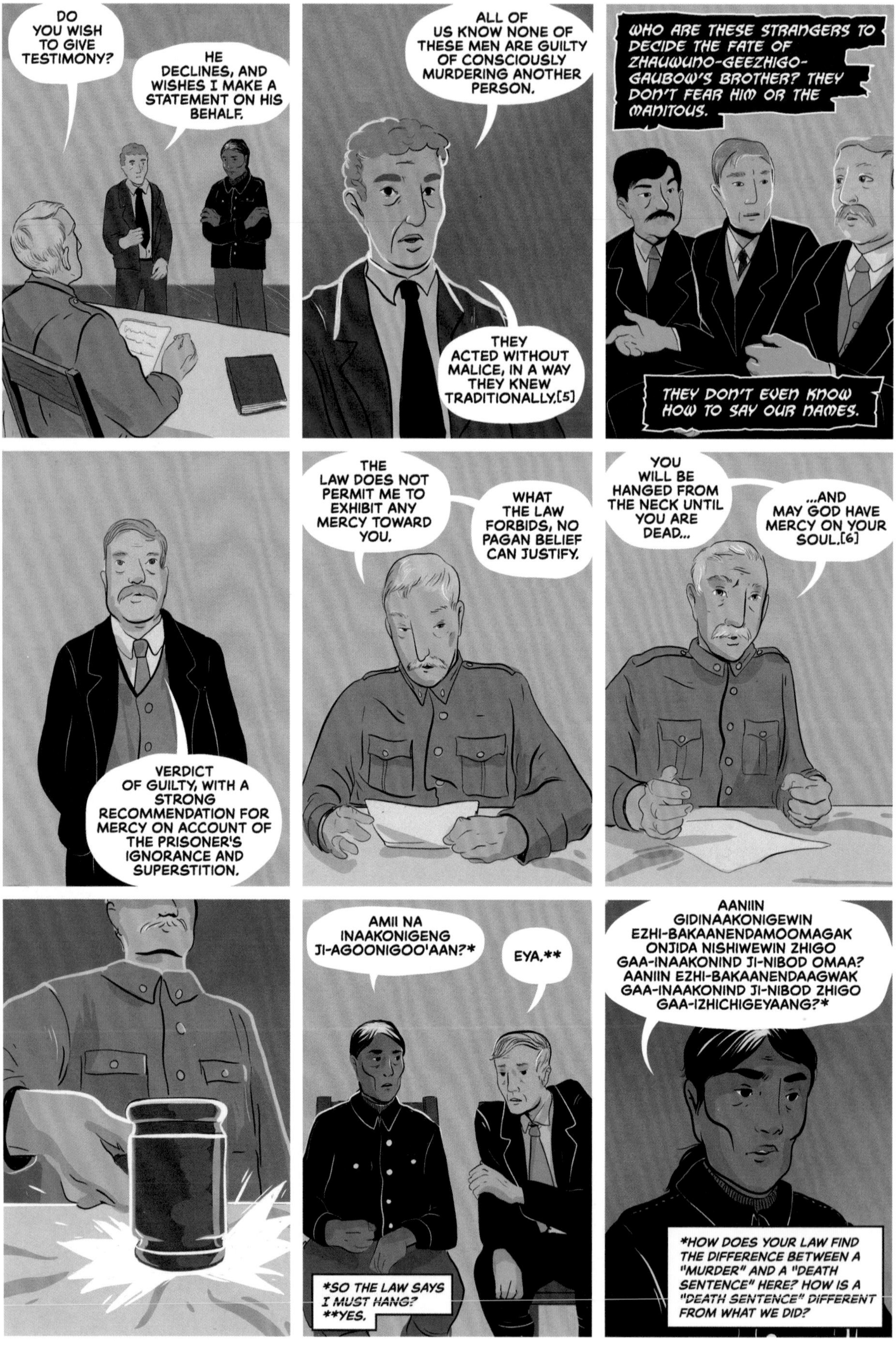

DO YOU WISH TO GIVE TESTIMONY?
HE DECLINES, AND WISHES I MAKE A STATEMENT ON HIS BEHALF.
ALL OF US KNOW NONE OF THESE MEN ARE GUILTY OF CONSCIOUSLY MURDERING ANOTHER PERSON.
THEY ACTED WITHOUT MALICE, IN A WAY THEY KNEW TRADITIONALLY.[5]
WHO ARE THESE STRANGERS TO DECIDE THE FATE OF ZHAUWUNO-GEEZHIGO-GAUBOW'S BROTHER? THEY DON'T FEAR HIM OR THE MANITOUS.
THEY DON'T EVEN KNOW HOW TO SAY OUR NAMES.
VERDICT OF GUILTY, WITH A STRONG RECOMMENDATION FOR MERCY ON ACCOUNT OF THE PRISONER'S IGNORANCE AND SUPERSTITION.
THE LAW DOES NOT PERMIT ME TO EXHIBIT ANY MERCY TOWARD YOU.
WHAT THE LAW FORBIDS, NO PAGAN BELIEF CAN JUSTIFY.
YOU WILL BE HANGED FROM THE NECK UNTIL YOU ARE DEAD...
...AND MAY GOD HAVE MERCY ON YOUR SOUL.[6]
AMII NA INAAKONIGENG JI-AGOONIGOO'AAN?*
EYA.**
*SO THE LAW SAYS I MUST HANG?
**YES.
AANIIN GIDINAAKONIGEWIN EZHI-BAKAANENDAMOOMAGAK ONJIDA NISHIWEWIN ZHIGO GAA-INAAKONIND JI-NIBOD OMAA? AANIIN EZHI-BAKAANENDAAGWAK GAA-INAAKONIND JI-NIBOD ZHIGO GAA-IZHICHIGEYAANG?*
*HOW DOES YOUR LAW FIND THE DIFFERENCE BETWEEN A "MURDER" AND A "DEATH SENTENCE" HERE? HOW IS A "DEATH SENTENCE" DIFFERENT FROM WHAT WE DID?

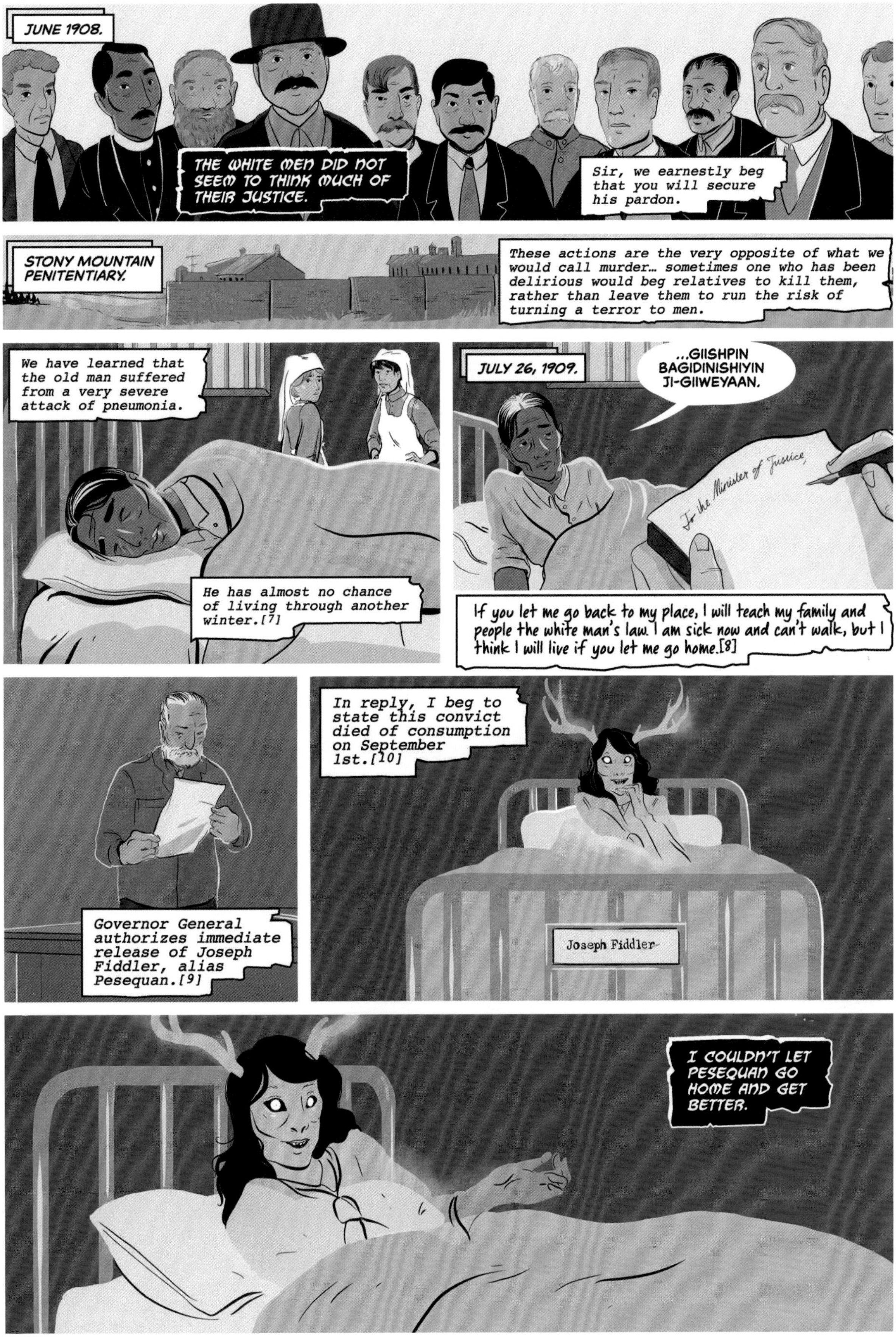
JUNE 1908.
THE WHITE MEN DID NOT SEEM TO THINK MUCH OF THEIR JUSTICE.
Sir, we earnestly beg that you will secure his pardon.
STONY MOUNTAIN PENITENTIARY.
These actions are the very opposite of what we would call murder… sometimes one who has been delirious would beg relatives to kill them, rather than leave them to run the risk of turning a terror to men.
We have learned that the old man suffered from a very severe attack of pneumonia.
He has almost no chance of living through another winter.[7]
JULY 26, 1909.
…GIISHPIN BAGIDINISHIYIN JI-GIIWEYAAN.
To the Minister of Justice,
If you let me go back to my place, I will teach my family and people the white man's law. I am sick now and can't walk, but I think I will live if you let me go home.[8]
Governor General authorizes immediate release of Joseph Fiddler, alias Pesequan.[9]
In reply, I beg to state this convict died of consumption on September 1st.[10]
Joseph Fiddler
I COULDN'T LET PESEQUAN GO HOME AND GET BETTER.

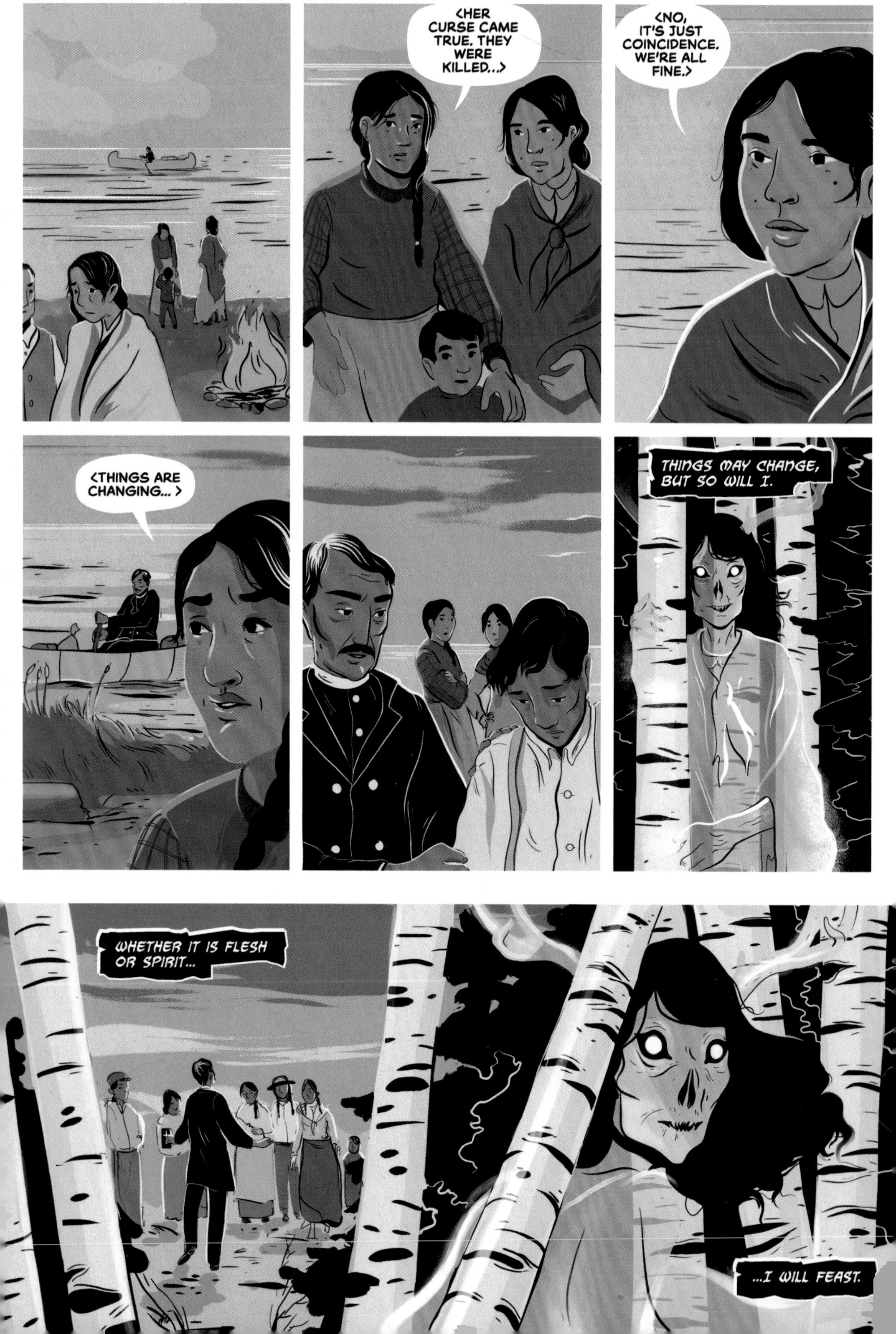
<HER CURSE CAME TRUE. THEY WERE KILLED...>
<NO, IT'S JUST COINCIDENCE. WE'RE ALL FINE.>
<THINGS ARE CHANGING...>
THINGS MAY CHANGE, BUT SO WILL I.
WHETHER IT IS FLESH OR SPIRIT...
...I WILL FEAST.

y work has often focused on representation—on how Indigenous Peoples now, and in the past, have been portrayed in popular culture. I also strive to find Indigenous heroes who have been underrepresented in literature. Often, I have used comics, an art form that spans all genres, and reaches all ages, genders, and cultures.

I've known about Francis Pegahmagabow for years, on a surface level. I knew that he was one of the most effective snipers in history, but I wanted to know more about him, and I thought it was important for Canadians to know more as well. Drawing on several texts, including Brian McInnes' excellent *Sounding Thunder*, I learned about Francis "Peggy" Pegahmagabow the man,

and the effectiveness of his work that extended beyond the battlefield.

Comics are engaging and powerful. Much like Francis himself. But, as with this story, they often serve as an introduction, and it is up to the reader to continue learning. There is so much more to Peggy, up to his retirement as Supreme Chief of the National Indian Government in 1950, and into his later life. These nuances, struggles, and victories are fascinating, and I hope this text catapults you into that life, and the teachings we can draw from it.

Ekosani,
David A. Robertson

1914-1918
World War I

1917
The Military Service Act introduces conscription in Canada. Indigenous men are included in the draft, despite not having the rights of citizenship.

1920
An Indian Act amendment makes attending day school or residential school mandatory.

1919
The League of Indians of Canada is formed. It is the first national organization of First Nations in Canada.

1917
The Soldier Settlement Act creates a fund to help WWI veterans obtain low-interest loans and establish farms.

1918
The Canadian government amends the Indian Act to allow expropriation of 'unused' Treaty lands for farming without Indigenous consent.

Peggy

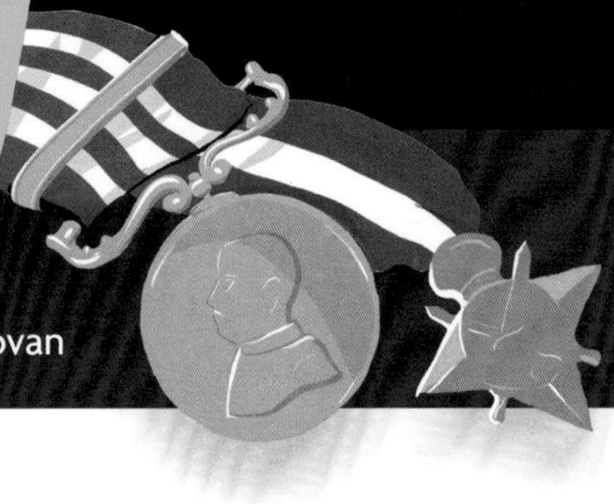

David A. Robertson

Illustration & colours: Natasha Donovan

1923-1924
Deskaheh, Cayuga Chief, lobbies the League of Nations to recognize the Six Nations as a sovereign state.

1925
An Indian Act amendment makes powwows, Sun Dances, and sweat lodges illegal.

1927
An Indian Act amendment prohibits hiring lawyers or filing land claims without prior government authorization.

1928
The Alberta government passes the Alberta Sexual Sterilization Act, targeting First Nations and Metis women for forced sterilization. British Columbia enacts a similar policy five years later.

1930
The Natural Resources Transfer Acts grant Indigenous peoples in the prairie provinces the right to hunt and fish on unoccupied Crown lands.

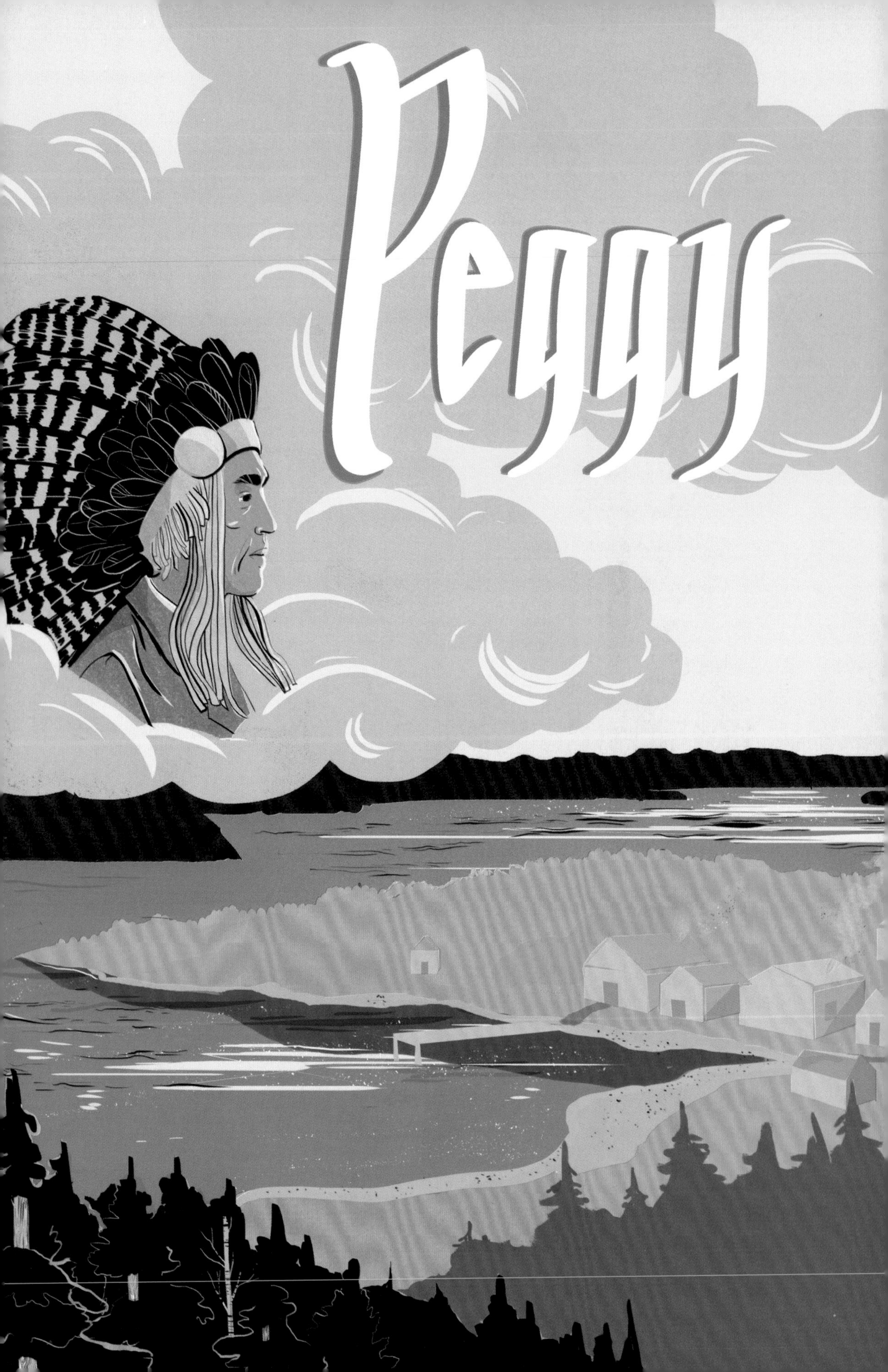
Peggy

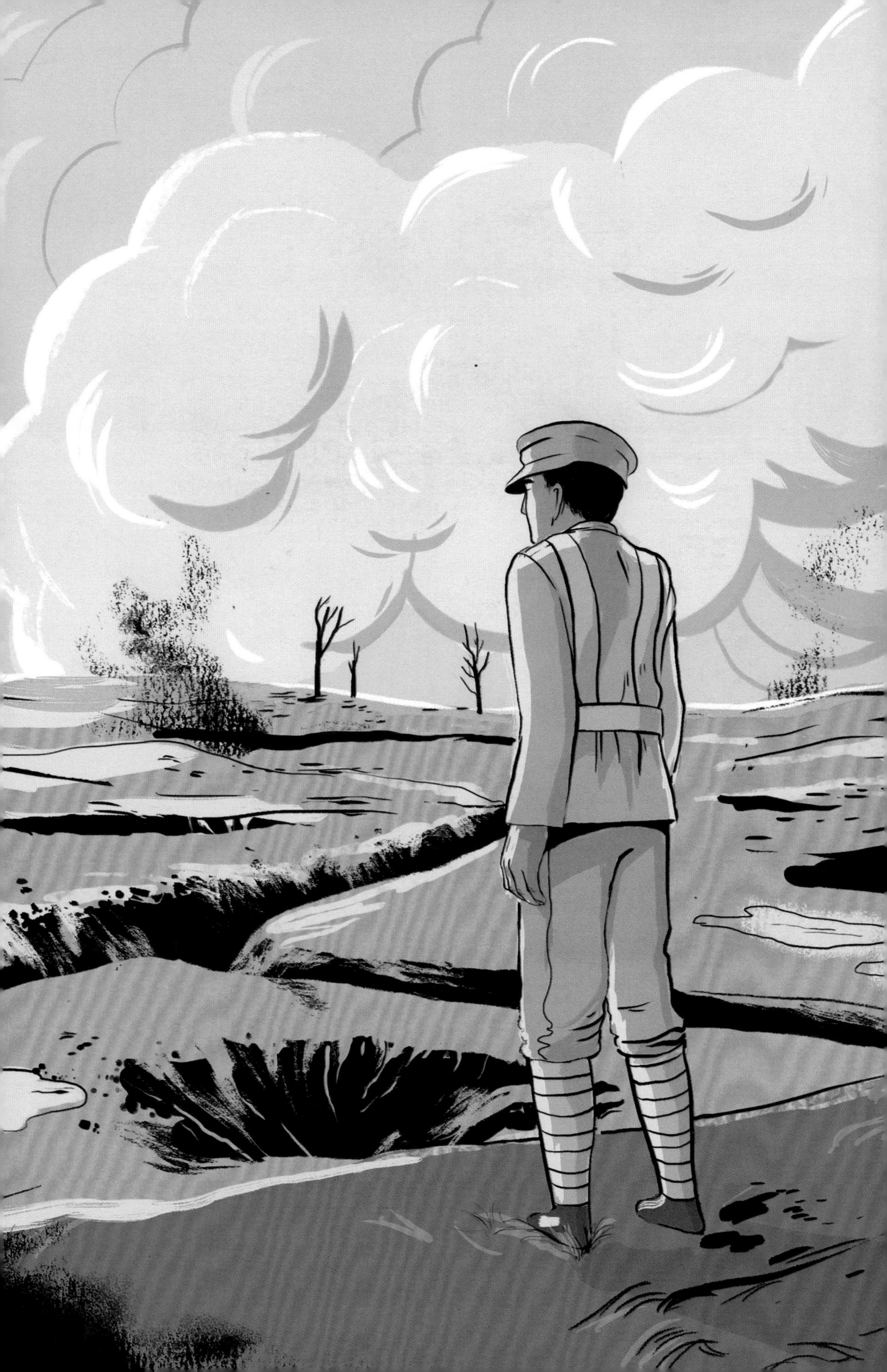

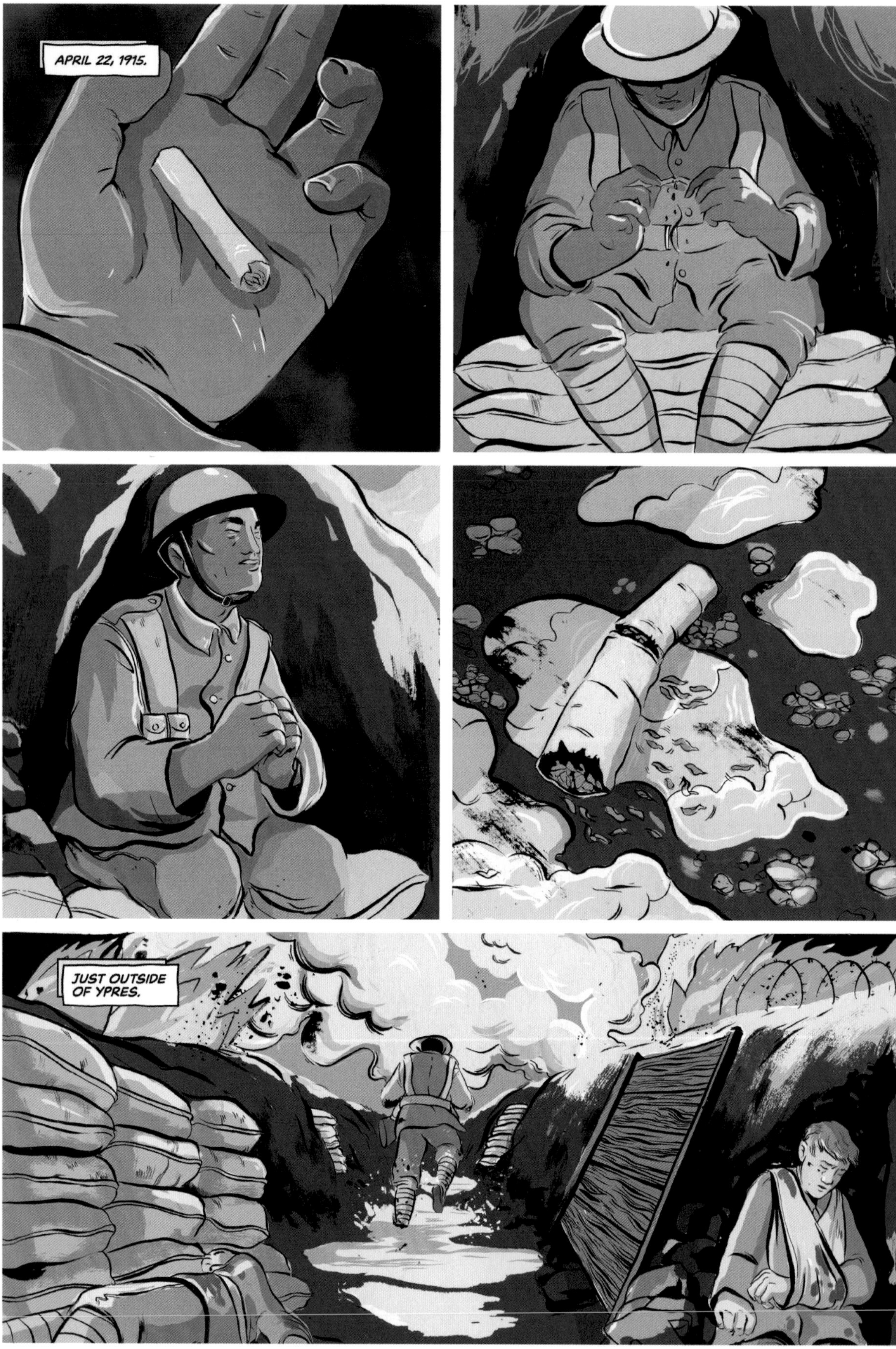
APRIL 22, 1915.
JUST OUTSIDE OF YPRES.

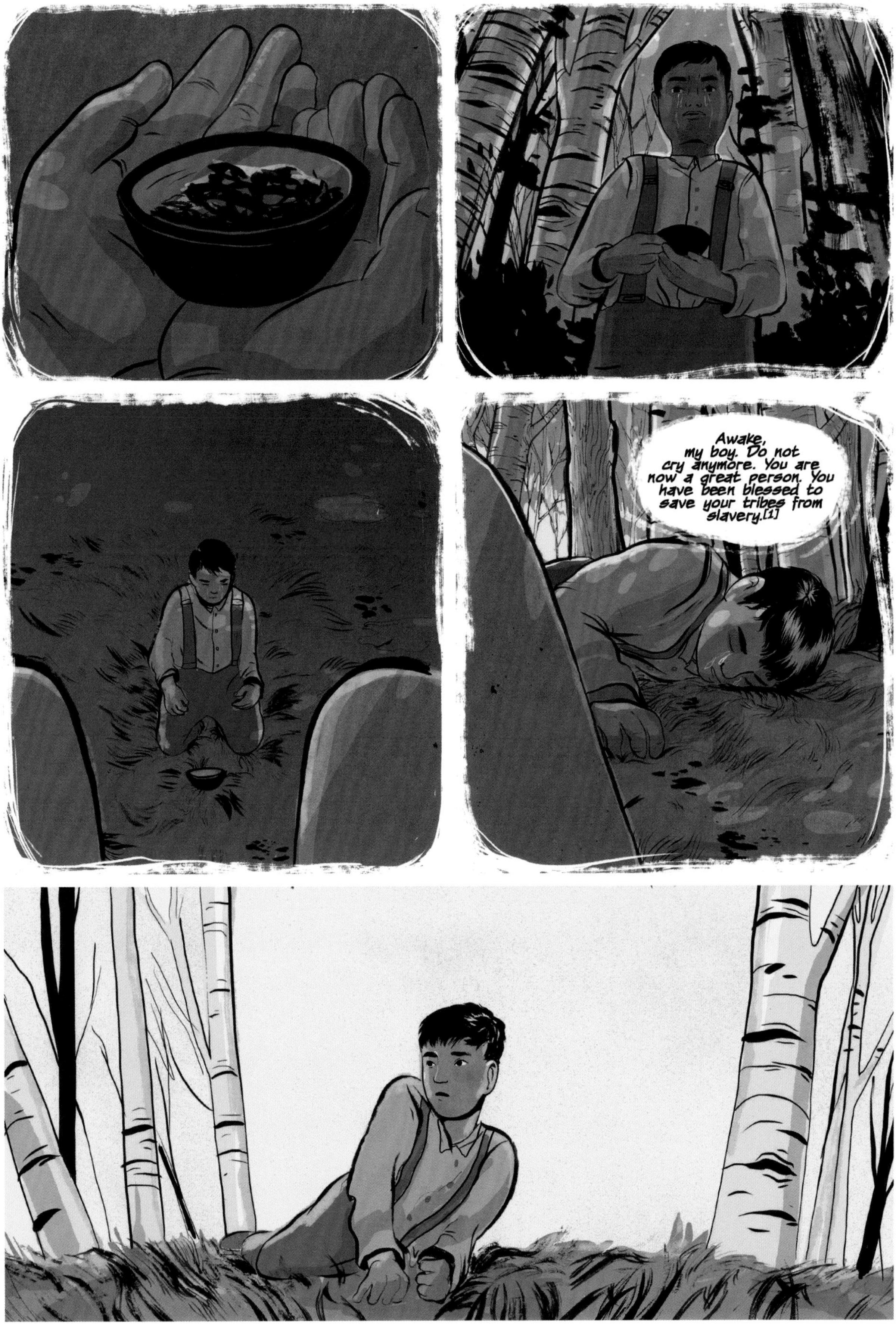
Awake, my boy. Do not cry anymore. You are now a great person. You have been blessed to save your tribes from slavery.[1]

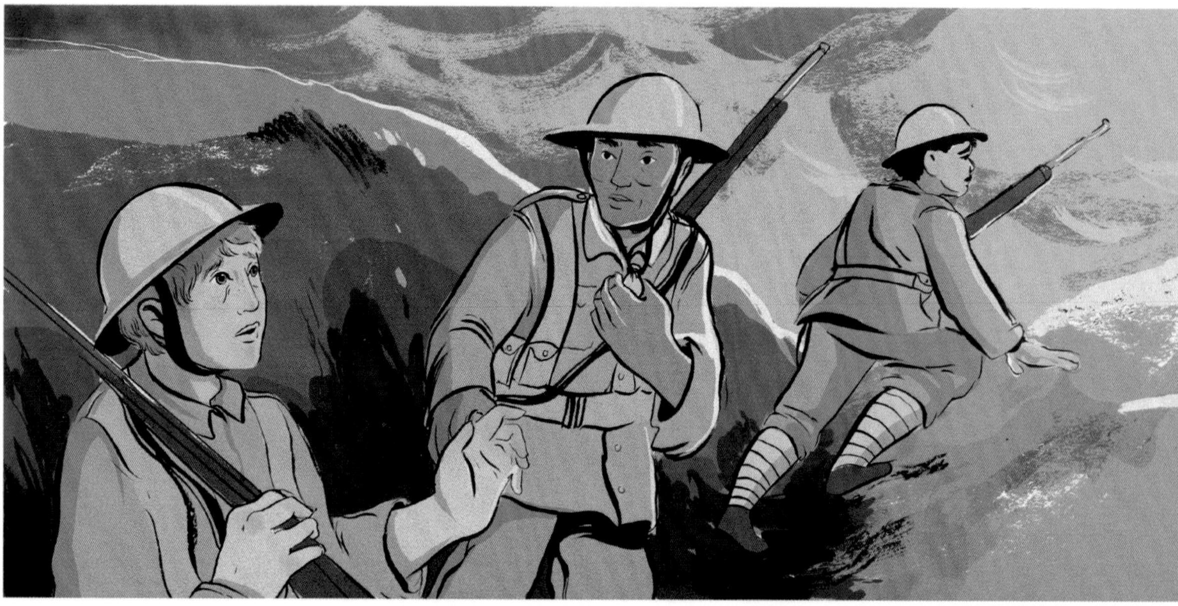

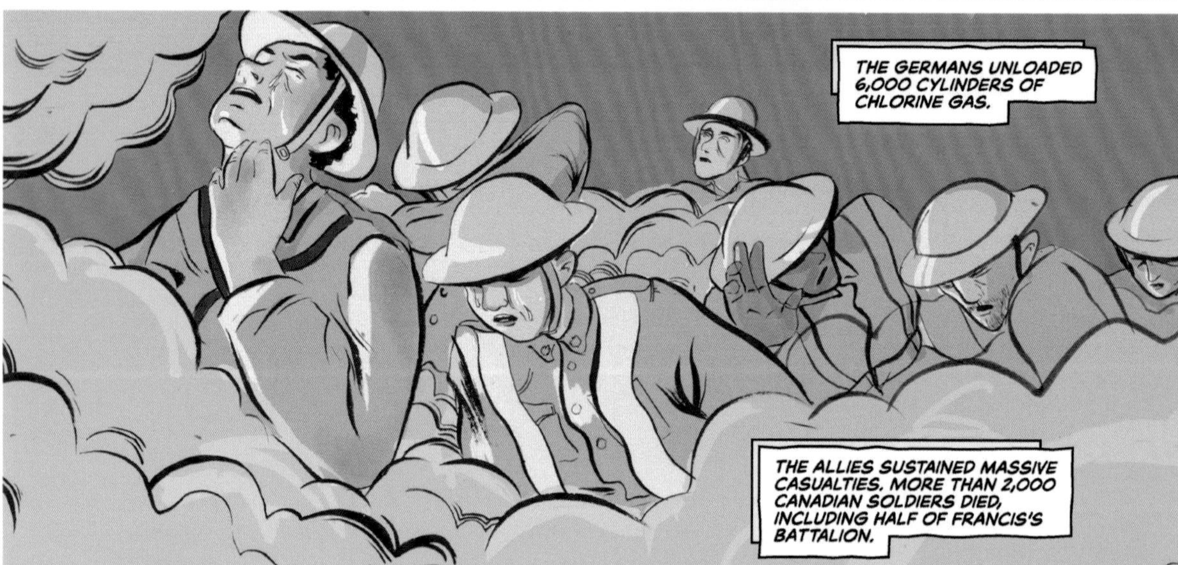
THE GERMANS UNLOADED 6,000 CYLINDERS OF CHLORINE GAS.
THE ALLIES SUSTAINED MASSIVE CASUALTIES. MORE THAN 2,000 CANADIAN SOLDIERS DIED, INCLUDING HALF OF FRANCIS'S BATTALION.

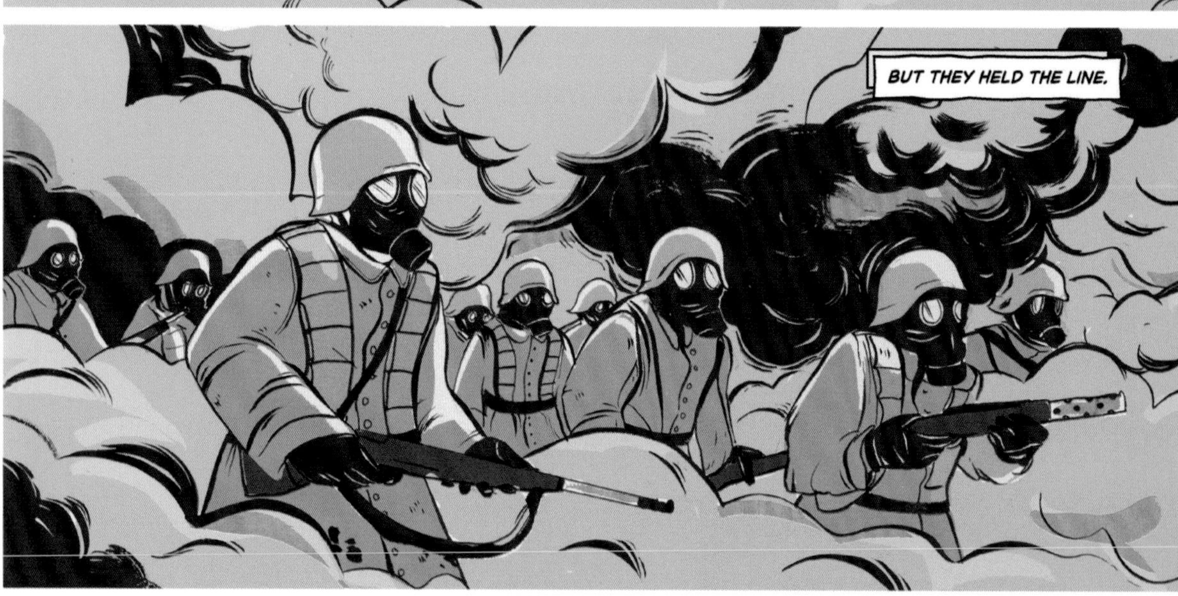
BUT THEY HELD THE LINE.

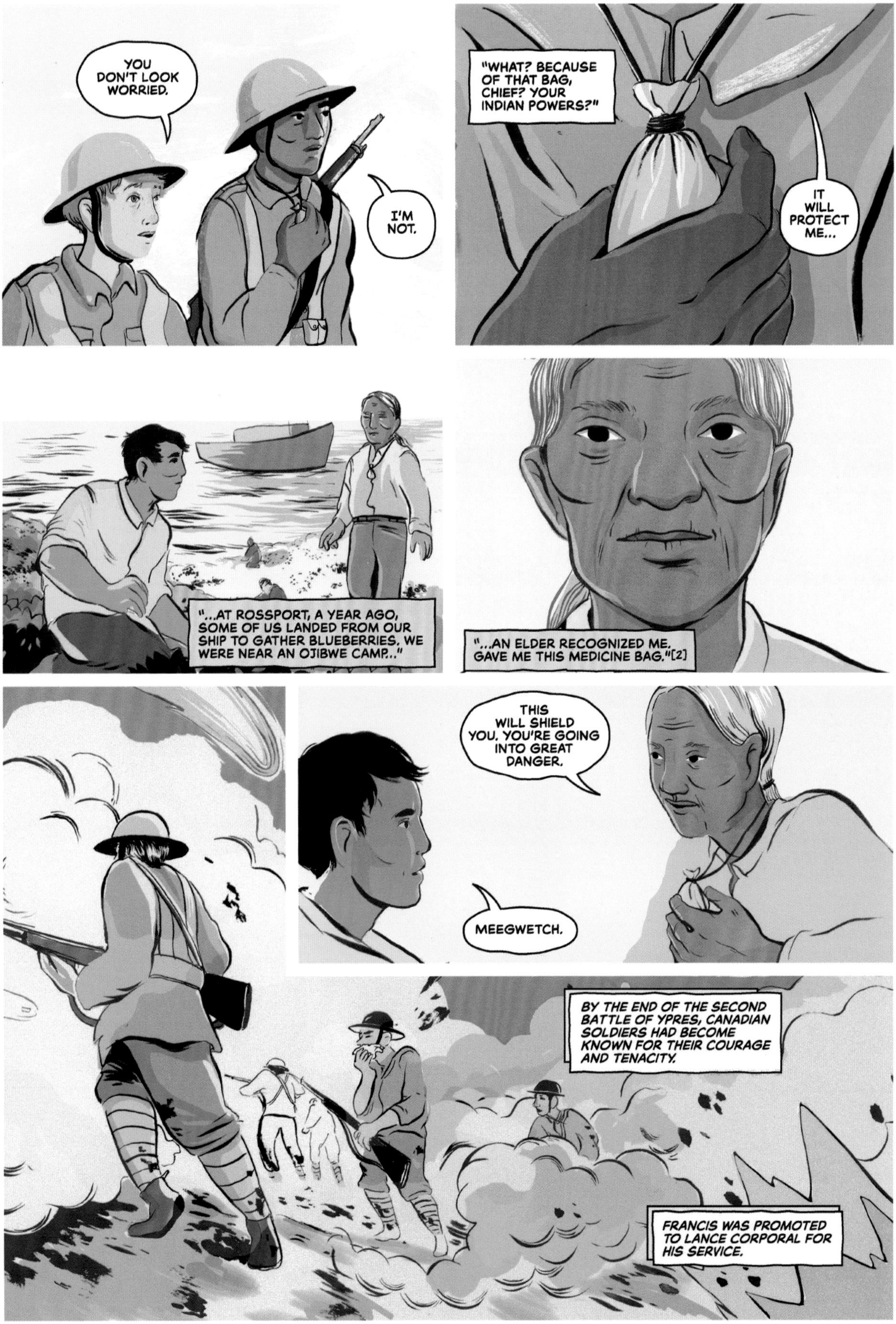
YOU DON'T LOOK WORRIED.
I'M NOT.
"WHAT? BECAUSE OF THAT BAG, CHIEF? YOUR INDIAN POWERS?"
IT WILL PROTECT ME...
"...AT ROSSPORT, A YEAR AGO, SOME OF US LANDED FROM OUR SHIP TO GATHER BLUEBERRIES. WE WERE NEAR AN OJIBWE CAMP..."
"...AN ELDER RECOGNIZED ME. GAVE ME THIS MEDICINE BAG."[2]
THIS WILL SHIELD YOU. YOU'RE GOING INTO GREAT DANGER.
MEEGWETCH.
BY THE END OF THE SECOND BATTLE OF YPRES, CANADIAN SOLDIERS HAD BECOME KNOWN FOR THEIR COURAGE AND TENACITY.
FRANCIS WAS PROMOTED TO LANCE CORPORAL FOR HIS SERVICE.

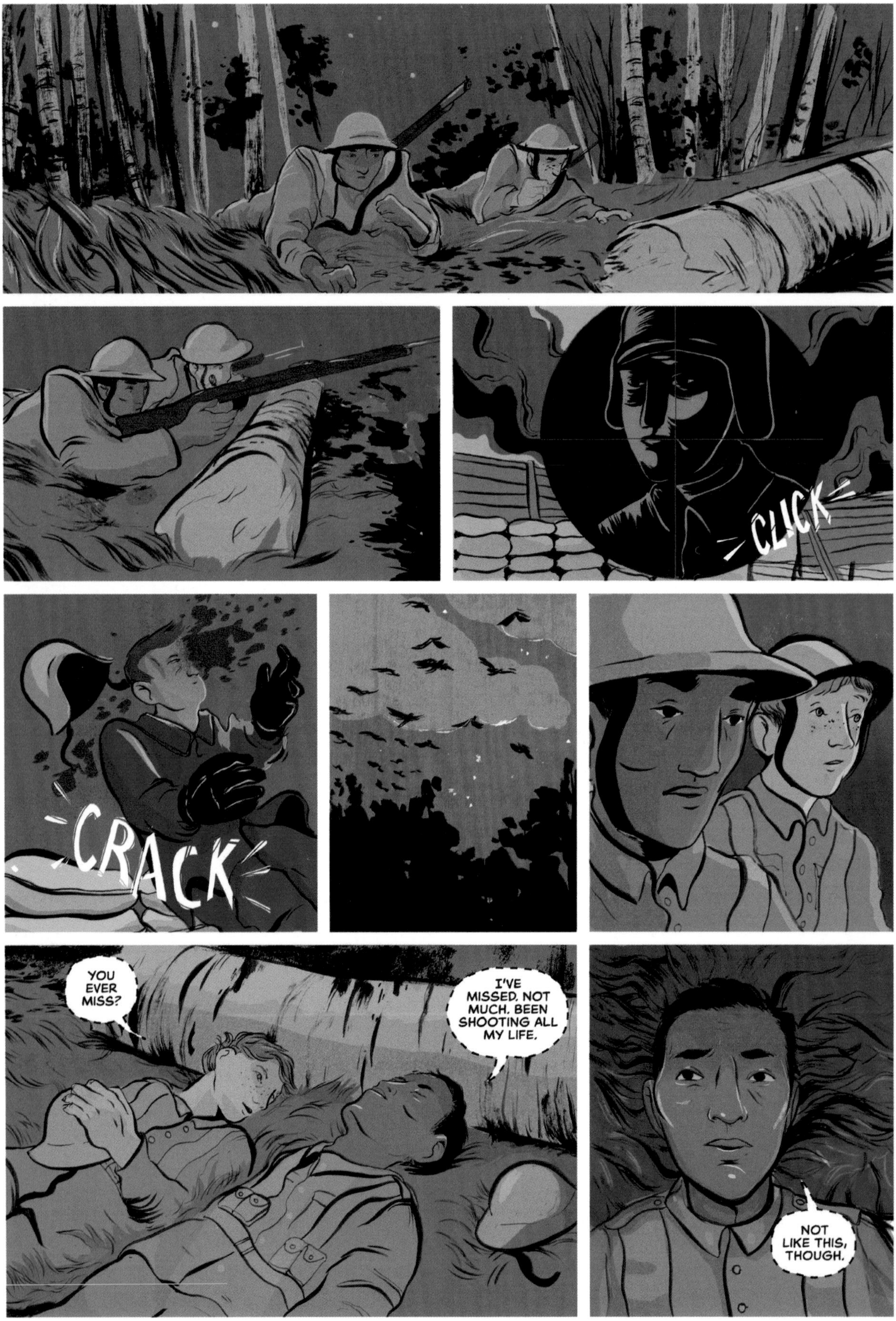
CLICK
CRACK
YOU EVER MISS?
I'VE MISSED. NOT MUCH. BEEN SHOOTING ALL MY LIFE.
NOT LIKE THIS, THOUGH.

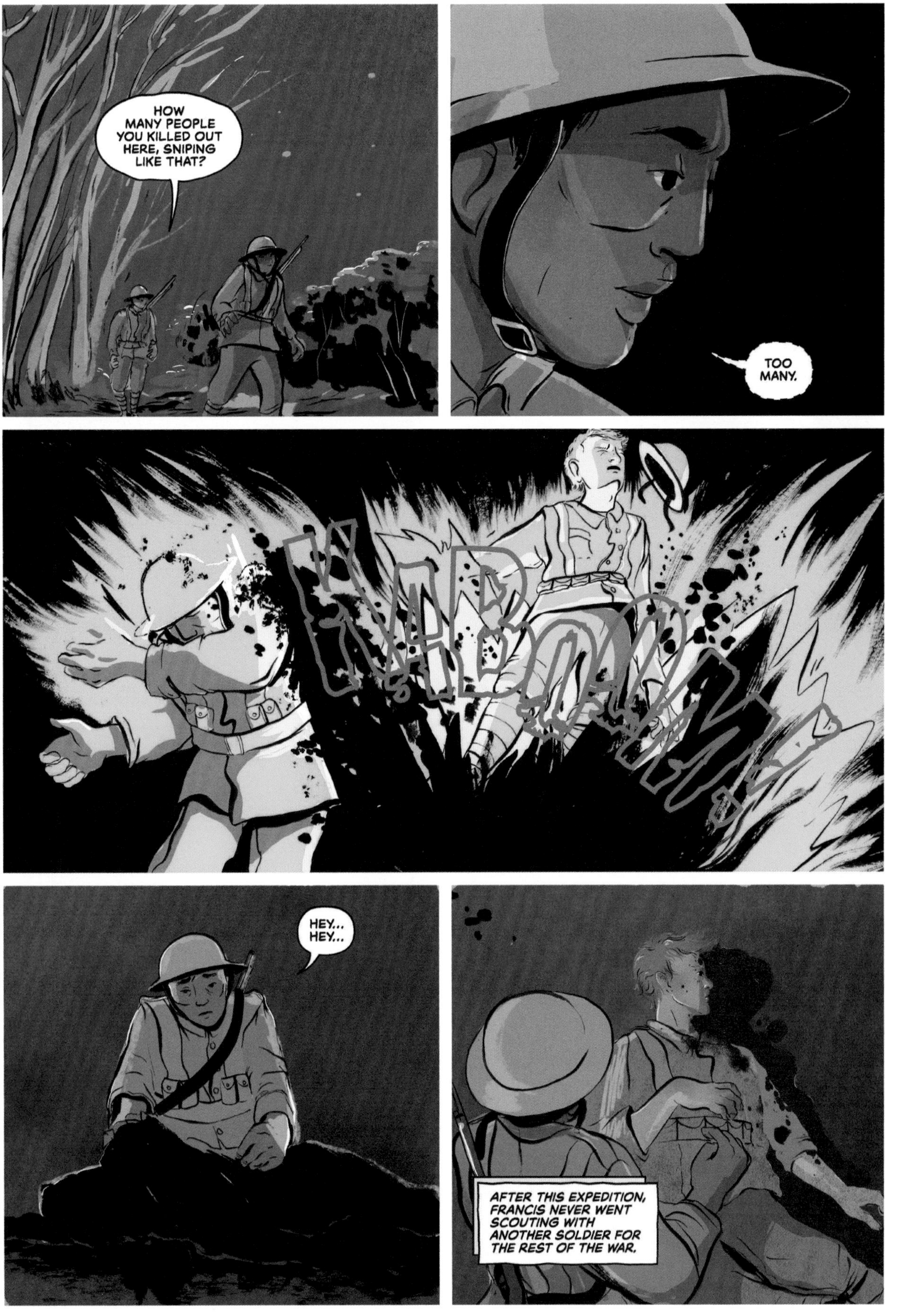
HOW MANY PEOPLE YOU KILLED OUT HERE, SNIPING LIKE THAT?
TOO MANY.
KABOOM!
HEY... HEY...
AFTER THIS EXPEDITION, FRANCIS NEVER WENT SCOUTING WITH ANOTHER SOLDIER FOR THE REST OF THE WAR.

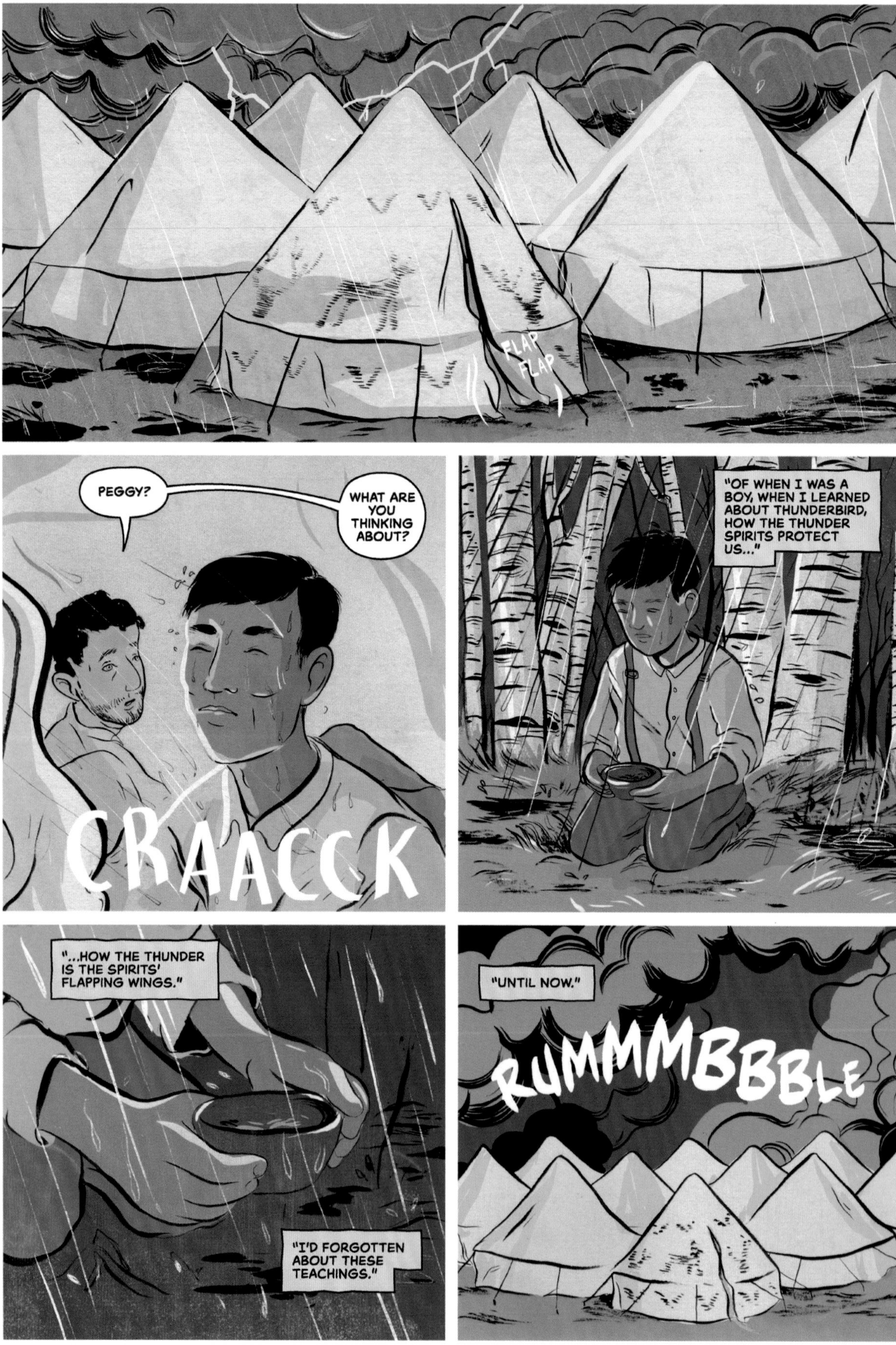
FLAP
FLAP
PEGGY?
WHAT ARE YOU THINKING ABOUT?
CRAACCK
"OF WHEN I WAS A BOY, WHEN I LEARNED ABOUT THUNDERBIRD, HOW THE THUNDER SPIRITS PROTECT US..."
"...HOW THE THUNDER IS THE SPIRITS' FLAPPING WINGS."
"I'D FORGOTTEN ABOUT THESE TEACHINGS."
"UNTIL NOW."
RUMMMBBBLE

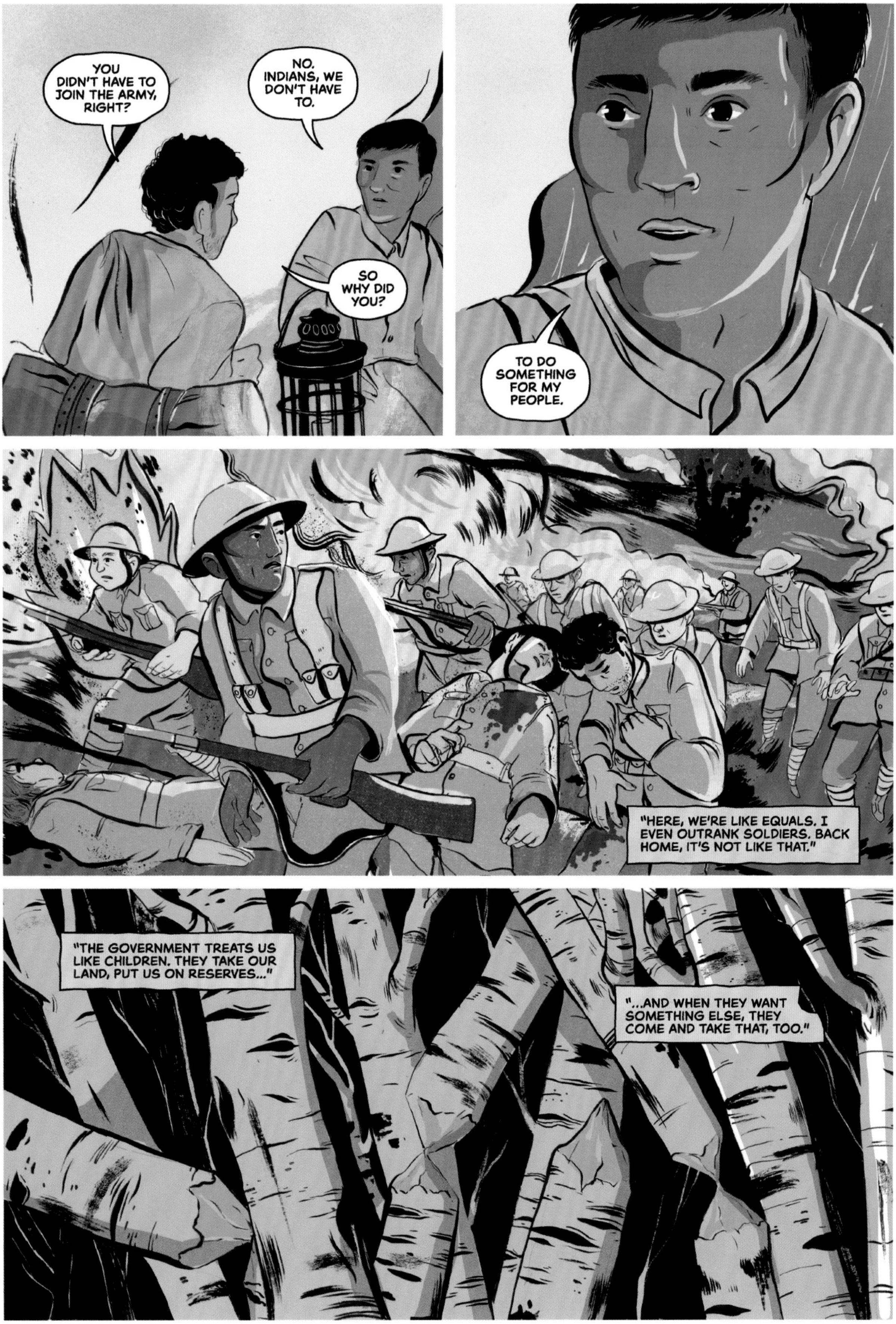
YOU DIDN'T HAVE TO JOIN THE ARMY, RIGHT?
NO. INDIANS, WE DON'T HAVE TO.
SO WHY DID YOU?
TO DO SOMETHING FOR MY PEOPLE.
"HERE, WE'RE LIKE EQUALS. I EVEN OUTRANK SOLDIERS. BACK HOME, IT'S NOT LIKE THAT."
"THE GOVERNMENT TREATS US LIKE CHILDREN. THEY TAKE OUR LAND, PUT US ON RESERVES..."
"...AND WHEN THEY WANT SOMETHING ELSE, THEY COME AND TAKE THAT, TOO."

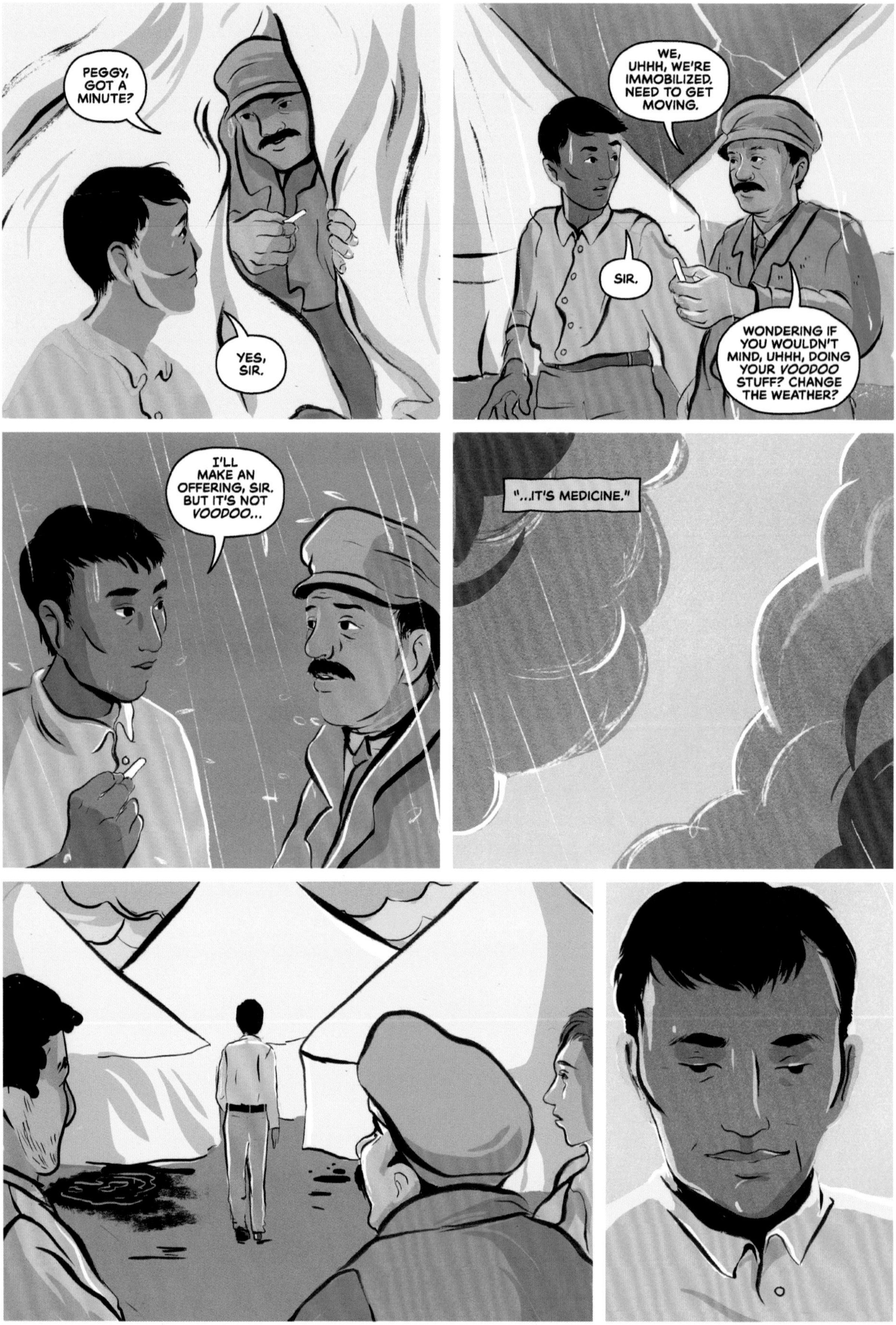
PEGGY, GOT A MINUTE?
YES, SIR.
WE, UHHH, WE'RE IMMOBILIZED. NEED TO GET MOVING.
SIR.
WONDERING IF YOU WOULDN'T MIND, UHHH, DOING YOUR *VOODOO* STUFF? CHANGE THE WEATHER?
I'LL MAKE AN OFFERING, SIR. BUT IT'S NOT *VOODOO*...
"...IT'S MEDICINE."

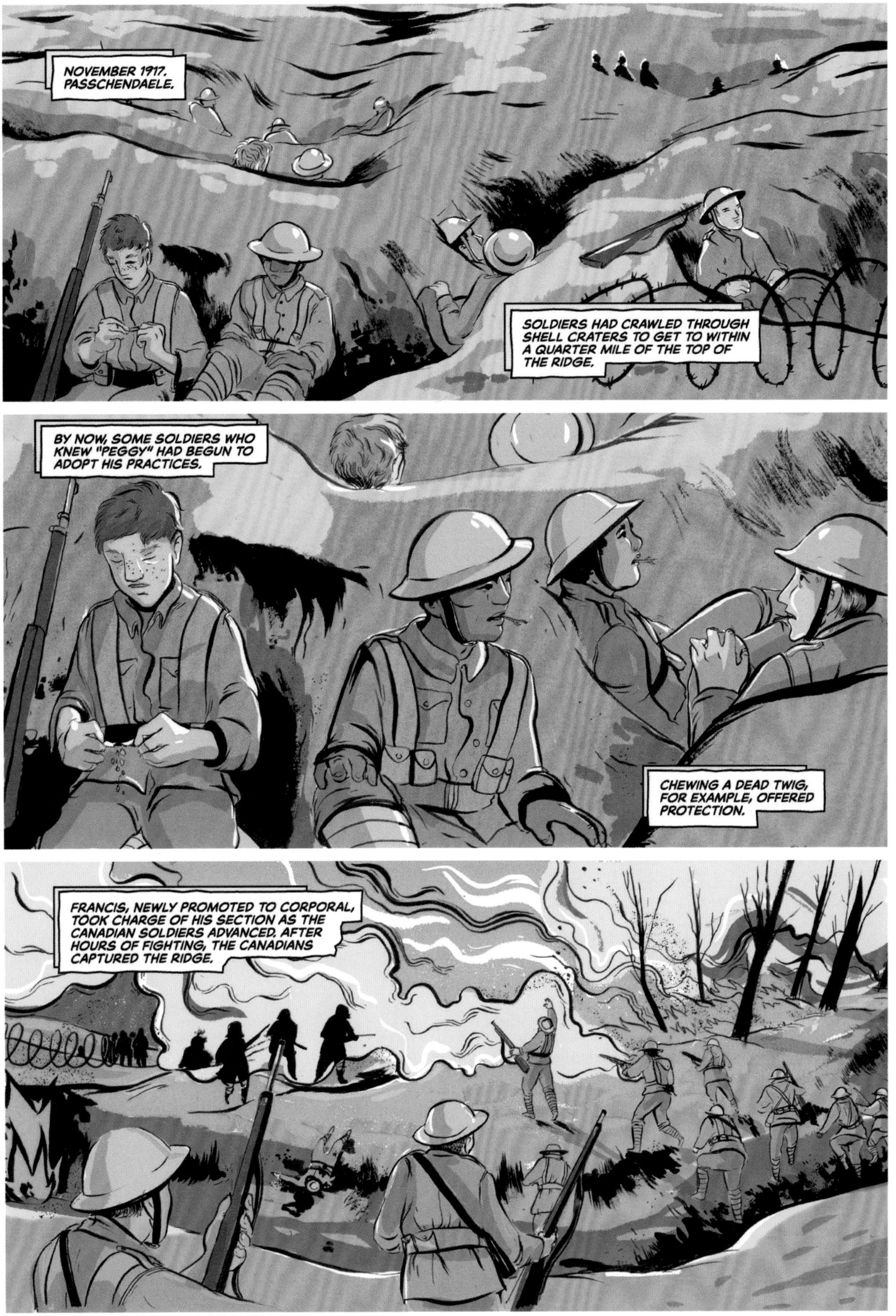
NOVEMBER 1917. PASSCHENDAELE.
SOLDIERS HAD CRAWLED THROUGH SHELL CRATERS TO GET TO WITHIN A QUARTER MILE OF THE TOP OF THE RIDGE.
BY NOW, SOME SOLDIERS WHO KNEW "PEGGY" HAD BEGUN TO ADOPT HIS PRACTICES.
CHEWING A DEAD TWIG, FOR EXAMPLE, OFFERED PROTECTION.
FRANCIS, NEWLY PROMOTED TO CORPORAL, TOOK CHARGE OF HIS SECTION AS THE CANADIAN SOLDIERS ADVANCED. AFTER HOURS OF FIGHTING, THE CANADIANS CAPTURED THE RIDGE.

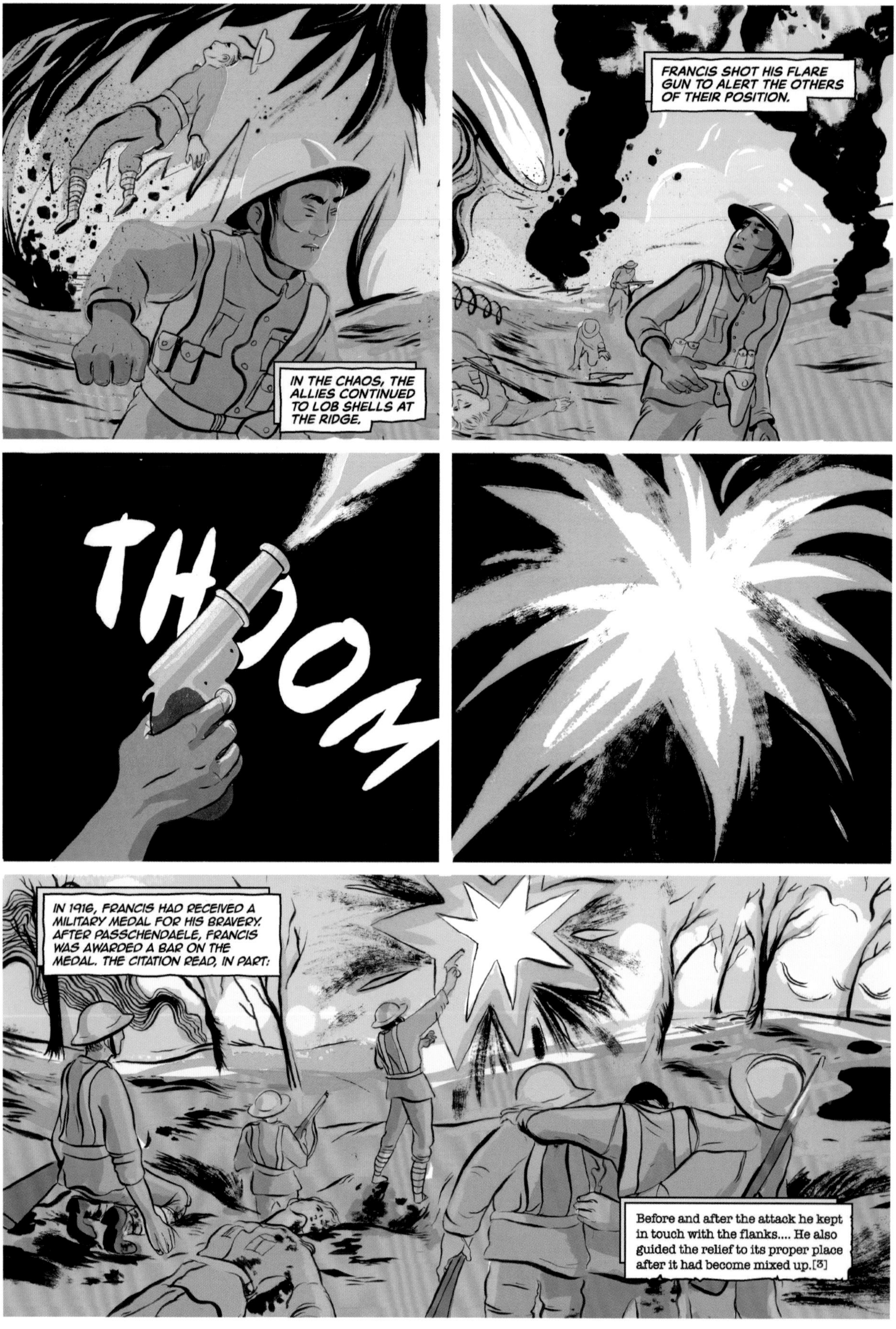
IN THE CHAOS, THE ALLIES CONTINUED TO LOB SHELLS AT THE RIDGE.
FRANCIS SHOT HIS FLARE GUN TO ALERT THE OTHERS OF THEIR POSITION.
THOOM
IN 1916, FRANCIS HAD RECEIVED A MILITARY MEDAL FOR HIS BRAVERY. AFTER PASSCHENDAELE, FRANCIS WAS AWARDED A BAR ON THE MEDAL. THE CITATION READ, IN PART:
Before and after the attack he kept in touch with the flanks.... He also guided the relief to its proper place after it had become mixed up.[3]

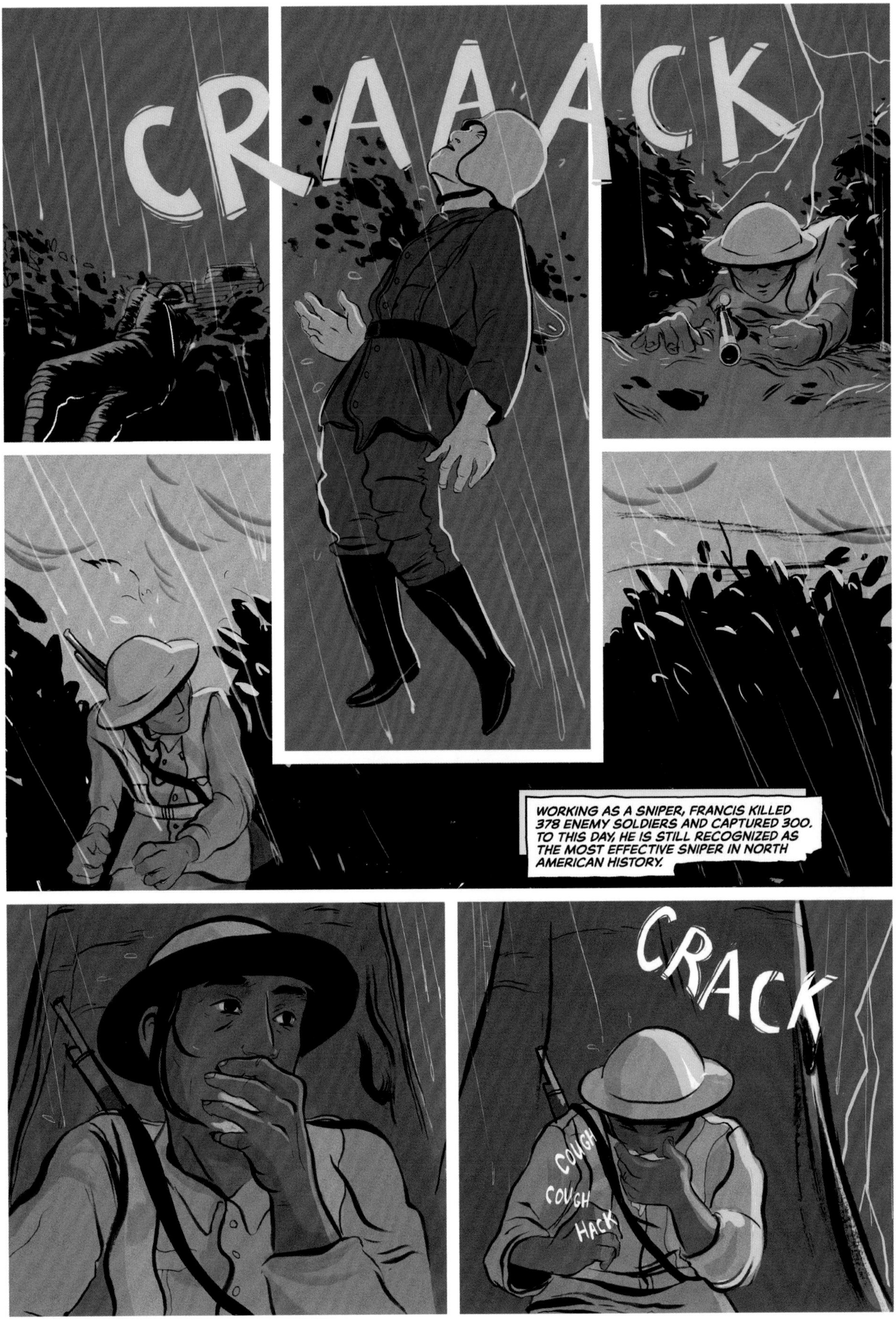
CRAAACK
WORKING AS A SNIPER, FRANCIS KILLED 378 ENEMY SOLDIERS AND CAPTURED 300. TO THIS DAY, HE IS STILL RECOGNIZED AS THE MOST EFFECTIVE SNIPER IN NORTH AMERICAN HISTORY.
CRACK
COUGH
COUGH
HACK

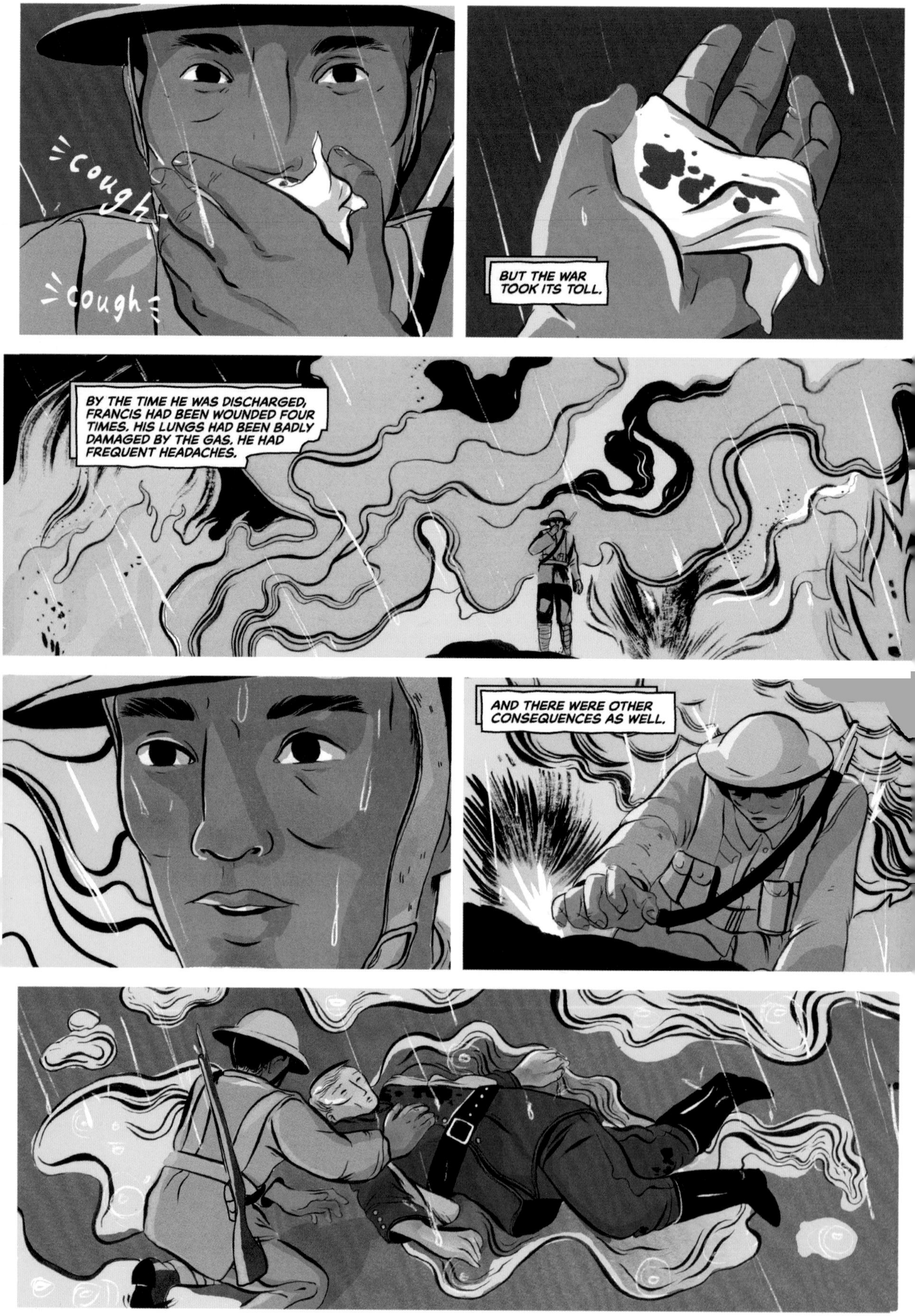
cough
cough
BUT THE WAR TOOK ITS TOLL.
BY THE TIME HE WAS DISCHARGED, FRANCIS HAD BEEN WOUNDED FOUR TIMES. HIS LUNGS HAD BEEN BADLY DAMAGED BY THE GAS. HE HAD FREQUENT HEADACHES.
AND THERE WERE OTHER CONSEQUENCES AS WELL.

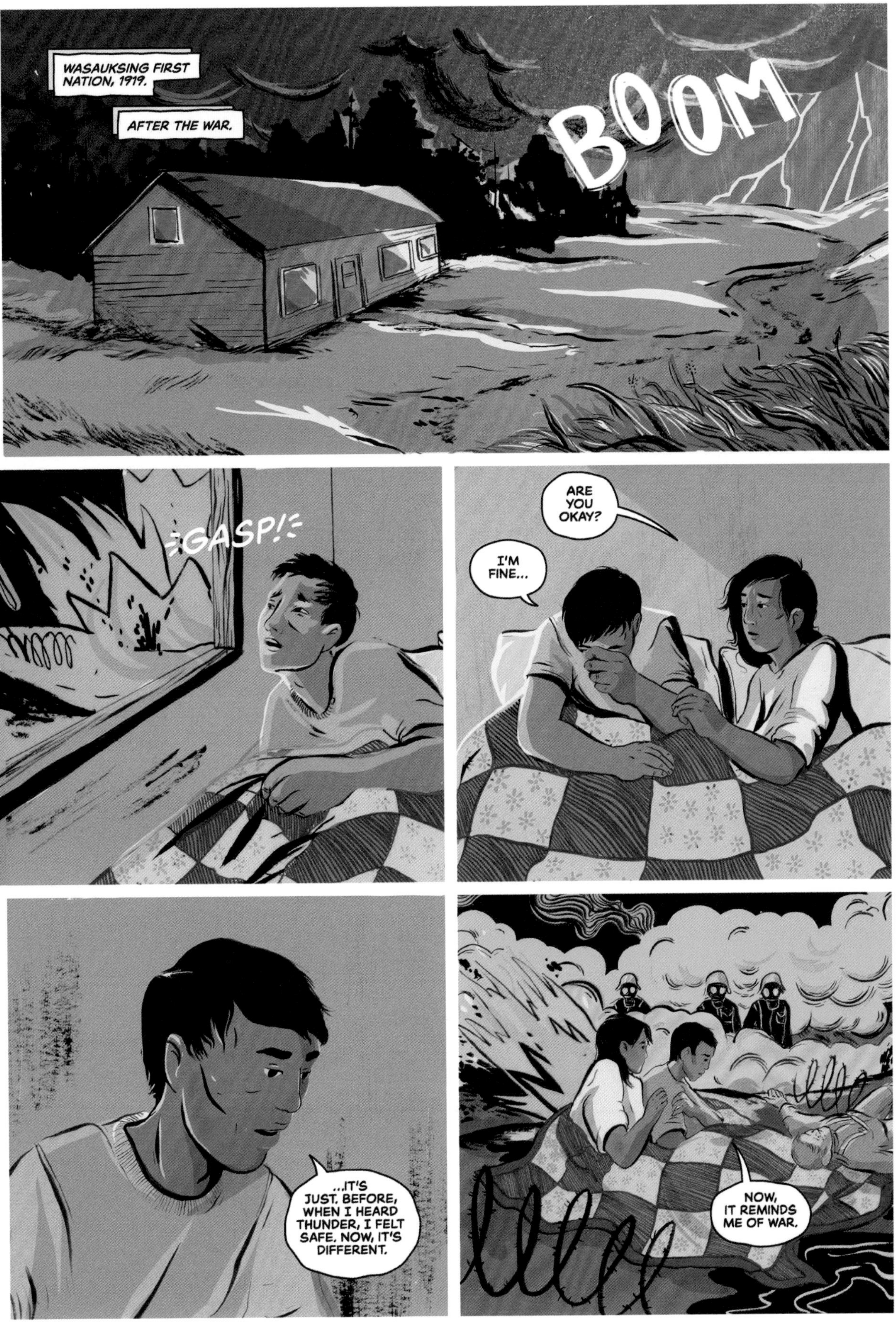
WASAUKSING FIRST NATION, 1919.
AFTER THE WAR.
BOOM
GASP!
ARE YOU OKAY?
I'M FINE...
...IT'S JUST. BEFORE, WHEN I HEARD THUNDER, I FELT SAFE. NOW, IT'S DIFFERENT.
NOW, IT REMINDS ME OF WAR.

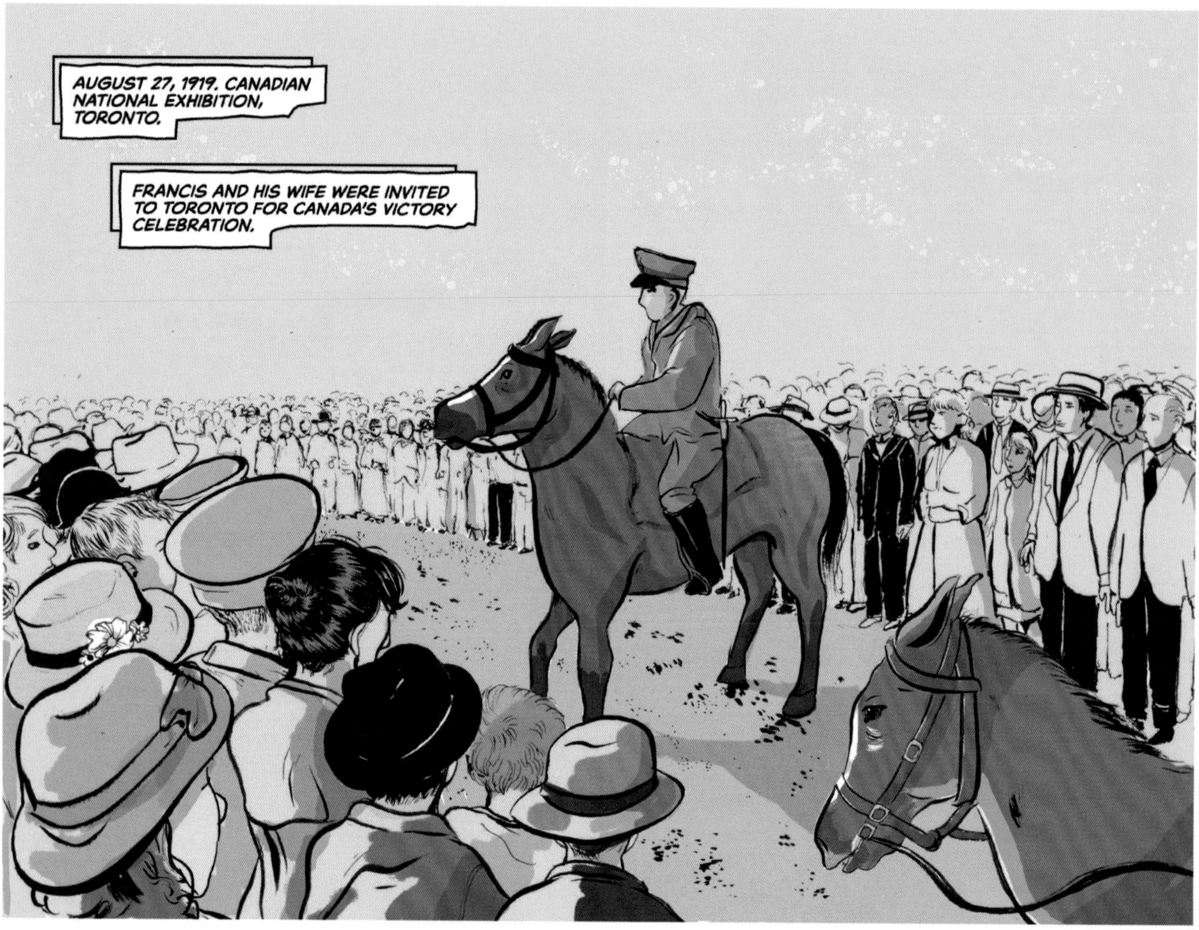
AUGUST 27, 1919. CANADIAN NATIONAL EXHIBITION, TORONTO.
FRANCIS AND HIS WIFE WERE INVITED TO TORONTO FOR CANADA'S VICTORY CELEBRATION.

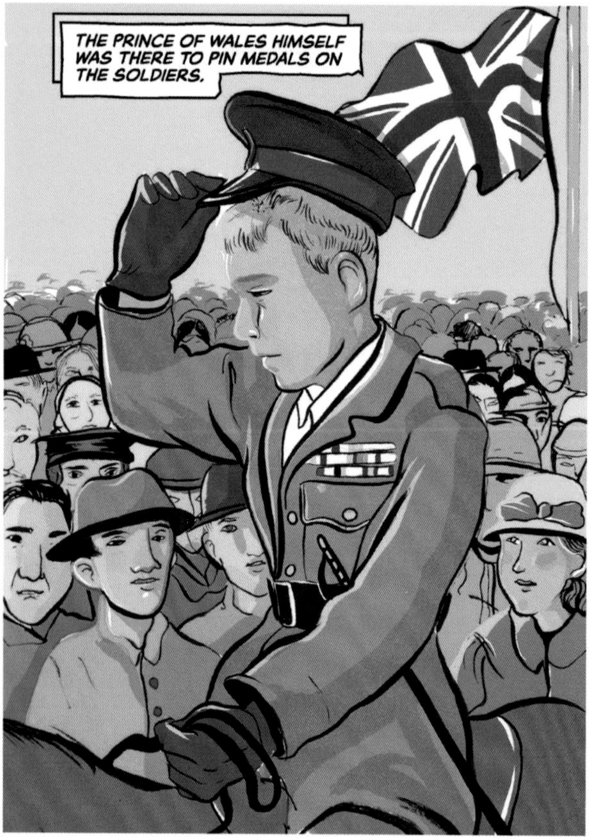
THE PRINCE OF WALES HIMSELF WAS THERE TO PIN MEDALS ON THE SOLDIERS.

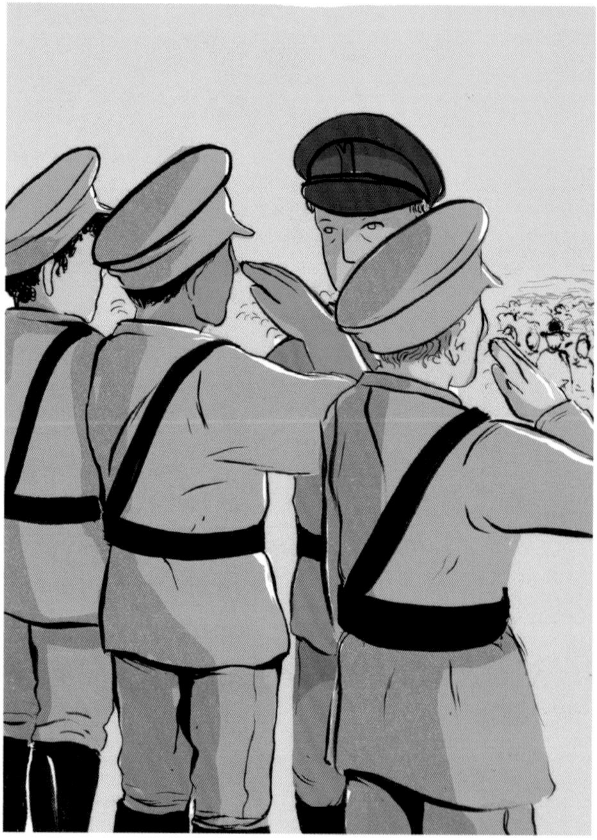

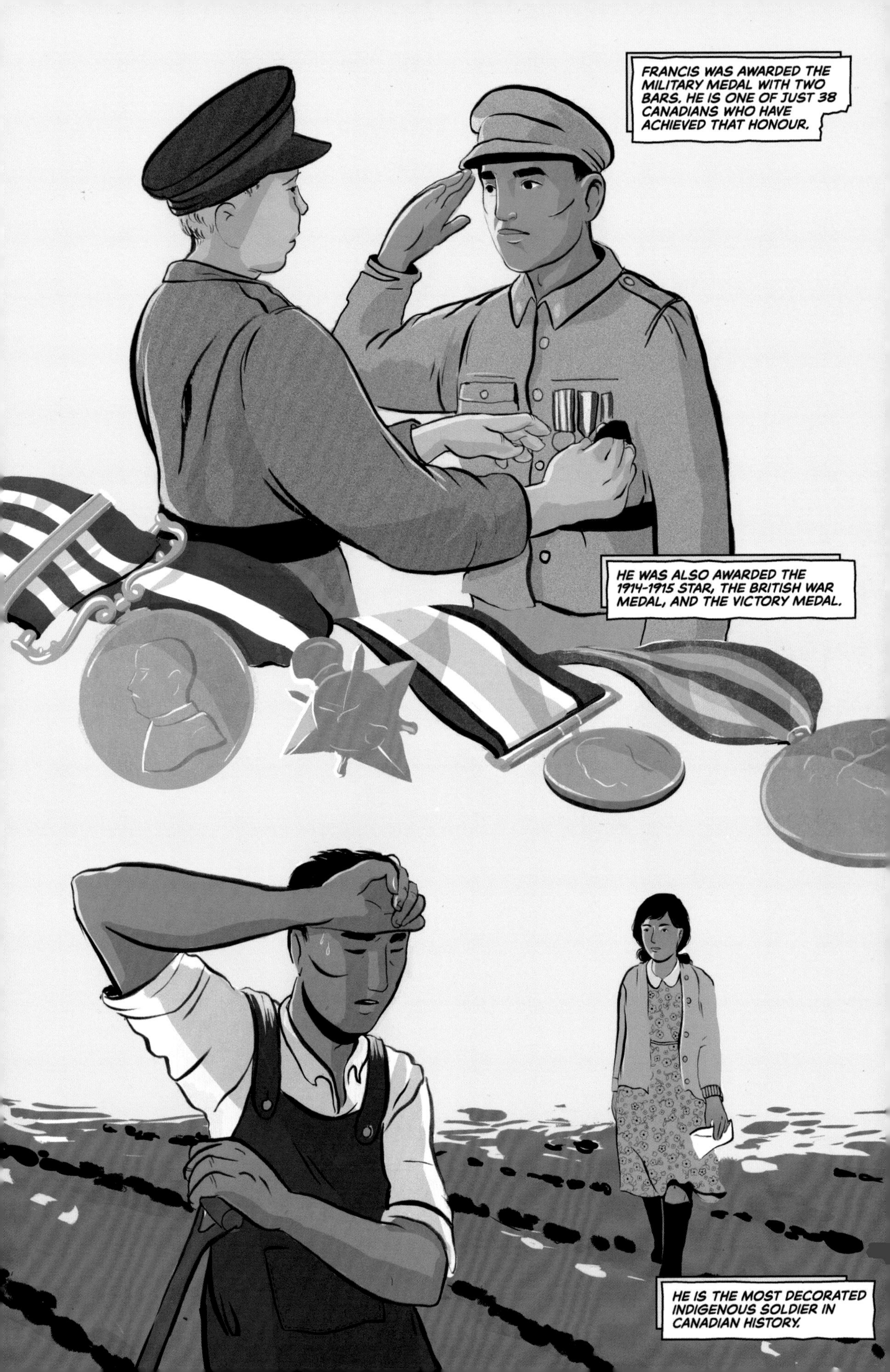
FRANCIS WAS AWARDED THE MILITARY MEDAL WITH TWO BARS. HE IS ONE OF JUST 38 CANADIANS WHO HAVE ACHIEVED THAT HONOUR.
HE WAS ALSO AWARDED THE 1914-1915 STAR, THE BRITISH WAR MEDAL, AND THE VICTORY MEDAL.
HE IS THE MOST DECORATED INDIGENOUS SOLDIER IN CANADIAN HISTORY.

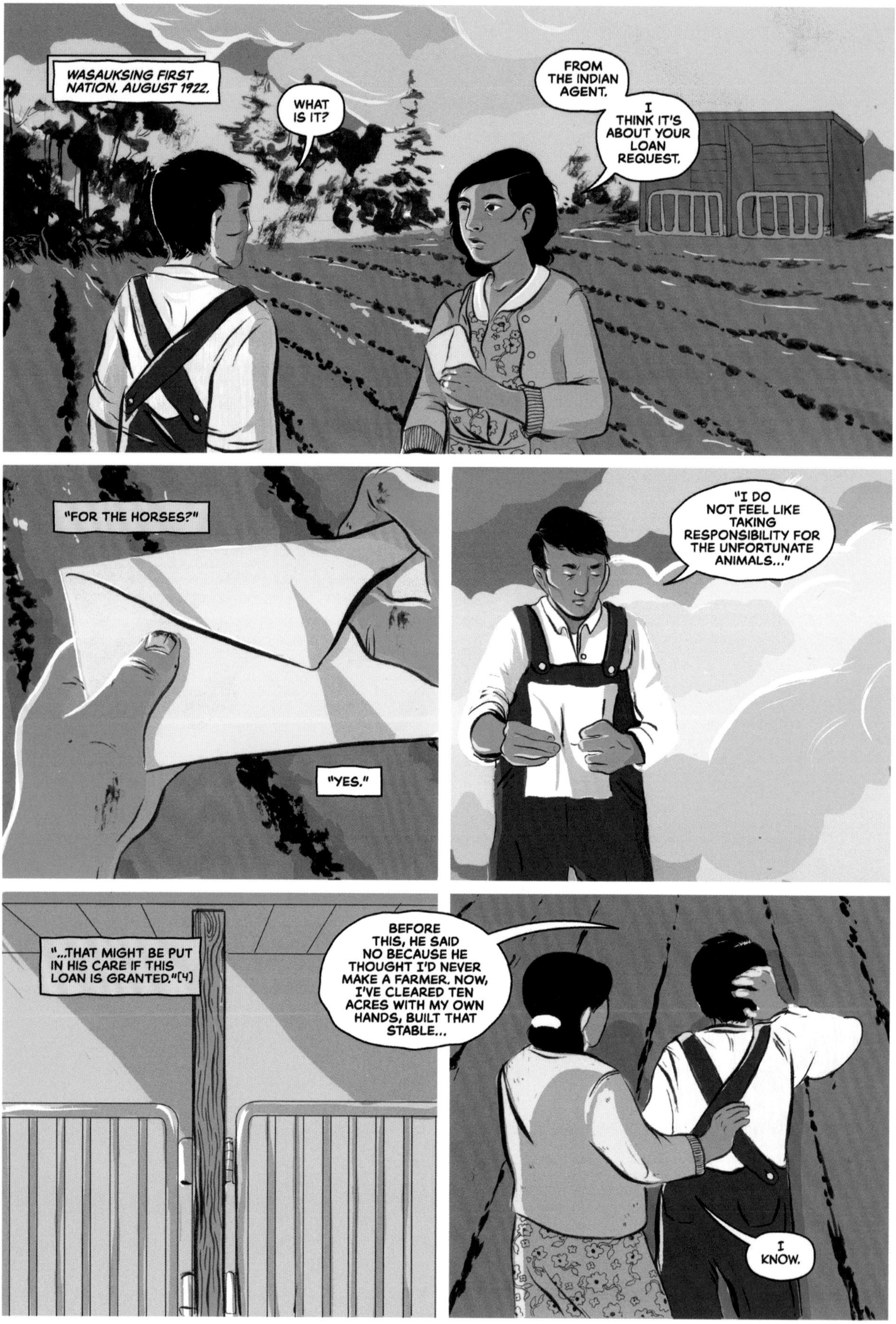
WASAUKSING FIRST NATION. AUGUST 1922.
WHAT IS IT?
FROM THE INDIAN AGENT.
I THINK IT'S ABOUT YOUR LOAN REQUEST.
"FOR THE HORSES?"
"YES."
"I DO NOT FEEL LIKE TAKING RESPONSIBILITY FOR THE UNFORTUNATE ANIMALS..."
"...THAT MIGHT BE PUT IN HIS CARE IF THIS LOAN IS GRANTED."[4]
BEFORE THIS, HE SAID NO BECAUSE HE THOUGHT I'D NEVER MAKE A FARMER. NOW, I'VE CLEARED TEN ACRES WITH MY OWN HANDS, BUILT THAT STABLE...
I KNOW.

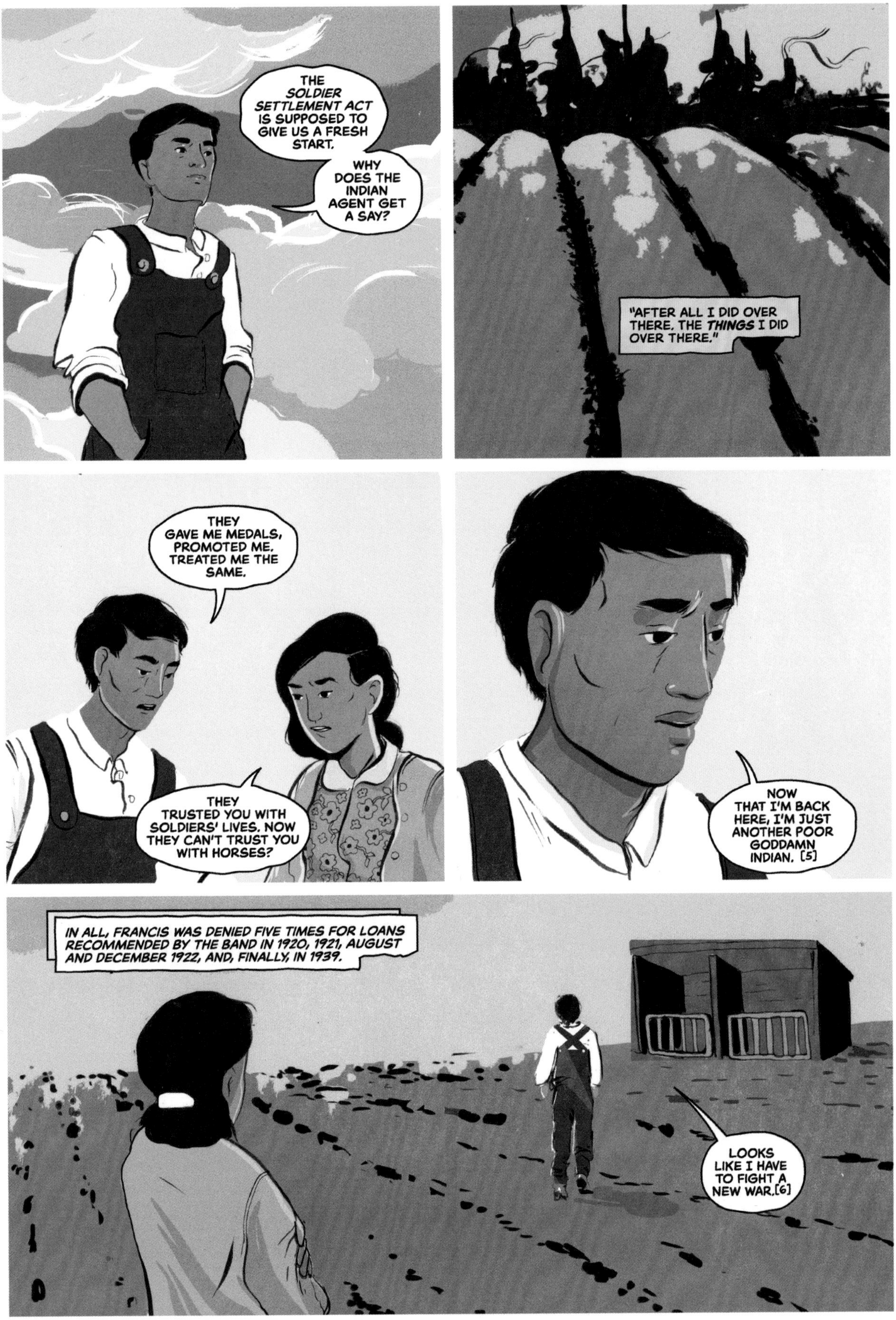
THE *SOLDIER SETTLEMENT ACT* IS SUPPOSED TO GIVE US A FRESH START.
WHY DOES THE INDIAN AGENT GET A SAY?
"AFTER ALL I DID OVER THERE, THE *THINGS* I DID OVER THERE."
THEY GAVE ME MEDALS, PROMOTED ME, TREATED ME THE SAME.
THEY TRUSTED YOU WITH SOLDIERS' LIVES. NOW THEY CAN'T TRUST YOU WITH HORSES?
NOW THAT I'M BACK HERE, I'M JUST ANOTHER POOR GODDAMN INDIAN. [5]
IN ALL, FRANCIS WAS DENIED FIVE TIMES FOR LOANS RECOMMENDED BY THE BAND IN 1920, 1921, AUGUST AND DECEMBER 1922, AND, FINALLY, IN 1939.
LOOKS LIKE I HAVE TO FIGHT A NEW WAR. [6]

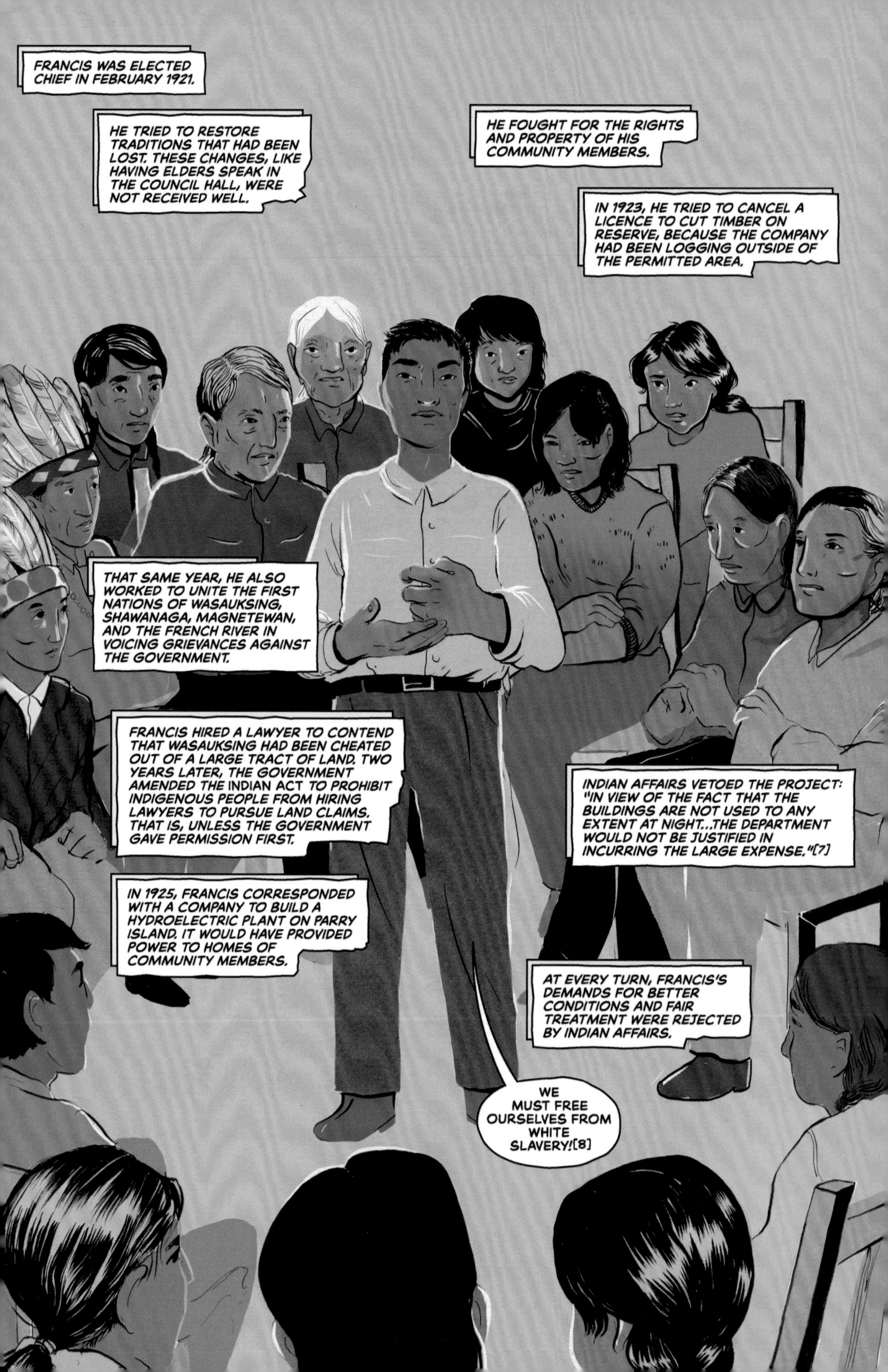
FRANCIS WAS ELECTED CHIEF IN FEBRUARY 1921.
HE TRIED TO RESTORE TRADITIONS THAT HAD BEEN LOST. THESE CHANGES, LIKE HAVING ELDERS SPEAK IN THE COUNCIL HALL, WERE NOT RECEIVED WELL.
HE FOUGHT FOR THE RIGHTS AND PROPERTY OF HIS COMMUNITY MEMBERS.
IN 1923, HE TRIED TO CANCEL A LICENCE TO CUT TIMBER ON RESERVE, BECAUSE THE COMPANY HAD BEEN LOGGING OUTSIDE OF THE PERMITTED AREA.
THAT SAME YEAR, HE ALSO WORKED TO UNITE THE FIRST NATIONS OF WASAUKSING, SHAWANAGA, MAGNETEWAN, AND THE FRENCH RIVER IN VOICING GRIEVANCES AGAINST THE GOVERNMENT.
FRANCIS HIRED A LAWYER TO CONTEND THAT WASAUKSING HAD BEEN CHEATED OUT OF A LARGE TRACT OF LAND. TWO YEARS LATER, THE GOVERNMENT AMENDED THE INDIAN ACT TO PROHIBIT INDIGENOUS PEOPLE FROM HIRING LAWYERS TO PURSUE LAND CLAIMS. THAT IS, UNLESS THE GOVERNMENT GAVE PERMISSION FIRST.
IN 1925, FRANCIS CORRESPONDED WITH A COMPANY TO BUILD A HYDROELECTRIC PLANT ON PARRY ISLAND. IT WOULD HAVE PROVIDED POWER TO HOMES OF COMMUNITY MEMBERS.
INDIAN AFFAIRS VETOED THE PROJECT: "IN VIEW OF THE FACT THAT THE BUILDINGS ARE NOT USED TO ANY EXTENT AT NIGHT...THE DEPARTMENT WOULD NOT BE JUSTIFIED IN INCURRING THE LARGE EXPENSE."[7]
AT EVERY TURN, FRANCIS'S DEMANDS FOR BETTER CONDITIONS AND FAIR TREATMENT WERE REJECTED BY INDIAN AFFAIRS.
WE MUST FREE OURSELVES FROM WHITE SLAVERY![8]

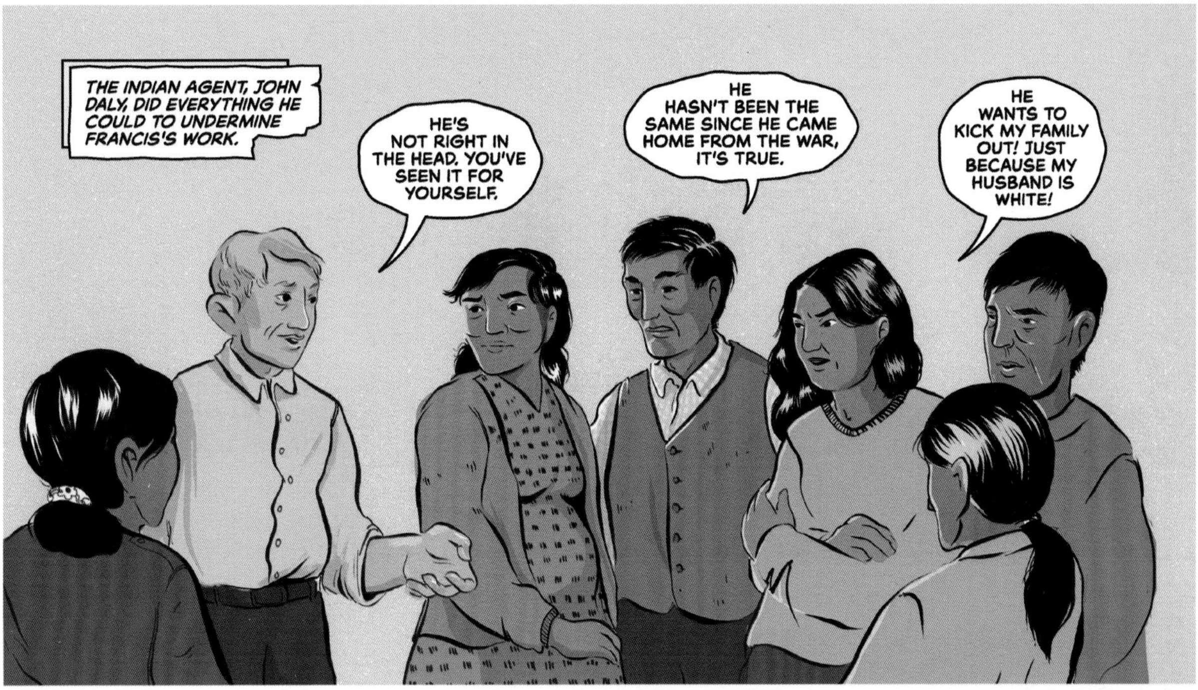
THE INDIAN AGENT, JOHN DALY, DID EVERYTHING HE COULD TO UNDERMINE FRANCIS'S WORK.
HE'S NOT RIGHT IN THE HEAD. YOU'VE SEEN IT FOR YOURSELF.
HE HASN'T BEEN THE SAME SINCE HE CAME HOME FROM THE WAR, IT'S TRUE.
HE WANTS TO KICK MY FAMILY OUT! JUST BECAUSE MY HUSBAND IS WHITE!

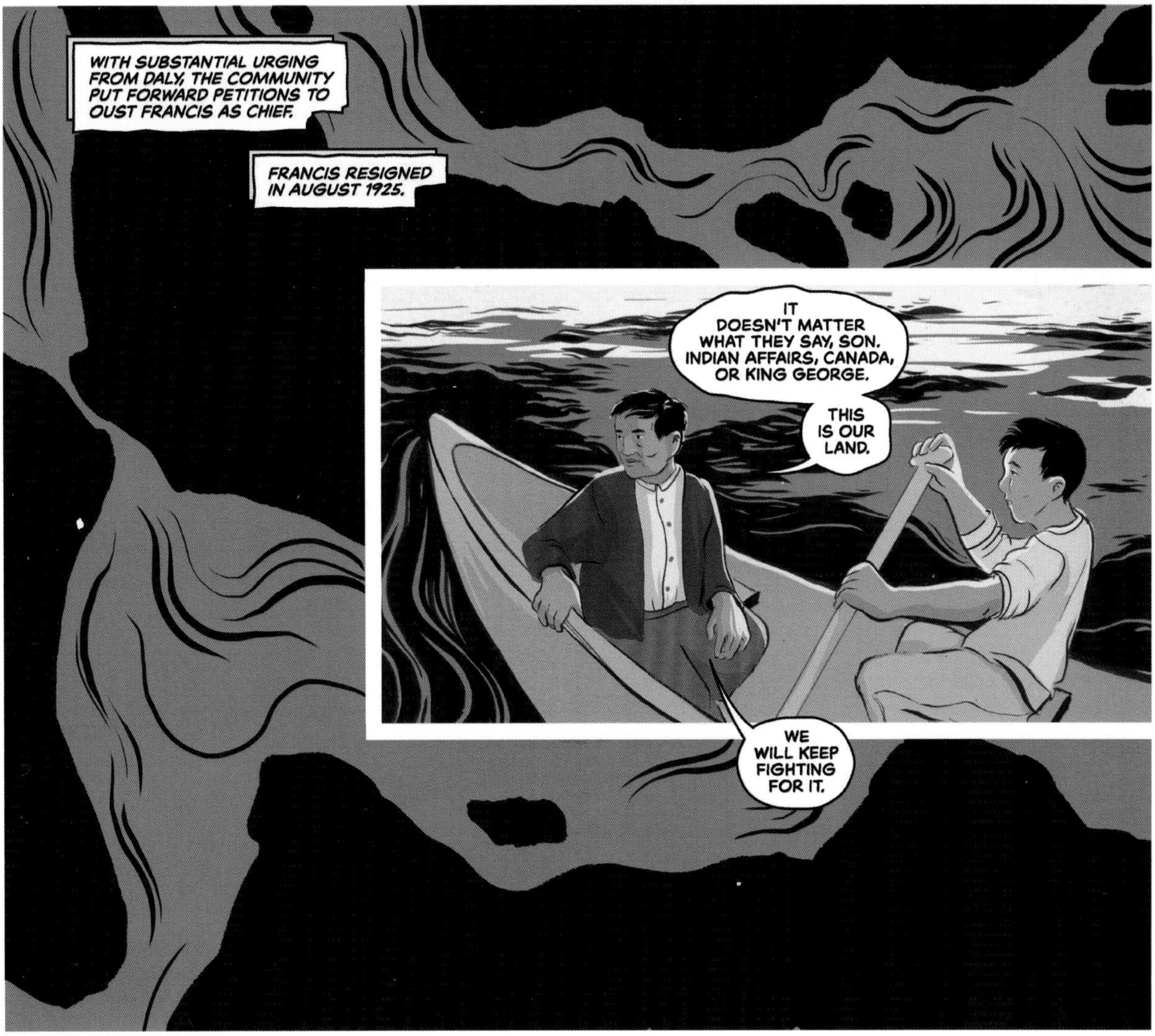
WITH SUBSTANTIAL URGING FROM DALY, THE COMMUNITY PUT FORWARD PETITIONS TO OUST FRANCIS AS CHIEF.
FRANCIS RESIGNED IN AUGUST 1925.
IT DOESN'T MATTER WHAT THEY SAY, SON. INDIAN AFFAIRS, CANADA, OR KING GEORGE.
THIS IS OUR LAND.
WE WILL KEEP FIGHTING FOR IT.

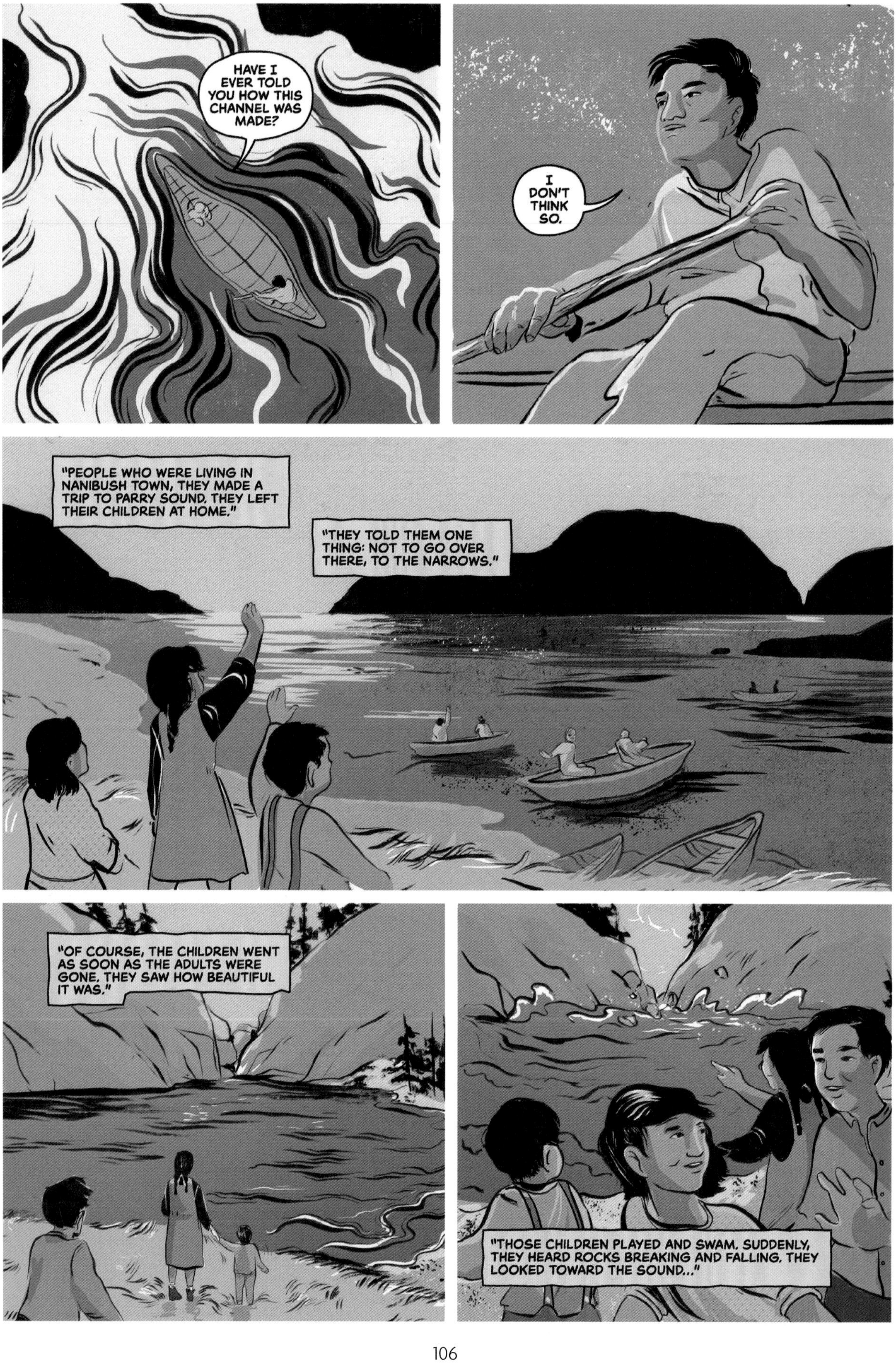
HAVE I EVER TOLD YOU HOW THIS CHANNEL WAS MADE?
I DON'T THINK SO.
"PEOPLE WHO WERE LIVING IN NANIBUSH TOWN, THEY MADE A TRIP TO PARRY SOUND. THEY LEFT THEIR CHILDREN AT HOME."
"THEY TOLD THEM ONE THING: NOT TO GO OVER THERE, TO THE NARROWS."
"OF COURSE, THE CHILDREN WENT AS SOON AS THE ADULTS WERE GONE. THEY SAW HOW BEAUTIFUL IT WAS."
"THOSE CHILDREN PLAYED AND SWAM. SUDDENLY, THEY HEARD ROCKS BREAKING AND FALLING. THEY LOOKED TOWARD THE SOUND..."

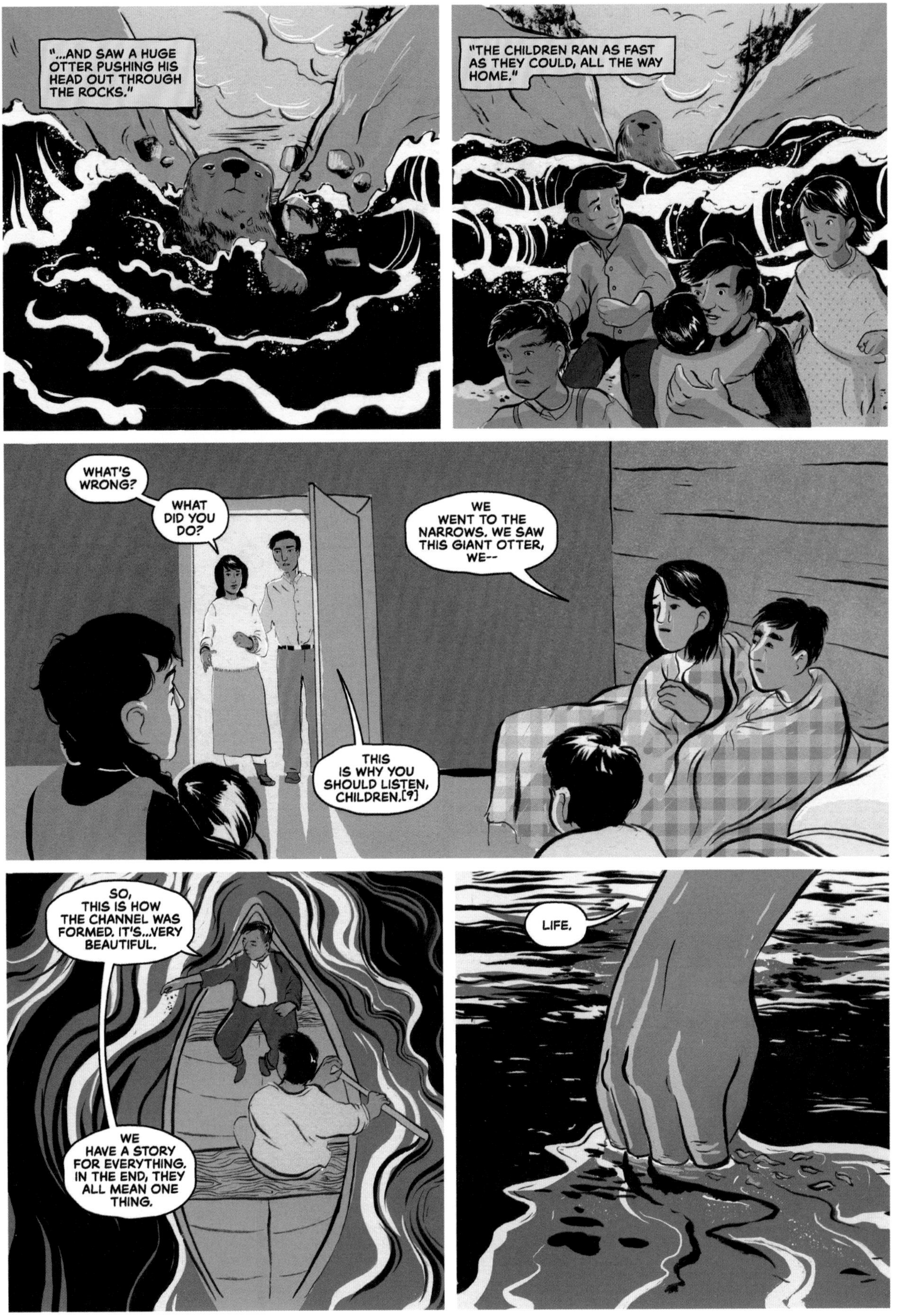
"...AND SAW A HUGE OTTER PUSHING HIS HEAD OUT THROUGH THE ROCKS."
"THE CHILDREN RAN AS FAST AS THEY COULD, ALL THE WAY HOME."
WHAT'S WRONG?
WHAT DID YOU DO?
WE WENT TO THE NARROWS. WE SAW THIS GIANT OTTER, WE--
THIS IS WHY YOU SHOULD LISTEN, CHILDREN.[9]
SO, THIS IS HOW THE CHANNEL WAS FORMED. IT'S...VERY BEAUTIFUL.
WE HAVE A STORY FOR EVERYTHING. IN THE END, THEY ALL MEAN ONE THING.
LIFE.

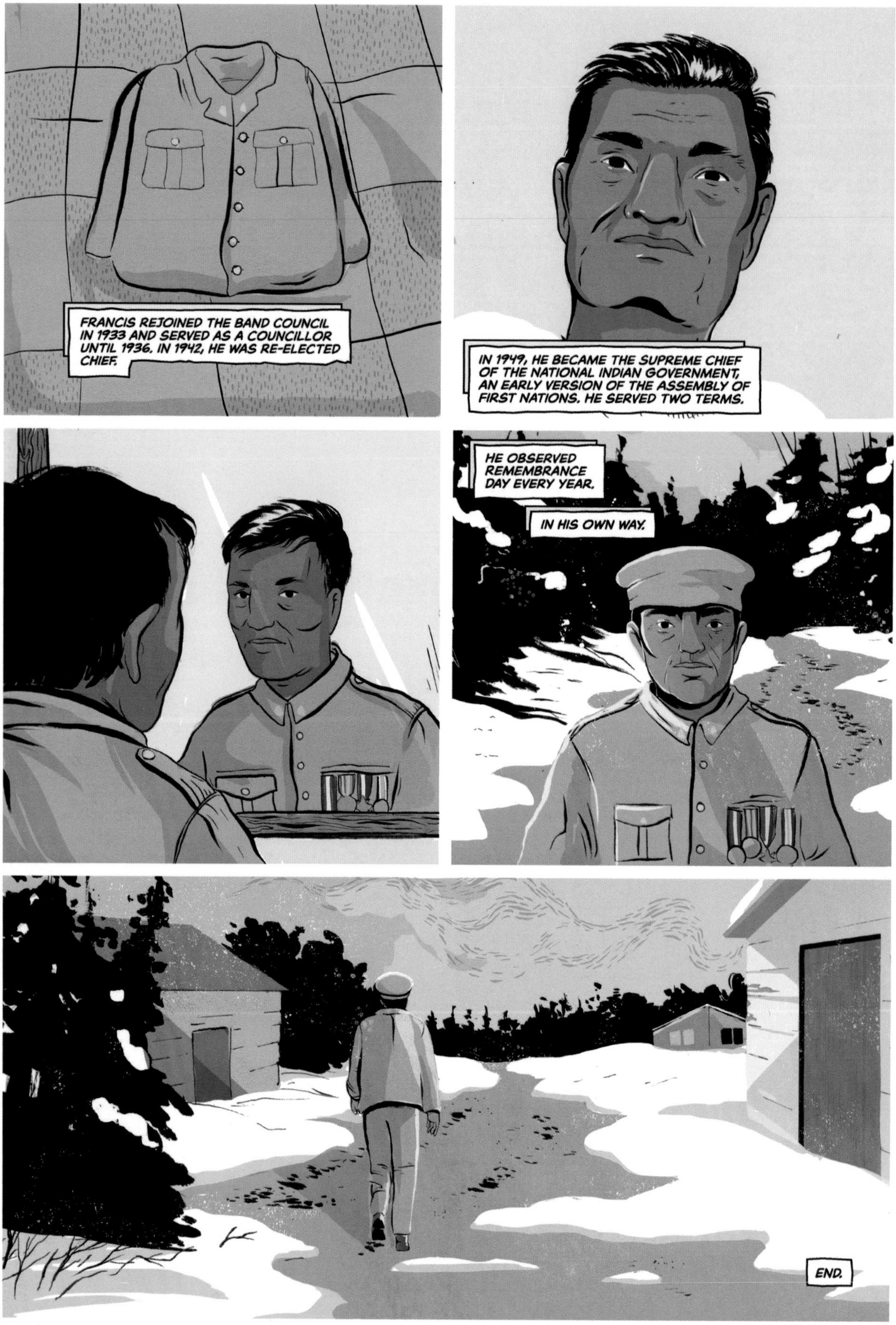
FRANCIS REJOINED THE BAND COUNCIL IN 1933 AND SERVED AS A COUNCILLOR UNTIL 1936. IN 1942, HE WAS RE-ELECTED CHIEF.
IN 1949, HE BECAME THE SUPREME CHIEF OF THE NATIONAL INDIAN GOVERNMENT, AN EARLY VERSION OF THE ASSEMBLY OF FIRST NATIONS. HE SERVED TWO TERMS.
HE OBSERVED REMEMBRANCE DAY EVERY YEAR.
IN HIS OWN WAY.
END.

Secrecy. Intuition. Isolation. These factors conspired to make Inuit latecomers to assimilation. The result is that Inuit retain specifics regarding their cosmogony and shamanism—traditions spanning the circumpolar Arctic and laughably huge compared to our tale set around Canada's "Foxe Basin."

Doing a search for "Inuit beliefs" can get pretty depressing. Inuit psychology, as rendered in many sources, is presented as chaotic. Crude. But most researchers failed to understand that shamans (Inuktitut, aangakkuit; eldritch word implying "ecstatic ones") were expressing a form of "imaginal intelligence" (praised by Einstein) necessary for physical and psychological survival. This is a vision of existence using layered, reiterating systems, whether in the human heart, or ice and wind.

"Rosie" is a nod to shamanism—a secret history of Inuit. To its layers. Much of this story is true. And while we're not going to pluck at fact over fiction, for those who think the idea of shamans versus Nazis is...over-the-top, well, that really did happen. The dolls were real, too. So don't be surprised at the rest.

Please note this, if nothing else: shamanism is different from spirituality. Aangakkuit are specialists in the soul (of any life), a membrane where mind meets spirit. The mind is temporary, while spirit is borrowed from a greater All, eternal and beyond expression. Shamans, in this sense, are not spiritual people. One might instead call them practitioners of "psychotechnology" (there's a nice made-up word for you). Not the Inuit religion, but a system. An understanding.

Of what?

(Inuit secrecy...)

Rachel & Sean Qitsualik-Tinsley

<1930
As Arctic nomads, Inuit represent interrelated cultures derived from an ancient, circumpolar super-culture, distinct from First Nations.

1931
Catholic and Protestant missionaries compete to convert the Inuit to Christianity. Many Inuit convert. Many secretly maintain shamanism. Many blend Christian and Inuit cosmogony.

1932
Inuit names are considered too chaotic to bureaucrats and Satanic to missionaries. The government suggests forcible, mass fingerprinting of the Inuit.

1933-1934
The forcible fingerprinting of all Inuit is a failure, sparking interagency conflict.

1935-1940
Non-Inuit complain that Inuit bear multiple individual names that defy alphabetization. Forcible wearing of "identity discs" and/or cards is recommended, along with mass Biblical renaming.

Rosie

Rachel & Sean Qitsualik-Tinsley
Illustration & Colours: GMB Chomichuk

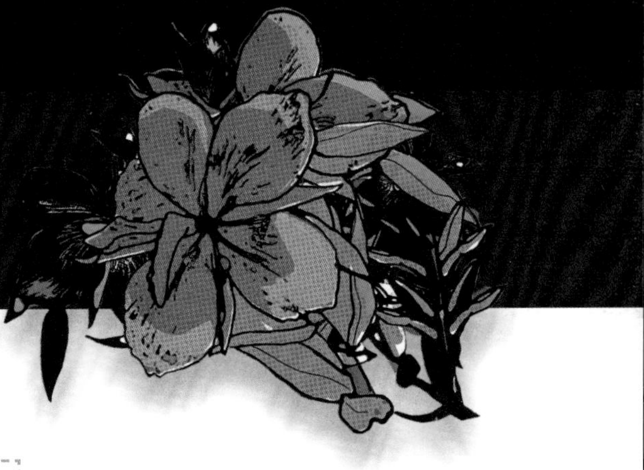

1941
Inuit are included in the census for the first time. Bureaucratic complaints of no "tribal system" finally spur federal allotment of disc necklaces.

1942
Disc distribution and usage sparks interagency squabbling. Inuit dispose of discs or wear them only with non-Inuit.

1943-1944
Government orders RCMP to make disc system work. Inuit still keep disc necklaces in tin cans. Mounting push to force paternal "family" names upon Inuit.

1945›
End of WWII, pre-nuclear era. Dawn, for Inuit, of forced dependency, social experimentation, and "velvet" genocide. Unconcluded.[1]

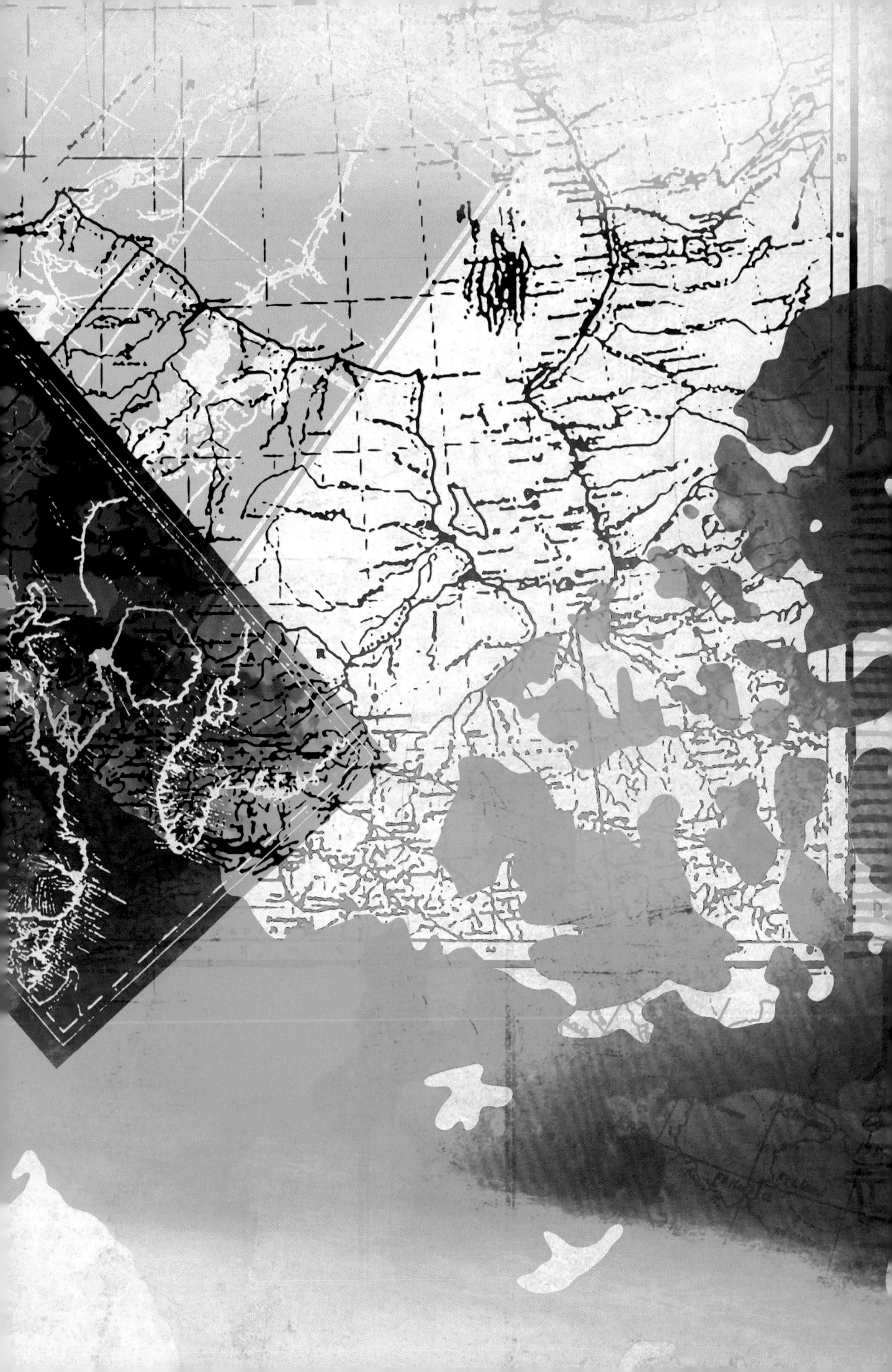

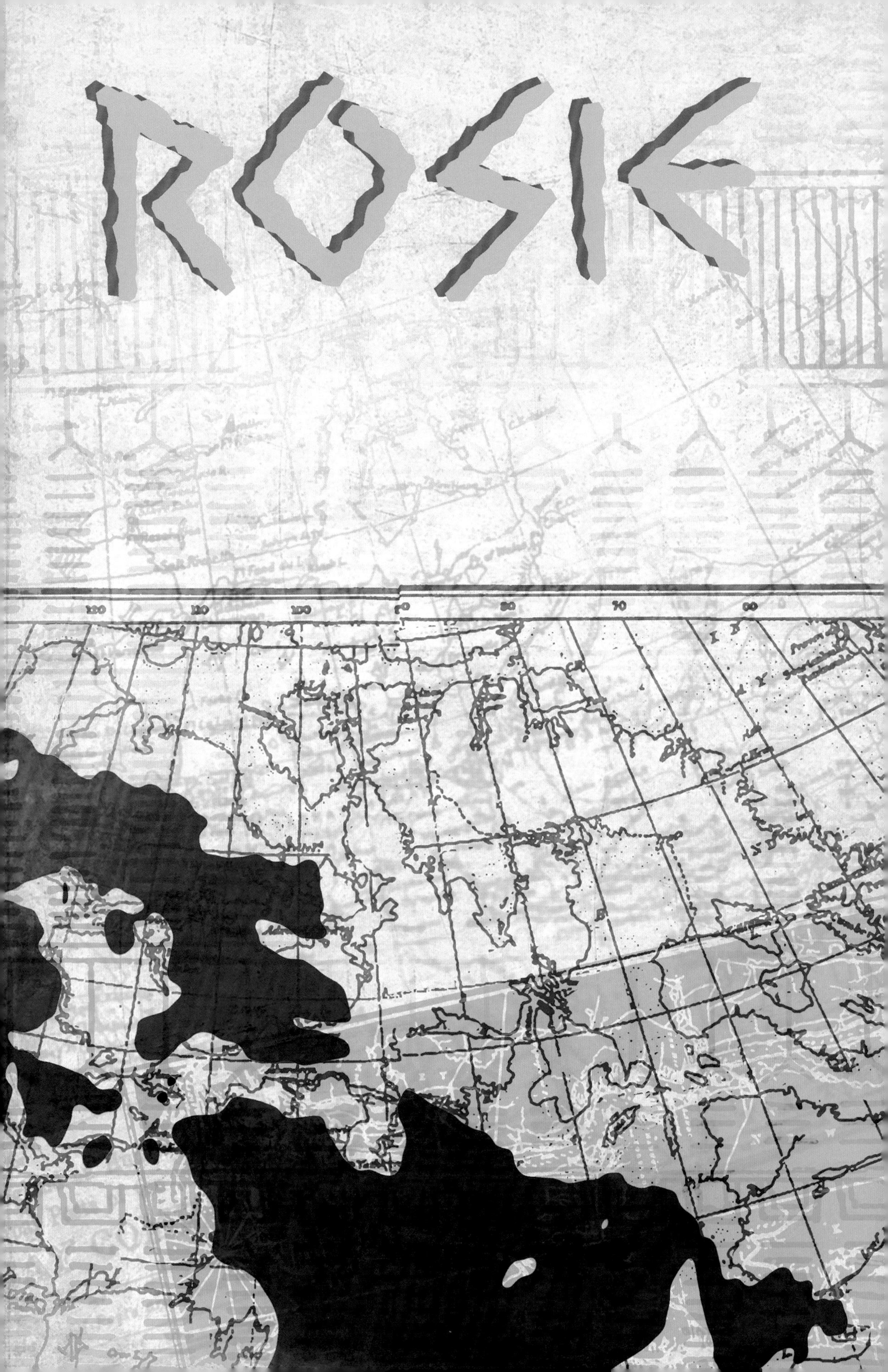
ROSIE

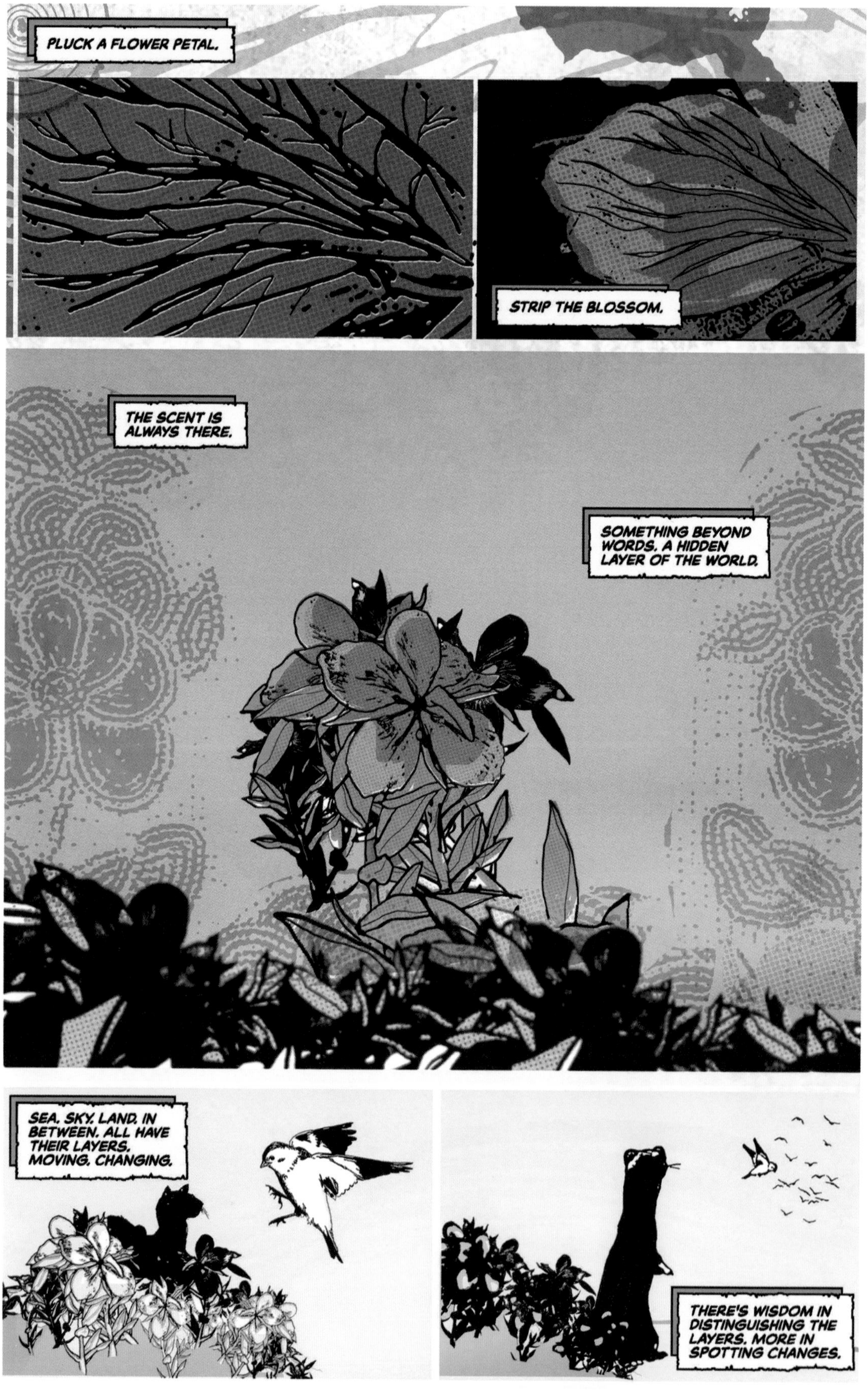
PLUCK A FLOWER PETAL.
STRIP THE BLOSSOM.
THE SCENT IS ALWAYS THERE.
SOMETHING BEYOND WORDS. A HIDDEN LAYER OF THE WORLD.
SEA. SKY. LAND. IN BETWEEN. ALL HAVE THEIR LAYERS. MOVING. CHANGING.
THERE'S WISDOM IN DISTINGUISHING THE LAYERS. MORE IN SPOTTING CHANGES.

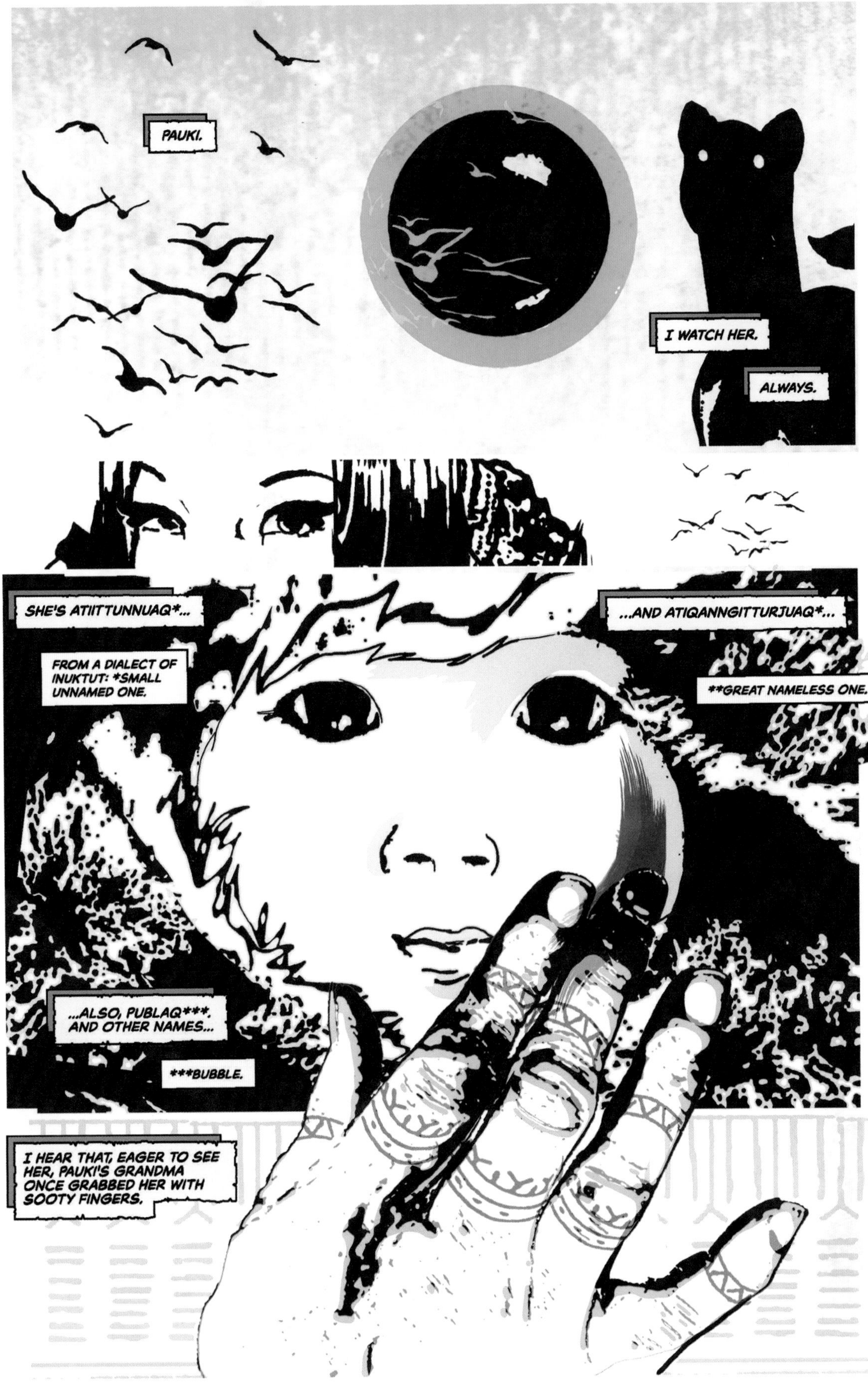
PAUKI.
I WATCH HER.
ALWAYS.
SHE'S ATIITTUNNUAQ*...
FROM A DIALECT OF INUKTUT: *SMALL UNNAMED ONE.
...AND ATIQANNGITTURJUAQ*...
**GREAT NAMELESS ONE.
...ALSO, PUBLAQ***. AND OTHER NAMES...
***BUBBLE.
I HEAR THAT, EAGER TO SEE HER, PAUKI'S GRANDMA ONCE GRABBED HER WITH SOOTY FINGERS.

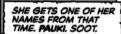
SHE GETS ONE OF HER NAMES FROM THAT TIME. PAUKI. SOOT.

TWO YEARS AGO. THAT'S WHEN WE MET.

IT WAS IQQAQ WHO GAVE ME OVER. HIS NAME MEANS SEA BOTTOM. BUT IN A SECRET TONGUE, IT MEANS LAND. AND HE COULD SEE.

HE WAS AFRAID SHE WOULDN'T ACCEPT ME. SHE DIDN'T UNDERSTAND, AND THERE WAS TOO MUCH TO EXPLAIN.

SHE THOUGHT I WAS A TOY. AND SHE WAS ALREADY GETTING TOO OLD FOR TOYS.

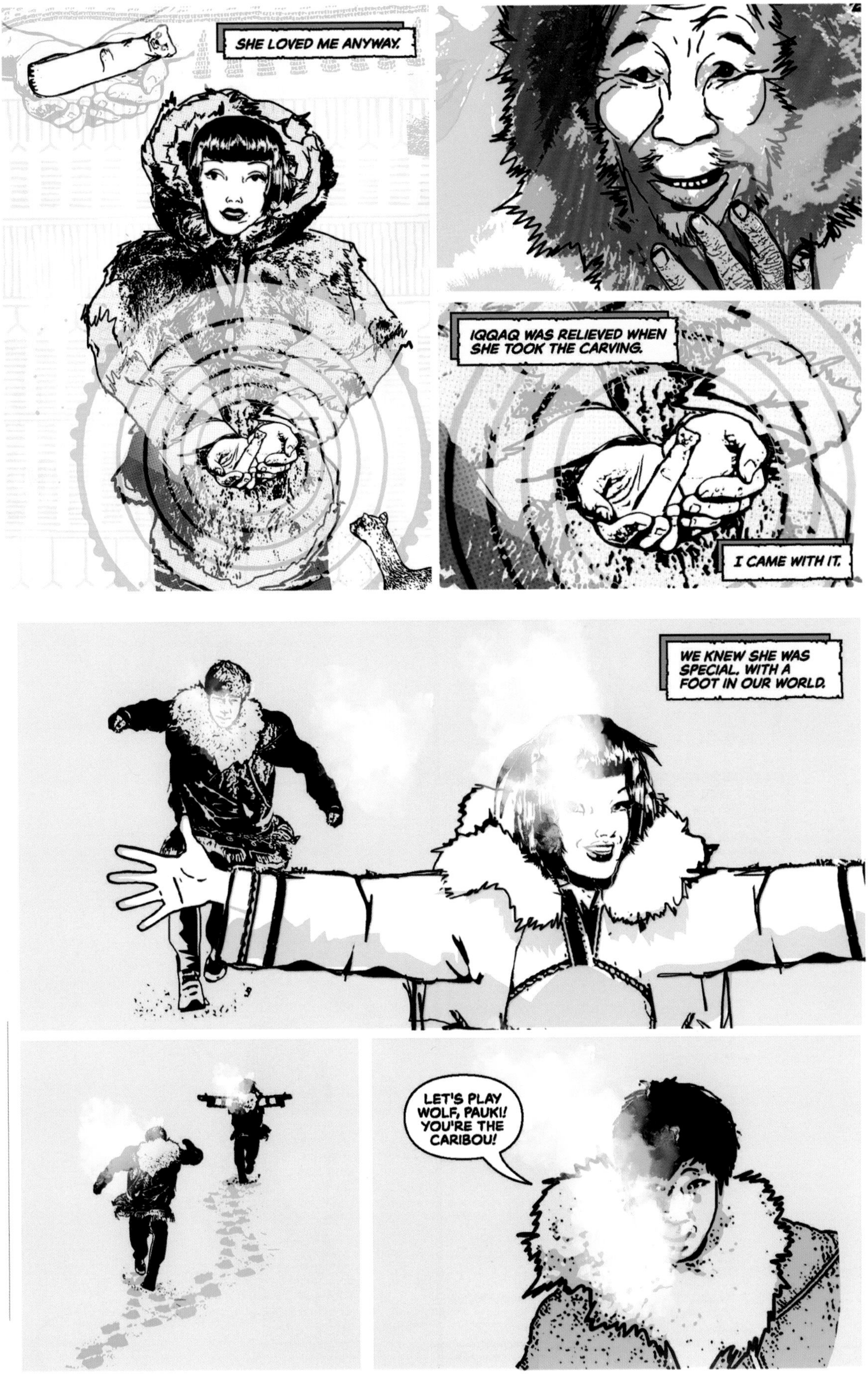
SHE LOVED ME ANYWAY.
IQQAQ WAS RELIEVED WHEN SHE TOOK THE CARVING.
I CAME WITH IT.
WE KNEW SHE WAS SPECIAL, WITH A FOOT IN OUR WORLD.
LET'S PLAY WOLF, PAUKI! YOU'RE THE CARIBOU!

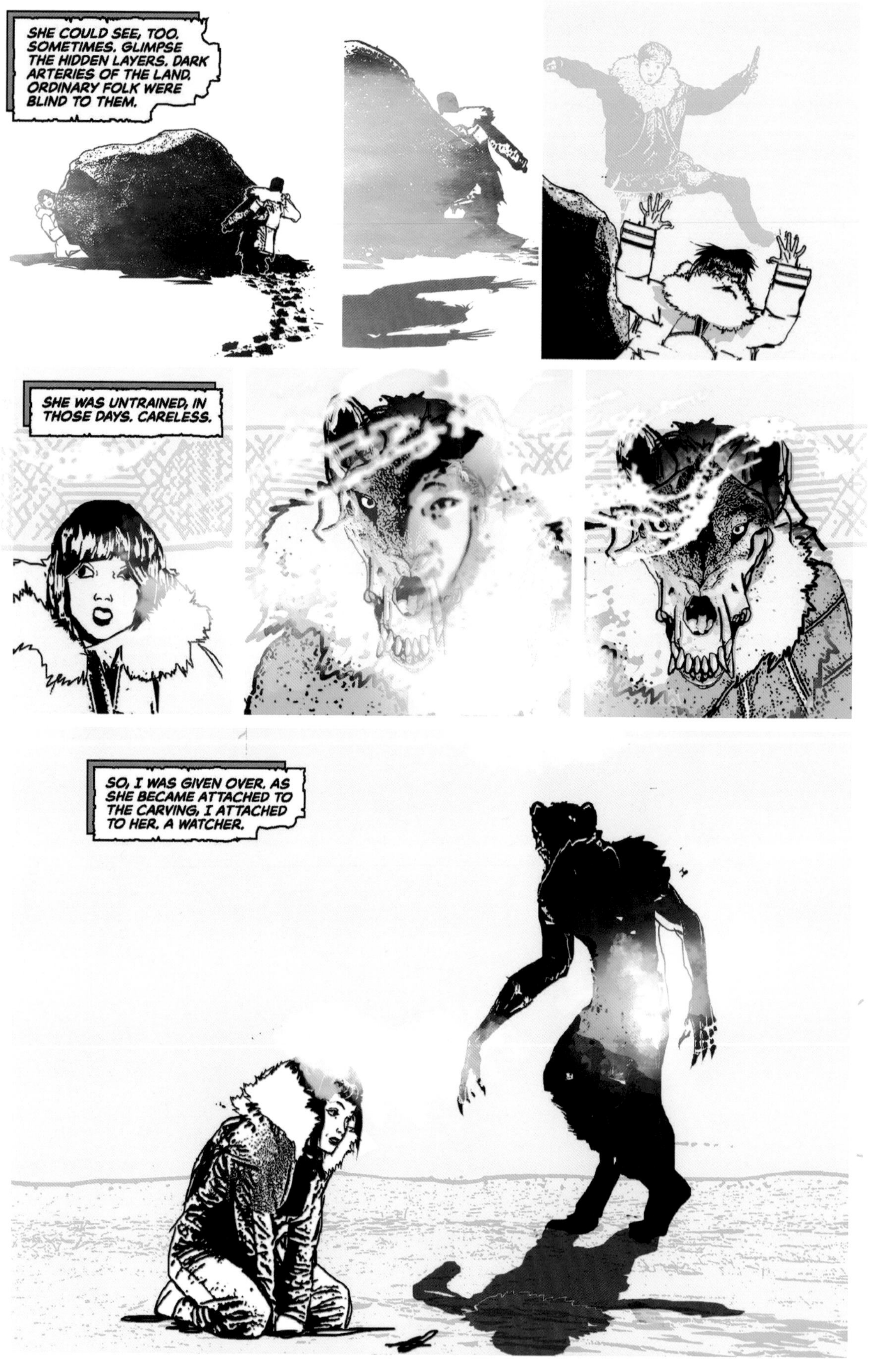
SHE COULD SEE, TOO. SOMETIMES. GLIMPSE THE HIDDEN LAYERS. DARK ARTERIES OF THE LAND. ORDINARY FOLK WERE BLIND TO THEM.
SHE WAS UNTRAINED, IN THOSE DAYS. CARELESS.
SO, I WAS GIVEN OVER. AS SHE BECAME ATTACHED TO THE CARVING, I ATTACHED TO HER. A WATCHER.

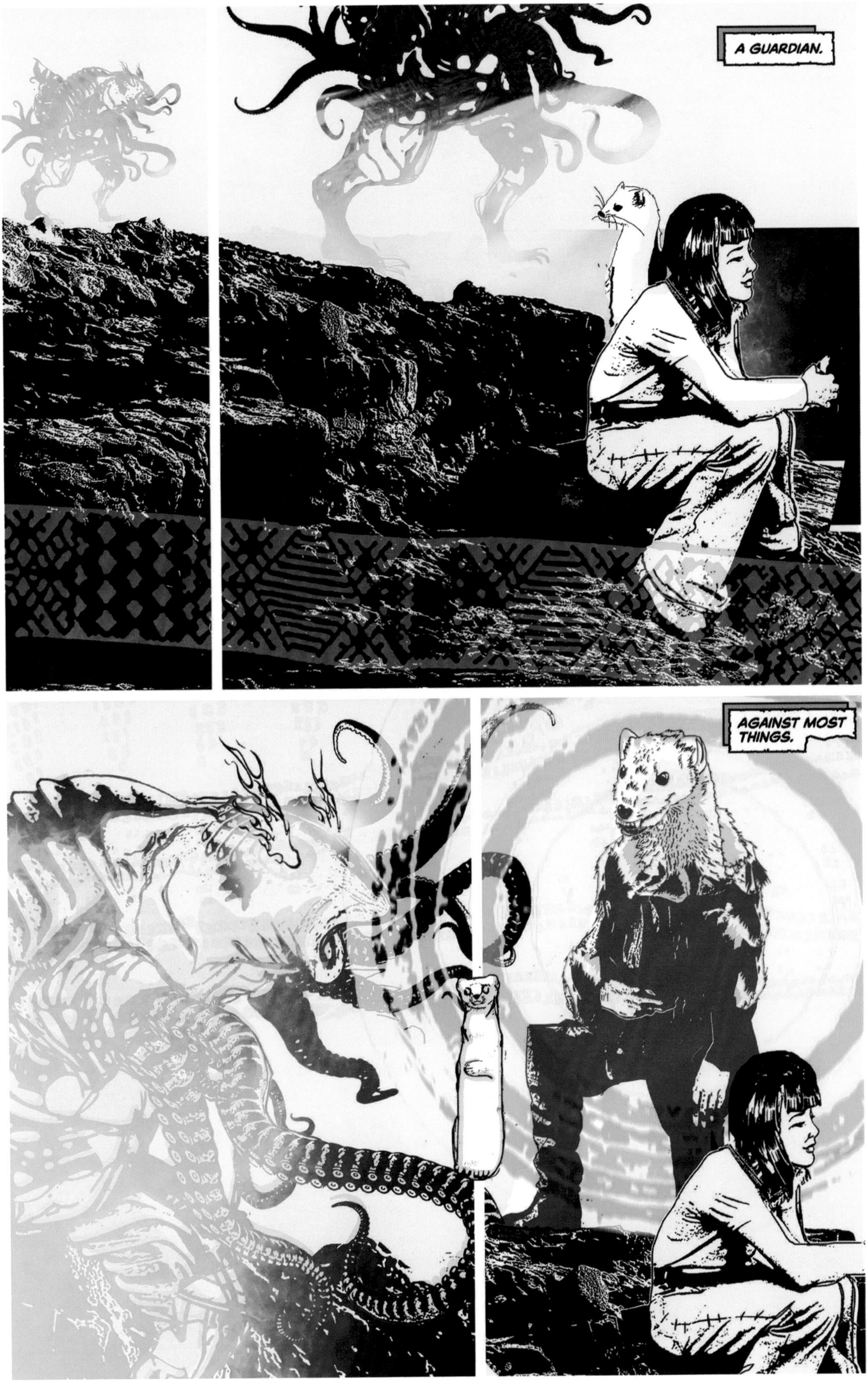
A GUARDIAN.
AGAINST MOST THINGS.

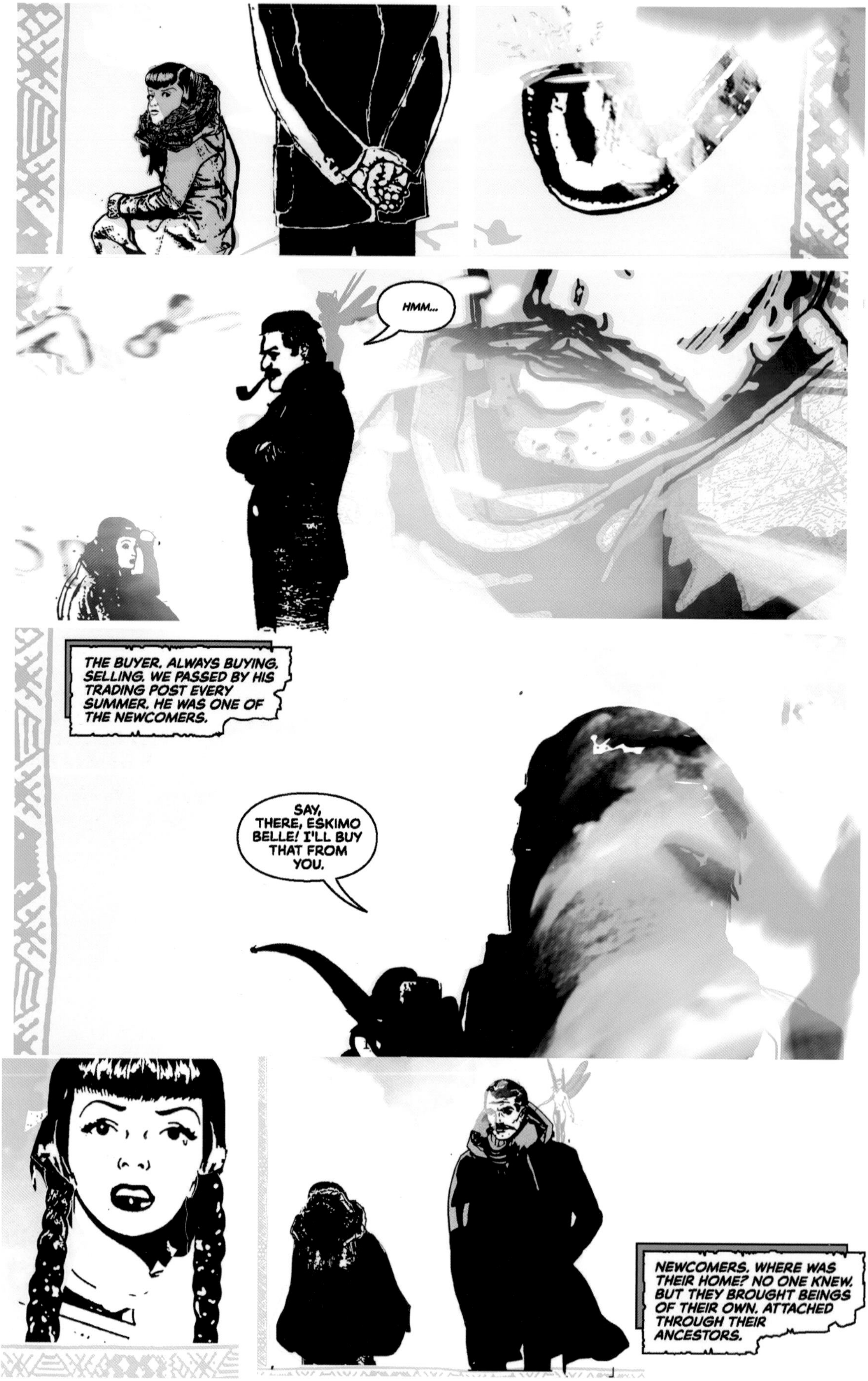
HMM...
THE BUYER. ALWAYS BUYING. SELLING. WE PASSED BY HIS TRADING POST EVERY SUMMER. HE WAS ONE OF THE NEWCOMERS.
SAY, THERE, ESKIMO BELLE! I'LL BUY THAT FROM YOU.
NEWCOMERS. WHERE WAS THEIR HOME? NO ONE KNEW. BUT THEY BROUGHT BEINGS OF THEIR OWN. ATTACHED THROUGH THEIR ANCESTORS.

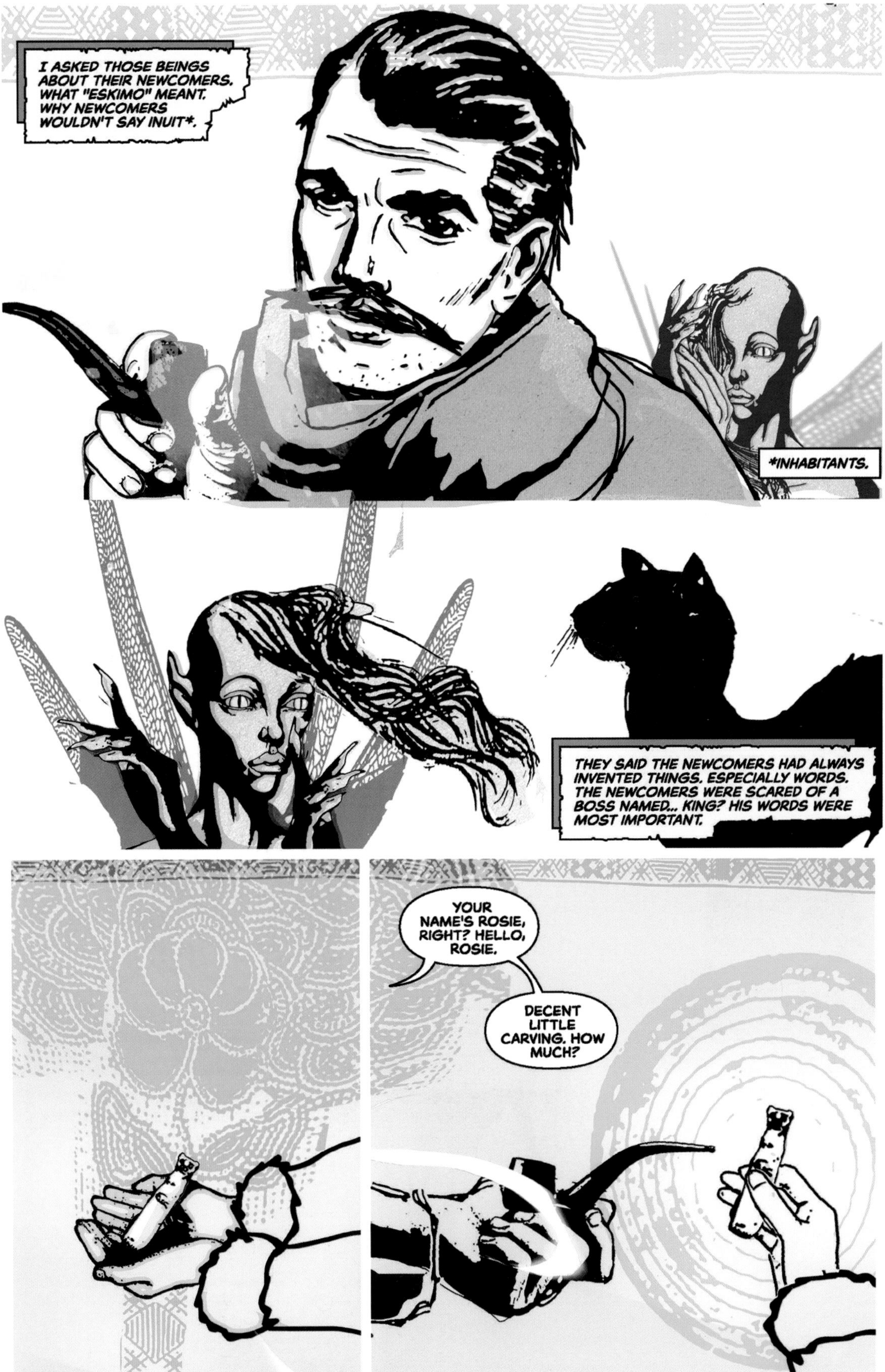
I ASKED THOSE BEINGS ABOUT THEIR NEWCOMERS. WHAT "ESKIMO" MEANT. WHY NEWCOMERS WOULDN'T SAY INUIT*.
*INHABITANTS.
THEY SAID THE NEWCOMERS HAD ALWAYS INVENTED THINGS. ESPECIALLY WORDS. THE NEWCOMERS WERE SCARED OF A BOSS NAMED... KING? HIS WORDS WERE MOST IMPORTANT.
YOUR NAME'S ROSIE, RIGHT? HELLO, ROSIE.
DECENT LITTLE CARVING. HOW MUCH?

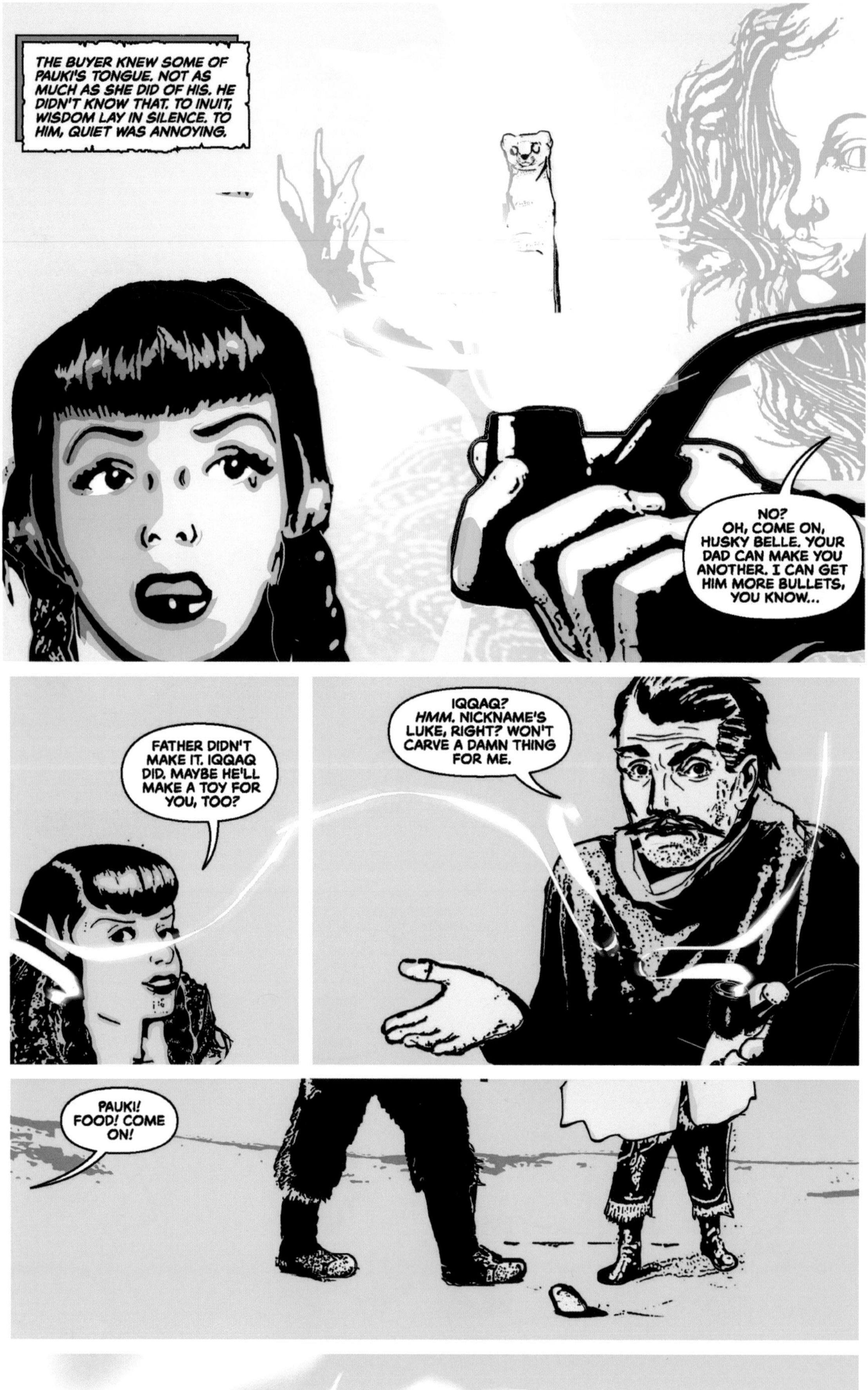
THE BUYER KNEW SOME OF PAUKI'S TONGUE. NOT AS MUCH AS SHE DID OF HIS. HE DIDN'T KNOW THAT. TO INUIT, WISDOM LAY IN SILENCE. TO HIM, QUIET WAS ANNOYING.
NO? OH, COME ON, HUSKY BELLE. YOUR DAD CAN MAKE YOU ANOTHER. I CAN GET HIM MORE BULLETS, YOU KNOW...
FATHER DIDN'T MAKE IT. IQQAQ DID. MAYBE HE'LL MAKE A TOY FOR YOU, TOO?
IQQAQ? HMM. NICKNAME'S LUKE, RIGHT? WON'T CARVE A DAMN THING FOR ME.
PAUKI! FOOD! COME ON!

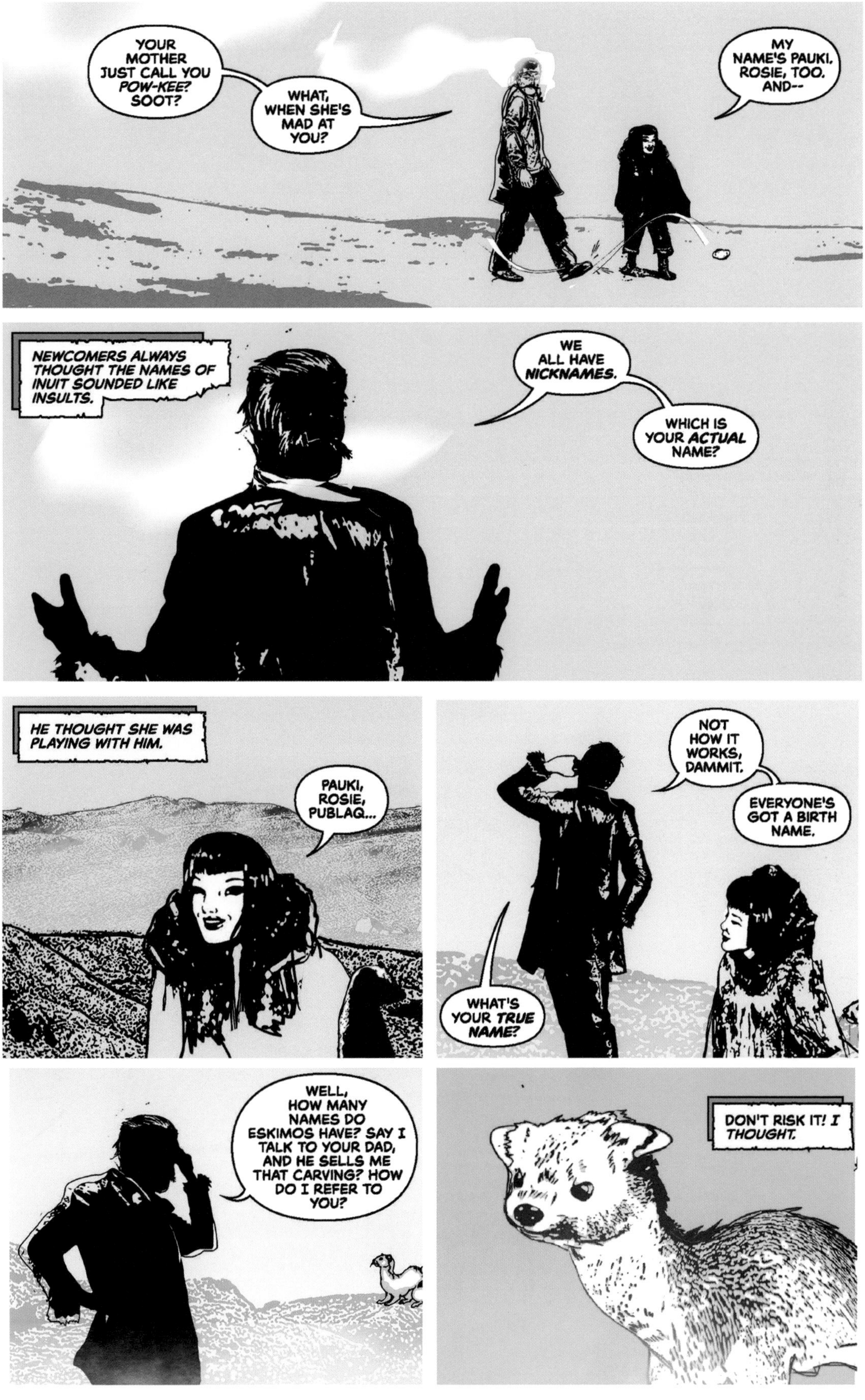
YOUR MOTHER JUST CALL YOU *POW-KEE?* SOOT?
WHAT, WHEN SHE'S MAD AT YOU?
MY NAME'S PAUKI. ROSIE, TOO. AND--
NEWCOMERS ALWAYS THOUGHT THE NAMES OF INUIT SOUNDED LIKE INSULTS.
WE ALL HAVE *NICKNAMES.*
WHICH IS YOUR *ACTUAL* NAME?
HE THOUGHT SHE WAS PLAYING WITH HIM.
PAUKI, ROSIE, PUBLAQ...
NOT HOW IT WORKS, DAMMIT.
EVERYONE'S GOT A BIRTH NAME.
WHAT'S YOUR *TRUE NAME?*
WELL, HOW MANY NAMES DO ESKIMOS HAVE? SAY I TALK TO YOUR DAD, AND HE SELLS ME THAT CARVING? HOW DO I REFER TO YOU?
DON'T RISK IT! I THOUGHT.

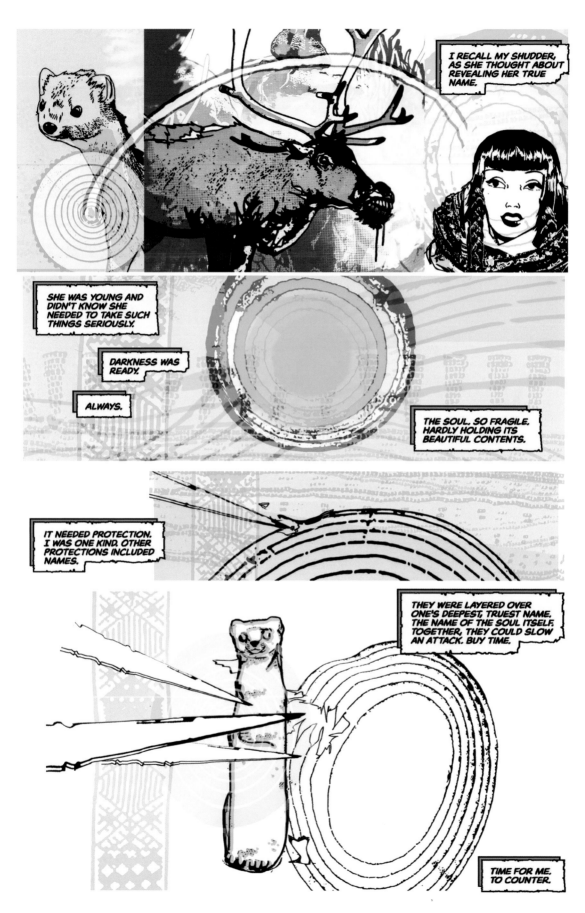

I RECALL MY SHUDDER, AS SHE THOUGHT ABOUT REVEALING HER TRUE NAME.

SHE WAS YOUNG AND DIDN'T KNOW SHE NEEDED TO TAKE SUCH THINGS SERIOUSLY.

DARKNESS WAS READY.

ALWAYS.

THE SOUL. SO FRAGILE. HARDLY HOLDING ITS BEAUTIFUL CONTENTS.

IT NEEDED PROTECTION. I WAS ONE KIND. OTHER PROTECTIONS INCLUDED NAMES.

THEY WERE LAYERED OVER ONE'S DEEPEST, TRUEST NAME. THE NAME OF THE SOUL ITSELF. TOGETHER, THEY COULD SLOW AN ATTACK. BUY TIME.

TIME FOR ME. TO COUNTER.

HOPED YOU WERE SMARTER.

JUST ANOTHER GODDAMN, STUPID ESKIMO.

TRUE NAME, THEN. BLURTED. LIKE A STRAY WORD...

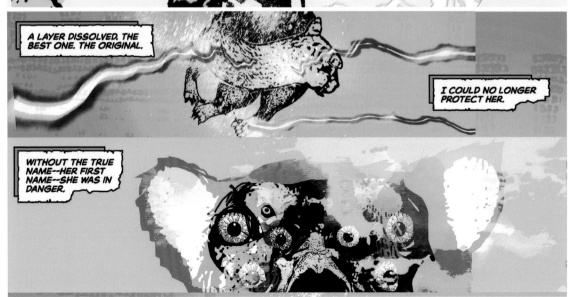

A LAYER DISSOLVED. THE BEST ONE. THE ORIGINAL.

I COULD NO LONGER PROTECT HER.

WITHOUT THE TRUE NAME--HER FIRST NAME--SHE WAS IN DANGER.

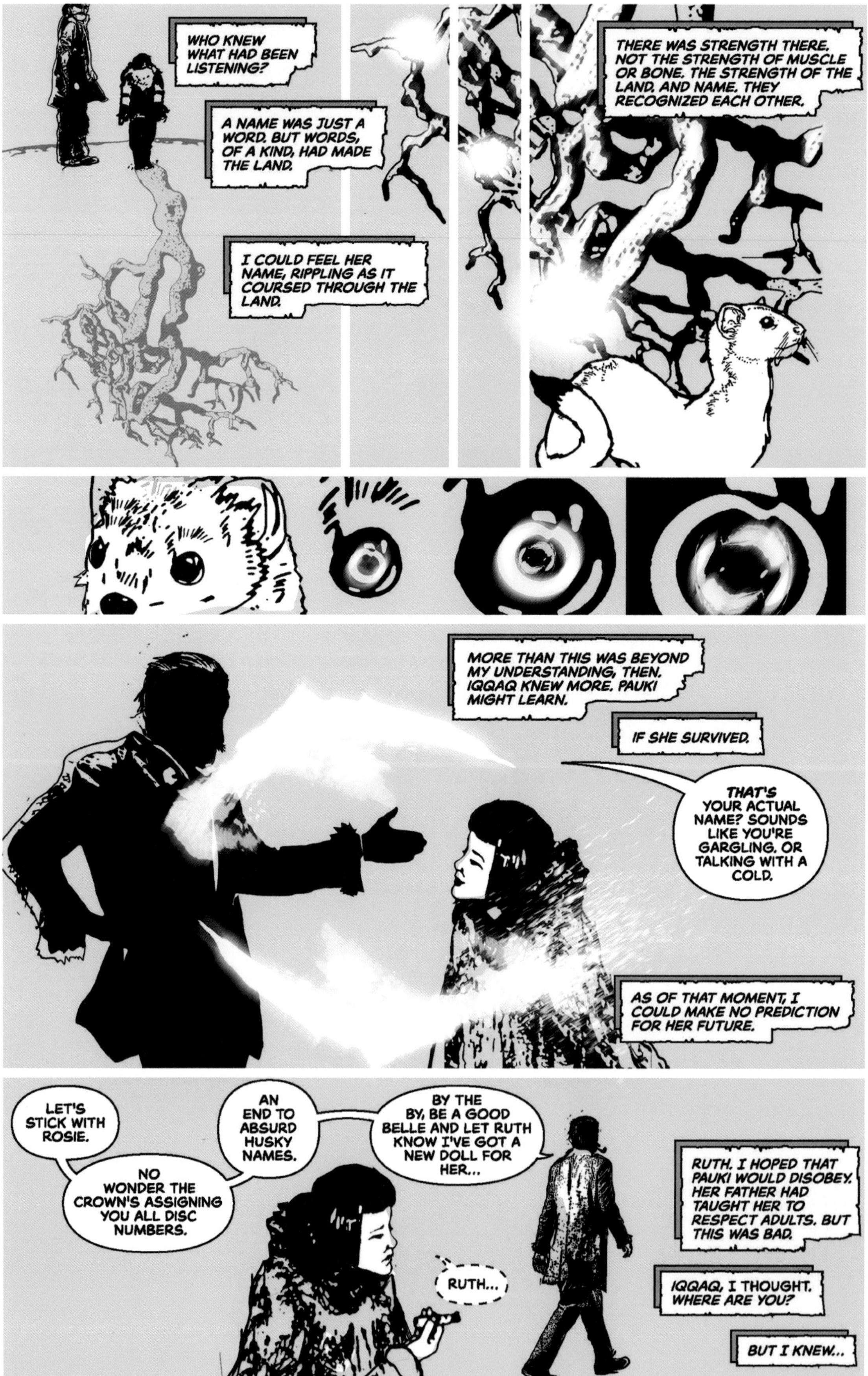
WHO KNEW WHAT HAD BEEN LISTENING?
A NAME WAS JUST A WORD. BUT WORDS, OF A KIND, HAD MADE THE LAND.
I COULD FEEL HER NAME, RIPPLING AS IT COURSED THROUGH THE LAND.
THERE WAS STRENGTH THERE. NOT THE STRENGTH OF MUSCLE OR BONE. THE STRENGTH OF THE LAND. AND NAME. THEY RECOGNIZED EACH OTHER.
MORE THAN THIS WAS BEYOND MY UNDERSTANDING, THEN. IQQAQ KNEW MORE. PAUKI MIGHT LEARN.
IF SHE SURVIVED.
THAT'S YOUR ACTUAL NAME? SOUNDS LIKE YOU'RE GARGLING. OR TALKING WITH A COLD.
AS OF THAT MOMENT, I COULD MAKE NO PREDICTION FOR HER FUTURE.
LET'S STICK WITH ROSIE.
NO WONDER THE CROWN'S ASSIGNING YOU ALL DISC NUMBERS.
AN END TO ABSURD HUSKY NAMES.
BY THE BY, BE A GOOD BELLE AND LET RUTH KNOW I'VE GOT A NEW DOLL FOR HER...
RUTH...
RUTH. I HOPED THAT PAUKI WOULD DISOBEY. HER FATHER HAD TAUGHT HER TO RESPECT ADULTS. BUT THIS WAS BAD.
IQQAQ, I THOUGHT. WHERE ARE YOU?
BUT I KNEW...

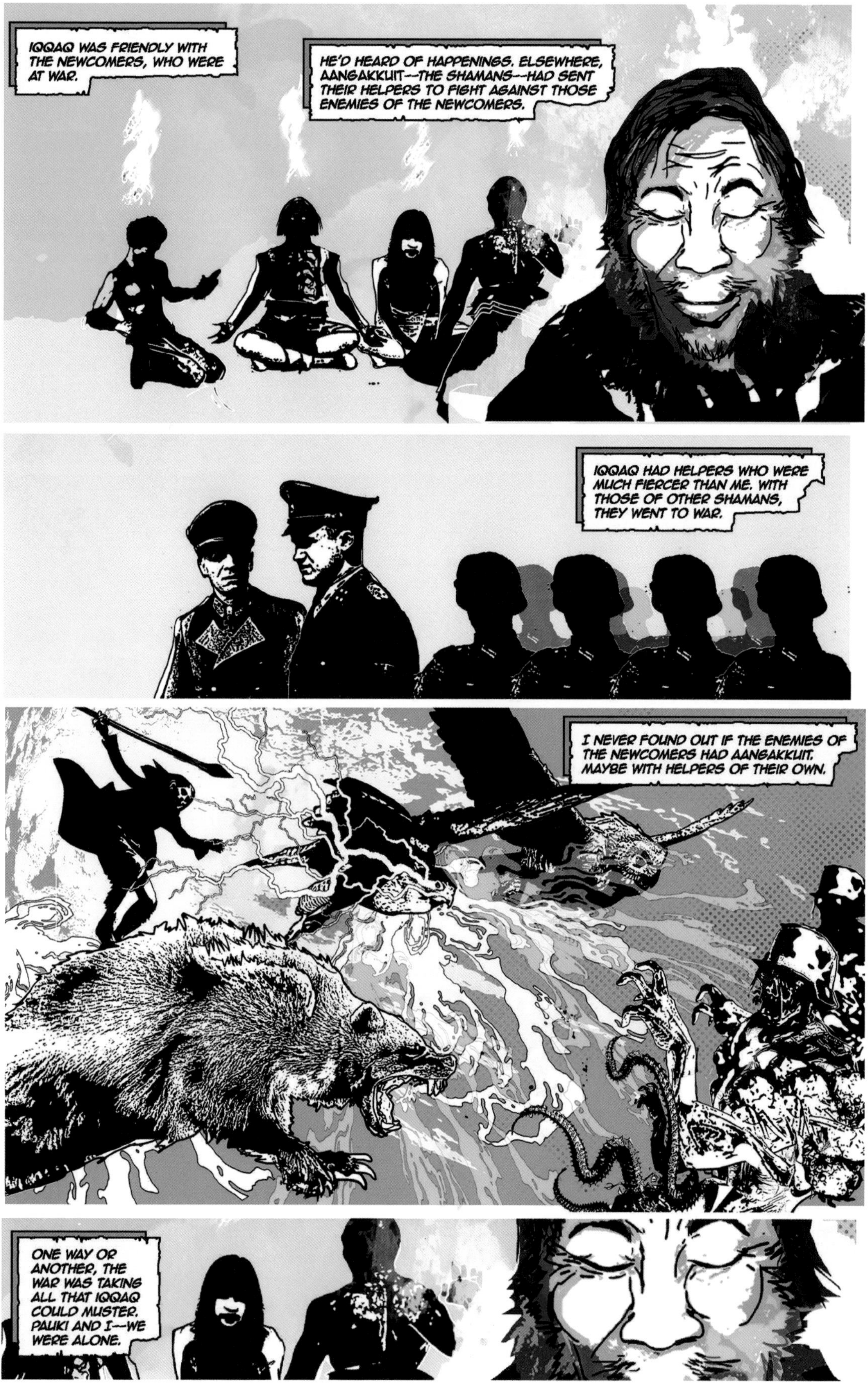
IQQAQ WAS FRIENDLY WITH THE NEWCOMERS, WHO WERE AT WAR.
HE'D HEARD OF HAPPENINGS. ELSEWHERE, AANGAKKUIT--THE SHAMANS--HAD SENT THEIR HELPERS TO FIGHT AGAINST THOSE ENEMIES OF THE NEWCOMERS.
IQQAQ HAD HELPERS WHO WERE MUCH FIERCER THAN ME. WITH THOSE OF OTHER SHAMANS, THEY WENT TO WAR.
I NEVER FOUND OUT IF THE ENEMIES OF THE NEWCOMERS HAD AANGAKKUIT. MAYBE WITH HELPERS OF THEIR OWN.
ONE WAY OR ANOTHER, THE WAR WAS TAKING ALL THAT IQQAQ COULD MUSTER. PAUKI AND I--WE WERE ALONE.

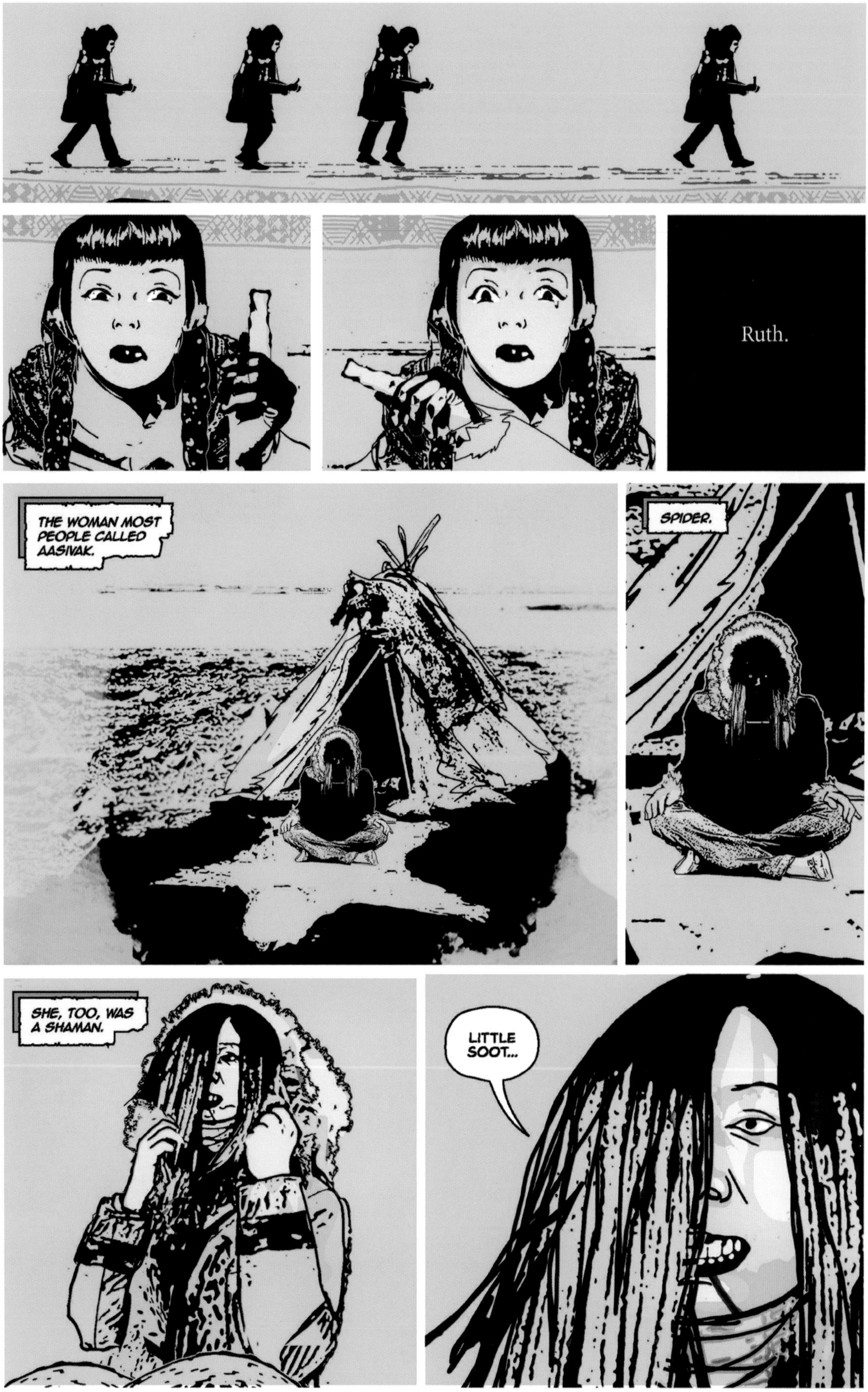
Ruth.
THE WOMAN MOST PEOPLE CALLED AASIVAK.
SPIDER.
SHE, TOO, WAS A SHAMAN.
LITTLE SOOT...

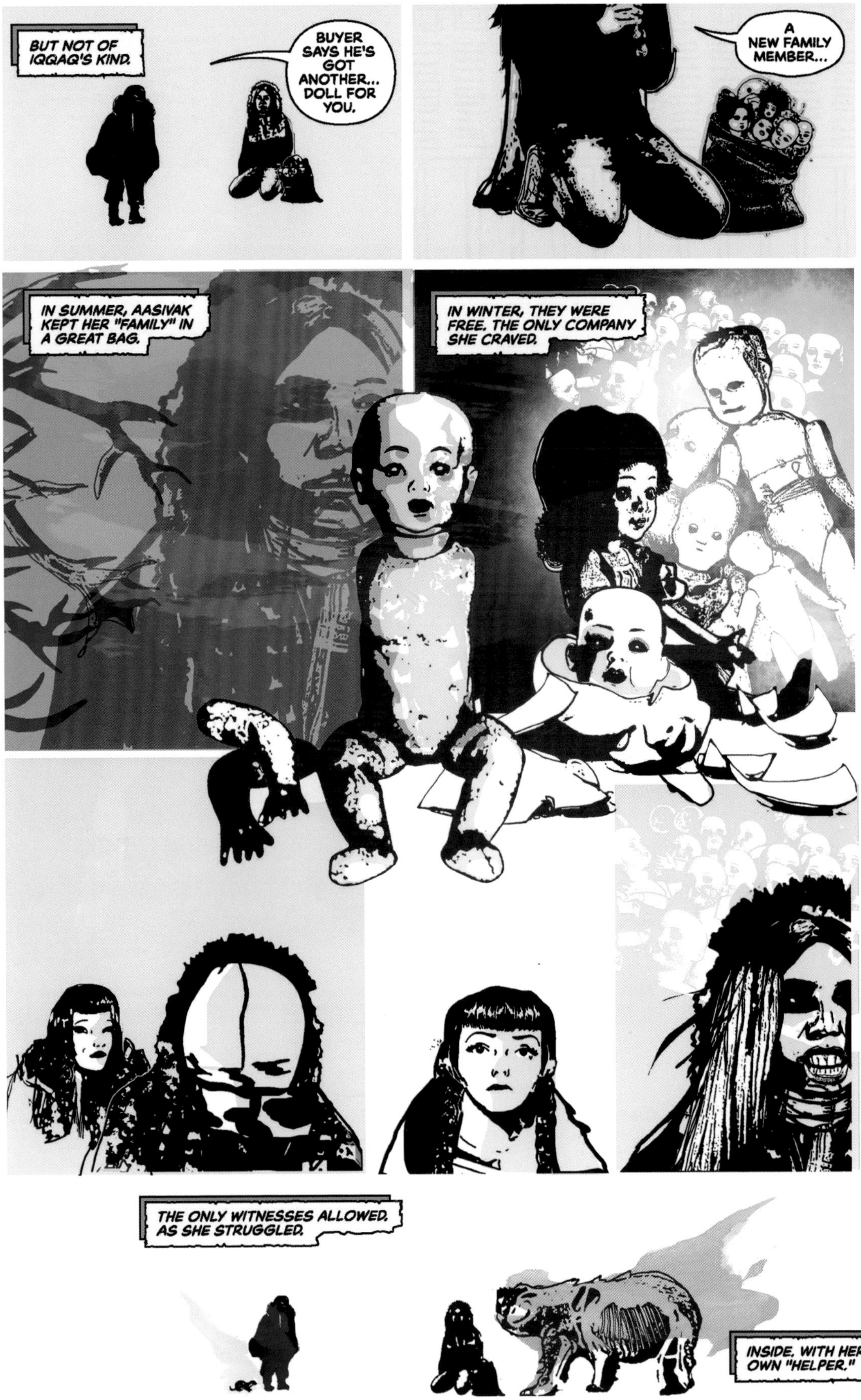
BUT NOT OF IQQAQ'S KIND.
BUYER SAYS HE'S GOT ANOTHER... DOLL FOR YOU.
A NEW FAMILY MEMBER...
IN SUMMER, AASIVAK KEPT HER "FAMILY" IN A GREAT BAG.
IN WINTER, THEY WERE FREE. THE ONLY COMPANY SHE CRAVED.
THE ONLY WITNESSES ALLOWED. AS SHE STRUGGLED.
INSIDE, WITH HER OWN "HELPER."

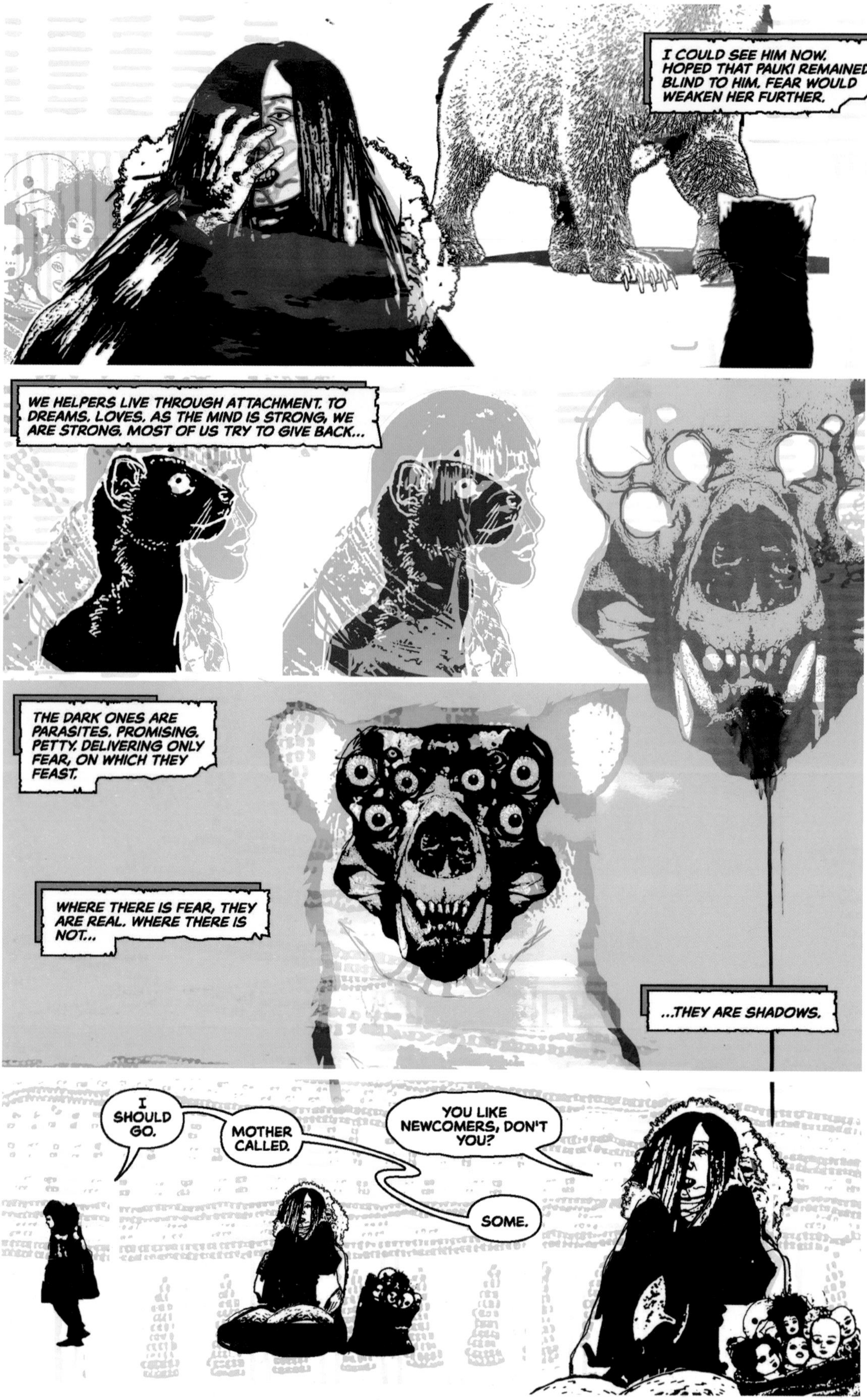

I COULD SEE HIM NOW. HOPED THAT PAUKI REMAINED BLIND TO HIM. FEAR WOULD WEAKEN HER FURTHER.
WE HELPERS LIVE THROUGH ATTACHMENT. TO DREAMS. LOVES. AS THE MIND IS STRONG, WE ARE STRONG. MOST OF US TRY TO GIVE BACK...
THE DARK ONES ARE PARASITES. PROMISING. PETTY. DELIVERING ONLY FEAR, ON WHICH THEY FEAST.
WHERE THERE IS FEAR, THEY ARE REAL. WHERE THERE IS NOT...
...THEY ARE SHADOWS.
I SHOULD GO.
MOTHER CALLED.
YOU LIKE NEWCOMERS, DON'T YOU?
SOME.

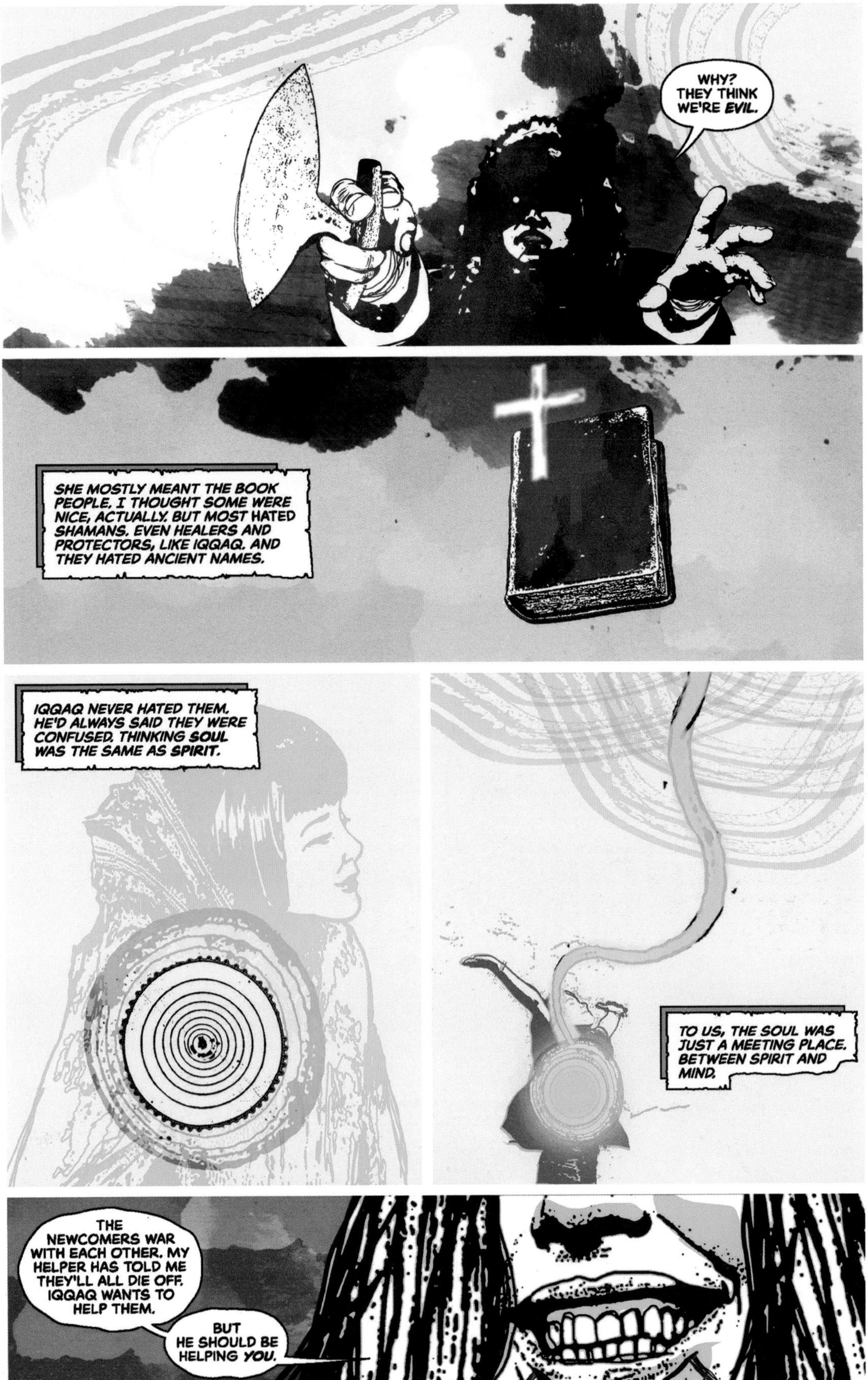
WHY? THEY THINK WE'RE EVIL.
SHE MOSTLY MEANT THE BOOK PEOPLE. I THOUGHT SOME WERE NICE, ACTUALLY. BUT MOST HATED SHAMANS. EVEN HEALERS AND PROTECTORS, LIKE IQQAQ. AND THEY HATED ANCIENT NAMES.
IQQAQ NEVER HATED THEM. HE'D ALWAYS SAID THEY WERE CONFUSED. THINKING SOUL WAS THE SAME AS SPIRIT.
TO US, THE SOUL WAS JUST A MEETING PLACE. BETWEEN SPIRIT AND MIND.
THE NEWCOMERS WAR WITH EACH OTHER. MY HELPER HAS TOLD ME THEY'LL ALL DIE OFF. IQQAQ WANTS TO HELP THEM.
BUT HE SHOULD BE HELPING YOU.

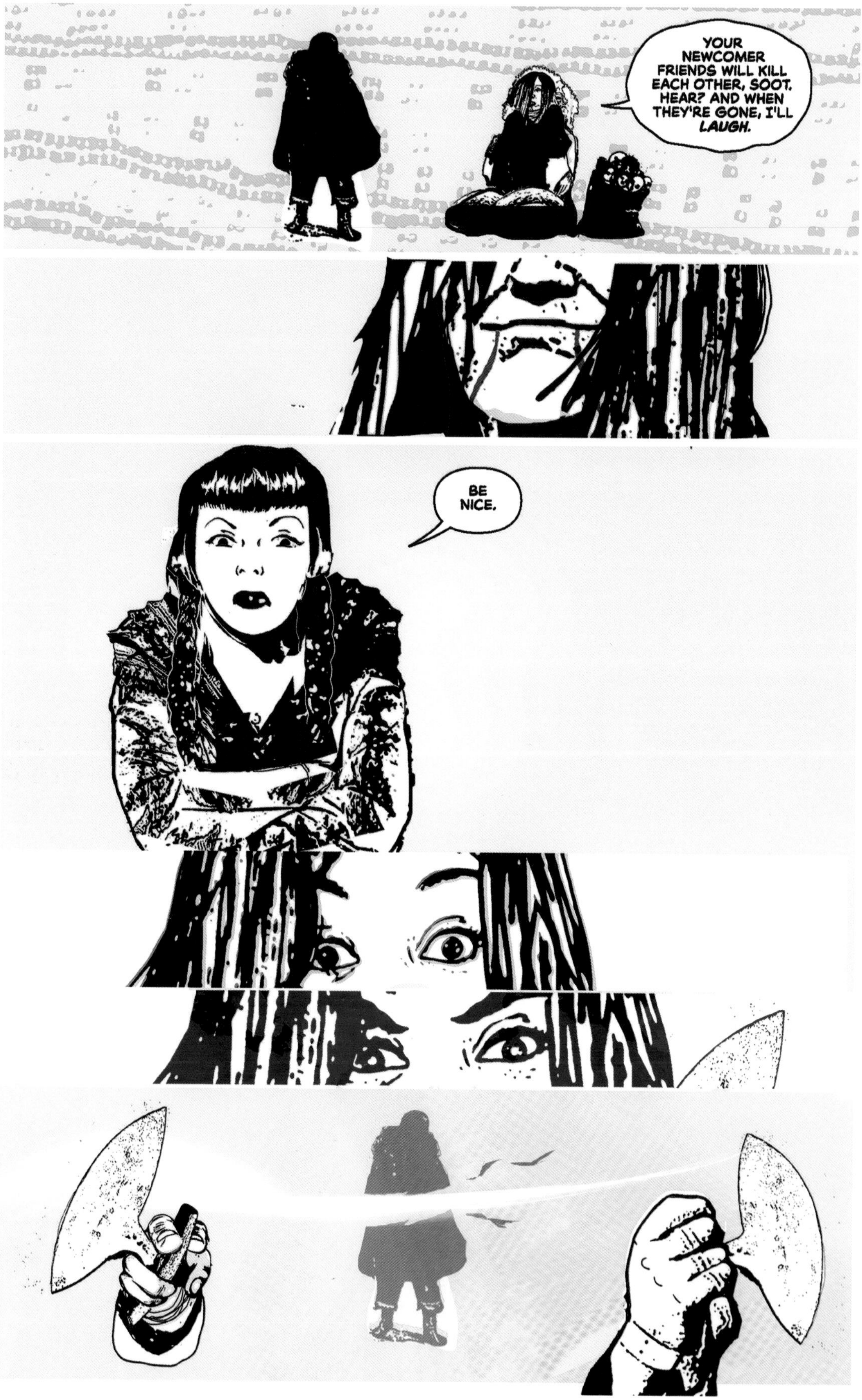
YOUR NEWCOMER FRIENDS WILL KILL EACH OTHER, SOOT. HEAR? AND WHEN THEY'RE GONE, I'LL LAUGH.
BE NICE.

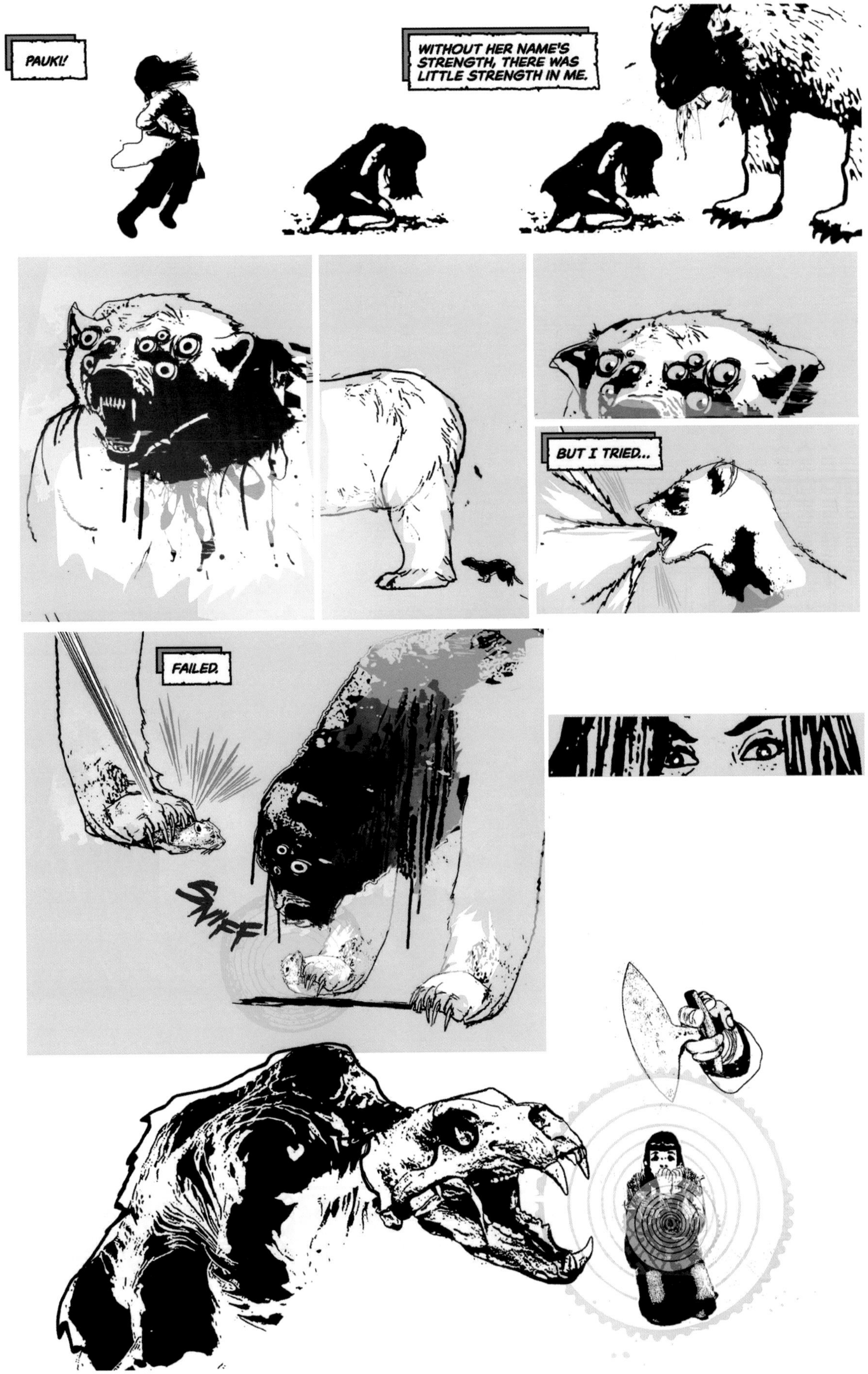
PAUKI!
WITHOUT HER NAME'S STRENGTH, THERE WAS LITTLE STRENGTH IN ME.
BUT I TRIED...
FAILED.
SNIFF

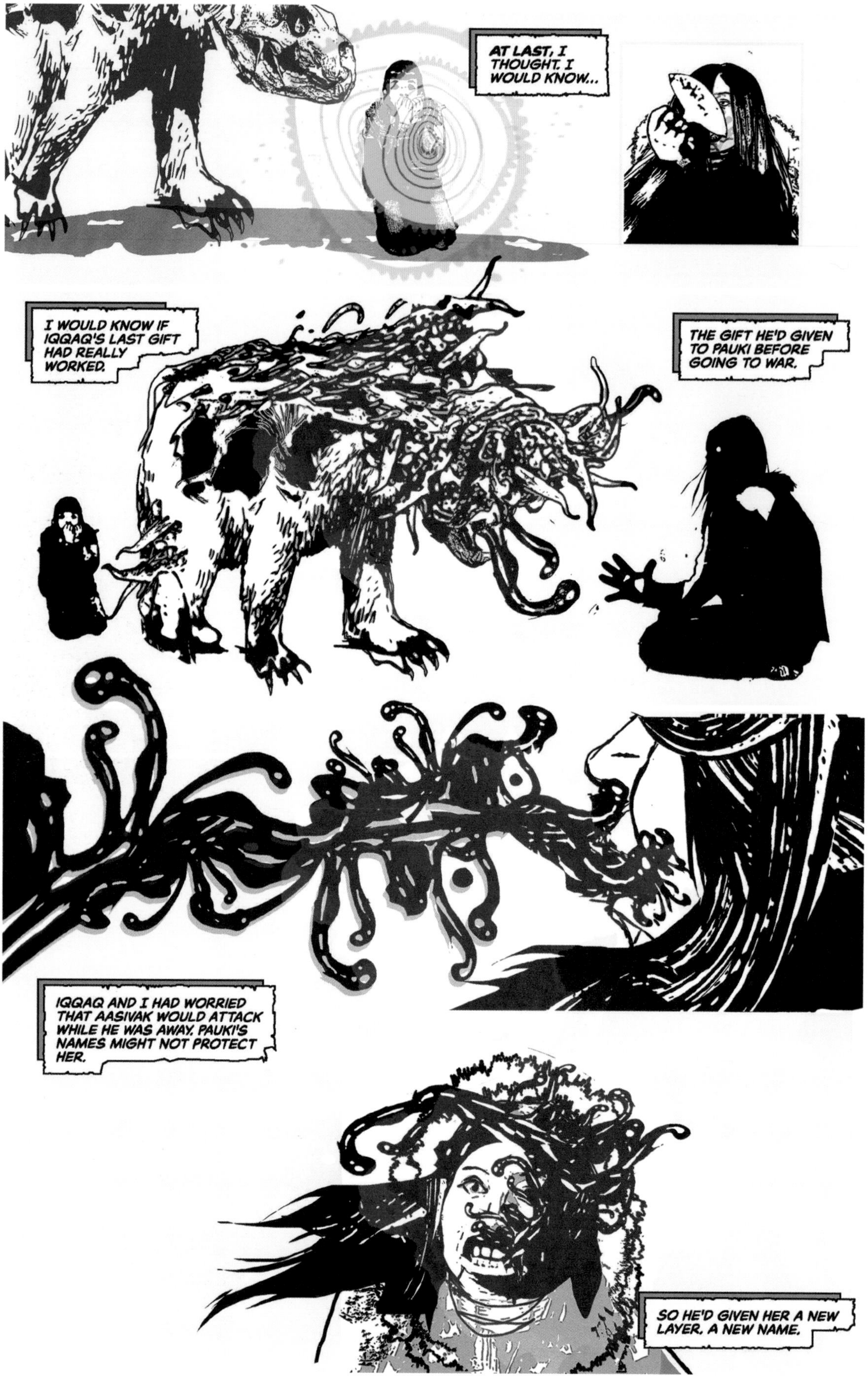
AT LAST, I THOUGHT, I WOULD KNOW...
I WOULD KNOW IF IQQAQ'S LAST GIFT HAD REALLY WORKED.
THE GIFT HE'D GIVEN TO PAUKI BEFORE GOING TO WAR.
IQQAQ AND I HAD WORRIED THAT AASIVAK WOULD ATTACK WHILE HE WAS AWAY. PAUKI'S NAMES MIGHT NOT PROTECT HER.
SO HE'D GIVEN HER A NEW LAYER. A NEW NAME.

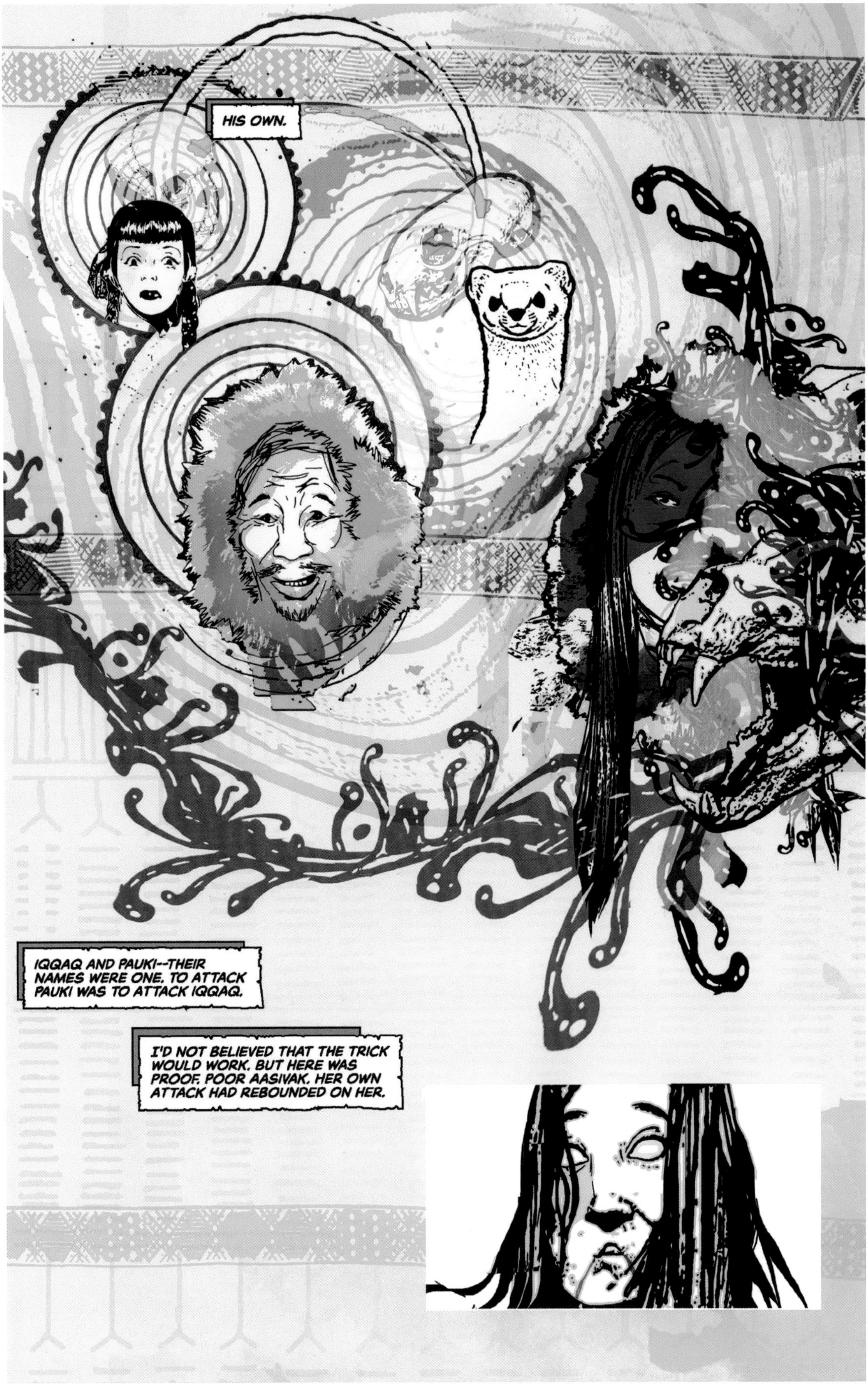
HIS OWN.
IQQAQ AND PAUKI--THEIR NAMES WERE ONE. TO ATTACK PAUKI WAS TO ATTACK IQQAQ.
I'D NOT BELIEVED THAT THE TRICK WOULD WORK. BUT HERE WAS PROOF. POOR AASIVAK. HER OWN ATTACK HAD REBOUNDED ON HER.

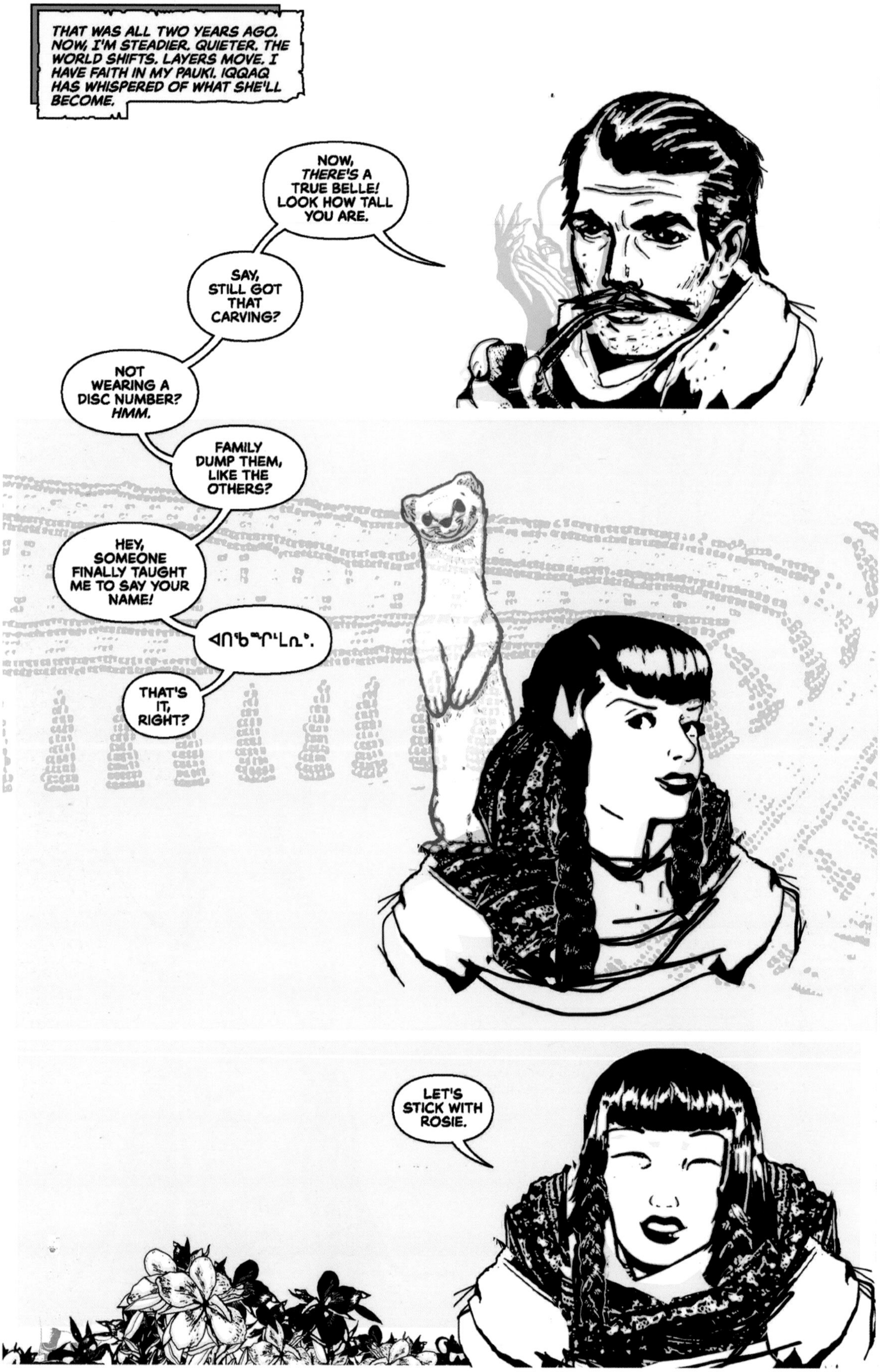
THAT WAS ALL TWO YEARS AGO. NOW, I'M STEADIER. QUIETER. THE WORLD SHIFTS. LAYERS MOVE. I HAVE FAITH IN MY PAUKI. IQQAQ HAS WHISPERED OF WHAT SHE'LL BECOME.
NOW, THERE'S A TRUE BELLE! LOOK HOW TALL YOU ARE.
SAY, STILL GOT THAT CARVING?
NOT WEARING A DISC NUMBER? HMM.
FAMILY DUMP THEM, LIKE THE OTHERS?
HEY, SOMEONE FINALLY TAUGHT ME TO SAY YOUR NAME!
ᐊᑎᖅᑲᖕᒋᓪᒪᓇᒃ.
THAT'S IT, RIGHT?
LET'S STICK WITH ROSIE.

"Nimkii" was inspired by the lives of a few specific children in care, the shocking statistics about Indigenous children in the system, and my own experience as an adoptive mother. In the late 1980s, I watched Alanis Obomsawin's documentary *Richard Cardinal: Cry from the Diary of a Metis Child* about a boy who took his own life after being placed in 28 different foster homes during his 14 years "in care." Richard's story lodged itself in my heart, changing the way I understood Indigenous history and what it means to be "in care." I resolved to adopt when I started a family. Later I heard about Teddy Bellingham, an Anishinaabe "Crown Ward" with roots in my community, who was brutally murdered in Smith Falls, Ontario. I learned about the Sixties Scoop and its devastating impacts on children, families, and communities, many of whom fought to bring their children home. When I eventually started my family, I did adopt. I have two beautiful, smart, loving, Anishinaabe boys who are the loves of my life, my family, my joy. It's heartbreaking to know that there are many other children, just as beautiful and deserving of love, who languish in the system, neglected, abused, placed in homes where they are simply a "meal ticket" or a "good deed," pawns in a power game by CFS workers and agencies exerting their control over Indigenous lives. There are Indigenous children "in care" who develop lifelong attachment issues, with no one to care or advocate for them, exposed to crime and addictions, taught to hate their Indigeneity. Of course, some Indigenous children are adopted into families bonded by love, respect, and caring. Some are fostered with kindness. Some thrive despite the system. They too inspire me and deserve to be celebrated. With "Nimkii," I have done my best to tell a story that lovingly honours all of these children.

Kateri Akiwenzie-Damm

1945

World War II ends. Residential Schools are in a state of grave disrepair. At the same time, the war had brought human rights and bigotry into public consciousness. Attention soon fell on First Nations communities and the poverty and social ills resulting from generations of colonialism and the Indian Residential School system.

1951

Major changes are made to the Indian Act, including a ban on alcohol consumption, greater autonomy for bands, and an end to the prohibition of ceremonies and dances. The changes also give the provinces jurisdiction over the welfare of Indigenous children. Child welfare workers begin removing Indigenous children from their families and communities.

1960, MARCH 10

Indigenous peoples are granted the right to vote in federal elections without relinquishing their Indian status.

LATE 1950S-1960s

The Sixties Scoop: As residential schools close, thousands of Indigenous children are removed from their families and placed in non-Indigenous foster or adoption homes. Many children are placed outside of Canada.

Nimkii

Kateri Akiwenzie-Damm

Illustration: Ryan Howe & Jen Storm

Colours: Donovan Yaciuk

1960
The 1960 Canadian Bill of Rights is passed. This affirmed the right to equality before the law for all Canadians, including Indigenous peoples.

1980s
For decades, the children of Wabaseemoong had been taken by the Children's Aid Society (CAS), sometimes by the bus load. By the end of the 1980s, a third of the community's children are in foster care.

1969, JANUARY 1
The Department of Indian Affairs assumes responsibility for the remaining residential schools.

1990
The federal government creates the First Nations Child and Family Services program, which gives local bands the power to administer child and family services according to provincial and territorial legislation.

1990s
Class action lawsuits on behalf of Sixties Scoop survivors are pursued against provincial governments in Ontario, Alberta, Saskatchewan, and Manitoba. These lawsuits are still before the courts.

1990
Wabaseemoong Band Council passes a resolution that forbids the Children's Aid Society from entering the reserve. Community members stand guard at the reserve boundary to prevent any more of their children from being taken.

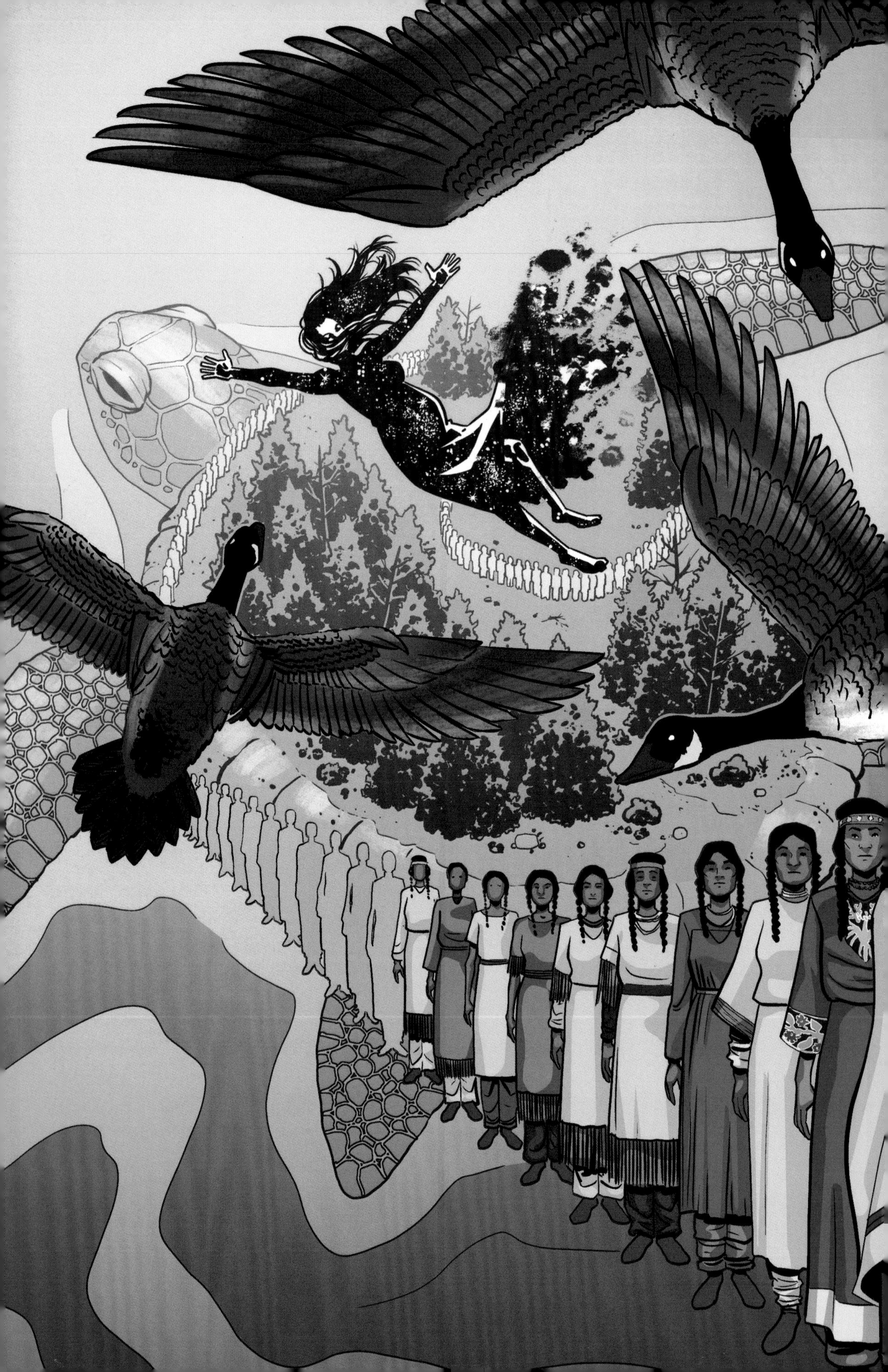

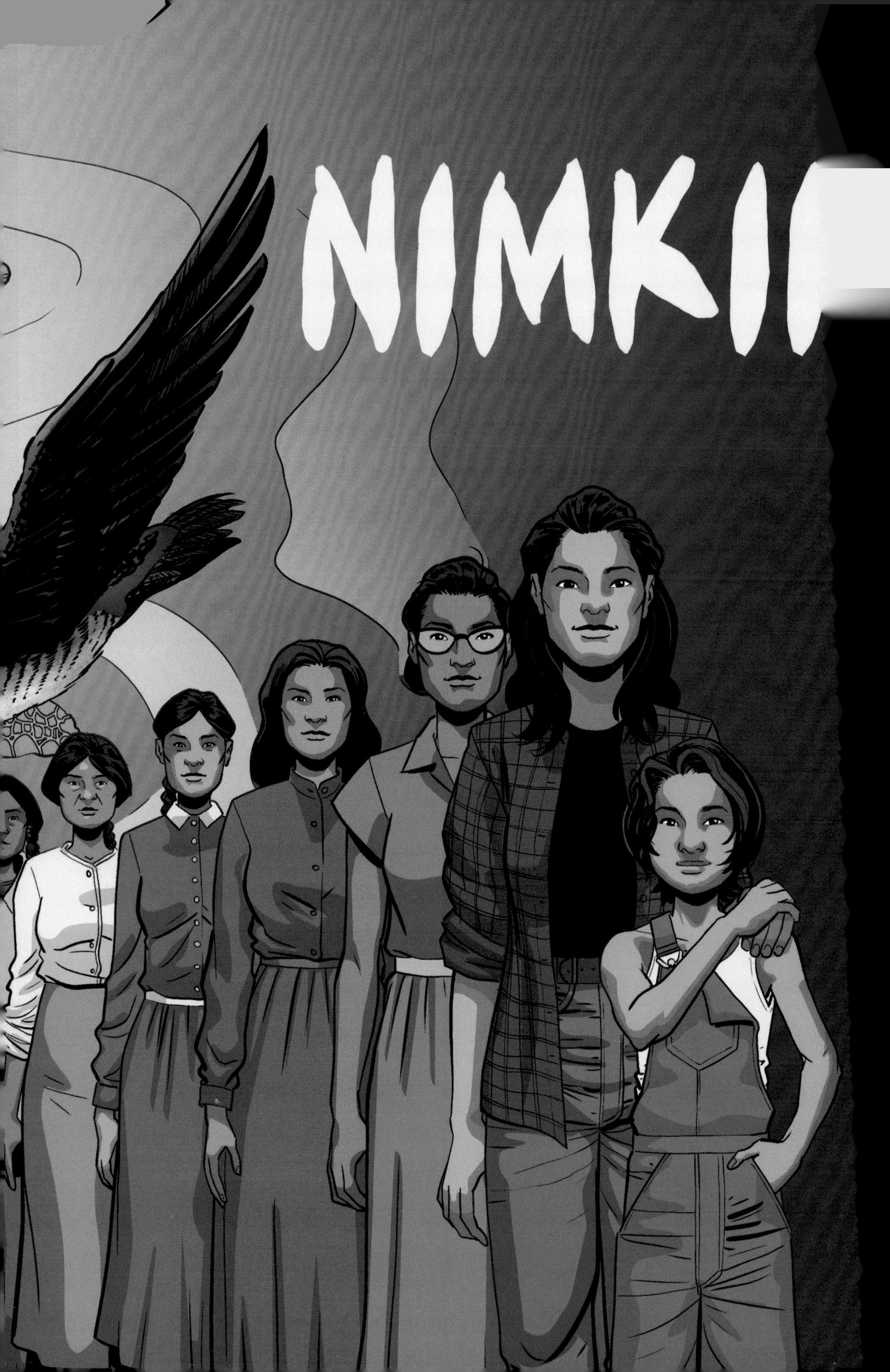
NIMKII

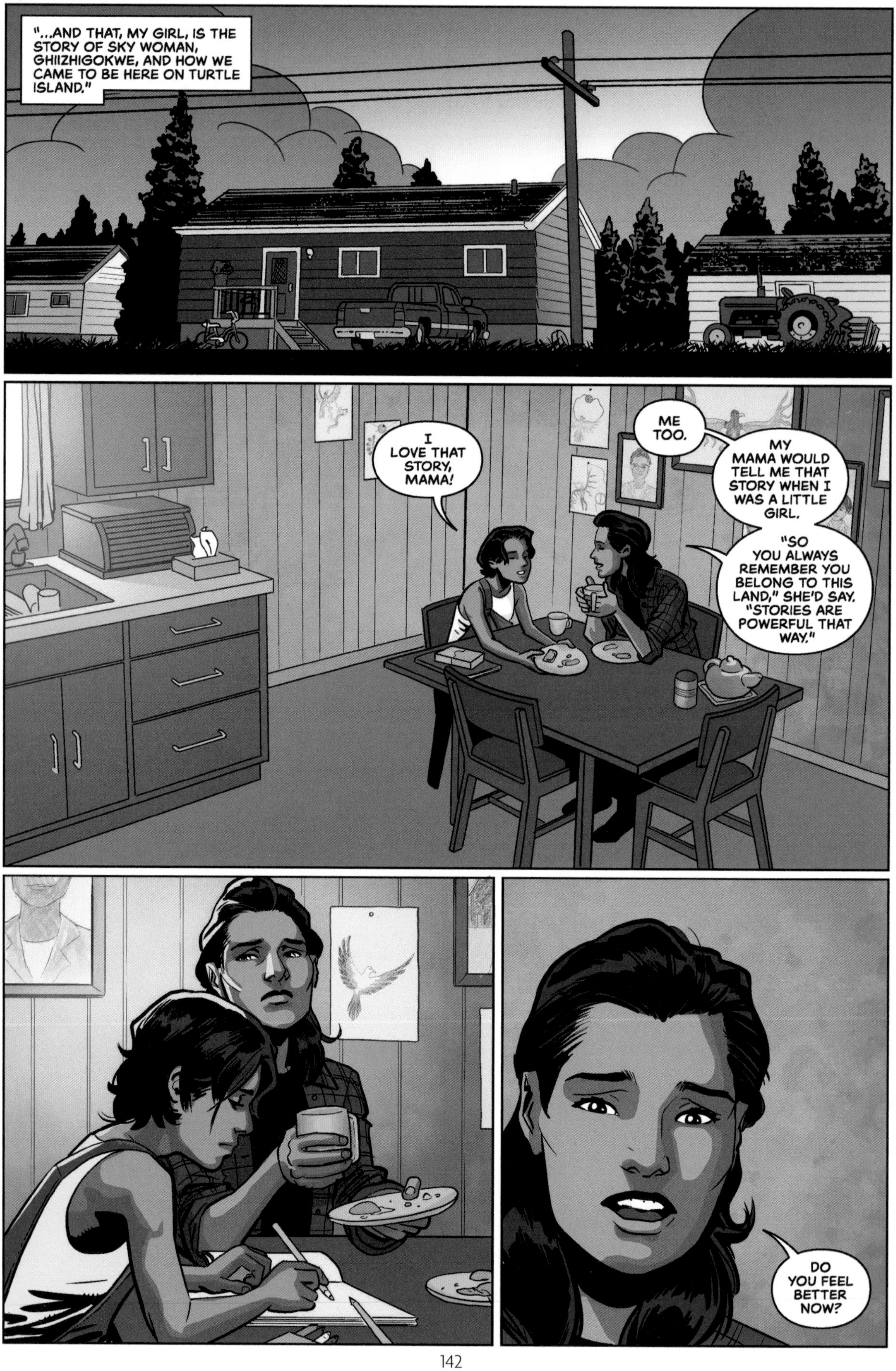
"...AND THAT, MY GIRL, IS THE STORY OF SKY WOMAN, GHIIZHIGOKWE, AND HOW WE CAME TO BE HERE ON TURTLE ISLAND."
I LOVE THAT STORY, MAMA!
ME TOO.
MY MAMA WOULD TELL ME THAT STORY WHEN I WAS A LITTLE GIRL.
"SO YOU ALWAYS REMEMBER YOU BELONG TO THIS LAND," SHE'D SAY. "STORIES ARE POWERFUL THAT WAY."
DO YOU FEEL BETTER NOW?

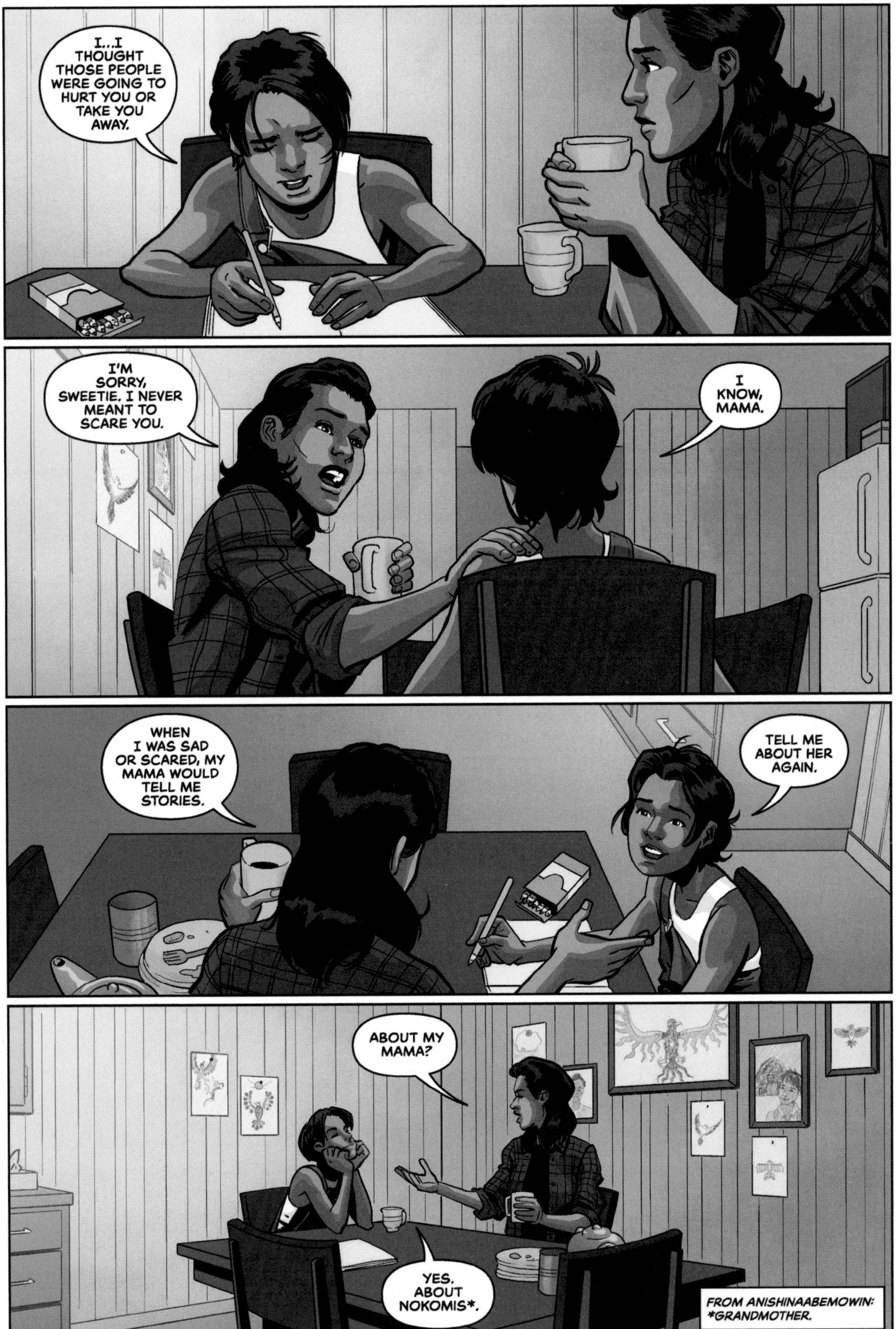
I...I THOUGHT THOSE PEOPLE WERE GOING TO HURT YOU OR TAKE YOU AWAY.
I'M SORRY, SWEETIE. I NEVER MEANT TO SCARE YOU.
I KNOW, MAMA.
WHEN I WAS SAD OR SCARED, MY MAMA WOULD TELL ME STORIES.
TELL ME ABOUT HER AGAIN.
ABOUT MY MAMA?
YES. ABOUT NOKOMIS*.
FROM ANISHINAABEMOWIN: *GRANDMOTHER.

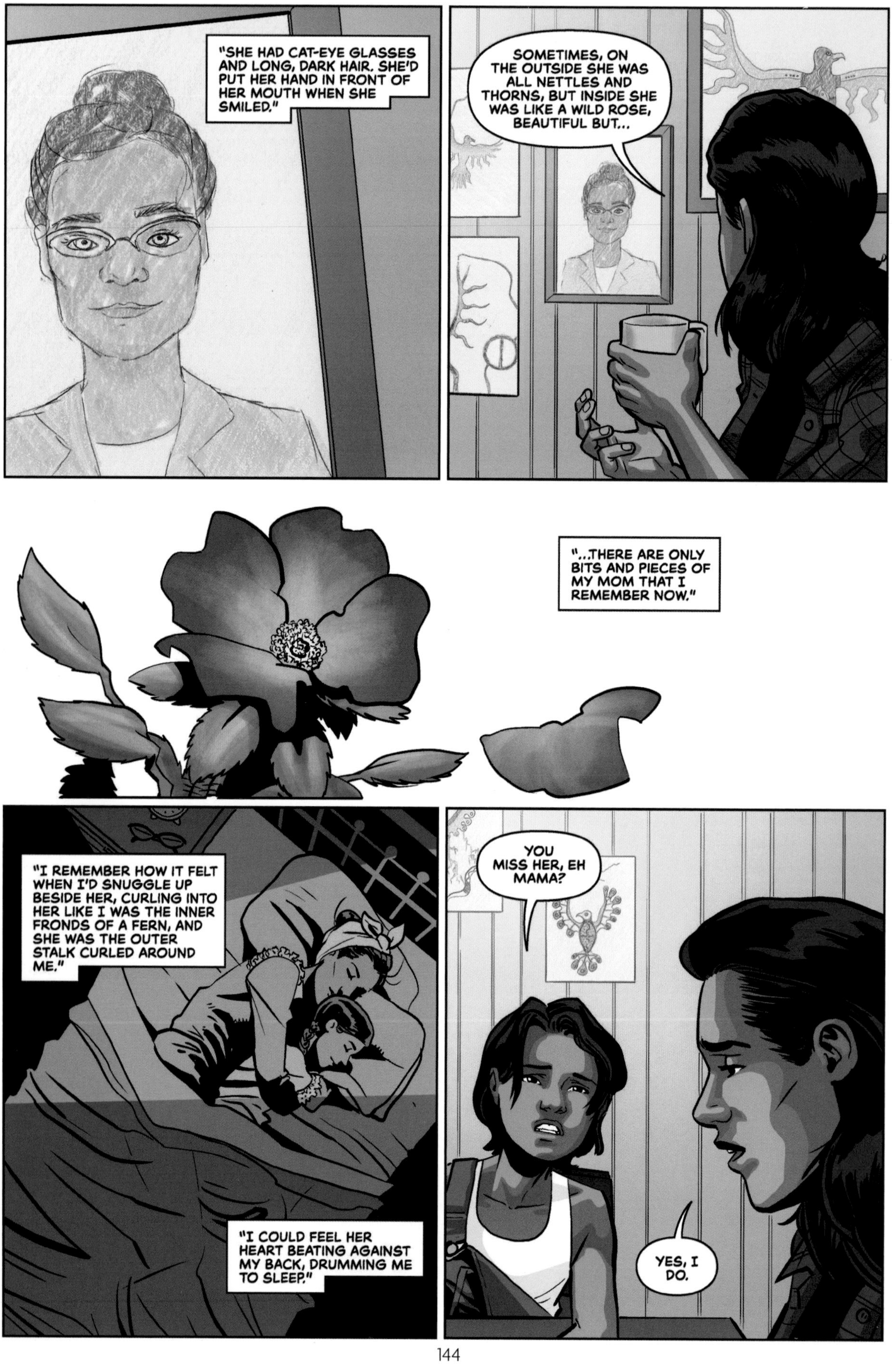
"SHE HAD CAT-EYE GLASSES AND LONG, DARK HAIR. SHE'D PUT HER HAND IN FRONT OF HER MOUTH WHEN SHE SMILED."
SOMETIMES, ON THE OUTSIDE SHE WAS ALL NETTLES AND THORNS, BUT INSIDE SHE WAS LIKE A WILD ROSE, BEAUTIFUL BUT...
"...THERE ARE ONLY BITS AND PIECES OF MY MOM THAT I REMEMBER NOW."
"I REMEMBER HOW IT FELT WHEN I'D SNUGGLE UP BESIDE HER, CURLING INTO HER LIKE I WAS THE INNER FRONDS OF A FERN, AND SHE WAS THE OUTER STALK CURLED AROUND ME."
"I COULD FEEL HER HEART BEATING AGAINST MY BACK, DRUMMING ME TO SLEEP."
YOU MISS HER, EH MAMA?
YES, I DO.

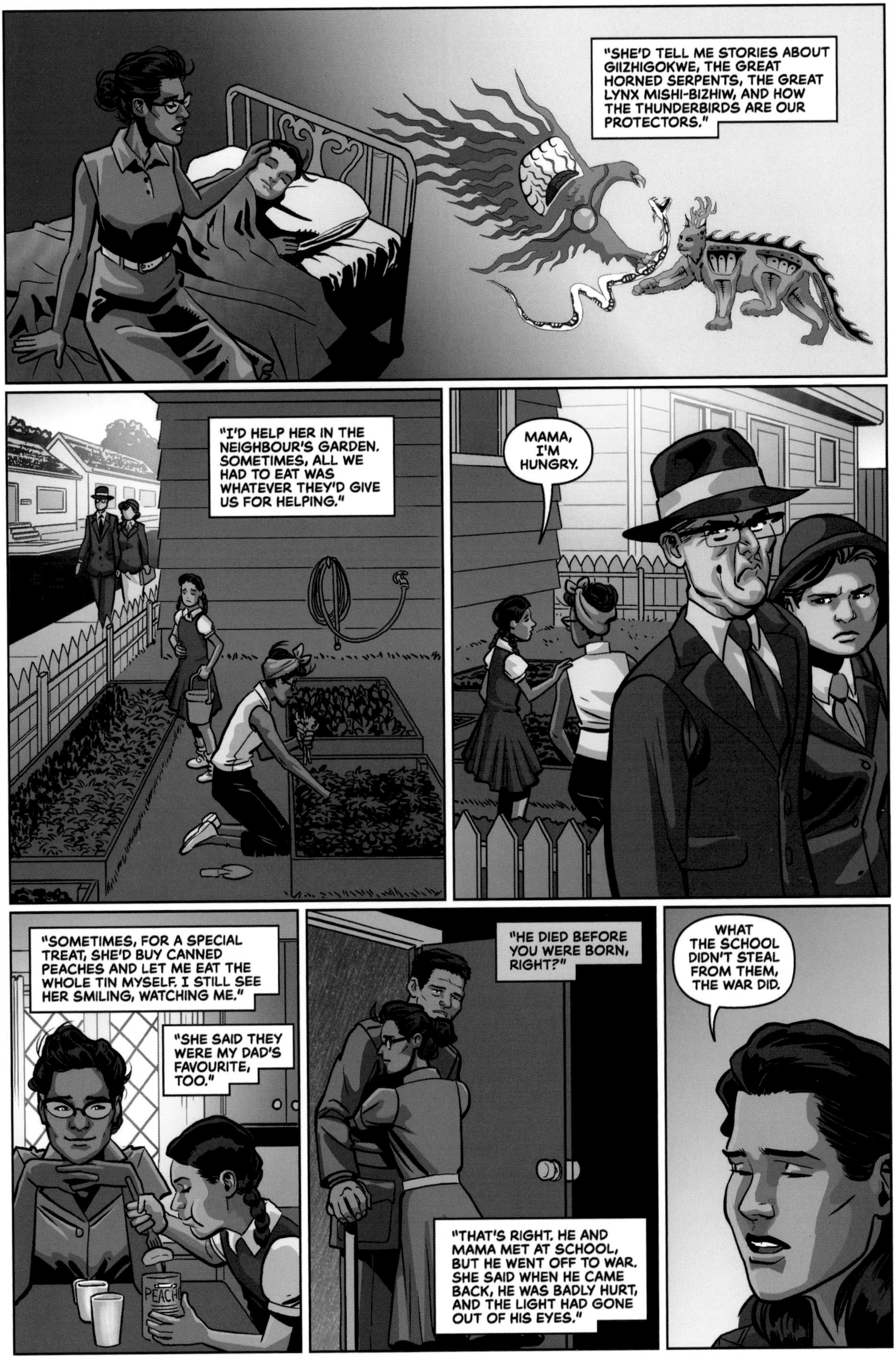
"SHE'D TELL ME STORIES ABOUT GIIZHIGOKWE, THE GREAT HORNED SERPENTS, THE GREAT LYNX MISHI-BIZHIW, AND HOW THE THUNDERBIRDS ARE OUR PROTECTORS."
"I'D HELP HER IN THE NEIGHBOUR'S GARDEN. SOMETIMES, ALL WE HAD TO EAT WAS WHATEVER THEY'D GIVE US FOR HELPING."
MAMA, I'M HUNGRY.
"SOMETIMES, FOR A SPECIAL TREAT, SHE'D BUY CANNED PEACHES AND LET ME EAT THE WHOLE TIN MYSELF. I STILL SEE HER SMILING, WATCHING ME."
"SHE SAID THEY WERE MY DAD'S FAVOURITE, TOO."
PEACH
"HE DIED BEFORE YOU WERE BORN, RIGHT?"
"THAT'S RIGHT. HE AND MAMA MET AT SCHOOL, BUT HE WENT OFF TO WAR. SHE SAID WHEN HE CAME BACK, HE WAS BADLY HURT, AND THE LIGHT HAD GONE OUT OF HIS EYES."
WHAT THE SCHOOL DIDN'T STEAL FROM THEM, THE WAR DID.

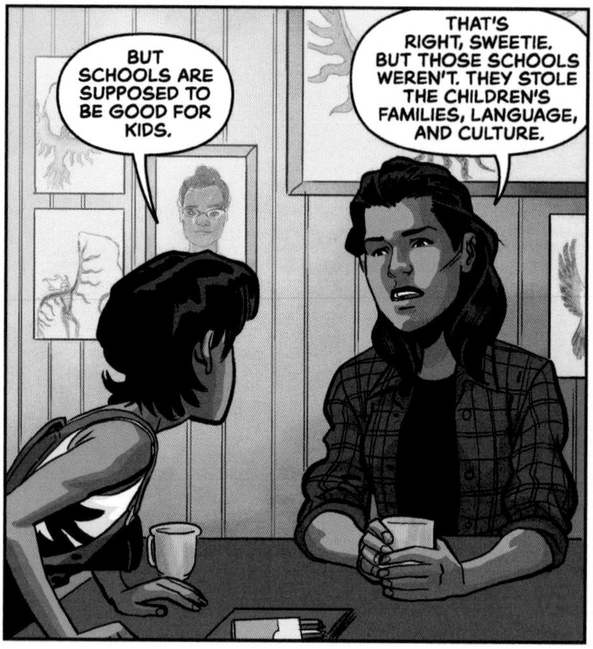
BUT SCHOOLS ARE SUPPOSED TO BE GOOD FOR KIDS.
THAT'S RIGHT, SWEETIE. BUT THOSE SCHOOLS WEREN'T. THEY STOLE THE CHILDREN'S FAMILIES, LANGUAGE, AND CULTURE.

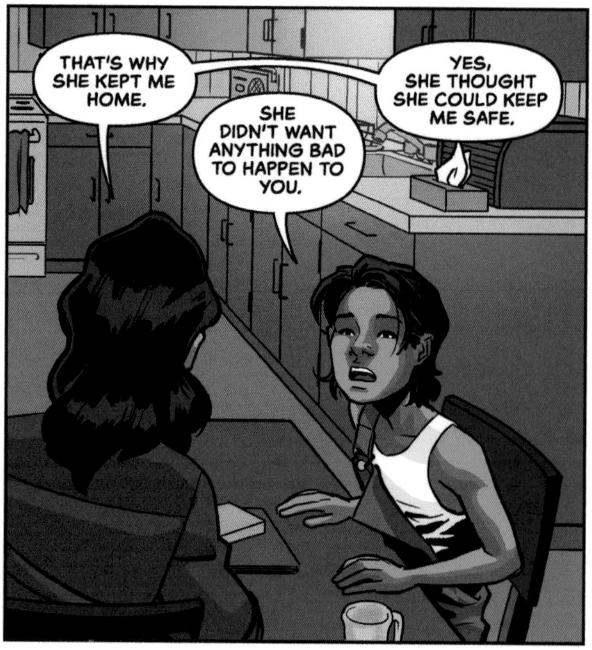
THAT'S WHY SHE KEPT ME HOME.
YES, SHE THOUGHT SHE COULD KEEP ME SAFE.
SHE DIDN'T WANT ANYTHING BAD TO HAPPEN TO YOU.

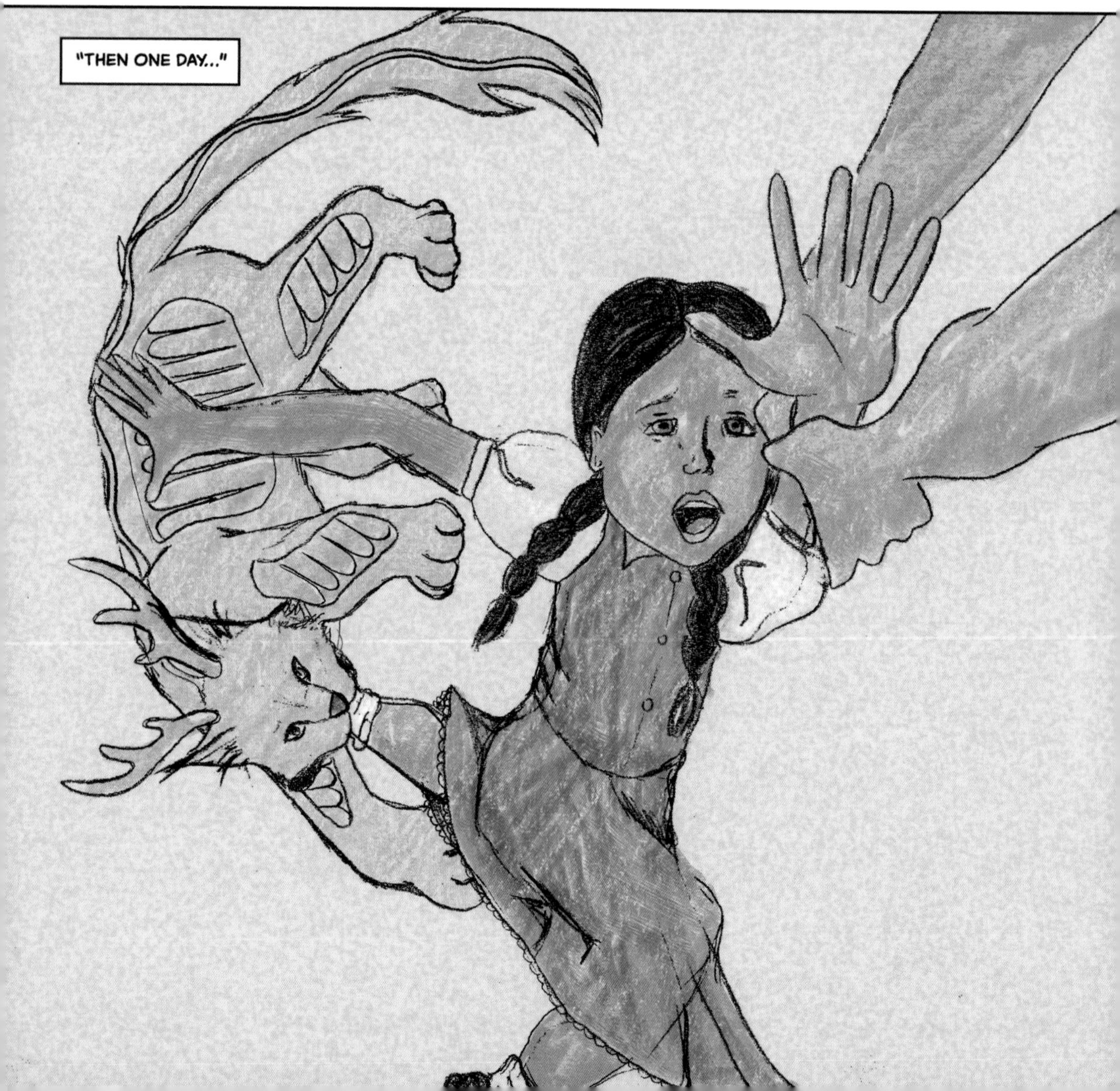
"THEN ONE DAY..."

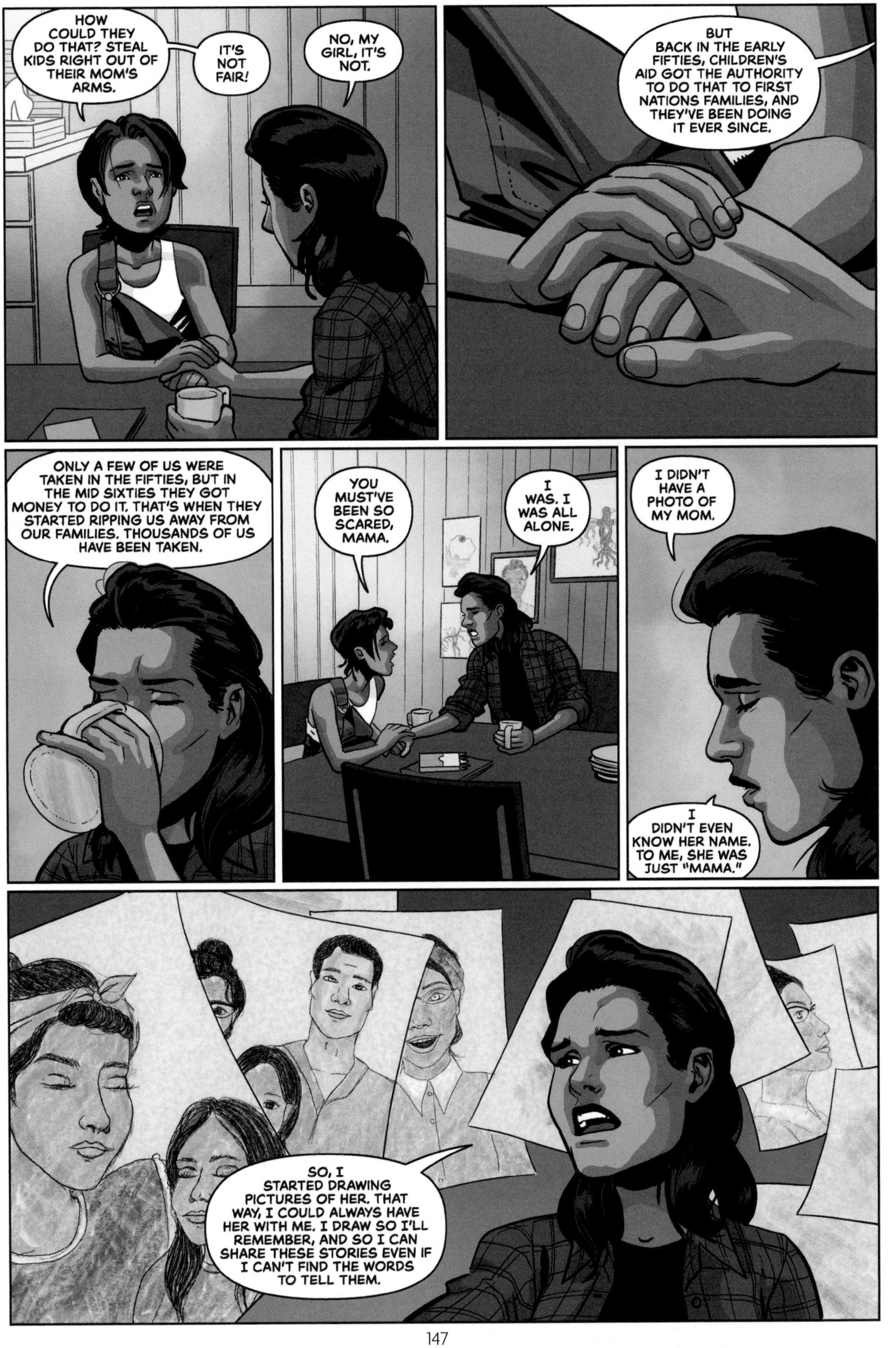
HOW COULD THEY DO THAT? STEAL KIDS RIGHT OUT OF THEIR MOM'S ARMS.
IT'S NOT FAIR!
NO, MY GIRL, IT'S NOT.
BUT BACK IN THE EARLY FIFTIES, CHILDREN'S AID GOT THE AUTHORITY TO DO THAT TO FIRST NATIONS FAMILIES, AND THEY'VE BEEN DOING IT EVER SINCE.
ONLY A FEW OF US WERE TAKEN IN THE FIFTIES, BUT IN THE MID SIXTIES THEY GOT MONEY TO DO IT. THAT'S WHEN THEY STARTED RIPPING US AWAY FROM OUR FAMILIES. THOUSANDS OF US HAVE BEEN TAKEN.
YOU MUST'VE BEEN SO SCARED, MAMA.
I WAS. I WAS ALL ALONE.
I DIDN'T HAVE A PHOTO OF MY MOM.
I DIDN'T EVEN KNOW HER NAME. TO ME, SHE WAS JUST "MAMA."
SO, I STARTED DRAWING PICTURES OF HER. THAT WAY, I COULD ALWAYS HAVE HER WITH ME. I DRAW SO I'LL REMEMBER, AND SO I CAN SHARE THESE STORIES EVEN IF I CAN'T FIND THE WORDS TO TELL THEM.

AND YOU KNOW WHAT ELSE?

I STILL LOVE CANNED PEACHES.

PEACHES ALWAYS REMIND ME OF MY MOM.

AND TEDDY.

THE LITTLE BOY YOU ALWAYS DRAW?

YES. I'VE WANTED TO TELL YOU ABOUT HIM FOR A LONG TIME.

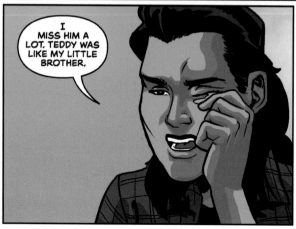

I MISS HIM A LOT. TEDDY WAS LIKE MY LITTLE BROTHER.

WHAT I DID TODAY WAS BECAUSE OF WHAT'S BEEN HAPPENING TO KIDS LIKE US, ME AND TEDDY.

TISSUE

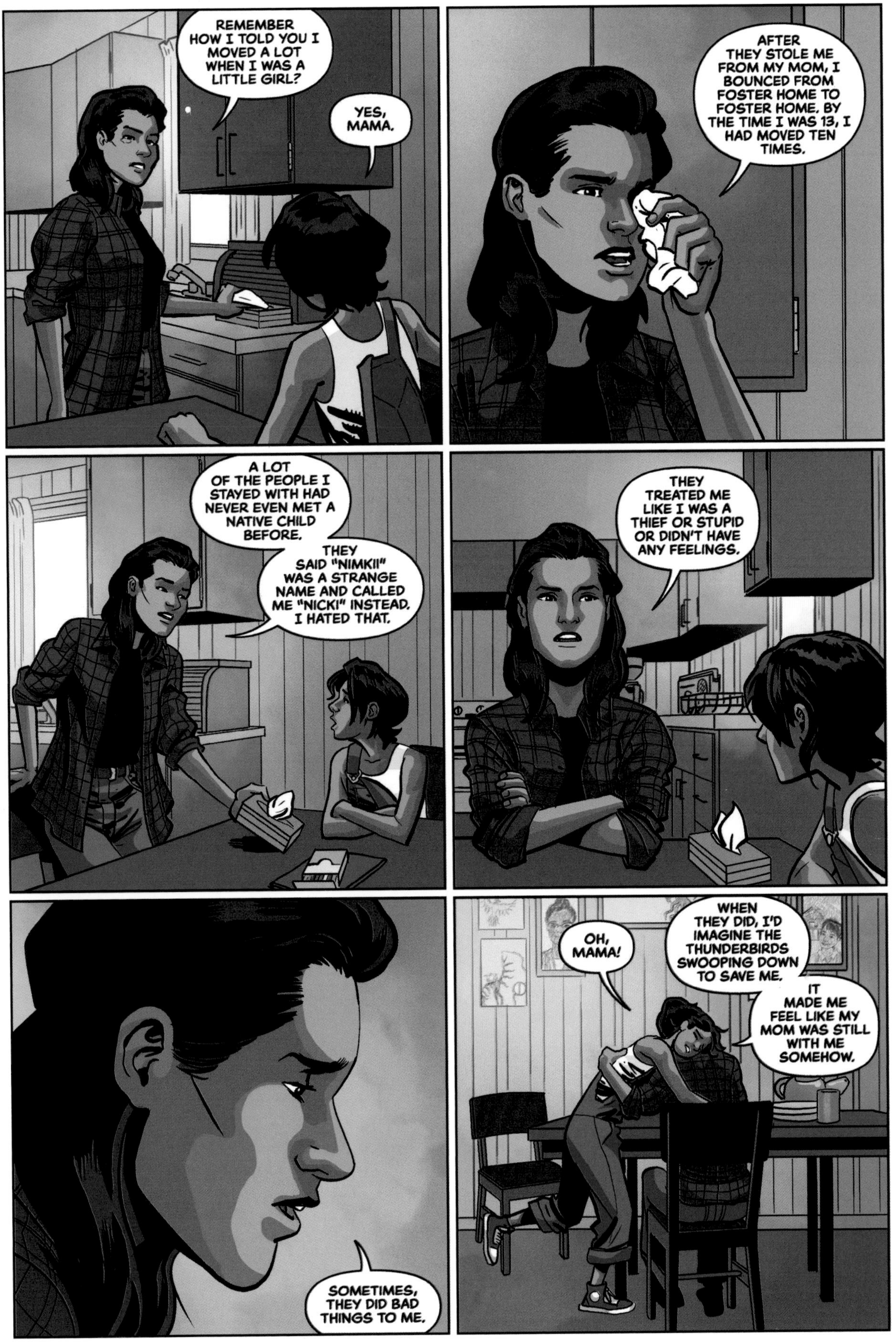
REMEMBER HOW I TOLD YOU I MOVED A LOT WHEN I WAS A LITTLE GIRL?
YES, MAMA.
AFTER THEY STOLE ME FROM MY MOM, I BOUNCED FROM FOSTER HOME TO FOSTER HOME. BY THE TIME I WAS 13, I HAD MOVED TEN TIMES.
A LOT OF THE PEOPLE I STAYED WITH HAD NEVER EVEN MET A NATIVE CHILD BEFORE.
THEY SAID "NIMKII" WAS A STRANGE NAME AND CALLED ME "NICKI" INSTEAD. I HATED THAT.
THEY TREATED ME LIKE I WAS A THIEF OR STUPID OR DIDN'T HAVE ANY FEELINGS.
SOMETIMES, THEY DID BAD THINGS TO ME.
OH, MAMA!
WHEN THEY DID, I'D IMAGINE THE THUNDERBIRDS SWOOPING DOWN TO SAVE ME.
IT MADE ME FEEL LIKE MY MOM WAS STILL WITH ME SOMEHOW.

"THEN ONE SPRING WHEN I WAS 13, I WAS SENT TO LIVE AT A FARM."

"THE COUPLE WHO LIVED THERE TREATED ME LIKE ONE OF THEIR WORK HORSES. IF I DID MY CHORES, THEY GAVE ME DECENT FOOD AND A WARM PLACE TO SLEEP."

"BUT I STAYED AWAY FROM THEM BY DOING EXTRA WORK OUTSIDE OR WITH THE ANIMALS. I LOVE ANIMALS--THEY NEVER LET YOU DOWN."

"THERE WAS ALSO A GARDEN. WHEN I WAS WEEDING, I PRETENDED I WAS HOME, WITH MY MOM BESIDE ME."

"THAT'S WHERE I MET TEDDY."

"I'D BEEN LIVING AT THE FARM FOR A FEW MONTHS WHEN THEY BROUGHT HIM HOME."

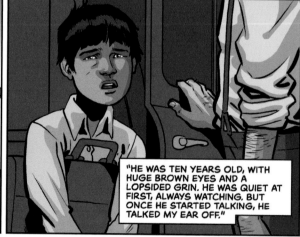

"HE WAS TEN YEARS OLD, WITH HUGE BROWN EYES AND A LOPSIDED GRIN. HE WAS QUIET AT FIRST, ALWAYS WATCHING, BUT ONCE HE STARTED TALKING, HE TALKED MY EAR OFF."

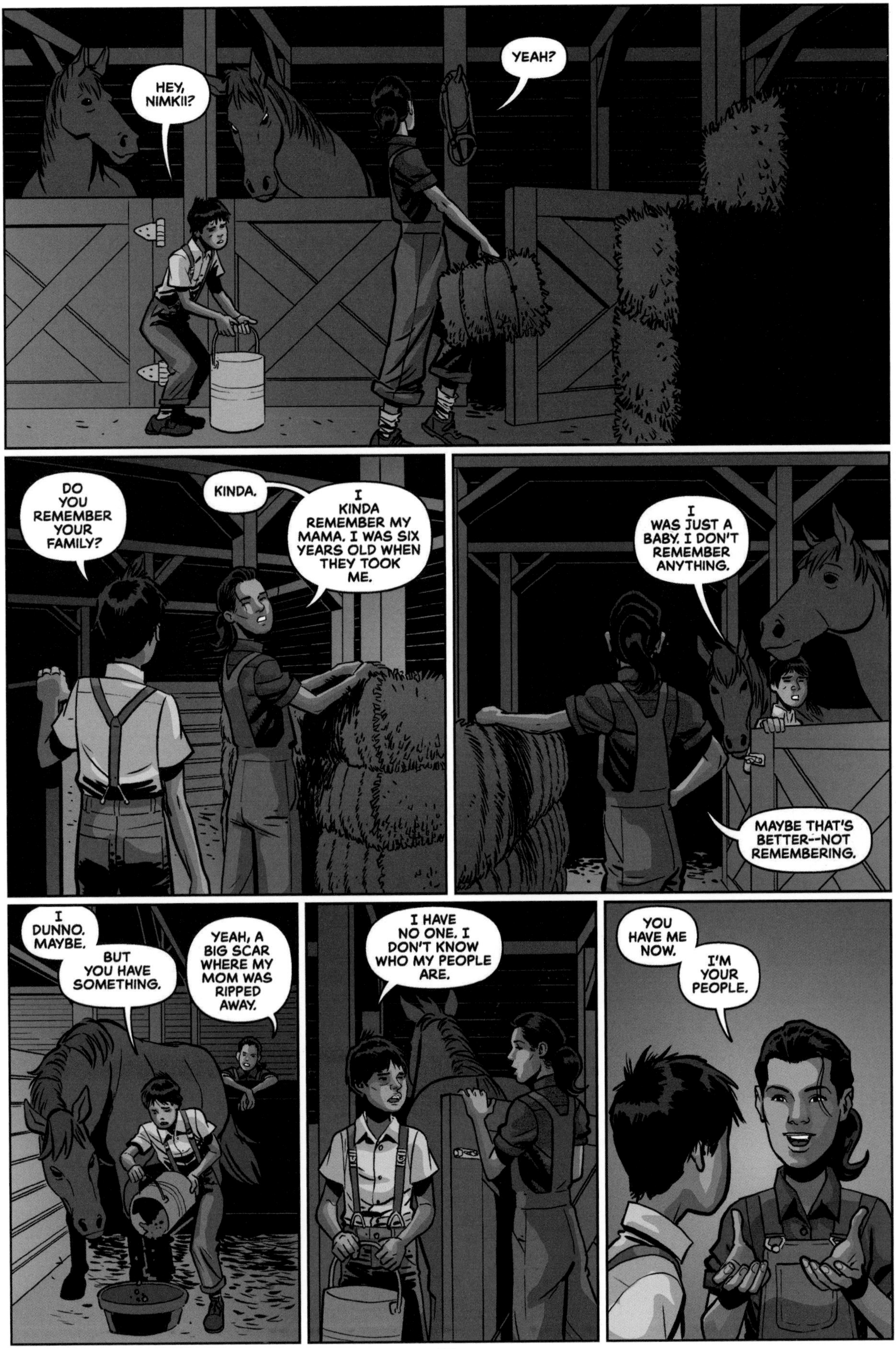
HEY, NIMKII?
YEAH?
DO YOU REMEMBER YOUR FAMILY?
KINDA.
I KINDA REMEMBER MY MAMA. I WAS SIX YEARS OLD WHEN THEY TOOK ME.
I WAS JUST A BABY. I DON'T REMEMBER ANYTHING.
MAYBE THAT'S BETTER--NOT REMEMBERING.
I DUNNO. MAYBE.
BUT YOU HAVE SOMETHING.
YEAH, A BIG SCAR WHERE MY MOM WAS RIPPED AWAY.
I HAVE NO ONE. I DON'T KNOW WHO MY PEOPLE ARE.
YOU HAVE ME NOW.
I'M YOUR PEOPLE.

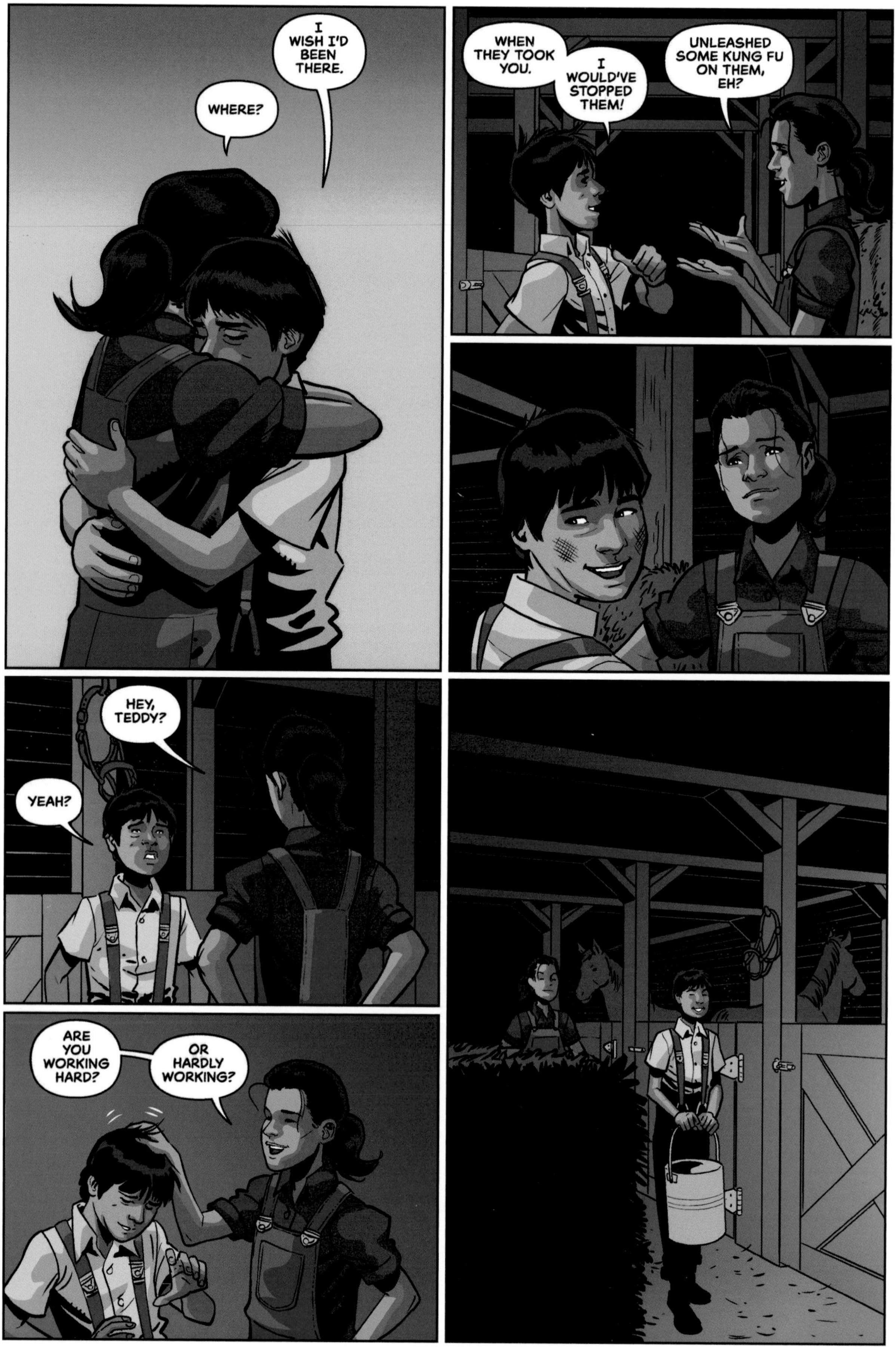

WHERE?
I WISH I'D BEEN THERE.
WHEN THEY TOOK YOU.
I WOULD'VE STOPPED THEM!
UNLEASHED SOME KUNG FU ON THEM, EH?
HEY, TEDDY?
YEAH?
ARE YOU WORKING HARD?
OR HARDLY WORKING?

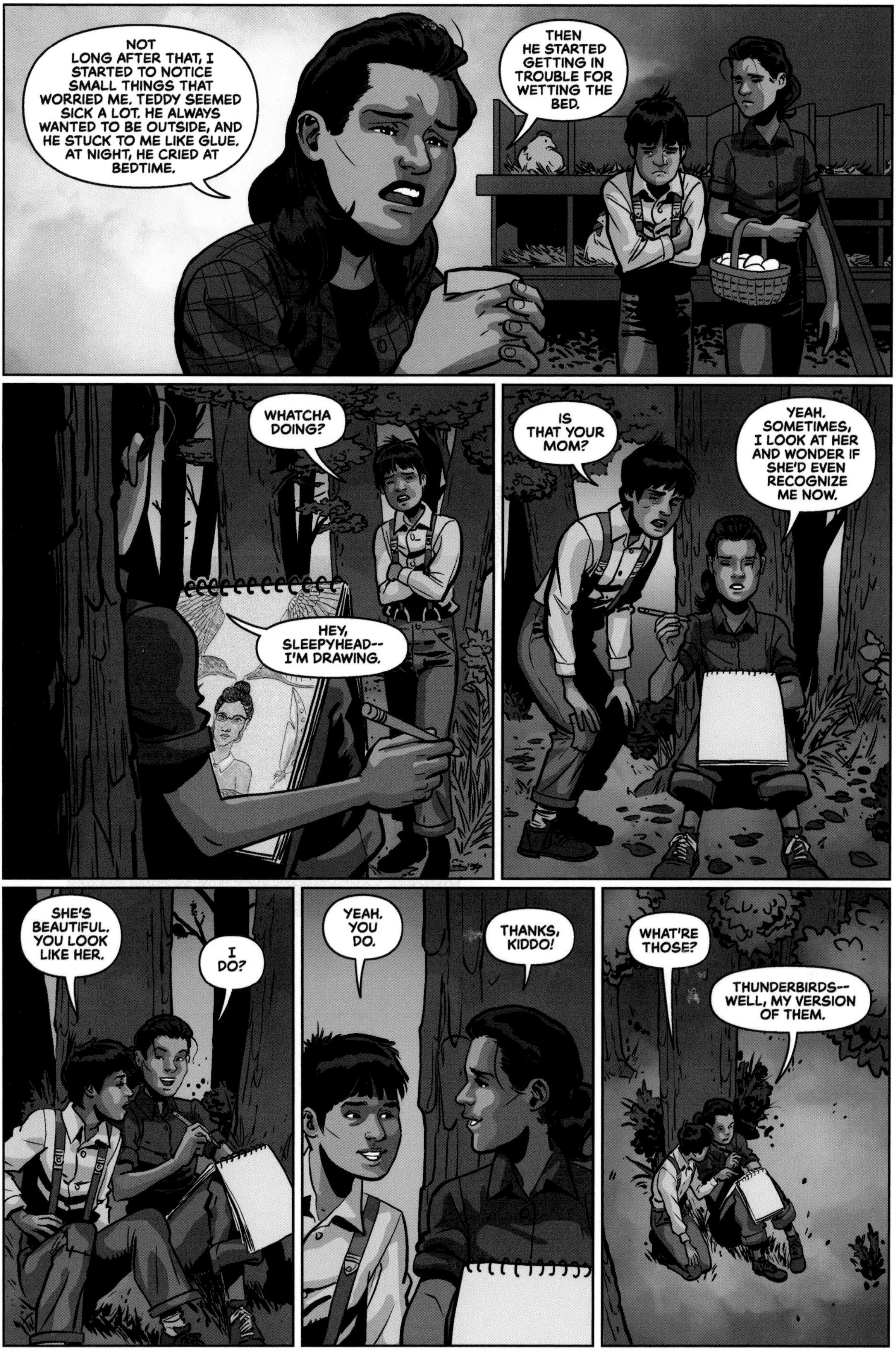
NOT LONG AFTER THAT, I STARTED TO NOTICE SMALL THINGS THAT WORRIED ME. TEDDY SEEMED SICK A LOT. HE ALWAYS WANTED TO BE OUTSIDE, AND HE STUCK TO ME LIKE GLUE. AT NIGHT, HE CRIED AT BEDTIME.
THEN HE STARTED GETTING IN TROUBLE FOR WETTING THE BED.
WHATCHA DOING?
HEY, SLEEPYHEAD-- I'M DRAWING.
IS THAT YOUR MOM?
YEAH. SOMETIMES, I LOOK AT HER AND WONDER IF SHE'D EVEN RECOGNIZE ME NOW.
SHE'S BEAUTIFUL. YOU LOOK LIKE HER.
I DO?
YEAH. YOU DO.
THANKS, KIDDO!
WHAT'RE THOSE?
THUNDERBIRDS-- WELL, MY VERSION OF THEM.

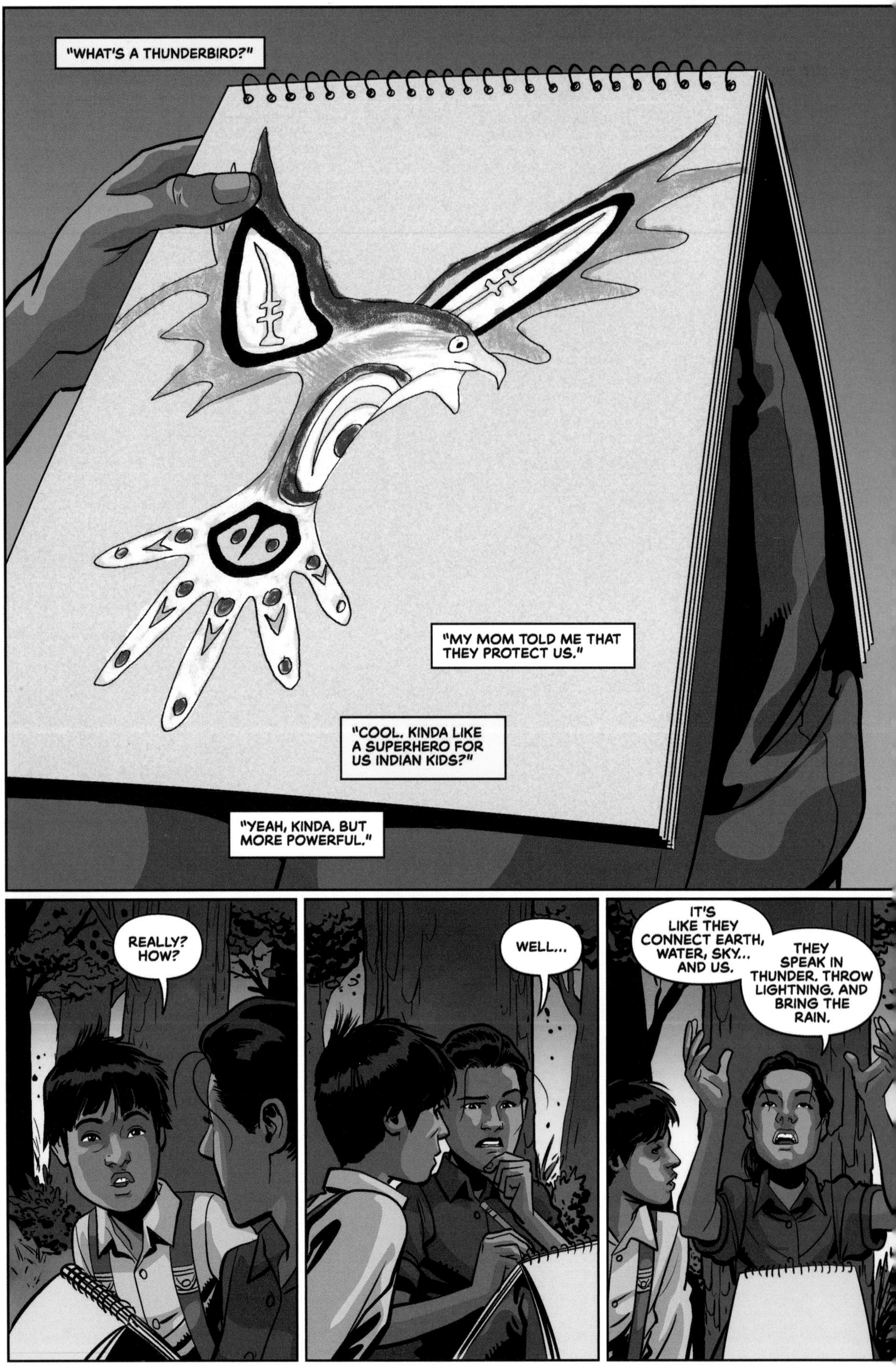
"WHAT'S A THUNDERBIRD?"
"MY MOM TOLD ME THAT THEY PROTECT US."
"COOL. KINDA LIKE A SUPERHERO FOR US INDIAN KIDS?"
"YEAH, KINDA. BUT MORE POWERFUL."
REALLY? HOW?
WELL...
IT'S LIKE THEY CONNECT EARTH, WATER, SKY... AND US.
THEY SPEAK IN THUNDER, THROW LIGHTNING, AND BRING THE RAIN.

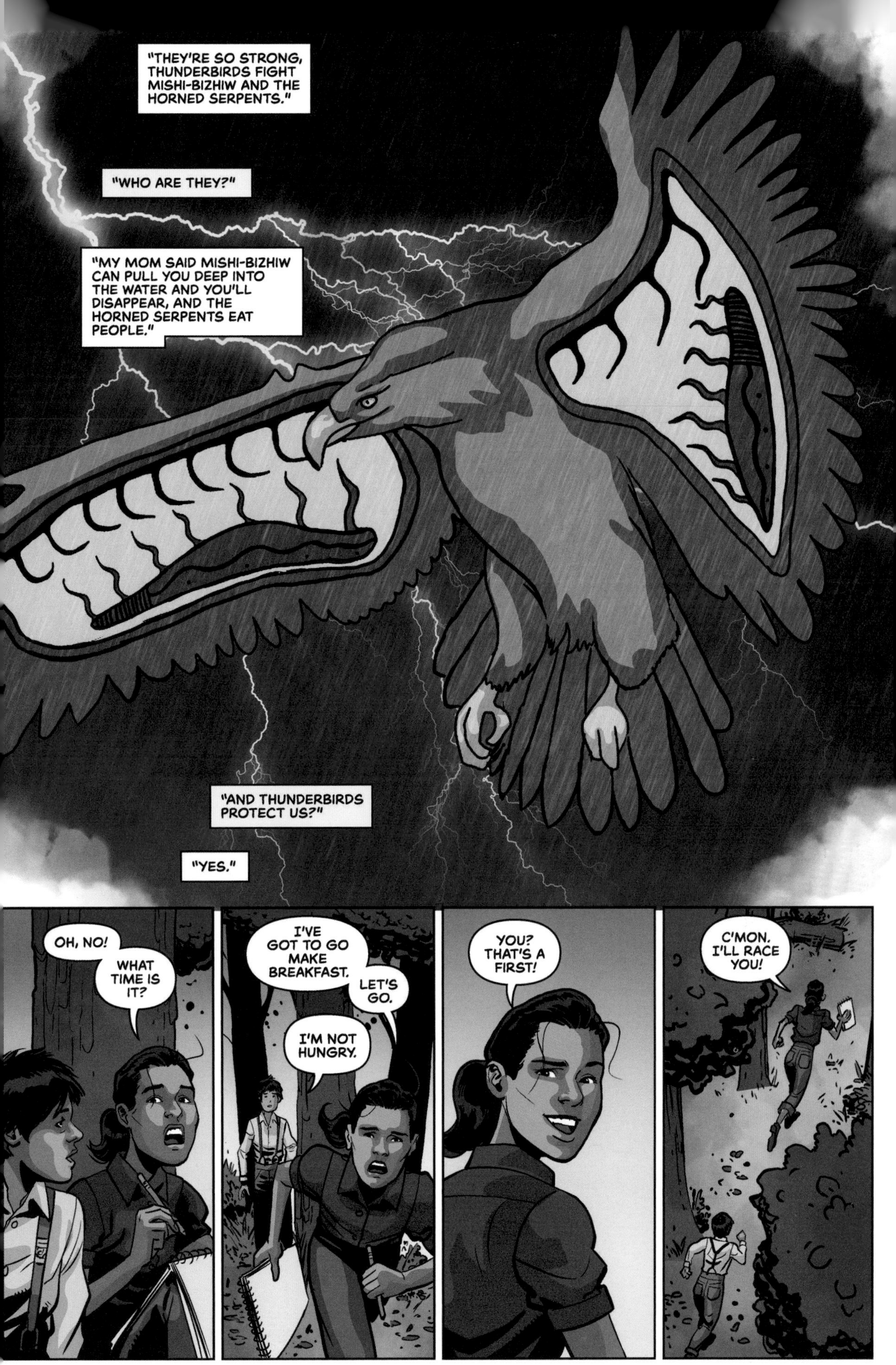
"THEY'RE SO STRONG, THUNDERBIRDS FIGHT MISHI-BIZHIW AND THE HORNED SERPENTS."
"WHO ARE THEY?"
"MY MOM SAID MISHI-BIZHIW CAN PULL YOU DEEP INTO THE WATER AND YOU'LL DISAPPEAR, AND THE HORNED SERPENTS EAT PEOPLE."
"AND THUNDERBIRDS PROTECT US?"
"YES."
OH, NO!
WHAT TIME IS IT?
I'VE GOT TO GO MAKE BREAKFAST.
LET'S GO.
I'M NOT HUNGRY.
YOU? THAT'S A FIRST!
C'MON. I'LL RACE YOU!

"THEN ONE DAY, I WAS WORKING IN THE BACK FIELD. I HADN'T SEEN TEDDY ALL MORNING. THEN I SAW HIM."

"EVEN FROM FAR AWAY, I COULD TELL SOMETHING WASN'T RIGHT."

WHAT'S WRONG?

TEDDY, WHAT HAPPENED?

"I TOUCHED HIS SHOULDER, AND HE FLINCHED AND SUCKED AIR BETWEEN HIS CLENCHED TEETH."

SHOW ME.

I...I CAN'T!

PLEASE, TEDDY. I'M YOUR FAMILY, REMEMBER? SHOW ME.

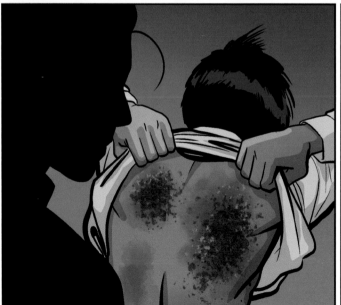

I'LL KILL HIM!

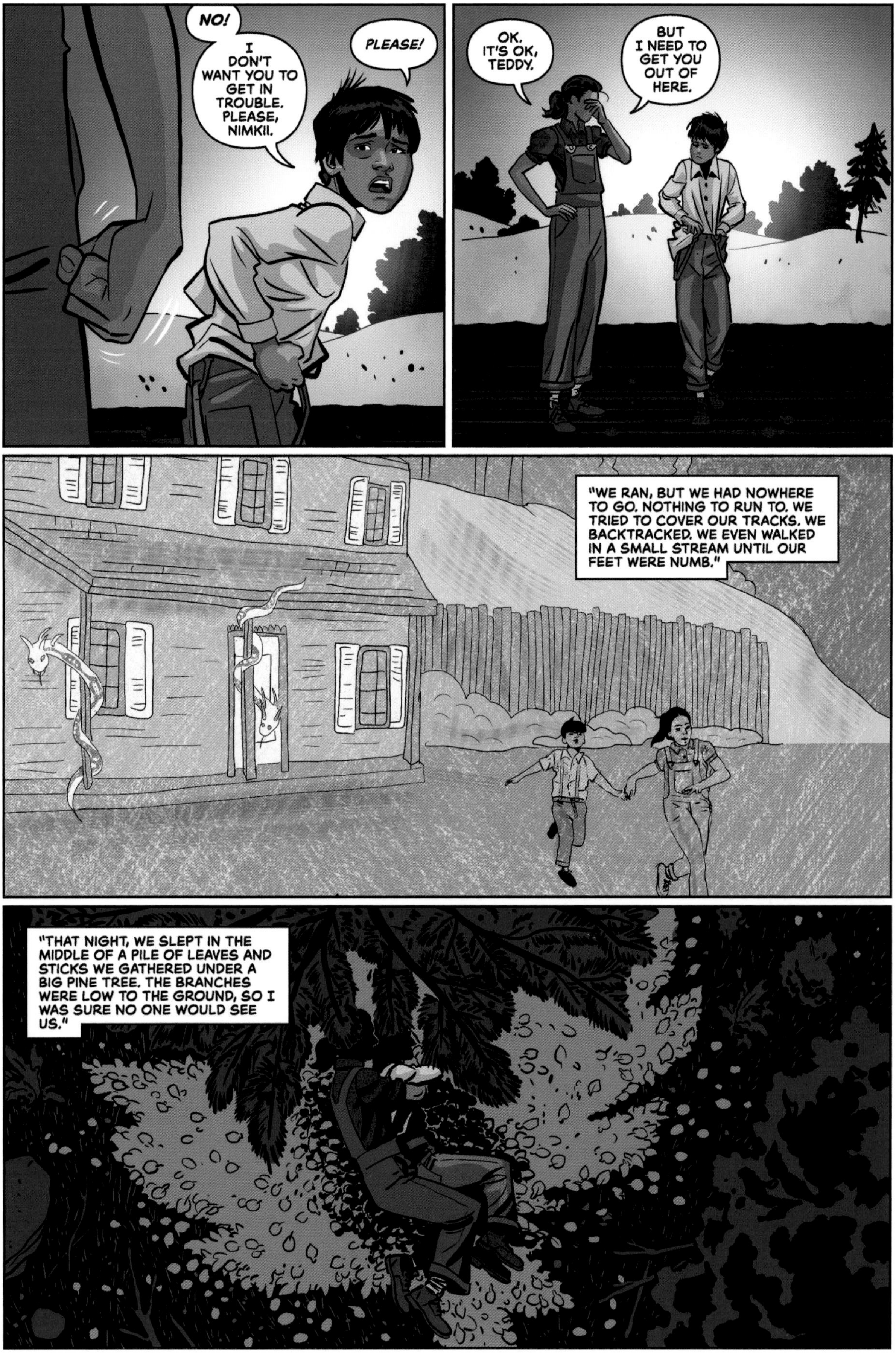
NO!
I DON'T WANT YOU TO GET IN TROUBLE. PLEASE, NIMKII.
PLEASE!
OK. IT'S OK, TEDDY.
BUT I NEED TO GET YOU OUT OF HERE.
"WE RAN, BUT WE HAD NOWHERE TO GO. NOTHING TO RUN TO. WE TRIED TO COVER OUR TRACKS. WE BACKTRACKED. WE EVEN WALKED IN A SMALL STREAM UNTIL OUR FEET WERE NUMB."
"THAT NIGHT, WE SLEPT IN THE MIDDLE OF A PILE OF LEAVES AND STICKS WE GATHERED UNDER A BIG PINE TREE. THE BRANCHES WERE LOW TO THE GROUND, SO I WAS SURE NO ONE WOULD SEE US."

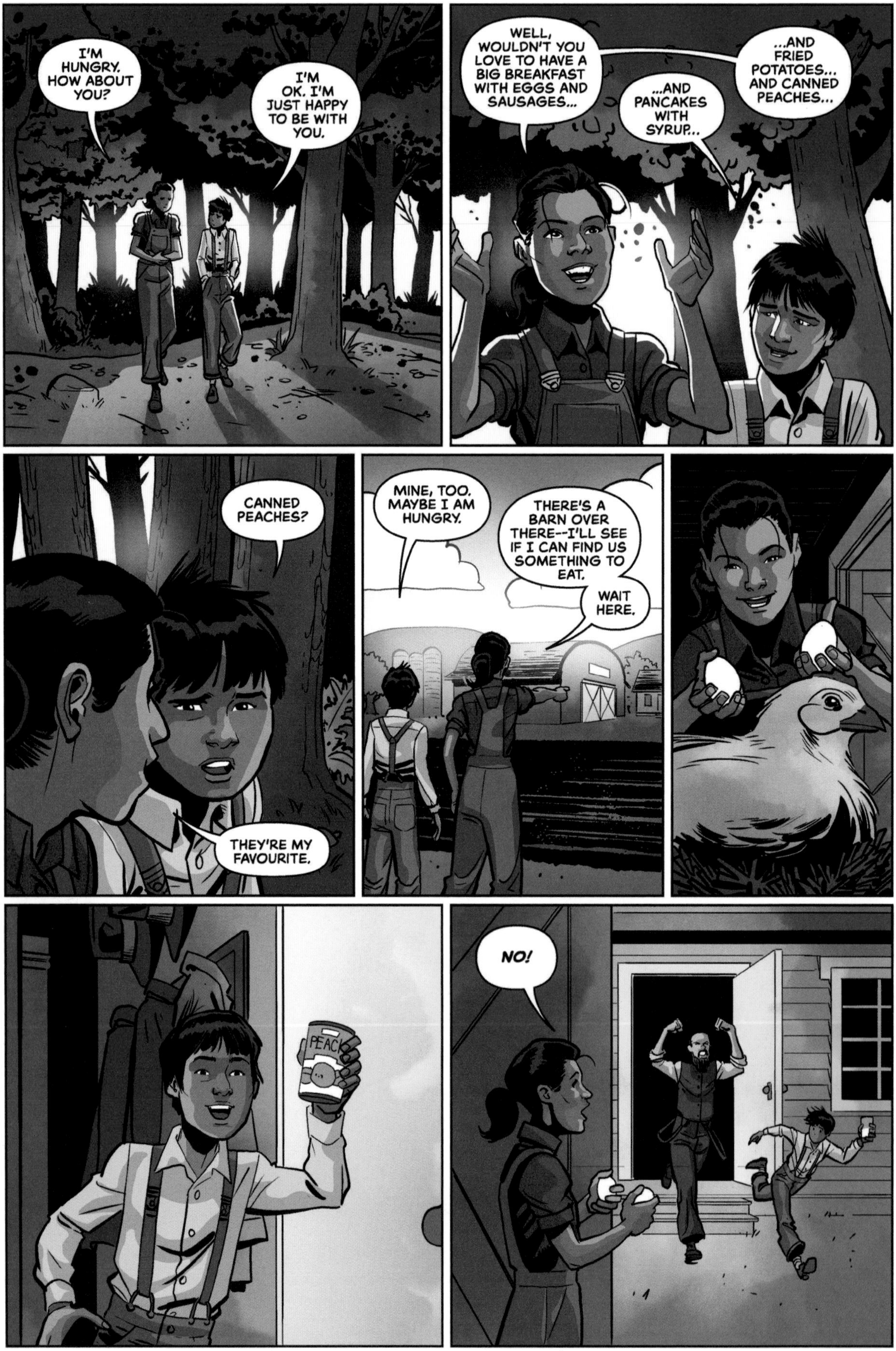
I'M HUNGRY. HOW ABOUT YOU?
I'M OK. I'M JUST HAPPY TO BE WITH YOU.
WELL, WOULDN'T YOU LOVE TO HAVE A BIG BREAKFAST WITH EGGS AND SAUSAGES...
...AND PANCAKES WITH SYRUP...
...AND FRIED POTATOES... AND CANNED PEACHES...
CANNED PEACHES?
THEY'RE MY FAVOURITE.
MINE, TOO. MAYBE I AM HUNGRY.
THERE'S A BARN OVER THERE--I'LL SEE IF I CAN FIND US SOMETHING TO EAT.
WAIT HERE.
PEACH
NO!

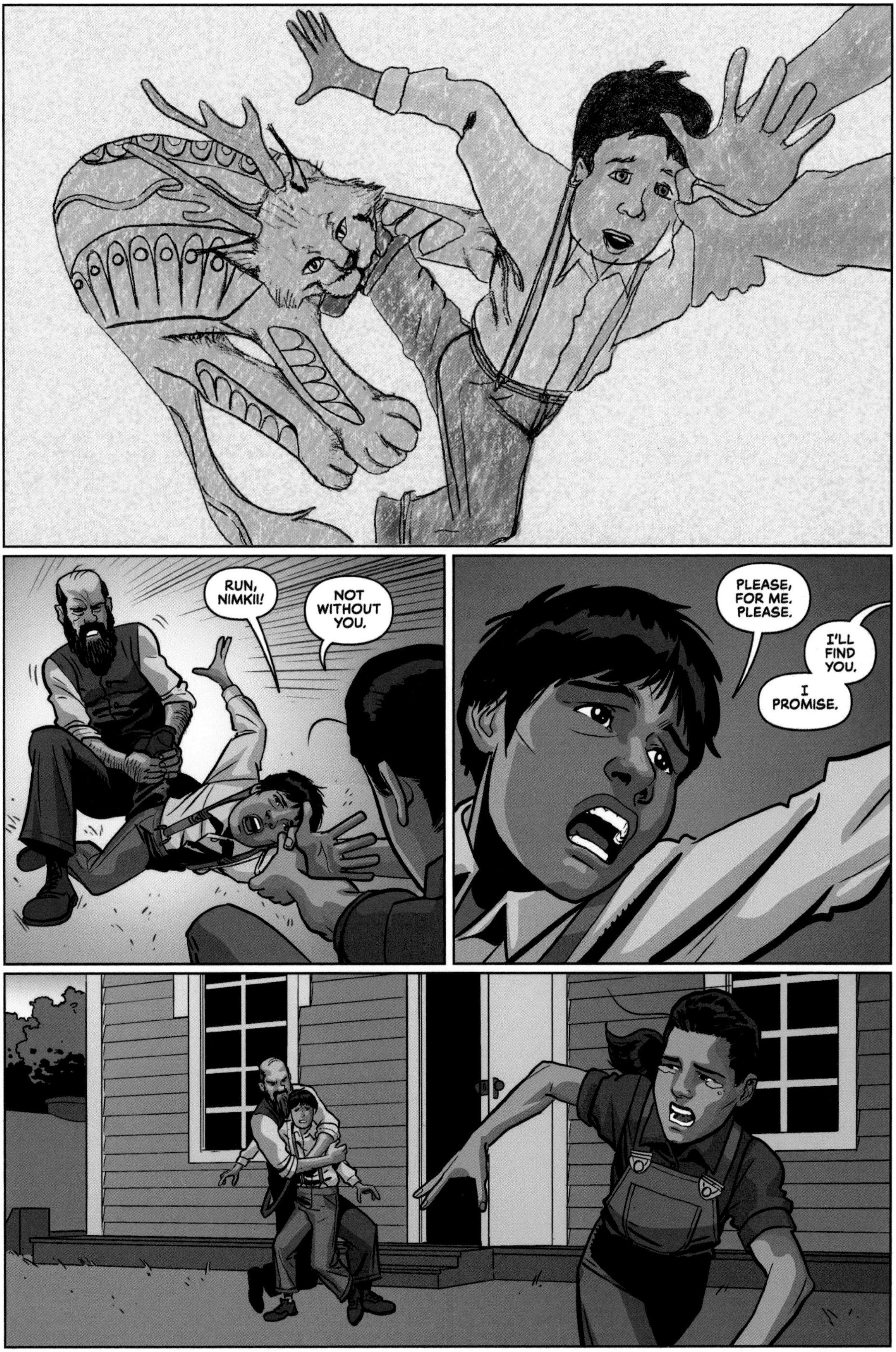

RUN, NIMKII!
NOT WITHOUT YOU.
PLEASE, FOR ME. PLEASE.
I'LL FIND YOU.
I PROMISE.

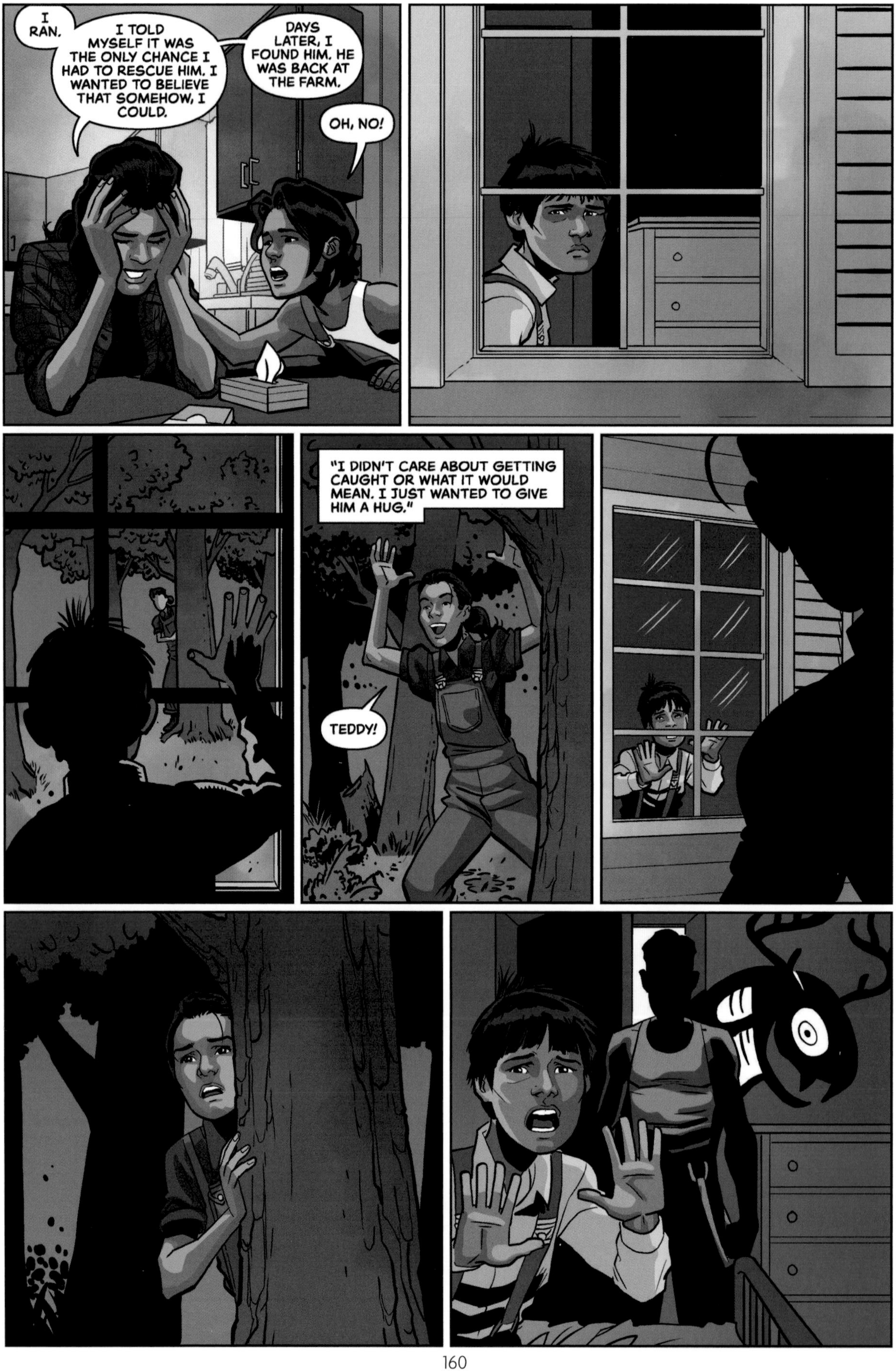
I RAN.
I TOLD MYSELF IT WAS THE ONLY CHANCE I HAD TO RESCUE HIM. I WANTED TO BELIEVE THAT SOMEHOW, I COULD.
DAYS LATER, I FOUND HIM. HE WAS BACK AT THE FARM.
OH, NO!
"I DIDN'T CARE ABOUT GETTING CAUGHT OR WHAT IT WOULD MEAN. I JUST WANTED TO GIVE HIM A HUG."
TEDDY!

"I WATCHED FOR HIM EVERY DAY, BUT THEY DIDN'T LET HIM OUTSIDE ALONE. I KEPT TRYING TO THINK OF A PLAN TO GET US BOTH SOMEWHERE SAFE."

"MEANWHILE, TEDDY GREW DIMMER AND DIMMER, LIKE THE LIGHT INSIDE HIM WAS GOING OUT."

TOMORROW, WHEN I COME BACK, I'M GOING TO BEG TO STAY HERE AGAIN. THEN I CAN PROTECT YOU.

NO, NIMKII! YOU CAN'T. THEY'LL TAKE YOU AWAY.

IT'LL BE OKAY.

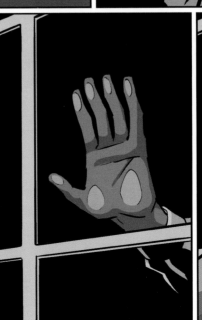

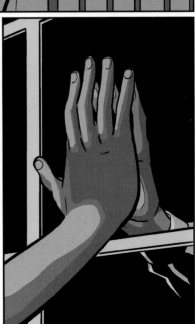

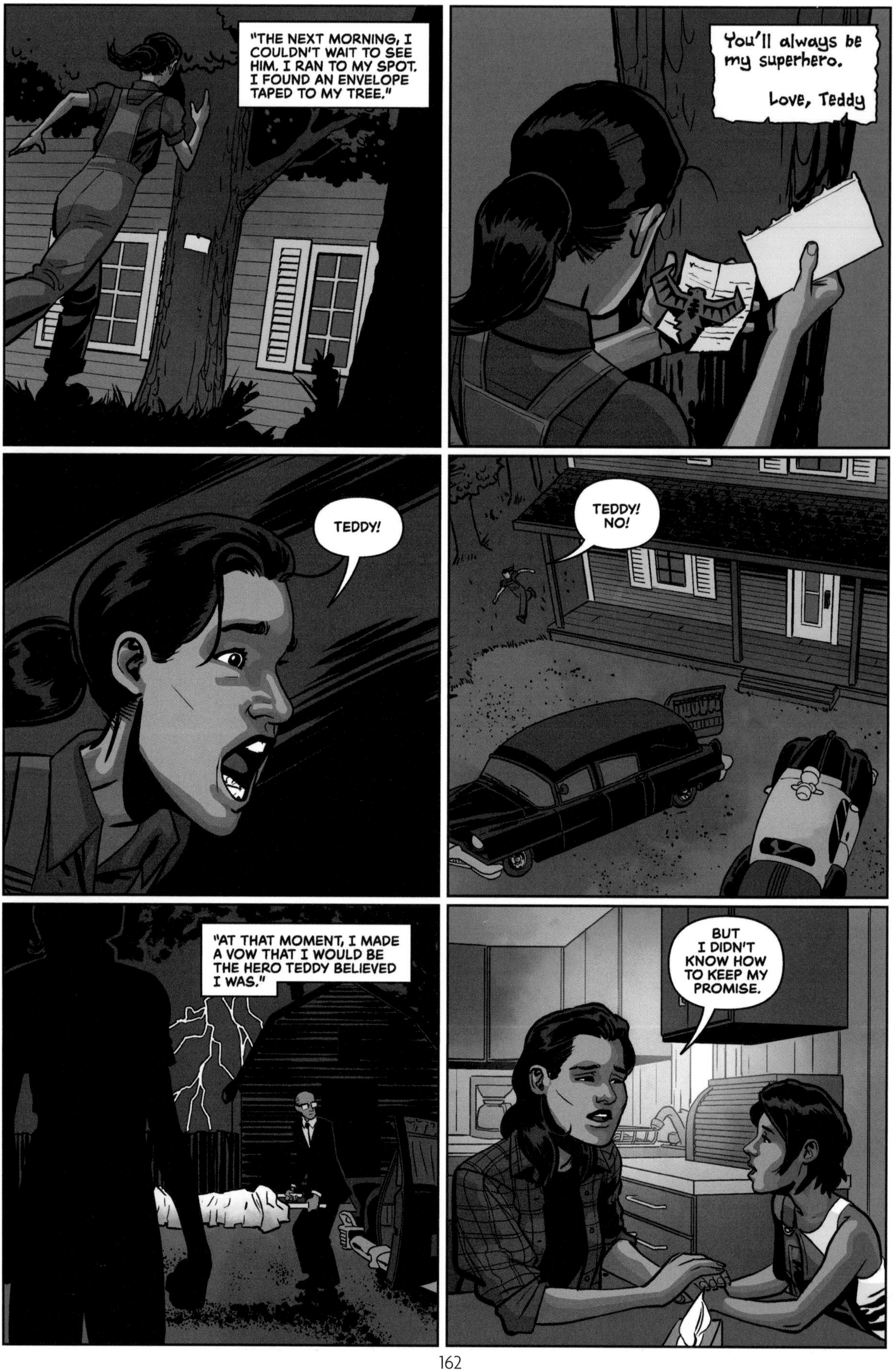
"THE NEXT MORNING, I COULDN'T WAIT TO SEE HIM. I RAN TO MY SPOT. I FOUND AN ENVELOPE TAPED TO MY TREE."
You'll always be my superhero.
Love, Teddy
TEDDY!
TEDDY! NO!
"AT THAT MOMENT, I MADE A VOW THAT I WOULD BE THE HERO TEDDY BELIEVED I WAS."
BUT I DIDN'T KNOW HOW TO KEEP MY PROMISE.

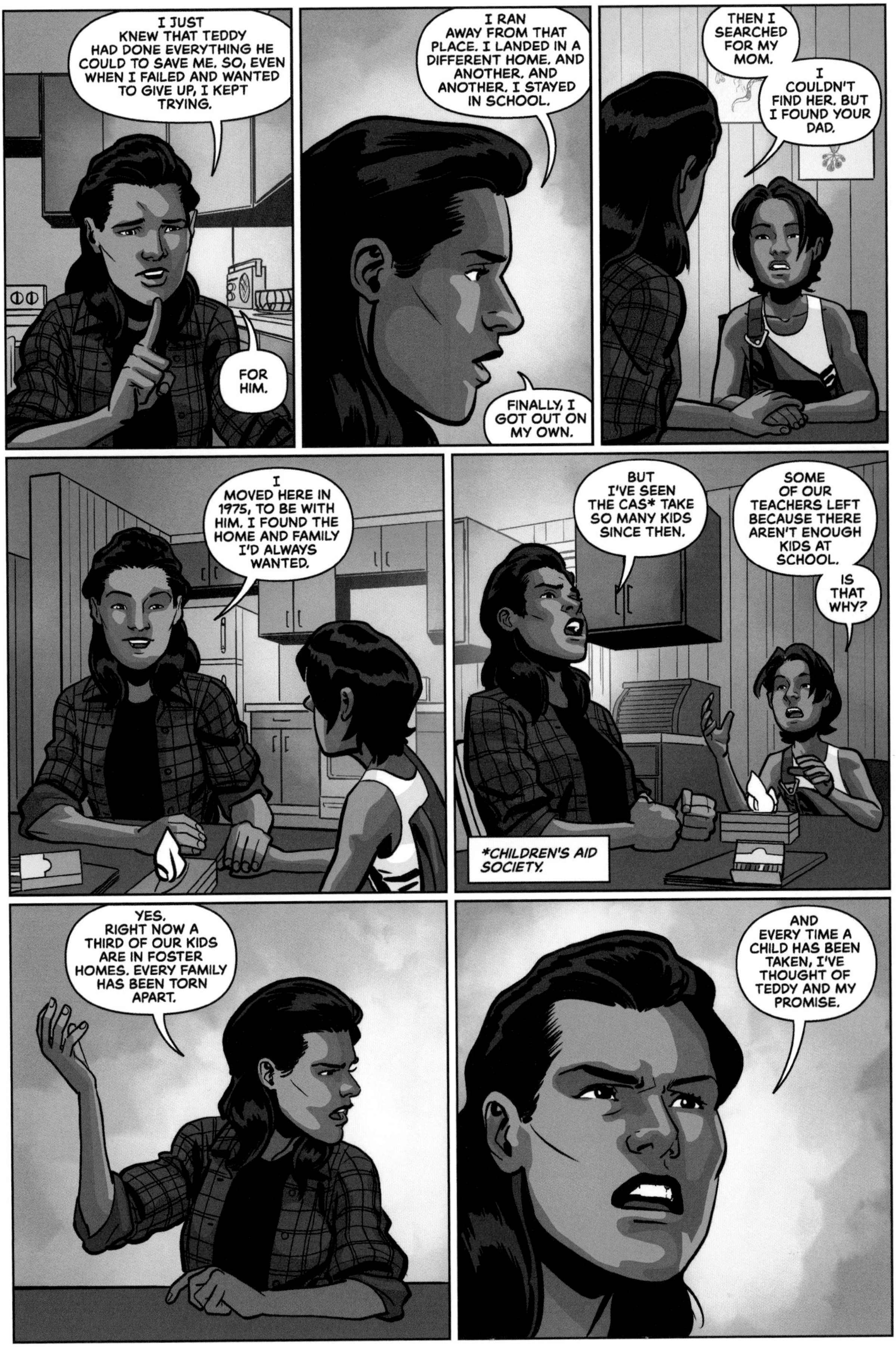
I JUST KNEW THAT TEDDY HAD DONE EVERYTHING HE COULD TO SAVE ME. SO, EVEN WHEN I FAILED AND WANTED TO GIVE UP, I KEPT TRYING.
FOR HIM.
I RAN AWAY FROM THAT PLACE. I LANDED IN A DIFFERENT HOME. AND ANOTHER. AND ANOTHER. I STAYED IN SCHOOL.
FINALLY, I GOT OUT ON MY OWN.
THEN I SEARCHED FOR MY MOM.
I COULDN'T FIND HER. BUT I FOUND YOUR DAD.
I MOVED HERE IN 1975, TO BE WITH HIM. I FOUND THE HOME AND FAMILY I'D ALWAYS WANTED.
BUT I'VE SEEN THE CAS* TAKE SO MANY KIDS SINCE THEN.
SOME OF OUR TEACHERS LEFT BECAUSE THERE AREN'T ENOUGH KIDS AT SCHOOL.
IS THAT WHY?
*CHILDREN'S AID SOCIETY.
YES, RIGHT NOW A THIRD OF OUR KIDS ARE IN FOSTER HOMES. EVERY FAMILY HAS BEEN TORN APART.
AND EVERY TIME A CHILD HAS BEEN TAKEN, I'VE THOUGHT OF TEDDY AND MY PROMISE.

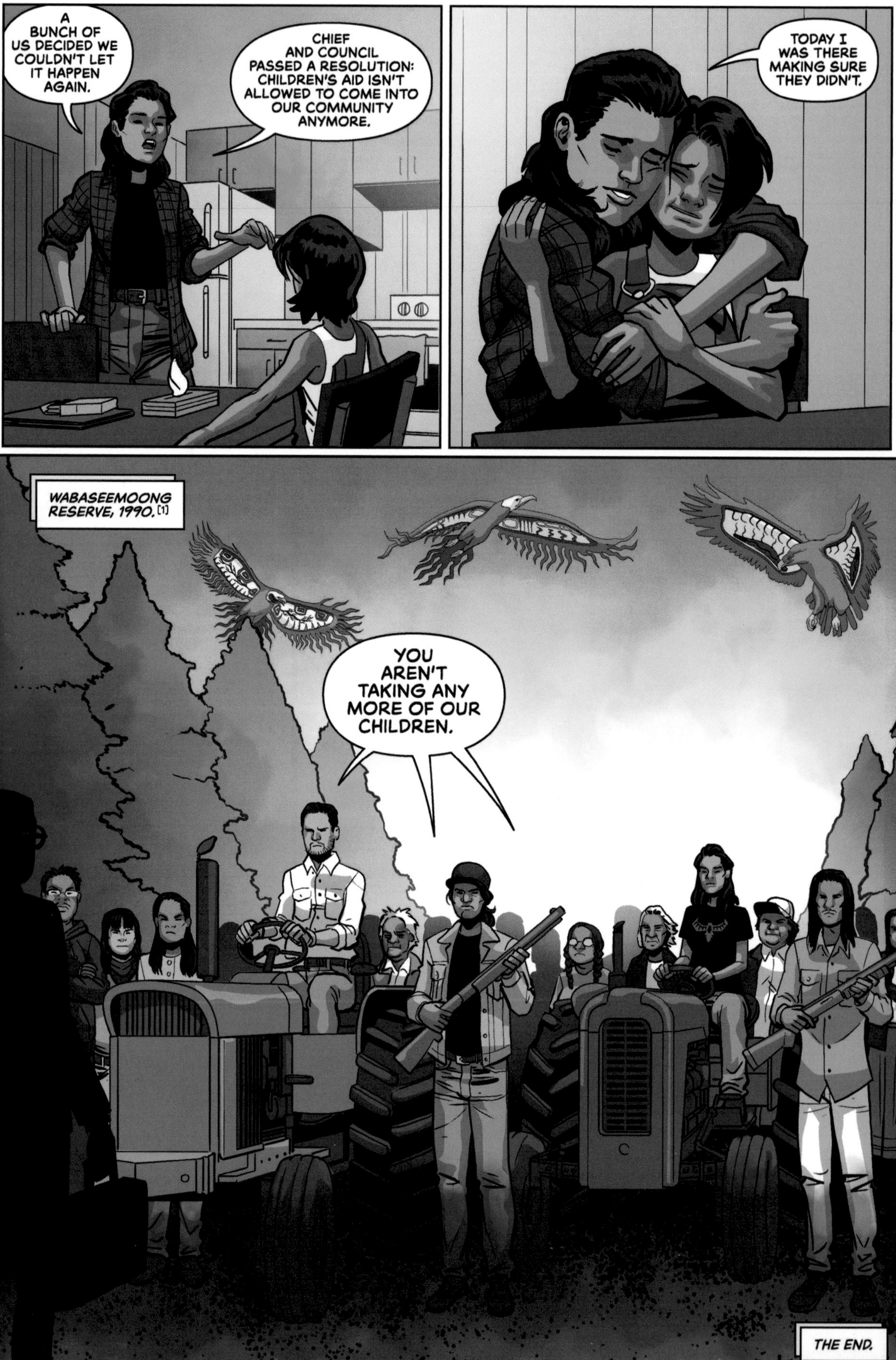
A BUNCH OF US DECIDED WE COULDN'T LET IT HAPPEN AGAIN.
CHIEF AND COUNCIL PASSED A RESOLUTION: CHILDREN'S AID ISN'T ALLOWED TO COME INTO OUR COMMUNITY ANYMORE.
TODAY I WAS THERE MAKING SURE THEY DIDN'T.
WABASEEMOONG RESERVE, 1990.[1]
YOU AREN'T TAKING ANY MORE OF OUR CHILDREN.
THE END.

was three years old when Chief Frank T'Seleie delivered one of the most important testimonies of our time in Fort Good Hope, NWT, defending the North against the proposed Mackenzie Valley Pipeline. You can watch the entire speech online and feel the tension grow in the room.[1]

I wanted to use this chapter to highlight Mr. T'Seleie's speech, but also to honour Justice Thomas Berger for his commitment to listening to almost 1,000 testimonies. He visited 35 communities along the Mackenzie River as well as other cities across Canada. This commitment took up three years of his life: listening, writing, deciding.

I feel that The Mackenzie Valley Pipeline laid the groundwork for the IdleNoMore movement and the strong activism we see against corporations and pipelines to this day. This is when we used our voice to let Canada know we would continue to proclaim our need for self-determination.

I feel that Mr. T'Seleie's speech is one of the finest speeches ever crafted. His words are eternal. I'm grateful that I had the opportunity to call Mr. T'Seleie in his home several times as I wrote this story. I was sad to learn that he, his mother, and his great aunt had all been to residential school. I decided to open this story by honouring Mr. T'Seleie as a young boy.

Mahsi cho to everyone involved with this project. It's not every day that you get to call one of your heroes and ask the questions that you've always wanted to.

Thank you. Mahsi cho.
Richard Van Camp

1961, DECEMBER 31
The National Indian Council, an umbrella group for Indigenous and Métis concerns, is established.

1969, JUNE
A government White Paper calls for the abolition of the Indian Department and the Indian Act, thus eliminating Indian status. The initiative is abandoned after the National Indian Brotherhood protests.

1970, APRIL 1
The NWT takes responsibility for governing the eastern and upper Arctic from the Department of Indian Affairs and Northern Development.

1970, SEPTEMBER 1
Blue Quills Residential School in Alberta becomes the first residential school run by Indigenous people.

1971
Inuit Tapirisat of Canada is formed to deal with issues such as the development of the Canadian North and the preservation of Inuit culture.

1970s
The Dene pursue land-claim settlements in court, on the grounds that Treaty 11 had no legal validity since the provisions were improperly implemented.

Like a Razor Slash

Richard Van Camp
Illustration: Scott B. Henderson
Colours: Scott A. Ford

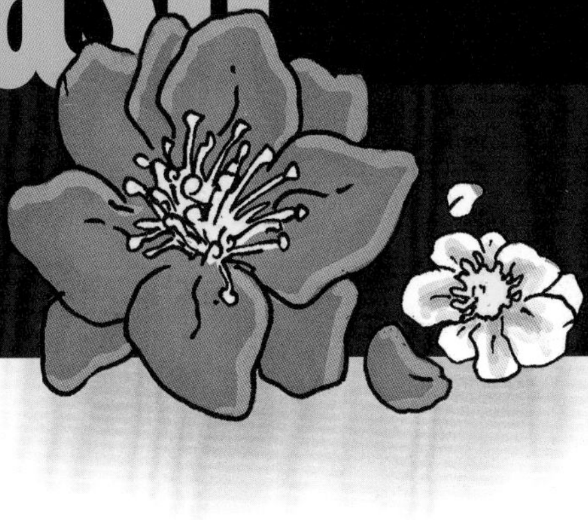

1973
The Supreme Court rules Aboriginal land rights exist.

1973, AUGUST 8
The federal government renews the right of Indigenous peoples to initiate land claim negotiations.

1973, SEPTEMBER 7
The Dene Nation files a claim for approximately a third of the land in the Northwest Territories.

1973
Court decisions recognize the Dene land title to the Mackenzie River Valley, and the title of the Cree and Inuit of Quebec. Both decisions are later overturned.

1975, NOVEMBER 11
The James Bay agreement in Quebec is the first treaty negotiated since 1923.

LIKE A RAZOR SLASH

Some dismissed the impact of a pipeline, saying it would be like a thread stretched across a football field. Those close to the land said the impact would be more like a razor slash across the Mona Lisa. [2]

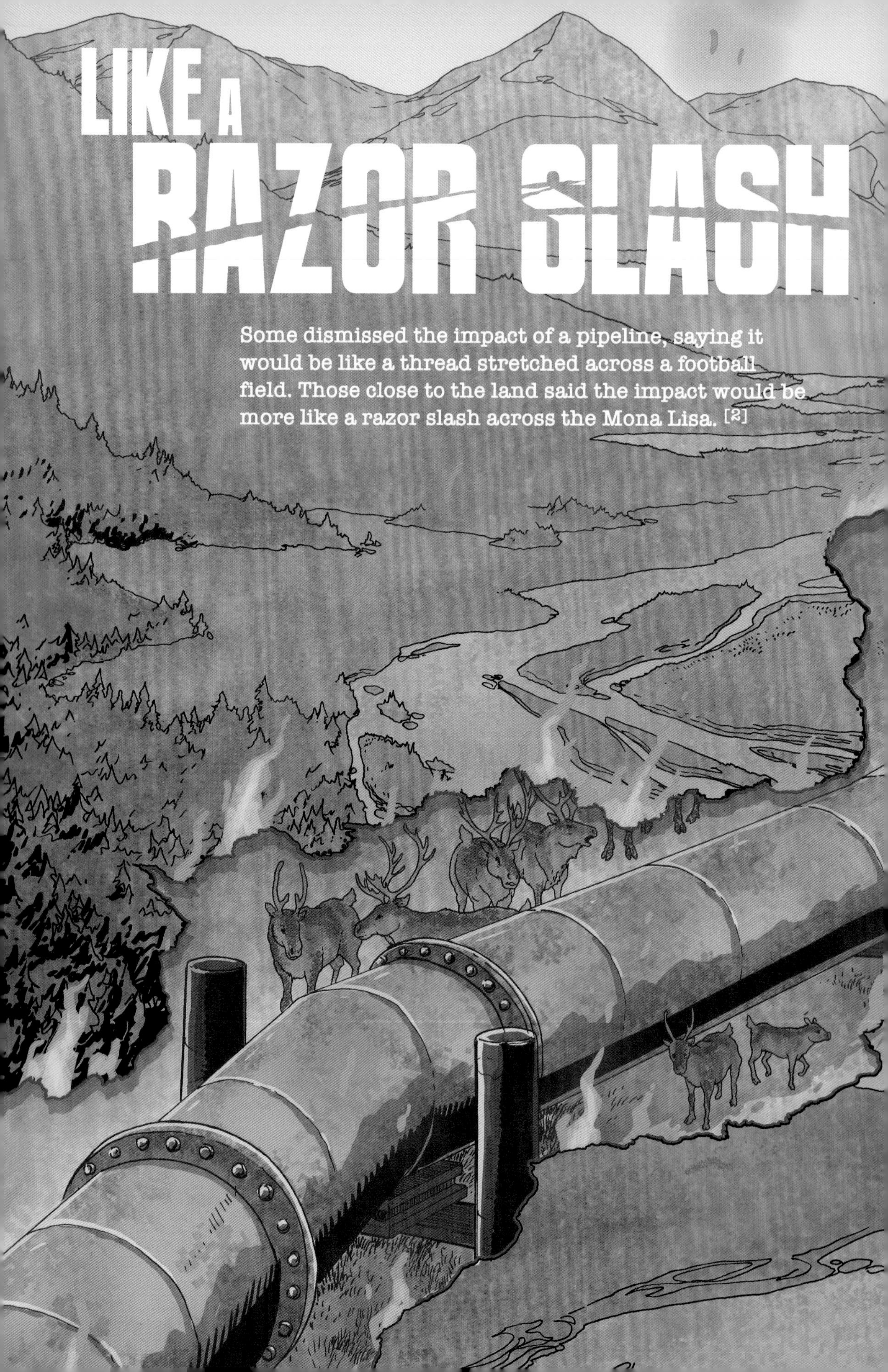

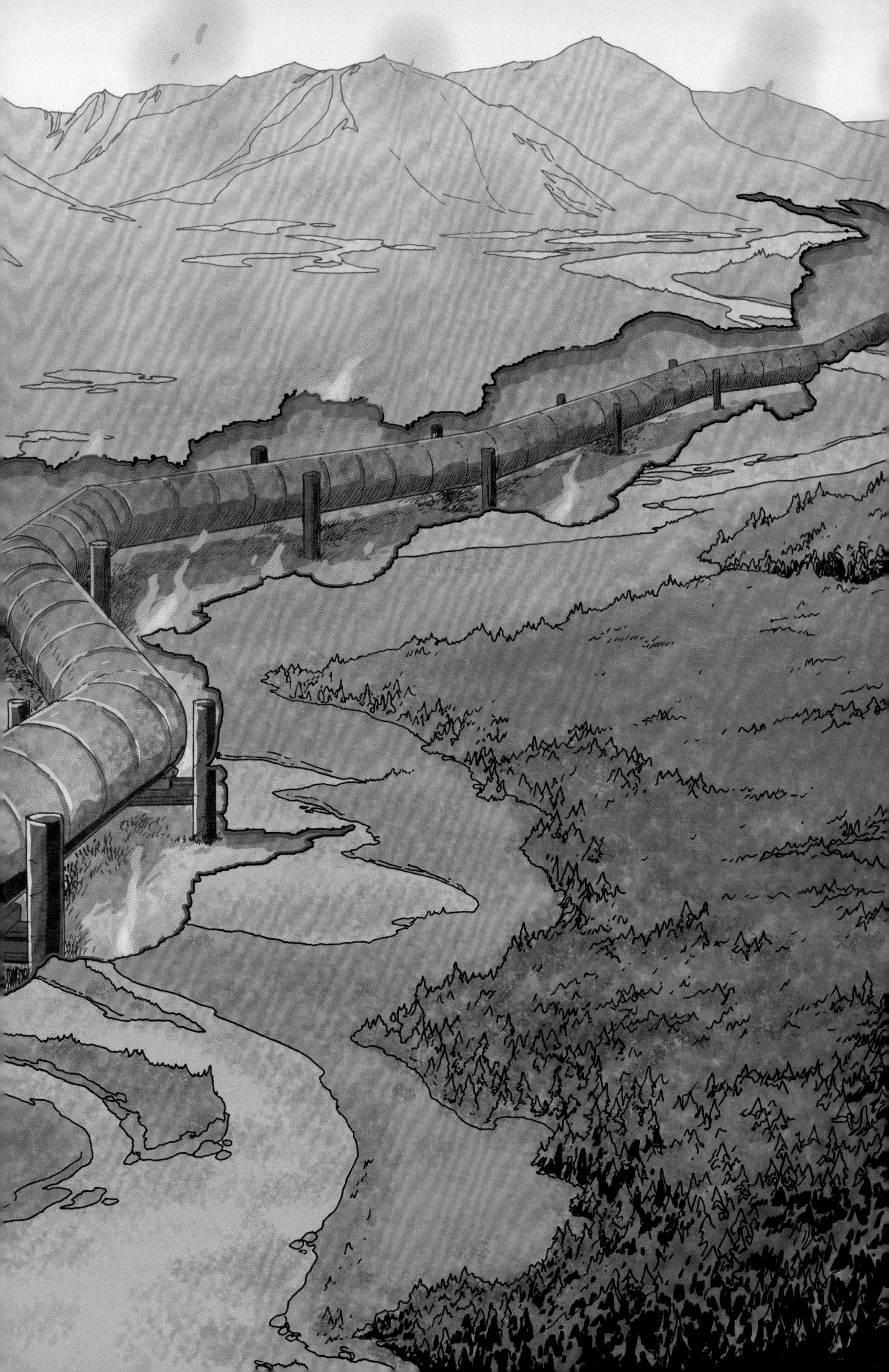

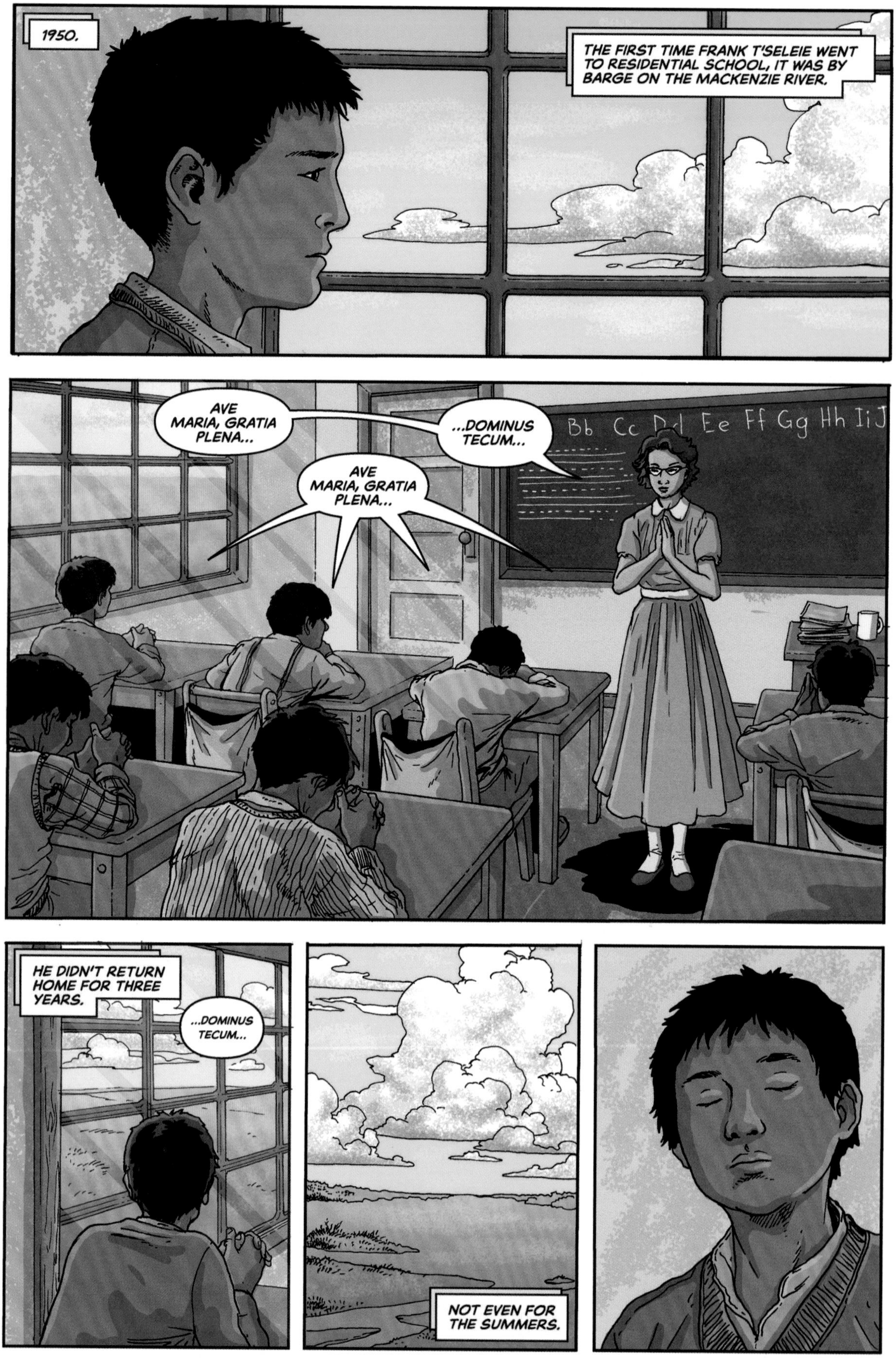

1950.
THE FIRST TIME FRANK T'SELEIE WENT TO RESIDENTIAL SCHOOL, IT WAS BY BARGE ON THE MACKENZIE RIVER.
AVE MARIA, GRATIA PLENA...
...DOMINUS TECUM...
AVE MARIA, GRATIA PLENA...
Bb Cc Dd Ee Ff Gg Hh Ii J
HE DIDN'T RETURN HOME FOR THREE YEARS.
...DOMINUS TECUM...
NOT EVEN FOR THE SUMMERS.

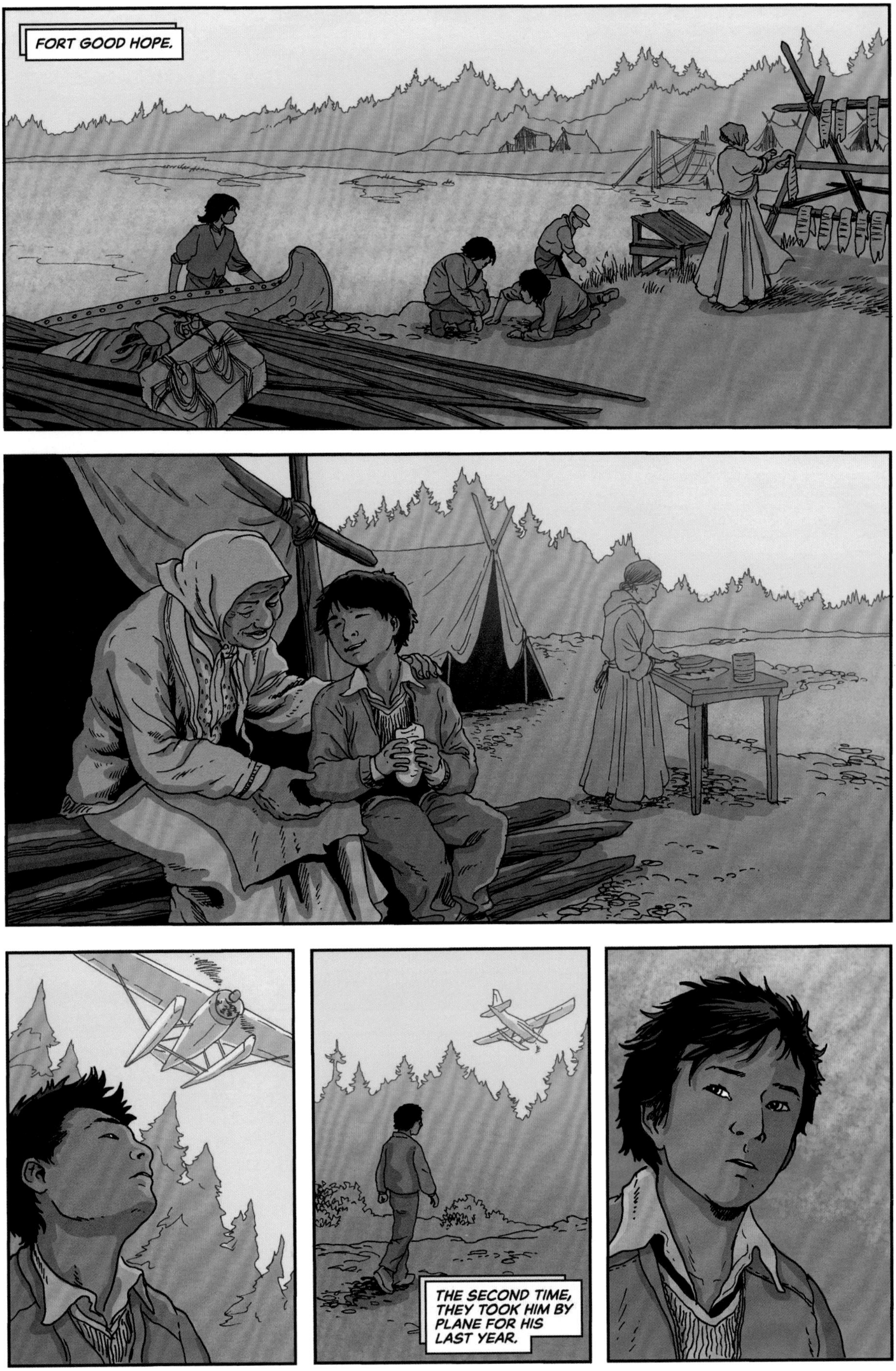
FORT GOOD HOPE.
THE SECOND TIME, THEY TOOK HIM BY PLANE FOR HIS LAST YEAR.

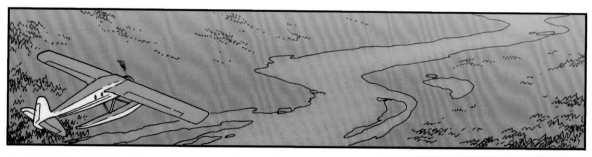

WHETHER HE WAS IN RESIDENTIAL SCHOOL, ON THE LAND, OR IN TOWN, FRANK T'SELEIE KNEW WHO HE WAS AND WHERE HE WAS FROM.

HE JOINED THE BAND COUNCIL AS AN ADMINISTRATOR IN 1971.

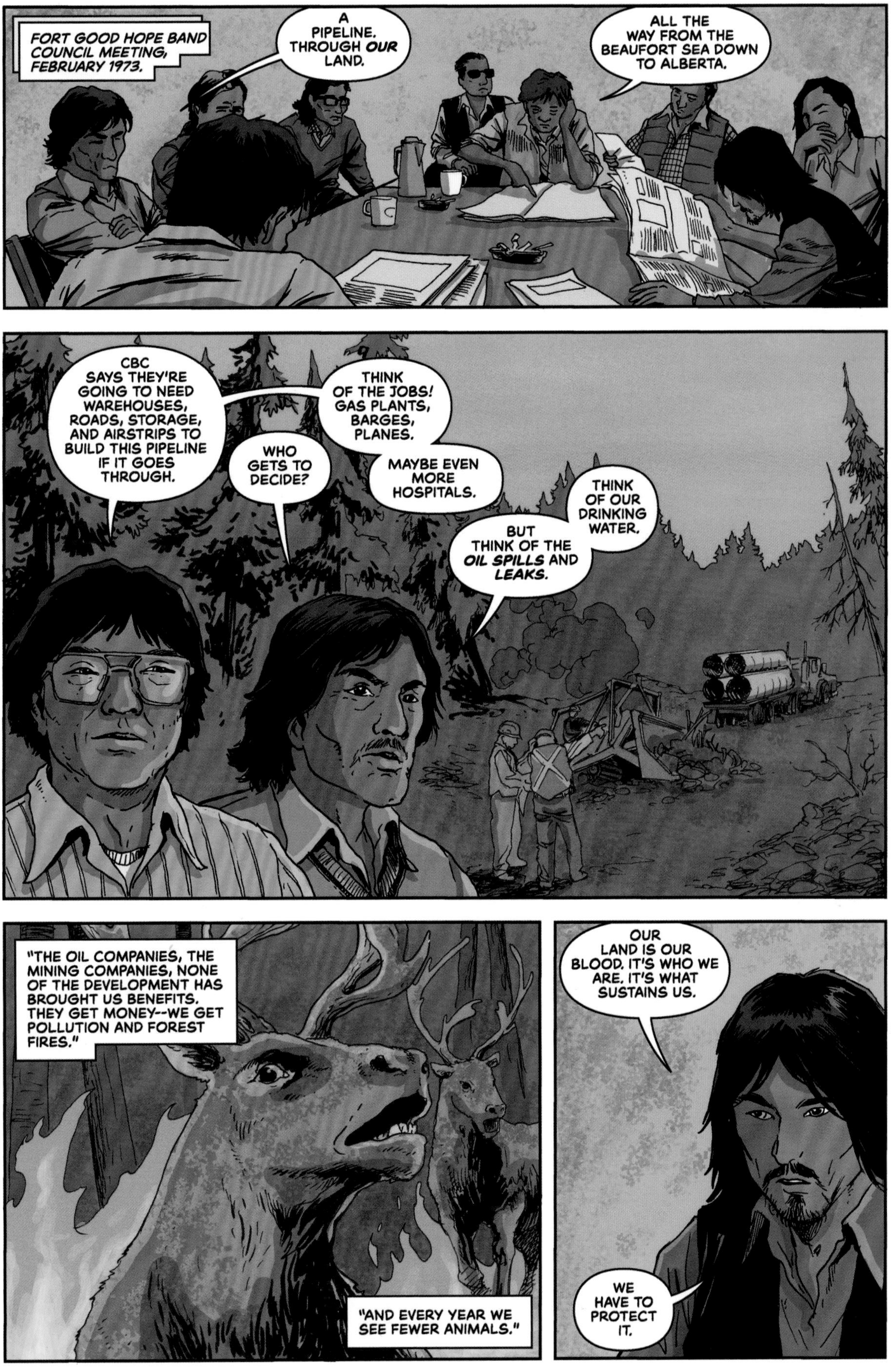
FORT GOOD HOPE BAND COUNCIL MEETING, FEBRUARY 1973.
A PIPELINE. THROUGH OUR LAND.
ALL THE WAY FROM THE BEAUFORT SEA DOWN TO ALBERTA.
CBC SAYS THEY'RE GOING TO NEED WAREHOUSES, ROADS, STORAGE, AND AIRSTRIPS TO BUILD THIS PIPELINE IF IT GOES THROUGH.
THINK OF THE JOBS! GAS PLANTS, BARGES, PLANES.
WHO GETS TO DECIDE?
MAYBE EVEN MORE HOSPITALS.
THINK OF OUR DRINKING WATER.
BUT THINK OF THE OIL SPILLS AND LEAKS.
"THE OIL COMPANIES, THE MINING COMPANIES, NONE OF THE DEVELOPMENT HAS BROUGHT US BENEFITS. THEY GET MONEY--WE GET POLLUTION AND FOREST FIRES."
"AND EVERY YEAR WE SEE FEWER ANIMALS."
OUR LAND IS OUR BLOOD. IT'S WHO WE ARE. IT'S WHAT SUSTAINS US.
WE HAVE TO PROTECT IT.

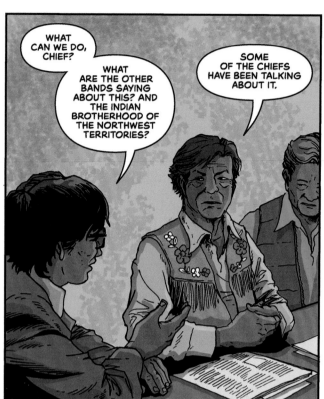

WHAT CAN WE DO, CHIEF?

WHAT ARE THE OTHER BANDS SAYING ABOUT THIS? AND THE INDIAN BROTHERHOOD OF THE NORTHWEST TERRITORIES?

SOME OF THE CHIEFS HAVE BEEN TALKING ABOUT IT.

WE ARE THINKING OF FILING A *CAVEAT*-- DECLARING OUR LEGAL INTEREST IN THE LAND.

NO PROJECTS COULD GO FORWARD UNTIL THE CAVEAT IS RESOLVED.

IT WON'T WORK. THE GOVERNMENT SAYS WE GAVE THEM OUR TITLE.

DID YOU HEAR ABOUT THE CALDER CASE? THE SUPREME COURT JUST ISSUED ITS RULING.

"THE NISGA'A GOT A LAWYER AND ARGUED THAT THEY HAD NEVER SURRENDERED THEIR TITLE TO THEIR LAND."

"THEY LOST THAT PART OF THE CASE ON A *TECHNICALITY*."

"BUT THE SUPREME COURT ESTABLISHED THAT 'ABORIGINAL TITLE' EXISTS IN CANADIAN LAW."

BUT THE NISGA'A DIDN'T HAVE TREATIES. WE DO.

THE TREATIES WE SIGNED WERE SUPPOSED TO KEEP THE PEACE AND PROTECT OUR WAY OF LIFE. WE NEVER AGREED TO GIVE UP OUR LAND.

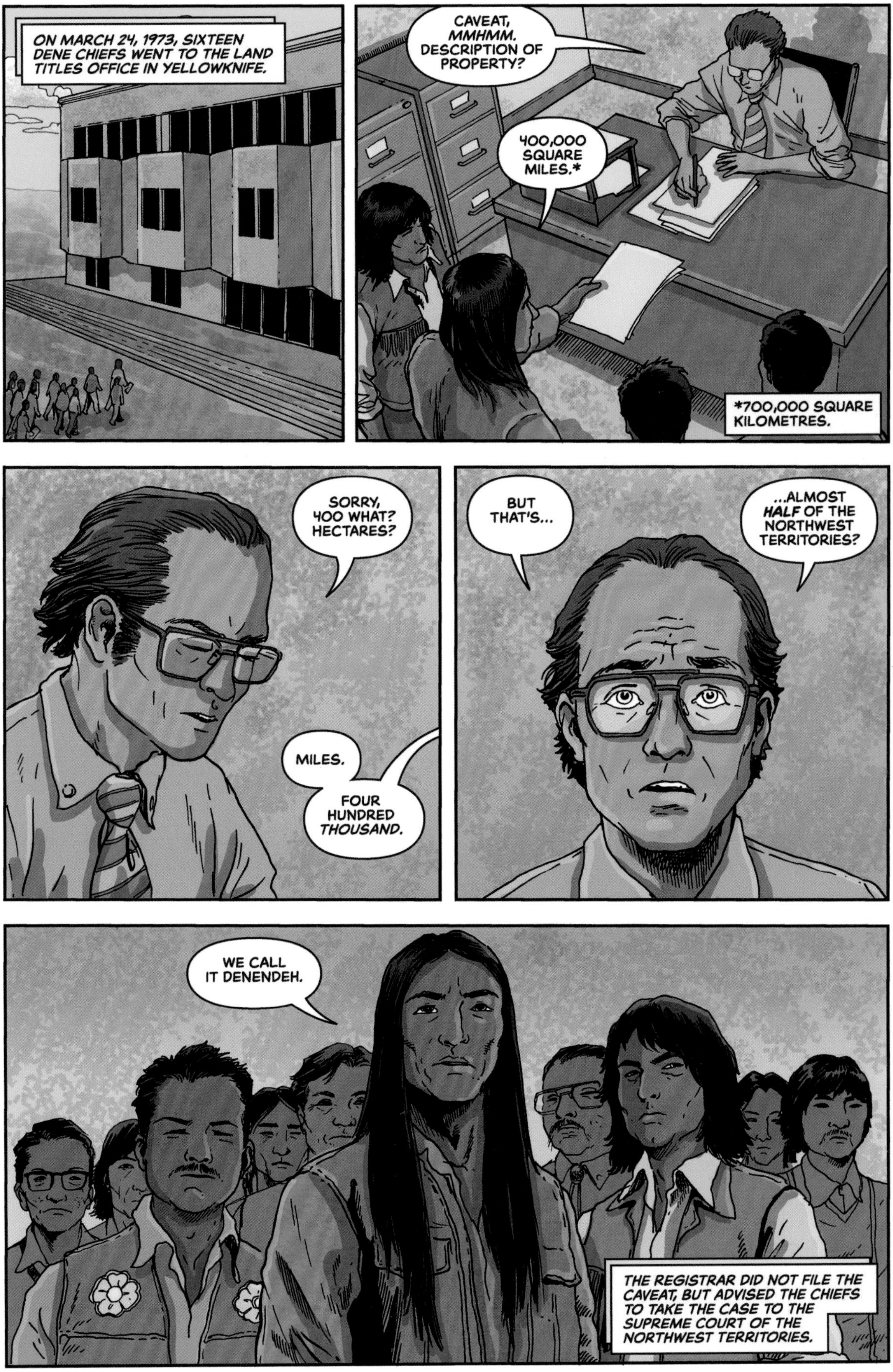
ON MARCH 24, 1973, SIXTEEN DENE CHIEFS WENT TO THE LAND TITLES OFFICE IN YELLOWKNIFE.
CAVEAT, MMHMM. DESCRIPTION OF PROPERTY?
400,000 SQUARE MILES.*
*700,000 SQUARE KILOMETRES.
SORRY, 400 WHAT? HECTARES?
MILES.
FOUR HUNDRED *THOUSAND.*
BUT THAT'S...
...ALMOST *HALF* OF THE NORTHWEST TERRITORIES?
WE CALL IT DENENDEH.
THE REGISTRAR DID NOT FILE THE CAVEAT, BUT ADVISED THE CHIEFS TO TAKE THE CASE TO THE SUPREME COURT OF THE NORTHWEST TERRITORIES.

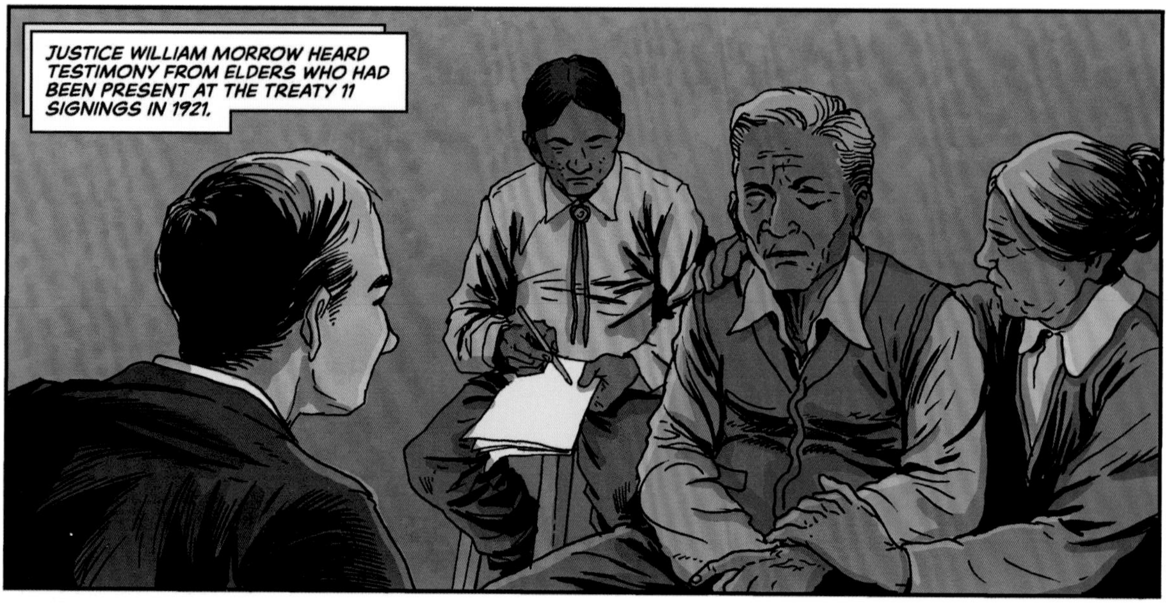
JUSTICE WILLIAM MORROW HEARD TESTIMONY FROM ELDERS WHO HAD BEEN PRESENT AT THE TREATY 11 SIGNINGS IN 1921.

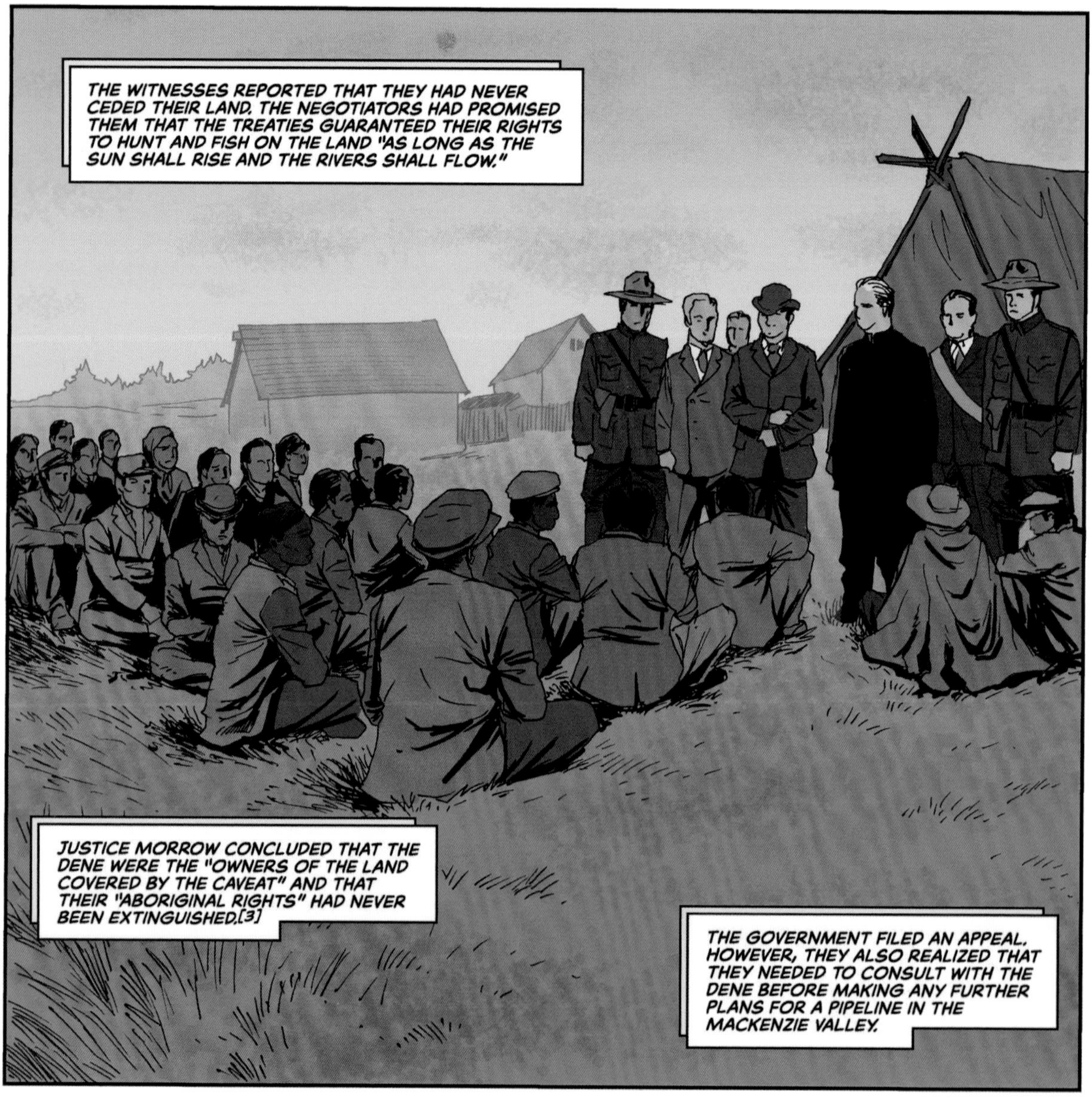
THE WITNESSES REPORTED THAT THEY HAD NEVER CEDED THEIR LAND. THE NEGOTIATORS HAD PROMISED THEM THAT THE TREATIES GUARANTEED THEIR RIGHTS TO HUNT AND FISH ON THE LAND "AS LONG AS THE SUN SHALL RISE AND THE RIVERS SHALL FLOW."
JUSTICE MORROW CONCLUDED THAT THE DENE WERE THE "OWNERS OF THE LAND COVERED BY THE CAVEAT" AND THAT THEIR "ABORIGINAL RIGHTS" HAD NEVER BEEN EXTINGUISHED.[3]
THE GOVERNMENT FILED AN APPEAL. HOWEVER, THEY ALSO REALIZED THAT THEY NEEDED TO CONSULT WITH THE DENE BEFORE MAKING ANY FURTHER PLANS FOR A PIPELINE IN THE MACKENZIE VALLEY.

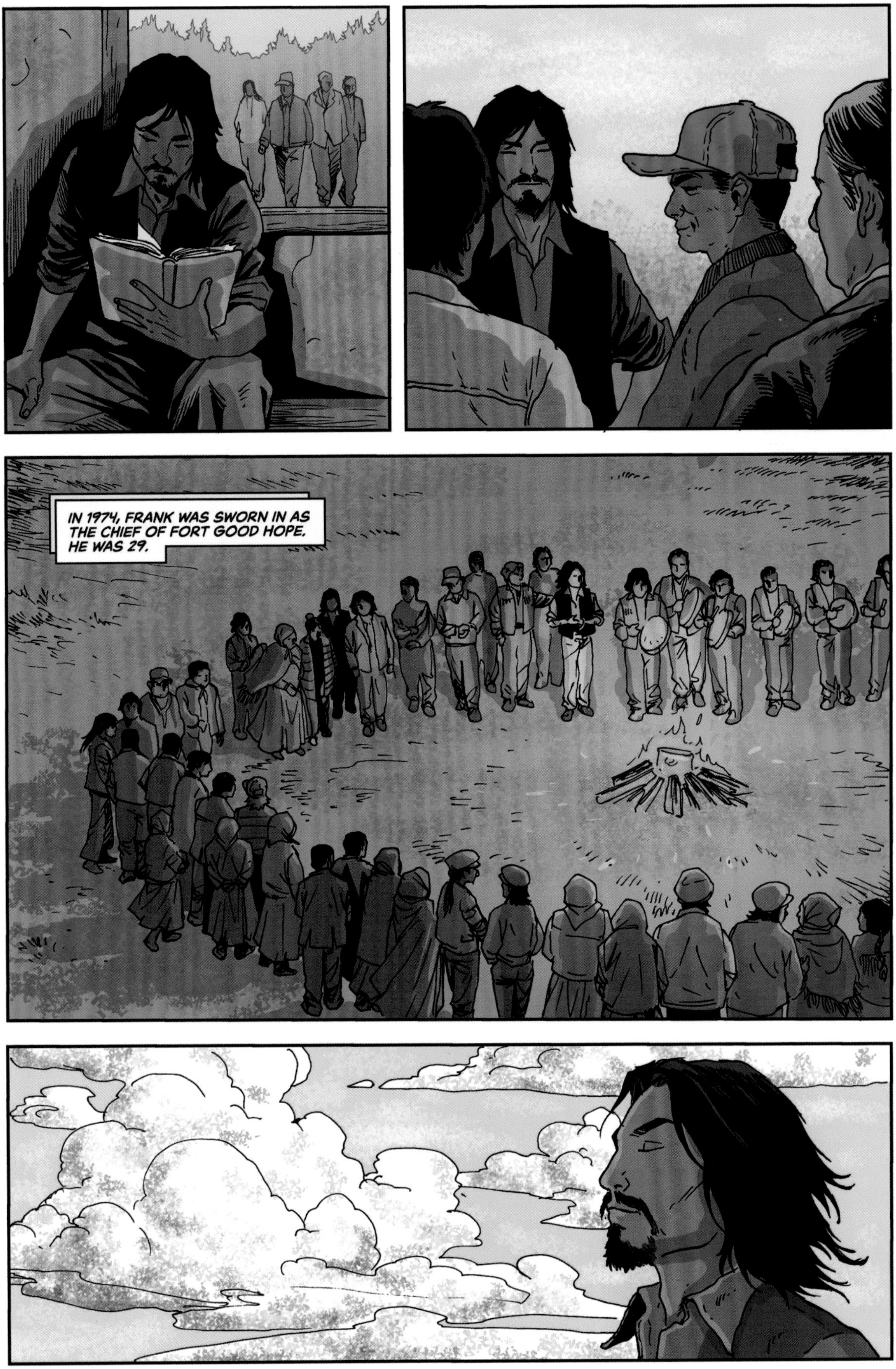
IN 1974, FRANK WAS SWORN IN AS THE CHIEF OF FORT GOOD HOPE. HE WAS 29.

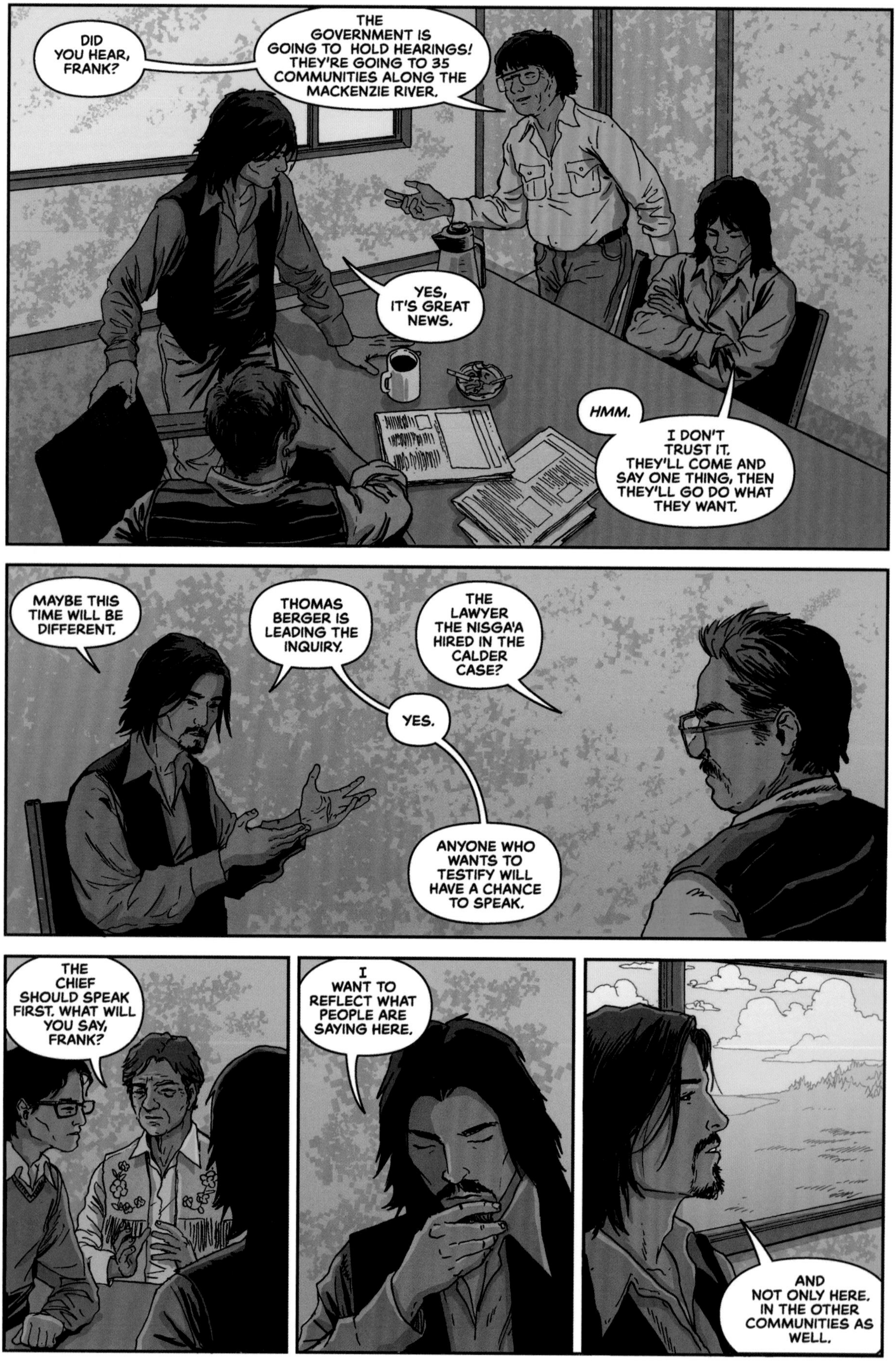
DID YOU HEAR, FRANK?
THE GOVERNMENT IS GOING TO HOLD HEARINGS! THEY'RE GOING TO 35 COMMUNITIES ALONG THE MACKENZIE RIVER.
YES, IT'S GREAT NEWS.
HMM.
I DON'T TRUST IT. THEY'LL COME AND SAY ONE THING, THEN THEY'LL GO DO WHAT THEY WANT.
MAYBE THIS TIME WILL BE DIFFERENT.
THOMAS BERGER IS LEADING THE INQUIRY.
THE LAWYER THE NISGA'A HIRED IN THE CALDER CASE?
YES.
ANYONE WHO WANTS TO TESTIFY WILL HAVE A CHANCE TO SPEAK.
THE CHIEF SHOULD SPEAK FIRST. WHAT WILL YOU SAY, FRANK?
I WANT TO REFLECT WHAT PEOPLE ARE SAYING HERE.
AND NOT ONLY HERE. IN THE OTHER COMMUNITIES AS WELL.

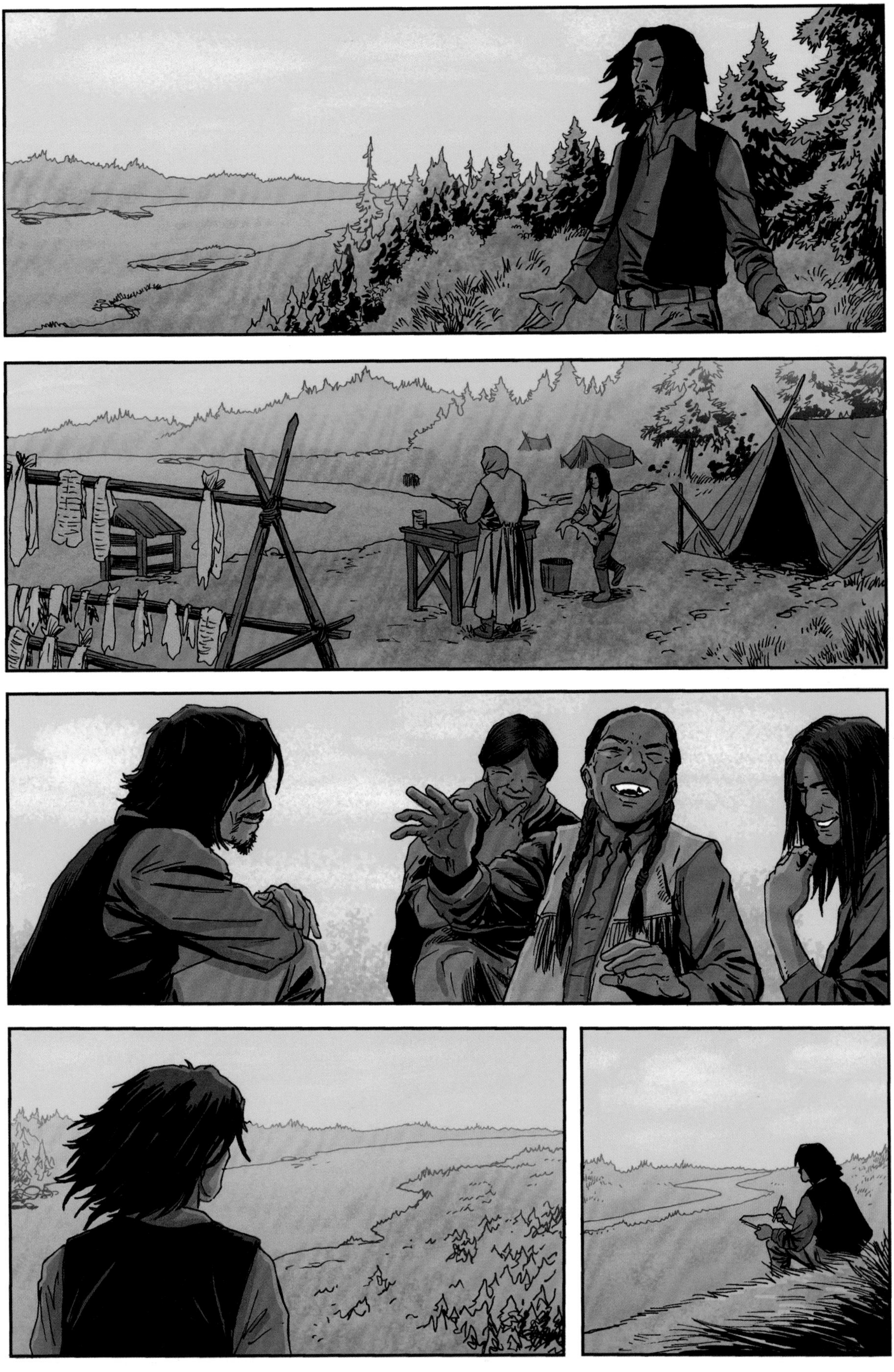

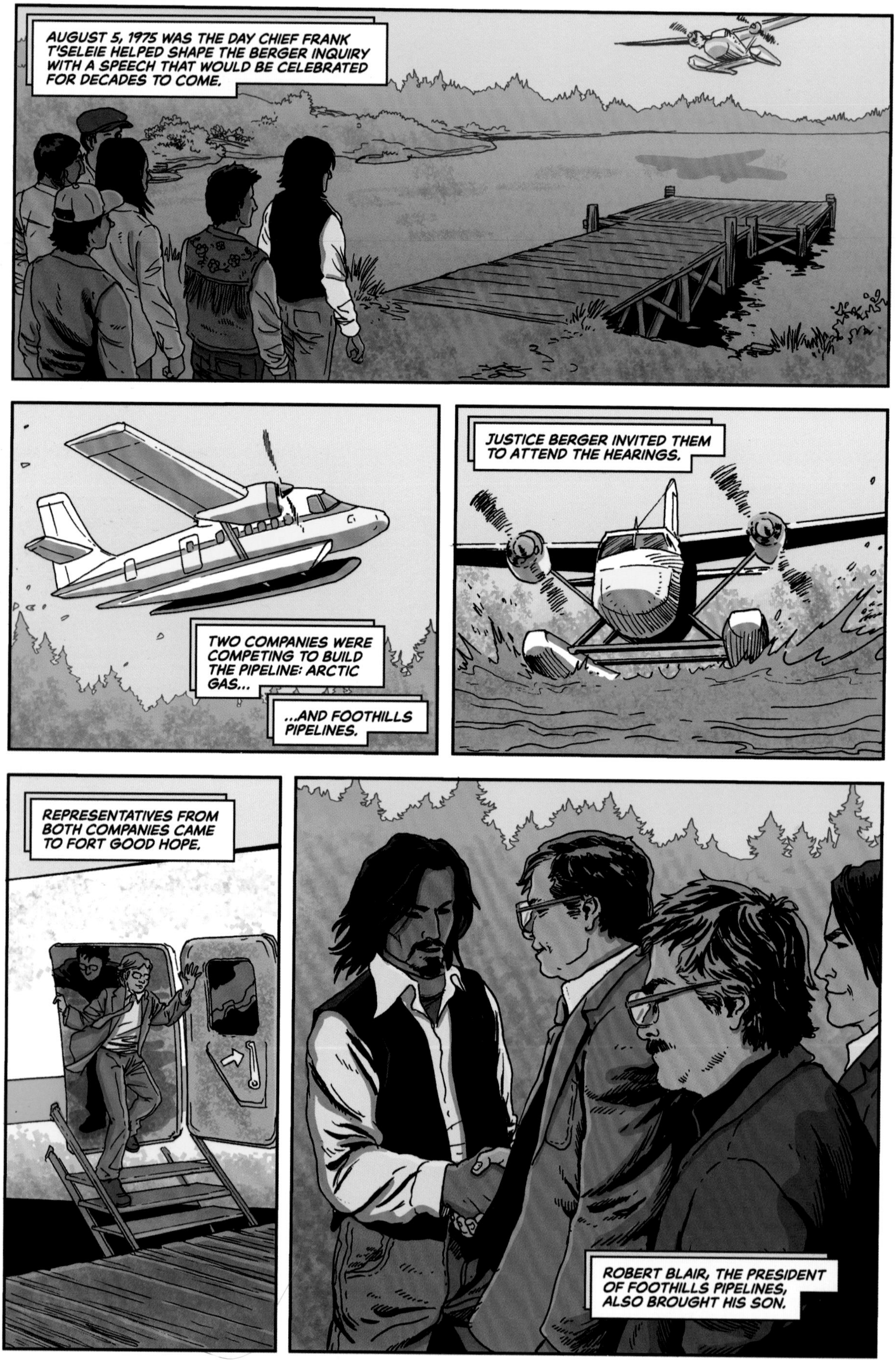
AUGUST 5, 1975 WAS THE DAY CHIEF FRANK T'SELEIE HELPED SHAPE THE BERGER INQUIRY WITH A SPEECH THAT WOULD BE CELEBRATED FOR DECADES TO COME.
TWO COMPANIES WERE COMPETING TO BUILD THE PIPELINE: ARCTIC GAS...
...AND FOOTHILLS PIPELINES.
JUSTICE BERGER INVITED THEM TO ATTEND THE HEARINGS.
REPRESENTATIVES FROM BOTH COMPANIES CAME TO FORT GOOD HOPE.
ROBERT BLAIR, THE PRESIDENT OF FOOTHILLS PIPELINES, ALSO BROUGHT HIS SON.

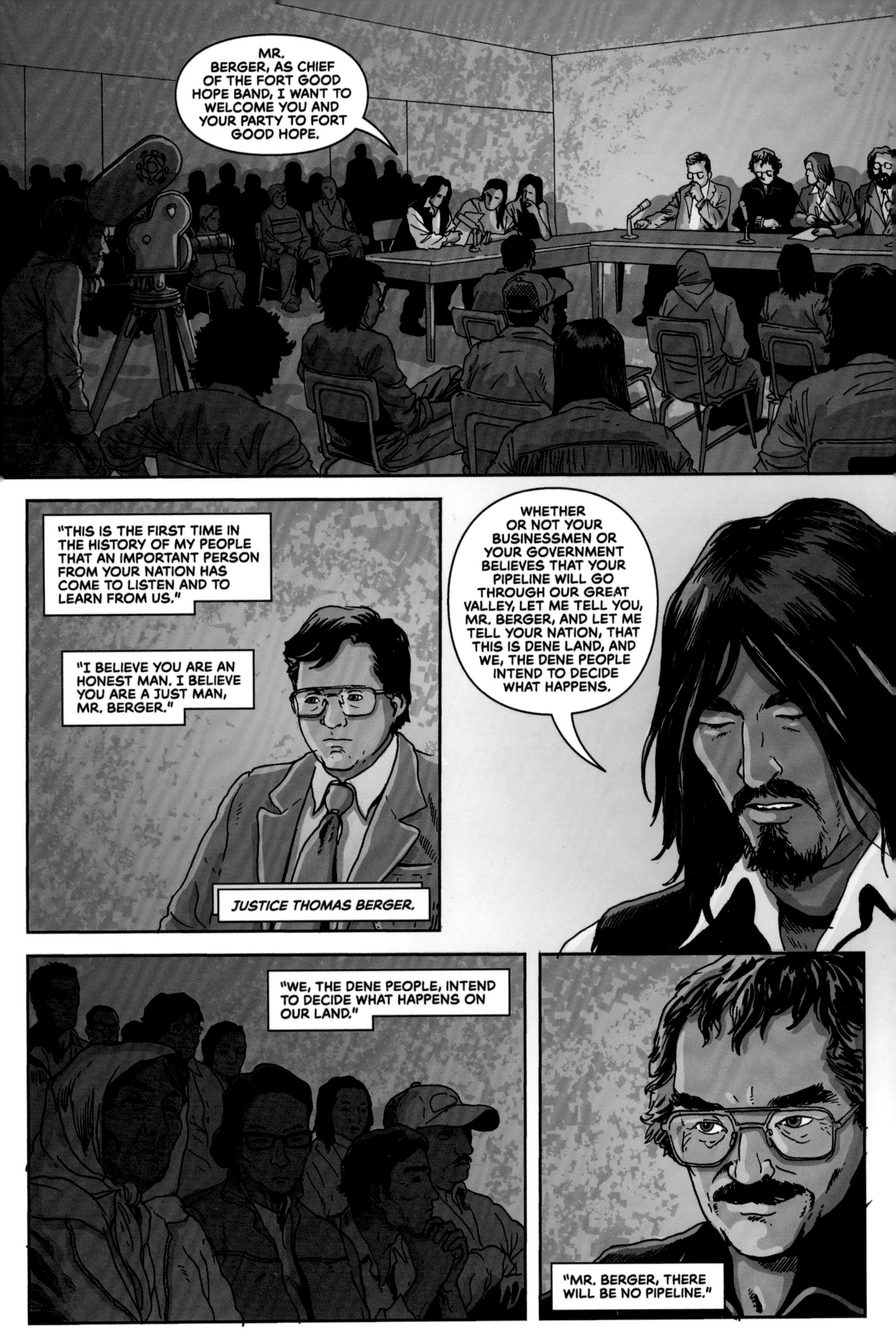
MR. BERGER, AS CHIEF OF THE FORT GOOD HOPE BAND, I WANT TO WELCOME YOU AND YOUR PARTY TO FORT GOOD HOPE.
"THIS IS THE FIRST TIME IN THE HISTORY OF MY PEOPLE THAT AN IMPORTANT PERSON FROM YOUR NATION HAS COME TO LISTEN AND TO LEARN FROM US."
"I BELIEVE YOU ARE AN HONEST MAN. I BELIEVE YOU ARE A JUST MAN, MR. BERGER."
JUSTICE THOMAS BERGER.
WHETHER OR NOT YOUR BUSINESSMEN OR YOUR GOVERNMENT BELIEVES THAT YOUR PIPELINE WILL GO THROUGH OUR GREAT VALLEY, LET ME TELL YOU, MR. BERGER, AND LET ME TELL YOUR NATION, THAT THIS IS DENE LAND, AND WE, THE DENE PEOPLE INTEND TO DECIDE WHAT HAPPENS.
"WE, THE DENE PEOPLE, INTEND TO DECIDE WHAT HAPPENS ON OUR LAND."
"MR. BERGER, THERE WILL BE NO PIPELINE."

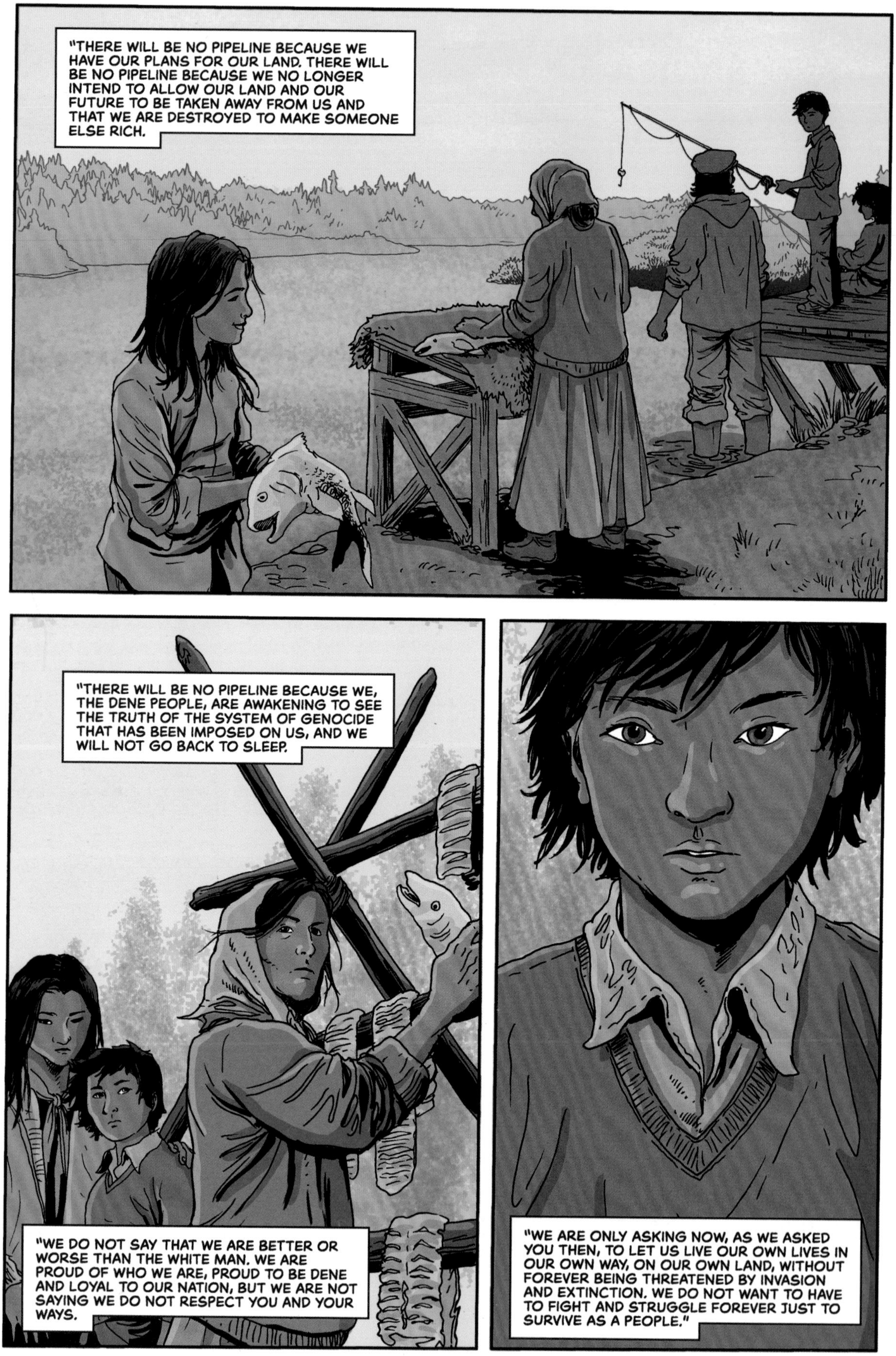
"THERE WILL BE NO PIPELINE BECAUSE WE HAVE OUR PLANS FOR OUR LAND. THERE WILL BE NO PIPELINE BECAUSE WE NO LONGER INTEND TO ALLOW OUR LAND AND OUR FUTURE TO BE TAKEN AWAY FROM US AND THAT WE ARE DESTROYED TO MAKE SOMEONE ELSE RICH.
"THERE WILL BE NO PIPELINE BECAUSE WE, THE DENE PEOPLE, ARE AWAKENING TO SEE THE TRUTH OF THE SYSTEM OF GENOCIDE THAT HAS BEEN IMPOSED ON US, AND WE WILL NOT GO BACK TO SLEEP.
"WE DO NOT SAY THAT WE ARE BETTER OR WORSE THAN THE WHITE MAN. WE ARE PROUD OF WHO WE ARE, PROUD TO BE DENE AND LOYAL TO OUR NATION, BUT WE ARE NOT SAYING WE DO NOT RESPECT YOU AND YOUR WAYS.
"WE ARE ONLY ASKING NOW, AS WE ASKED YOU THEN, TO LET US LIVE OUR OWN LIVES IN OUR OWN WAY, ON OUR OWN LAND, WITHOUT FOREVER BEING THREATENED BY INVASION AND EXTINCTION. WE DO NOT WANT TO HAVE TO FIGHT AND STRUGGLE FOREVER JUST TO SURVIVE AS A PEOPLE."

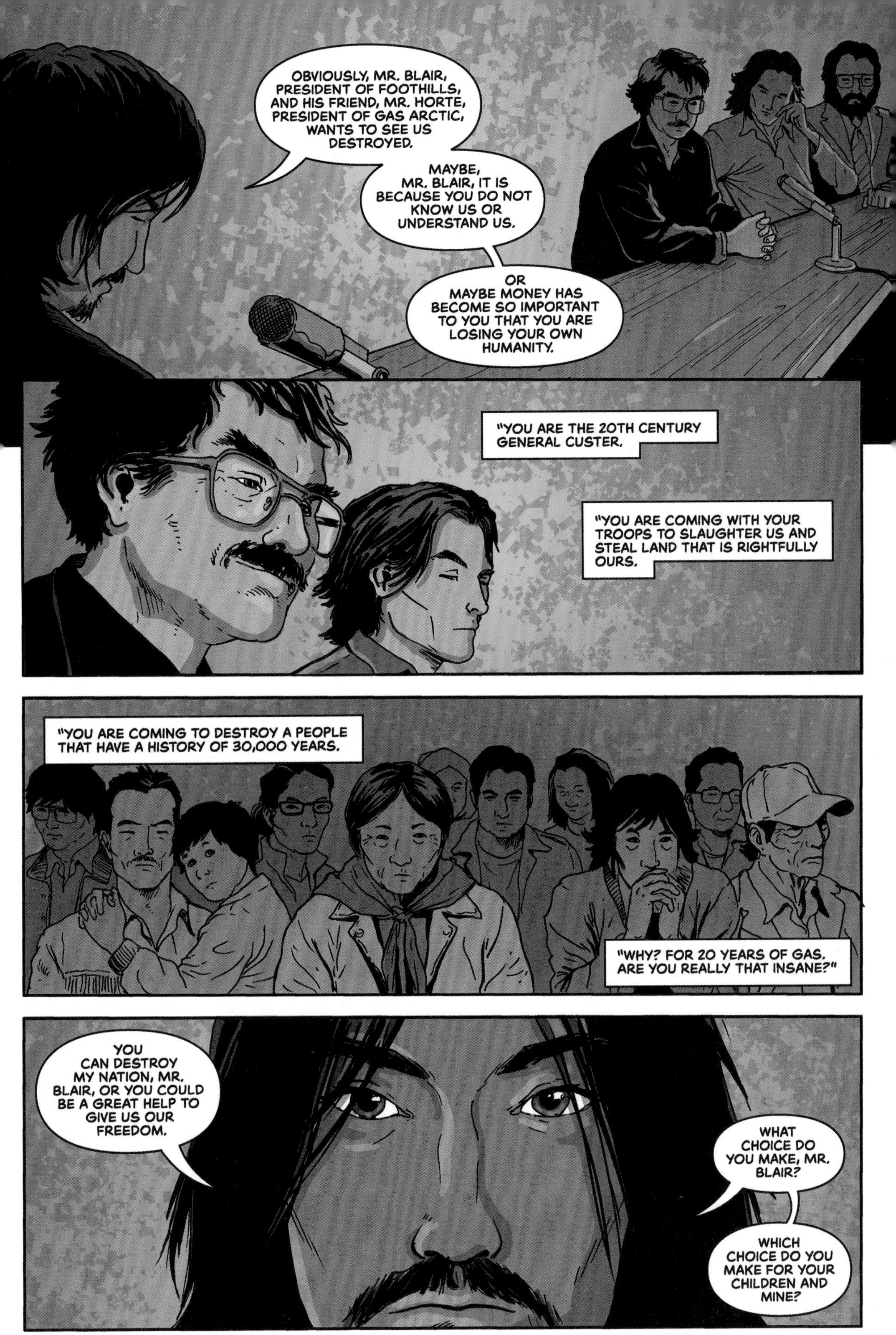
OBVIOUSLY, MR. BLAIR, PRESIDENT OF FOOTHILLS, AND HIS FRIEND, MR. HORTE, PRESIDENT OF GAS ARCTIC, WANTS TO SEE US DESTROYED.
MAYBE, MR. BLAIR, IT IS BECAUSE YOU DO NOT KNOW US OR UNDERSTAND US.
OR MAYBE MONEY HAS BECOME SO IMPORTANT TO YOU THAT YOU ARE LOSING YOUR OWN HUMANITY.
"YOU ARE THE 20TH CENTURY GENERAL CUSTER.
"YOU ARE COMING WITH YOUR TROOPS TO SLAUGHTER US AND STEAL LAND THAT IS RIGHTFULLY OURS.
"YOU ARE COMING TO DESTROY A PEOPLE THAT HAVE A HISTORY OF 30,000 YEARS.
"WHY? FOR 20 YEARS OF GAS. ARE YOU REALLY THAT INSANE?"
YOU CAN DESTROY MY NATION, MR. BLAIR, OR YOU COULD BE A GREAT HELP TO GIVE US OUR FREEDOM.
WHAT CHOICE DO YOU MAKE, MR. BLAIR?
WHICH CHOICE DO YOU MAKE FOR YOUR CHILDREN AND MINE?

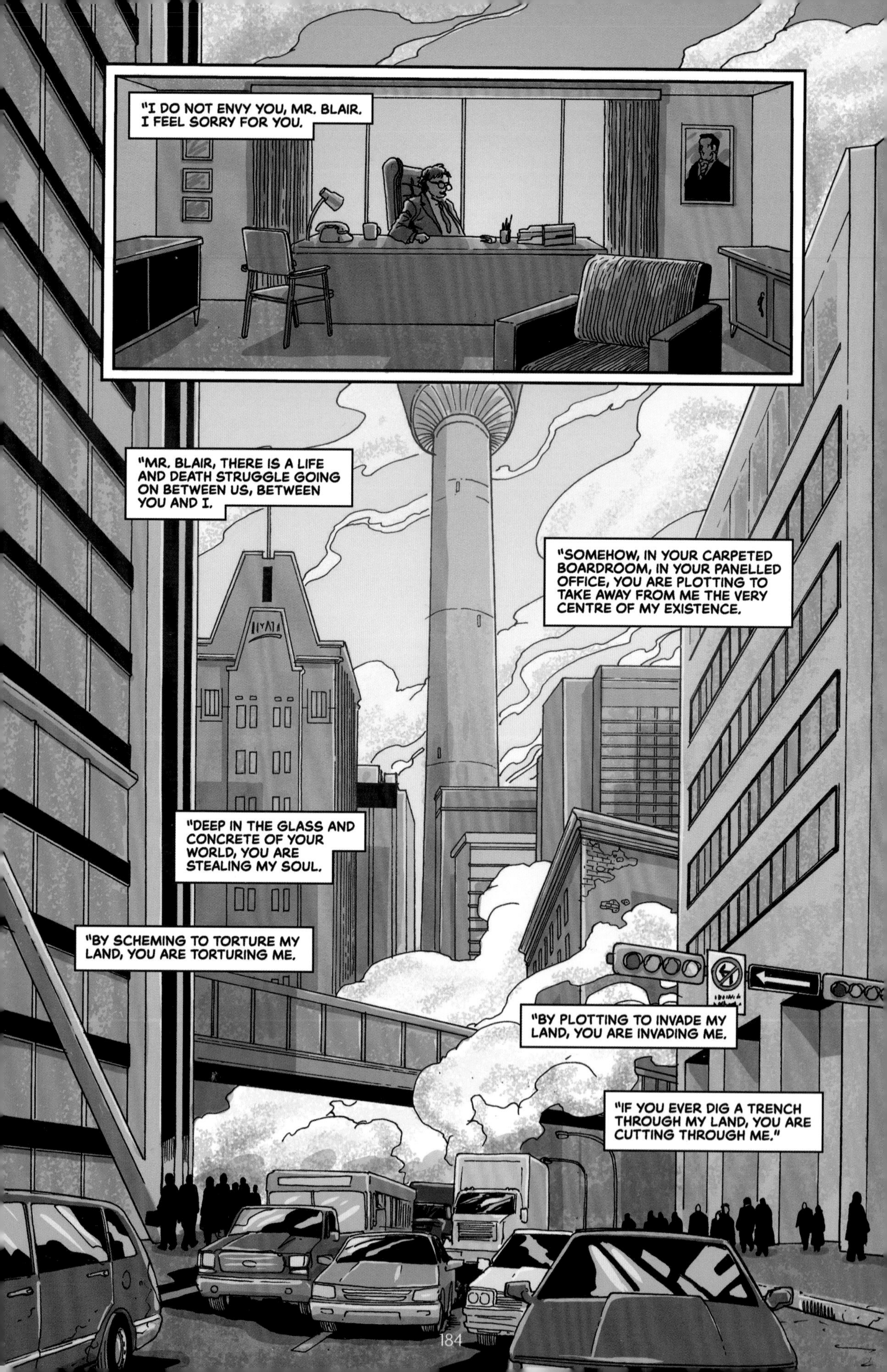
"I DO NOT ENVY YOU, MR. BLAIR. I FEEL SORRY FOR YOU.
"MR. BLAIR, THERE IS A LIFE AND DEATH STRUGGLE GOING ON BETWEEN US, BETWEEN YOU AND I.
"SOMEHOW, IN YOUR CARPETED BOARDROOM, IN YOUR PANELLED OFFICE, YOU ARE PLOTTING TO TAKE AWAY FROM ME THE VERY CENTRE OF MY EXISTENCE.
"DEEP IN THE GLASS AND CONCRETE OF YOUR WORLD, YOU ARE STEALING MY SOUL.
"BY SCHEMING TO TORTURE MY LAND, YOU ARE TORTURING ME.
"BY PLOTTING TO INVADE MY LAND, YOU ARE INVADING ME.
"IF YOU EVER DIG A TRENCH THROUGH MY LAND, YOU ARE CUTTING THROUGH ME."

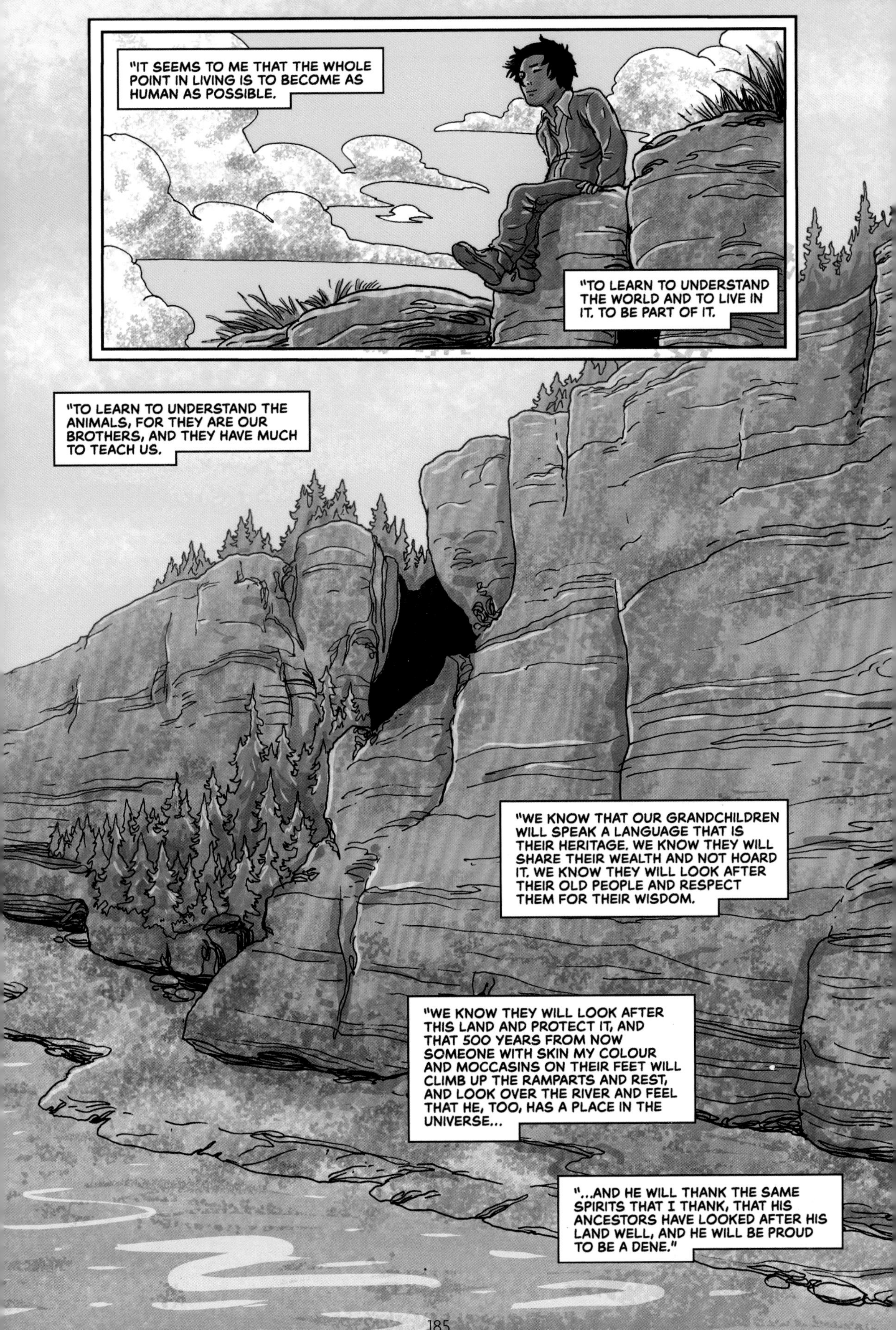
"IT SEEMS TO ME THAT THE WHOLE POINT IN LIVING IS TO BECOME AS HUMAN AS POSSIBLE.
"TO LEARN TO UNDERSTAND THE WORLD AND TO LIVE IN IT. TO BE PART OF IT.
"TO LEARN TO UNDERSTAND THE ANIMALS, FOR THEY ARE OUR BROTHERS, AND THEY HAVE MUCH TO TEACH US.
"WE KNOW THAT OUR GRANDCHILDREN WILL SPEAK A LANGUAGE THAT IS THEIR HERITAGE. WE KNOW THEY WILL SHARE THEIR WEALTH AND NOT HOARD IT. WE KNOW THEY WILL LOOK AFTER THEIR OLD PEOPLE AND RESPECT THEM FOR THEIR WISDOM.
"WE KNOW THEY WILL LOOK AFTER THIS LAND AND PROTECT IT, AND THAT 500 YEARS FROM NOW SOMEONE WITH SKIN MY COLOUR AND MOCCASINS ON THEIR FEET WILL CLIMB UP THE RAMPARTS AND REST, AND LOOK OVER THE RIVER AND FEEL THAT HE, TOO, HAS A PLACE IN THE UNIVERSE...
"...AND HE WILL THANK THE SAME SPIRITS THAT I THANK, THAT HIS ANCESTORS HAVE LOOKED AFTER HIS LAND WELL, AND HE WILL BE PROUD TO BE A DENE."

"IT IS FOR THIS UNBORN CHILD, MR. BERGER, THAT MY NATION WILL STOP THE PIPELINE, IT IS SO THIS UNBORN CHILD CAN KNOW THE FREEDOM OF THIS LAND THAT I AM WILLING TO LAY DOWN MY LIFE."[4]

JUDGE BERGER MADE SEVERAL HUGE RECOMMENDATIONS IN HIS MAY 1977 REPORT, INCLUDING THE CREATION OF A NATIONAL WILDERNESS PARK, BIRD SANCTUARIES, AND A SANCTUARY FOR THE ESTIMATED 5,000 WHITE WHALES OF THE BEAUFORT SEA.

If a pipeline were built now, it would bring limited economic benefits, its social impact would be devastating, and it would frustrate the goals of native claims.[5]

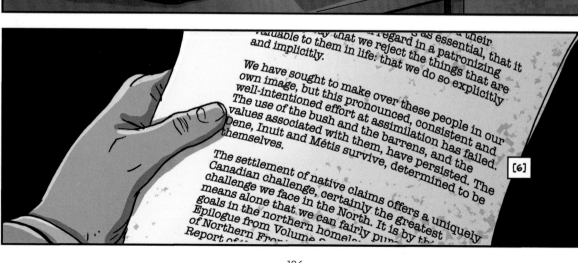

valuable to them in life: that we do so explicitly and implicitly.

We have sought to make over these people in our own image, but this pronounced, consistent and well-intentioned effort at assimilation has failed. The use of the bush and the barrens, and the values associated with them, have persisted. The Dene, Inuit and Métis survive, determined to be themselves.

The settlement of native claims offers a uniquely Canadian challenge, certainly the greatest challenge we face in the North. It is by the means alone that we can fairly p... goals in the northern homel... Epilogue from Volume ... of Northern Fr... Report of...

[6]

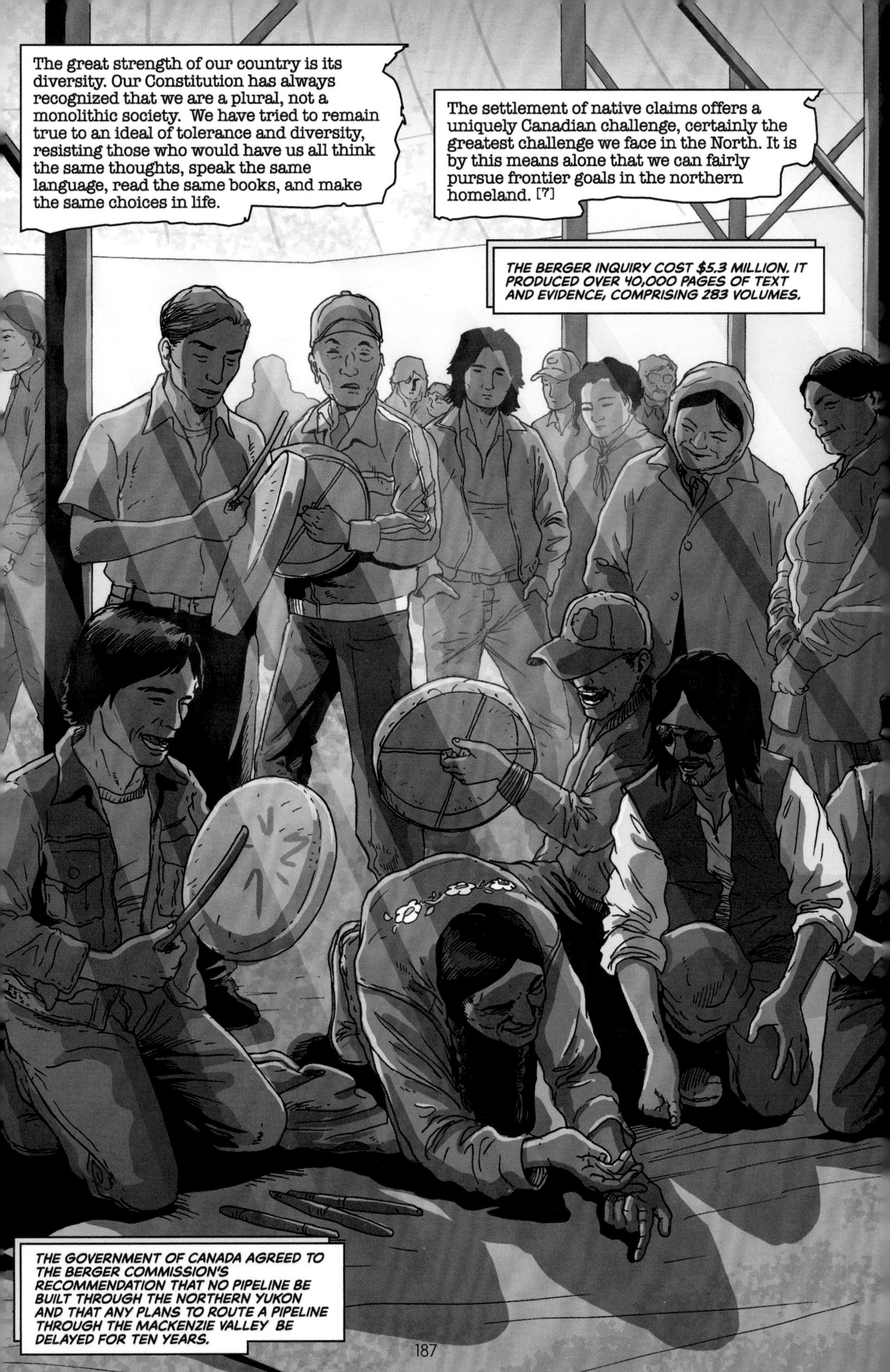
The great strength of our country is its diversity. Our Constitution has always recognized that we are a plural, not a monolithic society. We have tried to remain true to an ideal of tolerance and diversity, resisting those who would have us all think the same thoughts, speak the same language, read the same books, and make the same choices in life.
The settlement of native claims offers a uniquely Canadian challenge, certainly the greatest challenge we face in the North. It is by this means alone that we can fairly pursue frontier goals in the northern homeland. [7]
THE BERGER INQUIRY COST $5.3 MILLION. IT PRODUCED OVER 40,000 PAGES OF TEXT AND EVIDENCE, COMPRISING 283 VOLUMES.
THE GOVERNMENT OF CANADA AGREED TO THE BERGER COMMISSION'S RECOMMENDATION THAT NO PIPELINE BE BUILT THROUGH THE NORTHERN YUKON AND THAT ANY PLANS TO ROUTE A PIPELINE THROUGH THE MACKENZIE VALLEY BE DELAYED FOR TEN YEARS.

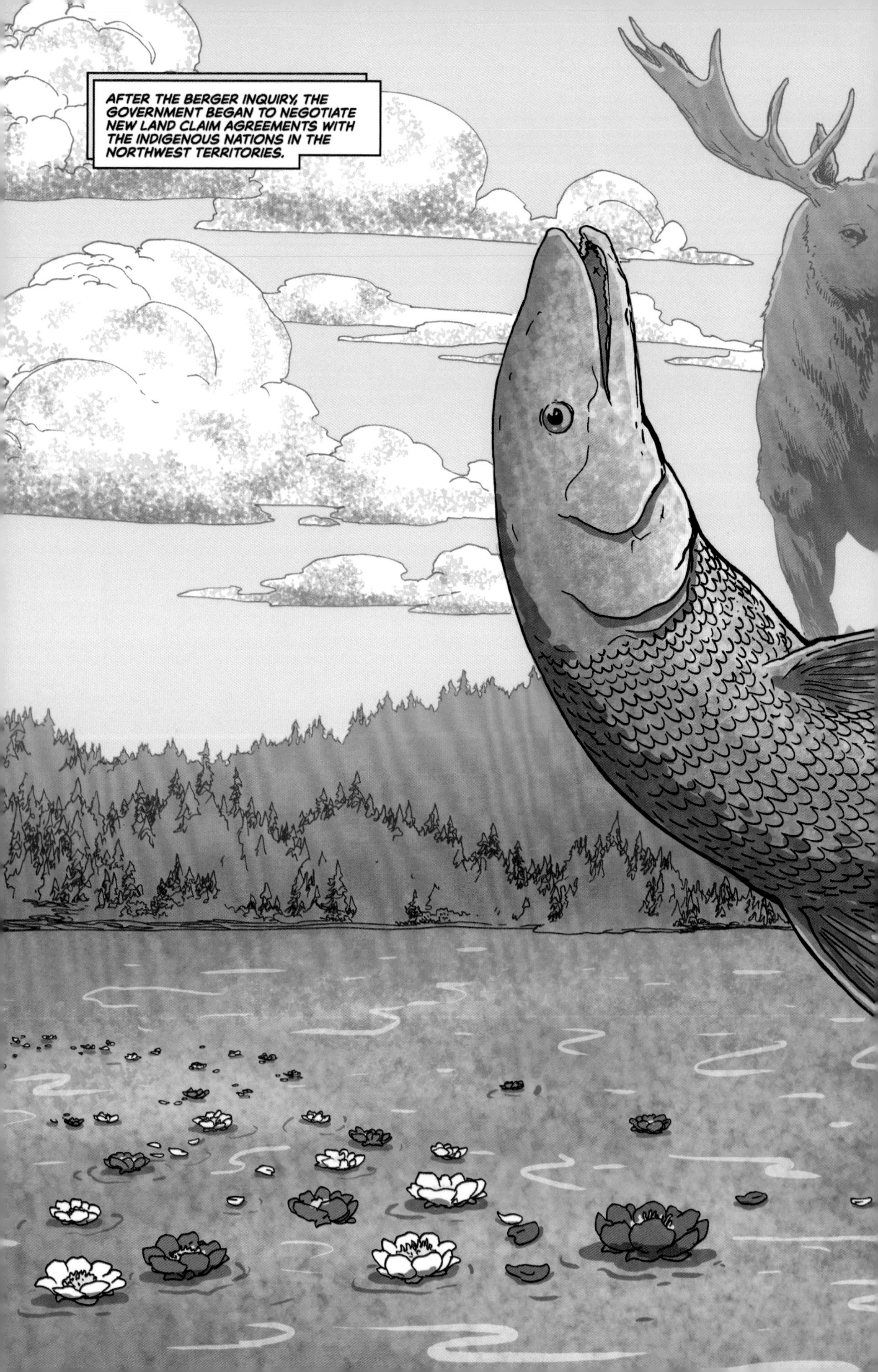
AFTER THE BERGER INQUIRY, THE GOVERNMENT BEGAN TO NEGOTIATE NEW LAND CLAIM AGREEMENTS WITH THE INDIGENOUS NATIONS IN THE NORTHWEST TERRITORIES.

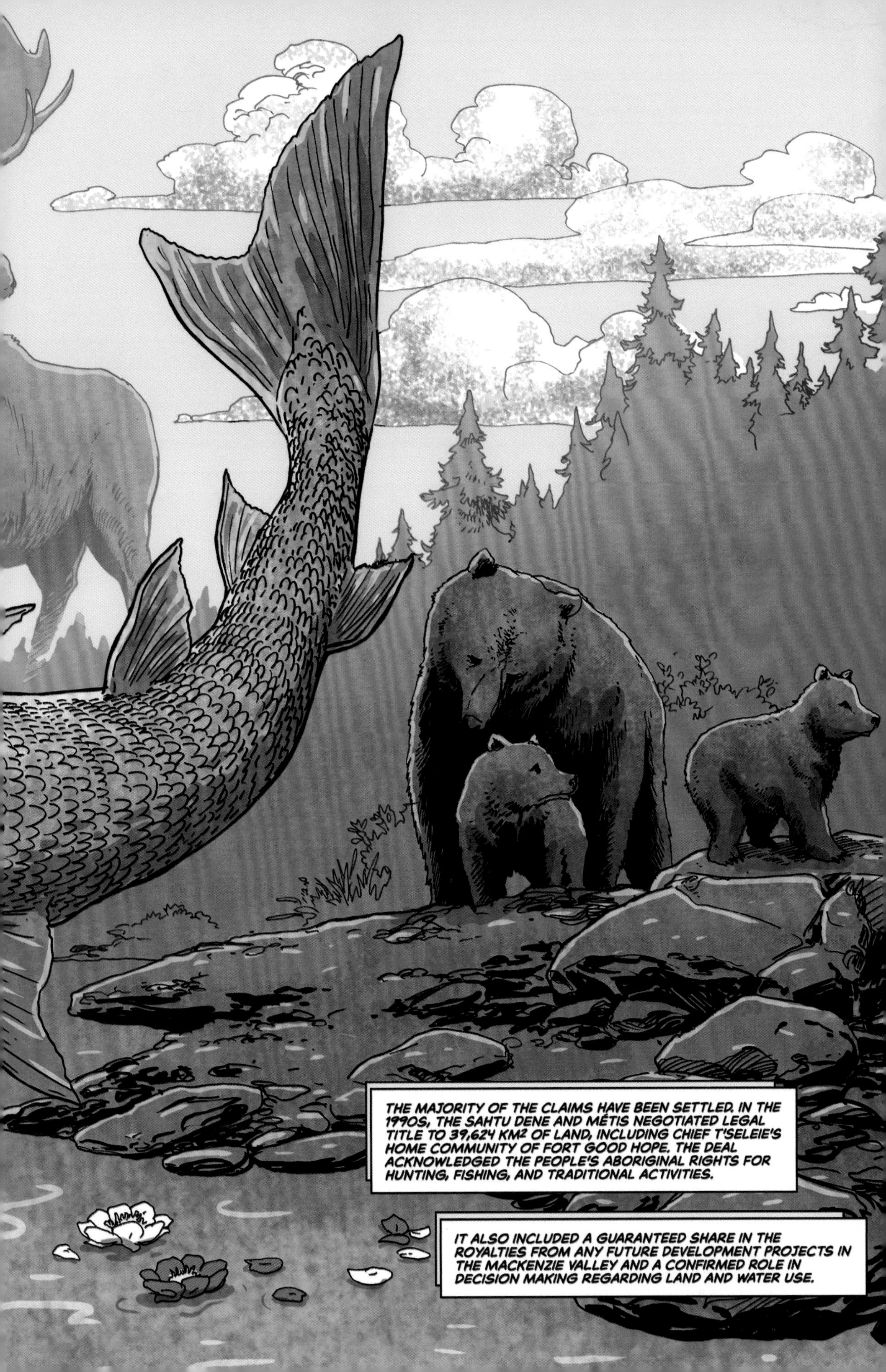
THE MAJORITY OF THE CLAIMS HAVE BEEN SETTLED. IN THE 1990S, THE SAHTU DENE AND MÉTIS NEGOTIATED LEGAL TITLE TO 39,624 KM² OF LAND, INCLUDING CHIEF T'SELEIE'S HOME COMMUNITY OF FORT GOOD HOPE. THE DEAL ACKNOWLEDGED THE PEOPLE'S ABORIGINAL RIGHTS FOR HUNTING, FISHING, AND TRADITIONAL ACTIVITIES.
IT ALSO INCLUDED A GUARANTEED SHARE IN THE ROYALTIES FROM ANY FUTURE DEVELOPMENT PROJECTS IN THE MACKENZIE VALLEY AND A CONFIRMED ROLE IN DECISION MAKING REGARDING LAND AND WATER USE.

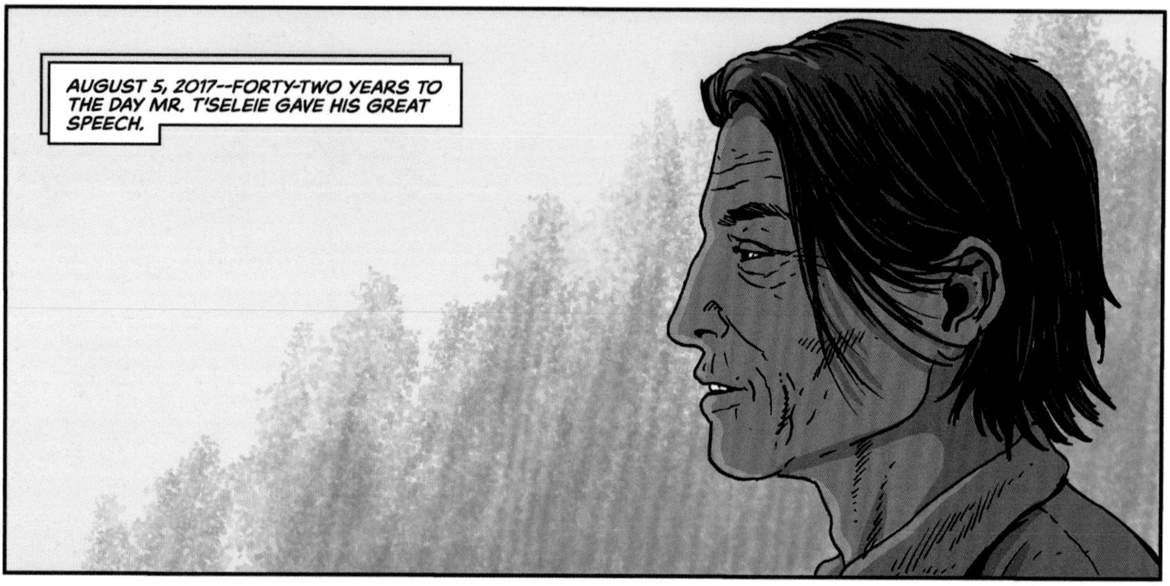
AUGUST 5, 2017--FORTY-TWO YEARS TO THE DAY MR. T'SELEIE GAVE HIS GREAT SPEECH.

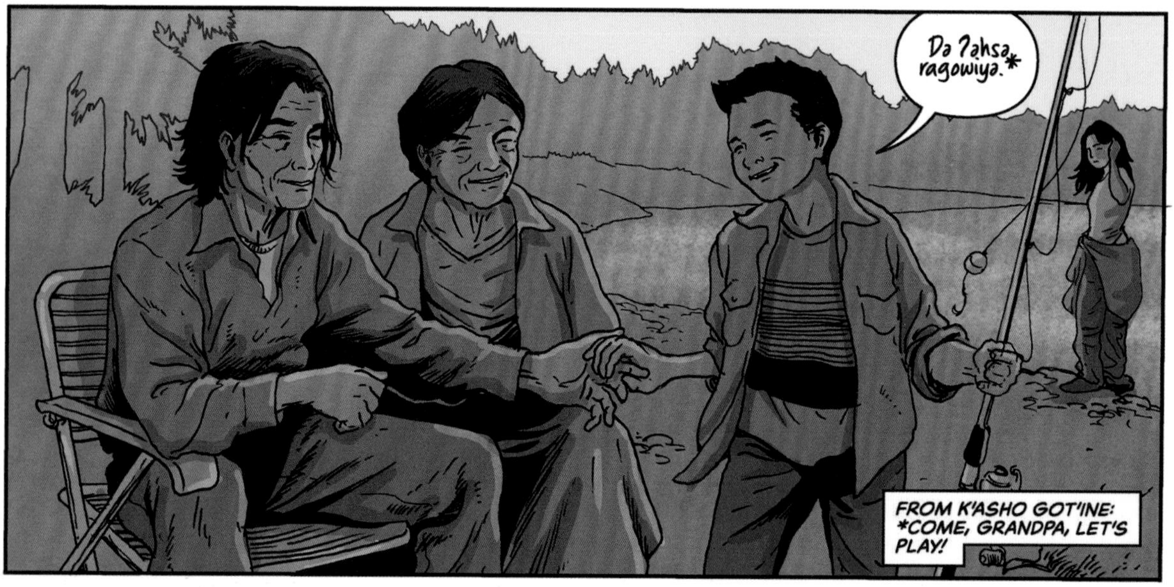
Də ʔə̨hsə̨ ragowiyə.*
FROM K'ASHO GOT'INE: *COME, GRANDPA, LET'S PLAY!

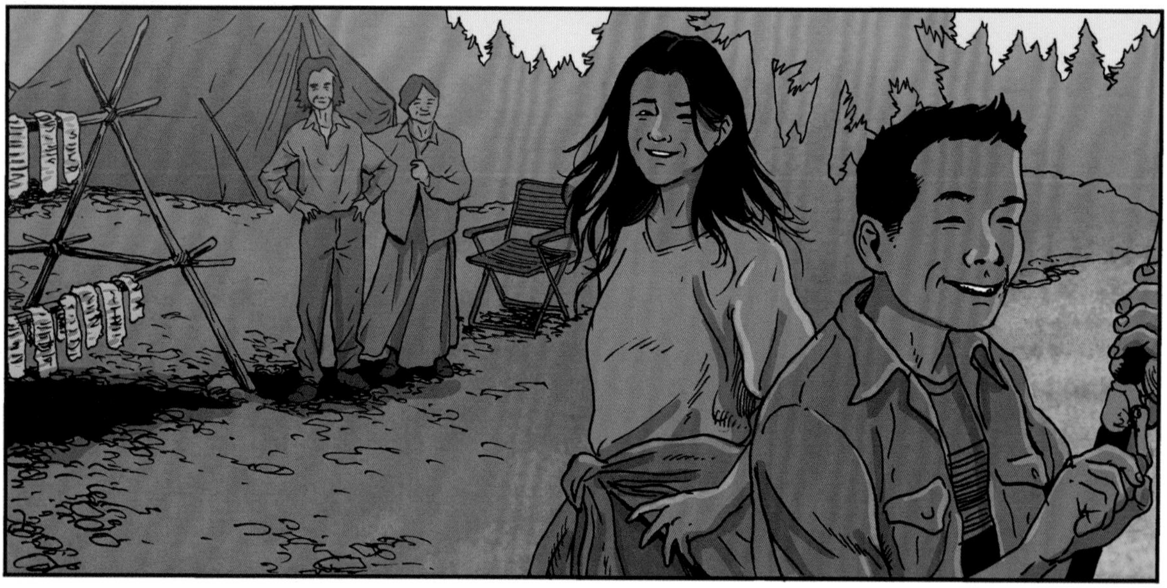

L istuguj is my home. My earliest memories are of rod-fishing on the river banks at sunrise with my father and younger brother. My father would talk to us about our right to fish, and our responsibility to respect the cycle of the salmon. We fish to feed ourselves and to share with those who can't.

The raids of 1981 were rarely mentioned growing up. As I grew older, when I told people from other First Nation communities that I was from Listuguj, I was surprised at how many replied with, "I remember being there in '81…". They shared vivid stories about supporting us during the raids.

When the opportunity came to share this story, I didn't know where to begin. I didn't want to cover the same ground as Alanis Obomsawin's compelling documentary, *Incident at Restigouche*[1]. I mentioned the project to my mother-in-law; she wanted me to start with the 1980 raid. I was confused—"There was an earlier raid?" I began researching, and found stories on the "salmon wars" of the 1970s. I discovered that there were many smaller raids that had taken place in Listuguj and other Indigenous communities in Quebec in the lead-up to 1981, including one larger raid in 1980. I found my direction.

This story is dedicated to everyone who shared their stories of the raids with me.

Brandon Mitchell

1975
James Bay and Northern Quebec agreements are signed.

1977
Montagnais people assert fishing rights by 'trespassing' on private fishing clubs.

1978
The Northeastern Quebec Agreement is signed between Quebec and the Naskapi.

1981, JUNE 11
500 Quebec Provincial Police (QPP) and fishing wardens raid Listiguj in a failed attempt to end Indigenous fishers' traditional, treaty-enshrined practices.

1983-1987
For the first time, Indigenous peoples are invited into constitutional negotiations at a series of ministers' conferences.

1982, APRIL 17
The Constitution Act affirms existing Indigenous and treaty rights and defines "the aboriginal peoples of Canada" as Indian, Inuit, and Métis.

1981, JUNE 20
The QPP and fishing wardens raid Listiguj a second time.

Migwite'tmeg: We Remember It

Brandon Mitchell

Illustration: Tara Audibert

Colours: Donovan Yaciuk

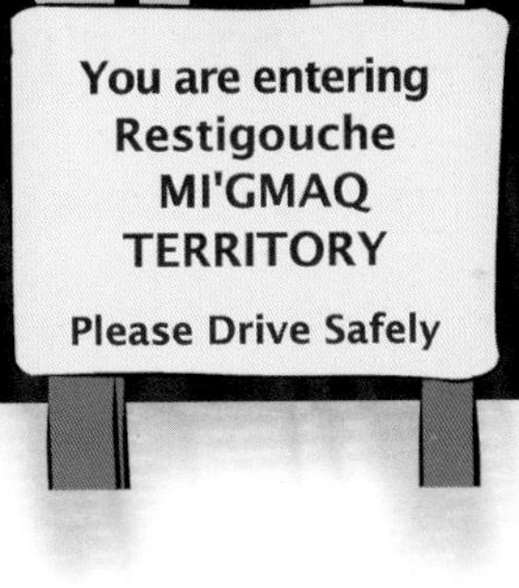
You are entering
Restigouche
MI'GMAQ
TERRITORY
Please Drive Safely

1983
The Constitution Act of 1982 is amended to ensure equal rights for Indigenous men and women.

1984
The Supreme Court confirms Mi'gmaq title to lands, as described in 18th century treaties.

1985
Amendments to the Indian Act extend formal status to the Métis, those who live off-reserve, and women who had lost status through marriage (Bill C-31).

1986, OCTOBER 9
Sechelt First Nation in British Columbia becomes the first to break from the Indian Act, with the passing of the Sechelt Indian Band Self-Government Act.

1987
Indigenous groups successfully argue at a First Ministers Conference that self-government is an inherent right.

1993
The Listiguj Mi'gmaq pass their own law to regulate fishing within their territories.

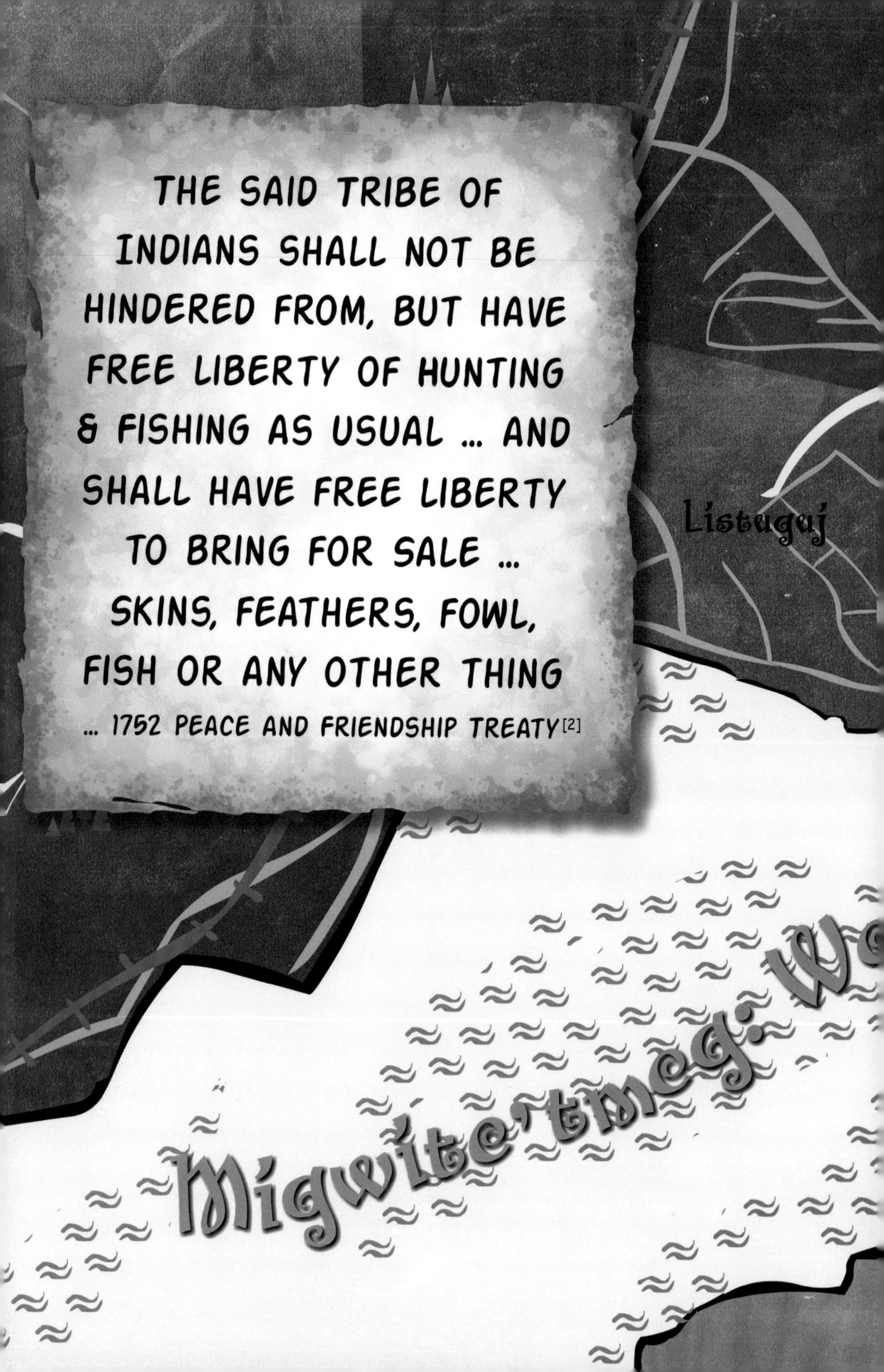
THE SAID TRIBE OF INDIANS SHALL NOT BE HINDERED FROM, BUT HAVE FREE LIBERTY OF HUNTING & FISHING AS USUAL ... AND SHALL HAVE FREE LIBERTY TO BRING FOR SALE ... SKINS, FEATHERS, FOWL, FISH OR ANY OTHER THING
... 1752 PEACE AND FRIENDSHIP TREATY[2]
Listuguj
Migwite'tmeg:

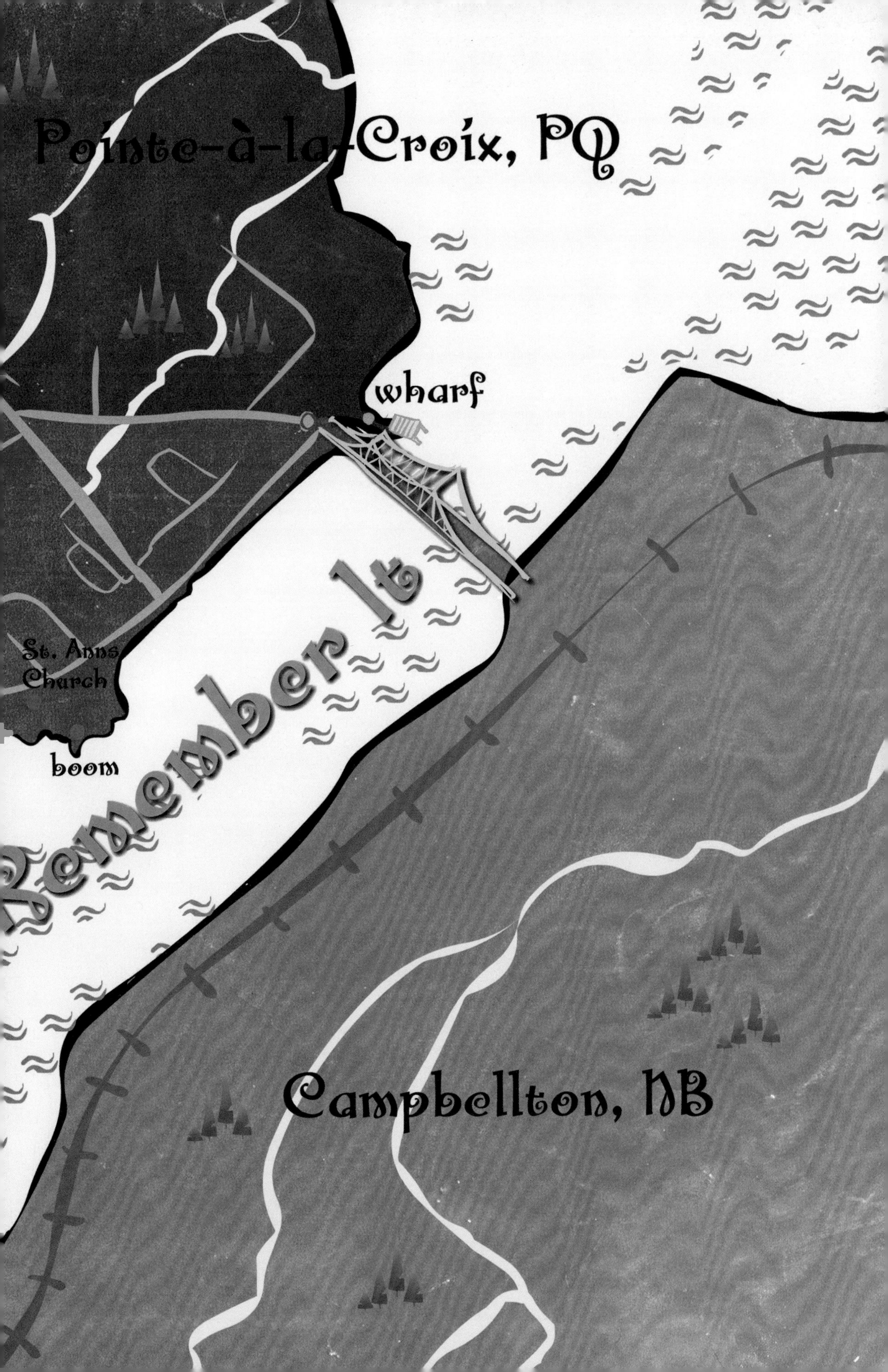
Pointe-à-la-Croix, PQ
wharf
St. Anns
Church
boom
Remember It
Campbellton, NB

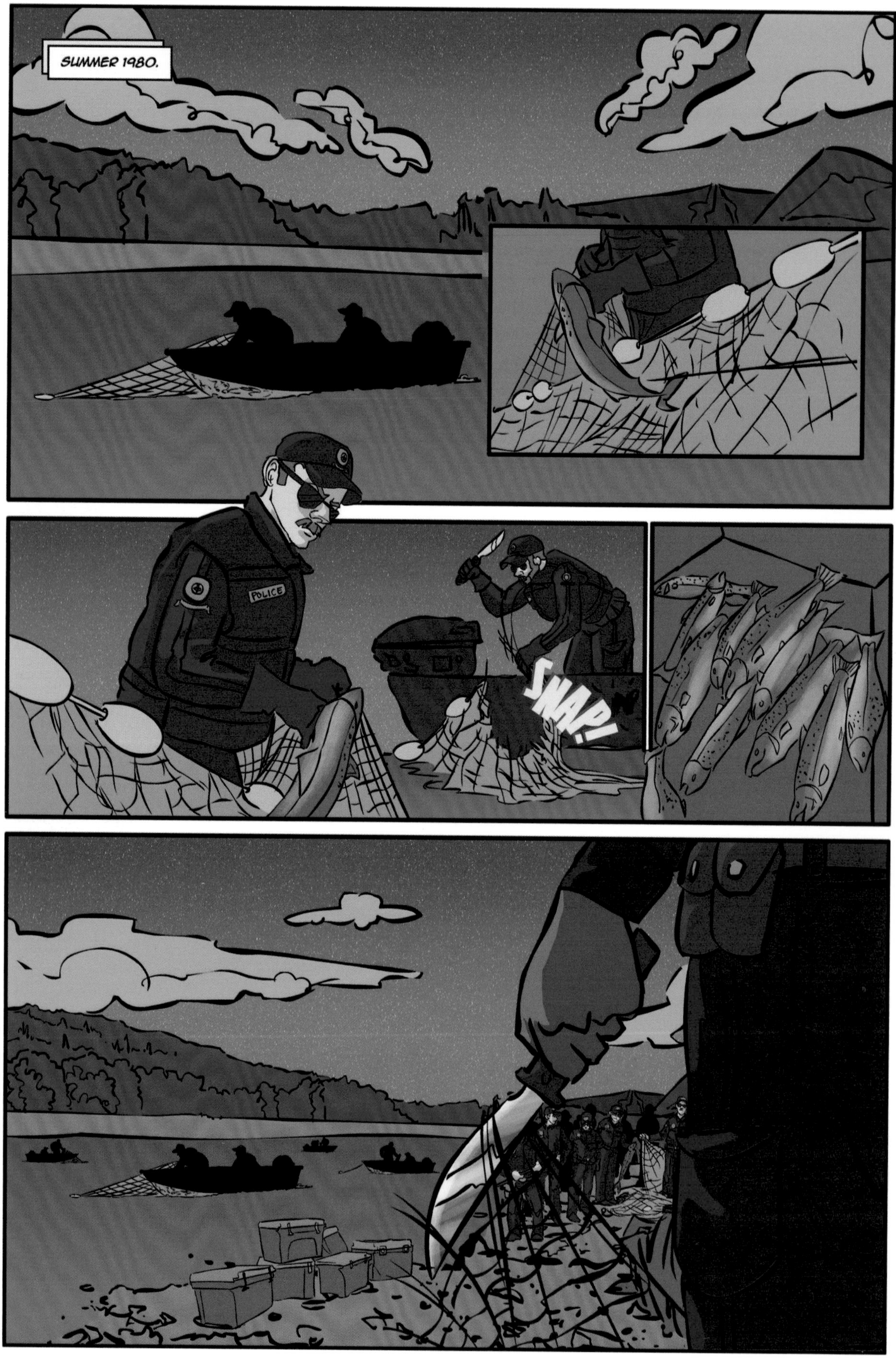
SUMMER 1980.
POLICE
SNAP!

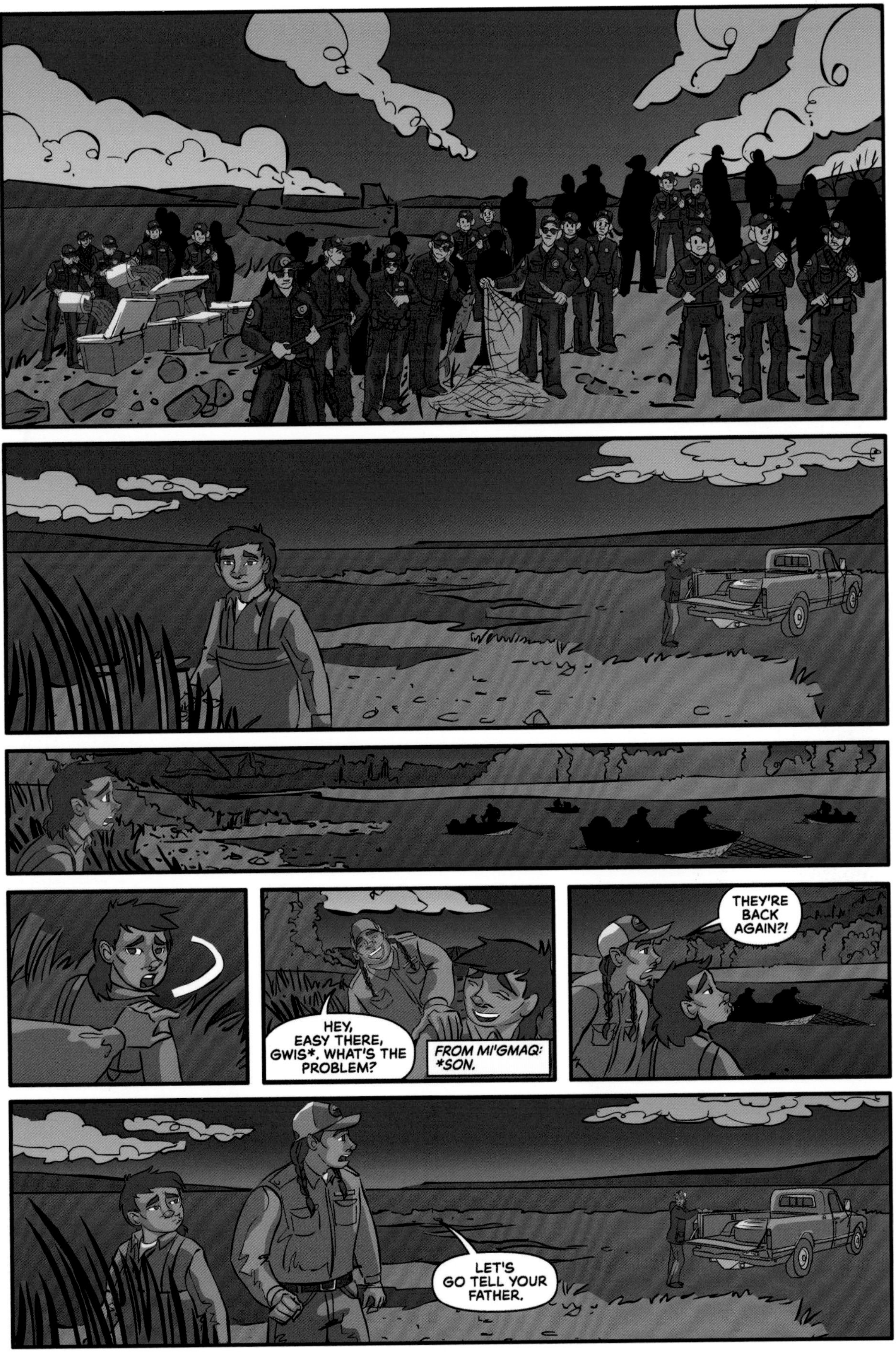
HEY, EASY THERE, GWIS*. WHAT'S THE PROBLEM?
FROM MI'GMAQ: *SON.
THEY'RE BACK AGAIN?!
LET'S GO TELL YOUR FATHER.

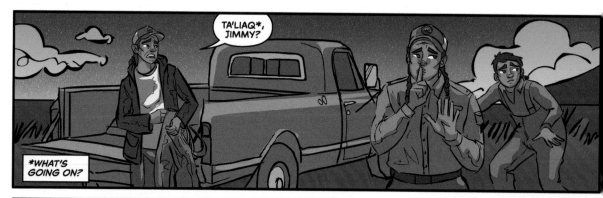

TA'LIAQ*, JIMMY?

*WHAT'S GOING ON?

HOW MANY THIS TIME?

MAYBE FIFTY. WARDENS AND QPP FROM THE LOOKS OF IT.

THEY'RE NOT GOING TO GET AWAY WITH IT THIS TIME.

WALTER, TELL AS MANY PEOPLE AS POSSIBLE TO COME MEET US BACK HERE. SEE IF YOU CAN RING THE CHURCH BELLS.

LEAVE THE TRUCK. WE DON'T WANT THEM TO HEAR US.

I'LL GO GET THE CHIEF.

GWIS, GO TO AUNTY'S HOUSE.

TELL THEM WHAT'S GOING ON.

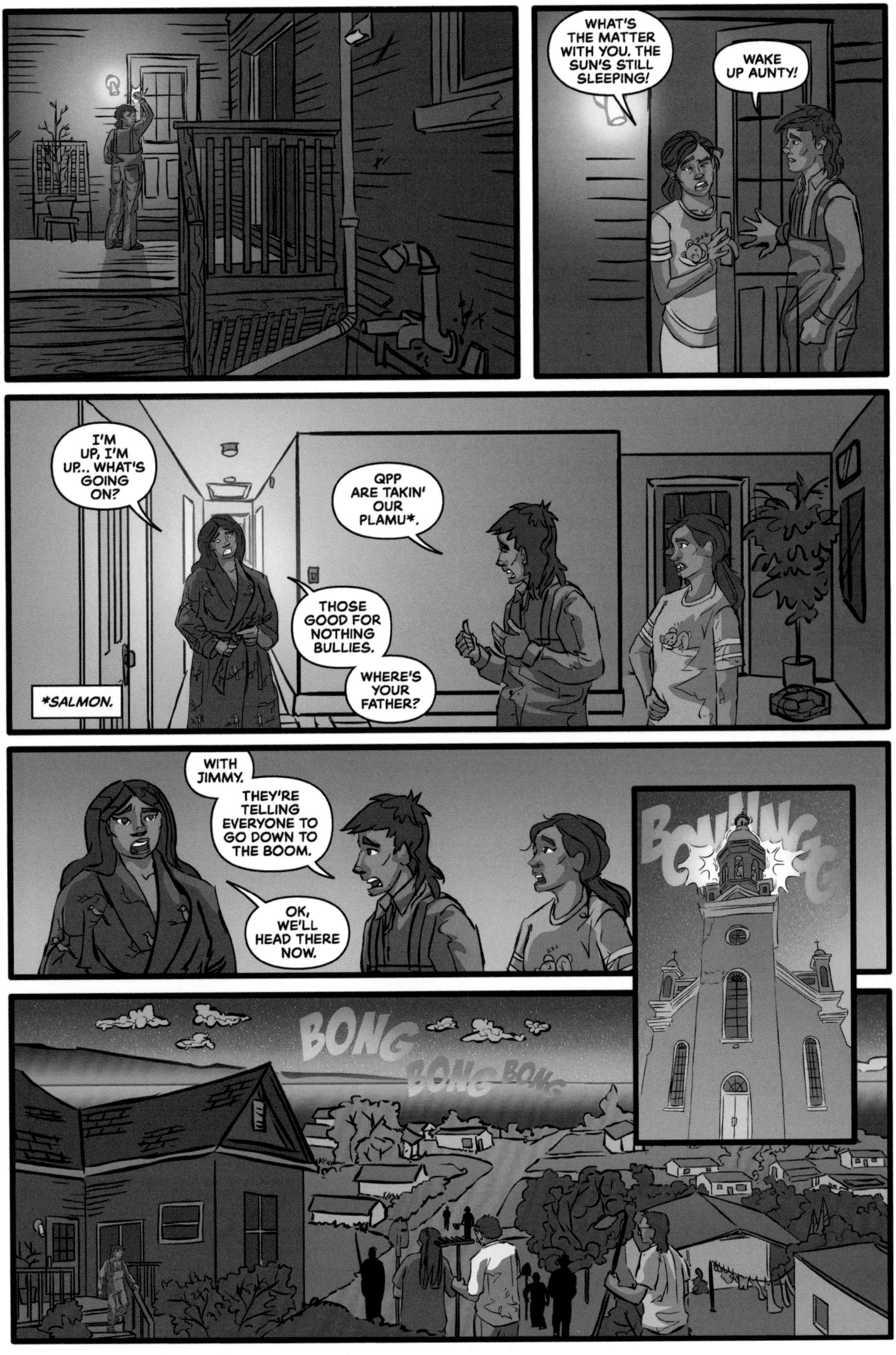
WHAT'S THE MATTER WITH YOU. THE SUN'S STILL SLEEPING!
WAKE UP AUNTY!
I'M UP, I'M UP... WHAT'S GOING ON?
QPP ARE TAKIN' OUR PLAMU*.
THOSE GOOD FOR NOTHING BULLIES.
WHERE'S YOUR FATHER?
*SALMON.
WITH JIMMY.
THEY'RE TELLING EVERYONE TO GO DOWN TO THE BOOM.
OK, WE'LL HEAD THERE NOW.
BONG
BONG BONG

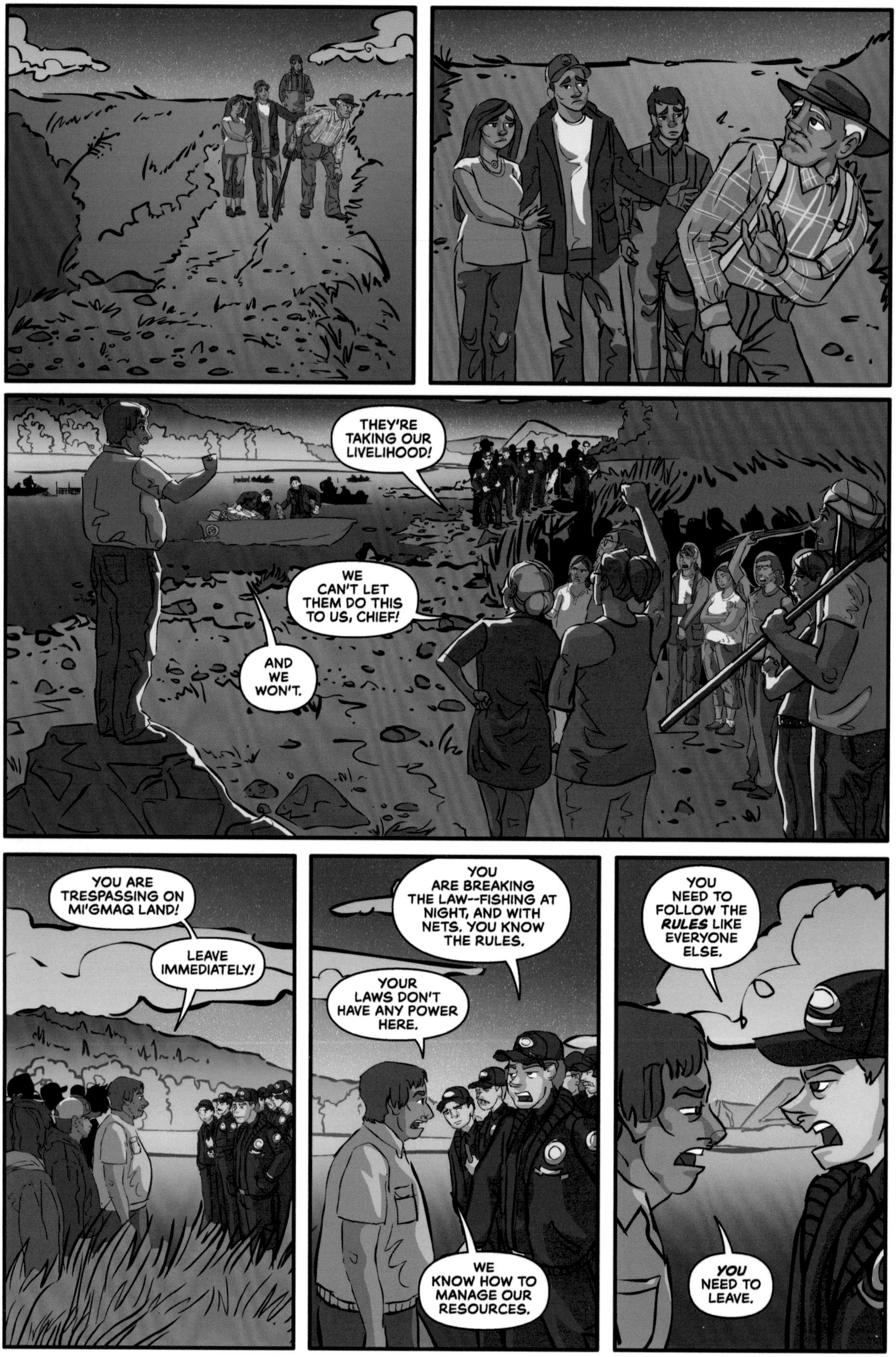
THEY'RE TAKING OUR LIVELIHOOD!
WE CAN'T LET THEM DO THIS TO US, CHIEF!
AND WE WON'T.
YOU ARE TRESPASSING ON MI'GMAQ LAND!
LEAVE IMMEDIATELY!
YOU ARE BREAKING THE LAW--FISHING AT NIGHT, AND WITH NETS. YOU KNOW THE RULES.
YOUR LAWS DON'T HAVE ANY POWER HERE.
WE KNOW HOW TO MANAGE OUR RESOURCES.
YOU NEED TO FOLLOW THE *RULES* LIKE EVERYONE ELSE.
YOU NEED TO LEAVE.

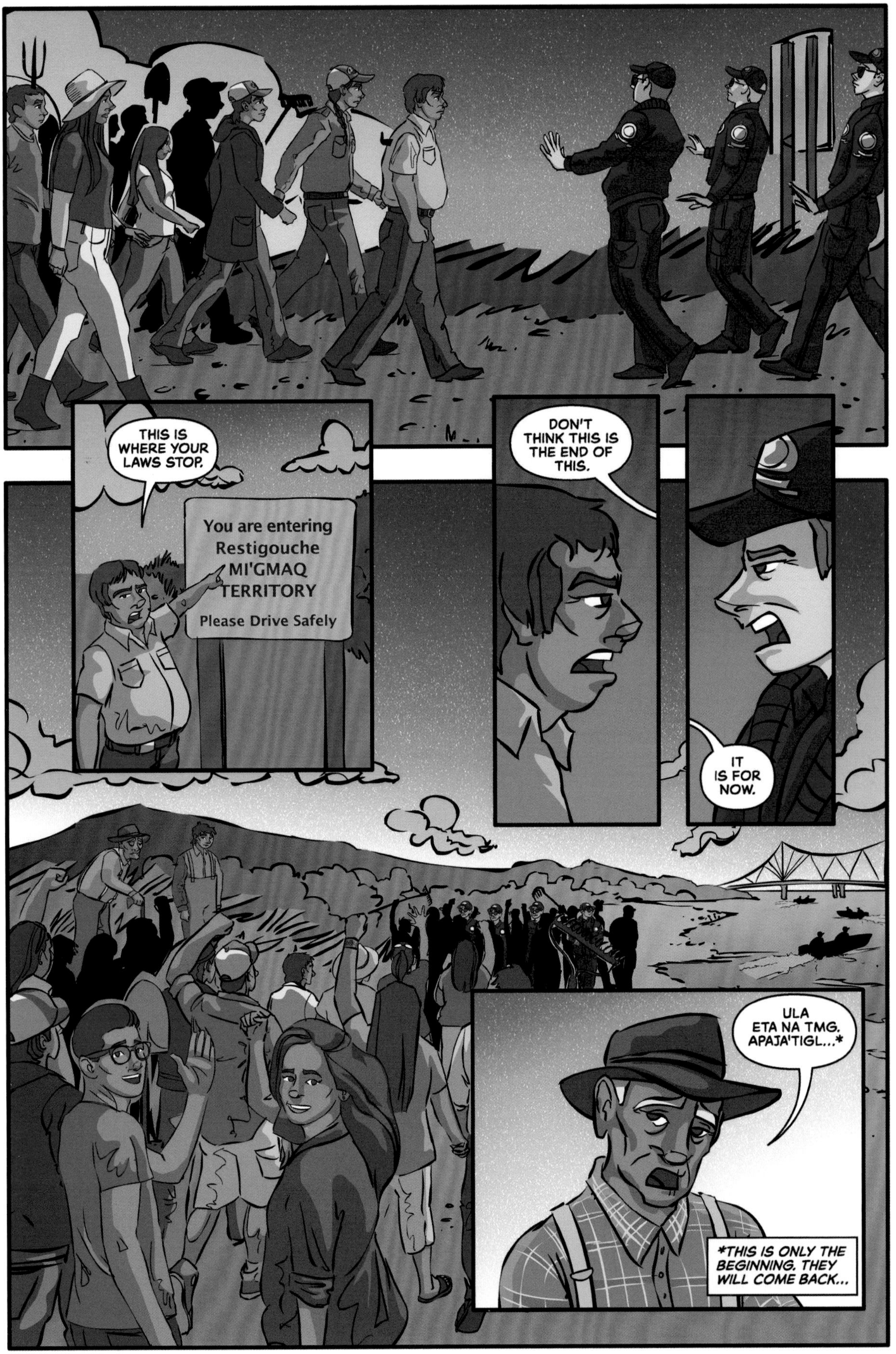
THIS IS WHERE YOUR LAWS STOP.
You are entering Restigouche MI'GMAQ TERRITORY Please Drive Safely
DON'T THINK THIS IS THE END OF THIS.
IT IS FOR NOW.
ULA ETA NA TMG. APAJA'TIGL...*
*THIS IS ONLY THE BEGINNING. THEY WILL COME BACK...

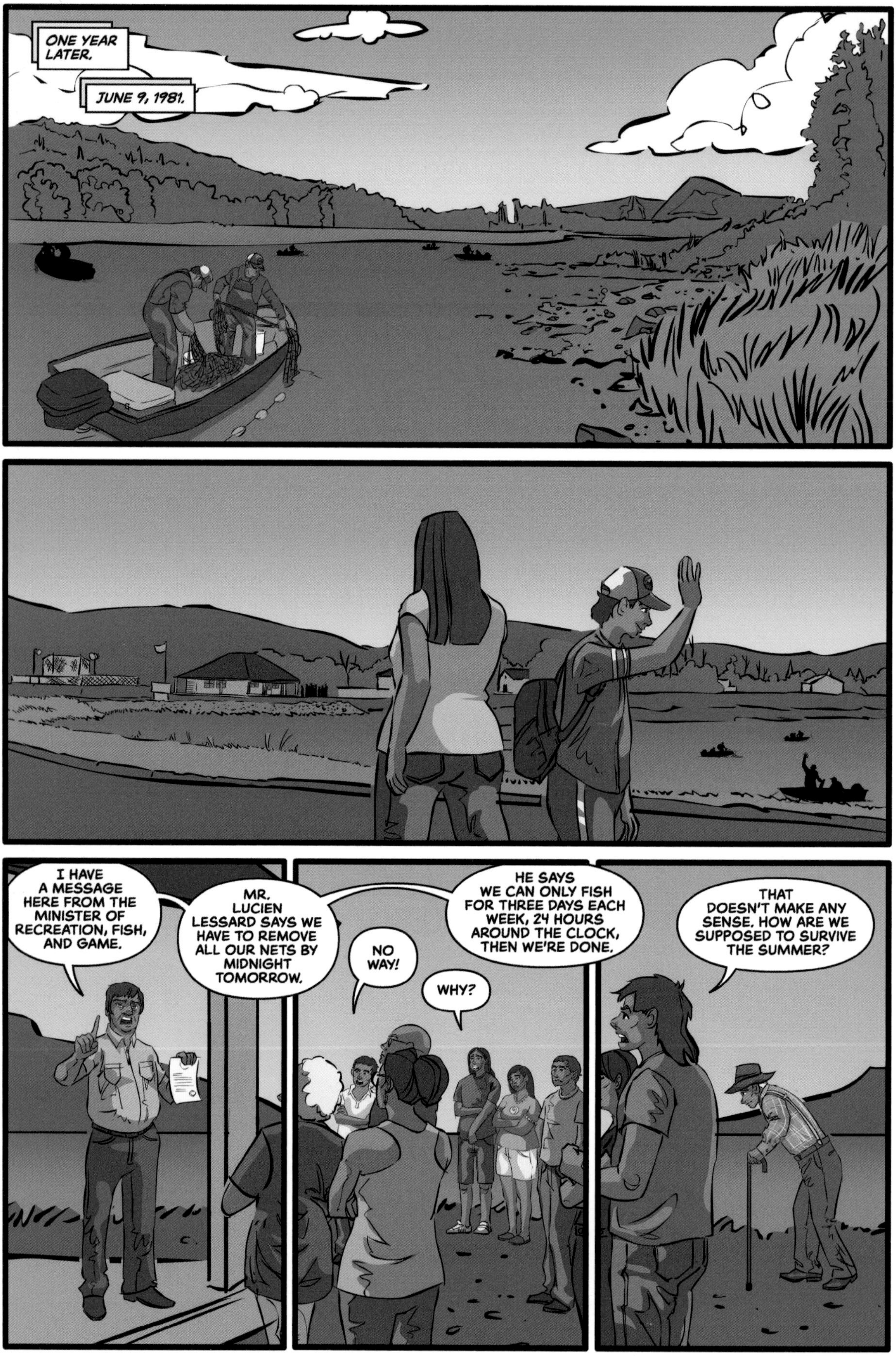
ONE YEAR LATER.
JUNE 9, 1981.
I HAVE A MESSAGE HERE FROM THE MINISTER OF RECREATION, FISH, AND GAME.
MR. LUCIEN LESSARD SAYS WE HAVE TO REMOVE ALL OUR NETS BY MIDNIGHT TOMORROW.
NO WAY!
WHY?
HE SAYS WE CAN ONLY FISH FOR THREE DAYS EACH WEEK, 24 HOURS AROUND THE CLOCK, THEN WE'RE DONE.
THAT DOESN'T MAKE ANY SENSE. HOW ARE WE SUPPOSED TO SURVIVE THE SUMMER?

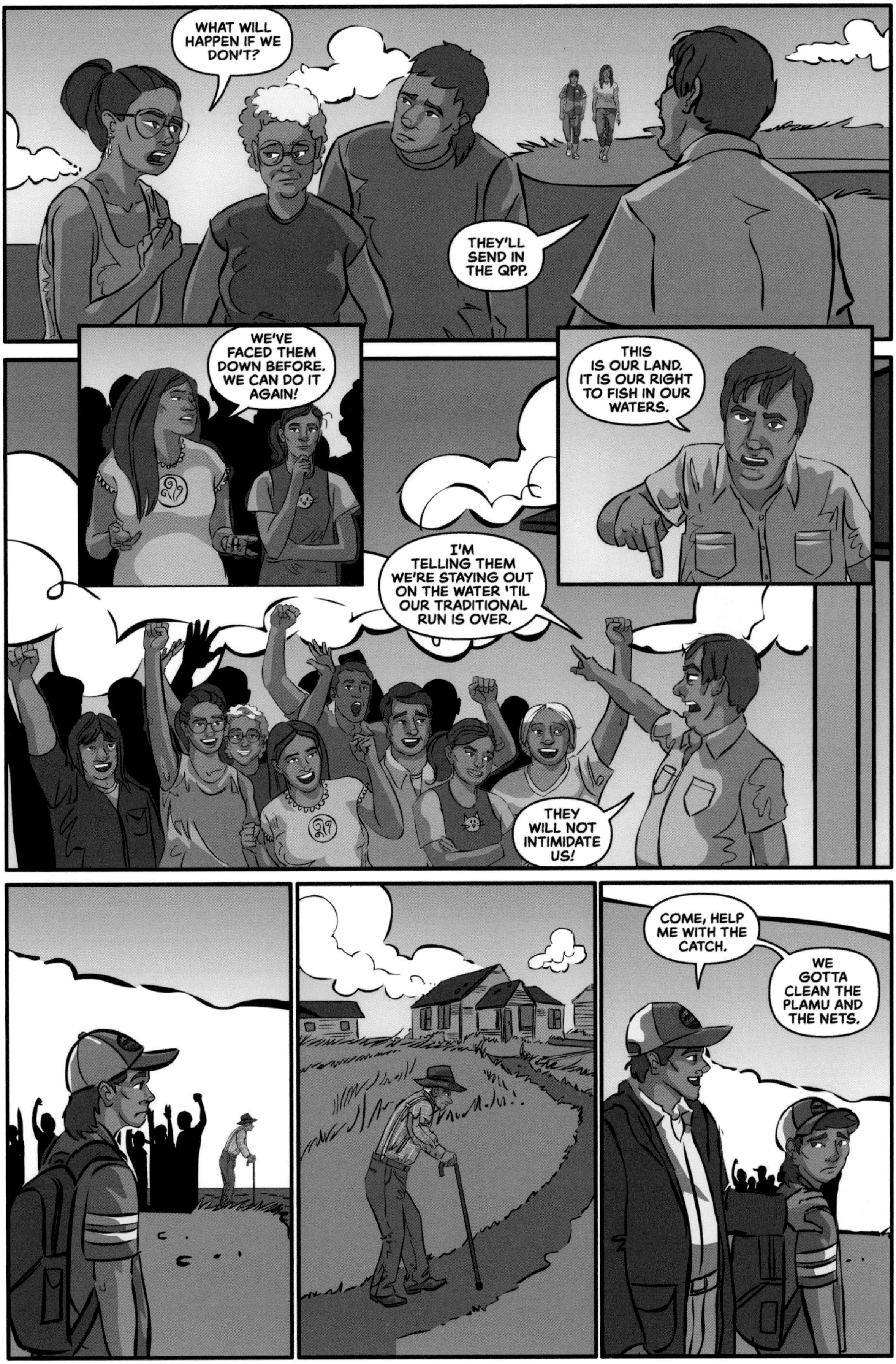
WHAT WILL HAPPEN IF WE DON'T?
THEY'LL SEND IN THE QPP.
WE'VE FACED THEM DOWN BEFORE. WE CAN DO IT AGAIN!
THIS IS OUR LAND. IT IS OUR RIGHT TO FISH IN OUR WATERS.
I'M TELLING THEM WE'RE STAYING OUT ON THE WATER 'TIL OUR TRADITIONAL RUN IS OVER.
THEY WILL NOT INTIMIDATE US!
COME, HELP ME WITH THE CATCH.
WE GOTTA CLEAN THE PLAMU AND THE NETS.

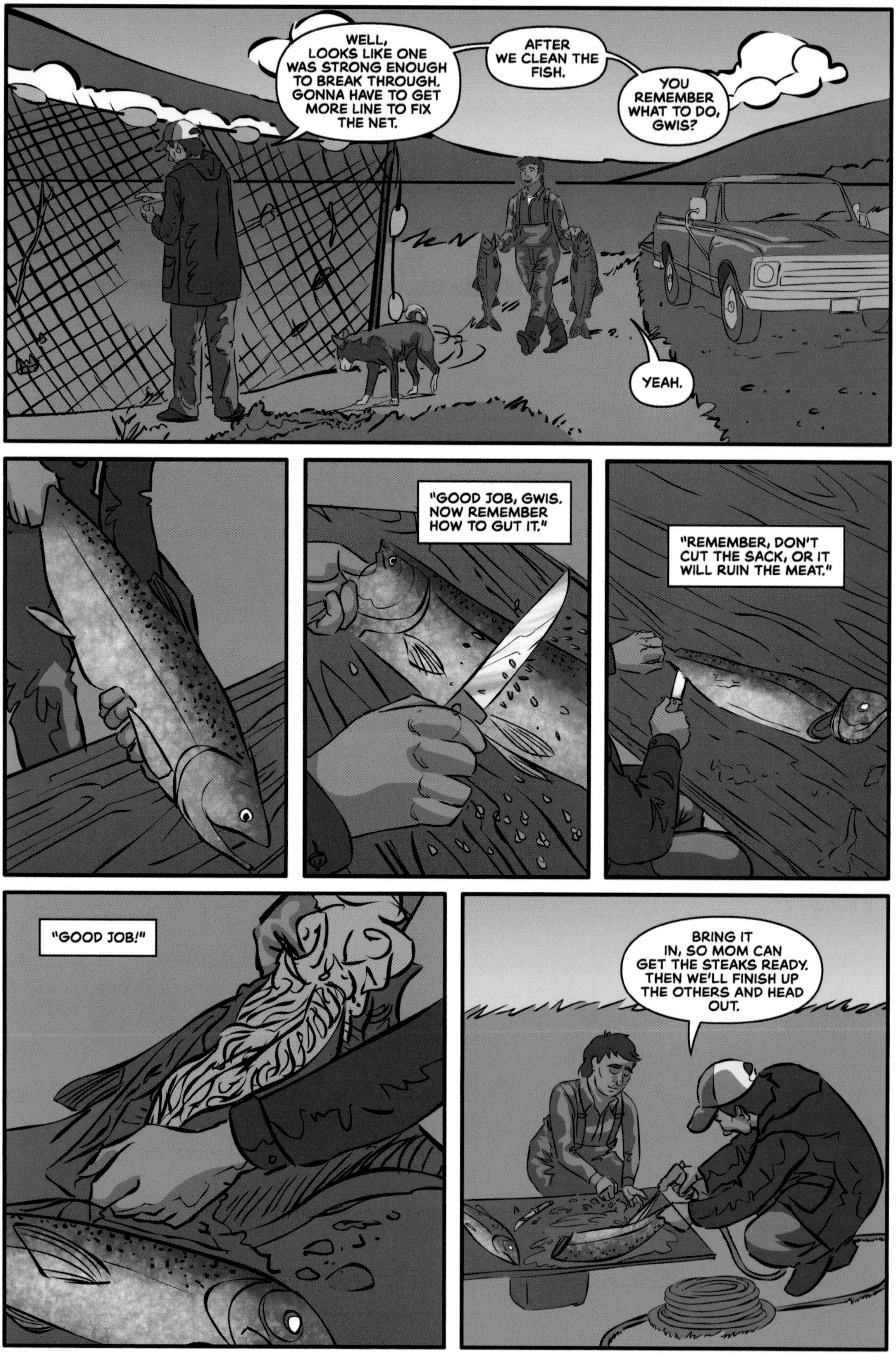
WELL, LOOKS LIKE ONE WAS STRONG ENOUGH TO BREAK THROUGH. GONNA HAVE TO GET MORE LINE TO FIX THE NET.
AFTER WE CLEAN THE FISH.
YOU REMEMBER WHAT TO DO, GWIS?
YEAH.
"GOOD JOB, GWIS. NOW REMEMBER HOW TO GUT IT."
"REMEMBER, DON'T CUT THE SACK, OR IT WILL RUIN THE MEAT."
"GOOD JOB!"
BRING IT IN, SO MOM CAN GET THE STEAKS READY. THEN WE'LL FINISH UP THE OTHERS AND HEAD OUT.

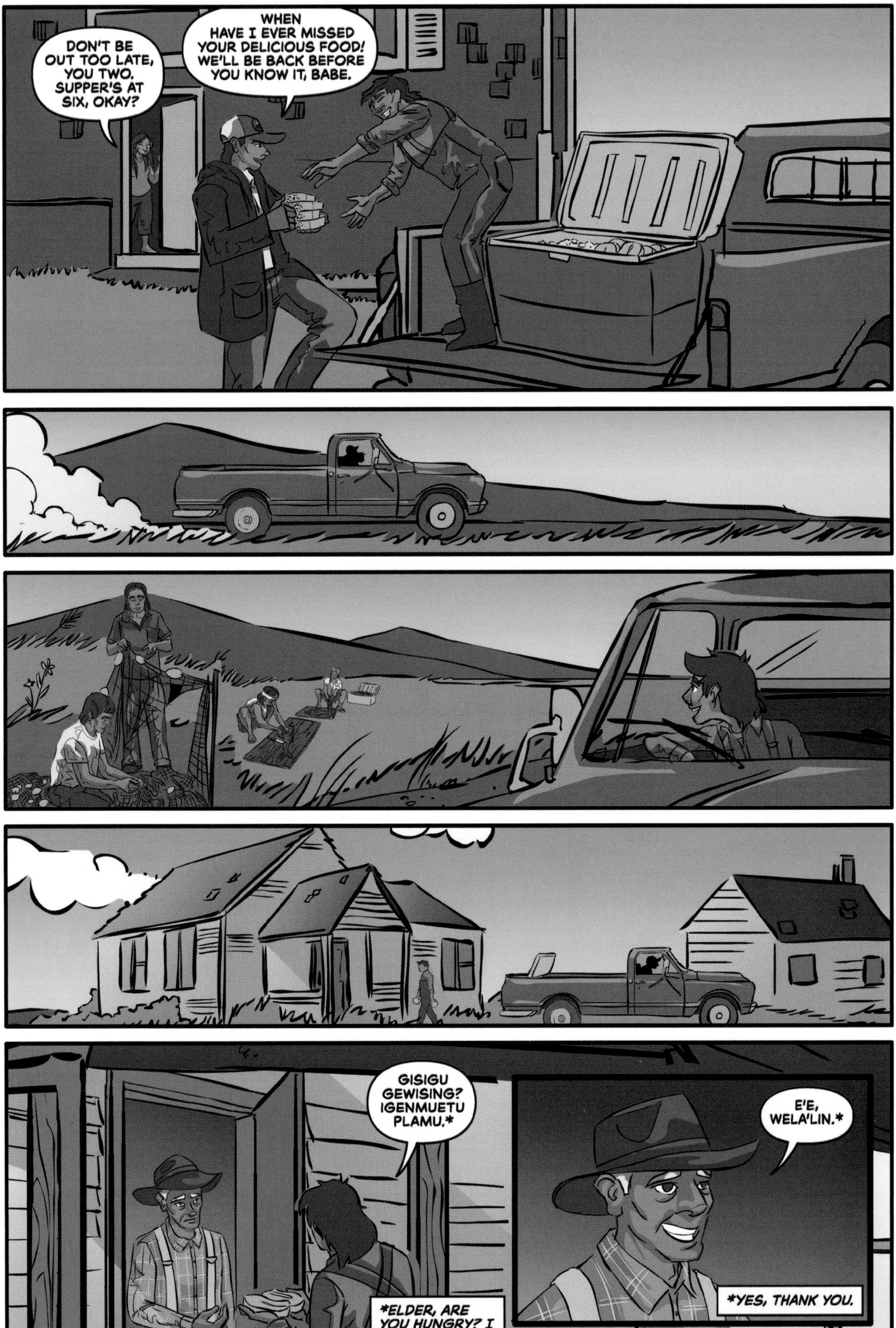
DON'T BE OUT TOO LATE, YOU TWO. SUPPER'S AT SIX, OKAY?
WHEN HAVE I EVER MISSED YOUR DELICIOUS FOOD! WE'LL BE BACK BEFORE YOU KNOW IT, BABE.
GISIGU GEWISING? IGENMUETU PLAMU.*
*ELDER, ARE YOU HUNGRY? I HAVE SALMON.
E'E, WELA'LIN.*
*YES, THANK YOU.

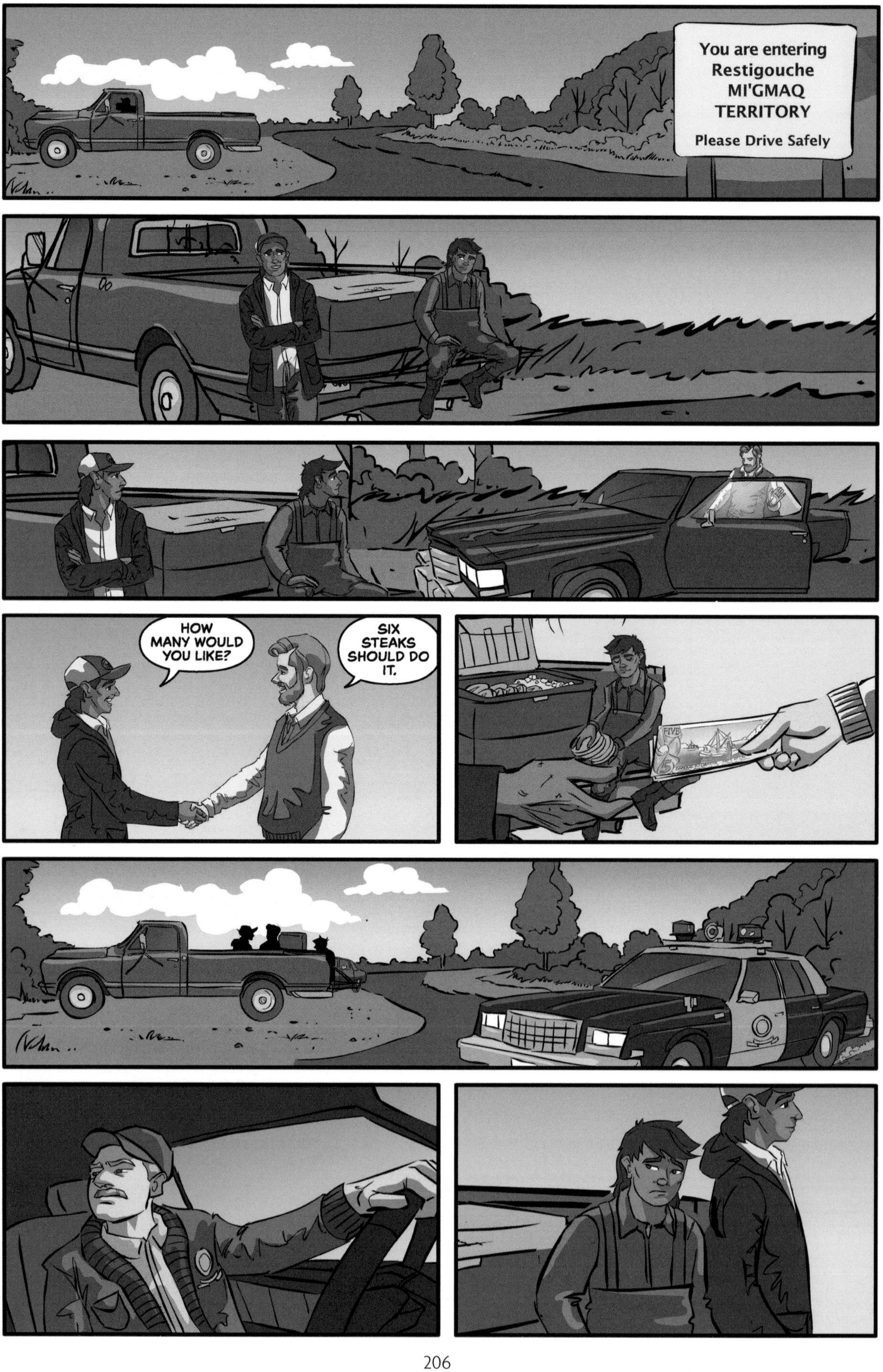
You are entering
Restigouche
MI'GMAQ
TERRITORY
Please Drive Safely
HOW MANY WOULD YOU LIKE?
SIX STEAKS SHOULD DO IT.

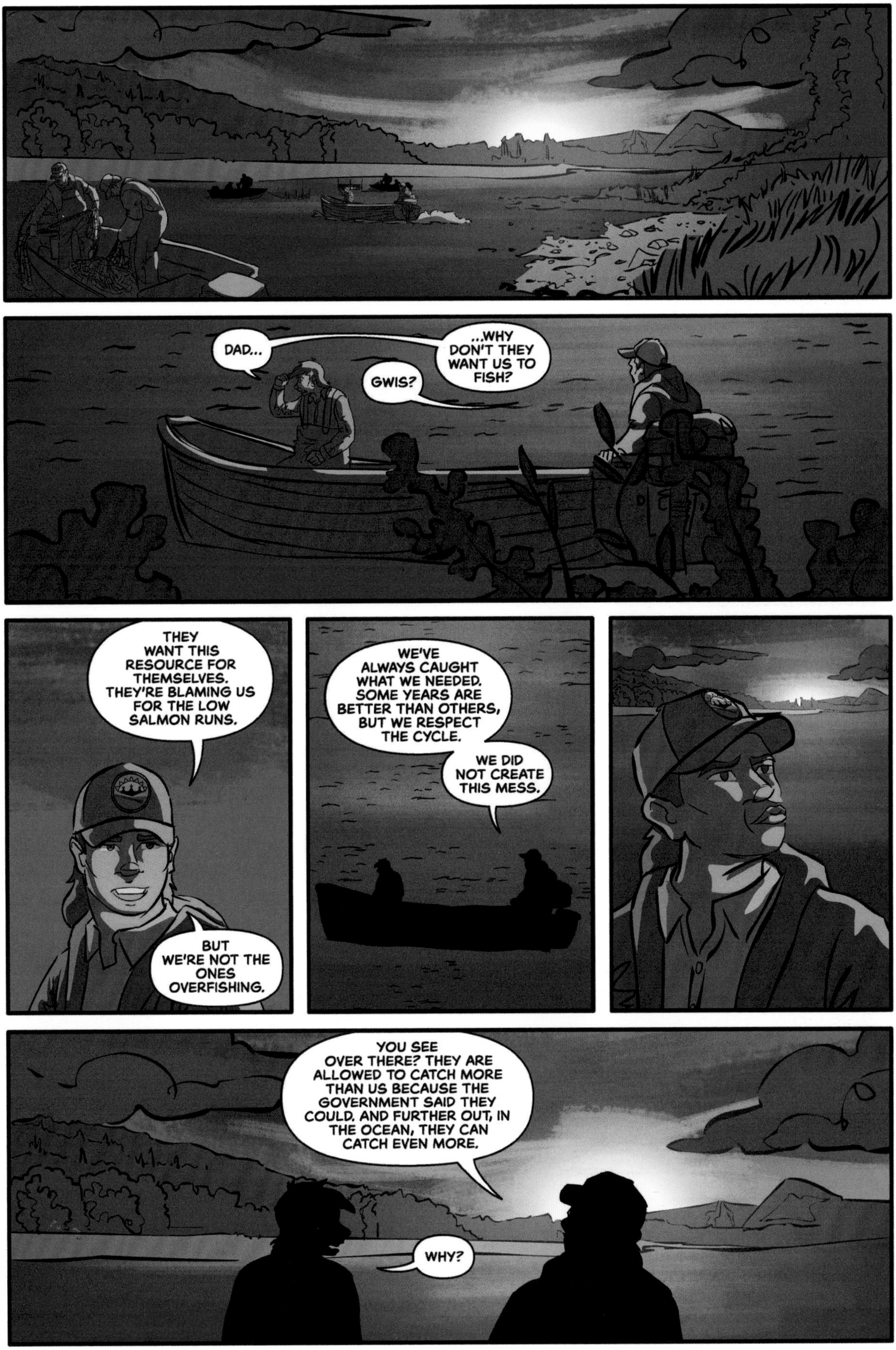
DAD...
...WHY DON'T THEY WANT US TO FISH?
GWIS?
THEY WANT THIS RESOURCE FOR THEMSELVES. THEY'RE BLAMING US FOR THE LOW SALMON RUNS.
BUT WE'RE NOT THE ONES OVERFISHING.
WE'VE ALWAYS CAUGHT WHAT WE NEEDED. SOME YEARS ARE BETTER THAN OTHERS, BUT WE RESPECT THE CYCLE.
WE DID NOT CREATE THIS MESS.
YOU SEE OVER THERE? THEY ARE ALLOWED TO CATCH MORE THAN US BECAUSE THE GOVERNMENT SAID THEY COULD. AND FURTHER OUT, IN THE OCEAN, THEY CAN CATCH EVEN MORE.
WHY?

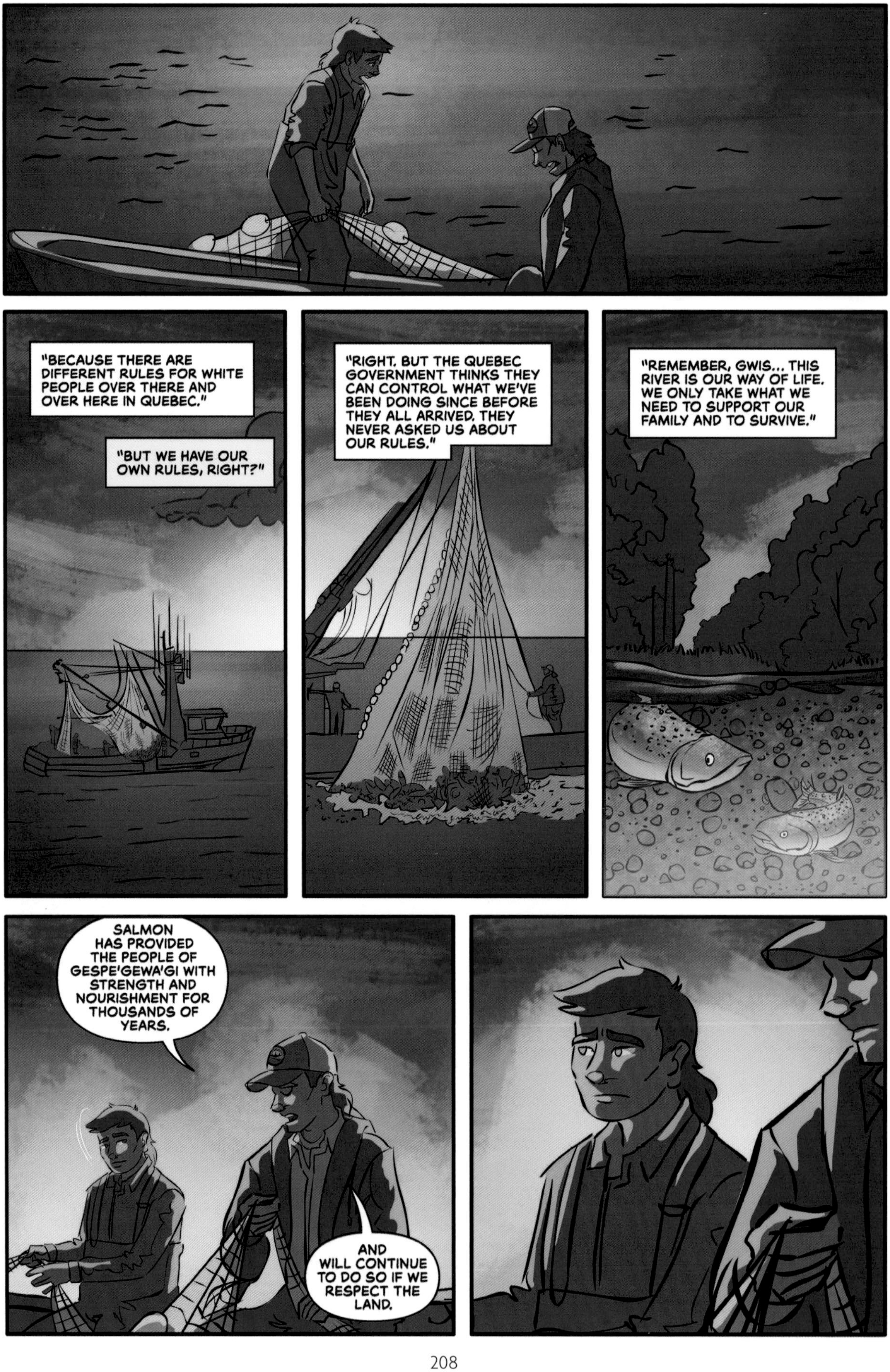
"BECAUSE THERE ARE DIFFERENT RULES FOR WHITE PEOPLE OVER THERE AND OVER HERE IN QUEBEC."
"BUT WE HAVE OUR OWN RULES, RIGHT?"
"RIGHT. BUT THE QUEBEC GOVERNMENT THINKS THEY CAN CONTROL WHAT WE'VE BEEN DOING SINCE BEFORE THEY ALL ARRIVED. THEY NEVER ASKED US ABOUT OUR RULES."
"REMEMBER, GWIS... THIS RIVER IS OUR WAY OF LIFE. WE ONLY TAKE WHAT WE NEED TO SUPPORT OUR FAMILY AND TO SURVIVE."
SALMON HAS PROVIDED THE PEOPLE OF GESPE'GEWA'GI WITH STRENGTH AND NOURISHMENT FOR THOUSANDS OF YEARS.
AND WILL CONTINUE TO DO SO IF WE RESPECT THE LAND.

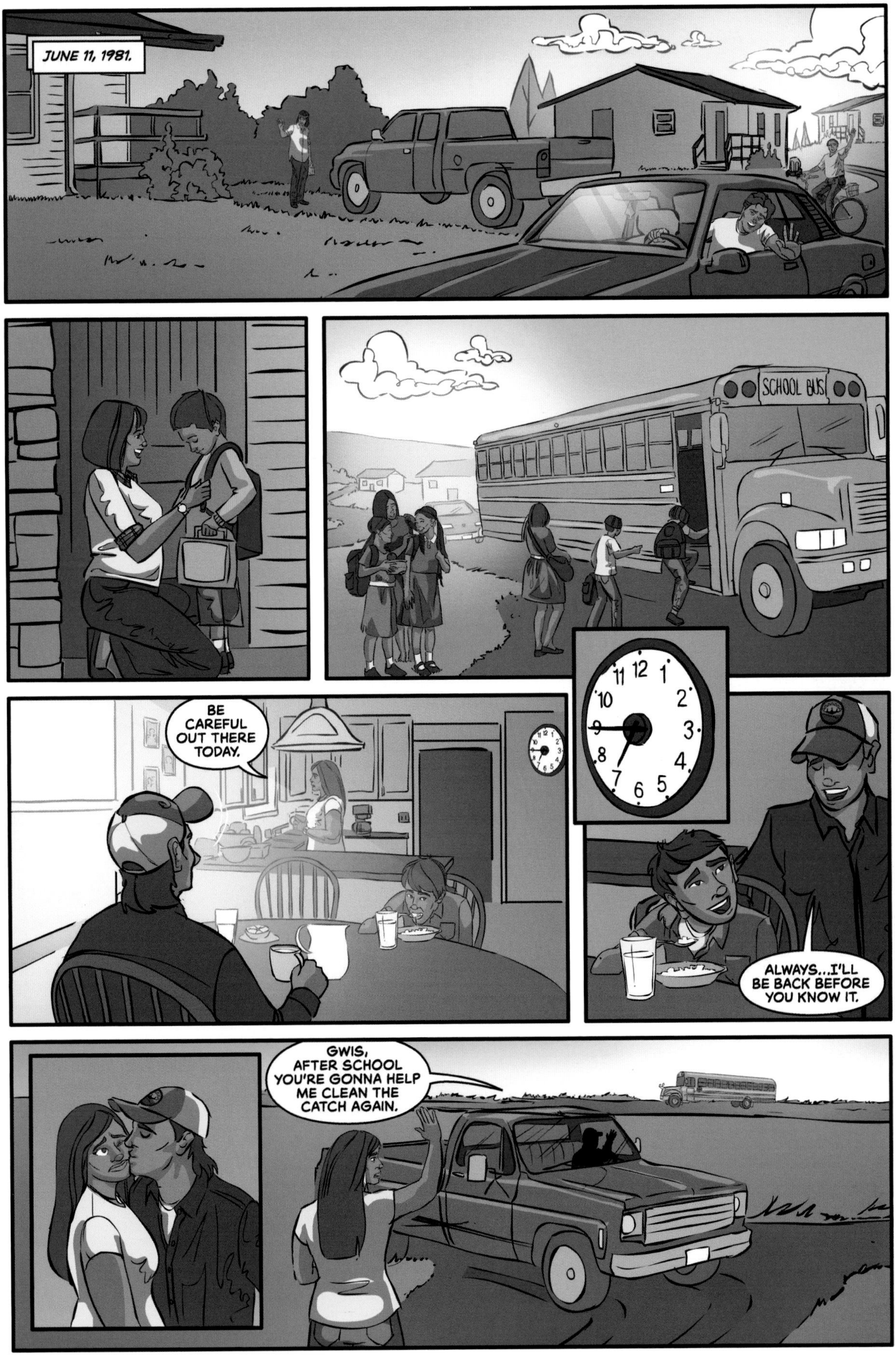
JUNE 11, 1981.
SCHOOL BUS
BE CAREFUL OUT THERE TODAY.
ALWAYS...I'LL BE BACK BEFORE YOU KNOW IT.
GWIS, AFTER SCHOOL YOU'RE GONNA HELP ME CLEAN THE CATCH AGAIN.

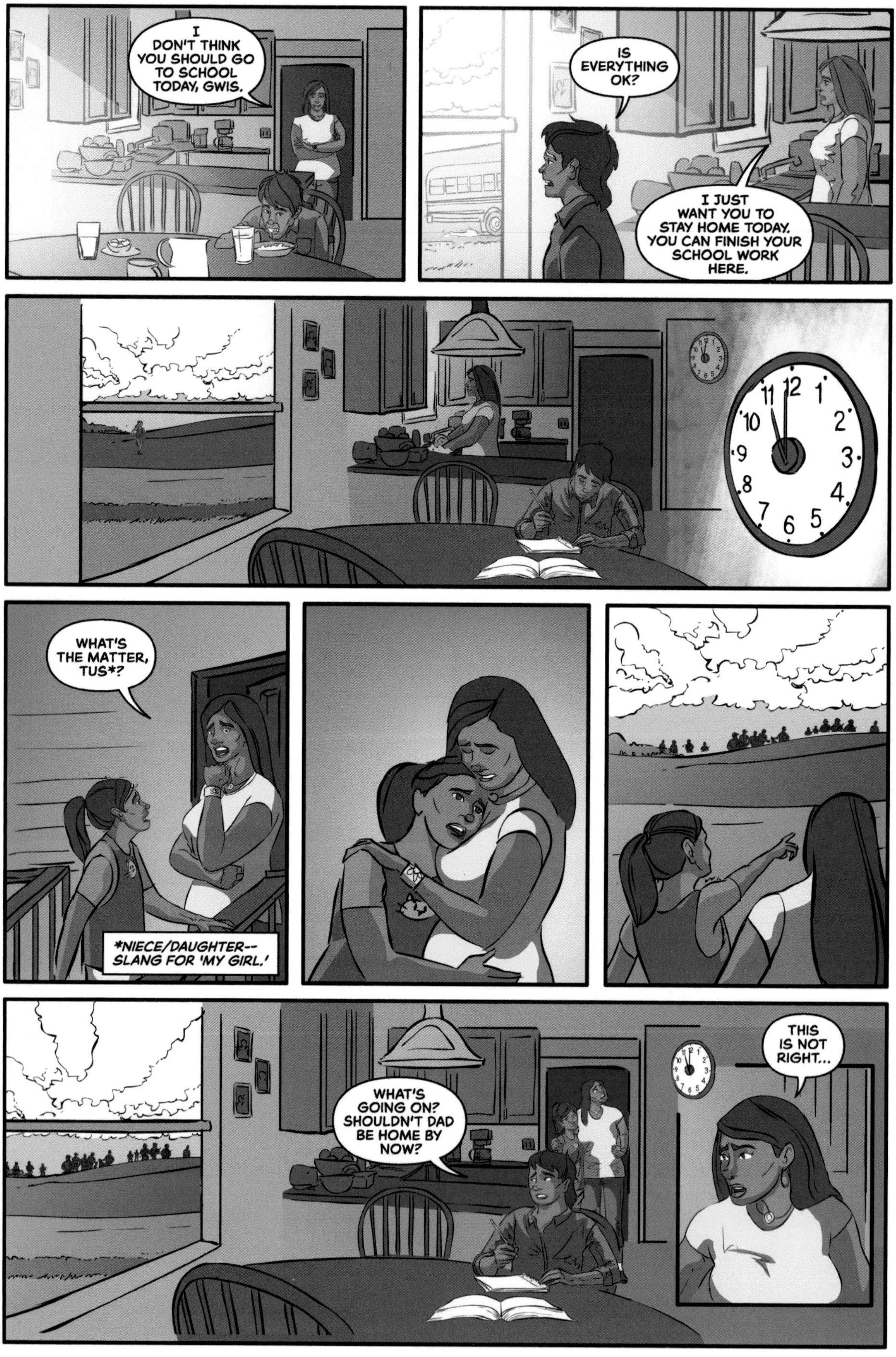
I DON'T THINK YOU SHOULD GO TO SCHOOL TODAY, GWIS.
IS EVERYTHING OK?
I JUST WANT YOU TO STAY HOME TODAY. YOU CAN FINISH YOUR SCHOOL WORK HERE.
11 12 1 2 3 4 5 6 7 8 9 10
WHAT'S THE MATTER, TUS*?
*NIECE/DAUGHTER-- SLANG FOR 'MY GIRL.'
WHAT'S GOING ON? SHOULDN'T DAD BE HOME BY NOW?
THIS IS NOT RIGHT...

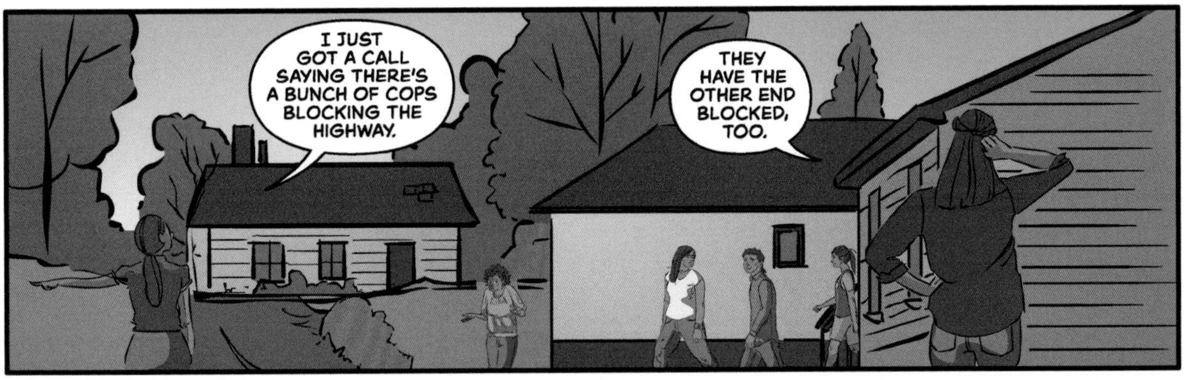
I JUST GOT A CALL SAYING THERE'S A BUNCH OF COPS BLOCKING THE HIGHWAY.
THEY HAVE THE OTHER END BLOCKED, TOO.

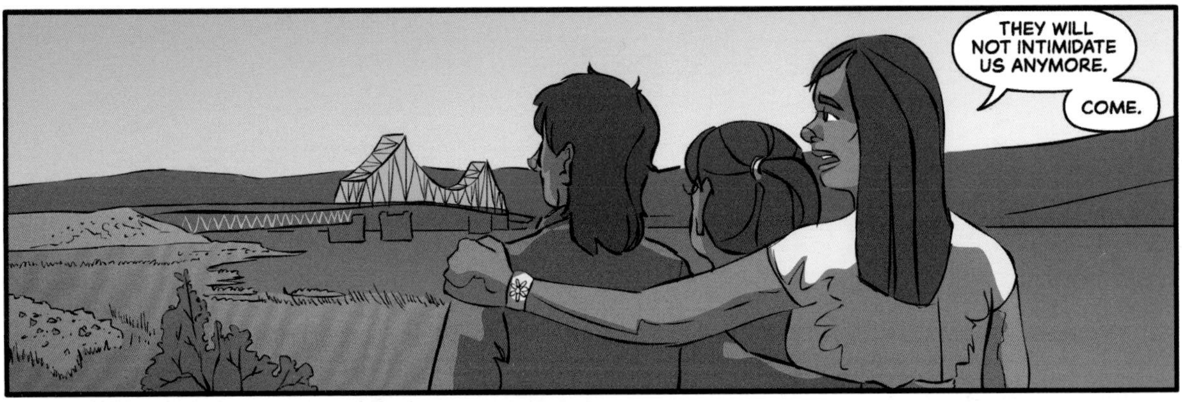
THEY WILL NOT INTIMIDATE US ANYMORE.
COME.

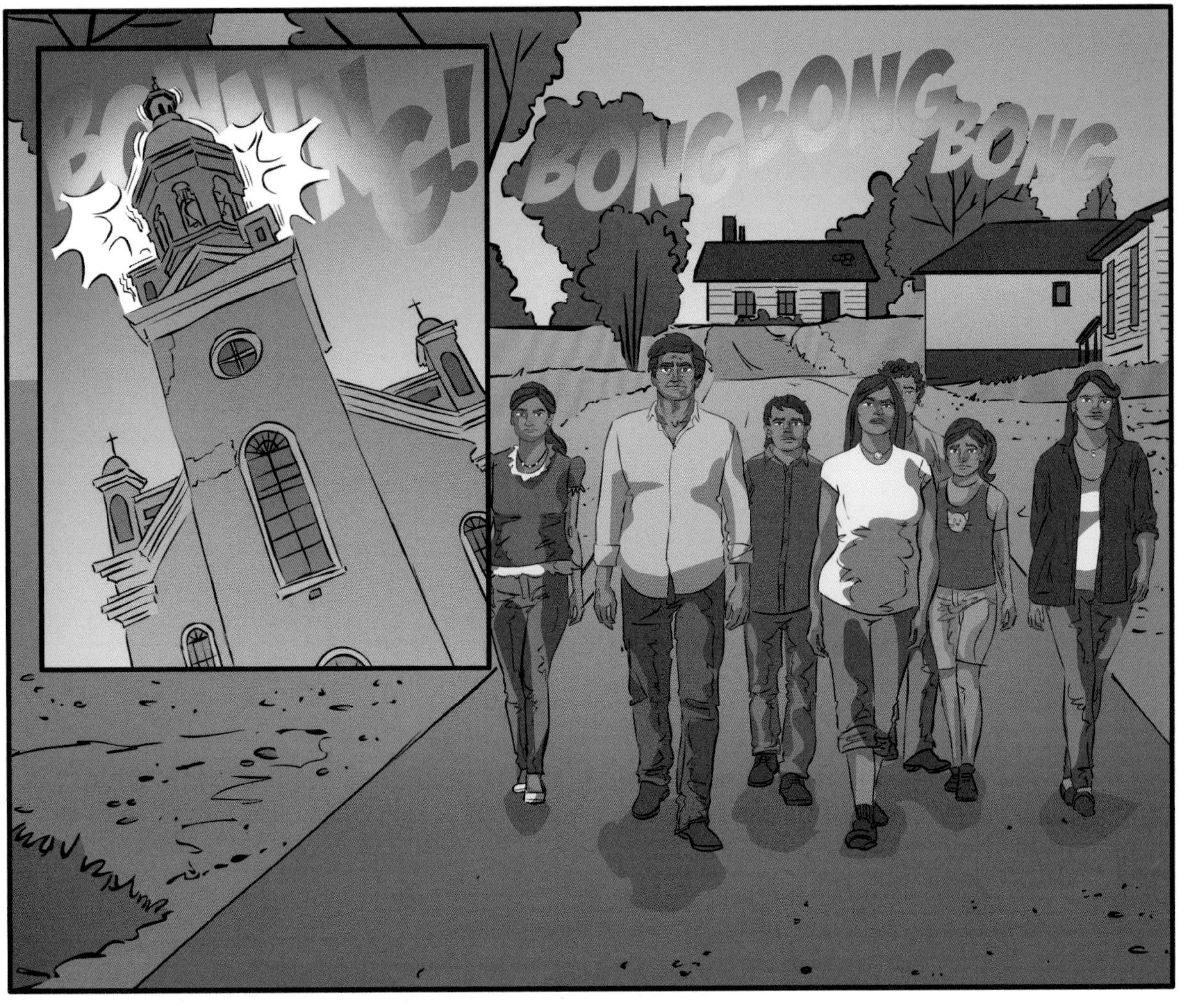
BONNNNG!
BONG BONG BONG

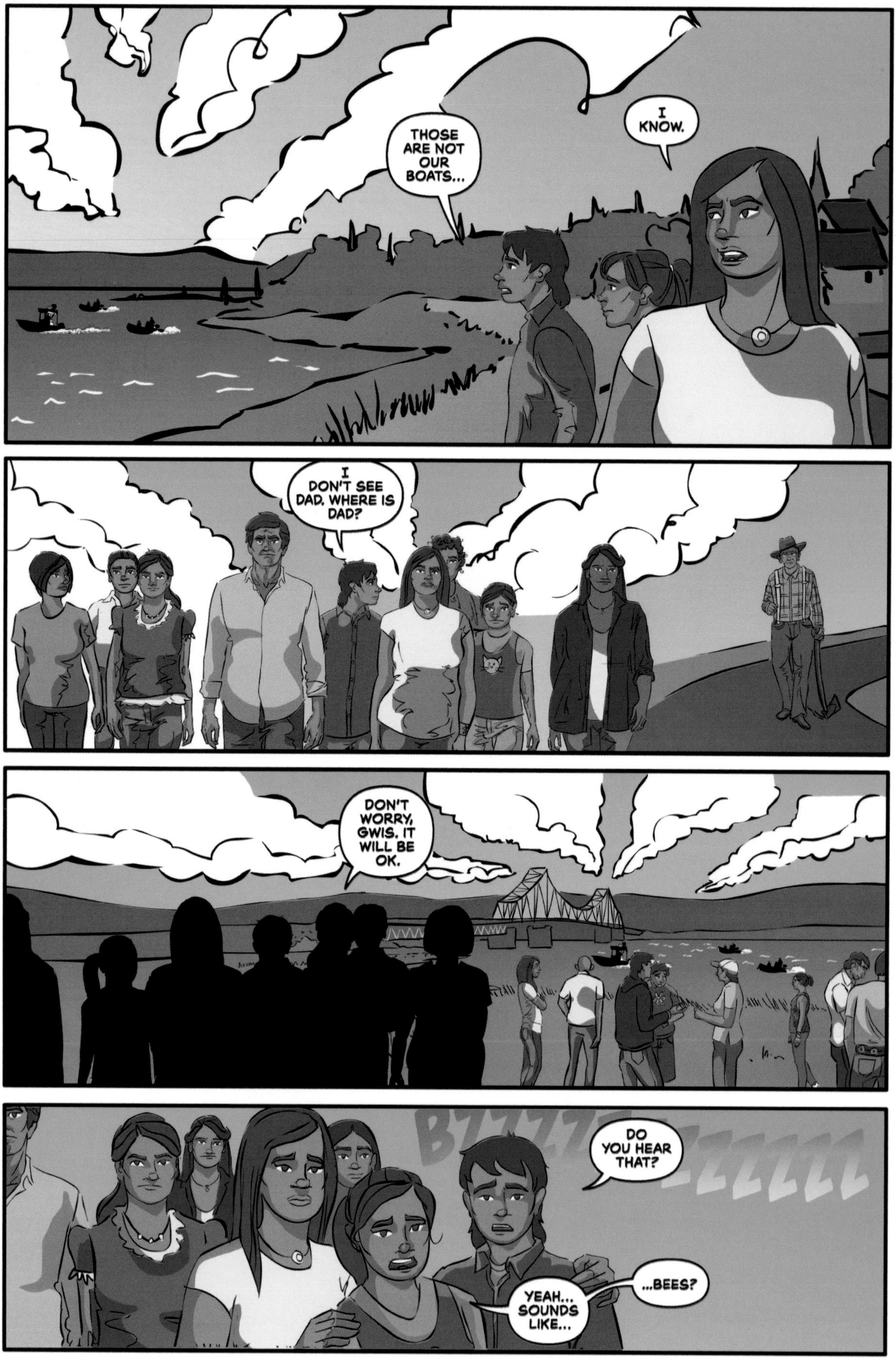
THOSE ARE NOT OUR BOATS...
I KNOW.
I DON'T SEE DAD, WHERE IS DAD?
DON'T WORRY, GWIS. IT WILL BE OK.
BZZZZZZZZZZZZ
DO YOU HEAR THAT?
YEAH... SOUNDS LIKE...
...BEES?

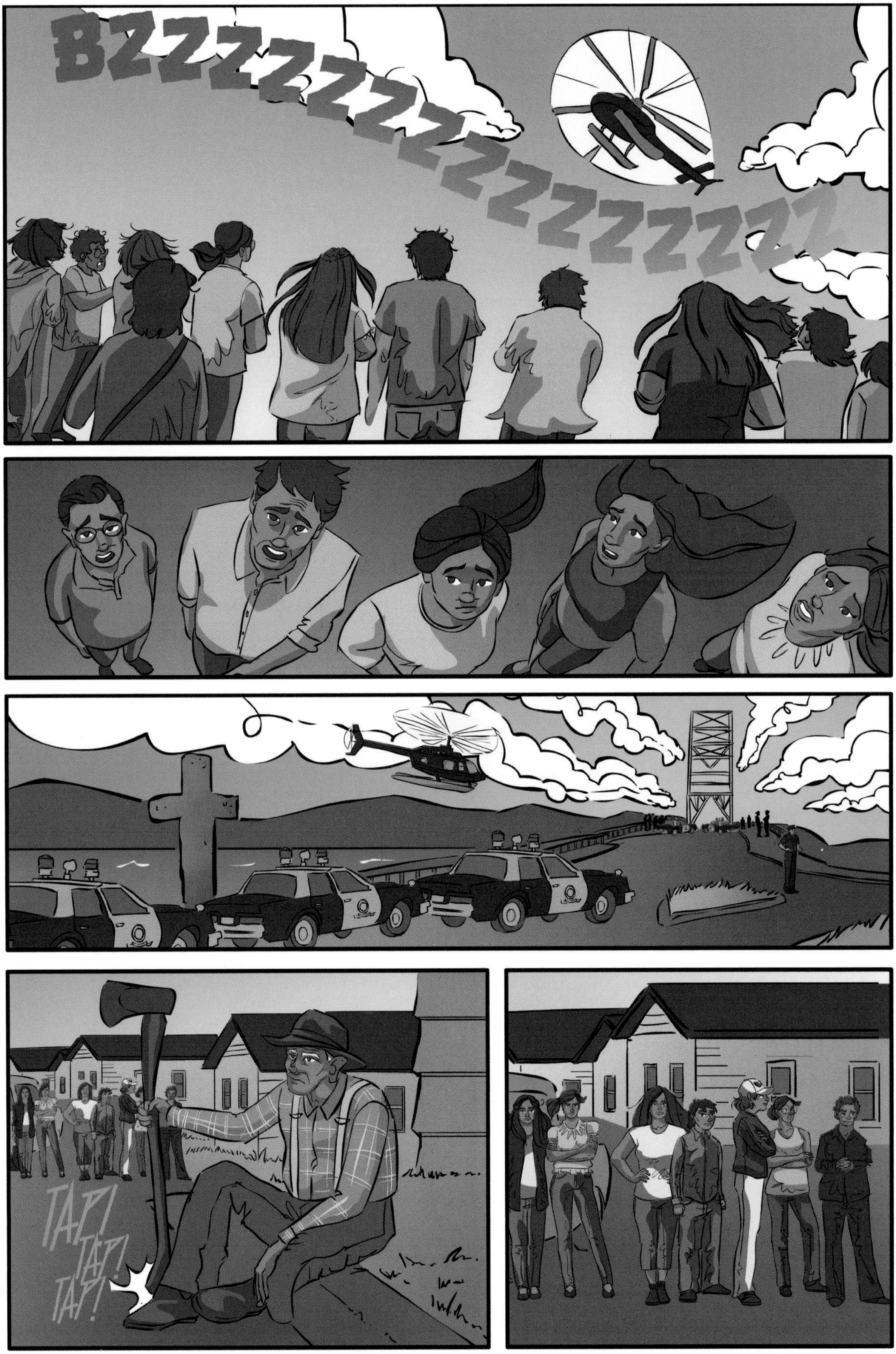
BZZZZZZZZZZZZZZZZZ
TAP! TAP! TAP!

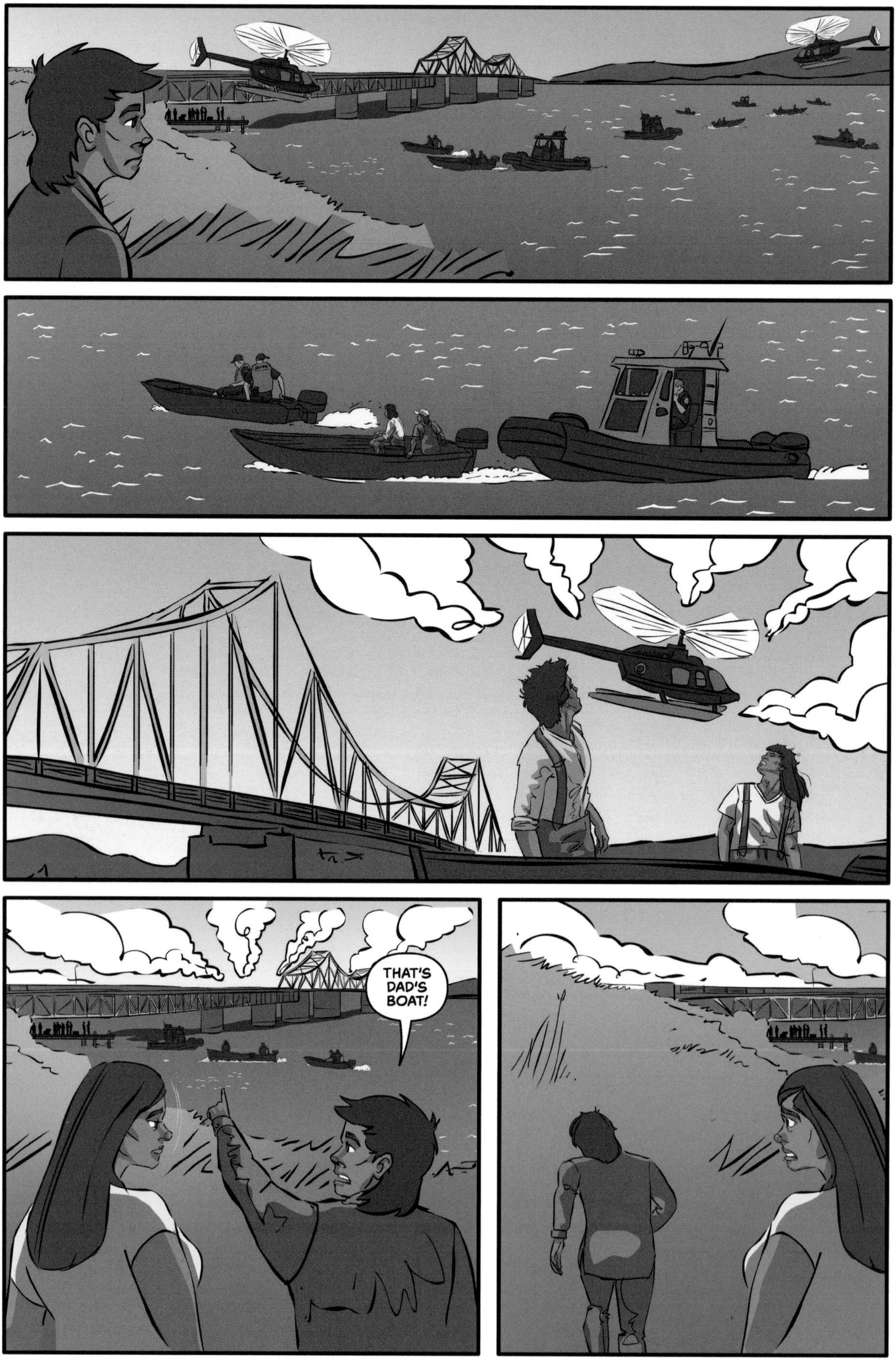
THAT'S DAD'S BOAT!

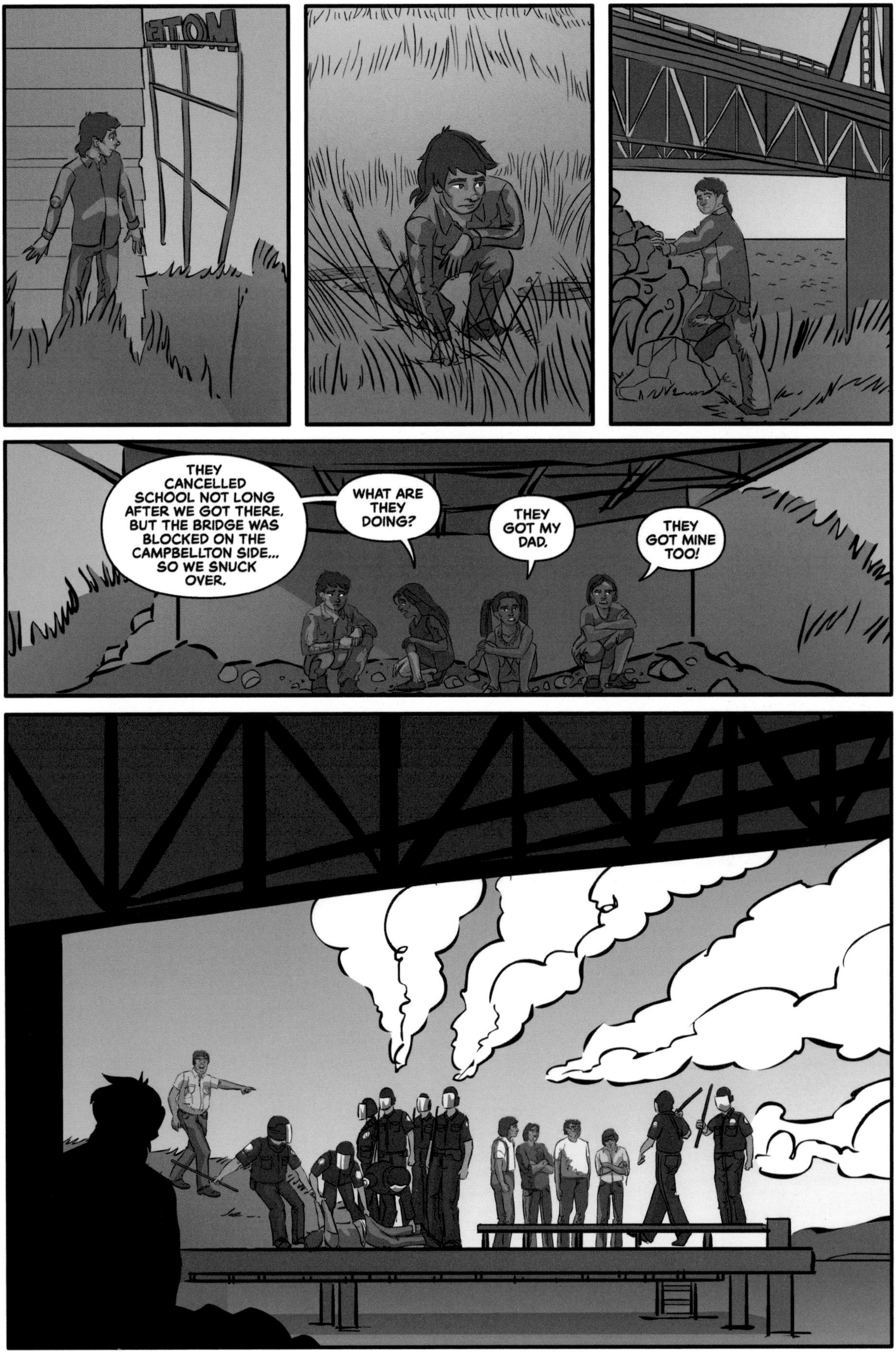
THEY CANCELLED SCHOOL NOT LONG AFTER WE GOT THERE, BUT THE BRIDGE WAS BLOCKED ON THE CAMPBELLTON SIDE... SO WE SNUCK OVER.
WHAT ARE THEY DOING?
THEY GOT MY DAD.
THEY GOT MINE TOO!

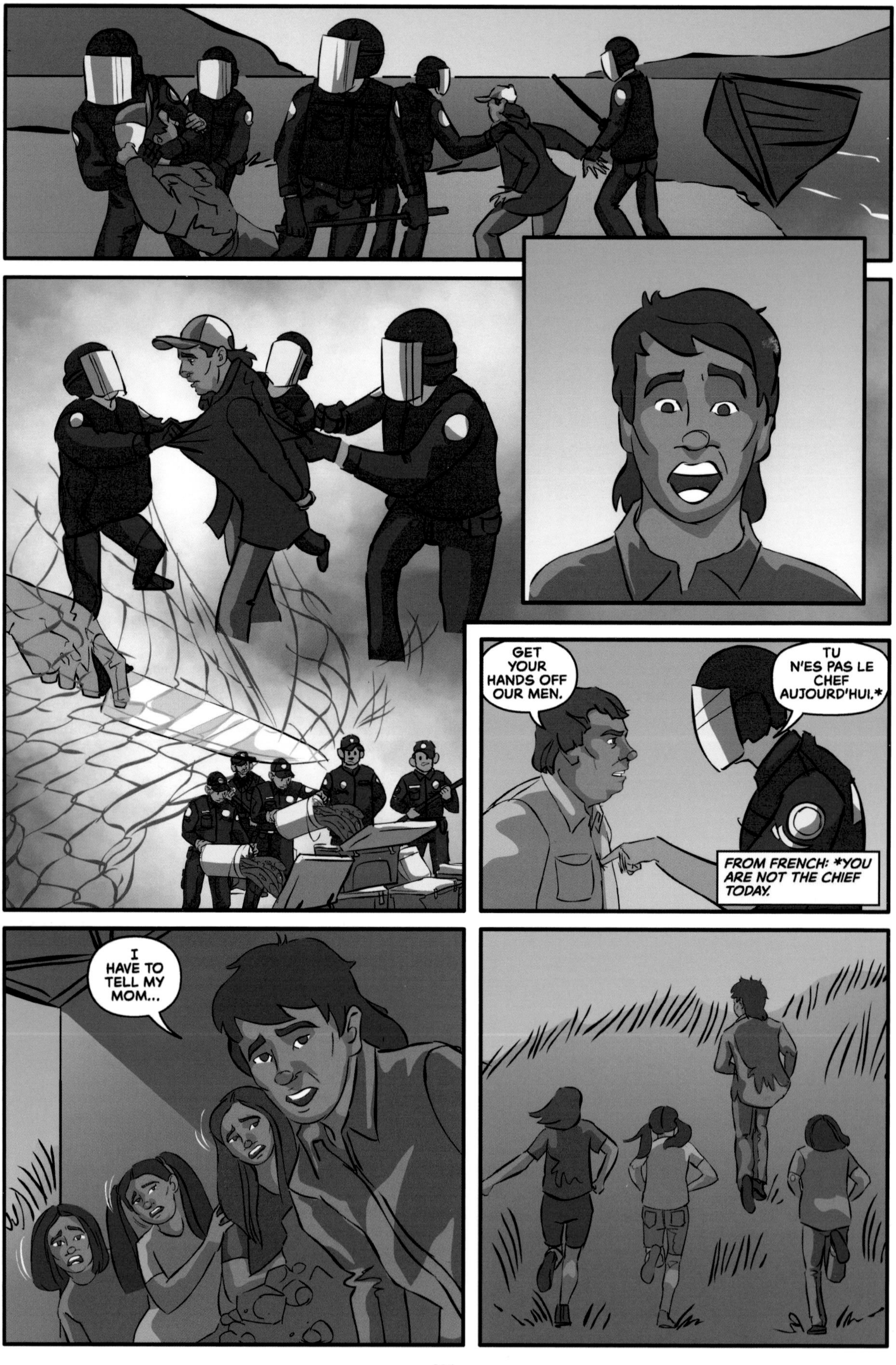
GET YOUR HANDS OFF OUR MEN.
TU N'ES PAS LE CHEF AUJOURD'HUI.*
FROM FRENCH: *YOU ARE NOT THE CHIEF TODAY.
I HAVE TO TELL MY MOM...

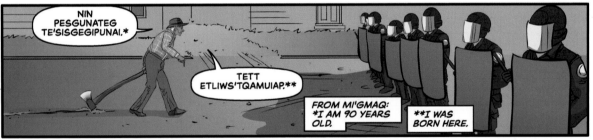

NIN PESGUNATEG TE'SISGEGIPUNAI.*

TETT ETLIWS'TQAMUIAP.**

FROM MI'GMAQ:
*I AM 90 YEARS OLD.

**I WAS BORN HERE.

MU EJIGLIWSIW UGJIT WEN PILUEI.*

*I'M NOT GOING TO MOVE FOR ANYBODY.

GI'MA' GISTLIMIWUN TA'N TUUJIW 'NP'T'S.*

*YOU ARE NOT THE PERSON WHO WILL TELL ME WHEN I'M GOING TO DIE.

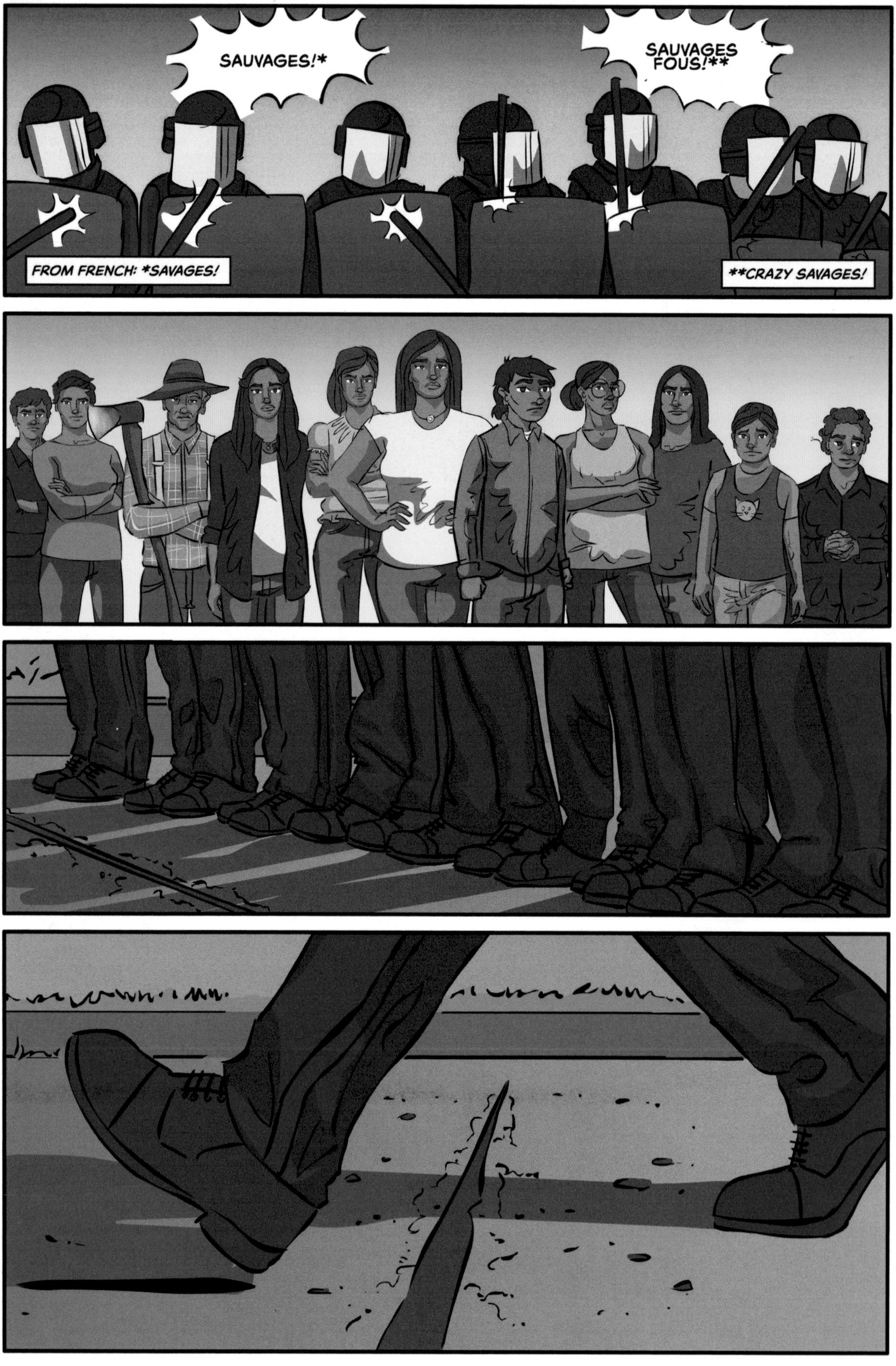
SAUVAGES!*
SAUVAGES FOUS!**
FROM FRENCH: *SAVAGES!
**CRAZY SAVAGES!

The years 1990–2005 were the most formative for me as an Anishinaabe and an inini, a man. It was these years when I learned much of what makes me today—particularly my fierce belief in the power of story. It is this spirit I hope to instill in Warrior Nation.

I was 14 when Elijah Harper bravely said "no" to Meech Lake and Ellen Gabriel and my Kanien'kehá:ka relations stood their ground at Oka—a time when a boy realizes he is a part of something bigger than himself. It should be no surprise that parts of me are inside Washashk (from ignorance to maturation), but Raven is a conglomeration of so many who helped, me along my journey who humbled, helped and taught me along the way. I walk in their footsteps now. This is also the reason why I ended the story hopefully.

While the Kelowna Accord was an abject failure, the resistance and unity Indigenous communities forged during this time is the ultimate story that needs to be told. It is this "warrior spirit" that I believe carried us into the world of today.

I want to take this opportunity to thank Ellen Gabriel who profoundly influenced me with the details of the Oka resistance and helped me re-frame the entire story due to her advice and direction. Miigwech Ellen and to all who helped me along this path and into the future.

Niigaanwewidam James Sinclair

1990
Meech Lake Accord; Cree MLA Elijah Harper refuses to consent, arguing it fails to recognize the rights of Indigenous peoples.

1990
The "Oka Crisis," a 78-day standoff over land between the Haudenosaunee people of Kanehsata:ke and the Canadian state near Oka, Québec, captures the world's attention.

1992
Phil Fontaine, Grand Chief of the Assembly of Manitoba Chiefs, first speaks publicly about experiencing physical and sexual abuse in residential school.

1995
Gustafson Lake Standoff

1991
The Royal Commission on Aboriginal Peoples is created.

1991
The Aboriginal Justice Inquiry report is released in Manitoba. It concludes that the provincial justice system is racist and abusive towards Indigenous people. The report recommends extensive structural changes, including a distinct Aboriginal justice system for First Nations and Métis people.

Warrior Nation

Niigaanwewidam James Sinclair

Illustration & Colours: Andrew Lodwick

1996
The final report of the Royal Commission on Aboriginal Peoples (RCAP) is tabled with 440 recommendations and sweeping changes.

2005
The Kelowna Accord is negotiated between federal, provincial, territorial, and Indigenous leaders—a $5 billion plan to address health, education, social, and economic improvements for Indigenous peoples.

1998, JANUARY 7
The federal government apologizes to residential school survivors and sets up a $350-million fund for community healing.

1998-2000
Nisaga'a Final Treaty Agreement is passed in British Columbia.

1999
Creation of Nunavut as a territory; under the 1993 Nunavut Land Agreement, the Inuit people of the region are granted self-government and a cash settlement.

2001
Violent confrontations take place between Indigenous and non-Indigenous fishers at Burnt Church, New Brunswick, over Indigenous hunting and fishing rights.

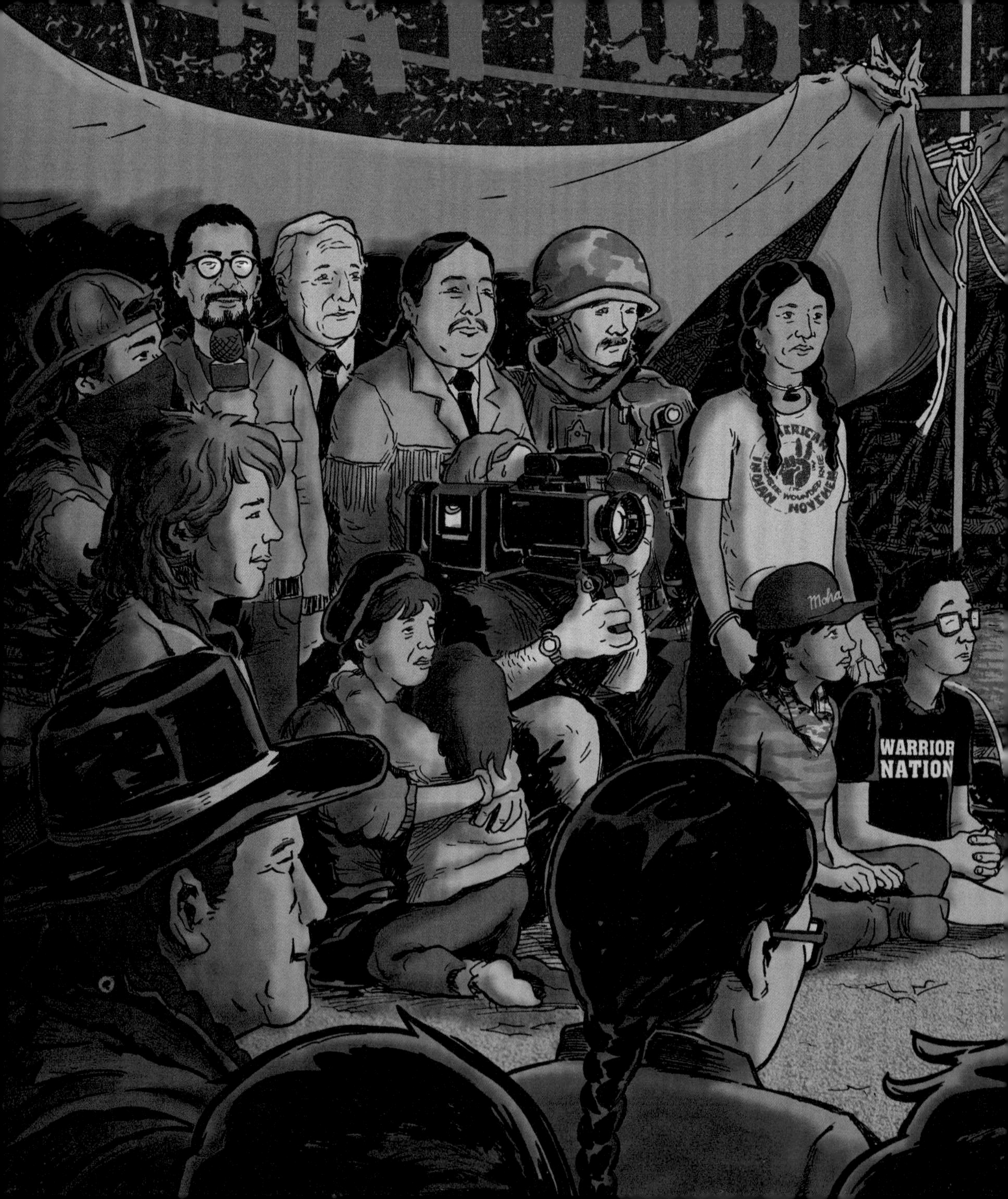
WARRIOR
NATION

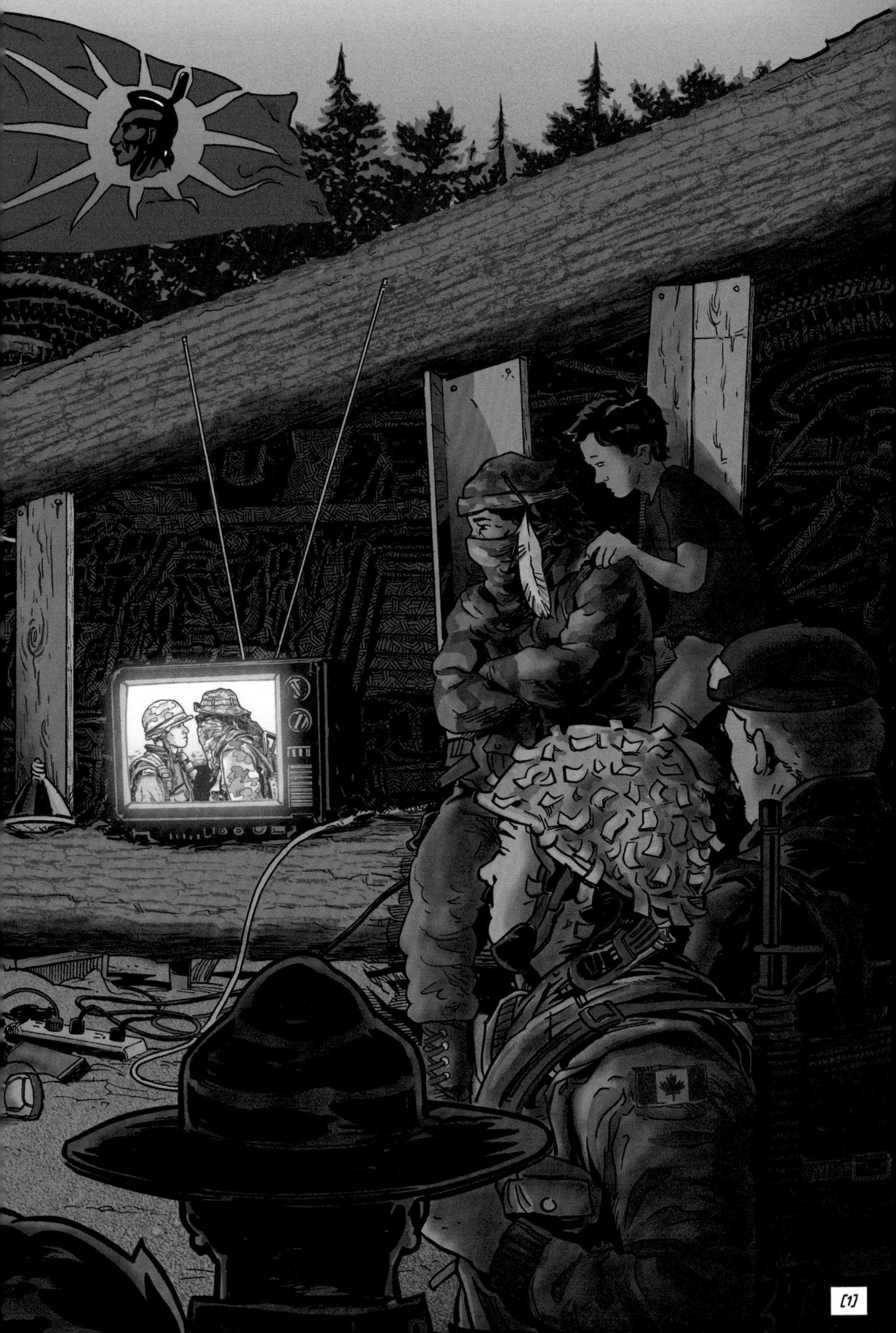
[1]

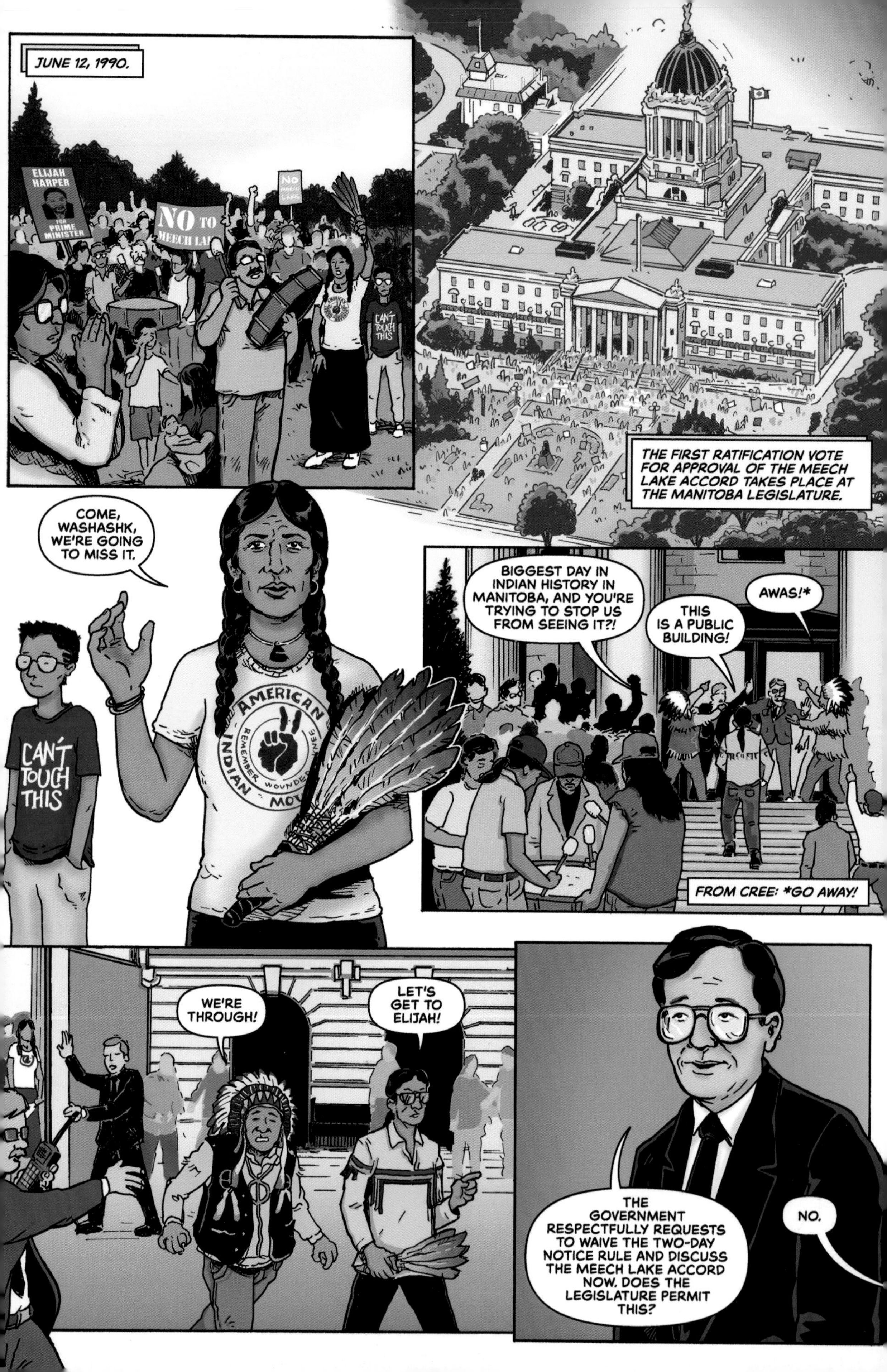
JUNE 12, 1990.
ELIJAH HARPER FOR PRIME MINISTER
NO TO MEECH LAKE
NO MEECH LAKE
CAN'T TOUCH THIS
THE FIRST RATIFICATION VOTE FOR APPROVAL OF THE MEECH LAKE ACCORD TAKES PLACE AT THE MANITOBA LEGISLATURE.
COME, WASHASHK, WE'RE GOING TO MISS IT.
CAN'T TOUCH THIS
AMERICAN INDIAN MOV
REMEMBER WOUNDED KNEE
BIGGEST DAY IN INDIAN HISTORY IN MANITOBA, AND YOU'RE TRYING TO STOP US FROM SEEING IT?!
THIS IS A PUBLIC BUILDING!
AWAS!*
FROM CREE: *GO AWAY!
WE'RE THROUGH!
LET'S GET TO ELIJAH!
THE GOVERNMENT RESPECTFULLY REQUESTS TO WAIVE THE TWO-DAY NOTICE RULE AND DISCUSS THE MEECH LAKE ACCORD NOW. DOES THE LEGISLATURE PERMIT THIS?
NO.

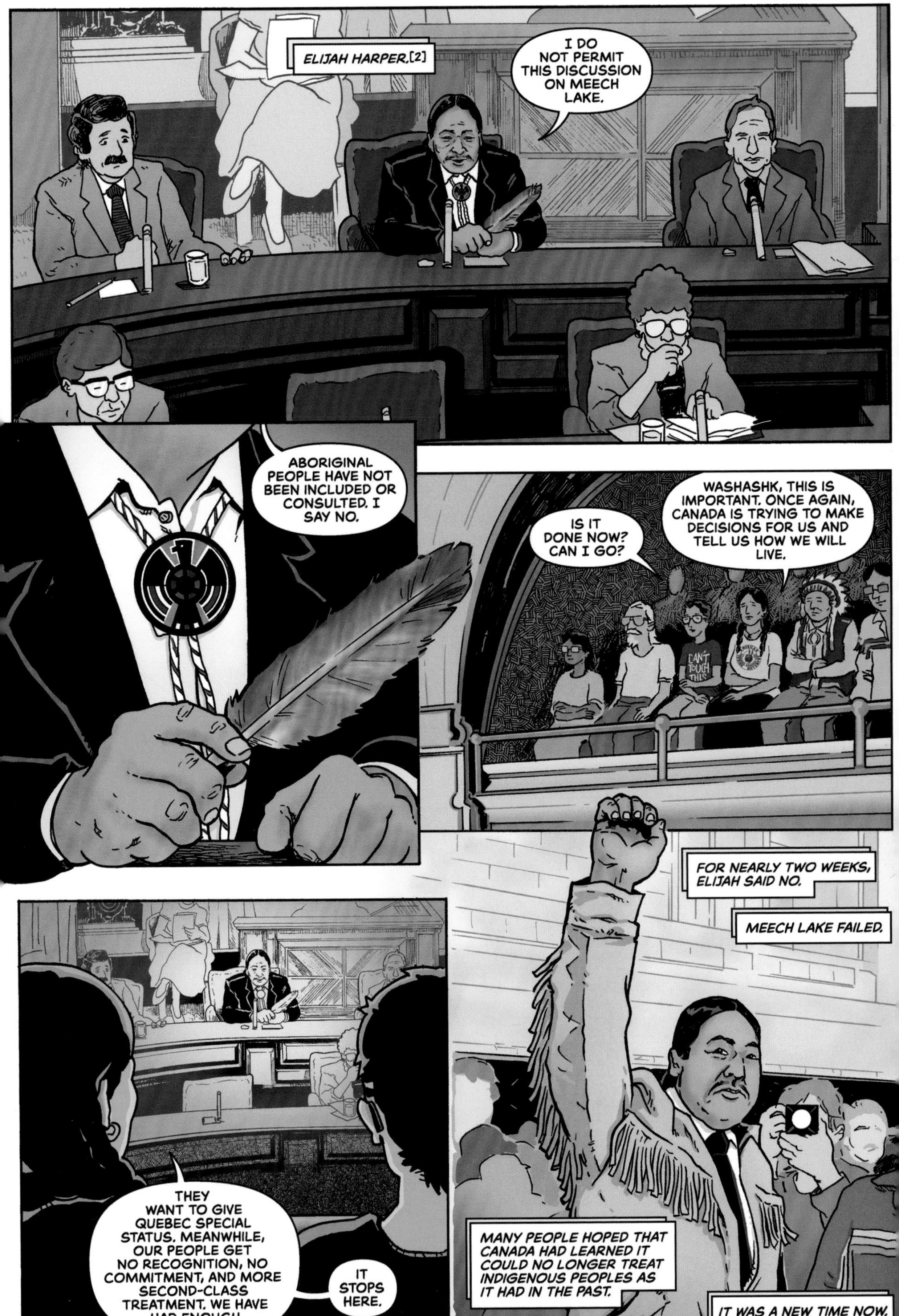

ELIJAH HARPER.[2]
I DO NOT PERMIT THIS DISCUSSION ON MEECH LAKE.
ABORIGINAL PEOPLE HAVE NOT BEEN INCLUDED OR CONSULTED. I SAY NO.
IS IT DONE NOW? CAN I GO?
WASHASHK, THIS IS IMPORTANT. ONCE AGAIN, CANADA IS TRYING TO MAKE DECISIONS FOR US AND TELL US HOW WE WILL LIVE.
CAN'T TOUCH THIS
THEY WANT TO GIVE QUEBEC SPECIAL STATUS. MEANWHILE, OUR PEOPLE GET NO RECOGNITION, NO COMMITMENT, AND MORE SECOND-CLASS TREATMENT. WE HAVE HAD ENOUGH.
IT STOPS HERE.
FOR NEARLY TWO WEEKS, ELIJAH SAID NO.
MEECH LAKE FAILED.
MANY PEOPLE HOPED THAT CANADA HAD LEARNED IT COULD NO LONGER TREAT INDIGENOUS PEOPLES AS IT HAD IN THE PAST.
IT WAS A NEW TIME NOW.

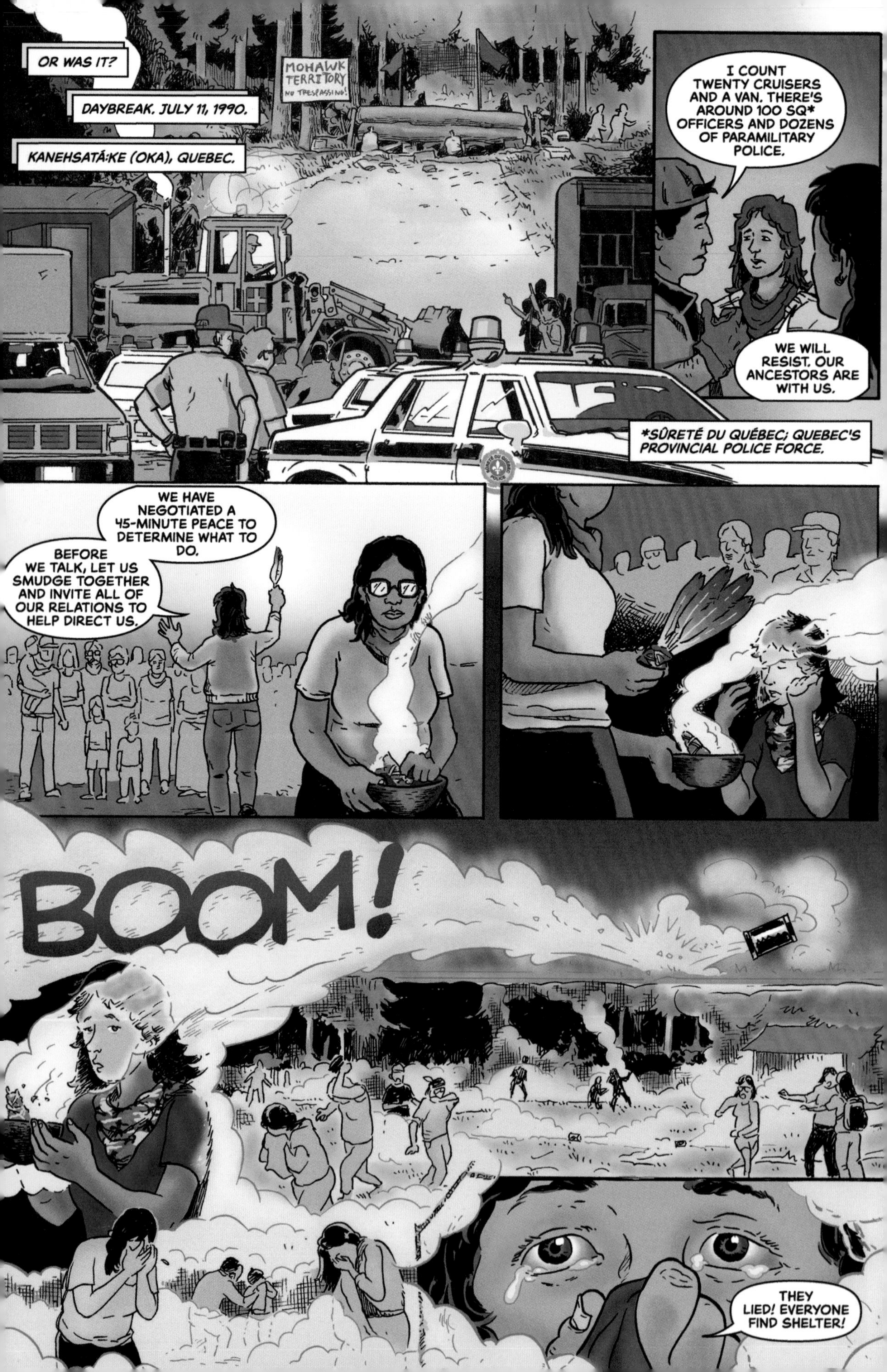
OR WAS IT?
DAYBREAK. JULY 11, 1990.
KANEHSATÁ:KE (OKA), QUEBEC.
MOHAWK TERRITORY NO TRESPASSING!
I COUNT TWENTY CRUISERS AND A VAN. THERE'S AROUND 100 SQ* OFFICERS AND DOZENS OF PARAMILITARY POLICE.
WE WILL RESIST. OUR ANCESTORS ARE WITH US.
*SÛRETÉ DU QUÉBEC; QUEBEC'S PROVINCIAL POLICE FORCE.
WE HAVE NEGOTIATED A 45-MINUTE PEACE TO DETERMINE WHAT TO DO.
BEFORE WE TALK, LET US SMUDGE TOGETHER AND INVITE ALL OF OUR RELATIONS TO HELP DIRECT US.
BOOM!
THEY LIED! EVERYONE FIND SHELTER!

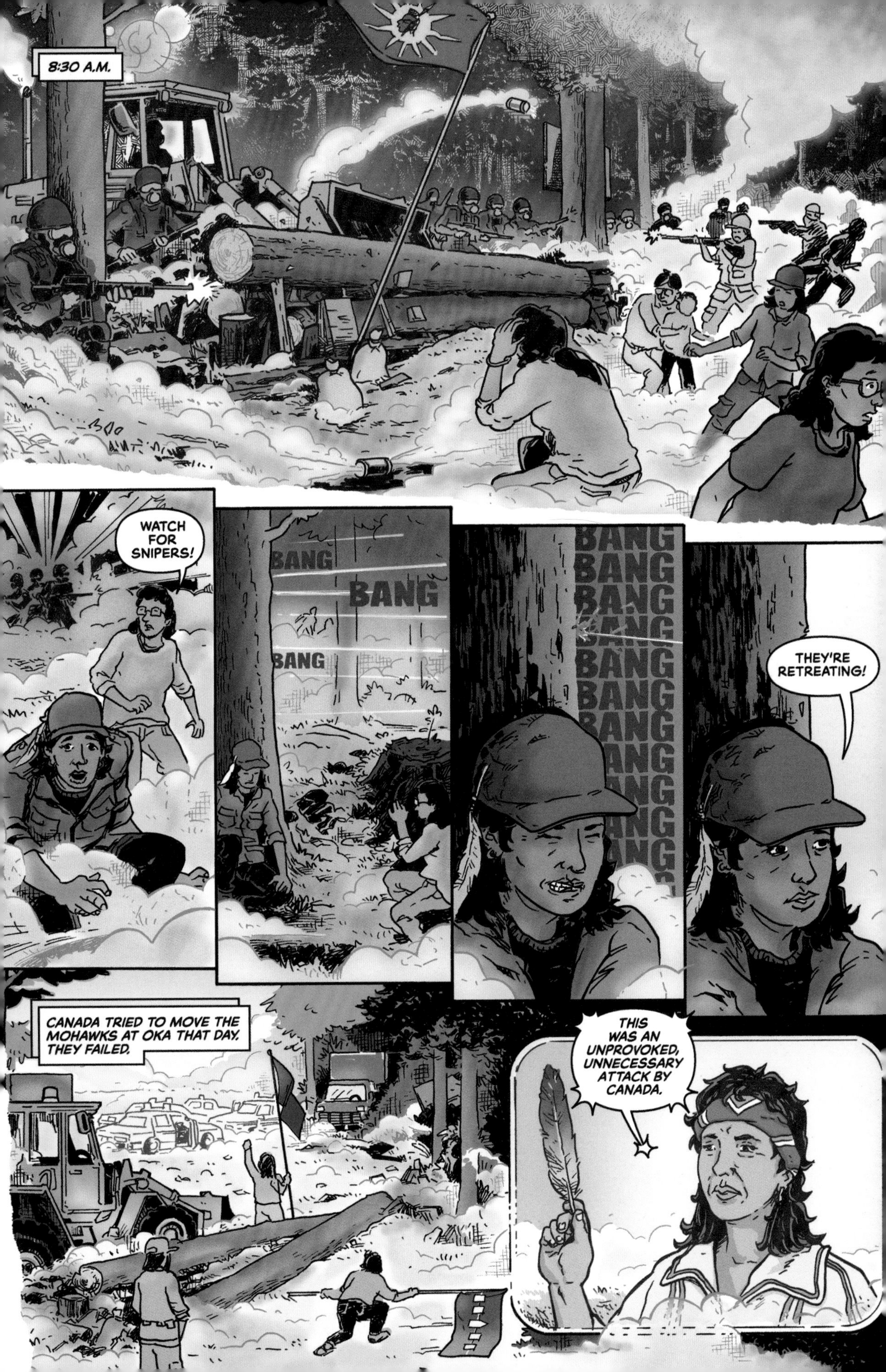
8:30 A.M.
WATCH FOR SNIPERS!
BANG
BANG
BANG
BANG
BANG
BANG
BANG
BANG
BANG
BANG
BANG
BANG
BANG
BANG
BANG
BANG
THEY'RE RETREATING!
CANADA TRIED TO MOVE THE MOHAWKS AT OKA THAT DAY. THEY FAILED.
THIS WAS AN UNPROVOKED, UNNECESSARY ATTACK BY CANADA.

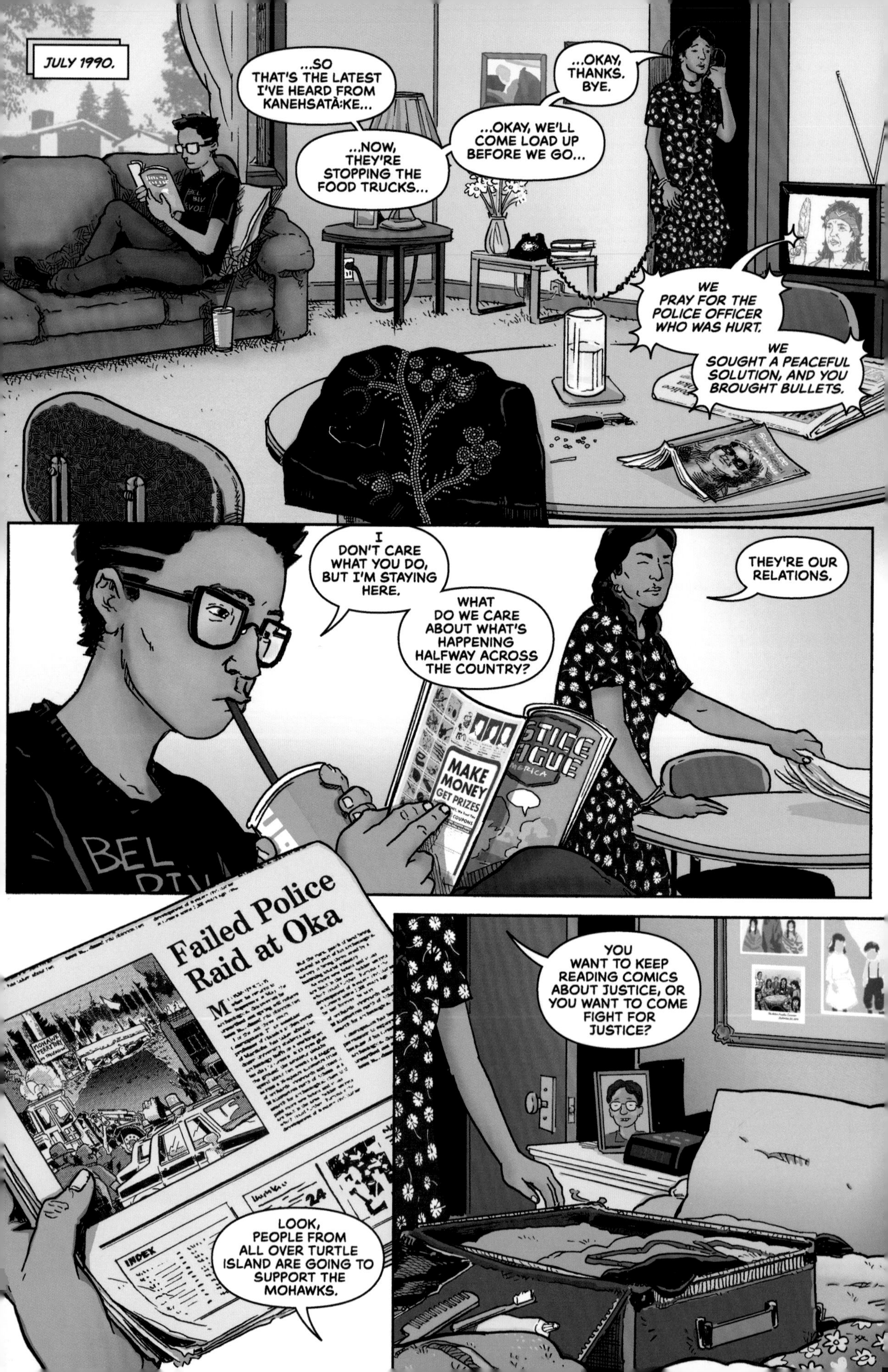
JULY 1990.
...SO THAT'S THE LATEST I'VE HEARD FROM KANEHSATÀ:KE...
...NOW, THEY'RE STOPPING THE FOOD TRUCKS...
...OKAY, WE'LL COME LOAD UP BEFORE WE GO...
...OKAY, THANKS. BYE.
WE PRAY FOR THE POLICE OFFICER WHO WAS HURT.
WE SOUGHT A PEACEFUL SOLUTION, AND YOU BROUGHT BULLETS.
I DON'T CARE WHAT YOU DO, BUT I'M STAYING HERE.
WHAT DO WE CARE ABOUT WHAT'S HAPPENING HALFWAY ACROSS THE COUNTRY?
THEY'RE OUR RELATIONS.
MAKE MONEY
GET PRIZES
Failed Police Raid at Oka
INDEX
LOOK, PEOPLE FROM ALL OVER TURTLE ISLAND ARE GOING TO SUPPORT THE MOHAWKS.
YOU WANT TO KEEP READING COMICS ABOUT JUSTICE, OR YOU WANT TO COME FIGHT FOR JUSTICE?

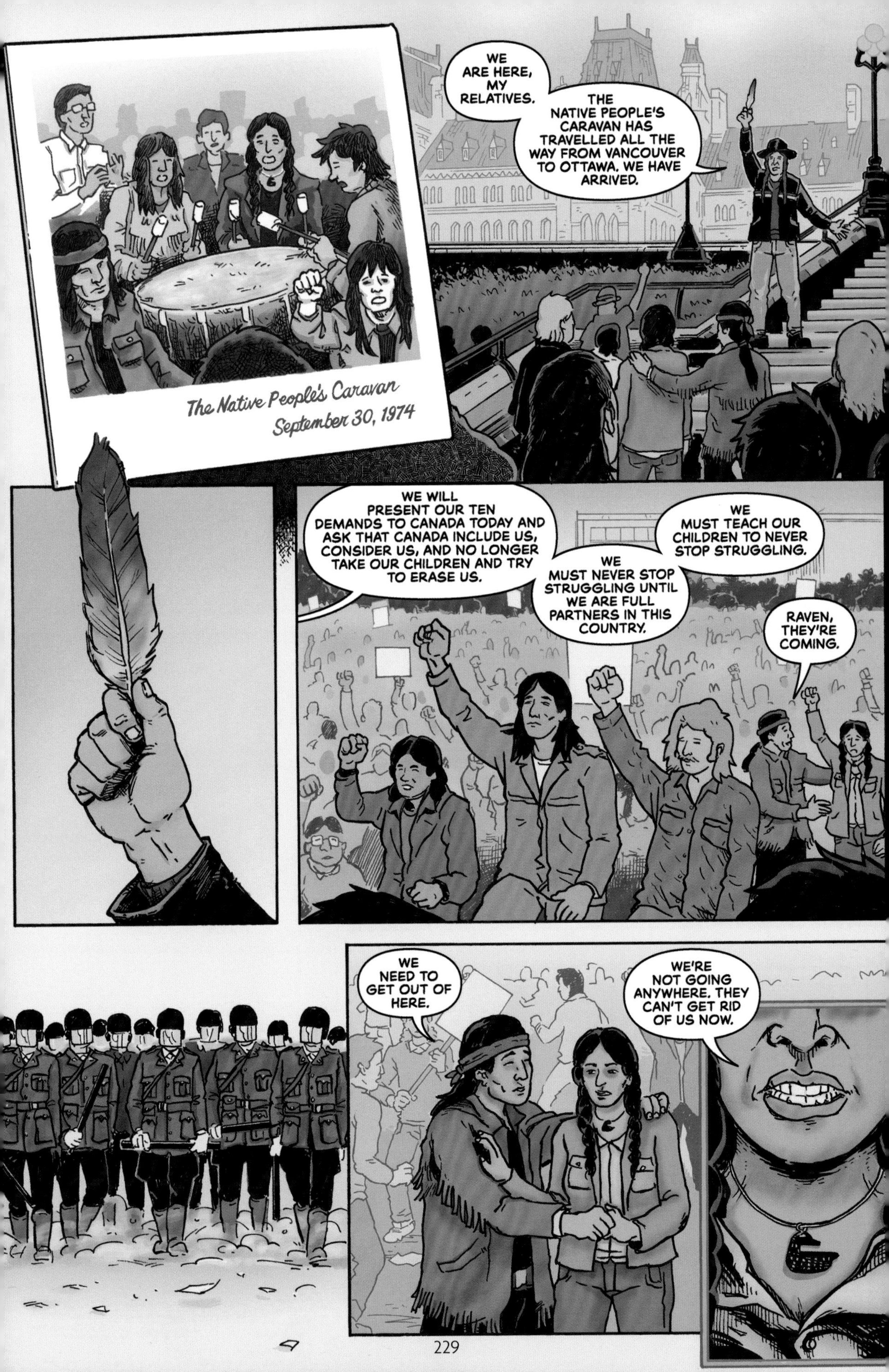
The Native People's Caravan
September 30, 1974
WE ARE HERE, MY RELATIVES.
THE NATIVE PEOPLE'S CARAVAN HAS TRAVELLED ALL THE WAY FROM VANCOUVER TO OTTAWA. WE HAVE ARRIVED.
WE WILL PRESENT OUR TEN DEMANDS TO CANADA TODAY AND ASK THAT CANADA INCLUDE US, CONSIDER US, AND NO LONGER TAKE OUR CHILDREN AND TRY TO ERASE US.
WE MUST NEVER STOP STRUGGLING UNTIL WE ARE FULL PARTNERS IN THIS COUNTRY.
WE MUST TEACH OUR CHILDREN TO NEVER STOP STRUGGLING.
RAVEN, THEY'RE COMING.
WE NEED TO GET OUT OF HERE.
WE'RE NOT GOING ANYWHERE. THEY CAN'T GET RID OF US NOW.

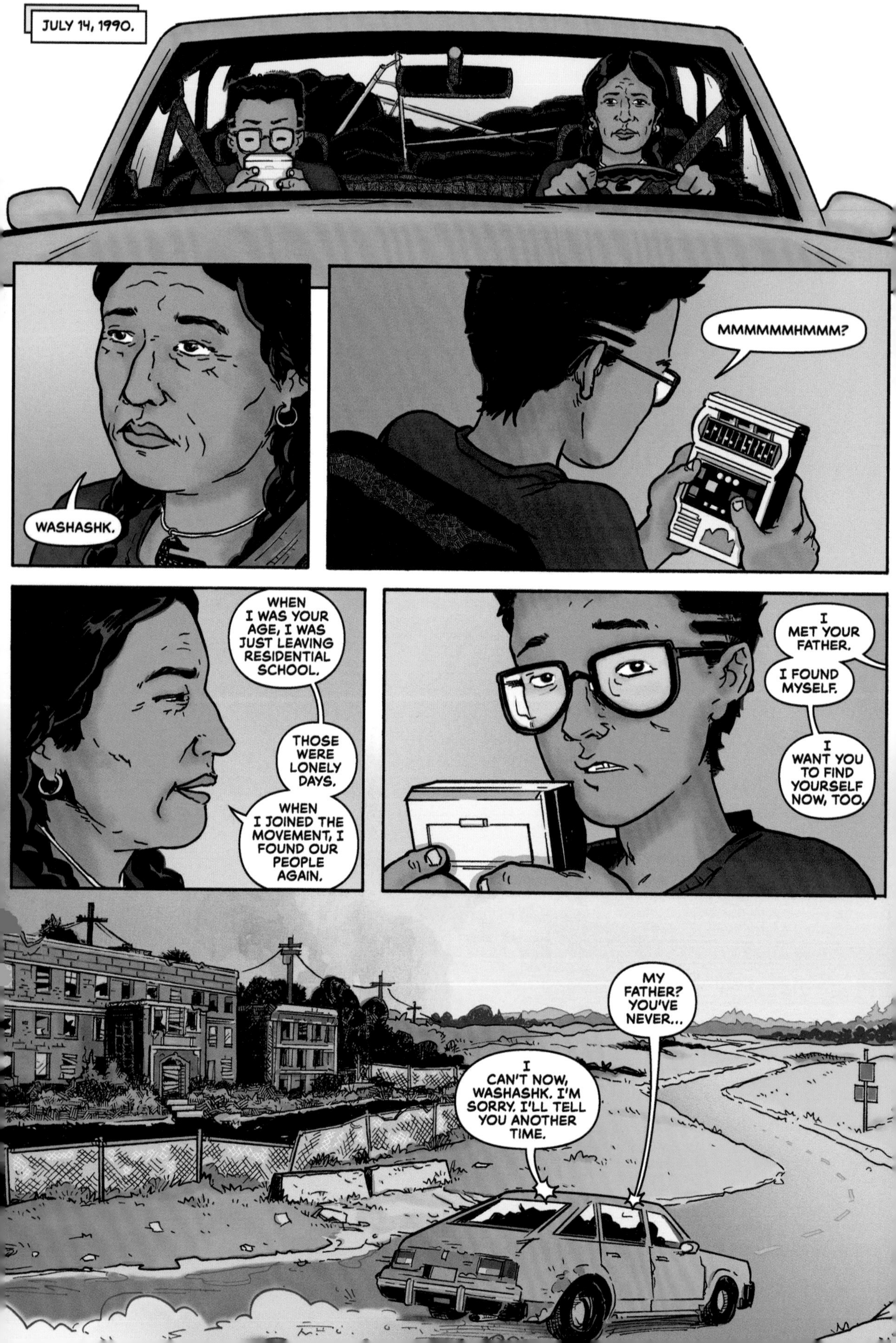
JULY 14, 1990.
WASHASHK.
MMMMMMHMMM?
WHEN I WAS YOUR AGE, I WAS JUST LEAVING RESIDENTIAL SCHOOL.
THOSE WERE LONELY DAYS.
WHEN I JOINED THE MOVEMENT, I FOUND OUR PEOPLE AGAIN.
I MET YOUR FATHER.
I FOUND MYSELF.
I WANT YOU TO FIND YOURSELF NOW, TOO.
MY FATHER? YOU'VE NEVER...
I CAN'T NOW, WASHASHK. I'M SORRY. I'LL TELL YOU ANOTHER TIME.

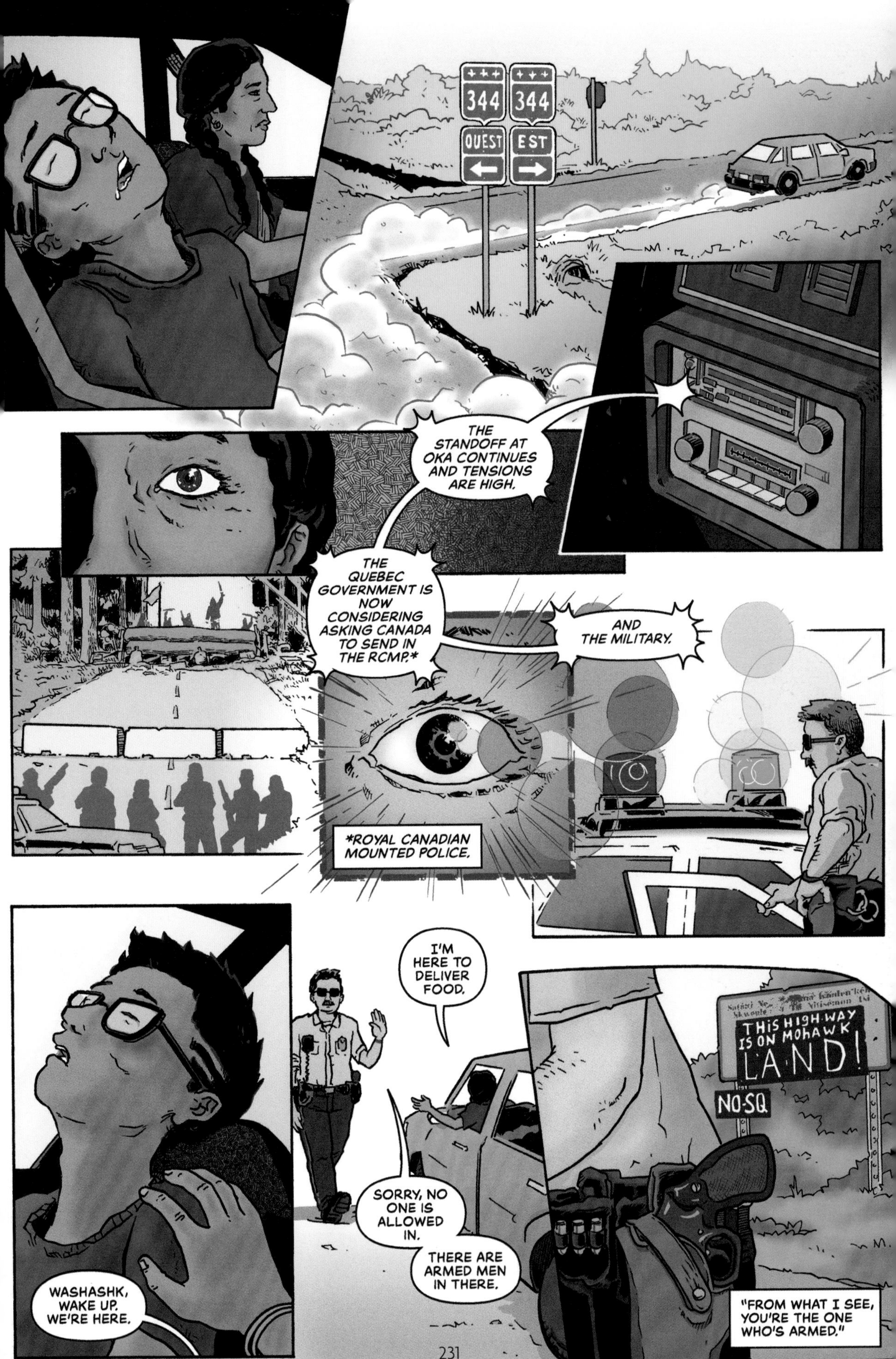
344
344
OUEST
EST
THE STANDOFF AT OKA CONTINUES AND TENSIONS ARE HIGH.
THE QUEBEC GOVERNMENT IS NOW CONSIDERING ASKING CANADA TO SEND IN THE RCMP.*
AND THE MILITARY.
*ROYAL CANADIAN MOUNTED POLICE.
WASHASHK, WAKE UP. WE'RE HERE.
I'M HERE TO DELIVER FOOD.
SORRY, NO ONE IS ALLOWED IN.
THERE ARE ARMED MEN IN THERE.
THIS HIGH WAY IS ON MOHAWK LAND!
NO-SQ
"FROM WHAT I SEE, YOU'RE THE ONE WHO'S ARMED."

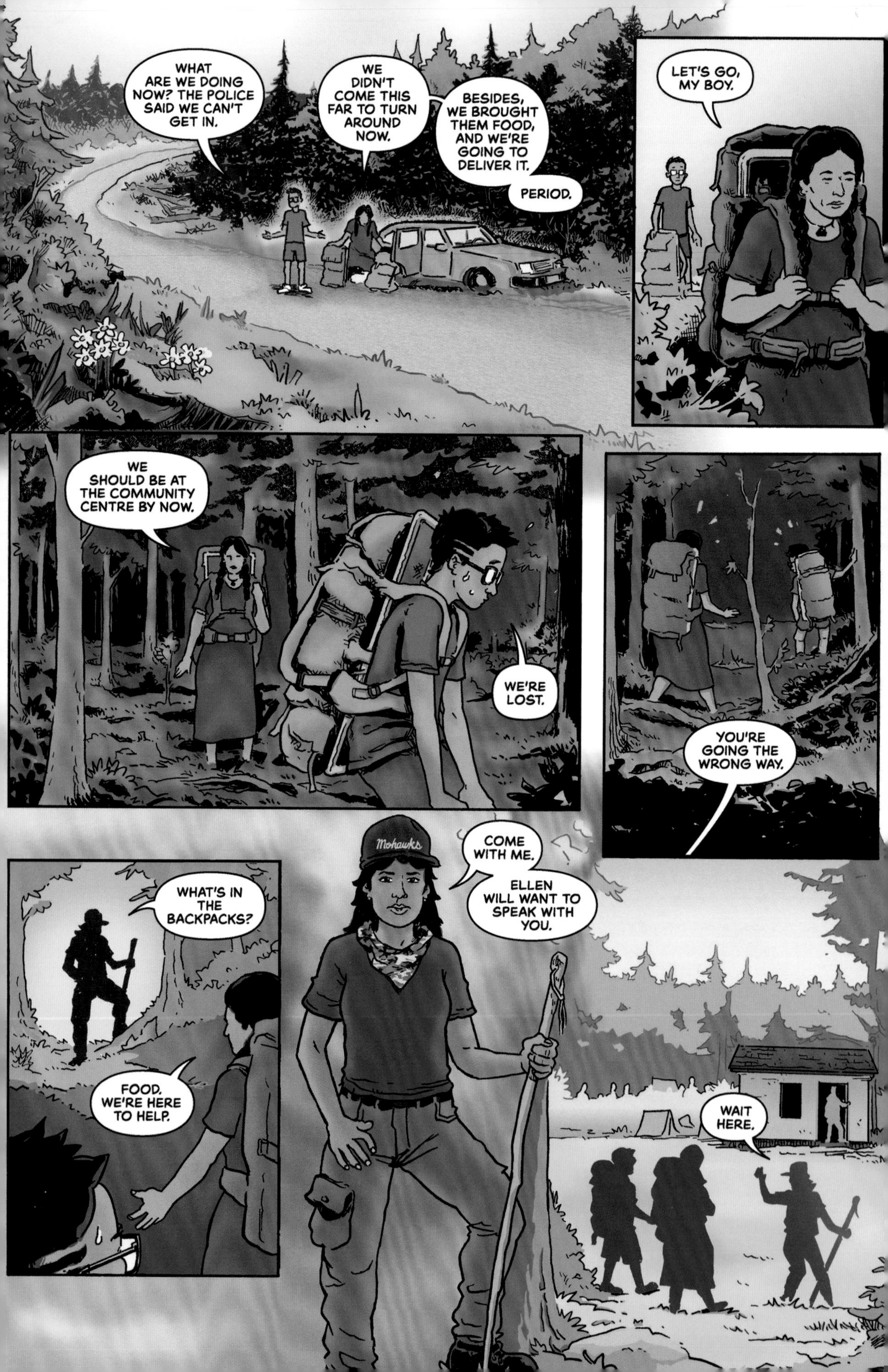
WHAT ARE WE DOING NOW? THE POLICE SAID WE CAN'T GET IN.
WE DIDN'T COME THIS FAR TO TURN AROUND NOW.
BESIDES, WE BROUGHT THEM FOOD, AND WE'RE GOING TO DELIVER IT.
PERIOD.
LET'S GO, MY BOY.
WE SHOULD BE AT THE COMMUNITY CENTRE BY NOW.
WE'RE LOST.
YOU'RE GOING THE WRONG WAY.
WHAT'S IN THE BACKPACKS?
FOOD. WE'RE HERE TO HELP.
Mohawks
COME WITH ME.
ELLEN WILL WANT TO SPEAK WITH YOU.
WAIT HERE.

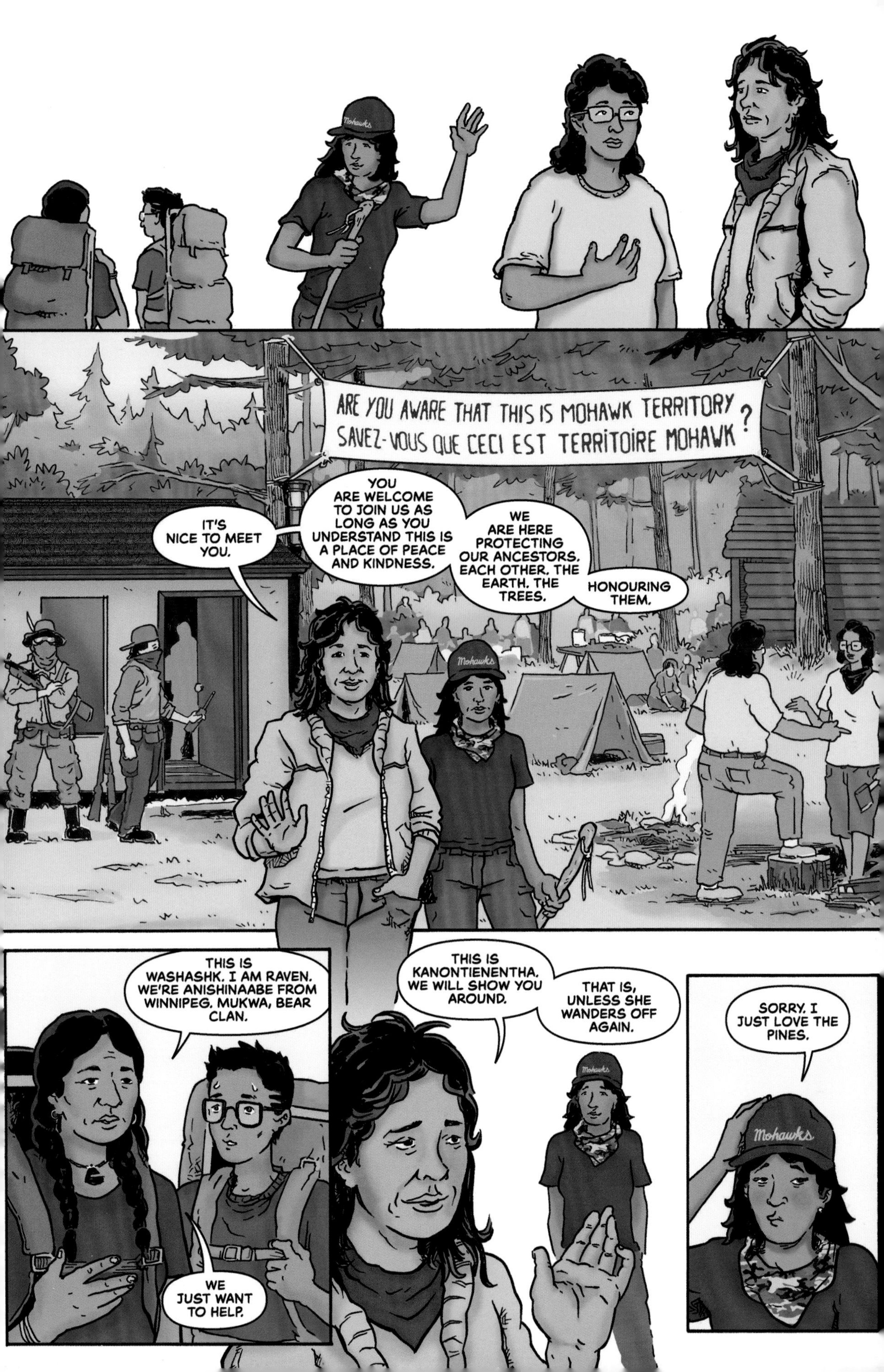
ARE YOU AWARE THAT THIS IS MOHAWK TERRITORY ?
SAVEZ-VOUS QUE CECI EST TERRITOIRE MOHAWK ?
IT'S NICE TO MEET YOU.
YOU ARE WELCOME TO JOIN US AS LONG AS YOU UNDERSTAND THIS IS A PLACE OF PEACE AND KINDNESS.
WE ARE HERE PROTECTING OUR ANCESTORS. EACH OTHER. THE EARTH. THE TREES.
HONOURING THEM.
Mohawks
THIS IS WASHASHK. I AM RAVEN. WE'RE ANISHINAABE FROM WINNIPEG. MUKWA, BEAR CLAN.
WE JUST WANT TO HELP.
THIS IS KANONTIENENTHA. WE WILL SHOW YOU AROUND.
THAT IS, UNLESS SHE WANDERS OFF AGAIN.
SORRY. I JUST LOVE THE PINES.

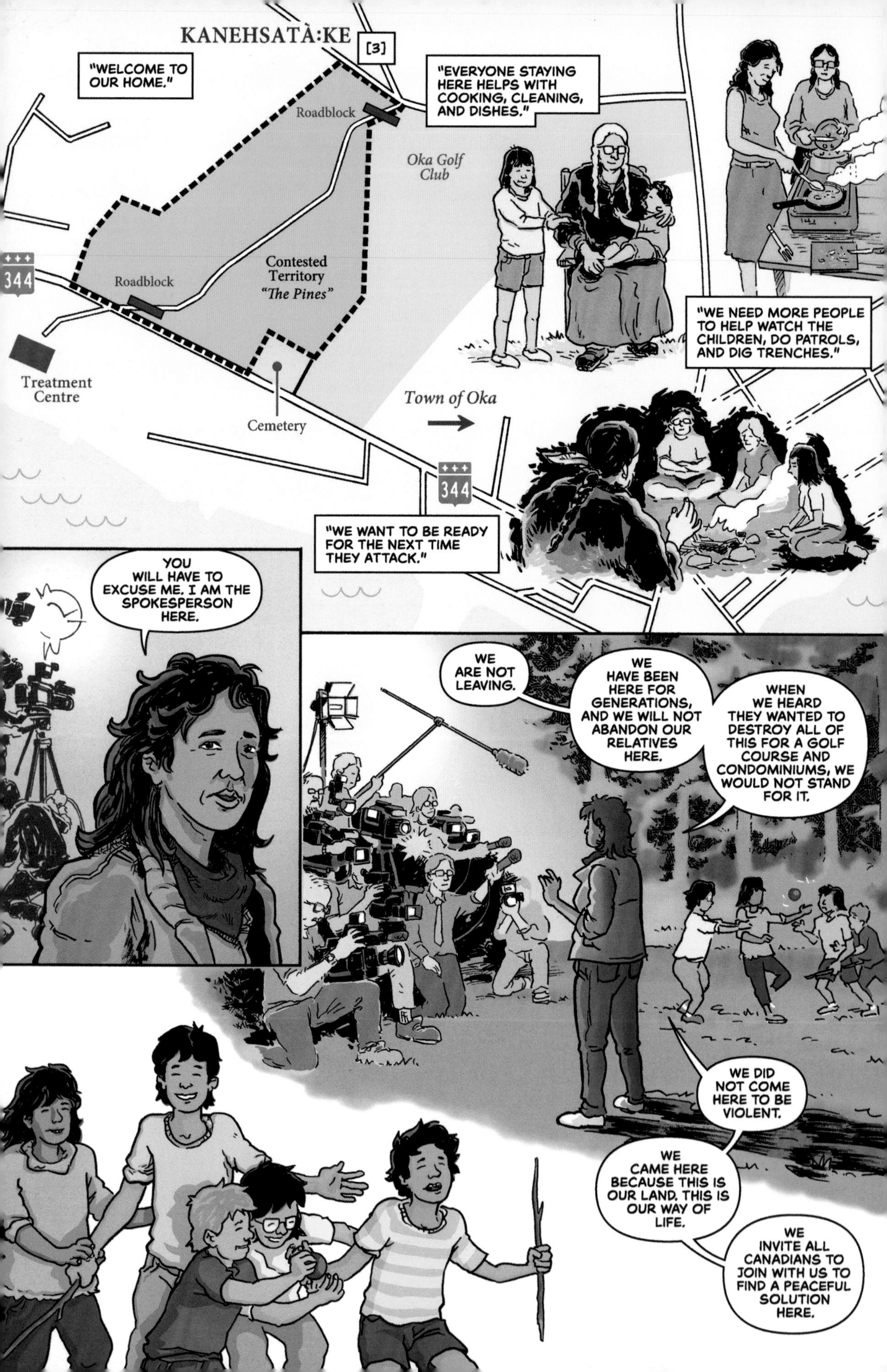

KANEHSATÀ:KE
[3]
"WELCOME TO OUR HOME."
Roadblock
"EVERYONE STAYING HERE HELPS WITH COOKING, CLEANING, AND DISHES."
Oka Golf Club
344
Roadblock
Contested Territory "The Pines"
Treatment Centre
Cemetery
Town of Oka
"WE NEED MORE PEOPLE TO HELP WATCH THE CHILDREN, DO PATROLS, AND DIG TRENCHES."
344
"WE WANT TO BE READY FOR THE NEXT TIME THEY ATTACK."
YOU WILL HAVE TO EXCUSE ME. I AM THE SPOKESPERSON HERE.
WE ARE NOT LEAVING.
WE HAVE BEEN HERE FOR GENERATIONS, AND WE WILL NOT ABANDON OUR RELATIVES HERE.
WHEN WE HEARD THEY WANTED TO DESTROY ALL OF THIS FOR A GOLF COURSE AND CONDOMINIUMS, WE WOULD NOT STAND FOR IT.
WE DID NOT COME HERE TO BE VIOLENT.
WE CAME HERE BECAUSE THIS IS OUR LAND. THIS IS OUR WAY OF LIFE.
WE INVITE ALL CANADIANS TO JOIN WITH US TO FIND A PEACEFUL SOLUTION HERE.

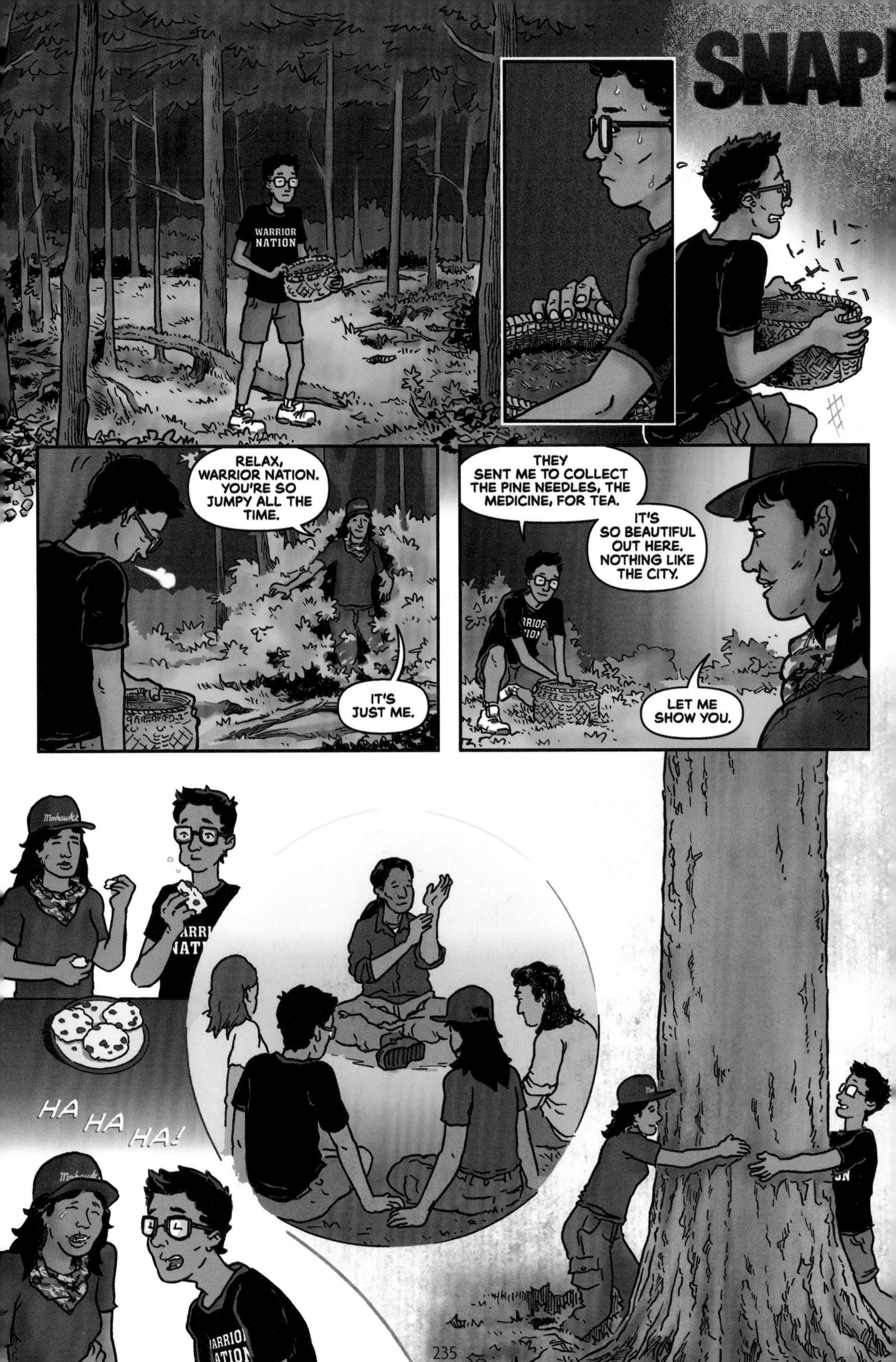
WARRIOR NATION
SNAP!
RELAX, WARRIOR NATION. YOU'RE SO JUMPY ALL THE TIME.
IT'S JUST ME.
THEY SENT ME TO COLLECT THE PINE NEEDLES, THE MEDICINE, FOR TEA.
IT'S SO BEAUTIFUL OUT HERE. NOTHING LIKE THE CITY.
LET ME SHOW YOU.
Mohawks
HA HA HA!

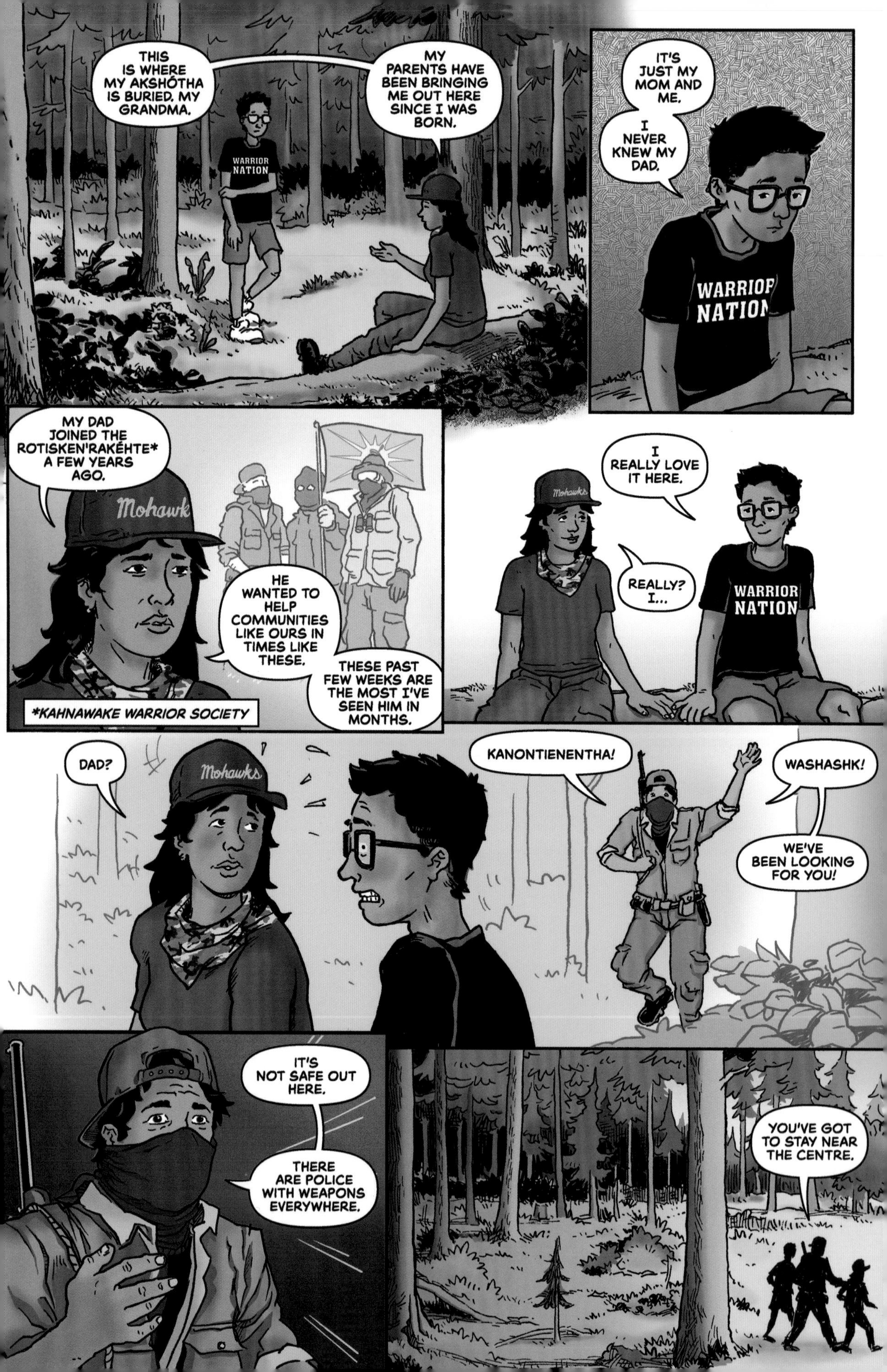
THIS IS WHERE MY AKSHÓTHA IS BURIED. MY GRANDMA.
MY PARENTS HAVE BEEN BRINGING ME OUT HERE SINCE I WAS BORN.
WARRIOR NATION
IT'S JUST MY MOM AND ME.
I NEVER KNEW MY DAD.
WARRIOR NATION
MY DAD JOINED THE ROTISKEN'RAKÉHTE* A FEW YEARS AGO.
Mohawk
HE WANTED TO HELP COMMUNITIES LIKE OURS IN TIMES LIKE THESE.
THESE PAST FEW WEEKS ARE THE MOST I'VE SEEN HIM IN MONTHS.
*KAHNAWAKE WARRIOR SOCIETY
I REALLY LOVE IT HERE.
Mohawks
REALLY? I...
WARRIOR NATION
DAD?
Mohawks
KANONTIENENTHA!
WASHASHK!
WE'VE BEEN LOOKING FOR YOU!
IT'S NOT SAFE OUT HERE.
THERE ARE POLICE WITH WEAPONS EVERYWHERE.
YOU'VE GOT TO STAY NEAR THE CENTRE.

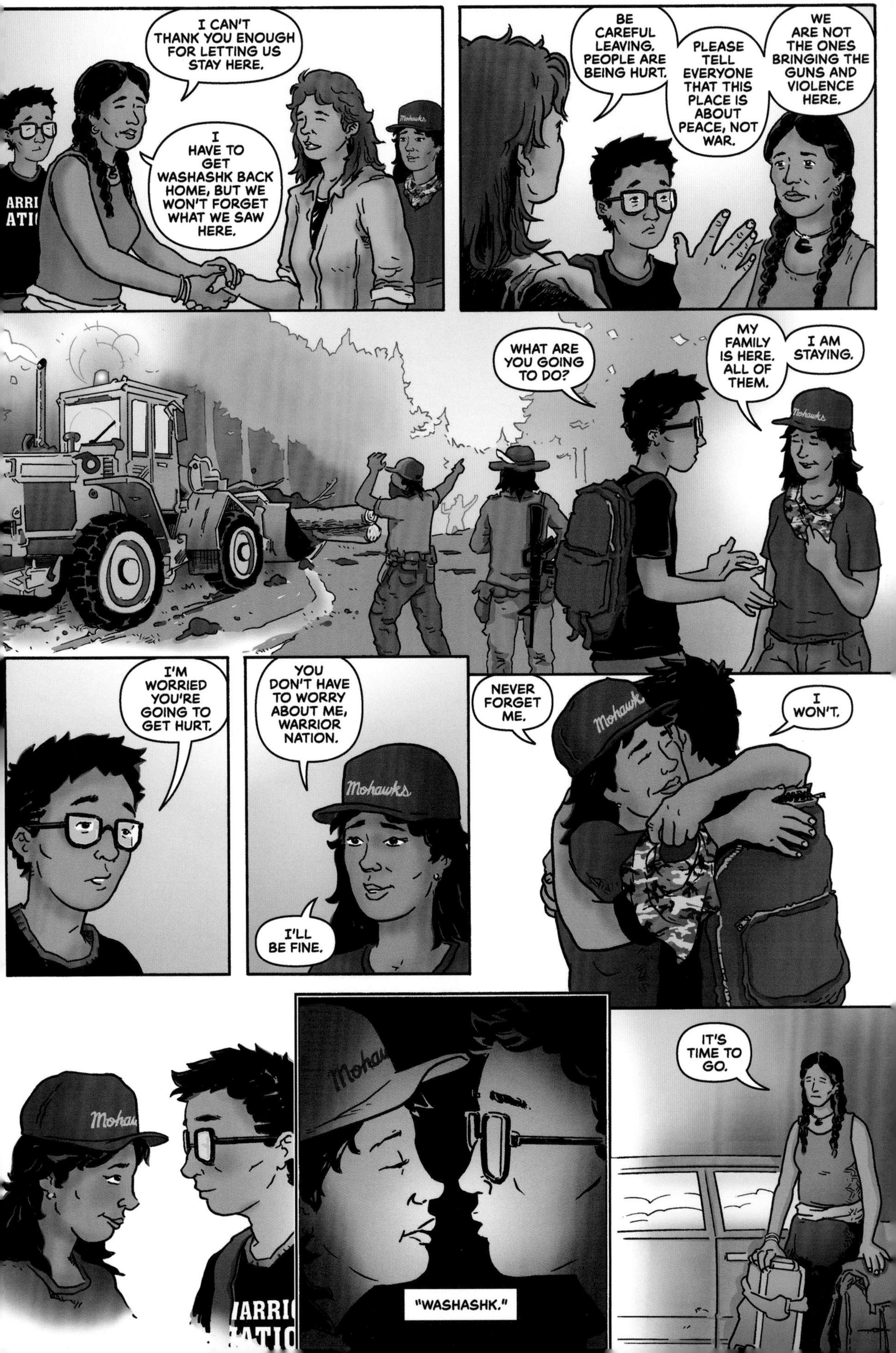
I CAN'T THANK YOU ENOUGH FOR LETTING US STAY HERE.
I HAVE TO GET WASHASHK BACK HOME, BUT WE WON'T FORGET WHAT WE SAW HERE.
ARRI ATI
BE CAREFUL LEAVING. PEOPLE ARE BEING HURT.
PLEASE TELL EVERYONE THAT THIS PLACE IS ABOUT PEACE, NOT WAR.
WE ARE NOT THE ONES BRINGING THE GUNS AND VIOLENCE HERE.
WHAT ARE YOU GOING TO DO?
MY FAMILY IS HERE. ALL OF THEM.
I AM STAYING.
Mohawks
I'M WORRIED YOU'RE GOING TO GET HURT.
YOU DON'T HAVE TO WORRY ABOUT ME, WARRIOR NATION.
Mohawks
I'LL BE FINE.
NEVER FORGET ME.
I WON'T.
"WASHASHK."
IT'S TIME TO GO.

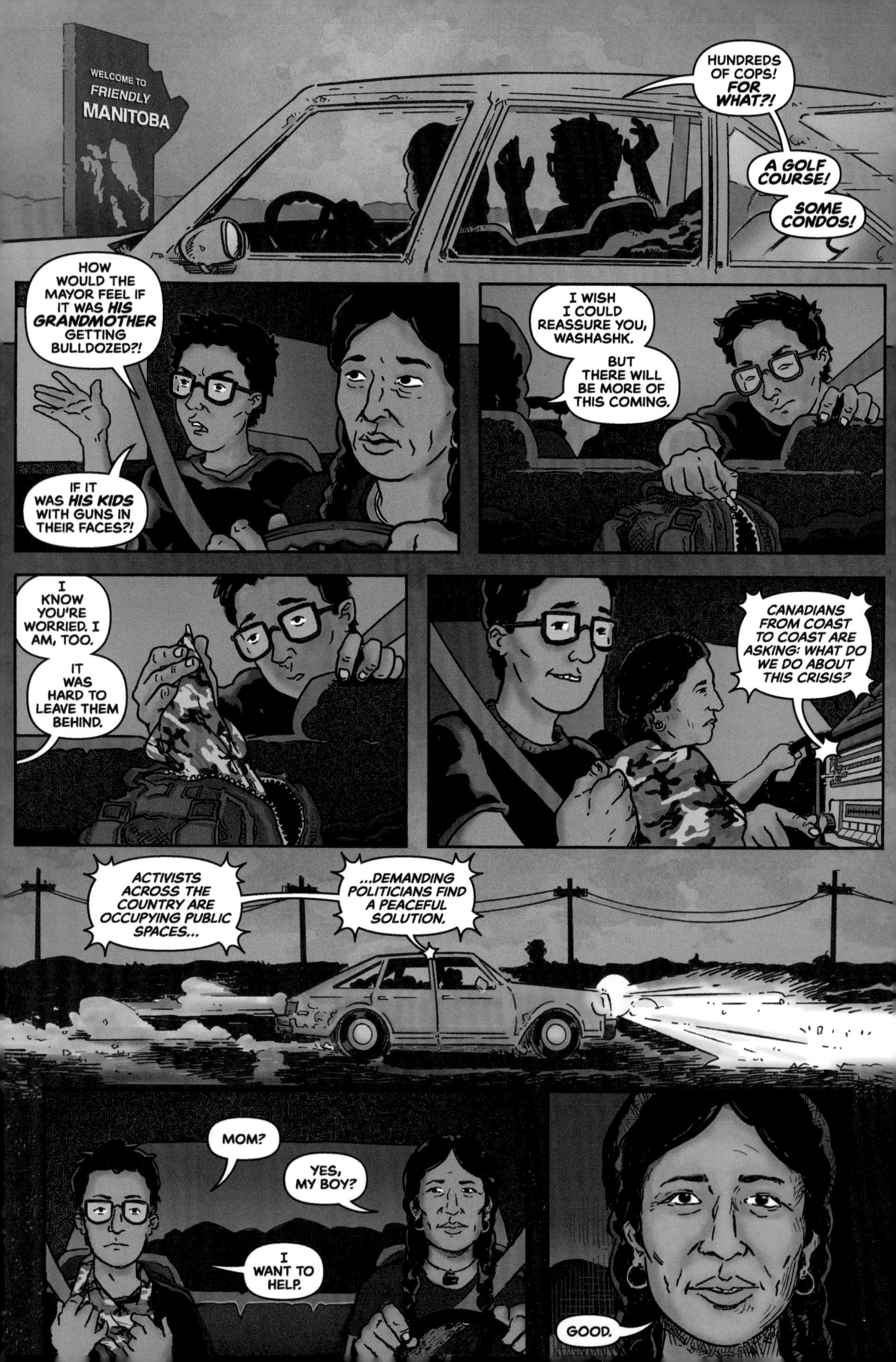
WELCOME TO
FRIENDLY
MANITOBA
HUNDREDS OF COPS! FOR WHAT?!
A GOLF COURSE!
SOME CONDOS!
HOW WOULD THE MAYOR FEEL IF IT WAS HIS GRANDMOTHER GETTING BULLDOZED?!
IF IT WAS HIS KIDS WITH GUNS IN THEIR FACES?!
I WISH I COULD REASSURE YOU, WASHASHK.
BUT THERE WILL BE MORE OF THIS COMING.
I KNOW YOU'RE WORRIED. I AM, TOO.
IT WAS HARD TO LEAVE THEM BEHIND.
CANADIANS FROM COAST TO COAST ARE ASKING: WHAT DO WE DO ABOUT THIS CRISIS?
ACTIVISTS ACROSS THE COUNTRY ARE OCCUPYING PUBLIC SPACES...
...DEMANDING POLITICIANS FIND A PEACEFUL SOLUTION.
MOM?
YES, MY BOY?
I WANT TO HELP.
GOOD.

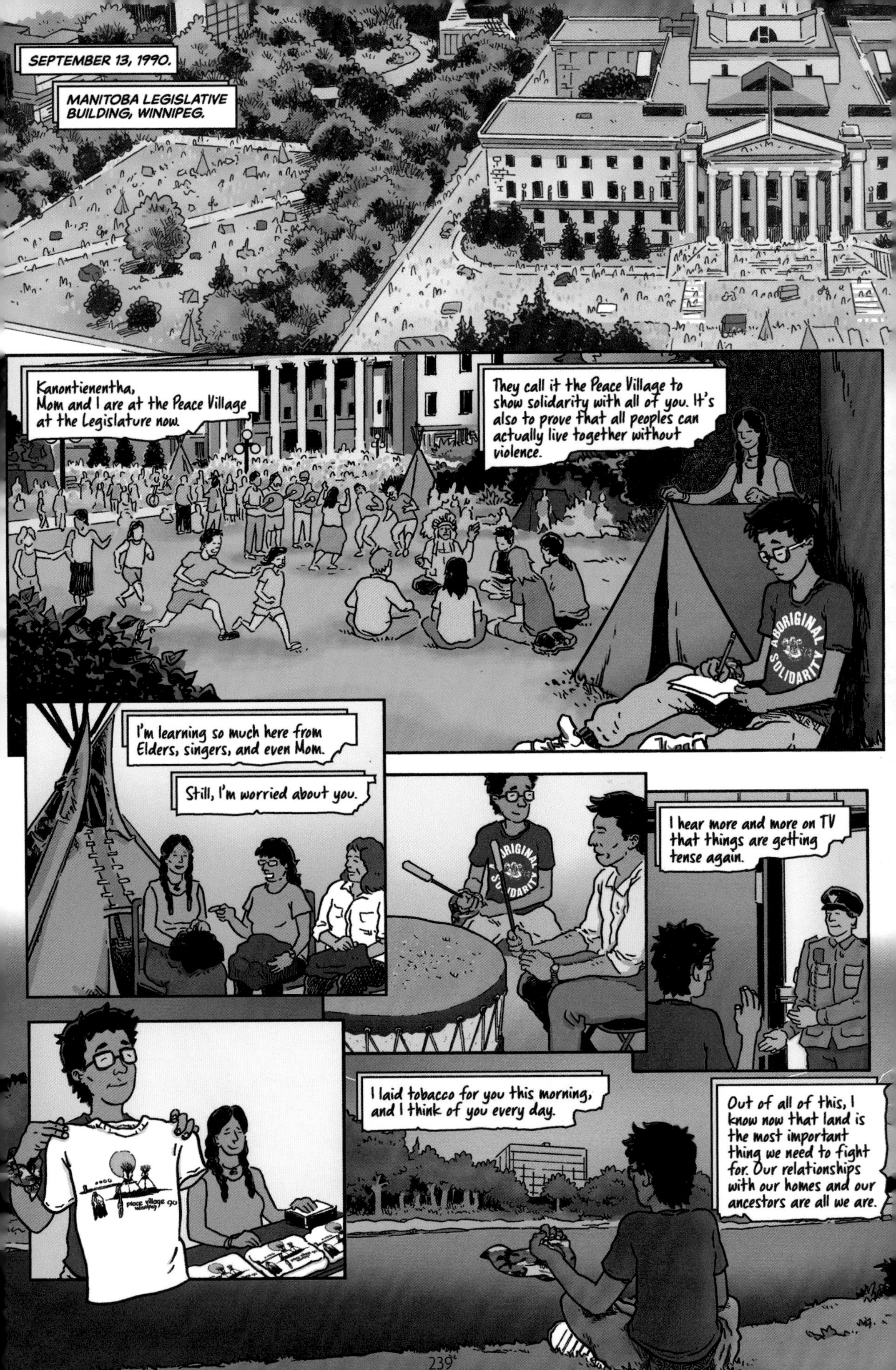
SEPTEMBER 13, 1990.
MANITOBA LEGISLATIVE BUILDING, WINNIPEG.
Kanontienentha, Mom and I are at the Peace Village at the Legislature now.
They call it the Peace Village to show solidarity with all of you. It's also to prove that all peoples can actually live together without violence.
ABORIGINAL SOLIDARITY
I'm learning so much here from Elders, singers, and even Mom.
Still, I'm worried about you.
ABORIGINAL SOLIDARITY
I hear more and more on TV that things are getting tense again.
peace village winnipeg 90
I laid tobacco for you this morning, and I think of you every day.
Out of all of this, I know now that land is the most important thing we need to fight for. Our relationships with our homes and our ancestors are all we are.

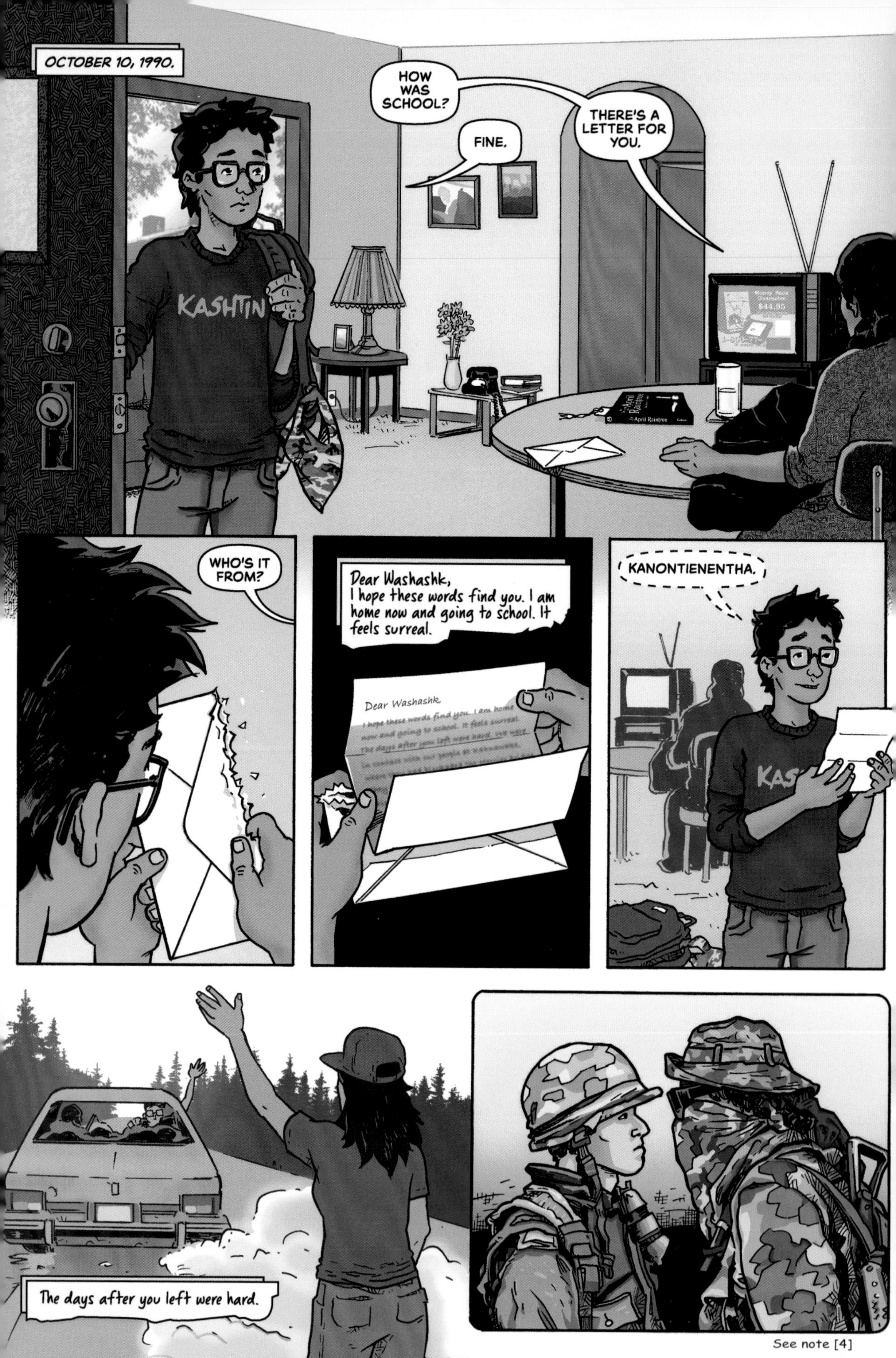
OCTOBER 10, 1990.
HOW WAS SCHOOL?
FINE.
THERE'S A LETTER FOR YOU.
KASHTIN
WHO'S IT FROM?
Dear Washashk,
I hope these words find you. I am home now and going to school. It feels surreal.
Dear Washashk
KANONTIENENTHA.
The days after you left were hard.

See note [4]

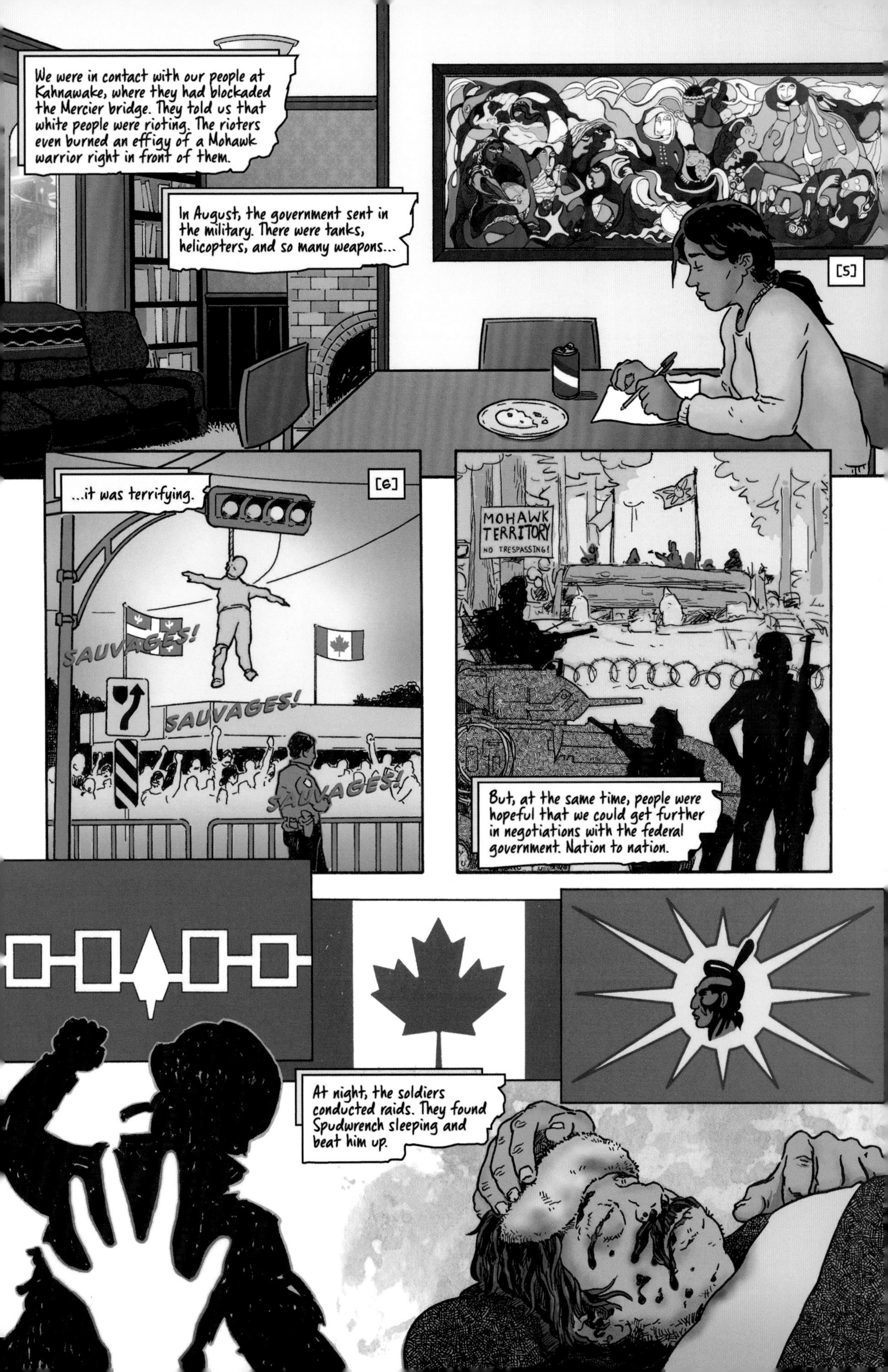

We were in contact with our people at Kahnawake, where they had blockaded the Mercier bridge. They told us that white people were rioting. The rioters even burned an effigy of a Mohawk warrior right in front of them.
In August, the government sent in the military. There were tanks, helicopters, and so many weapons...
[5]
...it was terrifying.
[6]
SAUVAGES!
SAUVAGES!
SAUVAGES!
MOHAWK TERRITORY
NO TRESPASSING!
But, at the same time, people were hopeful that we could get further in negotiations with the federal government. Nation to nation.
At night, the soldiers conducted raids. They found Spudwrench sleeping and beat him up.

The army cut off our food supply. Some of us wore the same clothes for months.

When you were with us, there were hundreds of people at the camp. By the end of September, there was only a handful of us left.

Many of us were scared for our lives. Winter was coming, too.

On September 26th, we decided to leave. We didn't surrender.

Then everything went crazy. The soldiers and police didn't want us to escape.

One soldier stabbed my friend Waneek with his bayonet. She was carrying her little sister.

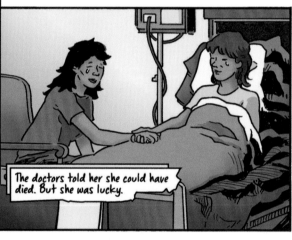

The doctors told her she could have died. But she was lucky.

The police arrested everyone. But most of us are back home now.

And it feels like nothing changed. Canada has gone back to ignoring us.

And they still have our land.

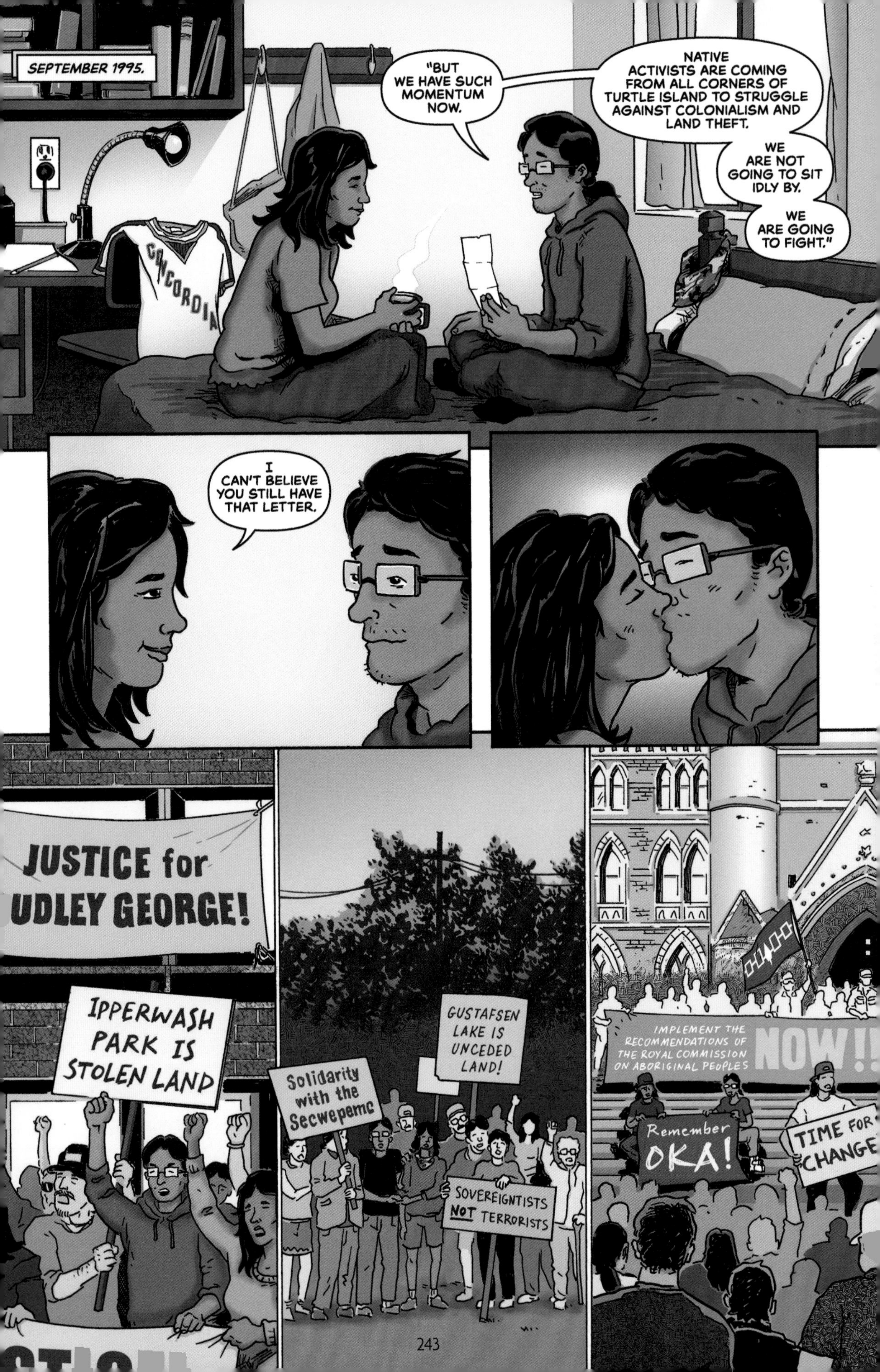

SEPTEMBER 1995.
"BUT WE HAVE SUCH MOMENTUM NOW.
NATIVE ACTIVISTS ARE COMING FROM ALL CORNERS OF TURTLE ISLAND TO STRUGGLE AGAINST COLONIALISM AND LAND THEFT.
WE ARE NOT GOING TO SIT IDLY BY.
WE ARE GOING TO FIGHT."
CONCORDIA
I CAN'T BELIEVE YOU STILL HAVE THAT LETTER.
JUSTICE for UDLEY GEORGE!
IPPERWASH PARK IS STOLEN LAND
GUSTAFSEN LAKE IS UNCEDED LAND!
Solidarity with the Secwepemc
SOVEREIGNTISTS NOT TERRORISTS
IMPLEMENT THE RECOMMENDATIONS OF THE ROYAL COMMISSION ON ABORIGINAL PEOPLES NOW!!
Remember OKA!
TIME FOR CHANGE

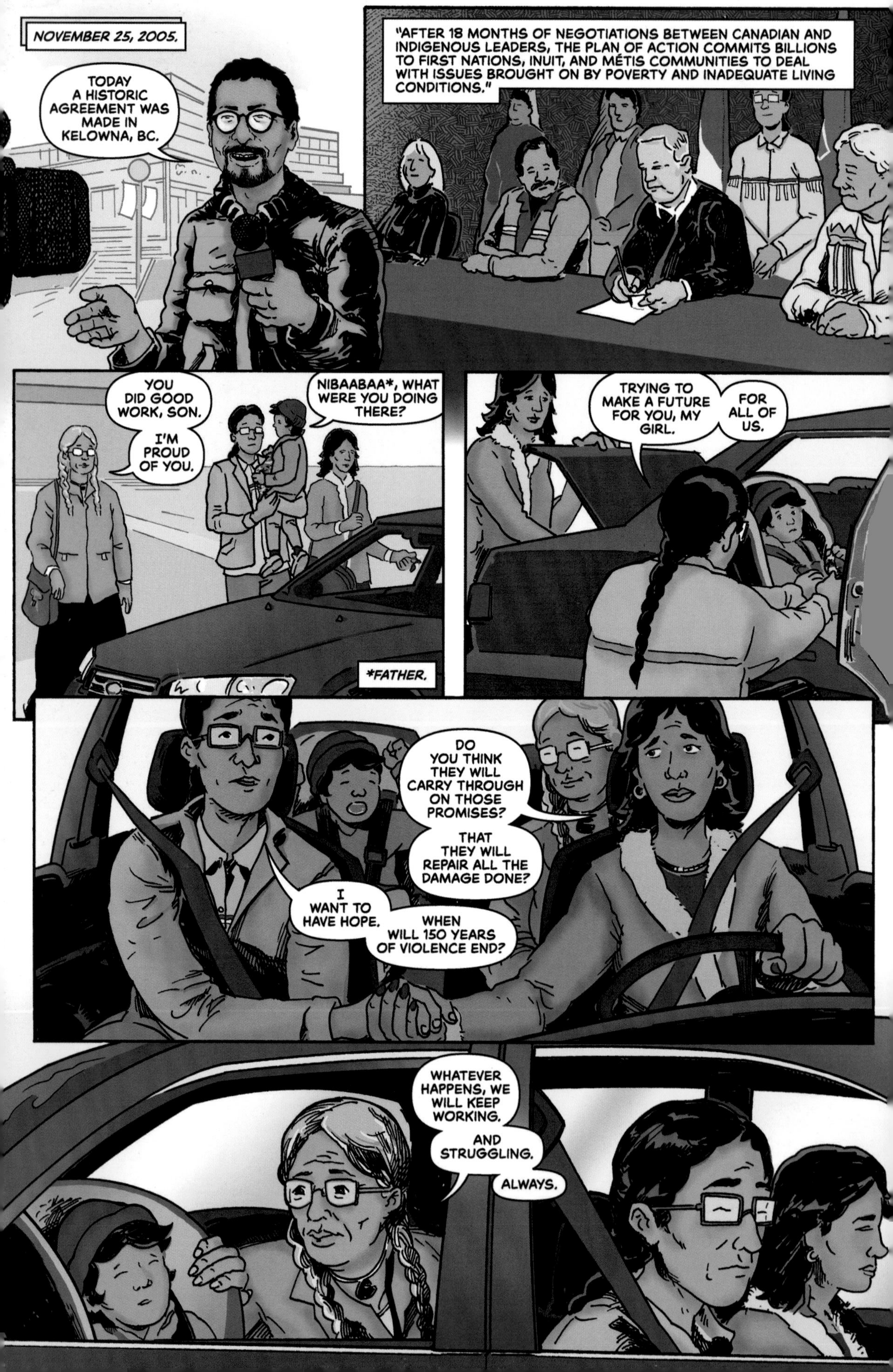
NOVEMBER 25, 2005.
TODAY A HISTORIC AGREEMENT WAS MADE IN KELOWNA, BC.
"AFTER 18 MONTHS OF NEGOTIATIONS BETWEEN CANADIAN AND INDIGENOUS LEADERS, THE PLAN OF ACTION COMMITS BILLIONS TO FIRST NATIONS, INUIT, AND MÉTIS COMMUNITIES TO DEAL WITH ISSUES BROUGHT ON BY POVERTY AND INADEQUATE LIVING CONDITIONS."
YOU DID GOOD WORK, SON.
I'M PROUD OF YOU.
NIBAABAA*, WHAT WERE YOU DOING THERE?
*FATHER.
TRYING TO MAKE A FUTURE FOR YOU, MY GIRL.
FOR ALL OF US.
DO YOU THINK THEY WILL CARRY THROUGH ON THOSE PROMISES?
THAT THEY WILL REPAIR ALL THE DAMAGE DONE?
I WANT TO HAVE HOPE.
WHEN WILL 150 YEARS OF VIOLENCE END?
WHATEVER HAPPENS, WE WILL KEEP WORKING.
AND STRUGGLING.
ALWAYS.

Dystopian or apocalyptic writing occupies an enormous amount of space in contemporary storytelling and in our social consciousness. We are told that the end is nigh, and that the world (or at least the world as we know it) will be destroyed, and that this is a Bad Thing. We are encouraged to imagine what life could be like during and after this supposedly inevitable destruction, but are steered away from dreaming up alternatives. Indigenous peoples have been living in a post-apocalyptic world since Contact. This entire anthology deals with events post-apocalypse! Why end on the same note?

In 2014, Molly Swain and I began an Indigenous feminist sci-fi podcast called *Métis in Space*. We explicitly rejected the idea that liberation necessarily proceeds from a period of even more intense oppression, of apocalypse as a catalyst for decolonization. Instead, we envisioned a future shaped by Indigenous peoples, a future in which the ways we relate to one another are fundamentally transformed.

This chapter is a love letter to my ancestors and my descendants. It is a refusal to lose hope, and a denial of oblivion. Indigenous peoples will continue to exist into the near and far future. We need space and time to imagine our relationships branching out, growing in spite of severances, becoming more firmly rooted and nourished. We can do that work wherever we are, in our communities, in the academy, at the bedside of our babies who demand just one. more. story.

Perhaps, after you finish this anthology, you will realize you too have been doing this work, and for that, I thank you.

Chelsea Vowel

nêhiyâwêwin translations by Chelsea Vowel

In the scenes set in the future, the characters are speaking Plains Cree Y Dialect (nêhiyâwêwin). For the 21st century reader's convenience, most of this dialogue has been translated into English.

2005
Kelowna Accord is agreed to between Indigenous and Canadian leaders. Meant to increase support for Indigenous communities, subsequent federal governments fail to enact the Accord.

2013
Members of Elsipogtog First Nation blockade to prevent fracking near their reserve, in the face of police violence and dozens of arrests.

2012
#IdleNoMore movement begins, using marches, blockades, and flash mob Round Dances to fight for Indigenous sovereignty, and against racialized inequality and ecological destruction.

2007
The United Nations votes to adopt the Declaration of the Rights of Indigenous Peoples; Canada is one of four states to vote against it.

2008
Prime Minister Stephen Harper offers a formal apology on behalf of Canada for the residential school system. The Truth and Reconciliation Commission (TRC) begins to document the impact of the schools.

kitaskînaw 2350

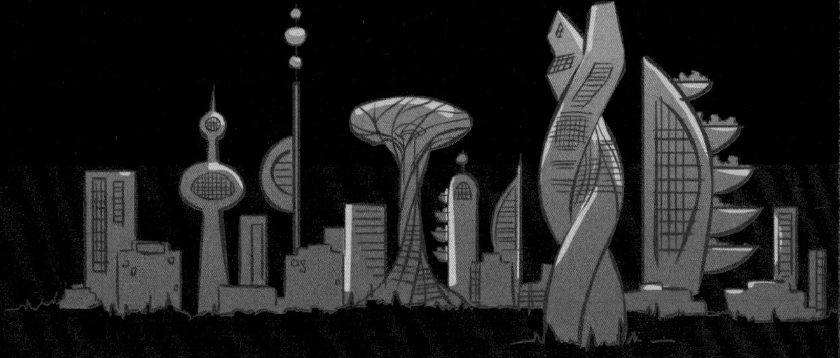

Chelsea Vowel
Illustration: Tara Audibert
Colours: Donovan Yaciuk

2015
The TRC ends. Subsequent Canadian governments are criticized for failing to enact meaningful change to colonialism's ongoing impact on Indigenous communities.

2015-PRESENT
Outcry over the 1200+ Indigenous women killed or missing between 1980-2012 leads to a national inquiry into Missing and Murdered Indigenous Women and Girls.

2018
Gerald Stanley and Raymond Cormier are found not guilty for the murders of Colten Boushie and Tina Fontaine. These verdicts prompt protests over the devaluing of Indigenous lives by the Canadian justice system.

2016-2017
Massive protests occur against pipeline development near Standing Rock Reservation, North Dakota.

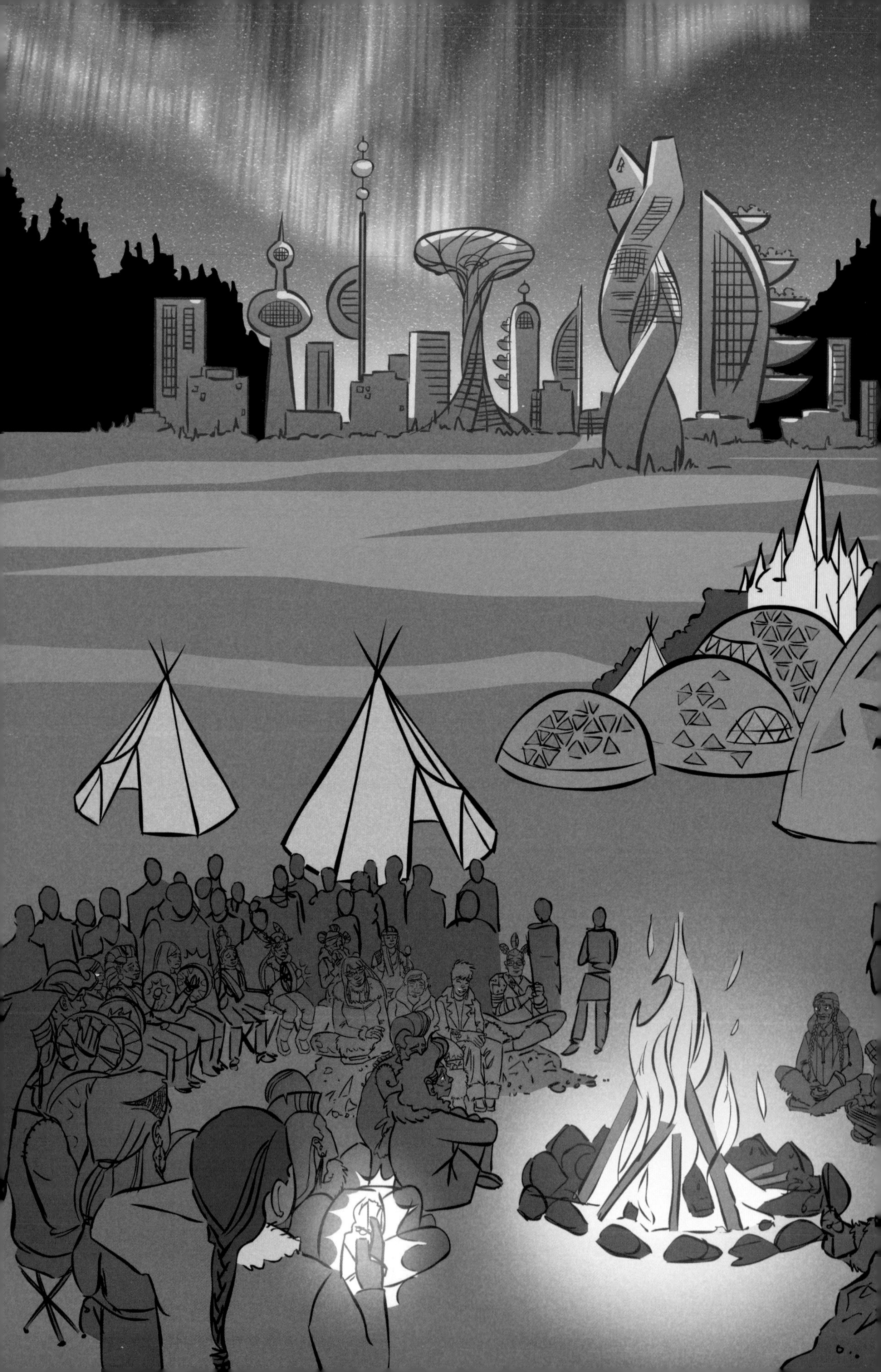

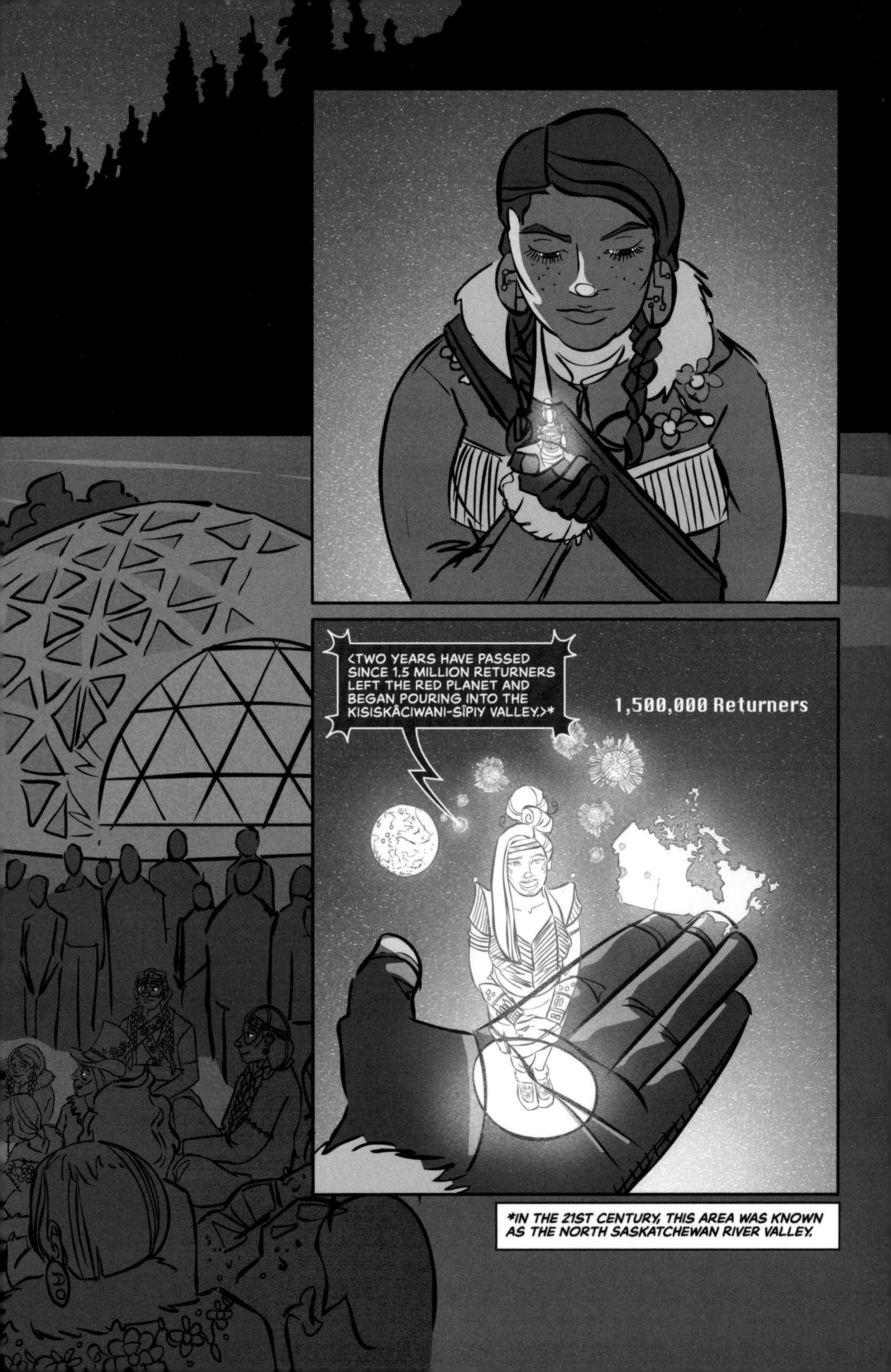
<TWO YEARS HAVE PASSED SINCE 1.5 MILLION RETURNERS LEFT THE RED PLANET AND BEGAN POURING INTO THE KISISKÂCIWANI-SÎPIY VALLEY.>*
1,500,000 Returners
*IN THE 21ST CENTURY, THIS AREA WAS KNOWN AS THE NORTH SASKATCHEWAN RIVER VALLEY.

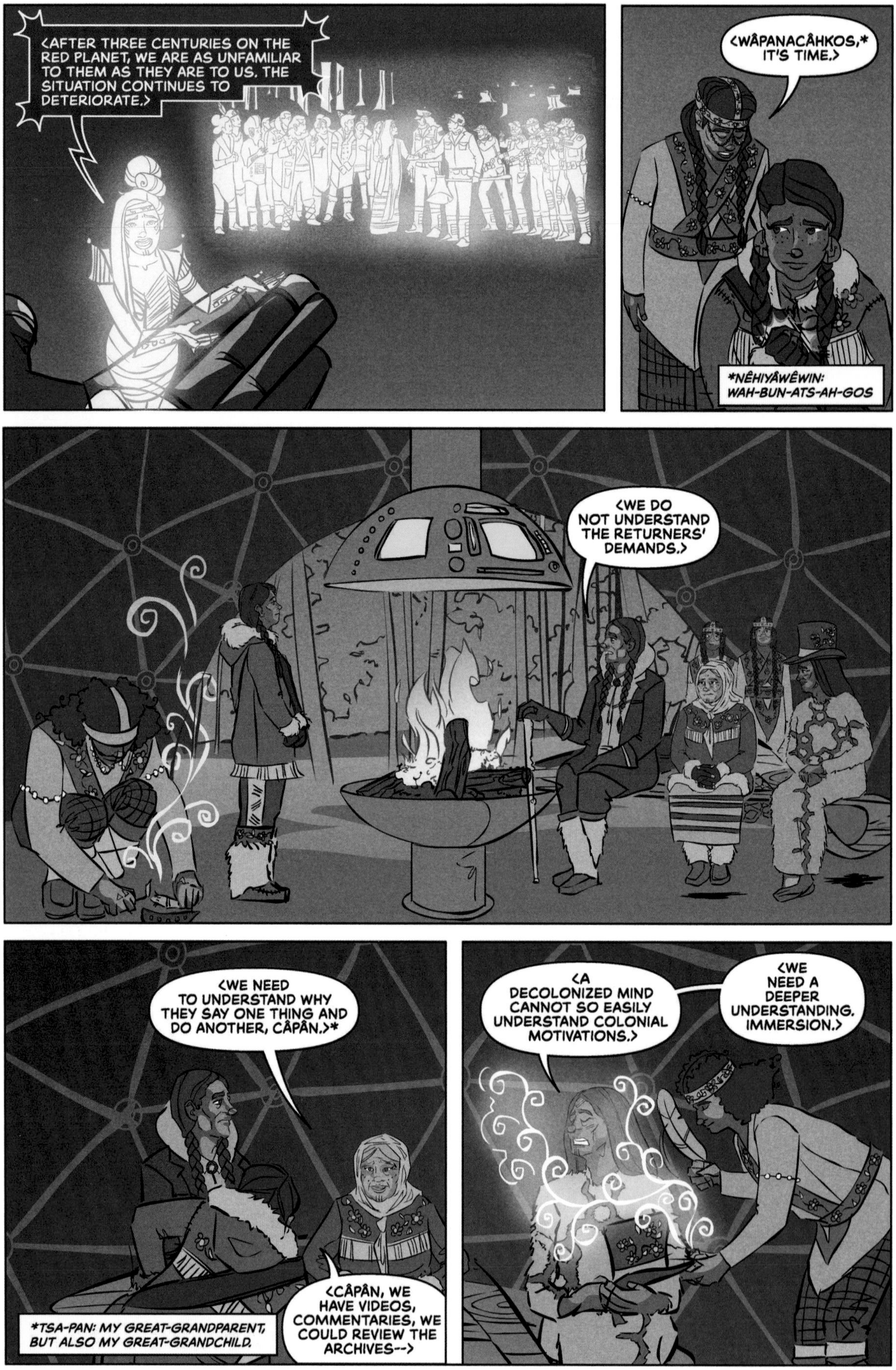
<AFTER THREE CENTURIES ON THE RED PLANET, WE ARE AS UNFAMILIAR TO THEM AS THEY ARE TO US. THE SITUATION CONTINUES TO DETERIORATE.>
<WÂPANACÂHKOS,* IT'S TIME.>
*NÊHIYÂWÊWIN: WAH-BUN-ATS-AH-GOS
<WE DO NOT UNDERSTAND THE RETURNERS' DEMANDS.>
<WE NEED TO UNDERSTAND WHY THEY SAY ONE THING AND DO ANOTHER, CÂPÂN.>*
*TSA-PAN: MY GREAT-GRANDPARENT, BUT ALSO MY GREAT-GRANDCHILD.
<CÂPÂN, WE HAVE VIDEOS, COMMENTARIES, WE COULD REVIEW THE ARCHIVES-->
<A DECOLONIZED MIND CANNOT SO EASILY UNDERSTAND COLONIAL MOTIVATIONS.>
<WE NEED A DEEPER UNDERSTANDING. IMMERSION.>

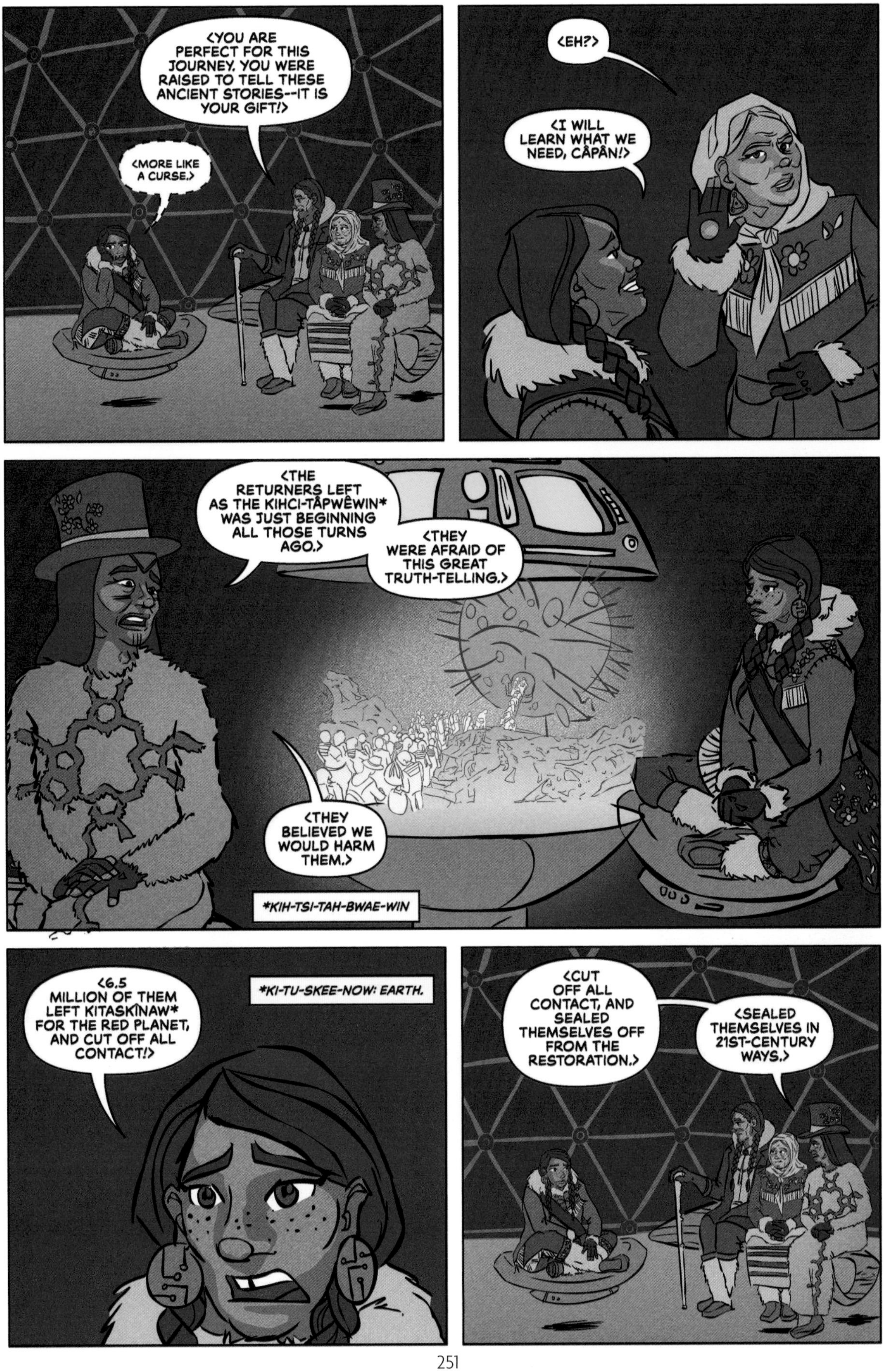
<YOU ARE PERFECT FOR THIS JOURNEY. YOU WERE RAISED TO TELL THESE ANCIENT STORIES--IT IS YOUR GIFT!>
<MORE LIKE A CURSE.>
<EH?>
<I WILL LEARN WHAT WE NEED, CÂPÂN!>
<THE RETURNERS LEFT AS THE KIHCI-TÂPWÊWIN* WAS JUST BEGINNING ALL THOSE TURNS AGO.>
<THEY WERE AFRAID OF THIS GREAT TRUTH-TELLING.>
<THEY BELIEVED WE WOULD HARM THEM.>
*KIH-TSI-TAH-BWAE-WIN
<6.5 MILLION OF THEM LEFT KITASKÎNAW* FOR THE RED PLANET, AND CUT OFF ALL CONTACT!>
*KI-TU-SKEE-NOW: EARTH.
<CUT OFF ALL CONTACT, AND SEALED THEMSELVES OFF FROM THE RESTORATION.>
<SEALED THEMSELVES IN 21ST-CENTURY WAYS.>

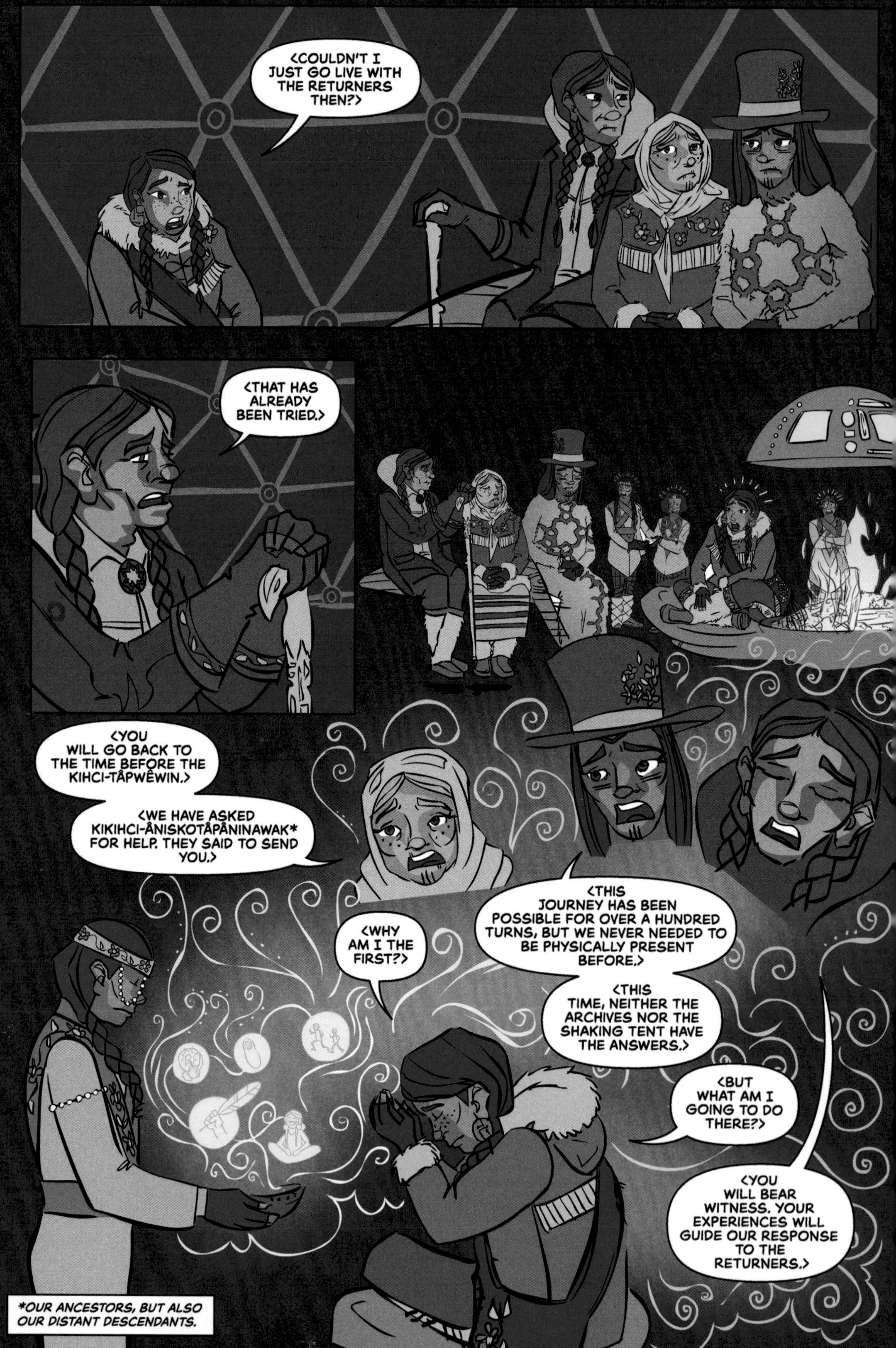

<COULDN'T I JUST GO LIVE WITH THE RETURNERS THEN?>
<THAT HAS ALREADY BEEN TRIED.>
<YOU WILL GO BACK TO THE TIME BEFORE THE KIHCI-TÂPWÊWIN.>
<WE HAVE ASKED KIKIHCI-ÂNISKOTÂPÂNINAWAK* FOR HELP. THEY SAID TO SEND YOU.>
<WHY AM I THE FIRST?>
<THIS JOURNEY HAS BEEN POSSIBLE FOR OVER A HUNDRED TURNS, BUT WE NEVER NEEDED TO BE PHYSICALLY PRESENT BEFORE.>
<THIS TIME, NEITHER THE ARCHIVES NOR THE SHAKING TENT HAVE THE ANSWERS.>
<BUT WHAT AM I GOING TO DO THERE?>
<YOU WILL BEAR WITNESS. YOUR EXPERIENCES WILL GUIDE OUR RESPONSE TO THE RETURNERS.>
*OUR ANCESTORS, BUT ALSO OUR DISTANT DESCENDANTS.

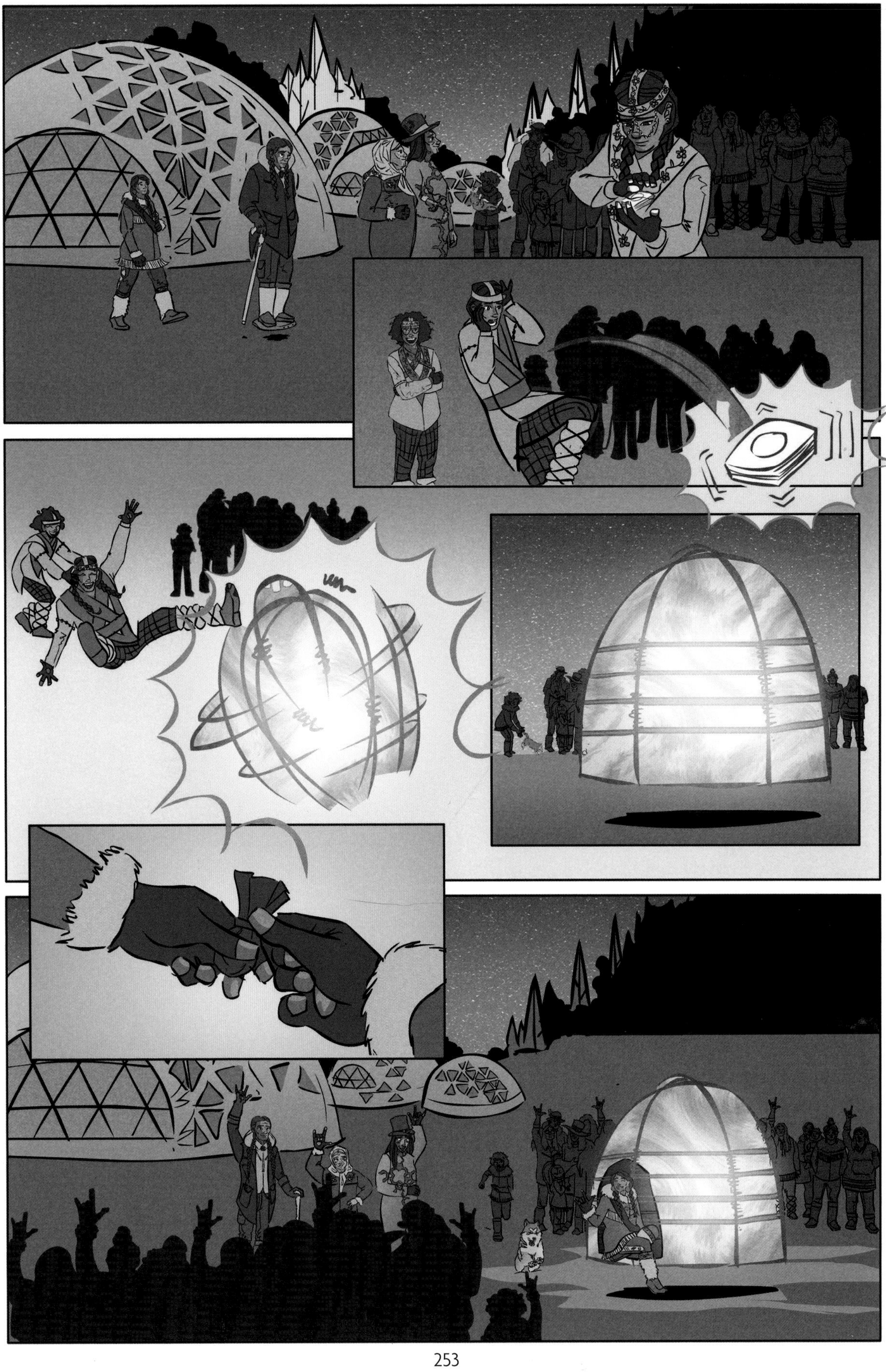

ᐃᑐᐦᑌᐃᐧᐤ
ᑖᐧᓂᐢᐲˣ
18ᐸᐚᒐᑭᓇᓰᓯ ᐲᓯᒼ2012
<WHERE...>
<...WHEN AM I?>
<THIS ISN'T RIGHT!>
<WHAT ARE YOU DOING HERE, ACIMOSIS*?>
*PUPPY.

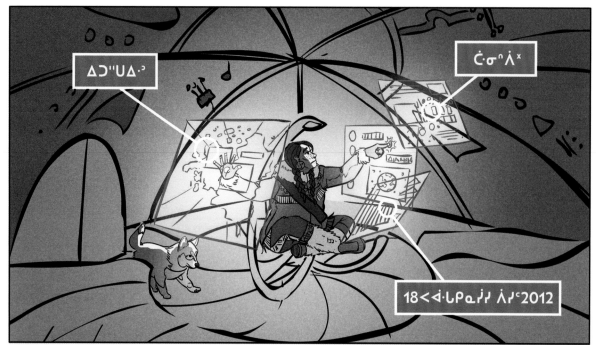

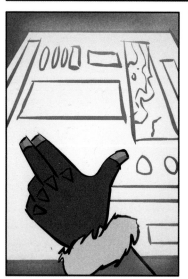

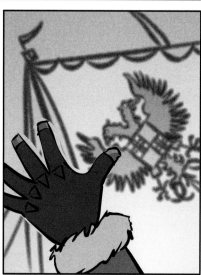

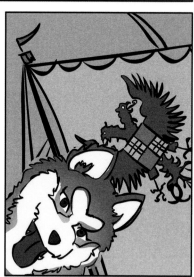

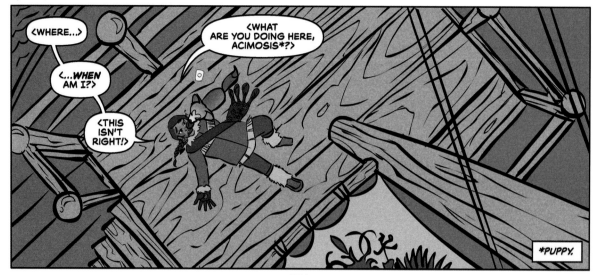

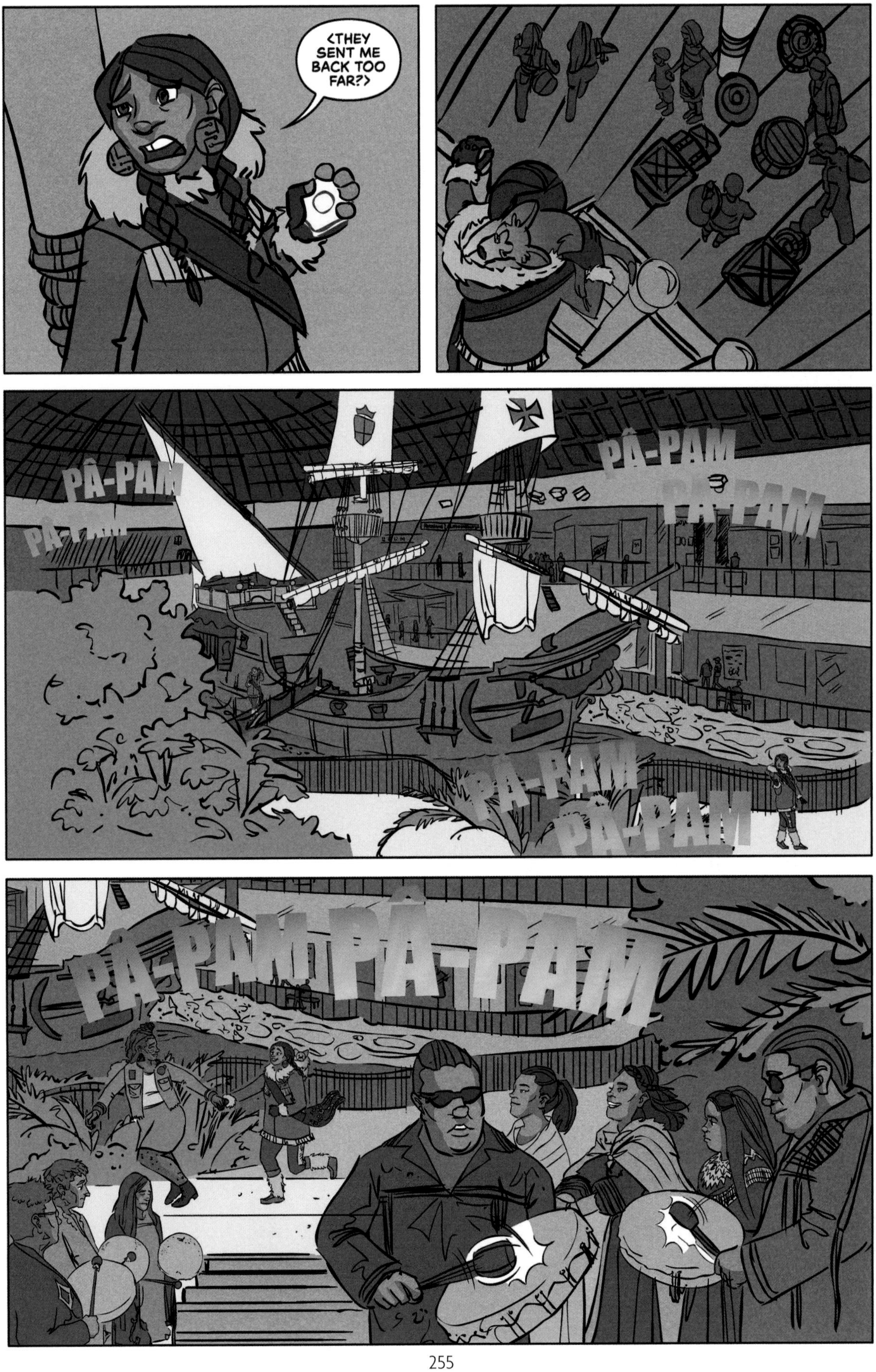
<THEY SENT ME BACK TOO FAR?>
PÂ-PAM
PÂ-PAM
PÂ-PAM
PÂ-PAM
PÂ-PAM
PÂ-PAM
PÂ-PAM PÂ-PAM

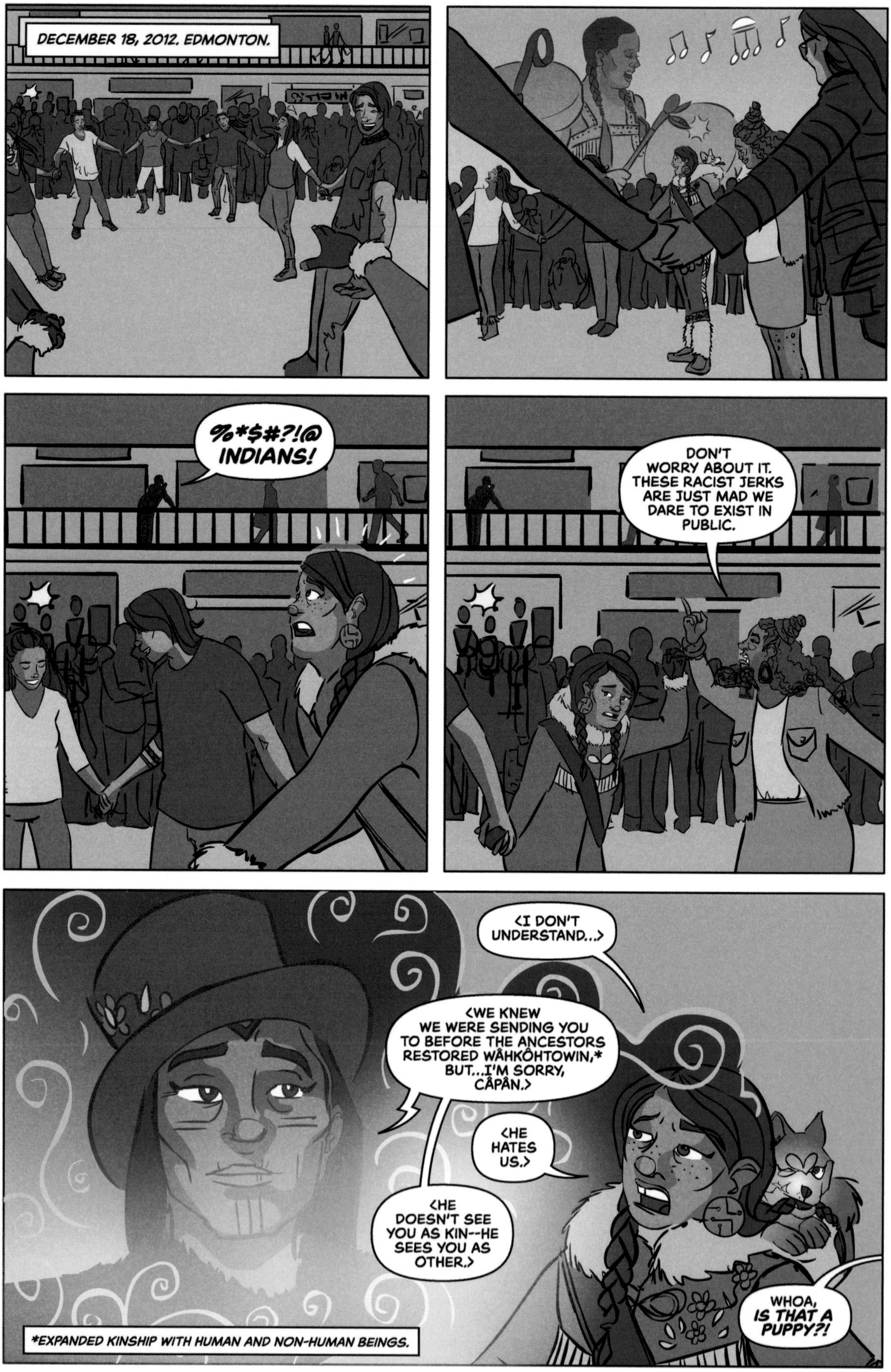

DECEMBER 18, 2012. EDMONTON.
%*$#?!@ INDIANS!
DON'T WORRY ABOUT IT. THESE RACIST JERKS ARE JUST MAD WE DARE TO EXIST IN PUBLIC.
<I DON'T UNDERSTAND...>
<WE KNEW WE WERE SENDING YOU TO BEFORE THE ANCESTORS RESTORED WÂHKÔHTOWIN,* BUT...I'M SORRY, CÂPÂN.>
<HE HATES US.>
<HE DOESN'T SEE YOU AS KIN--HE SEES YOU AS OTHER.>
WHOA, IS THAT A PUPPY?!
*EXPANDED KINSHIP WITH HUMAN AND NON-HUMAN BEINGS.

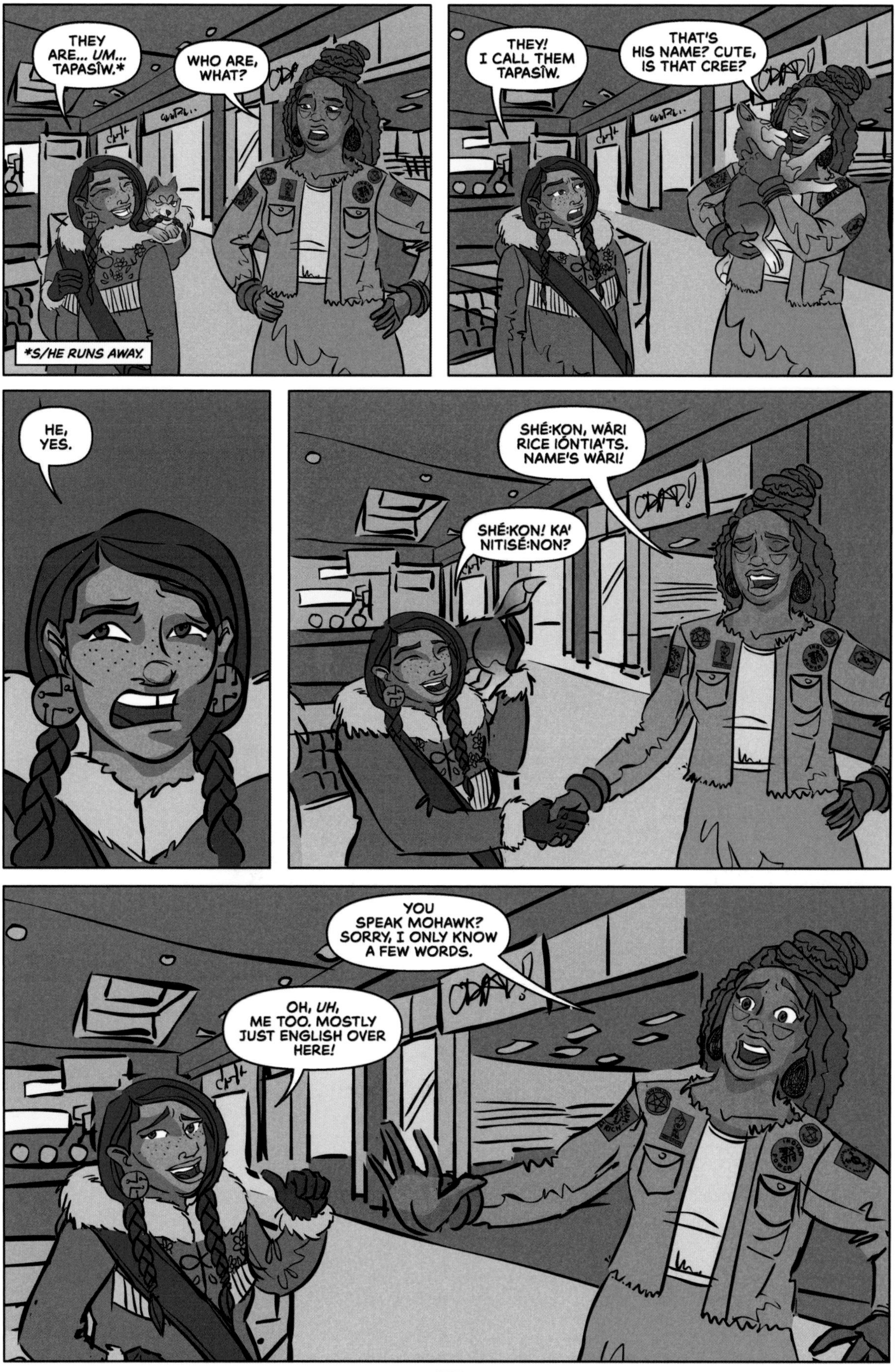
THEY ARE... *UM*... TAPASÎW.*
WHO ARE, WHAT?
*S/HE RUNS AWAY.
THEY! I CALL THEM TAPASÎW.
THAT'S HIS NAME? CUTE, IS THAT CREE?
HE, YES.
SHÉ:KON, WÂRI RICE IÓNTIA'TS. NAME'S WÂRI!
SHÉ:KON! KA' NITISÉ:NON?
YOU SPEAK MOHAWK? SORRY, I ONLY KNOW A FEW WORDS.
OH, *UH*, ME TOO. MOSTLY JUST ENGLISH OVER HERE!

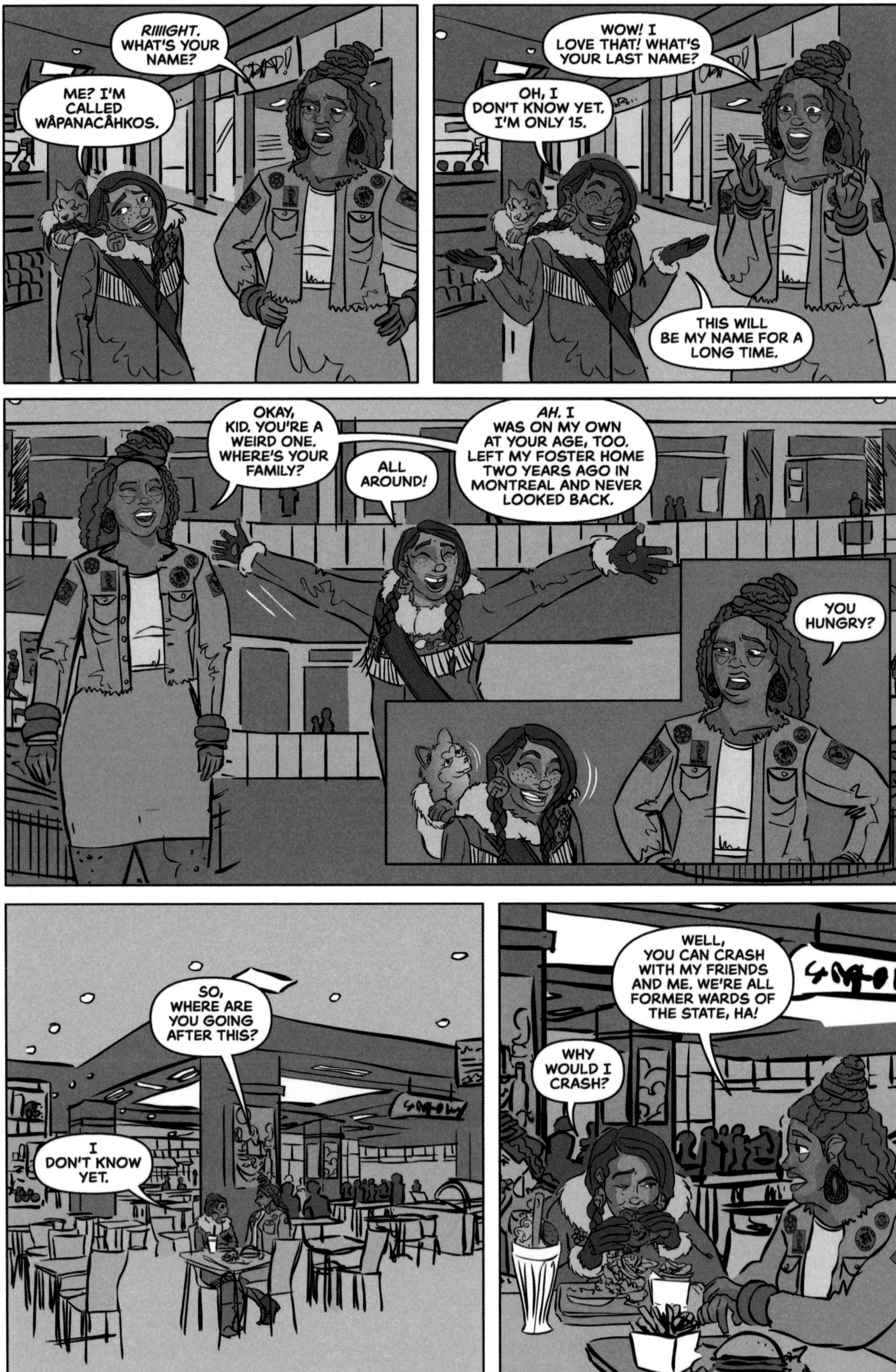
RIIIIGHT. WHAT'S YOUR NAME?
ME? I'M CALLED WÂPANACÂHKOS.
WOW! I LOVE THAT! WHAT'S YOUR LAST NAME?
OH, I DON'T KNOW YET. I'M ONLY 15.
THIS WILL BE MY NAME FOR A LONG TIME.
OKAY, KID. YOU'RE A WEIRD ONE. WHERE'S YOUR FAMILY?
ALL AROUND!
AH. I WAS ON MY OWN AT YOUR AGE, TOO. LEFT MY FOSTER HOME TWO YEARS AGO IN MONTREAL AND NEVER LOOKED BACK.
YOU HUNGRY?
SO, WHERE ARE YOU GOING AFTER THIS?
I DON'T KNOW YET.
WELL, YOU CAN CRASH WITH MY FRIENDS AND ME. WE'RE ALL FORMER WARDS OF THE STATE, HA!
WHY WOULD I CRASH?

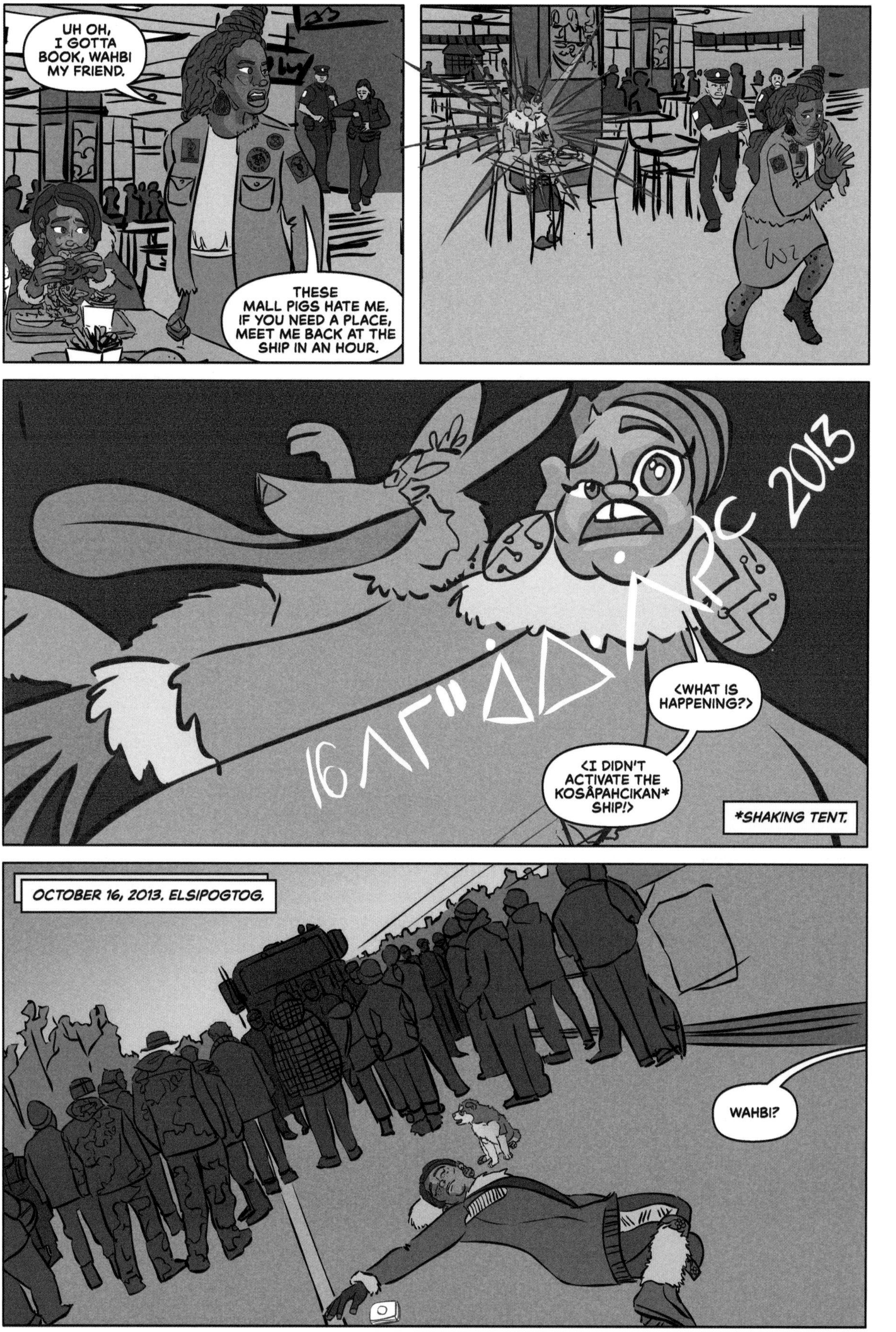
UH OH, I GOTTA BOOK, WAHBI MY FRIEND.
THESE MALL PIGS HATE ME. IF YOU NEED A PLACE, MEET ME BACK AT THE SHIP IN AN HOUR.
<WHAT IS HAPPENING?>
<I DIDN'T ACTIVATE THE KOSÂPAHCIKAN* SHIP!>
*SHAKING TENT.
OCTOBER 16, 2013. ELSIPOGTOG.
WAHBI?

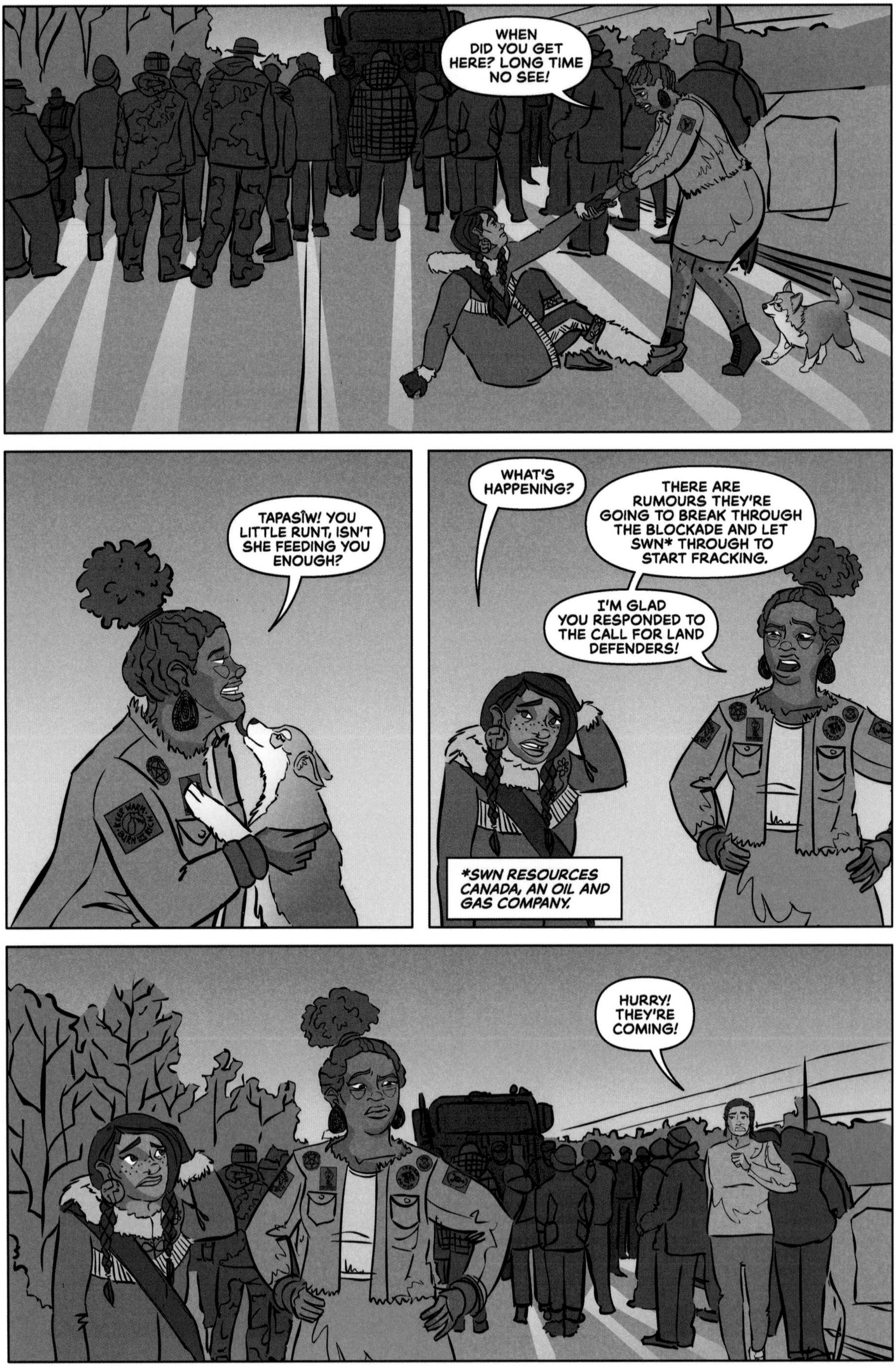
WHEN DID YOU GET HERE? LONG TIME NO SEE!
TAPASÎW! YOU LITTLE RUNT, ISN'T SHE FEEDING YOU ENOUGH?
WHAT'S HAPPENING?
THERE ARE RUMOURS THEY'RE GOING TO BREAK THROUGH THE BLOCKADE AND LET SWN* THROUGH TO START FRACKING.
I'M GLAD YOU RESPONDED TO THE CALL FOR LAND DEFENDERS!
*SWN RESOURCES CANADA, AN OIL AND GAS COMPANY.
HURRY! THEY'RE COMING!

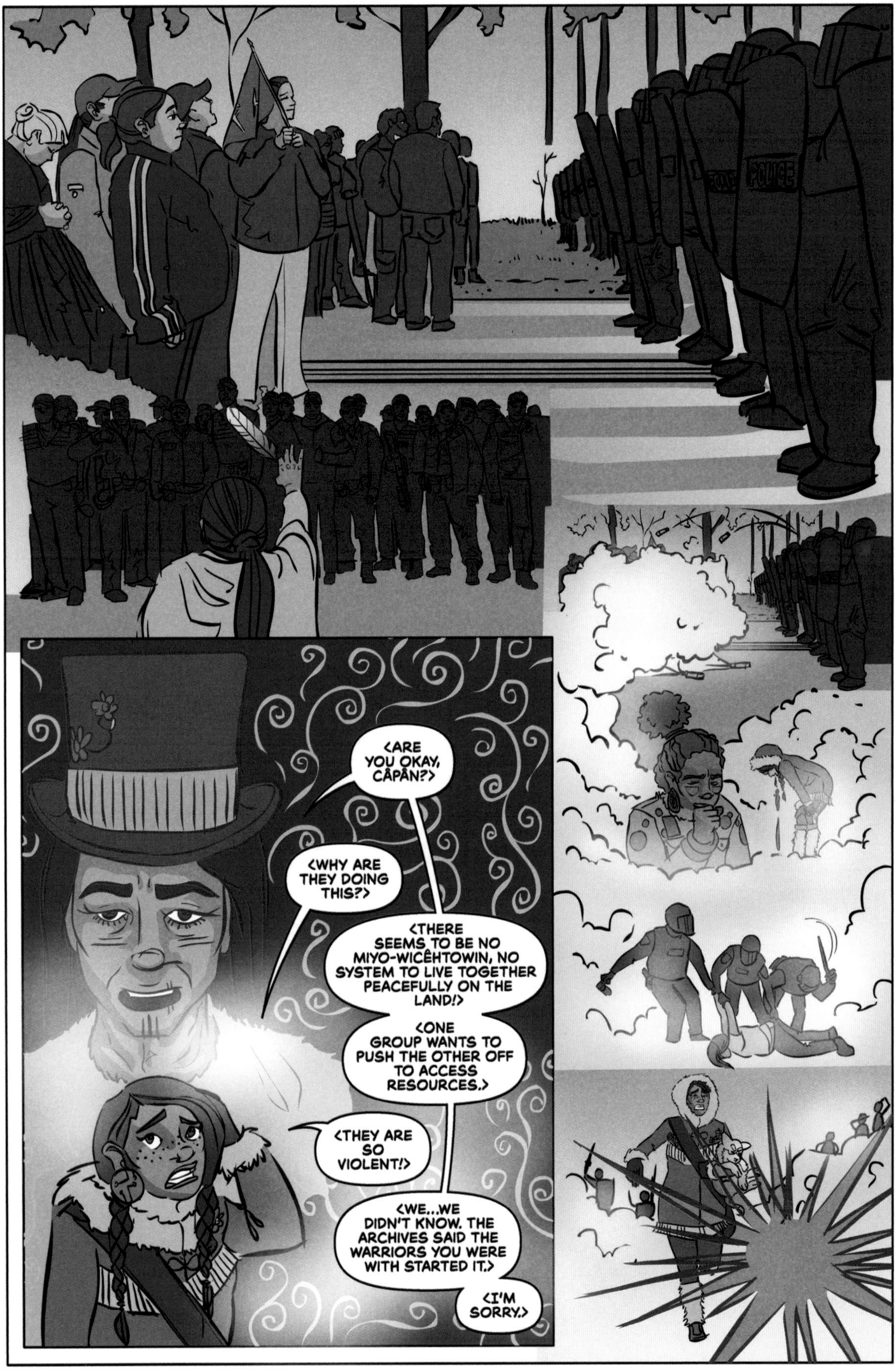
POLICE
<ARE YOU OKAY, CÂPÂN?>
<WHY ARE THEY DOING THIS?>
<THERE SEEMS TO BE NO MIYO-WICÊHTOWIN, NO SYSTEM TO LIVE TOGETHER PEACEFULLY ON THE LAND!>
<ONE GROUP WANTS TO PUSH THE OTHER OFF TO ACCESS RESOURCES.>
<THEY ARE SO VIOLENT!>
<WE...WE DIDN'T KNOW. THE ARCHIVES SAID THE WARRIORS YOU WERE WITH STARTED IT.>
<I'M SORRY.>

See note [1]

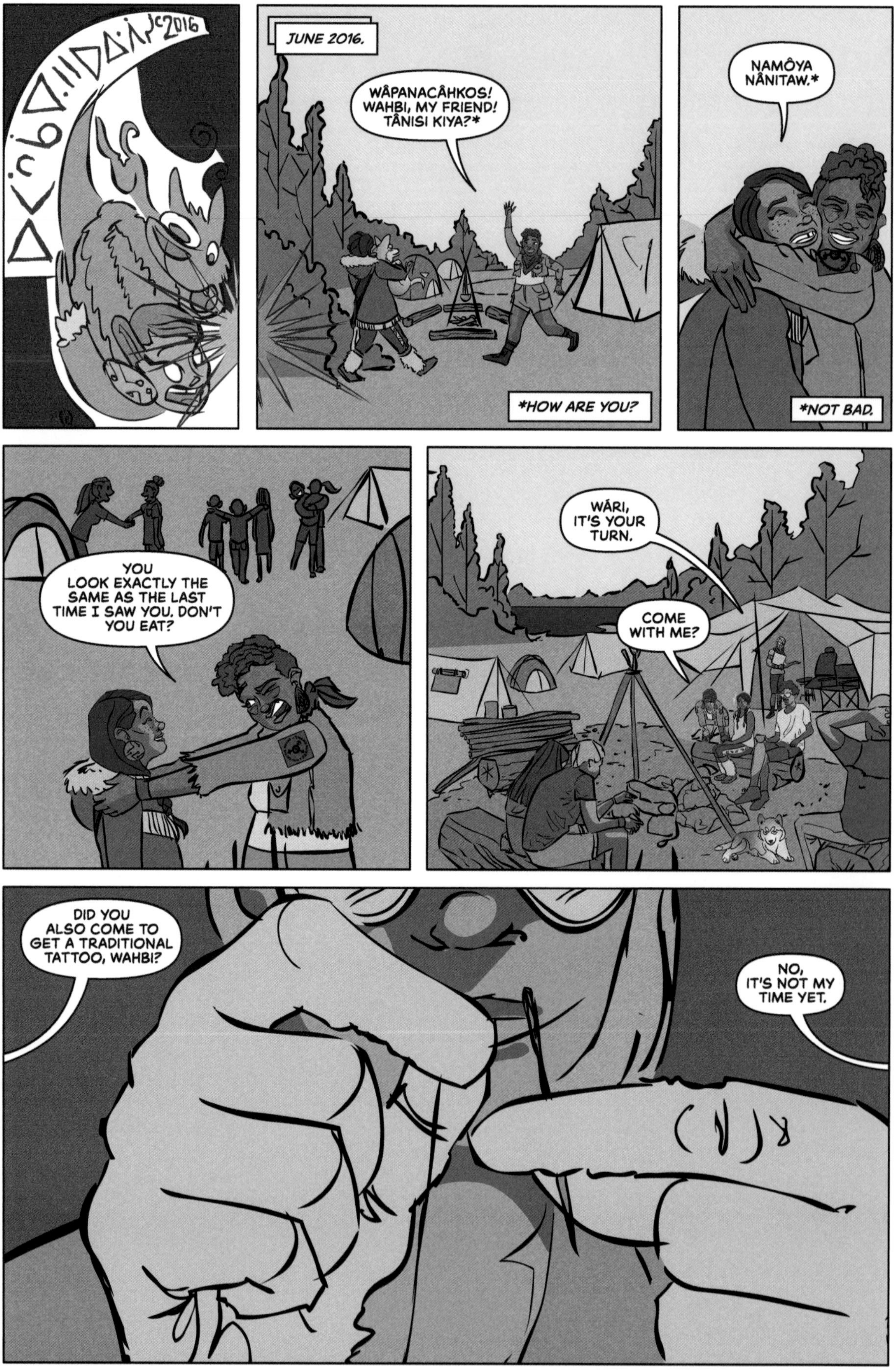
JUNE 2016.
WÂPANACÂHKOS! WAHBI, MY FRIEND! TÂNISI KIYA?*
*HOW ARE YOU?
NAMÔYA NÂNITAW.*
*NOT BAD.
YOU LOOK EXACTLY THE SAME AS THE LAST TIME I SAW YOU. DON'T YOU EAT?
WÂRI, IT'S YOUR TURN.
COME WITH ME?
DID YOU ALSO COME TO GET A TRADITIONAL TATTOO, WAHBI?
NO, IT'S NOT MY TIME YET.

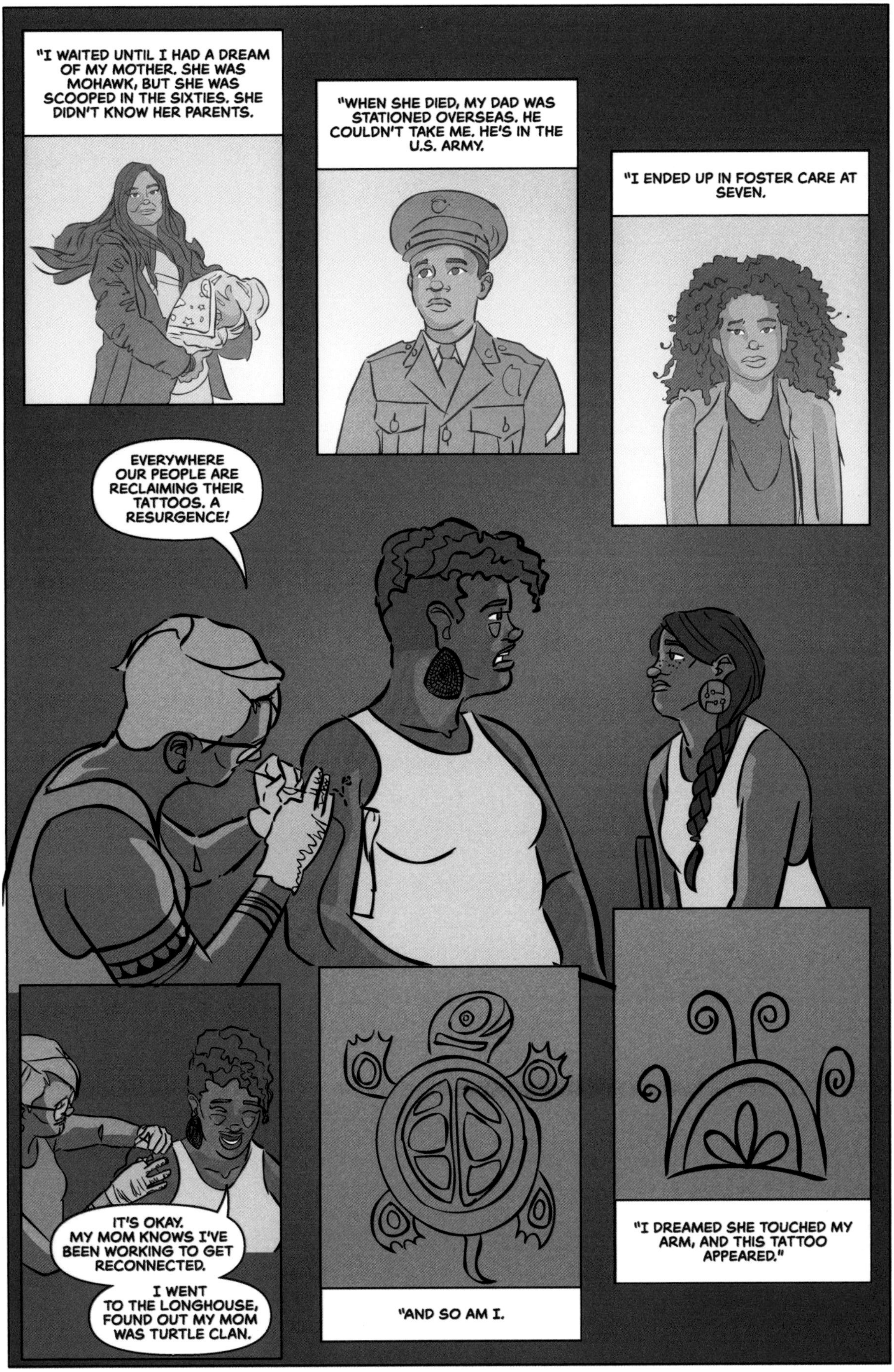
"I WAITED UNTIL I HAD A DREAM OF MY MOTHER. SHE WAS MOHAWK, BUT SHE WAS SCOOPED IN THE SIXTIES. SHE DIDN'T KNOW HER PARENTS.
"WHEN SHE DIED, MY DAD WAS STATIONED OVERSEAS. HE COULDN'T TAKE ME. HE'S IN THE U.S. ARMY.
"I ENDED UP IN FOSTER CARE AT SEVEN.
EVERYWHERE OUR PEOPLE ARE RECLAIMING THEIR TATTOOS. A RESURGENCE!
IT'S OKAY. MY MOM KNOWS I'VE BEEN WORKING TO GET RECONNECTED.
I WENT TO THE LONGHOUSE, FOUND OUT MY MOM WAS TURTLE CLAN.
"AND SO AM I.
"I DREAMED SHE TOUCHED MY ARM, AND THIS TATTOO APPEARED."

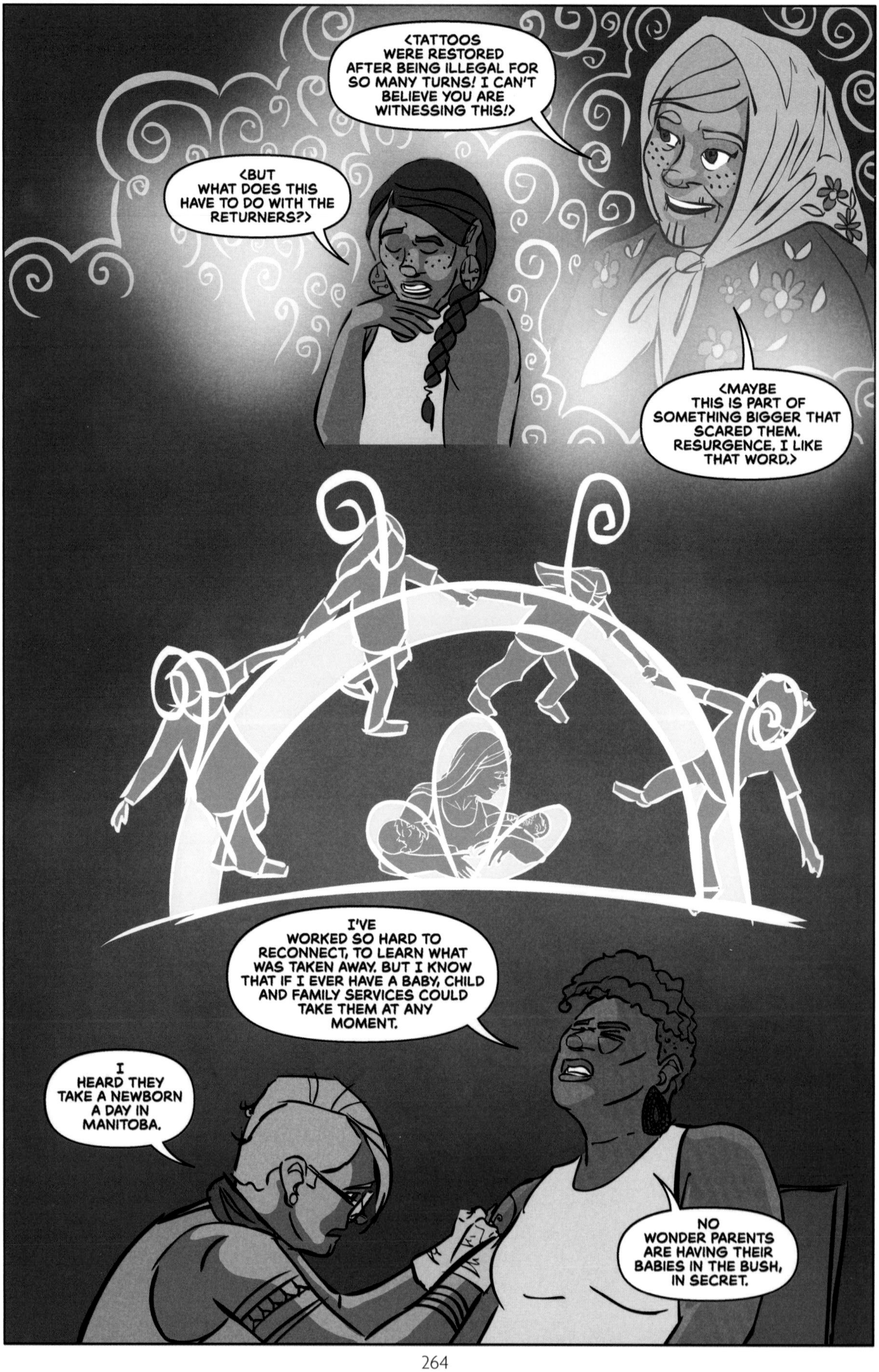
<TATTOOS WERE RESTORED AFTER BEING ILLEGAL FOR SO MANY TURNS! I CAN'T BELIEVE YOU ARE WITNESSING THIS!>
<BUT WHAT DOES THIS HAVE TO DO WITH THE RETURNERS?>
<MAYBE THIS IS PART OF SOMETHING BIGGER THAT SCARED THEM. RESURGENCE. I LIKE THAT WORD.>
I'VE WORKED SO HARD TO RECONNECT, TO LEARN WHAT WAS TAKEN AWAY. BUT I KNOW THAT IF I EVER HAVE A BABY, CHILD AND FAMILY SERVICES COULD TAKE THEM AT ANY MOMENT.
I HEARD THEY TAKE A NEWBORN A DAY IN MANITOBA.
NO WONDER PARENTS ARE HAVING THEIR BABIES IN THE BUSH, IN SECRET.

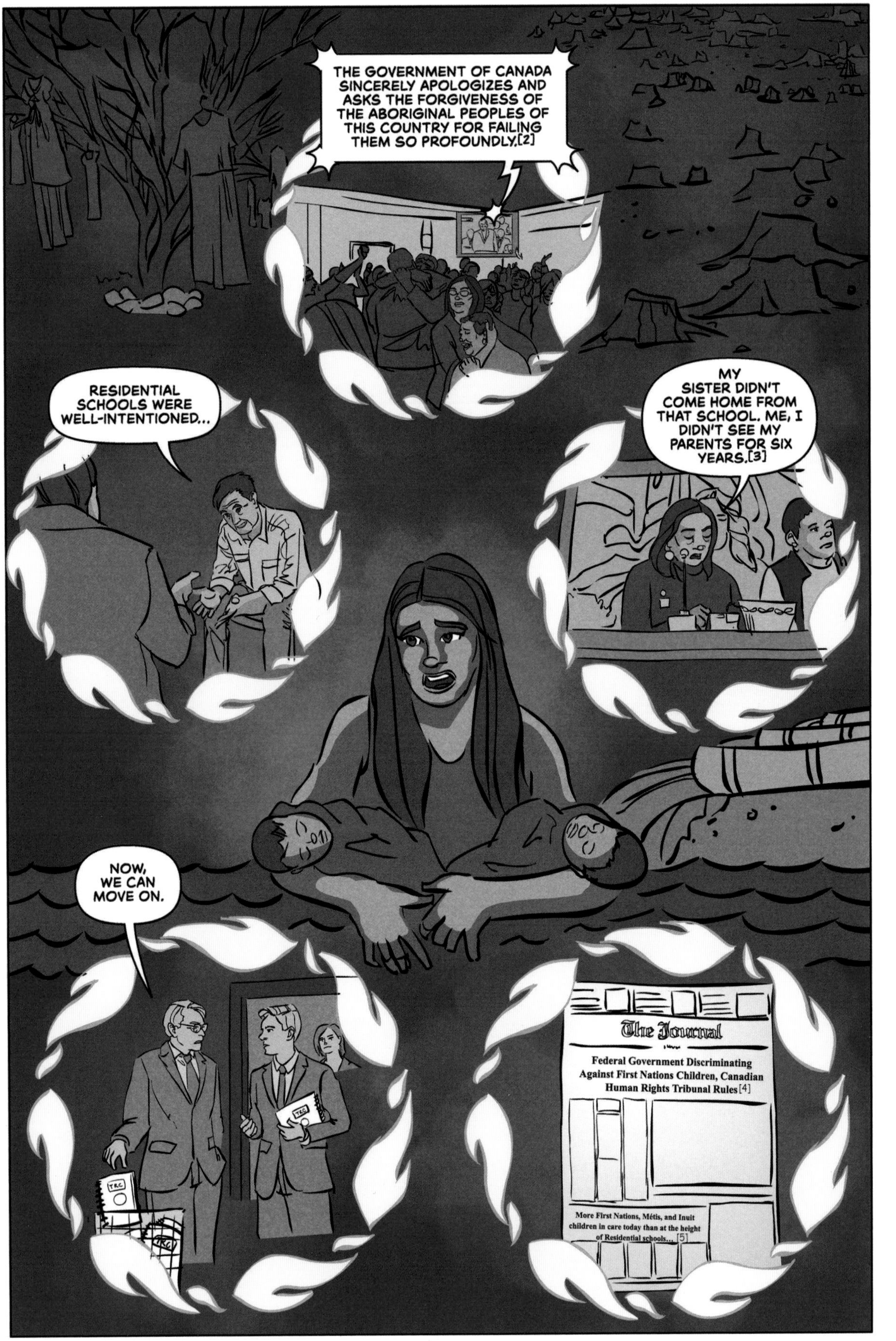
THE GOVERNMENT OF CANADA SINCERELY APOLOGIZES AND ASKS THE FORGIVENESS OF THE ABORIGINAL PEOPLES OF THIS COUNTRY FOR FAILING THEM SO PROFOUNDLY.[2]
RESIDENTIAL SCHOOLS WERE WELL-INTENTIONED...
MY SISTER DIDN'T COME HOME FROM THAT SCHOOL. ME, I DIDN'T SEE MY PARENTS FOR SIX YEARS.[3]
NOW, WE CAN MOVE ON.
TRC
The Journal
Federal Government Discriminating Against First Nations Children, Canadian Human Rights Tribunal Rules[4]
More First Nations, Métis, and Inuit children in care today than at the height of Residential schools...[5]

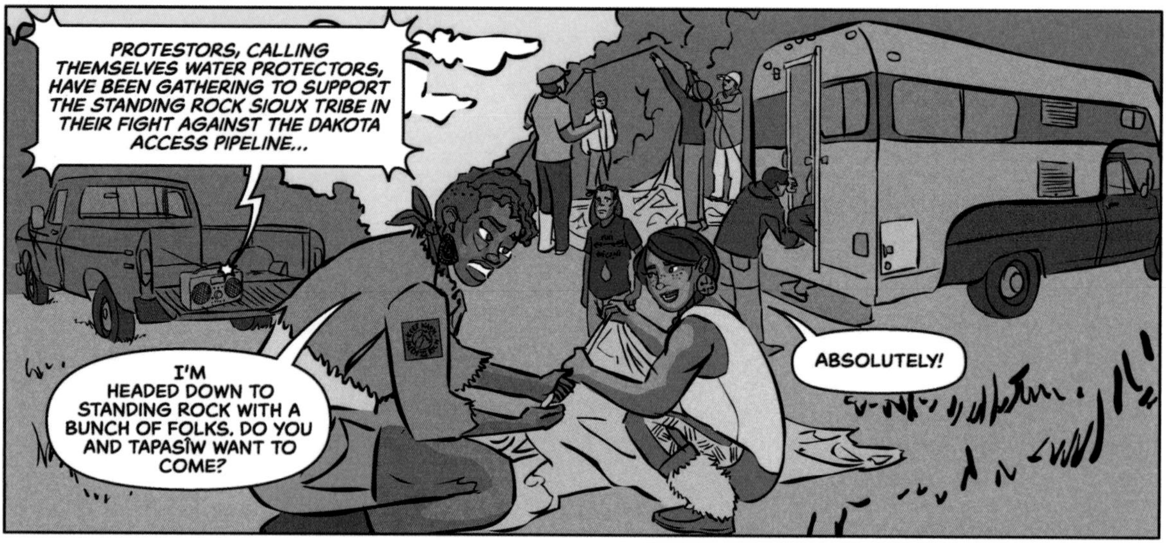
PROTESTORS, CALLING THEMSELVES WATER PROTECTORS, HAVE BEEN GATHERING TO SUPPORT THE STANDING ROCK SIOUX TRIBE IN THEIR FIGHT AGAINST THE DAKOTA ACCESS PIPELINE...
I'M HEADED DOWN TO STANDING ROCK WITH A BUNCH OF FOLKS. DO YOU AND TAPASÎW WANT TO COME?
ABSOLUTELY!

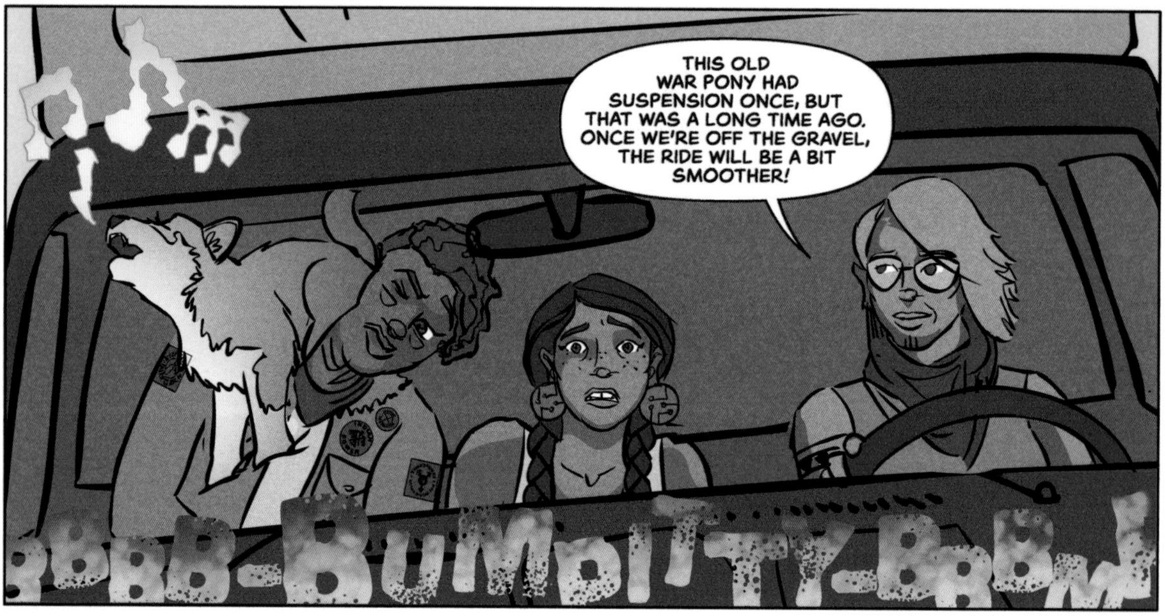
THIS OLD WAR PONY HAD SUSPENSION ONCE, BUT THAT WAS A LONG TIME AGO. ONCE WE'RE OFF THE GRAVEL, THE RIDE WILL BE A BIT SMOOTHER!
BBB-BUMPITY-BBM

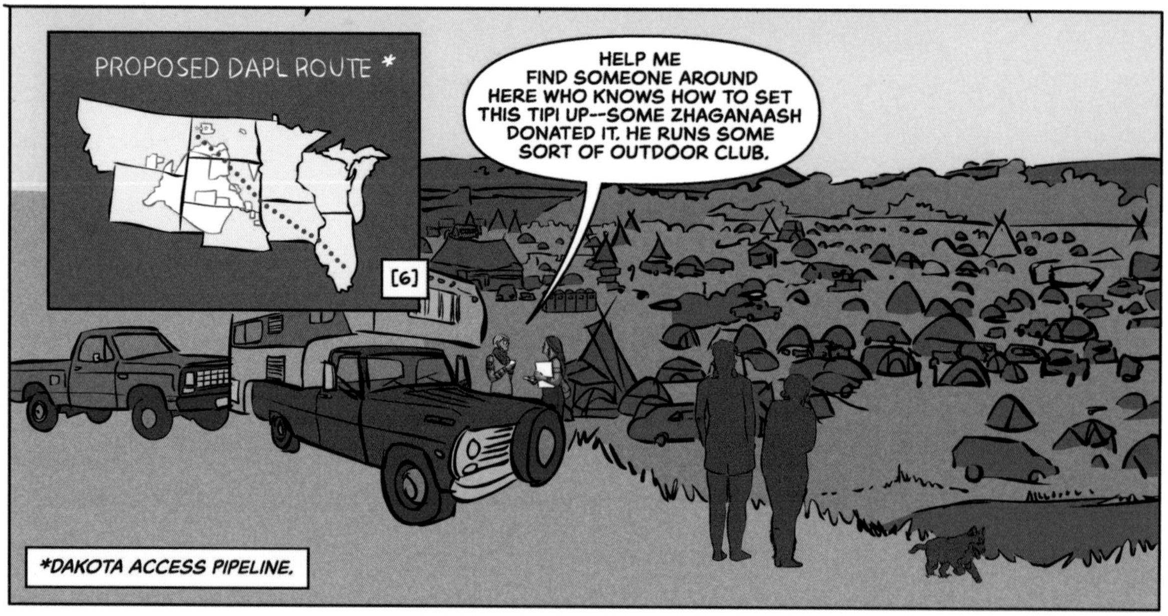
PROPOSED DAPL ROUTE *
[6]
HELP ME FIND SOMEONE AROUND HERE WHO KNOWS HOW TO SET THIS TIPI UP--SOME ZHAGANAASH DONATED IT. HE RUNS SOME SORT OF OUTDOOR CLUB.
*DAKOTA ACCESS PIPELINE.

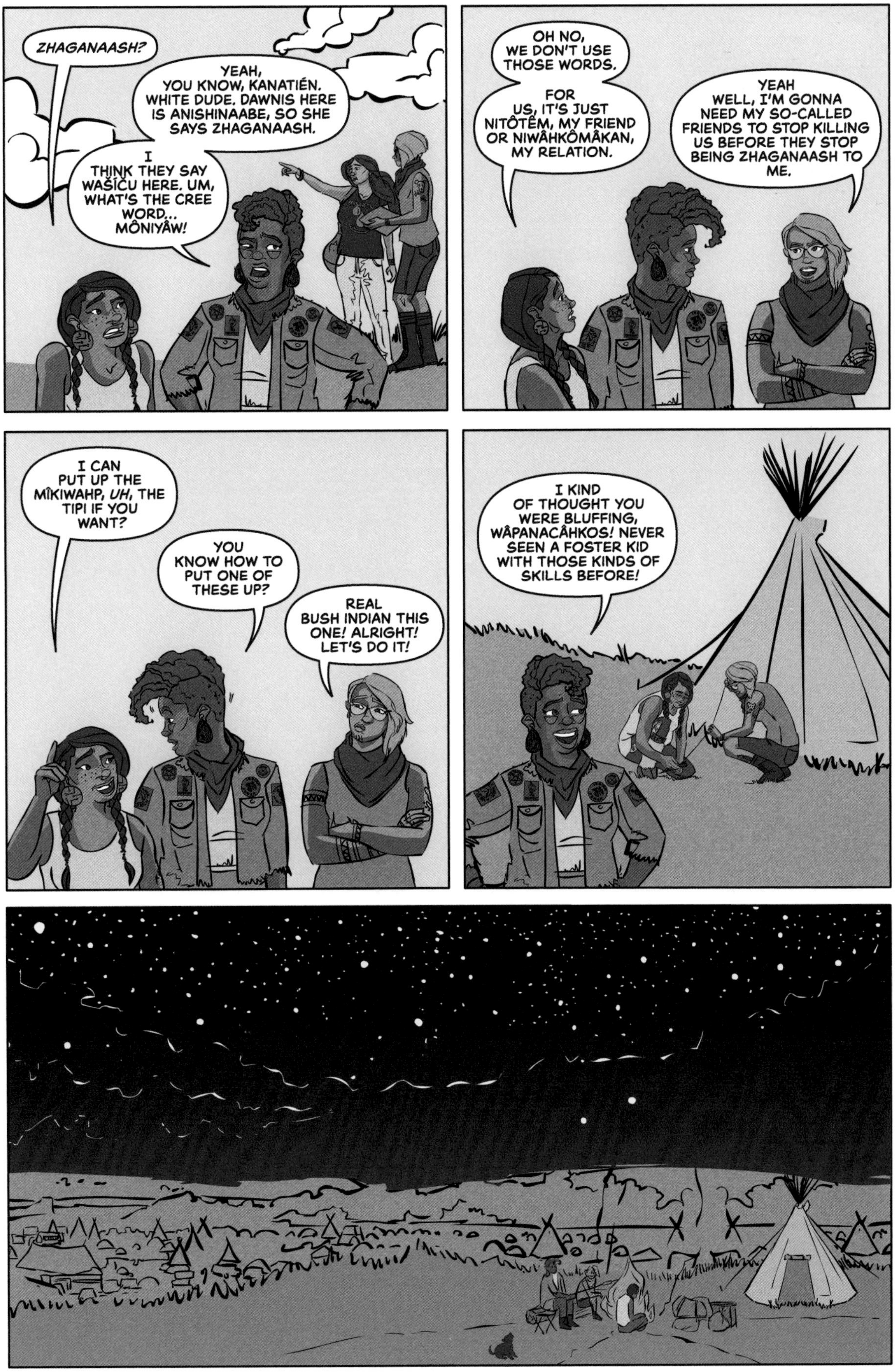
ZHAGANAASH?
YEAH, YOU KNOW, KANATIÉN. WHITE DUDE. DAWNIS HERE IS ANISHINAABE, SO SHE SAYS ZHAGANAASH.
I THINK THEY SAY WAŠÍČU HERE. UM, WHAT'S THE CREE WORD... MÔNIYÂW!
OH NO, WE DON'T USE THOSE WORDS.
FOR US, IT'S JUST NITÔTÊM, MY FRIEND OR NIWÂHKÔMÂKAN, MY RELATION.
YEAH WELL, I'M GONNA NEED MY SO-CALLED FRIENDS TO STOP KILLING US BEFORE THEY STOP BEING ZHAGANAASH TO ME.
I CAN PUT UP THE MÎKIWAHP, *UH*, THE TIPI IF YOU WANT?
YOU KNOW HOW TO PUT ONE OF THESE UP?
REAL BUSH INDIAN THIS ONE! ALRIGHT! LET'S DO IT!
I KIND OF THOUGHT YOU WERE BLUFFING, WÂPANACÂHKOS! NEVER SEEN A FOSTER KID WITH THOSE KINDS OF SKILLS BEFORE!

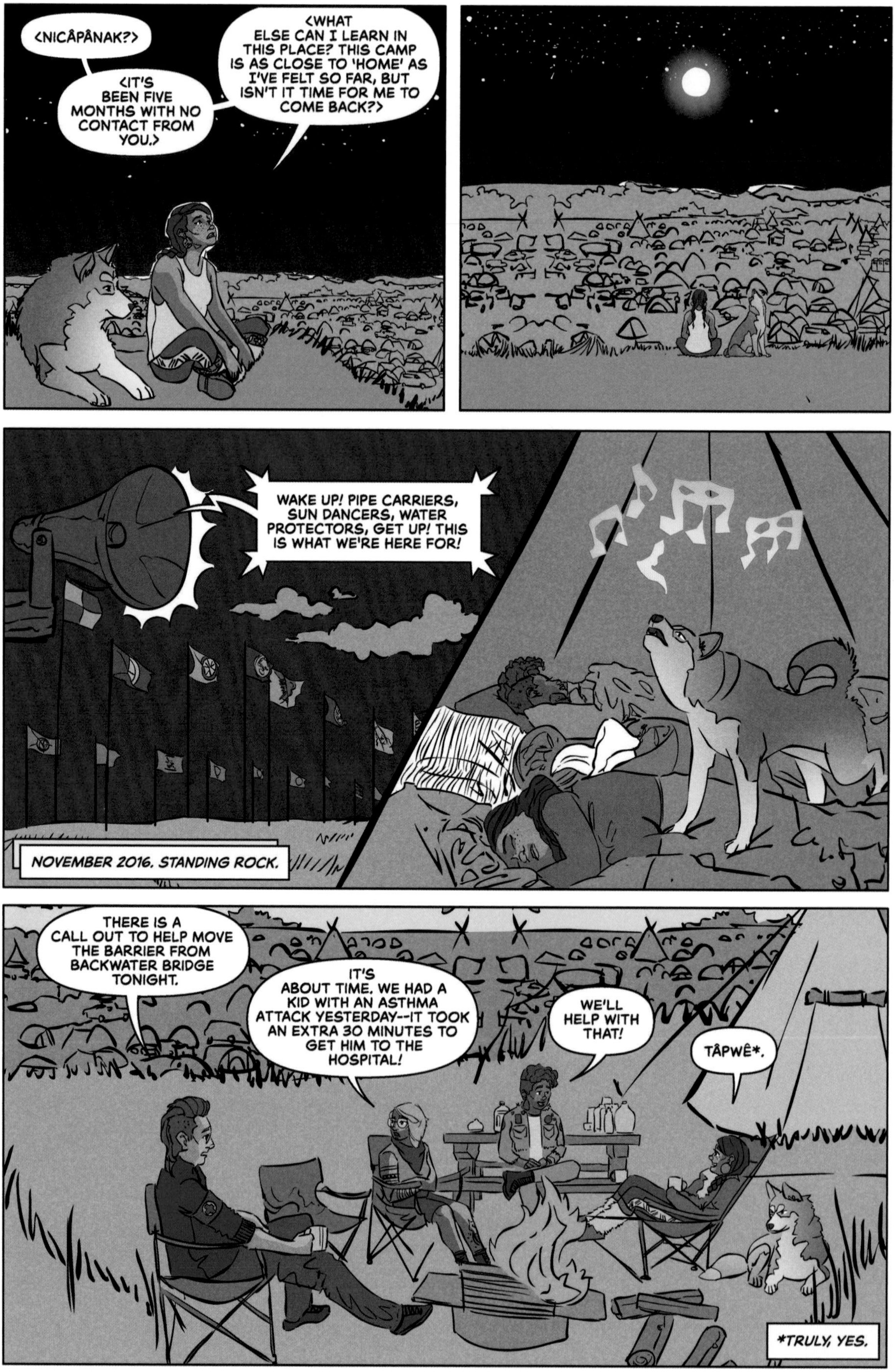
<NICÂPÂNAK?>
<IT'S BEEN FIVE MONTHS WITH NO CONTACT FROM YOU.>
<WHAT ELSE CAN I LEARN IN THIS PLACE? THIS CAMP IS AS CLOSE TO 'HOME' AS I'VE FELT SO FAR, BUT ISN'T IT TIME FOR ME TO COME BACK?>
WAKE UP! PIPE CARRIERS, SUN DANCERS, WATER PROTECTORS, GET UP! THIS IS WHAT WE'RE HERE FOR!
NOVEMBER 2016. STANDING ROCK.
THERE IS A CALL OUT TO HELP MOVE THE BARRIER FROM BACKWATER BRIDGE TONIGHT.
IT'S ABOUT TIME. WE HAD A KID WITH AN ASTHMA ATTACK YESTERDAY--IT TOOK AN EXTRA 30 MINUTES TO GET HIM TO THE HOSPITAL!
WE'LL HELP WITH THAT!
TÂPWÊ*.
*TRULY, YES.

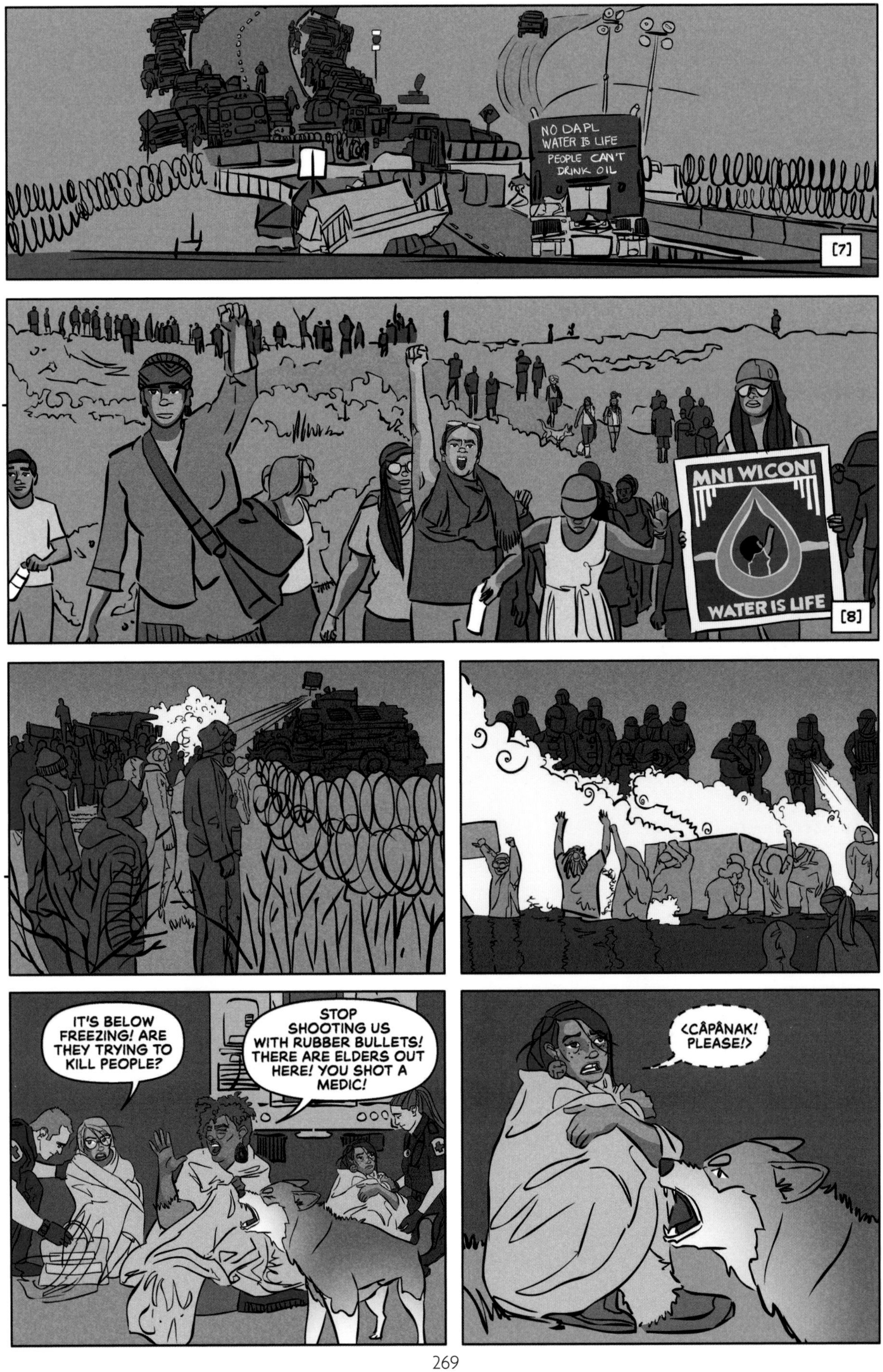
NO DAPL
WATER IS LIFE
PEOPLE CAN'T DRINK OIL
[7]
MNI WICONI
WATER IS LIFE
[8]
IT'S BELOW FREEZING! ARE THEY TRYING TO KILL PEOPLE?
STOP SHOOTING US WITH RUBBER BULLETS! THERE ARE ELDERS OUT HERE! YOU SHOT A MEDIC!
<CÂPÂNAK! PLEASE!>

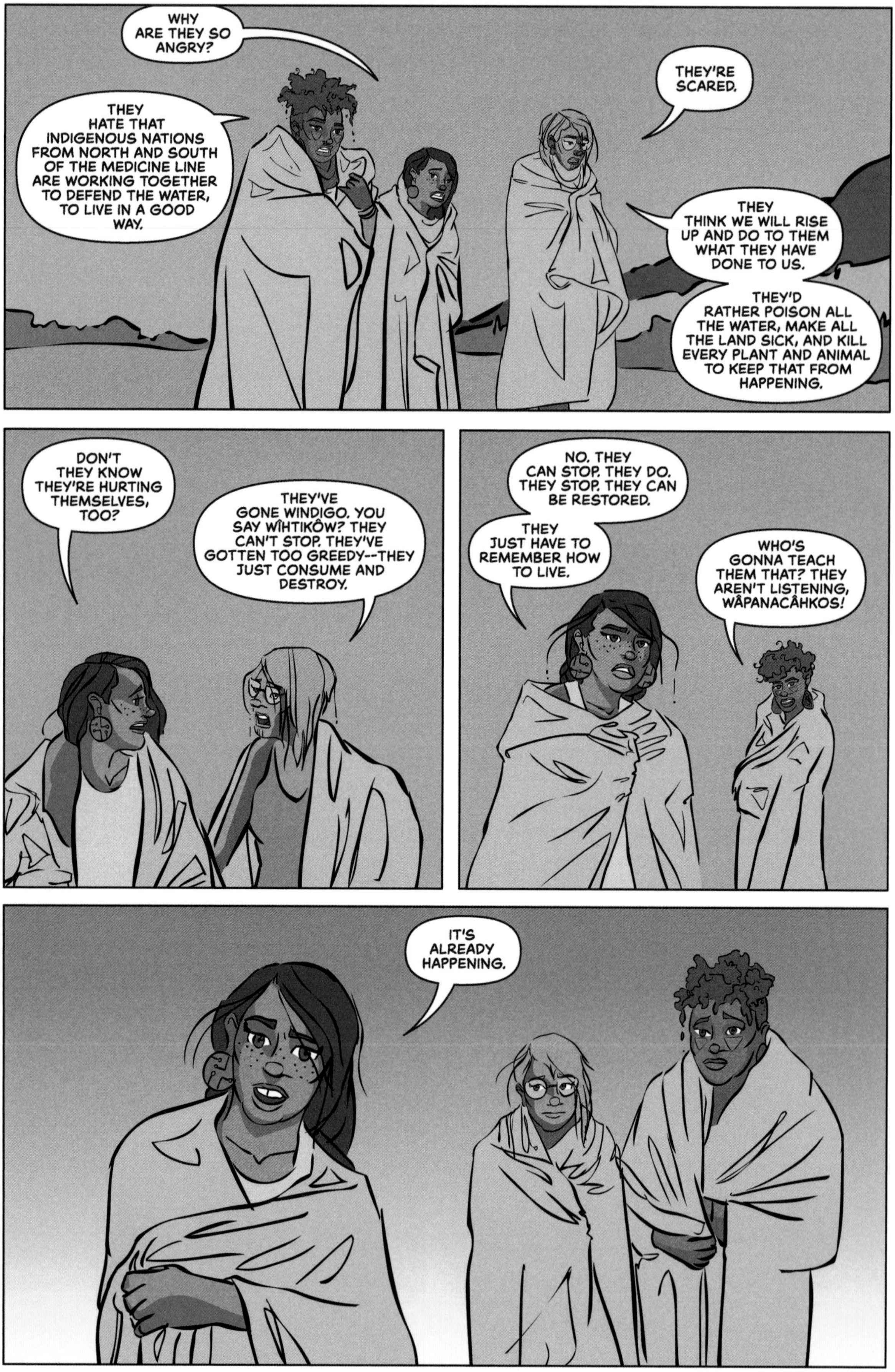
WHY ARE THEY SO ANGRY?
THEY HATE THAT INDIGENOUS NATIONS FROM NORTH AND SOUTH OF THE MEDICINE LINE ARE WORKING TOGETHER TO DEFEND THE WATER, TO LIVE IN A GOOD WAY.
THEY'RE SCARED.
THEY THINK WE WILL RISE UP AND DO TO THEM WHAT THEY HAVE DONE TO US.
THEY'D RATHER POISON ALL THE WATER, MAKE ALL THE LAND SICK, AND KILL EVERY PLANT AND ANIMAL TO KEEP THAT FROM HAPPENING.
DON'T THEY KNOW THEY'RE HURTING THEMSELVES, TOO?
THEY'VE GONE WINDIGO. YOU SAY WÎHTIKÔW? THEY CAN'T STOP. THEY'VE GOTTEN TOO GREEDY--THEY JUST CONSUME AND DESTROY.
NO. THEY CAN STOP. THEY DO. THEY STOP. THEY CAN BE RESTORED.
THEY JUST HAVE TO REMEMBER HOW TO LIVE.
WHO'S GONNA TEACH THEM THAT? THEY AREN'T LISTENING, WÂPANACÂHKOS!
IT'S ALREADY HAPPENING.

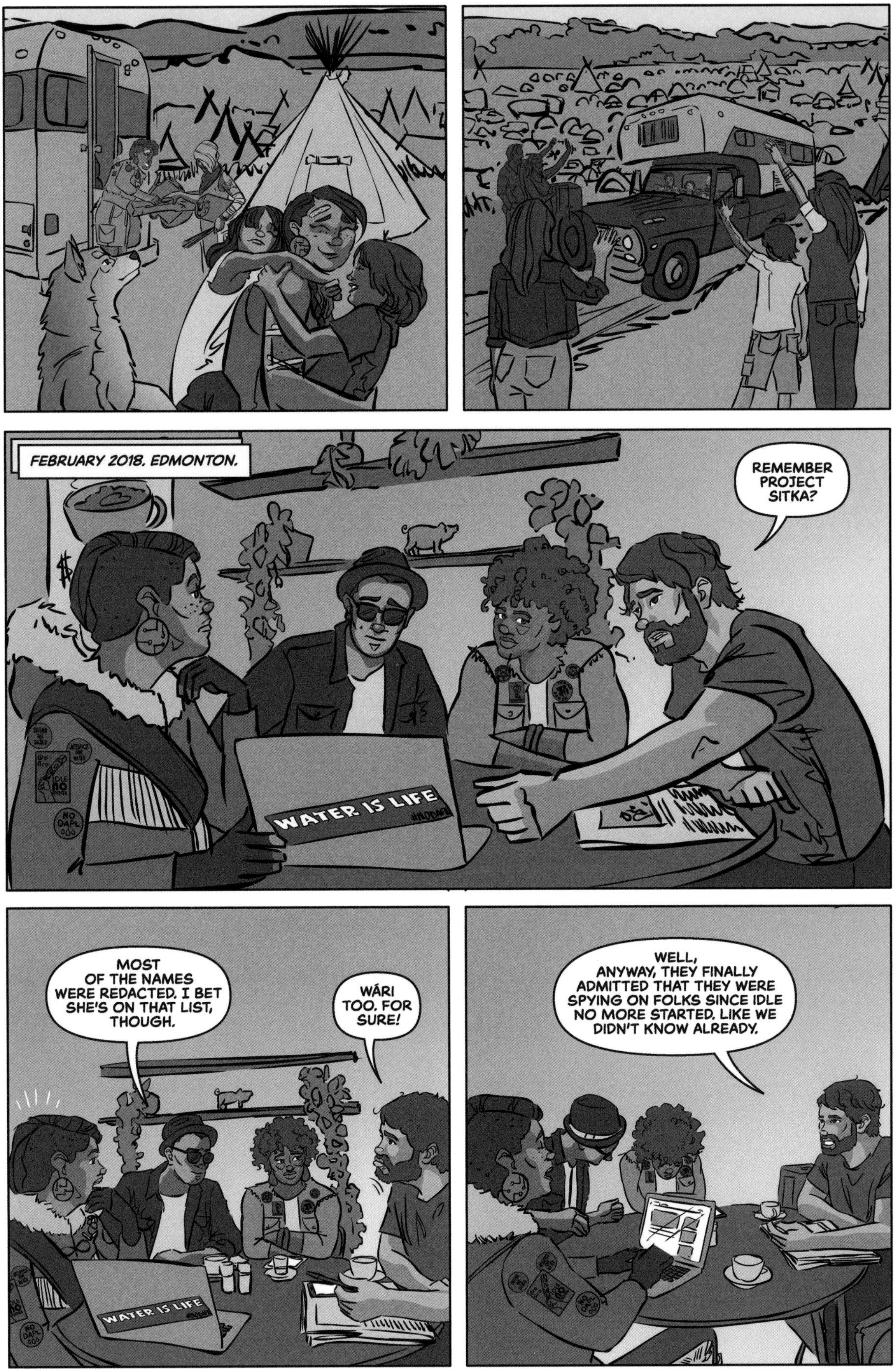

FEBRUARY 2018. EDMONTON.
REMEMBER PROJECT SITKA?
WATER IS LIFE
MOST OF THE NAMES WERE REDACTED. I BET SHE'S ON THAT LIST, THOUGH.
WÁRI TOO. FOR SURE!
WELL, ANYWAY, THEY FINALLY ADMITTED THAT THEY WERE SPYING ON FOLKS SINCE IDLE NO MORE STARTED. LIKE WE DIDN'T KNOW ALREADY.

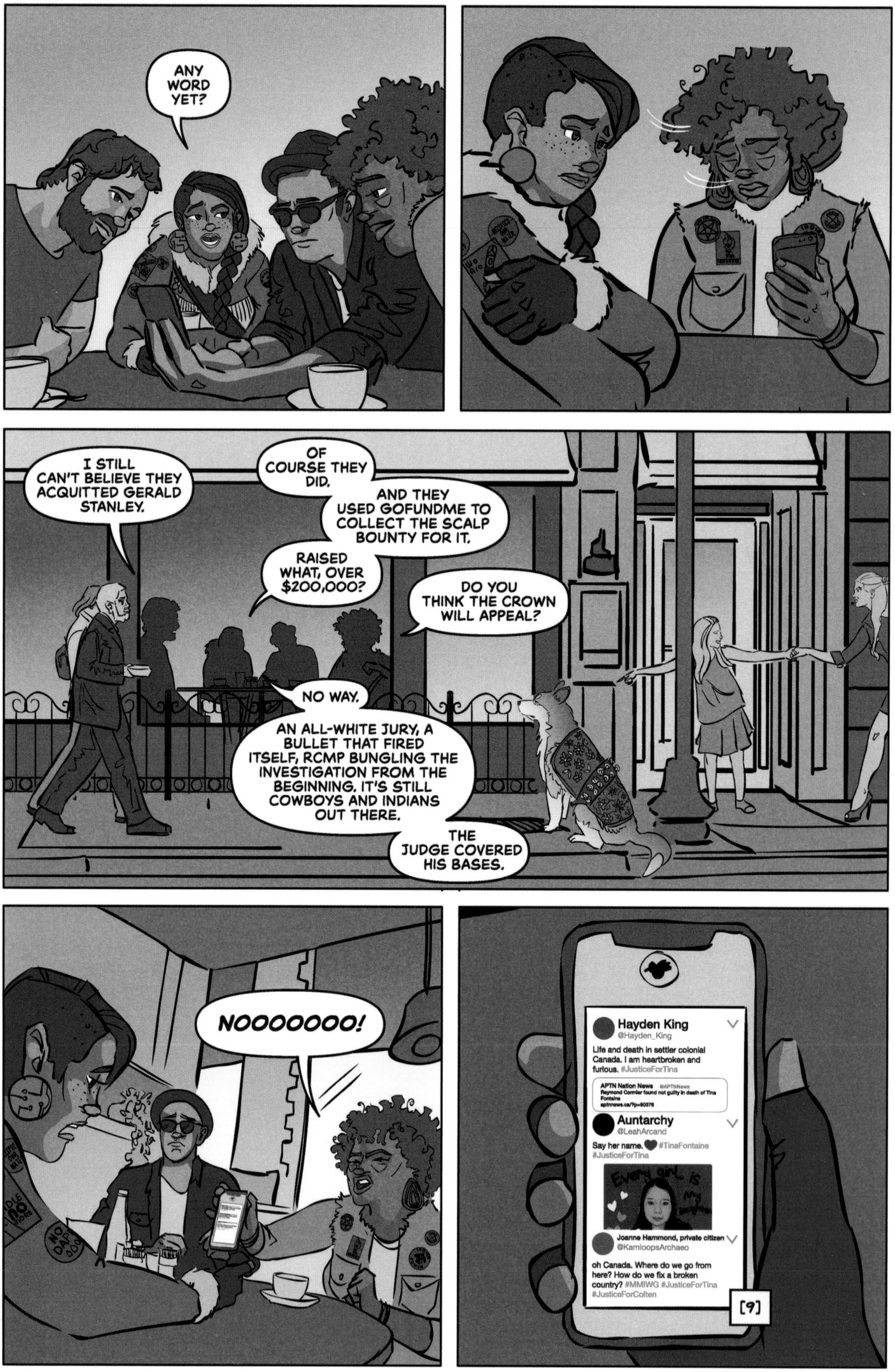
ANY WORD YET?
I STILL CAN'T BELIEVE THEY ACQUITTED GERALD STANLEY.
OF COURSE THEY DID.
AND THEY USED GOFUNDME TO COLLECT THE SCALP BOUNTY FOR IT.
RAISED WHAT, OVER $200,000?
DO YOU THINK THE CROWN WILL APPEAL?
NO WAY.
AN ALL-WHITE JURY, A BULLET THAT FIRED ITSELF, RCMP BUNGLING THE INVESTIGATION FROM THE BEGINNING. IT'S STILL COWBOYS AND INDIANS OUT THERE.
THE JUDGE COVERED HIS BASES.
NOOOOOOO!
Hayden King
@Hayden_King
Life and death in settler colonial Canada. I am heartbroken and furious. #JusticeForTina
APTN Nation News @APTNNews
Raymond Cormier found not guilty in death of Tina Fontaine
aptnnews.ca/?p=90376
Auntarchy
@LeahArcand
Say her name. #TinaFontaine #JusticeForTina
Every girl is
Joanne Hammond, private citizen
@KamloopsArchaeo
oh Canada. Where do we go from here? How do we fix a broken country? #MMIWG #JusticeForTina #JusticeForColten
[9]

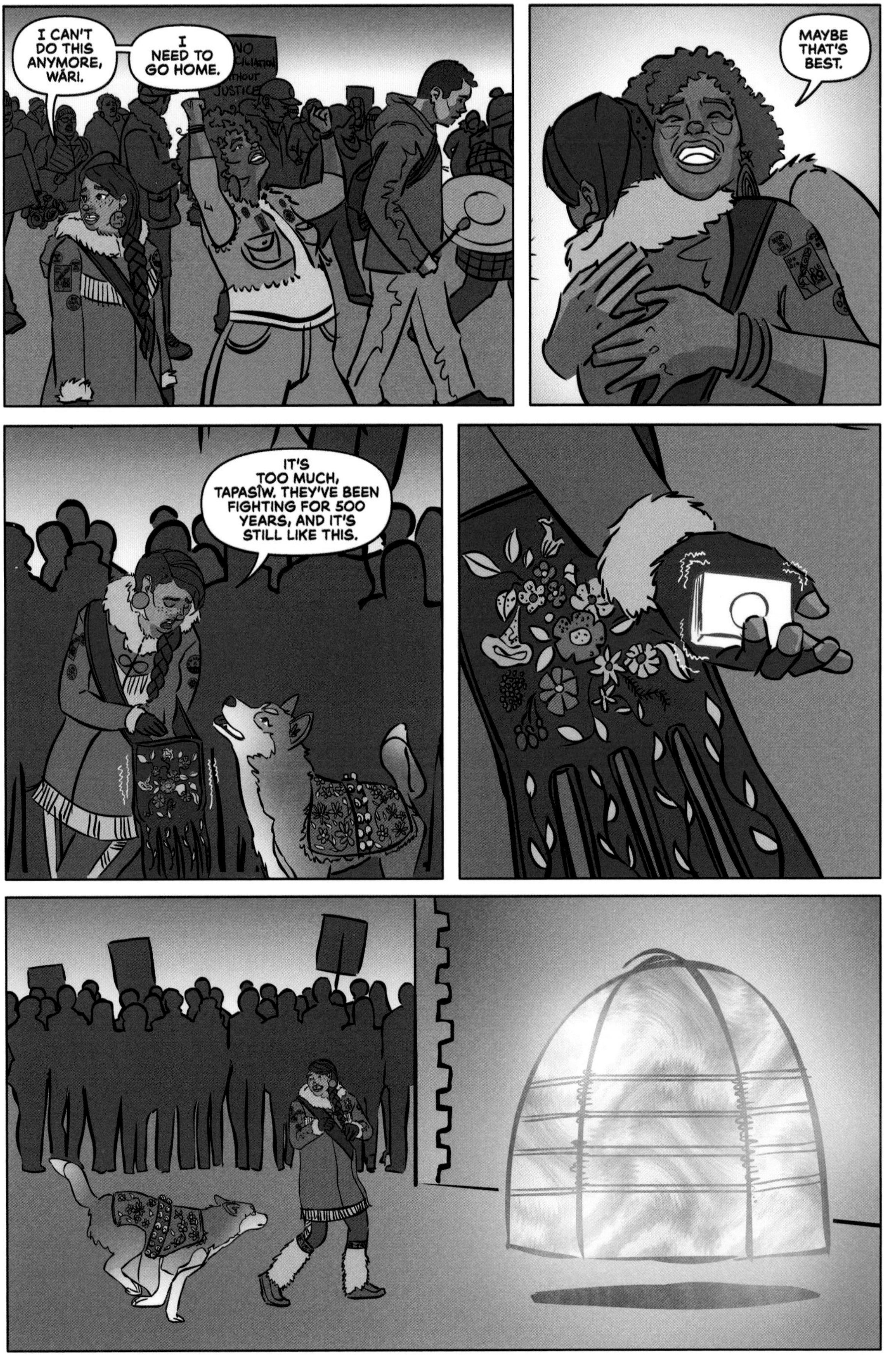
I CAN'T DO THIS ANYMORE, WĀRI.
I NEED TO GO HOME.
MAYBE THAT'S BEST.
IT'S TOO MUCH, TAPASÎW. THEY'VE BEEN FIGHTING FOR 500 YEARS, AND IT'S STILL LIKE THIS.

<THREE YEARS?! YOU LEFT ME FOR THREE YEARS!>

<WE NEEDED YOU TO DO MORE THAN SKIM, CÂPÂN. THE HISTORY BOOKS AND FEEDS COULD HAVE TOLD US AS MUCH AS THAT.>

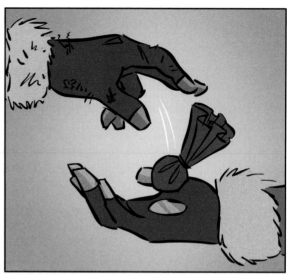

<THEY PUSHED US OFF OUR LANDS, PUNISHED US FOR TRYING TO MAINTAIN OUR RECIPROCAL OBLIGATION TO THE LAND, CALLED US CRIMINALS, AND ARRESTED US.>

<THE RETURNERS REMEMBER THOSE BOUNDARIES AND BELIEVE WE HAVE STOLEN THEIR TERRITORIES!>

<ANCESTORS, THE RETURNERS MUST LEARN WÎTASKÊWIN, LIVING TOGETHER ON THE LAND.>

<NEITHER NEEDS TO DOMINATE THE OTHER.>

<NOW, WE SEE THAT THEY FEARED WE WOULD TREAT THEM HARSHLY OUT OF REVENGE, BUT WE MADE PEACE WITH THEIR ANCESTORS.>

<WE WILL HAVE PEACE AGAIN.>

<THEY ALSO NEED TO BE RESTORED TO WÂHKÔHTOWIN, EXPANDED KINSHIP. THEIR ANCESTORS EVENTUALLY LEARNED THAT THEY ARE KIN TO US, TO THESE LANDS, THE ANIMALS, AND THE WATERS.>

<OUR RESPONSIBILITIES AND OUR FATES ARE LINKED. THESE ONES WILL LEARN IT, TOO.>

<FIRST, THEY MUST BE SHOWN MIYO-WÎCÊHTOWIN.>

<THEY NEED TO BE IN GOOD RELATION WITH ONE ANOTHER AS WELL AS WITH US. THREE CENTURIES OF SUSTAINABLE LIVING WILL BE THE PROOF THAT WORKING TOGETHER IS POSSIBLE.>

<BUT FOR NOW, WÂPANACÂHKOS, YOU NEED TO HEAL.>

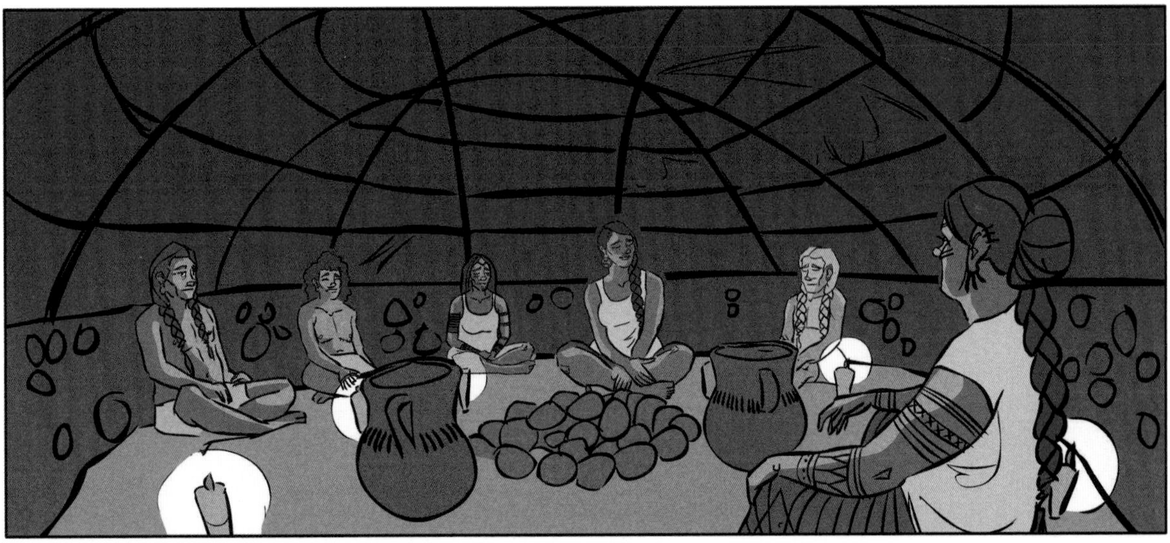

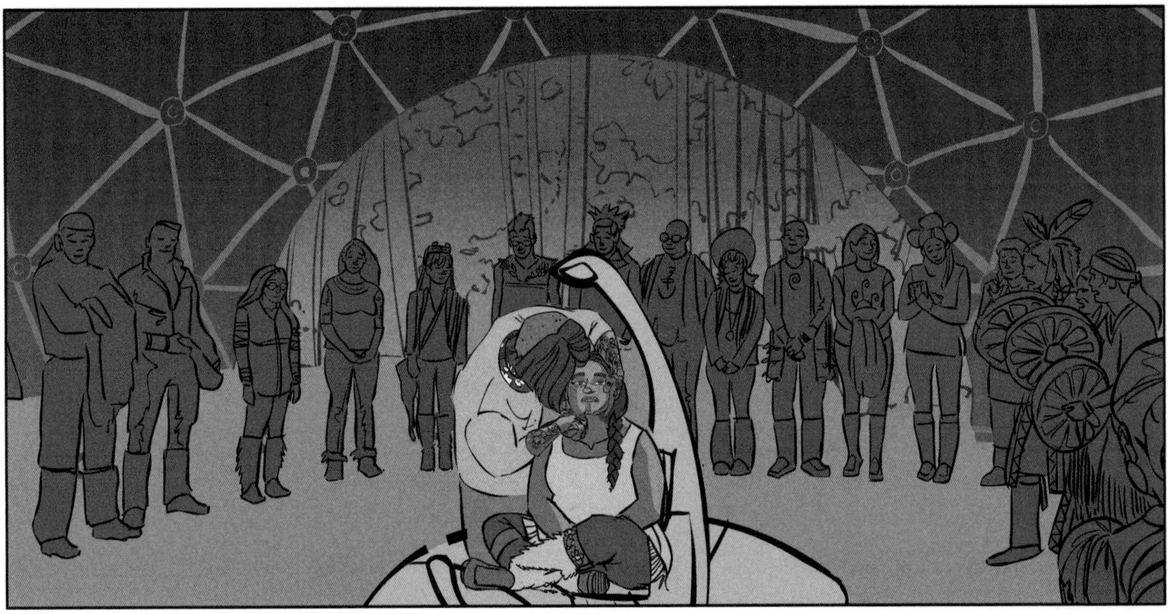

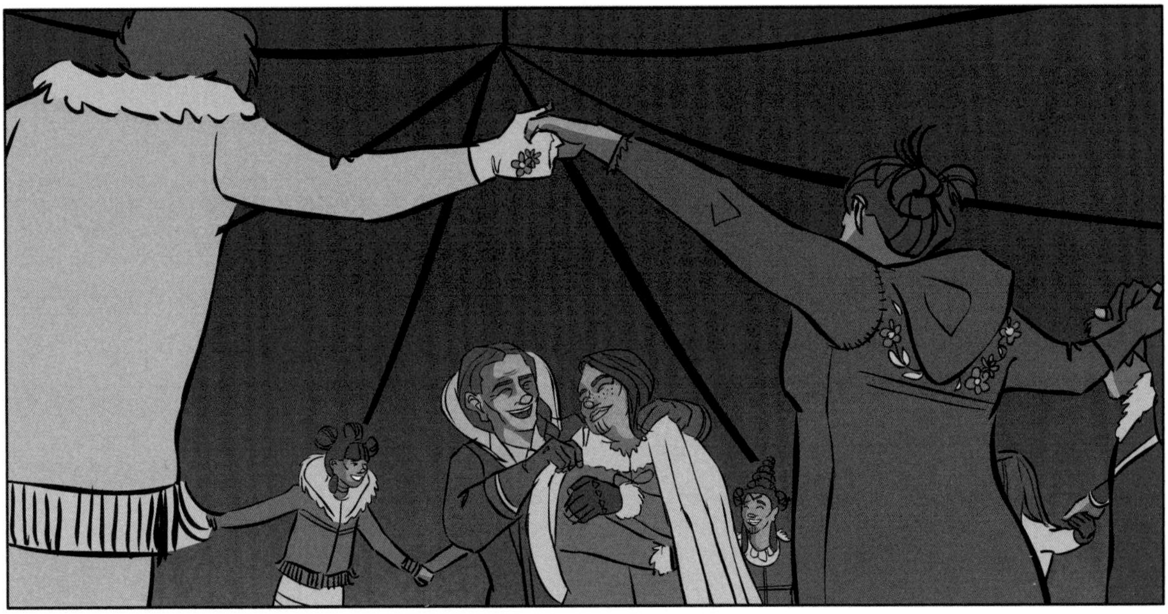

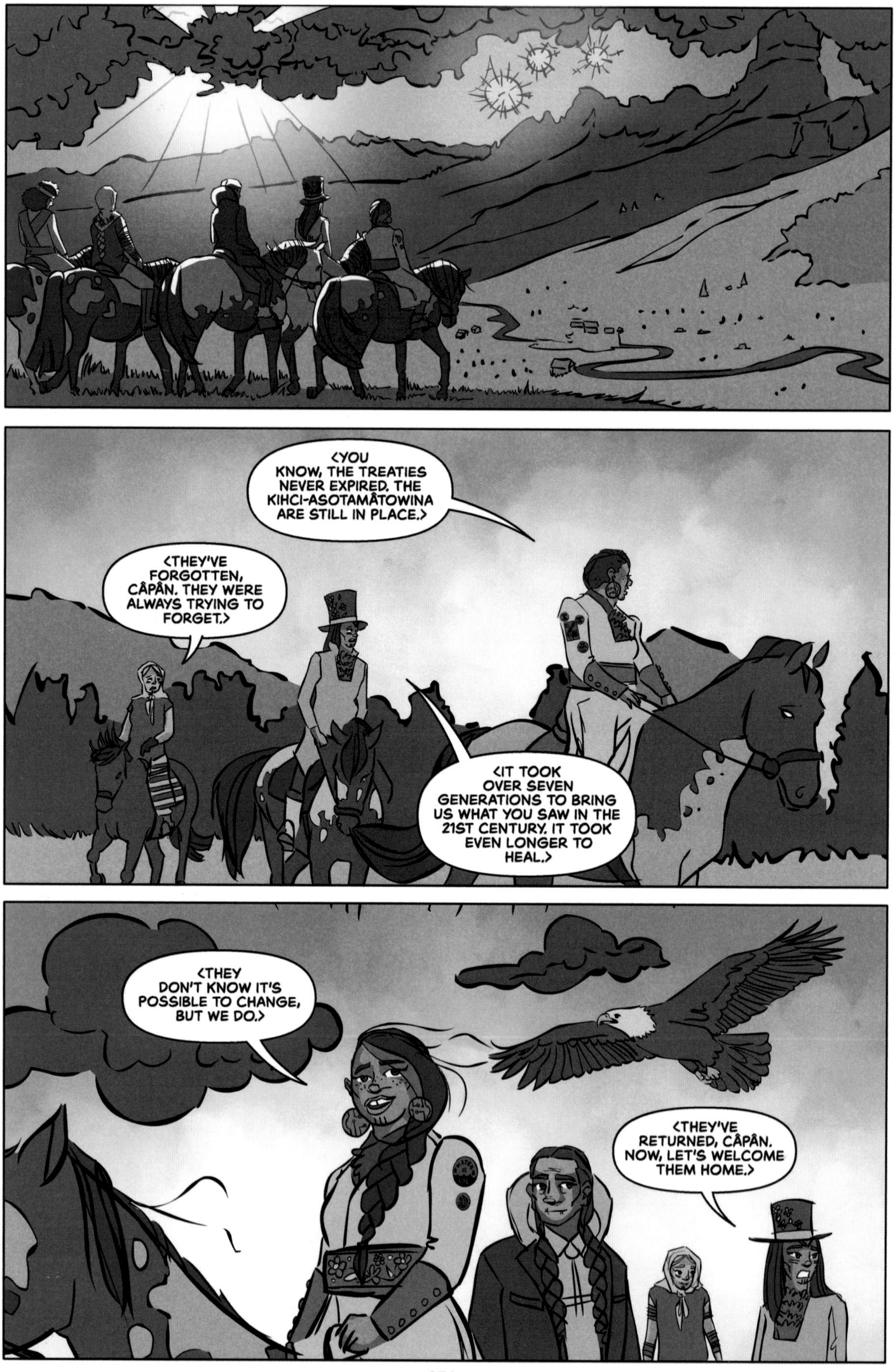
<YOU KNOW, THE TREATIES NEVER EXPIRED. THE KIHCI-ASOTAMÂTOWINA ARE STILL IN PLACE.>
<THEY'VE FORGOTTEN, CÂPÂN. THEY WERE ALWAYS TRYING TO FORGET.>
<IT TOOK OVER SEVEN GENERATIONS TO BRING US WHAT YOU SAW IN THE 21ST CENTURY. IT TOOK EVEN LONGER TO HEAL.>
<THEY DON'T KNOW IT'S POSSIBLE TO CHANGE, BUT WE DO.>
<THEY'VE RETURNED, CÂPÂN. NOW, LET'S WELCOME THEM HOME.>

Notes

"Annie of Red River"

[1] Todd Lamirande, "Annie McDermot (Bannatyne) (c.1830-1908)", Louis Riel Institute, 2008, http://www.metismuseum.ca/media/db/07426.

[2] Charles Mair, "From Red River," (January 4, 1869), Provisional Government of Assiniboia, 2011, https://hallnjean2.wordpress.com/the-red-river-resistence/the-documentary-record/transcripts-the-red-river-letters-of-charles-mair/.

"Tilted Ground"

[1] "U'mista Cultural Society," 2019. www.umista.ca/pages/kwakwakawakw-tribes. Abbreviated excerpt from the "WiweÐÐam" origin story told by Chief Billy Assu, recorded by Phillip Drucker.

[2] Government of Canada, Department of the Interior. Israel Wood Powell, *Annual Report of the Department of the Interior for the Fiscal Year Ending 30th June, 1876.*), Ottawa: MacLean, Roger & Co, 1877, 36. Israel Wood Powell, abbreviated excerpt.

[3] *Report of the Superintendent of Indian Affairs, for British Columbia, for 1872 & 1873*, Ottawa: I.B. Taylor, 1873, 8. Israel Wood Powell, excerpt.

[4] All Powell quotes from the previous two pages are from [3].

[5] Douglas Cole, Ira Chaikin, *An Iron Hand upon the People: The Law Against the Potlatch on the Northwest Coast* (Vancouver: Douglas & McIntyre, 1990),15. This phrase is not Sir John A. MacDonald's own. It comes from an 1879 letter from Indian Reserve Commissioner Gilbert Malcolm Sproat that advised lawmakers to "lay an iron hand upon the shoulders of the people" to end the practice of potlatching.

[6] Prime Minister Sir John A. MacDonald, House of Commons Debate, Second Reading of the amendment to the Indian Act, March 24, 1884.

[7] Bruce Clark, *Justice in Paradise* (Kingston: McGill-Queen's University Press, 1999), 308. These words were written by the author. However, MacDonald did state that the focus of this legislation was "to do away with the tribal system and assimilate the Indian people" (*Return to an Order of House of Commons*, May 2, 1887 (20b).

[8] *An Act further to amend* "The Indian Act, 1880," sc. 1884, c. 27, s. 3. http://kopiwadan.ca/wp-content/uploads/2017/01/1884-An-Act-further-to-amend-«The-Indian-Act-1880»-1.pdf.

[9] Franz Boas, "The Indians Of British Columbia," *Popular Science Monthly*, 32 (1888).

[10] Paraphrased excerpt from [9].

[11] Chief O'waxalagalis, quoted by Boas in [9].

"Red Clouds"

[1] Thomas Fiddler, James R. Stevens, *Killing the Shamen* (Moonbeam, Ontario: Penumbra Press, 2003 [1985]), 75. Zhauwuno-geezhigo-gaubow's words in panels 1 and 2 on this page are direct quotes attributed to him.

[2] Fiddler and Stevens, *Killing the Shamen*, 77. Robert & Constable O'Neil's exchange in this panel is a direct quote.

[3] Fiddler and Stevens, *Killing the Shamen*, 77. The exchange between Robert & Constable O'Neil in the first three panels is paraphrased from the original.

[4] Fiddler and Stevens, *Killing the Shamen*, 77. All words exchanged between D.W. McKerchar and Minowapawin (Norman Rae) on this page are direct quotes from the transcript from the trial.

[5] The trial transcript records that Calverley made a statement defending Joseph's actions, but it does not record what he said.

[6] Fiddler and Stevens, *Killing the Shamen*, 107–109. The jury's verdict and Commissioner Perry's lines are direct quotes from the trial transcript.

[7] Fiddler and Stevens, *Killing the Shamen*, 111-113. The original quote from the letter of the men at Norway House has been shortened to meet space requirements. The signatories to the letter were: the trader who initially told Sergeant Smith about the windigo killings (William Campbell) and seven other traders; three jurors from the trial; C. Crompton Calverley (Indian Department "observer" at trial); and four Methodist missionaries.

[8] Fiddler and Stevens, *Killing the Shamen*, 115. The text of Joseph's letter, as written down for him by an unnamed translator.

[9] Fiddler and Stevens, *Killing the Shamen*, 116. Telegram from Thomas Mulvey, Under-Secretary of State Canada, September 4, 1909, on behalf of the Governor General.

[10] Fiddler and Stevens, *Killing the Shamen*, 116. Letter from A. Irving, Warden of Stony Mountain Penitentiary, September 5, 1909.

"Peggy"

[1] Adrian Hayes, *Pegahmagabow: Life-Long Warrior* (Toronto: Blue Butterfly Books, 2009), 20. Vision recounted by Francis Pegahmagabow.

[2] Brian McInnes, *Sounding Thunder: The Stories of Francis Pegahmagabow* (Winnipeg: University of Manitoba Press, 2016), 28. Francis Pegahmagabow, paraphrased from the story recounted in the above.

[3] Hayes, *Pegahmagabow: Life-Long Warrior*, 20. Military citation quoted.

[4] Hayes, *Pegahmagabow: Life-Long Warrior*, 2. Indian Agent Alexander Logan's letter to Indian Affairs (August 17, 1922).

[5] Hayes, *Pegahmagabow: Life-Long Warrior*, 2. Francis Pegahmagabow is not recorded as saying these exact words, but they are in keeping with his disappointment and anger at his treatment upon returning home from the war. This remark is attributed to Lance-Sergeant Joseph Flavien St. Germain, a Cree man from Northern Alberta. In 1943, when his commanding officer complimented him on his bravery and skills, he said, "It's fine, sir, but if I get back to Canada, I'll be treated just like another poor goddamn Indian."

[6] Brian McInnes, *Sounding Thunder: The Stories of Francis Pegahmagabow*, 189. According to Duncan Pegahmagabow, Francis's son, Francis called his political work and advocacy his "last war."

[7] Hayes, *Pegahmagabow: Life-Long Warrior*, 67. Indian Affairs acting assistant deputy minister A.F. Mackenzie's letter to Indian Agent John M. Daly (March 11, 1925).

[8] Robin Brownlie, *A Fatherly Eye: Indian Agents, Government Power, and Aboriginal Resistance in Ontario, 1918–1939* (University of Toronto Press, 2003), 65. Francis Pegahmagabow, quoted in the above. See also Hayes, p. 64.

[9] Brian McInnes, *Sounding Thunder: The Stories of Francis Pegahmagabow*, 92-97. The Great Otter story is paraphrased from Duncan Pegahmagabow's retelling in the above.

"Rosie"

[1] Government of Canada, Social Development Division, Department of Indian and Northern Affairs Canada. *Eskimo Identification and Disc Numbers: A Brief History*, by Barry A. Roberts. (Social Development Division, 1975.) The 1931–44 entries in the timeline are based on this document.

"Nimkii"

[1] Adrian Humphreys. "'A lost tribe': Child welfare system accused of repeating residential school history," National Post. December 15, 2014, Paraphrased quote credited to Wabaseemoong First Nation community members by Theresa Stevens, quoted in the above.

"Like A Razor Slash"

[1] CBC Digital Archives. "Dene Chief: 'My Nation Will Stop the Pipeline.'" Video. CBC Television News Broadcast, August 5, 1975, Fort Good Hope, Northwest Territories. http://www.cbc.ca/archives/entry/dene-chief-my-nation-will-stop-the-pipeline (also available as "Dene Chief Frank T'Seleie - Mackenzie Valley pipeline/Gas Project in 1975" at https://www.youtube.com/watch?v=pohp-gYL1I0)

[2] This quote is from the "Submission to the Joint Review Panel investigating the proposed McKenzie Valley Pipeline," written by David J. Parker on behalf of the Edmonton Friends of the North Environmental Society on February 1, 2007. A copy of the letter was provided to the editor by David J. Parker.

[3] "1973: The Morrow Decision: The Birth of Land Claims in the Northwest Territories": http://www.nwttimeline.ca/1950/1973Morrow.html. Dene witnesses' testimony and Justice William Morrow's decision quoted here.

[4] Mackenzie Valley Pipeline Inquiry, *Proceedings at Community Hearing*, Volume 18, 1768–1779: Fort Good Hope, August 5, 1975. All text from "Mr. Berger, as chief ..." to "... lay down my life" are excerpts from Chief Frank T'Seleie's statement. They appear as they were transcribed.

[5] Justice Thomas Berger, *Northern Frontier, Northern Homeland: The Report of The Mackenzie Valley Pipeline Inquiry*, Volume 1, 1977, xxvii.

[6] Berger, Volume 2, 218–219.

[7] Berger, Volume 1, 197.

"Migwite'tmeg: We Remember It"

[1] Alanis Obomsawin, *Incident at Restigouche*, National Film Board of Canada, 1984: https://www.nfb.ca/film/incident_at_restigouche/.

[2] 1752 Peace and Friendship Treaty Between His Majesty the King and the Jean Baptiste Cope: https://www.aadnc-aandc.gc.ca/eng/1100100029037/1100100029038

"Warrior Nation"

[1] The title page spread is adapted from a photo taken by Benoît Aquin (Library and Archives Canada). The people in the original image have been replaced by characters from this story. The image on the TV is a reproduction of the iconic photograph of the face-off between soldier Patrick Cloutier and Anishinaabe warrior Brad Larocque, a University of Saskatchewan economics student. The photograph was taken on September 1, 1990, by Shaney Komulainen of the Canadian Press. Both photographs may be seen at: https://www.thecanadianencyclopedia.ca/en/article/oka-crisis/.

[2] This image of Elijah Harper is based on a photograph taken on June 22, 1990, by Wayne Glowacki of the Winnipeg Free Press. The original is available at: https://www.winnipegfreepress.com/local/Elijah-Harper-The-humble-man-who-said-no-207988151.html.

[3] This map was created using three references: (a) a map created by Jonathon Rivait for the *National Post*, currently available online at: https://warriorpublications.files.wordpress.com/2015/07/oka-maps.jpg; (b) an uncredited map published in "The Indian Summer – Oka 1990," *istormnews*, May 16, 2015: https://istormnews.wordpress.com/2015/05/16/the-indian-summer-oka-1990/; and (c) Google Maps Satellite.

[4] Reproduction of photograph by Shaney Komulainen (Canadian Press). See [1] for details.

[5] Reproduction of Daphne Odjig's 1978 mural *The Indian in Transition*. To view a photograph of the original, please see: http://www.arthistoryarchive.com/arthistory/canadian/images/DaphneOdjig-Unknown-Title-DateUnknown.jpg.

[6] Image based on a photograph taken by Ellen Gabriel.

"kitaskinaw 2350"

[1] The image of the woman with a feather is based on a photograph that reporter Ossie Michelin took of Amanda Polchies on October 17, 2013, published by APTN: http://aptnnews.ca/2013/12/12/elsipogtog-anti-fracking-fight-fallout-putting-strain-rcmp-first-nation-relations/.

[2] Government of Canada. Indigenous Services Canada. *Statement of apology to former students of Indian Residential Schools* (Ottawa: Indigenous and Northern Affairs Canada, 2008). Stephen Harper, excerpt quoted.

[3] "The Survivors Speak," Truth and Reconciliation Commission of Canada, 2015. www.trc.ca/websites/trcinstitution/File/2015/Findings/Survivors_Speak_2015_05_30_web_o.pdf. The testimony here is not a direct quote from a specific individual.

[4] Tim Fontaine, "Canada discriminates against children on reserves, tribunal rules," CBC News, January 26, 2016.

[5] Cindy Blackstock, "The long history of discrimination against First Nations children," Policy Options, October 6, 2016.

[6] "Dakota Access Pipeline."Camp of the Sacred Stones. http://sacredstonecamp.org/dakota-access-pipeline. This map is adapted from the site.

[7] This image is based on a photograph taken by Mike McCleary and published by the *Bismarck Tribune* on November 21, 2016: http://www.brainerddispatch.com/news/4164386-police-and-protesters-face-backwater-bridge.

[8] "Mní Wíconí" sign designed by Joey Montoya: http://www.urbannativeera.com.

[9] Hayden King, Twitter post, February 22, 2018, 5:49 p.m., https://twitter.com/Hayden_King.

Joanne Hammond, Twitter post, February 22, 2018, 5:36 p.m., https://twitter.com/KamloopsArchaeo.

Leah Arcand, Twitter post, February 22, 2018, 6:28 p.m., https://twitter.com/LeahArcand.

These Tweets are reproduced here with permission from their authors.

Select Bibliography

"Annie of Red River"

Charlebois, Peter. *The Life of Louis Riel*. Toronto: New Canada Publications, 1975.

Hall, Norma J. "Anne 'Annie' McDermot Bannatyne". The Provisional Government of Assiniboia. November 28, 2012. https://hallnjean2.wordpress.com/the-red-river-resistence/women-and-the-resistance/annie-mcdermot-bannatyne/

Lamirande, Todd. "Annie McDermot, (Bannatyne). (C.1830-1908)". Edited by Lawrence Barkwell. Louis Riel Institute. June 17, 2008. http://www.metismuseum.ca/media/db/07426

Mair, Charles. "From Red River". *The Daily Globe*. January 4, 1869.

Rea, J.E. "BANNATYNE, ANDREW GRAHAM BALLENDEN." Dictionary of Canadian Biography, vol. 11. University of Toronto/Université Laval. 1982.

Stanley, George F.G. "Louis Riel." Revised by Adam Gaudry. The Canadian Encyclopedia. April 22, 2013. https://www.thecanadianencyclopedia.ca/en/article/louis-riel/

"Tilted Ground"

Assu, Frank. *Lekwiltok Anthology: A Collection of Essays about the We Wai Kai People of Cape Mudge*. Nuyem, Comox, and Quadra Island: First Choice Books, 2009.

Assu, Harry, Joy Inglis. Assu of Cape Mudge: Recollections of a Coastal Indian Chief. Vancouver: UBC Press, 1989.

Berman, Judith. "HUNT, GEORGE (Xawe, 'Maxwalagalis, K'ixitasu, Notq'ołala)." *Dictionary of Canadian Biography*, vol. 16. University of Toronto/Université Laval. 2017.

Boas, Franz, dir. *The Kwakiutl of British Columbia*. 1930-1931. Seattle: University of Washington Press, 2016. DVD, 25 min.

Boas, Franz. "The Social Organization and the Secret Societies of the Kwakiutl Indians." *The Report of the U.S. National Museum for 1895*. Washington: Government Printing Office (1987): 311-737.

Boas, Franz. "The Indians Of British Columbia," *Popular Science Monthly*, Vol. 32 (1888).

Cole, Douglas, Ira Chaikin. *An Iron Hand upon the People: The Law Against the Potlatch on the Northwest Coast*. Vancouver: Douglas & McIntyre, 1990.

Frogner, R. "Assu, Billy." *BC Archives, Royal BC Museum*, 2015. http://search-bcarchives.royalbcmuseum. bc.ca/assu-billy-1867-1965.

Government of Canada. *An Act to further amend "The Indian Act, 1880."* Chapter 27. April 19, 1884.

Halpern, Ida ed. *Indian Music of the Pacific Northwest Coast*. Folkways Records. 1967. CD.

"Museum at Campbell River." Chameleon CreativeGraphic & Web Design. 2011. http://campbellriver.crmuseum.ca

"Nuyumbalees Cultural Centre, Museum at Cape Mudge." (n.d.) https://www.museumatcapemudge.com

Sewid, James, James P. Spradley. *Guests Never Leave Hungry: The Autobiography of James Sewid, a Kwakiutl Indian*. Revised edition. Montreal and Kingston: McGill-Queen's University Press, 1995.

Sparks, Sevda. "Incited to Potlatch". Library and Archives Canada, December 7, 2017. https://thediscoverblog.com/2017/12/07/incited-to-potlatch/

"The Man Behind the Masks: The Legacy of Chief Billy Assu." (n.d.) Nuyumbalees Cultural Centre, Museum at Cape Mudge: https://www.museumatcapemudge.com/the-man-behind-the-masks.

Thornton, Mildred Valley. *Potlatch People: Indian Lives & Legends of British Columbia*. Surrey: Hancock House Publishing, 2003.

"U'mista Cultural Society" 2019. https://www.umista.ca/

"Red Clouds"

Fiddler, Thomas, James R. Stevens. *Killing the Shamen*. Moonbeam, Ontario: Penumbra Press, 1985.

Stevens, James R., Carl Ray. *Sacred Legends of the Sandy Lake Cree*. Toronto: McClelland and Stewart, 1971.

Stevens, James R. "ZHAUWUNO-GEEZHIGO-GAUBOW." *Dictionary of Canadian Biography*, vol. 13. University of Toronto/Université Laval. 1994.

"Timeline: Residential Schools," *The Canadian Encyclopedia* https://www.thecanadianencyclopedia.ca/en/timeline/residential-schools.

"Peggy"

Hayes, Adrian. *Pegahmagabow: Life-Long Warrior*. Toronto: Blue Butterfly Books, 2009.

Koennecke, Franz M. "Francis Pegahmagabow." The Canadian Encyclopedia. February 4, 2008. https://www.thecanadianencyclopedia.ca/en/article/francis-pegahmagabow.

McInnes, Brian D. *Sounding Thunder: The Stories of Francis Pegahmagabow*. Winnipeg: University of Manitoba Press, 2016.

McInnes, Brian. "Indigenous War Heroes Project." Wasauksing First Nation, 2016. http://indigenouswarhero.org.

Library and Archives Canada. "Francis Pegahmagabow." Military Heritage Collection, First World War. 2017.

"Rosie"

Aupilaarjuk, Mariano, Tulimaaq Aupilaarjuk, Lucassie Nutaraaluk, Rose Iqallijuq, Johanasi Ujarak, Isidore Ijituuq, and Michel Kupaaq. *Interviewing Inuit Elders, Volume 4: Cosmology & Shamanism*. Ed. Bernard Saladin d'Anglure. Iqaluit: Nunavut Arctic College, 2001. http://tradition-orale.ca/english/pdf/ Cosmology-And-Shamanism-E.pdf.

Potter, Russell A. *Finding Franklin: The Untold Story of a 165-year Search*. Montreal and Kingston: McGill-Queen's University Press, 2016.

Government of Canada. Social Development Division, Department of Indian and Northern Affairs Canada. *Eskimo Identification and Disc Numbers: A Brief History*. Roberts, A. Barry. Social Development Division, 1975.

Qitsualik-Tinsley, Rachel and Sean. *Why the Monster*. Iqaluit: Inhabit Media, 2017.

"Nimkii"

Humphreys, Adrian. "'A lost tribe': Child welfare system accused of repeating residential school history." *National Post*. December 15, 2014,

Obamsawin, Alanis, dir. *Richard Cardinal: Cry from a Diary of a Métis Child*. National Film Board of Canada, 1986. DVD, 29 min. https://www.nfb.ca/film/richard_cardinal/

"Like a Razor Slash"

Berger, Thomas. "Northern Frontier, Northern Homeland: The Report of The Mackenzie Valley Pipeline Inquiry, Volumes 1 and 2." Prince of Wales Northern Heritage Centre, 2018.

CBC Digital Archives. "Dene Chief: 'My Nation Will Stop the Pipeline.'" Video. CBC Television News Broadcast, August 5, 1975, Fort Good Hope, Northwest Territories. http://www.cbc.ca/archives/entry/dene-chief-my-nation-will-stop-the-pipeline

CBC Digital Archives. "The Berger Pipeline Inquiry." Last updated November 14, 2017. http://www.cbc.ca/archives/topic/the-berger-pipeline-inquiry

Jaremko, Gordon. "Greens Pan Northern Pipeline: Mackenzie Valley Proposal like 'Razor Slash' on Mona Lisa." *Calgary Herald*, February 26, 2007, sec. B,7.

Nishihata, Jesse, dir. *The Inquiry Film*. Prince of Wales Northern Heritage Centre, 1976. https://www.pwnhc.ca/ item/the-inquiry-film/

Supreme Court of Canada. "Paulette et al. vs. The Queen." *Supreme Court of Canada Reporter (SCR)*, Vol. 2 (1977): 628–645.

Prince of Wales Northern Heritage Centre (PWNHC). "Inquiry: Berger Inquiry Educational Resource Archive." (n.d.) https://www.pwnhc.ca/exhibitions/berger/

Prince of Wales Northern Heritage Centre (PWNHC). "1994 Sahtu Land Claim." Historical Timeline of the Northwest Territories. (n.d.)http://www.nwttimeline.ca/1975/1994SahtuClaim.html

Sparks, Sevda. "Incited to Potlatch". Library and Archives Canada, December 7, 2017. https://thediscoverblog.com/2017/12/07/incited-to-potlatch/

Ryen, Tind Shepper. "*The Mackenzie Gas Pipeline: The Berger Inquiry*." Mackenzie Gas Pipeline and the Boreal Environment Information Project. Ed. Peter Blanken. Boulder: University of Colorado, (n.d.)

Scott, Patrick. *Talking Tools: Faces of Aboriginal Oral Tradition in Contemporary Society*. Solstice Series. Edmonton: University of Alberta Press, 2012.

"Migwite'tmeg: We Remember It"

Government of Canada. Department of Indian and Northern Affairs Canada. *1752 Peace and Friendship Treaty Between His Majesty the King and the Jean Baptiste Cope*. Supreme Court of Canada, 1985.

Cornell, Stephen, Miriam Jorgensen, Rachel Rose Starks, Renee Goldtooth, Sheldon Tetreault, Michele Guerin, Beaver Paul, and Anisa White. *Making First Nation Law: The Listuguj Mi'gmaq Fishery*. National Centre for First Nations Governance (NCFNG) and Native Nations Institute for Leadership, Management, and Policy (NNI), August, 2010.

McKenzie, Gérald, Thierry Vincent. "La « guerre du saumon » des années 1970–1980: Entrevue avec Pierre Lepage." *Recherches Amérindiennes au Québec* 40, no. 1–2 (2010)): 103–111.

"Mi'gwite'tm." *Nujignua'tegeg*. June 9, 2016.

Obamsawin, Alanis, dir. *Incident at Restigouche*. National Film Board of Canada, 1984. DVD, 45 min. https://www.nfb.ca/film/incident_at_restigouche/

"Warrior Nation"

CBC Digital Archives, "Elijah Harper's vote of protest, June 12, 1990". http://www.cbc.ca/player/play/1751911434

CBC Digital Archives, "The Oka Crisis". http://www.cbc.ca/archives/topic/the-oka-crisis

Deerchild, Rosanna. "Sisters Recall the Brutal Last Day of Oka Crisis." *Unreserved*. CBC Radio (Winnipeg), February 19, 2016.

"Federal government seeking end to long-running Ipperwash dispute offers $95M, return of land." *The National Post*. August 14, 2015 calls for an inquiry." *CBC News*. January 18, 2016.

Harper, Vern. *Following the Red Path: The Native People's Caravan*, 1974. Raleigh: NC Press, 1979.

Obamsawin, Alanis, dir. *Incident at Restigouche*. National Film Board of Canada, 1984. DVD, 45 min. https://www.nfb.ca/film/incident_at_restigouche/

Obamsawin, Alanis, dir. *Kanehsatake: 270 Years of Resistance*. National Film Board of Canada, 1993. DVD, 1h 29 min. https://www.nfb.ca/film/kanehsatake_270_years_of_resistance/

Ridd, Karen. "Peace Camps in Quebec and Manitoba to support the Mohawks in the 'Oka Crisis'". Global Nonviolent Action Database. August 17, 2012. https://nvdatabase.swarthmore.edu/content/peace-camps-quebec-and-manitoba-support-mohawks-oka-crisis-canada-1990

Scott, Marian. "Revisiting the Pines: Oka's Legacy." *Montreal Gazette*, July 10, 2015.

Simpson, Leanne, Kiera L. Ladner, eds. *This is an Honour Song: Twenty Years Since the Blockades, an anthology of writing on the "Oka crisis."* Winnipeg: ARP Books, 2010.

Zig Zag. "Oka Crisis, 1990." Warrior Publications. June 11, 2014. https://warriorpublications.wordpress.com/2014/06/11/oka-crisis-1990/

"kitaskinaw 2350"

Barrera, Jorge. "Elsipogtog anti-fracking fight fallout putting strain on RCMP-First Nation relations." *APTN National News*, December 12, 2013.

"Dakota Access Pipeline." Camp of the Sacred Stones. http://sacredstonecamp.org/dakota-access-pipeline

Government of Canada. Indigenous Services Canada. *Statement of apology to former students of Indian Residential Schools*. Ottawa: Indigenous and Northern Affairs Canada, 2008. http://www.aadnc-aandc.gc.ca/eng/1100100015644/1100100015649

"Idle No More." http://www.idlenomore.ca/

Kirman, Paula. "Idle No More – Round Dance Flash Mob at WEM [West Edmonton Mall] in Edmonton." Radical Citizen Media. December 18, 2012. Video, 7:41. https://www.youtube.com/watch?v=x2Nx4jUEZfc

"National Centre for Truth and Reconciliation (NCTR), University of Manitoba." http://nctr.ca

"National Inquiry into Missing and Murdered Indigenous Women and Girls (MMIWG)." http://www.mmiwg-ffada.ca

"Police and protesters face off at Backwater Bridge." *Bismarck Tribune*, November 21, 2016.

"Raymond Cormier not guilty in death of Tina Fontaine." *APTN National News*, February 22, 2018.

Vowel, Chelsea. "The often-ignored facts about Elsipogtog." *The Toronto Star*, November 14, 2013.

Wong, Julia Carrie. November 21, 2016. "Dakota Access pipeline: 300 protesters injured after police use water cannons." The Guardian.

About the Contributors

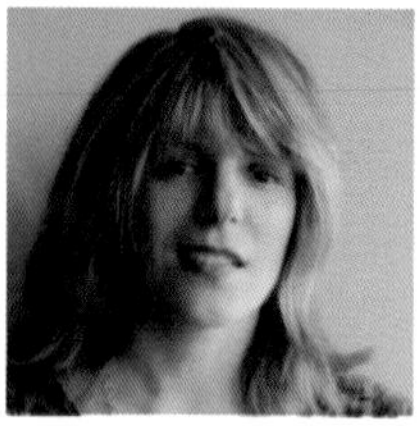

Kateri Akiwenzie-Damm is a writer, poet, spoken-word performer, librettist, and activist from the Chippewas of Nawash First Nation at Neyaashiinigmiing, Ontario. In 1993, she founded Kegedonce Press to publish the work of Indigenous creators. She has written two books of poetry, edited the award-winning *Skins: Contemporary Indigenous Writing*, and has also released two CDs. Kateri's work has been published internationally, and she has performed and spoken around the world.

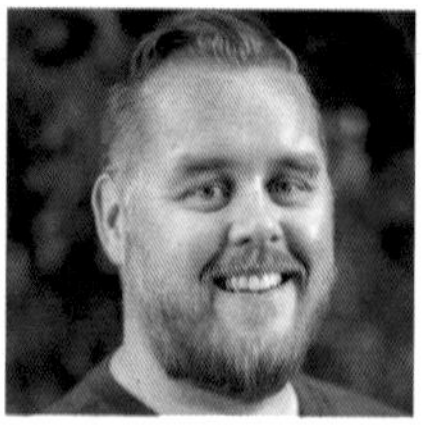

Sonny Assu is an interdisciplinary artist whose diverse practice is informed by Kwakwa̱ka̱'wakw culture melded with Western/pop art principles. His work has been shown at the National Gallery of Canada, Seattle Art Museum, Vancouver Art Gallery and in various public and private collections across Canada, the US, and the UK. He currently resides in unceded Ligwiłda'xw territory (Campbell River, BC).

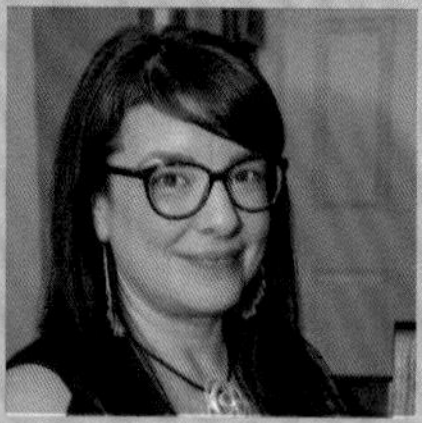

Tara Audibert is a Wolatoqiyik artist, filmmaker, and illustrator with 20 years' experience in animation, comics, and fine art. Tara combines traditional First Nations art and storytelling with contemporary design and digital mediums. She runs Moxy Fox Studio and her first independent animated film, *The Importance of Dreaming*, was released in 2017. She is also a founder of the Ni'gweg Collective and the app "NITAP: Legends of the First Nations."

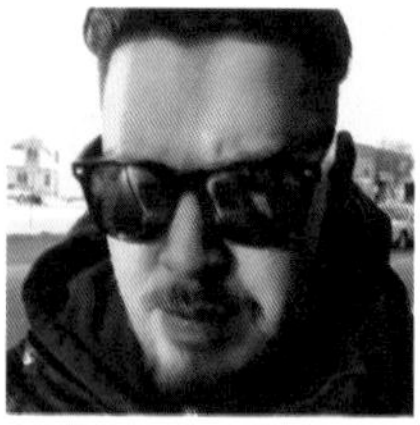

Kyle Charles is a writer/illustrator living in Edmonton, Alberta. He has drawn for several series including Roche Limit: Clandestiny and Her Infernal Descent. He has also written and illustrated short stories for publishers like Heavy Metal and OnSpec Magazine. When not busy at the drawing table, Kyle spends much of his time teaching comics to local students. He is a member of Whitefish Lake First Nation.

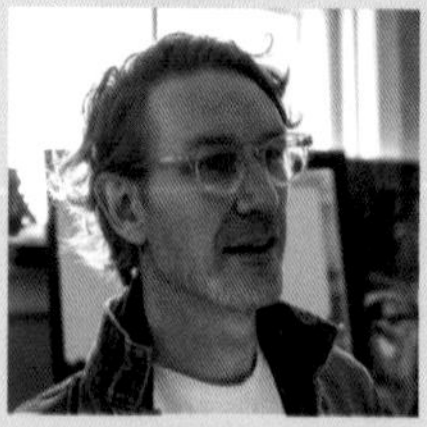

GMB Chomichuk is an award-winning writer and illustrator whose work has appeared in film, television, books, and comics. His most recent work with HighWater Press, *Will I See?*, was a collaboration with writer David A. Robertson and singer/songwriter Iskwē. His works include occult suspense (*Midnight City*), science fiction (*Red Earth*), and inspirational all-ages adventure (*Cassie and Tonk*). He is the host of *Super Pulp Science*, a podcast about how genre gets made. His newest full-length graphic novel, *Apocrypha: The Legend of Babymetal*, was featured on *The Hollywood Reporter*, *The Nerdist*, and *Billboard Magazine*.

Natasha Donovan is a freelance artist and illustrator from Vancouver, British Columbia. Her sequential work has been published in *The Other Side* anthology and *Surviving the City*. She is the illustrator of the award-winning children's book, *The Sockeye Mother* (shortlisted for the Norma Fleck Award for Canadian Children's Non-Fiction). Natasha is a member of the Métis Nation of British Columbia.

Alicia Elliott is a Tuscarora writer from Six Nations of the Grand River living in Brantford, Ontario. Her writing has been published in *The Malahat Review*, CBC, *The Globe and Mail*, and *Macleans*. Her essay, "A Mind Spread Out on the Ground," won Gold at the National Magazine Awards (2017). She was the 2017-2018 Geoffrey and Margaret Andrew Fellow at UBC, and received the RBC Taylor Emerging Writer Prize in 2018.

Scott A. Ford is an award-winning comic creator, illustrator, and designer from Winnipeg, Manitoba. His comic projects include *Romulus + Remus*, *Giant's Well*, and *Ark Land*. His work has been featured in galleries and publications, on beer cans and book covers. He has also spoken about his artistic practice at numerous public presentations about art and design. Check out all of Scott's art and comic projects at scottafordart.com.

Scott B. Henderson is the author/illustrator of the sci-fi/fantasy comic series, The Chronicles of Era. He has illustrated *Betty: The Helen Betty Osborne Story*, and the Eisner-nominated *A Blanket of Butterflies*, as well as the For Valour, Tales from Big Spirit and 7 Generations series. Scott is also the recipient of the 2016 C4 Central Canada Comic Con Storyteller Award.

Ryan Howe is a prairie Canadian cartoonist and graphic designer who fell in love with comics' unique storytelling language early in life and has been hooked ever since. He's been collaborating with other comics creators since 2003, providing art for a wide variety of projects and genres on both the web and in print. Ryan has recently tried his hand at writing as well as drawing, the Daisy Blackwood: Pilot for Hire series being the rip roarin' result.

Andrew Lodwick is a lifelong resident of Winnipeg and has a B.F.A. (Hons) from the University of Manitoba School of Art. He has worked for many years at Martha Street Studio as technician, custom screen printer, and studio manager. He maintains a personal art practice that includes printmaking and design work. In 2014, Andrew cofounded the Riso print collective, Parameter Press (parameter-press.com), of which he remains a member.

Of Inuit-Cree ancestry, **Rachel Qitsualik-Tinsley** was born in a tent on northernmost Baffin Island. She learned Inuit survival lore from her father, survived residential school and attended university. In 2012, she was awarded a Queen Elizabeth II Diamond Jubilee Medal for her numerous cultural writings. Of Scottish-Mohawk ancestry, **Sean Qitsualik-Tinsley** was born in southern Ontario, learning woodcraft and stories from his father. Training as an artist and writer, Sean's sci-fi work won 2nd place in the California-based Writers of the Future contest, published by Galaxy Press. Rachel and Sean have worked for decades as Arctic researchers and consultants. In writing together, they have published 10 successful books and many shorter works, celebrating the history and uniqueness of Arctic shamanism, cosmology, and cosmogony. Their novel, *Skraelings: Clashes in the Old Arctic*, was a Governor General Awards Finalist and First Prize Burt Award winner.

From Listuguj, Quebec, **Brandon Mitchell** is the founder of Birch Bark Comics and creator of the Sacred Circles comic series, which draws on his Mi'kmaq heritage. He has also written five books with the Healthy Aboriginal Network, (*Lost Innocence*, *Drawing Hope*, *River Run*, *Making it Right*, and *Emily's Choice*) and wrote and illustrated *Jean-Paul's Daring Adventure: Stories from Old Mobile* for the University of Alabama.

David A. Robertson is an award-winning writer. His books include *When We Were Alone* (winner Governor General's Literary Award), *Betty: The Helen Betty Osborne Story* (listed In The Margins), and the award-winning YA novels *Strangers* and *Monsters*. David educates as well as entertains through his writings about Indigenous peoples in Canada, reflecting their cultures, histories, communities, as well as illuminating many contemporary issues. David is a member of Norway House Cree Nation. He lives in Winnipeg.

Niigaanwewidam James Sinclair, PhD., is Anishinaabe (St. Peter's/Little Peguis) and an assistant professor at the University of Manitoba. He regularly speaks and writes about Indigenous issues for CTV, CBC, *The Guardian*, and APTN, as well as in *The Exile Edition of Native Canadian Fiction and Drama*. Niigaan is co-editor of the award-winning *Manitowapow: Aboriginal Writings from the Land of Water* and *Centering Anishinaabeg Studies: Understanding the World Through Stories*. He is also editorial director of The Debwe Series, published by HighWater Press.

Jen Storm is an Ojibway writer from the Couchiching First Nation in Northwestern Ontario. Born and raised in Winnipeg, Manitoba, Jennifer completed *Deadly Loyalties*, her first novel, at age fourteen. *Fire Starters* (AIYLA Honor Book) is her first graphic novel. Jen was a 2017 recipient for the CBC Manitoba's Future 40. Jen's updates on current and future projects can be found on Instagram @jenstorm_art where she shares her passion for creating art.

Richard Van Camp is a proud member of the Tlicho Nation from Fort Smith, Northwest Territories. He is the author of 22 books including *The Lesser Blessed* (also a feature film), the Eisner nominated graphic novel, *A Blanket of Butterflies* (with Scott B. Henderson), and *Three Feathers* (also a feature film). Richard is also the author of four collections of short stories, including *Night Moves*, and five baby books, including the award-winning *Little You* (with Julie Flett).

Katherena Vermette is a Métis writer of poetry, fiction, and children's literature. Her first book, *North End Love Songs*, won the 2013 Governor General Literary Award for Poetry. Her debut novel, *The Break*, was featured on Canada Reads 2017 and has gone on to win numerous awards, including the Amazon.ca First Novel Award. She holds a Master of Fine Arts from the University of British Columbia, and lives in Winnipeg, Manitoba.

Chelsea Vowel is Métis from manitow-sâkahikan (Lac Ste. Anne) Alberta, currently residing in amiskwacîwâskahikan (Edmonton). Mother to six girls, she has a BEd and LLB, and is currently a graduate student and Cree language curriculum developer. Chelsea is also a public intellectual, writer, speaker, and educator whose work intersects language, gender, Métis self-determination, and resurgence. Her collection of essays, *Indigenous Writes*, is a national bestseller (HighWater Press, 2016). She co-hosts the Indigenous feminist sci-fi podcast with Molly Swain, blogs at apihtawikosisan.com, and makes auntie-approved legendary bannock.

Since 1998, **Donovan Yaciuk** has done colouring work on books published by Marvel, DC, Dark Horse comics, and HighWater Press including the A Girl Called Echo series. Donovan holds a Bachelor of Fine Arts (Honours) from the University of Manitoba and began his career as a part of the legendary, now-defunct Digital Chameleon colouring studio. He lives in Winnipeg with his wife and daughter.